Five Nights at Freddy's
THE SILVER EYES

Five Nights at Freddy's

THE SILVER EYES

by

SCOTT CAWTHON
KIRA BREED-WRISLEY

Scholastic Inc.

Copyright © 2016 Scott Cawthon. All rights reserved.

Photo of tv static: © Klikk/Dreamstime

All rights reserved. Published by Scholastic Inc., *Publishers since 1920.* SCHOLASTIC and associated logos are trademarks and/or registered trademarks of Scholastic Inc.

The publisher does not have any control over and does not assume any responsibility for author or third-party websites or their content.

No part of this publication may be reproduced, stored in a retrieval system, or transmitted in any form or by any means, electronic, mechanical, photocopying, recording, or otherwise, without written permission of the publisher. For information regarding permission, write to Scholastic Inc., Attention: Permissions Department, 557 Broadway, New York, NY 10012.

This book is a work of fiction. Names, characters, places, and incidents are either the product of the author's imagination or are used fictitiously, and any resemblance to actual persons, living or dead, business establishments, events, or locales is entirely coincidental.

Library of Congress Cataloging-in-Publication Data available

ISBN 978-1-338-13437-7

20 19 18 17 16 15 14   20 21 22 23 24

Printed in the U.S.A.   40

First edition, October 2016

Book design by Rick DeMonico

CHAPTER ONE

He sees me.

Charlie dropped to her hands and knees. She was wedged behind a row of arcade games, cramped in the crawl space between the consoles and the wall, tangled electrical cords and useless plugs strewn beneath her. She was cornered; the only way out was past the thing, and she wasn't fast enough to make it. She could see him stalking back and forth, catching flickers of movement through the gaps between the games. There was scarcely enough room to move, but she tried to crawl backward. Her foot caught on a cord. She stopped, contorting herself to carefully dislodge it.

She heard the clash of metal on metal, and the farthest console rocked back against the wall. He hit it again, shattering the display, then attacked the next, crashing against them almost rhythmically, tearing through the machinery, coming closer.

I have to get out, I have to! The panicked thought was of no help; there was no way out. Her arm ached, and she wanted to sob aloud. Blood soaked through the tattered bandage, and it seemed as though she could feel it draining out of her.

The console a few feet away crashed against the wall, and Charlie flinched. He was getting closer; she could hear the grinding of gears and the clicking of servos, ever louder. Eyes closed, she could still see the way he looked at her, see the matted fur and the exposed metal beneath the synthetic flesh.

Suddenly the console in front of her was wrenched away. It toppled over, thrown down like a toy. The power cords beneath her hands and knees were yanked away, and Charlie slipped, almost falling. She caught herself and looked up just in time to see the downward swing of a hook . . .

WELCOME TO HURRICANE, UTAH.

Charlie smiled wryly at the sign and kept driving. The world didn't look any different from one side of the sign to the other, but she felt a nervous anticipation as she passed it. She didn't recognize anything. Then again, she hadn't really expected to, not this far at the edge of town where it was all highway and empty space.

She wondered what the others would look like, who they were now. Ten years ago they'd been best friends. And then *it* happened, and everything ended, at least for Charlie. She hadn't seen any of them since she was seven years old. They had written all the time as kids, especially Marla, who wrote like she talked: fast and incoherent. But as they got older they had grown apart, the letters had grown fewer and further between, and the conversations leading up to this trip had been perfunctory and full of awkward pauses. Charlie repeated their names as though to reassure herself that she still remembered them: *Marla. Jessica. Lamar. Carlton. John. And Michael . . .* Michael was the reason for this trip, after all. It was ten years since he'd died, ten years since *it* happened, and now his parents wanted them all together for the dedication ceremony. They wanted all his old friends there when they announced the scholarship they were creating in his name. Charlie knew it was a good thing to do, but the gathering still felt slightly macabre. She shivered and turned down the air-conditioning, even though she knew it was not the cold.

As she drove into the town center, Charlie began to recognize things: a few stores and the movie theater, which was now advertising the summer's blockbuster hit. She felt a brief moment of surprise, then smiled at herself. *What did you expect, that the whole place would be unchanged? A monument to the moment of your departure, frozen forever in July 1985?* Well, that was exactly what she had expected. She looked at her watch. Still a few hours to kill before they all met up. She thought about going to the movie, but she knew what she really wanted to do. Charlie made a left turn and headed out of town.

Ten minutes later, she pulled to a stop and got out.

The house loomed up before her, its dark outline a wound in the bright-blue sky. Charlie leaned back against the car, slightly dizzy. She took a moment to steady herself with deep breaths. She had known it would be here. An illicit look through her aunt's bank books a few years before had told her that the mortgage was paid off and that Aunt Jen was still paying property taxes. It had only been ten years; there was no reason it should have changed at all. Charlie climbed the steps slowly, taking in the peeling paint. The third stair still had a loose board, and the rosebushes had taken over one side of the porch, their thorns biting hungrily into the wood. The door was locked, but Charlie still had her key. She had never actually used it. As she took it from around her neck and slid it into the lock, she remembered her father putting its chain around her neck. *In case you ever need it.* Well, she needed it now.

The door opened easily, and Charlie looked around. She didn't remember much about the first couple of years here. She had been only three years old, and all the memories had faded together in the blur of a child's grief and loss, of not understanding why her mother had to go away, clinging to her father every moment, not trusting the world around her unless he was there, unless she was holding tightly to him, burying herself in his flannel shirts and the smell of grease and hot metal and him.

The stairs stretched straight up in front of her, but she did not move directly to them. Instead she went into the living room, where all the furniture was still in place. She had not really noticed it as a child, but the house was a little too large for the furniture they had. Things were spread out too widely in order to fill the space: The coffee table was too far from the couch to reach, the easy chair too far across the room to carry on a conversation. There was a dark stain in the wooden floorboards near the center of the room. Charlie stepped around it quickly and went to the kitchen, where the cupboards held only a few pots, pans, and dishes. Charlie had never felt a lack of anything as a child, but it seemed now that the unnecessary enormity of the house was a sort of apology, the attempt of a man who had lost so much to give his daughter what he could. He'd always had a way of over-doing whatever he did.

The last time she was here the house had been dark and everything felt wrong. She was carried up the stairs to her bedroom although she was seven years old and could have gone quicker on her own two feet. But Aunt Jen had stopped on the front porch, picked her up, and carried her, shielding her face as though she were a baby in the glaring sun.

In her room, Aunt Jen set Charlie down and closed the bedroom door behind them. She told her to pack her suitcase, and Charlie had cried because all her things could never fit into that small case.

"We can come back for the rest later," Aunt Jen said, her impatience leaking through as Charlie hovered indecisively at her dresser, trying to decide which T-shirts to bring along. They had never come back for the rest.

Charlie mounted the stairs, heading to her old bedroom. The door was partially cracked, and as she opened it she had a giddy feeling of displacement, as though her younger self might be sitting there among her toys, might look up and ask Charlie, *Who are you?* Charlie went in.

Like the rest of the house, her bedroom was untouched. The walls were pale pink, and the ceiling, which sloped dramatically on one side to follow the line of the roof, was painted to match. Her old bed still stood against the wall beneath a large window; the mattress was still intact, though the sheets were gone. The window was cracked slightly open, and rotting lace curtains wavered in the gentle breeze from outside. There was a dark water stain in the paint beneath the window where the weather had gotten in over the years, betraying the house's neglect. Charlie climbed onto the bed and forced the window shut. It obeyed with a screech, and Charlie stepped back and turned her attention to the rest of the room, to her father's creations.

Their first night in the house, Charlie had been afraid to sleep alone. She did not remember the night, but her father had told her about it often enough that the story had taken on the quality of memory. She sat up and wailed until her father came to find her, until he scooped her up and held her and promised her he would make sure she was never alone again. The next morning, he took her by the hand and led her to the garage, where he set to work keeping that promise.

The first of his inventions was a purple rabbit, now gray with age from years of sitting in the sunlight. Her father had named him Theodore. He was the size of a three-year-old child—her size at the time—and he had plush fur, shining eyes, and a dapper red bow tie. He didn't do much, only waved a hand, tilted his head to the side, and said in her father's voice, "I love you, Charlie." But it was enough to give her a night watcher, someone to keep her company when she could not sleep. Right now Theodore sat in a white wicker chair in the far corner of the room. Charlie waved at him, but, not activated, he did not wave back.

After Theodore, the toys got more complex. Some worked and some did not; some seemed to have permanent glitches, while others simply did not appeal to Charlie's childish imagination. She knew her father took those back to his workshop and recycled them for parts, though she did not like to watch them be dismantled. But the ones that were kept, those she loved, they were here now, looking at her expectantly. Smiling, Charlie pushed a button beside her bed. It gave way stiffly, but nothing happened. She pushed it again, holding it down longer, and this time, across the room and with the weary creak of metal on metal, the unicorn began to move.

The unicorn (Charlie had named him Stanley for some reason she could no longer remember) was made of metal and had been painted glossy white. He trundled around the room on a circular track, bobbing his head stiffly up and down. The track squealed as Stanley rounded the corner and came to a stop beside the bed. Charlie knelt beside him on the floor and patted his flank. His glossy paint was chipped and peeling, and his face had given over to rust. His eyes were lively, gazing out of the decay.

"You need a new coat of paint, Stanley," Charlie said. The unicorn stared ahead, unresponsive.

At the foot of the bed, there was a wheel. Made of patched-together metal, it had always reminded her of something she might find on a submarine. Charlie turned it. It stuck for a moment, then gave way, rotating as it always did, and across the room the smallest closet door swung open. Out sailed Ella on her track, a child-size doll bearing a teacup and saucer in her tiny hands like an offering. Ella's plaid dress was still crisp, and her patent leather shoes still shone; perhaps the closet had protected her from the damage of the damp. Charlie had had an identical outfit, back when she and Ella were the same height.

"Hi, Ella," she said softly. As the wheel unwound, Ella retreated to the closet again, the door closing behind her. Charlie followed her. The closets had been built to align with the slant of the ceiling, and there were three of them. Ella lived in the short one, which was about three and a half feet tall. Next to it was one a foot or so taller, and a third, closest to the bedroom door, was the same height as the rest of the room. She smiled, remembering.

"Why do you have three closets?" John had demanded the first time he came over. She looked at him blankly, confused by the question.

"'Cause that's how many there are," she said finally. She pointed defensively to the littlest one. "That one's Ella's anyway," she added. John nodded, satisfied.

Charlie shook her head and opened the door to the middle closet—or tried to. The knob stopped with a jolt: It was locked. She rattled it a few times but gave up without much conviction. She stayed crouched low to the floor and glanced up at the tallest closet, her *big-girl closet* that she would some-day grow into. *"You won't need it until you're bigger,"* her father would say, but that day never came. The door now hung open slightly, but Charlie didn't disturb it. It hadn't opened for her; it had only given way to time.

As she moved to stand, she noticed something shiny, half-hidden under the rim of the locked middle door. She leaned forward to pick it up. It looked like a broken-off piece of a circuit board. She smiled slightly. Nuts, bolts, scraps, and parts had turned up all over the place, once upon a time. Her father always had stray parts in his pockets. He would carry around something he was working on, set it down, and forget where it was, or worse, put something aside "for safe-keeping," never to be seen again. There was also a strand of her hair clinging to it; she unwound it carefully from the tiny lip of metal it was stuck on.

Finally, as though she had been putting it off, Charlie crossed the room and picked up Theodore. His back had not faded in the sun like the front of his body, and it was the same rich, dark purple she remembered. She pressed the button at the base of his neck, but he remained lifeless. His fur was threadbare, one ear hanging loose by a single rotting thread, and through the hole she could see the green plastic of his circuit board. Charlie held her breath, listening fearfully for something.

"I—ou—lie—" the rabbit said with a barely audible halting noise, and Charlie set him down, her face hot and her chest pinched tight. She had not really expected to hear her father's voice again. *I love you, too.*

Charlie looked around the room. When she was a child it had been her own magical world, and she was possessive of it. Only a few chosen friends were ever even allowed inside. She went to her bed and set Stanley moving on his track again. She left, closing the door behind her before the little unicorn came to a halt.

She went out the back door to the driveway and stopped in front of the garage that had been her father's workshop. Half-buried in the gravel a few feet away was a piece of metal, and Charlie went to pick it up. It was jointed in the middle, and she held it in her hands, smiling a little as she bent it back and forth. *An elbow joint,* she thought. *I wonder who that was going to belong to?*

She had stood in this exact spot many times before. She closed her eyes, and the memory overwhelmed her. She was a little girl again, sitting on the floor of her father's workshop, playing with scraps of wood and metal as though they were toy blocks, trying to build a tower with the uneven pieces. The shop was hot, and she was sweaty, grime sticking to her legs as she sat in her shorts and sneakers. She could almost smell the sharp, metallic odor of the soldering iron. Her father was nearby, never out of sight, working on Stanley the unicorn.

Stanley's face was still unfinished: one side white and shining and friendly, with a gleaming brown eye that seemed almost to see. The other half of the toy's face was all exposed circuit boards and metal parts. Charlie's father looked at her and smiled, and she smiled back, beloved. In a darkened corner behind her father, barely visible, hung a jumble of metal limbs, a twisted skeleton with burning silver eyes. Every once in a while, it gave an uncanny twitch. Charlie tried never to look at it, but as her father worked, as she played with her makeshift toys, her eye was drawn back to it again and again. The limbs, contorted, seemed almost mocking, the thing a ghastly jester, and yet there was something about it that suggested enormous pain.

"Daddy?" Charlie said, and her father did not look up from his work. "Daddy?" she said again, more urgently, and this time he turned to her slowly, as though not fully present in the world.

"What do you need, sweetie?"

She pointed at the metal skeleton. *Does it hurt?* She wanted to ask the question, but when she looked into her father's eyes she found she could not. She shook her head.

"Nothing."

He nodded at her with an absent smile and went back to his work. Behind him, the creature gave another awful twitch, and its eyes still burned.

Charlie shivered and drew herself back to the present. She glanced behind her, feeling exposed. She looked down, and her gaze fixed on something: three widely spaced grooves in the ground. She knelt, thoughtful, and ran her finger over one of them. The gravel was scattered away, the marks worn heavily into the dirt. *A camera tripod of some sort?* It was the first unfamiliar thing she'd seen. The door to the workshop was cracked open slightly, inviting, but she felt no desire to go inside. Quickly, she headed back to her car, but she stopped as soon as she settled into the driver's seat. Her keys were gone, having probably fallen out of her pocket somewhere inside the house.

She retraced her steps, merely glancing into the living room and kitchen before heading up to her bedroom. The keys were on the wicker chair, beside Theodore the rabbit. She picked them up and jangled them for a moment, not quite ready to leave the room behind. She sat down on the bed. Stanley the unicorn had stopped beside the bed as he always did, and as she sat, she patted him absently on the head. It had grown dark while she was outside, and the room was now cast in shadows. Somehow, without the bright sunlight, the toys' flaws and deterioration were thrown into sharp relief. Theodore's eyes no longer shone, and his thin fur and hanging ear made him look like a sickly vagabond. When she looked down at Stanley, the rust around his eyes made them look like hollow sockets, and his bared teeth, which she had always thought of as a smile, became the awful, knowing grin of a skull. Charlie stood up, careful not to touch him, and hurried toward the door, but her foot caught on the wheel beside the bed. She tripped on the tracks and fell sprawling to the floor. There was a whir of spinning metal, and as she raised her head, a small pair of feet appeared under her nose, clad in shining patent leather. She looked up.

There above her was Ella, staring down at her, silent and uninvited, her glassy eyes almost appearing to see. The teacup and saucer were held out before her with a military stiffness. Charlie got up cautiously, taking care not to disturb the doll. She left the room, stepping carefully to avoid accidentally activating any other toys. As Charlie went, Ella retreated to her closet, almost matching her pace.

Charlie hurried down the stairs, seized by an urgency to get away. In the car, she fumbled the key three times before sliding it into place. She backed too fast down the driveway, running recklessly over the grass of the front yard, and sped away. After about a mile, Charlie pulled over on the shoulder and turned the car off, staring straight ahead through the windshield, her eyes focused on nothing. She forced herself to breathe slowly. She reached up and adjusted the rearview mirror so she could see herself.

She always expected to see pain, anger, and sorrow written on her face, but they never were. Her cheeks were pink, and her round face looked almost cheerful, like always. Her first weeks living with Aunt Jen, she heard the same things over and over when Aunt Jen introduced her: *What a pretty child. What a happy-looking child she is.* Charlie always looked like she was about to smile, her brown eyes wide and sparkling, her thin mouth ready to curve up, even when she wanted to sob. The incongruity was a mild betrayal. She ran her fingers through her light brown hair as though that would magically fix its slight frizziness and put the mirror back into position.

She turned the car back on and searched for a radio station, hoping music might bring her fully back to reality. She flipped from station to station, not really hearing what any of them were playing, and finally settled on an AM broadcast with a host who seemed to be yelling condescendingly at his audience. She had no idea what he was talking about, but the brash and annoying sound was enough to jar her back into the present. The clock in the car was always wrong, so she checked her watch. It was almost time to meet her friends at the diner they had chosen, near the center of town.

Charlie pulled back onto the road and drove, letting the sound of the angry talk radio host soothe her mind.

When she reached the restaurant, Charlie pulled into the lot and stopped, but did not park. The front of the diner had a long picture window all across it, and she could see right inside. Though she had not seen them for years, it took her only a moment to spot her friends through the glass.

Jessica was easiest to pick out from the crowd. She always enclosed pictures with her letters, and right now she looked exactly like her last photo. Even seated, she was clearly taller than either of the boys, and very thin. Though Charlie could not see her whole outfit, she was wearing a loose white shirt with an embroidered vest, and she had a brimmed hat perched on her glossy, shoulder-length brown hair, with an enormous flower threatening to tip it off her head. She was gesturing excitedly about something as she spoke.

The two boys were sitting next to each other, facing her. Carlton looked like an older version of his red-headed childhood self. He still had a bit of a baby face, but his features had refined, and his hair was carefully tousled and held in place by some alchemical hair product. He was almost pretty, for a boy, and he wore a black workout shirt, though she doubted he'd ever worked out a day in his life. He slouched forward on the table, resting his chin in his hands. Beside him, John sat closest to the window. John had been the kind of child who got dirty before he even went outside: There would be paint on his shirt before the teacher handed out the watercolors, grass stains on his knees before they came near a playground, and dirt under his fingernails just after he washed his hands. Charlie knew it was him because it had to be, but he looked completely different. The grubbiness of childhood had been replaced by something crisp and clean. He was wearing a neatly pressed, light-green button-down shirt, the sleeves rolled up and the collar open, preventing him from looking too uptight. He was leaning back confidently in the booth, nodding enthusiastically, apparently absorbed in whatever Jessica was saying. The only concession to his former self was his hair, sticking up all over his head, and he had a five-o'clock shadow, a smug, adult version of the dirt he was always covered in as a kid.

Charlie smiled to herself. John had been something like her childhood crush, before either of them really understood what that meant. He gave her cookies from his Transformers lunchbox, and once in kindergarten he took the blame when she broke the glass jar that held colored beads for arts and crafts. She remembered the moment when it slipped from her hands, and she watched it fall. She could not have moved fast enough to catch it, but she would not have tried. She wanted to see it break. The glass hit the wood floor and shattered into a thousand pieces, and the beads scattered, many colored, among the shards. She thought it was beautiful, and then she started to cry. John had a note sent home to his parents, and when she told him "thank you" he had winked at her with an irony beyond his years and simply said, "For what?"

After that, John was allowed to come to her room. She let him play with Stanley and Theodore, watching anxiously the first time he learned to press the buttons and make them move. She would be crushed if he didn't like them, knowing instinctively that it would make her think less of him. They were her family. But John was fascinated as soon as he saw them; he loved her mechanical toys, and so she loved him. Two years later, behind a tree beside her father's workshop, she almost let him kiss her. And then *it* happened, and everything ended, at least for Charlie.

Charlie shook herself, forcing her mind back to the present. Looking again at Jessica's polished appearance, she glanced down at herself. Purple T-shirt, denim jacket, black jeans, and combat boots. It had felt like a good choice this morning, but now she wished she had chosen something else. *This is all you ever wear,* she reminded herself. She parked and locked the car behind her, even though people in Hurricane did not usually lock their cars. Then she went into the diner to meet her friends for the first time in ten years.

The warmth, noise, and light of the restaurant hit her in a wave as she entered. For a moment she was overwhelmed, but Jessica saw her pause in the doorway and shouted her name. Charlie smiled and went over.

"Hi," she said awkwardly, flicking her eyes at each of them but not fully making contact. Jessica scooted over on the red vinyl bench and patted the seat beside her.

"Here, sit," she said. "I was just telling John and Carlton about my glamorous life." She rolled her eyes as she said it, managing to convey both self-deprecation and the sense that her life was truly something exciting.

"Did you know Jessica lives in New York?" Carlton said. There was something careful about the way he spoke, like he was thinking about his words before he formed them. John was silent, but he smiled at Charlie anxiously.

Jessica rolled her eyes again, and with a flash of déjà vu Charlie suddenly recalled that this had been a habit even when they were children.

"Eight million people live in New York, Carlton. It's not exactly an achievement," Jessica said. Carlton shrugged.

"I've never been anywhere," he said.

"I didn't know you still lived in town," Charlie said.

"Where else am I going to live? My family has been here since 1896," he added, deepening his voice to mimic his father.

"Is that even true?" Charlie asked.

"I don't know," Carlton said in his own register. "Could be. Dad ran for mayor two years ago. I mean, he lost, but still, who runs for mayor?" He made a face. "I swear, the day I turn eighteen I am out of here."

"Where are you going to go?" John asked, looking seriously at Carlton.

Carlton met his eyes, just as serious for a moment. Abruptly, he broke away and pointed out the window, closing one eye as if to get his aim true. John raised an eyebrow as he looked out the window, trying to follow the line Carlton was pointing to. Charlie looked, too. Carlton wasn't pointing at anything. John opened his mouth to say something, but Carlton interrupted.

"Or," he said as he smoothly pointed in the opposite direction.

"Okay." John scratched his head, looking slightly embarrassed. "Anywhere, right?" he added with a laugh.

"Where's everyone else?" Charlie asked, peering out the window and searching the parking lot for new arrivals.

"Tomorrow," John said.

"They're coming tomorrow morning," Jessica jumped in to clarify. "Marla's bringing her little brother. Can you believe it?"

"Jason?" Charlie smiled. She remembered Jason as a little bundle of blankets with a tiny red face peeking out.

"I mean, who wants a baby around?" Jessica adjusted her hat primly.

"I'm pretty sure he's not a baby anymore," Charlie said, stifling a laugh.

"Practically a baby," Jessica said. "Anyway, I booked us a room at the motel down by the highway. It was all I could find. The boys are staying with Carlton."

"Okay," Charlie said. She was vaguely impressed by Jessica's organization, but she wasn't happy about the plan. She was loath to share a room with Jessica, who now seemed like a stranger. Jessica had become the kind of girl who intimidated her: polished and immaculate, speaking as though she had everything in life figured out. For a moment Charlie considered going back to her old house for the night, but as soon as she thought it, the idea repelled her. That house, at night, was no longer the province of the living.

Don't be dramatic, she scolded herself, but now John was speaking. He had a way of commanding attention with his voice, probably because he spoke less often than everyone else. He spent most of his time listening, but not out of reticence. He was gathering information, speaking only when he had wisdom or sarcasm to dispense. Often it was both at once.

"Does anyone know what's happening tomorrow?"

They were all silent for a moment, and the waitress took the opportunity to come over for their order. Charlie flipped quickly through the menu, her eyes not really focusing on the words. Her turn to order came much faster than she was expecting, and she froze.

"Um, eggs," she said at last. The woman's hard expression was still fixed on her, and she realized she had not finished. "Scrambled. Wheat toast," she added, and the woman went away. Charlie looked back down at the menu. She hated this about herself. When she was caught off guard she seemed to lose all ability to act or process what was going on around her. People were incomprehensible, their demands alien. *Ordering dinner shouldn't be hard,* she thought. The others had begun their conversation again, and she turned her attention to them, feeling like she had fallen behind.

"What do we even say to his parents?" Jessica was saying.

"Carlton, do you ever see them?" Charlie asked.

"Not really," he said. "Around, I guess. Sometimes."

"I'm surprised they stayed in Hurricane," Jessica said with a note of worldly disapproval in her voice.

Charlie said nothing, but she thought, *How could they not?*

His body had never been found. How could they not have secretly hoped he might come home, no matter how impossible they knew it was? How could they leave the only home Michael knew? It would mean really, finally giving up on him. Maybe that was what this scholarship was: an admission that he was never coming home.

Charlie was acutely aware that they were in a public place, where talking about Michael felt inappropriate. They were, in a sense, both insiders and outsiders. They had been closer to Michael, probably more than anyone in this restaurant, but, with the exception of Carlton, they were no longer from Hurricane. They did not belong.

She saw the tears falling on her paper placemat before she felt them, and she hurriedly wiped her eyes, looking down and hoping no one had noticed. When she looked up, John appeared to be studying his silverware, but she knew he had seen. She was grateful to him for not trying to offer comfort.

"John, do you still write?" Charlie asked.

John had declared himself "an author" when they were about six, having learned to read and write when he was four, a year ahead of the rest of them. At the age of seven, he completed his first "novel" and pressed his poorly spelled, inscrutably illustrated creation on his friends and family, demanding reviews. Charlie remembered that she had given him only two stars.

John laughed at the question. "I actually do my *E*s the right way these days," he said. "I can't believe you remember that. But I do actually, yeah." He stopped, clearly wanting to say more.

"What do you write?" Carlton obliged, and John looked down at his placemat, speaking mostly to the table.

"Um, short stories, mostly. I actually had one published last year. I mean, it was just in a magazine, nothing big." They all made suitable noises of being impressed, and he looked up again, embarrassed but pleased.

"What was the story about?" Charlie asked.

John hesitated, but before he could speak or decide not to, the waitress returned with their food. They had all ordered from the breakfast menu: coffee, eggs, and bacon; blueberry pancakes for Carlton. The brightly colored food looked hopeful, like a fresh start to the day. Charlie took a bite of her toast, and they all ate silently for a moment.

"Hey, Carlton," John said suddenly. "What ever happened to Freddy's anyway?"

There was a brief hush. Carlton looked nervously at Charlie, and Jessica stared up at the ceiling. John flushed red, and Charlie spoke hastily.

"It's okay, Carlton. I'd like to know, too."

Carlton shrugged, stabbing at his pancakes nervously with his fork.

"They built over it," he said.

"What did they build?" Jessica asked.

"Is there something else there now? Was it built over, or just torn down?" John asked. Carlton shrugged again, quick, like a nervous tic.

"Like I said, I don't know. It's too far back from the road to see, and I haven't exactly investigated. It might have been leased to someone, but I don't know what they did. It's all been blocked off for years, under construction. You can't even tell if the building is still there."

"So it could still be there?" Jessica asked with a spark of excitement breaking through.

"Like I said, I don't know," Carlton answered.

Charlie felt the diner's fluorescent lights glaring down on her face, suddenly too bright. She felt exposed. She had barely eaten, but she found herself rising from the booth, pulling a few crumpled bills from her pocket, and dropping them on the table.

"I'm going to go outside for a minute," she said. "Smoke break," she added hastily. *You don't smoke.* She chided herself for the clumsy lie as she made her way to the door, jostling past a family of four without saying "excuse me," and stepped out into the cool evening. She walked to her car and sat on the hood, the metal denting slightly under her weight. She took in breaths of the cool air as if it were water and closed her eyes. *You knew it would come up. You knew you would have to talk about it,* she reminded herself. She had practiced on the drive here, had forced herself to think back to happy memories, to smile and say, *"Remember when?"* She thought she was prepared for this. But of course she had been wrong. Why else would she have run out of the restaurant like a child?

"Charlie?"

She opened her eyes and saw John standing next to the car, holding her jacket out in front of him like an offering.

"You forgot your jacket," he said, and she made herself smile at him.

"Thanks," she said. She took it and draped it over her shoulders, then slid over on the car's hood for him to sit.

"Sorry about that," she said. In the dim lights of the parking lot she could still see him blush to the ears. He joined her on the car's hood, leaving a deliberate space between them.

"I haven't learned to think before I talk. I'm sorry." John watched the sky as a plane passed overhead.

Charlie smiled, this time unforced.

"It's okay. I knew it was going to come up; it had to. I just—it sounds stupid, but I never think about it. I don't let myself. No one knows what happened except my aunt, and we never talk about it. Then I come here, and suddenly it's everywhere. I was just surprised, that's all."

"Uh-oh." John pointed, and Charlie saw Jessica and Carlton hesitating in the doorway of the diner. She waved them over, and they came.

"Remember that time at Freddy's when the merry-go-round got stuck, and Marla and that mean kid Billy had to keep riding it until their parents plucked them off?" Charlie said.

John laughed, and the sound made her smile.

"Their faces were bright red, crying like babies." She covered her face, guilty that it was so funny to her.

There was a brief, surprised silence, then Carlton started laughing. "Then Marla puked all over him!"

"Sweet justice!" Charlie said.

"Actually, I think it was nachos," John added.

Jessica wrinkled her nose. "So gross. I never rode it again, not after that."

"Oh, come on, Jessica, they cleaned it," said Carlton. "I'm pretty sure kids puked all over that place; those wet floor signs weren't there for nothing. Right, Charlie?"

"Don't look at me," she said. "I never puked."

"We used to spend so much time there! Privileges of knowing the owner's daughter," Jessica said, looking at Charlie with mock accusation.

"I couldn't help who my dad was!" Charlie said, laughing.

Jessica looked thoughtful for a moment before she continued. "I mean, how could you have a better childhood than spending all day at Freddy Fazbear's Pizza?"

"I dunno," said Carlton. "I think that music got to me over the years." He hummed a few bars of the familiar song. Charlie dipped her head to it, recalling the tune.

"I loved those animals so much," Jessica said suddenly. "What's the proper term for them? Animals, robots, mascots?"

"I think those are all accurate." Charlie leaned back.

"Well, anyway, I used to go and talk to the bunny, what was his name?"

"Bonnie," Charlie said.

"Yeah," said Jessica. "I used to complain to him about my parents. I always thought he had an understanding look about him."

Carlton laughed. "Animatronic therapy! Recommended by six out of seven crazy people."

"Shut up," Jessica retorted. "I knew he wasn't real. I just liked talking to him."

Charlie smiled a little. "I remember that," she said. Jessica in her prim little dresses, her brown hair in two tight braids like a little kid out of an old book, walking up to the stage when the show was over, whispering earnestly to the life-size animatronic rabbit. If anyone came up beside her, she went instantly silent and still, waiting for them to go away so she could resume her one-sided conversations. Charlie had never talked to the animals at her father's restaurant or felt close to them like some kids seemed to; although she liked

27

them, they belonged to the public. She had her own toys, mechanical friends waiting for her at home, that belonged only to her.

"I liked Freddy," said John. "He always seemed the most relatable."

"You know, there are a lot of things about my childhood that I can't remember at all," Carlton said, "but I swear I can close my eyes and see every last detail of that place. Even the gum I used to stick under the tables."

"Gum? Yeah, right; those were boogers." Jessica took a tiny step away from Carlton.

He grinned. "I was seven; what do you want? You all picked on me back then. Remember when Marla wrote 'Carlton smells like feet' on the wall outside?"

"You did smell like feet." Jessica laughed with a sudden outburst.

Carlton shrugged, unperturbed. "I used to try to hide when it was time to go home. I wanted to be stuck in there overnight so I could have the whole place to myself."

"Yeah, you always kept everyone waiting," said John, "and you always hid under the same table."

Charlie spoke slowly, and when she did everyone turned to her, as though they had been waiting.

"Sometimes I feel like I remember every inch of it, like Carlton," she said. "But sometimes it's like I hardly remember it at all. It's all in pieces. Like, I remember the carousel, and that time it got stuck. I remember drawing on the place-mats. I remember little things: eating that greasy pizza, hugging Freddy in the summer and his yellow fur getting stuck all over my clothes. But a lot of it is like pictures, like it happened to someone else."

They were all looking at her oddly.

"Freddy was brown, right?" Jessica looked to the others for confirmation.

"I guess you really don't remember it that well after all," Carlton teased Charlie, and she laughed briefly.

"Right. I meant brown," she said. *Brown, Freddy was brown.* Of course he was; she could see him in her mind now. But somewhere in the depths of her recall, there was a flash of something else.

Carlton launched into another story, and Charlie tried to turn her attention to him, but there was something disturbing, worrisome, about that lapse in memory. *It was ten years ago; it's not like you've got dementia at seventeen*, she told herself, but it was such a basic detail to have misremembered. Out of the corner of her eye, she caught John looking at her, a pensive expression on his face, as though she had said something important.

"You really don't know what happened to it?" she asked Carlton with more urgency in her voice than she intended. He stopped talking, surprised. "Sorry," she said. "Sorry, I didn't mean to interrupt you."

"It's okay," he said. "But yeah—or no, I really don't know what happened."

"How can you not know? You live here."

"Charlie, come on," said John.

"It's not like I hang around that part of town. Things are different; the town has grown," Carlton said mildly, seeming unruffled by her outburst. "And I honestly don't look for reasons to go around there, you know? Why would I? There isn't any reason, not anymore."

"We could go there," John said suddenly, and Charlie's heart skipped.

Carlton looked nervously at Charlie. "What? Seriously, it's a mess. I don't know if you can even get to it."

Charlie found herself nodding. She felt as though she had spent the whole day weighed down by memory, seeing everything through a filter of years, and now she felt suddenly alert, her mind fully present. She wanted to go.

"Let's do it," she said. "Even if there's nothing there. I want to see." They were all silent. Suddenly, John smiled with a reckless confidence.

"Yeah. Let's do it."

CHAPTER TWO

Charlie pulled to a stop, feeling the soft give of dirt under her tires, and turned off the car. She got out and surveyed their surroundings. The sky was a rich, dark blue, the last trails of the sunset streaking off to the west. The parking lot was unpaved, and before them lay a sprawling monster of a building, a rising acre of glass and concrete. There were lamps in the parking lot that had never been used, and no lights shone out onto the lot. The building itself looked like an abandoned sanctuary, entombed in black trees amid the distant roar of civilization. She looked at Jessica in the passenger seat, who was craning her neck out the window.

"Is this the right place?" Jessica asked.

Charlie shook her head slowly, not quite certain what she was seeing. "I don't know," she whispered.

Charlie got out of the car and stood in silence as John and Carlton pulled up beside her.

"What is this?" John stepped out of the car cautiously and stared blankly at the monument. "Does anyone have a flashlight?" He looked at each of them.

Carlton held up his key chain and waved around the feeble glow of a penlight for a minute.

"Great," John muttered, walking away with resignation.

"Hold on a sec," Charlie said and went around to her trunk. "My aunt makes me carry around a bunch of stuff for emergencies."

Aunt Jen, loving but severe, had taught Charlie self-reliance above almost anything else. Before she let Charlie have her old blue Honda, she had insisted that Charlie know how to change a tire, check the oil, and know the basic parts of the engine. In the trunk, in a black box tucked in next to the jack, spare tire, and small crowbar; she had a blanket, a heavy police-issue flashlight, bottled water, granola bars, matches, and emergency flares. Charlie grabbed the flashlight; Carlton grabbed a granola bar.

Almost by silent agreement, they began to walk the building's perimeter, Charlie holding up the light in a steady beam in front of them. The building itself looked mostly finished, but the ground was all dirt and rock, uneven and soft. Charlie shone the light on the ground, where grass had grown patchy in the dirt, inches long.

"No one has been digging for a while," Charlie said.

The place was massive, and it took a long time to circum-navigate. It wasn't long before the rich blue of the evening was overtaken by a blanket of scattered silver clouds and stars. The surfaces of the building were all the same smooth, beige concrete, with windows too high up on the walls to see inside.

"Did they really build this whole thing and then just leave?" Jessica said.

"Carlton," said John, "you really don't know anything about what happened?"

Carlton shrugged expansively. "I told you, I knew there was construction, but I don't know anything else."

"Why would they do this?" John seemed almost paranoid, scouting the trees as though eyes might be looking back at him. "It just goes on and on." He squinted, gazing along the outside wall of the building, which seemed to stretch endlessly into the distance. He glanced back to the trees as if making sure they hadn't missed a building somehow. "No, it was here." He placed his hand on the drab concrete facing. "It's gone."

After a moment, he gestured to the others and began to walk back the way they came. Reluctantly, Charlie turned back, following the group. They kept going until they could see their cars again up ahead in the darkness.

"Sorry, guys; I hoped there would at least be something familiar," Carlton said exhaustedly.

"Yeah," Charlie said. She had known it would be, but seeing that Freddy's had been razed to the ground was still a shock. It was so paramount, sometimes, in her mind, that she wanted to get rid of it, wanted to scrub the memories—good and bad—from her head, as if they had never been. Now someone had scrubbed it from the landscape, and it felt like a violation. It should have been up to her. *Right,* she thought, *because you had the money to buy it and preserve it, like Aunt Jen did with the house.*

"Charlie?" John was saying her name, and it sounded like he was repeating it.

"Sorry," she said. "What were you saying?"

"Do you want to go inside?" Jessica asked.

Charlie was surprised they were only now considering this, but then again none of them was usually prone to criminal activity. The thought was a release, and she took a deep breath, speaking on her exhale. "Why not?" she said, almost laughing. She hefted the flashlight. Her arms were getting tired. "Anyone else want a turn?" She waved it back and forth like a pendulum.

Carlton grabbed it and took a moment to appreciate its weight.

"Why is this so heavy?" he said, passing it off to John. "Here you go."

"It's a police flashlight," Charlie said absently. "You can hit people with it."

Jessica wrinkled her nose. "Your aunt really wasn't kidding around, huh? Ever used it?"

"Not yet." Charlie winked and made a half-threatening glance at John, who returned an uncertain half smile, unsure how to react.

The wide entrances were sealed with hammered metal doors, no doubt intended to be temporary until construction was finished. Still, it wasn't difficult to find a way in, since many large mounds of gravel and sand scaled the walls, leading right up to the edges of the large, gaping windows.

"Not trying hard to keep people out," John said.

"What's anyone going to steal?" Charlie said, staring at the blank, towering walls.

They climbed the hills slowly, the gravel shifting and sliding beneath their feet as they went. Carlton reached the window first and peered through. Jessica looked over his shoulder.

"Can we drop down?" John asked.

"Yes," said Carlton.

"No," Jessica said at precisely the same time.

"I'll go," Charlie said. She felt reckless. Without looking through to see how far the fall was, she put her feet through the opening and let herself drop. She landed, knees bent; the impact rocked her, but it did not hurt. She looked up at her friends staring down. "Oh. Hang on!" Charlie called, pulling a short stepladder from a wall nearby and setting it under the window. "Okay," she said. "Come on!"

They dropped down one by one, and looked around them. Inside was an atrium, or maybe it would have become a food court, with metal benches and plastic tables scattered around, some bolted to the floor. The ceiling rose up high above them, with a glass roof where they could see the stars peering down at them.

"Very postapocalyptic," Charlie joked, her voice echoing in the open space.

Jessica sang a brief, wordless scale suddenly, startling them all into silence. Her voice rang out pure and clear, something beautiful in the emptiness.

"Very nice, but let's not call too much attention to ourselves," John said.

"Right," Jessica said, still very happy with herself. As they walked on, Carlton swept up and took her arm.

"Your voice is amazing," he said.

"It's just good acoustics," Jessica said, attempting humility but not meaning a word of it.

They walked the empty halls, peering into each of the massive cavities where a department store might have been. Some parts of the mall had been almost finished, while others were in shambles. Some hallways were littered with piles of dusty concrete bricks and stacks of wood; others were lined with glass-paneled storefronts, lights hanging in perfect rows above their heads.

"It's like a lost city," John said.

"Like Pompeii," said Jessica, "just without the volcano."

"No," Charlie said, "there's nothing here." The whole place had a sterile feel to it. It was not abandoned—it had never sustained life at all.

She looked in a store window across from her, one of the few with glass, wondering what would have been displayed. She imagined mannequins, dressed in bright clothing, but when she tried to picture them, all she could see was blank faces, concealing something. She suddenly felt out of place, unwelcomed by the building itself. Charlie began to feel restless, some of the luster wearing off the adventure. They had come; Freddy's was gone, and so was the shrine she had kept in her thoughts, where she could still find Michael playing where she last saw him.

John stopped suddenly, turning off the flashlight as carefully as he could. He put a finger to his lips, motioning for silence. He gestured back the way they had come. In the distance, they saw a small light bobbing in the darkness like a ship in the fog.

"Someone else is here," he hissed.

"A night guard, maybe?" Carlton whispered.

"Why would an abandoned building need a guard?" Charlie wondered.

"Kids probably come here to party," Carlton said, then grinned. "I would have come here to party, too, if I'd known about it, or if I partied."

"Okay, well, let's backtrack slowly," John said. "Jessica . . ." he started, then made a *zip-it* motion across his lips.

They continued down the hallway, this time with only the dimmer light of Carlton's key chain.

"Wait." Jessica stopped with a whisper, looking intently at the walls surrounding them. "Something's not right."

"Yeah, no giant pretzels. I know." Carlton seemed sincere. Jessica waved a hand at him impatiently.

"No, something isn't right about the architecture." She took several steps back, trying to see the whole of it. "Something is definitely not right," she repeated. "It's bigger on the outside."

"Bigger on the outside?" Charlie repeated, sounding puzzled.

"I mean there's a big difference between where the inside wall is and where the outside wall is. Look." Jessica ran along a length of wall between where two stores would have been.

"There would have been a store here and a store there." John pointed to the obvious, not understanding the problem.

"But there's something in the middle!" Jessica exclaimed, beating her hands against an empty portion of the wall. "This part juts out into the parking lot like the stores on each side, but there's no way into it."

"You're right." Charlie started walking toward Jessica, studying the walls. "There should be another entrance here."

"And"—Jessica dropped her voice so that only Charlie could hear her—"about the same size as Freddy's, don't you think?" Charlie's eyes widened, and she took a quick step back from Jessica.

"What are you two whispering about?" Carlton stepped closer.

"We're talking about you," Jessica said sharply, and they walked into one of the vacant department stores that seemed to sandwich the sealed space. "Come on," she said, "let's take a look." They started combing the wall as a group, clustered around the tiny light.

Charlie was not sure what to hope for. Aunt Jen had warned her about coming back. She didn't encourage Charlie to skip the memorial, not directly, but she wasn't pleased that Charlie was returning to Hurricane.

Just be careful, Aunt Jen had said. *Some things, some memories, are best left undisturbed.*

Is that why you kept Dad's house? Charlie thought now. *Is that why you kept paying for it, leaving it untouched like some kind of shrine, but never visiting?*

"Hey!" John was gesturing wildly, running inside to catch up to the rest of them. "Hide!"

The light was out in the hall again, bobbing up and down, and it was coming closer. Charlie glanced around. They were already too deep inside the massive store to get out in time, and there seemed to be nowhere to hide.

"Here, here!" Jessica whispered. There was a break in the wall beside a rig of scaffolding, and they hurried into it, squeezing past stacks of open boxes and sheets of plastic hanging from the ceiling.

They made their way down what appeared to be a make-shift hallway just on the other side of the department store wall. It was really more like an alley; it was incongruous with the rest of the mall, not shiny and new but dank and musty. One wall was made of the same concrete as the outside of the building, though it was rough and unfinished, and the other was exposed brick, some parts faded smooth with age, others with the mortar crumbling, leaving chinks and holes. Heavy wooden shelves of cleaning equipment stood against the wall, listing to the side, their boards sinking under the weight of old paint cans and mysterious buckets. Something was dripping from uncovered pipes overhead, leaving puddles that they all stepped carefully around. A mouse scuttled by, almost running over Carlton's foot. Carlton made a strangled sound, hand over his mouth.

They crouched down behind one of the wooden shelving units, pressing up against the wall. Charlie doused the light and waited.

She took shallow breaths, perfectly still, watching and wishing she had picked a better position to freeze into. After a few minutes, her legs started to feel numb under her, and Carlton was so close that she could smell the light, pleasant scent of his shampoo. "That's nice," she whispered.

"Thanks," Carlton said, knowing immediately what she was referring to. "It comes in Ocean Breeze and Tropical Paradise. I prefer Ocean Breeze, but it dries the scalp."

"Hush!" John hissed.

Charlie wasn't sure why she was so worried. It was just a night guard, and at the worst they would be asked to leave, maybe yelled at a little. She had an overblown aversion to getting in trouble.

The bobbing light came closer. Charlie was acutely aware of her body, holding every muscle motionless. Suddenly she could make out a thin figure leaning in from the great room outside. He shone his light in a long beam down the hallway, sweeping it up and down the walls. *He's got us,* Charlie thought, but inexplicably he turned and went, apparently satisfied.

They waited another few minutes, but there was nothing. He was gone. They all moved slowly out of their crouched positions, stretching limbs that had gone to sleep. Carlton shook one foot vigorously until he could stand on it. Charlie looked down at Jessica, who was still hunched over, as if frozen in time.

"Jessica, are you okay?" she whispered.

Jessica looked up, smiling.

"You won't believe this."

She was pointing at the wall, and Charlie leaned over to see. There, etched in the worn brick, were clumsy letters, almost illegible in a child's handiwork:

Carlton smells like feet.

"You have to be kidding me," John whispered in awe, turning to face the wall and placing both hands against it. "I recognize these bricks." He laughed. "These are the same bricks!" His smile faded. "They didn't tear it down; they built around it."

"It's still here!" Jessica unsuccessfully tried to keep her voice down. "There has to be a way in," she added, her eyes wide with an almost childish excitement.

Charlie shone the flashlight up and down the hallway, playing the light off each wall, but there was no break, no door.

"There was a back door to Freddy's," John said. "Marla wrote that right next to the back door, right?"

"Why didn't they just knock it down?" Charlie pondered.

"Does this hallway just lead nowhere?" Jessica said, puzzled.

"It's the story of my life," Carlton said lightly.

"Wait . . ." Charlie ran her fingers along the edge of a shelf, peering through the odds and ends crammed onto it. The wall behind it looked different; it was metal, not brick.

"Right here." She stepped back and looked at the others. "Help me move it."

John and Jessica pressed against one side in a unified effort, and she and Carlton pulled on the other. It was immensely heavy, laden with cleaning supplies and large buckets of nails and tools, but it slid farther down the hall almost easily, without incident.

Jessica stepped back, breathing hard. "John, give me the big light again." He handed it over, and she turned it back on, aiming where the shelf had stood. "This is it," she said.

It was metal and rusting, spattered with paint, a stark contrast to the walls around it. There was only a hole where the handle had been; someone must have removed it so the shelf could lie flush against the door.

Silently Charlie handed the flashlight back to John, and he held it above her head so she could see. She slipped around the others and tried to squeeze her fingers into the hole where the doorknob once was, trying to pull it open to no avail.

"It's not going to open," she said. John was behind her, peering over her shoulder.

"Just a second." He squeezed himself into the space beside her and knelt carefully. "I don't think it's locked or anything," he said. "I think it's just rusty. Look at it."

The door extended all the way to the floor, its bottom ragged and unfinished. The hinges were on the other side, and the edges were caked in rust. It looked as though it had not been opened in years. John and Charlie pulled on it together, and it moved a fraction of an inch.

"Yay!" Jessica exclaimed, almost shouting, then covered her mouth. "Sorry," she said in a whisper. "Containing my excitement."

They took turns pulling on it, leaning over one another, the metal scraping their fingers. The door held for a long moment, and then it came loose under their weight, swinging open slowly with an unearthly screech. Charlie looked nervously over her shoulder, but the guard did not appear. The door opened only about a foot wide, and they went one by one, until all four were through.

Inside, the air changed, and they all stopped short. Ahead of them was a dark hallway, familiar to them all.

"Is this . . . ?" Jessica whispered, not taking her eyes from the dark expanse.

It's here, Charlie thought. She held out her hand for the flashlight, and John handed it to her wordlessly. She shone the light ahead of them, sweeping the walls. They were covered in children's drawings, crayon on yellowing, curling paper. She started forward, and the others followed, feet shuffling on old tile.

It seemed to take forever to traverse the hall, or perhaps it was just that they were moving slowly, with methodical, deliberate steps. Eventually the hallway opened up into a larger expanse—the dining room. It was just as they remembered it, completely preserved. The flashlight beam bounced off a thousand little things reflective, glittered, or topped with foil ribbon.

The tables were still in place, covered in their silver-and-white checked cloths; the chairs were pulled up to them haphazardly, some tables with too many and others with too few. It looked as though the room had been abandoned in the middle of the lunch hour: Everyone had gotten up expecting to return, but never did. They walked in cautiously, breathing cold, stale air that had been trapped inside for a decade. The whole restaurant gave off a sense of abandonment—no one was coming back. There was a small merry-go-round barely visible in the distant corner, with four child-size ponies still at rest from their last song. In an instant, Charlie froze in place, as did the others.

There they were. Eyes stared back from the dark, large and lifeless. An illogical panic pulsed through her; time held still. No one spoke; no one breathed, as though a predatory animal was stalking them. But as the moments passed, the fear waned, until she was back again, as a child, and with old friends, separated from one another for far too long. Charlie walked toward the eyes in a straight line. Behind her the others were motionless; hers were the only footsteps. As Charlie walked, she touched the cold back of an old party chair without looking at it, guiding it out of her path. She took one final step, and the eyes in the dark became clear. It was them. Charlie smiled.

"Hi," she whispered, too soft for the others to hear.

Before her stood three animatronic animals: a bear, a rabbit, and a chicken, all standing as tall as adults, maybe taller. Their bodies were segmented like artists' models, each limb made of distinct, squarish pieces, separate at the joints. They belonged to the restaurant, or maybe the restaurant belonged to them, and there had been a time when everyone knew them by name. There was Bonnie, the rabbit. His fur was a bright blue, his squared-off muzzle held a permanent smile, and his wide and chipped pink eyes were thick-lidded, giving him a perpetually worn-out expression. His ears stuck up straight, crinkling over at the top, and his large feet splayed out for balance. He held a red bass guitar, blue paws poised to play, and around his neck was a bow tie that matched the instrument's fiery color.

Chica the Chicken was more bulky and had an apprehensive look, thick black eyebrows arching over her purple eyes and her beak slightly open, revealing teeth, as she held out a cupcake on a platter. The cupcake itself was somewhat disturbing, with eyes set into its pink frosting and teeth hanging out over the cake, a single candle sticking out the top.

"I always expected the cupcake to jump off the plate." Carlton gave a half laugh and cautiously stepped up to

46

Charlie's side. "They seem taller than I remember," he added in a whisper.

"That's because you never got this close as a kid." Charlie smiled, at ease, and stepped closer.

"You were busy hiding under tables," Jessica said from behind them, still some distance away.

Chica wore a bib around her neck with the words LET'S EAT! set out in purple and yellow against a confetti-covered background. A tuft of feathers stuck up in the middle of her head.

Standing between Bonnie and Chica was Freddy Fazbear himself, namesake of the restaurant. He was the most genial looking of the three, seeming at ease where he was. A robust, if lean, brown bear, he smiled down at the audience, holding a microphone in one paw, sporting a black bow tie and top hat. The only incongruity in his features was the color of his eyes, a bright blue that surely no bear had ever had before him. His mouth hung open, and his eyes were partially closed, as though he had been frozen in song.

Carlton drew closer to the stage until his knees pressed against the rim of it. "Hey, Freddy," he whispered. "Long time no see."

He reached out and grabbed at the microphone, wiggling it to see if he could get it loose.

"Don't!" Charlie blurted, looking up into Freddy's fixed gaze as though making sure he hadn't noticed.

Carlton pulled his hand back like he had touched something hot. "Sorry."

"Come on," John said, cracking a smile. "Don't you want to see the rest of the place?"

They spread out across the room, peering into corners and carefully trying doors, acting as though everything might be breakable to the touch. John went over to the small carousel, and Carlton disappeared into the dark arcade off the main room.

"I remember it being a lot brighter and noisier in here." Carlton smiled as though at home again, running his hands over the aging knobs and flat plastic buttons. "I wonder if my high scores are still in there," he muttered to himself.

To the left of the stage was a small hallway. Half hoping no one would notice where she had gone, Charlie started down it silently as the others occupied themselves with their own curiosities. At the end of the short, plain corridor was her father's office. It had been Charlie's favorite place in the restaurant. She liked to play with her friends in the main area, but she loved the singular privilege of coming back here when her father was doing paperwork. She paused outside the closed door, her hand poised over the knob, remembering. Most of the room was filled with his desk, his filing cabinets, and small boxes of uninteresting parts. In one corner was a smaller filing cabinet, painted a salmon color that Charlie had always insisted was pink. That had been

Charlie's. The bottom drawer held toys and crayons, and the top had what she liked to call "my paperwork." It was mostly coloring books and drawings, but occasionally she would go over to her father's desk and try to copy down whatever he was writing in a childish, crayoned hand. Charlie tried the door, but it was locked. *Better this way,* she thought. The office was personal, and she did not really want it opened tonight.

She headed back into the main dining room and found John looking pensively at the merry-go-round. He eyed her with curiosity but did not ask where she had gone.

"I used to love this thing." Charlie smiled, approaching warmly. Yet now the painted figures seemed odd and lifeless to her.

John made a face, as though he knew what she was thinking.

"Not the same," he said. He rubbed his hand over the top of a polished pony as though to scratch it behind the ear. "Just not the same," he repeated, removing his hand and gazing elsewhere. Charlie glanced over to see where the others were—in the arcade, she could see Jessica and Carlton wandering among the games.

The consoles stood still and unlit like massive tombstones, their screens blank. "I never liked playing the games," Jessica said, smiling. "They moved too fast, and just when I'd start to figure out what to do, I'd die and it would be someone else's turn." She wiggled a joystick that squeaked from neglect.

"They were rigged anyway," Carlton said with a wink.

"When's the last time you played one of these?" Jessica asked, peering closely into one of the screens to see what image was burned into it from too many years of use. Carlton was busy rocking a pinball machine back and forth, trying to get a ball to come loose.

"Uh, there's a pizza place I visit sometimes." He set the table back on four legs carefully and glanced at Jessica. "But it's no Freddy's," he added.

John was roaming through the dining room again amid the tables, flicking the stars and spirals hanging overhead. He plucked a red party hat from the table, stretched the rubber band hanging loosely from its base, and snapped it around his head, red-and-white tassels hanging down over his face.

"Oh, let's check out the kitchen," he said. Charlie followed as he bounded off toward it.

Although the kitchen had been off-limits to her friends, she'd spent a lot of time there, so much so that the chefs chased her out by name, or at least by the name they heard her father call her: Charlotte. John overheard someone calling her Charlotte one day when they were in kindergarten and persisted in teasing her with it constantly. He could always get a rise out of her with that. It wasn't that Charlie didn't like her full name, but Charlie was who she was to the world. Her father called her Charlotte, and it was like a secret between them, something no one else was allowed to share. The day she left Hurricane for good, the day they said good-bye, John had hesitated.

"Bye, Charlie," he said. In their cards, letters, and phone calls, he had never called her Charlotte again. She never asked why, and he never told her.

The kitchen was still fully stocked with pots and pans, but it held little interest for Charlie in the midst of her memories. She headed back out into the open space of the dining room, and John followed. At the same time, Jessica and Carlton stumbled out of the arcade, tripping into each other as they crossed the thresholds between rooms in the dark.

"Anything interesting?" John asked.

"Uh, a gum wrapper, thirty cents, and Jessica, so no, not really," Carlton said. Jessica playfully gave him a punch in the shoulder.

"Oh, have we all forgotten?" Jessica gave an evil smile, pointing to another hallway on the opposite side of the dining room. She headed toward it swiftly before anyone could answer, and they followed her. The hallway was long and narrow, and the farther they went, the less the flashlight seemed to illuminate. At last the passage opened out into a small room for private parties, set up with its own tables and chairs. As they entered, there was a collective hush. There in front of them was a small stage, the curtain drawn. A sign was strung across the front. OUT OF ORDER, it read in neat, handwritten letters. They stood still for a minute, then Jessica went up to it and poked the sign.

"Pirate's Cove," she said. "Ten years later and it's still out of order."

Don't touch it, Charlie thought.

"I had one birthday back here," John said. "It was out of order then, too." He took hold of the edge of the curtain and rubbed the glittered fabric between his fingers.

No, Charlie wanted to say again, but stopped. *You're being silly*, she chided herself.

"Do you think he's still back there?" Jessica said playfully, threatening to make the reveal with one giant swing on the curtain.

"I'm sure he is." John gave a false smile, seeming uncomfortable for the first time.

Yes, he's still there, Charlie thought. She stepped back cautiously, suddenly becoming aware of the drawings and posters surrounding them like spiders on the wall. Charlie's flashlight carefully inched from picture to picture, all depicting different variations of the same character: a large and energetic pirate fox with a patch over one eye and a hook for a hand, usually swinging in to deliver a pizza to hungry children.

"This is the room where you were the one hiding under tables," Jessica said to Charlie, trying to laugh. "But you're a big girl now, right?" Jessica climbed up on the stage unsteadily, almost losing her footing. John reached out a hand to steady her as she righted herself. She giggled nervously, looking down at the others as though for guidance, than grabbed hold of the tasseled edge of the fabric. She waved her other hand in front of her face as dust fell from the cloth.

"Maybe this isn't a good idea?" She laughed, but there was an edge to her voice, like she really meant it, and she looked down at the stage for a moment, as though poised to climb back down. Still, she didn't move, taking the edge of the curtain again.

"Wait," John said. "Can you hear that?"

They were all dead quiet, and in the silence Charlie could hear them all breathing. John's breaths were deliberate and calm, Jessica's quick and nervous. As she thought about it, her own breathing began to feel odd, like she had forgotten how to do it.

"I don't hear anything," she said.

"Me neither," Jessica echoed. "What is it?"

"Music. It's coming from—" He gestured back the way they had come.

"From the stage?" Charlie cocked her head to the side. "I don't hear it."

"It's like a music box," he said. Charlie and Jessica listened carefully, but their blank expressions didn't change. "It stopped, I guess." John returned his gaze forward.

"Maybe it was an ice cream truck," Jessica whispered.

"Hey, that wouldn't be so bad right now." John appreciated the levity.

Jessica turned her attention back to the curtain, but John began to hum a tune to himself. "It reminded me of something," he mumbled.

"Okay, here I go!" Jessica announced. She did not move. Charlie found her eyes drawn to Jessica's hand on the curtain, her pink, manicured nails pale against the dark, glittery fabric. It was almost like the hushed moment in a theater crowd, when the lights went dark but the curtain had not yet risen. They were all still, all anticipating, but they were not watching a play, no longer playing a game. All the mirth had gone out of Jessica's face; her cheekbones stood out stark in the shadows, and her eyes looked grim as though the simple thing she was about to do might be of terrible consequence. As Jessica hesitated, Charlie realized her hand hurt; she was making a fist so tight her nails dug into her flesh, but she could not force her grip to loosen.

A crash sounded from back the way they came, a cascading, clanging noise ringing out and filling the whole space. John and Charlie froze, meeting each other's eyes in sudden panic. Jessica dropped the curtain and leaped off the stage, bumping into Charlie and knocking the light out of her hands.

"Where's the way out?!" she exclaimed, and John came over to help. They hurriedly searched the walls, and Charlie chased the light beam spiraling across the floor. Just as they were all back to their feet, Carlton came trotting in.

"I knocked over a bunch of pots in the kitchen!" he exclaimed, an apology amid the panic.

"I thought you were with us," Charlie said.

"I wanted to see if there was any food left," Carlton said, not making it clear if he'd found anything or not.

"Seriously?" John laughed.

"That guard might have heard," Jessica said anxiously. "We have to get out of here."

They started for the door, and Jessica started running. The rest took off after her, picking up speed as they reached the hallway until they were racing as though something were behind them.

"Run, run!" John called out, and they all burst into giggles, the panic feigned but the urgency real.

They squeezed back through the door one by one and pushed it shut with the same painful squeal, Carlton and John leaning on it until it sealed. They all took hold of the shelf, hefting it back into place and replacing the tools so that it appeared undisturbed.

"Look good?" Jessica said, and John tugged her arm, guiding her away.

They made their way quickly but carefully back the way they came using only Carlton's penlight, back through the empty hallways and the open atrium to the parking lot. The guard's light did not appear again.

"Little anticlimactic," Carlton said with disappointment, checking back one more time in hopes they were being chased.

"Are you kidding?" Charlie said as she went to her car, already pulling the keys free from her pocket. She felt as though something locked deep inside her had been disturbed, and she was not sure if that was a good thing or not.

"That was fun!" John exclaimed, and Jessica laughed.

"That was terrifying!" she cried.

"It can be both," Carlton said, grinning widely. Charlie began to laugh, and John joined in.

"What?" Jessica said. Charlie shook her head, still laughing a little.

"It's just . . . we're all exactly the same as we were. I mean, we're totally different and older and everything. But we're the same. You and Carlton sound exactly like you did when we were six."

"Right," Jessica said, rolling her eyes again, but John nodded.

"I know what you mean," he said. "And so does Jessica, she just doesn't like to admit it." He glanced back at the mall. "Is everybody sure that guard didn't see us?"

"We can outrun him now," Carlton said reasonably, his hand resting on the car.

"I guess," John said, but he did not sound convinced.

"You haven't changed, either, you know," Jessica said with a certain satisfaction. "Stop looking for problems where there aren't any."

"Still," John said, glancing back again. "We should get out of here. I don't want to push our luck."

"See you all tomorrow, then?" Jessica said as they parted ways. Carlton gave a little wave over his shoulder.

Charlie's heart sank a little as Jessica settled herself into the passenger seat, tidily buckling herself in. She had not been looking forward to this. It wasn't that she didn't like Jessica, just that being alone with her was uncomfortable. She still wasn't much more than a stranger. Yet Charlie was still exhilarated from the night's adventure, and the lingering adrenaline gave her a new confidence. She smiled at Jessica. After tonight, they suddenly had something very much in common.

"Do you know which way the motel is?" she asked, and Jessica nodded and reached for the purse down at her feet. It was small and black with a long strap, and on the drive to the construction site Charlie had already seen her remove a lip gloss, a mirror, a pack of breath mints, a sewing kit, and a tiny hairbrush. Now she pulled out a small notebook and pen. Charlie smiled.

"Sorry, how much stuff do you have in that thing?" she asked, and Jessica looked at her with a grin.

"The secrets of The Purse must not be disclosed," she said playfully, and they both laughed. Jessica started reading Charlie the directions, and Charlie obeyed, turning left and right without paying much attention to her surroundings.

Jessica had already checked in, so they went straight to their room, a small beige box of a room with two double beds covered in shiny brown spreads. Charlie set her bags on the bed closest to the door, and Jessica went to the window.

"As you can see, I splurged on the room with the view," she said and flung the curtains open dramatically to reveal two Dumpsters and a dried-out hedge. "I want to have my wedding here."

"Right," Charlie said, amused. Jessica's prim demeanor and fashion-model looks made it easy to forget that she was smart as well. As a child she remembered being slightly intimidated every time they got together to play before realizing after the first few minutes how much she liked Jessica. She wondered if it was hard for Jessica to make friends, looking the way she did, but it wasn't the kind of thing you could really ask someone.

Jessica flopped down on the bed, lying across it to face

Charlie. "So tell me about you," she said confidentially, mocking a talk-show host or someone's nosy mother.

Charlie shrugged awkwardly, put on the spot. "What does that mean?" she said.

Jessica laughed. "I don't know! What an awful thing to ask, right? I mean, how do you answer that? Um, how about school? Any cute boys?"

Charlie lay down across the bed, mimicking Jessica's position. "Cute boys? What are we, twelve?"

"Well?" Jessica said impatiently.

"I don't know," she said. "Not really." Her class was too small. She had known most of the people in it since she moved in with Aunt Jen, and dating anyone, liking them "like that," seemed forced and altogether unappealing. She told Jessica as much. "Most of the girls, if they want to date, they date older guys," she said.

"And you don't have an older guy?" Jessica teased.

"Nah," Charlie said. "I figured I'd wait around for our batch to grow up."

"Right!" Jessica burst out laughing before quickly thinking of something to share. "Last year there was this guy, Donnie," she said. "I was gaga for him, like, really. He was so sweet to everyone. He wore all black all the time, and he had this black curly hair so thick all I could think about when I sat behind him was burying my face in it. I was so distracted I ended up with an A minus in trig. He was super artistic, a poet, and he carried around one of those black leather notebooks, and he was always scribbling something in it, but he would never show anybody." She sighed dreamily. "I figured if I could get him to show me his poetry, I would really come to know his soul, you know?"

"So did he ever?" Charlie said.

"Oh yeah," she said, nodding emphatically. "I asked him out finally, you know, 'cause he was shy and he was never gonna ask me, and we went to the movies and made out a little, and then we went and hung out on the roof of his apartment building and I told him all about how I want to study ancient civilizations and go on archaeological digs and stuff. And he showed me his poems."

"And did you come to know his soul?" Charlie said, excited to be included in girl talk, something she felt like she'd never really gotten to participate in before. Charlie nodded eagerly. *But not too eagerly.* She calmed herself as Jessica scooted forward on the bed to whisper.

"The poems were *awful*. I didn't know it was possible to be both melodramatic and boring at the same time. I mean, like, just reading them made me embarrassed for him." She covered her face in her hands. Charlie laughed.

"What did you do?"

"What could I do? I told him it wasn't gonna work out and went home."

"Wait, right after you read his poetry?"

"I still had the notebook in my hand."

"Oh no, Jessica, that's awful! You must have broken his heart!"

"I know! I felt so bad, but it was like the words just came out of my mouth. I couldn't stop myself."

"Did he ever speak to you again?"

"Oh yeah, he's perfectly nice. But now he takes statistics and economics and wears sweater vests."

"You broke him!" Charlie threw a pillow at Jessica, who sat up and caught it.

"I know! He'll probably be a millionaire stockbroker instead of a starving artist, and it's all my fault." She grinned. "Come on, he'll thank me someday."

Charlie shook her head. "Do you really want to be an archaeologist?"

"Yeah," Jessica said.

"Huh," said Charlie. "Sorry, I thought—" She shook her head. "Sorry, that is really cool."

"You thought I'd want to do something in fashion," Jessica said.

"Well, yeah."

"It's okay," Jessica said. "I did, too. I mean, I do, I love fashion, but there's only so much to it, you know? I think it's amazing to think about how people lived a thousand years ago, or two thousand, or ten. They were just like us, but so different. I like to imagine living in other times, other places, wonder who I would have been. Anyway, what about you?"

Charlie rolled over onto her back, looking up at the ceiling. The tiles were made of loose, stained Styrofoam, and the one above her head was askew. *I hope there aren't any bugs up in there,* she thought.

"I don't know," she said slowly. "I think it's really cool that you know who you want to be, but I have just never had that kind of a plan."

"Well, it's not like you have to figure it out now," Jessica said.

"Maybe," Charlie said. "But I don't know, you know what you want to do, John's known since he could hold a pencil that he wanted to be a writer and he's already getting published, even Carlton—I don't know what he has planned, but you can just see that there's a scheme brewing behind all his kidding around. But I just don't have that kind of direction."

"It really doesn't matter," Jessica said. "I don't think most people know at our age. Plus, I might change my mind, or not get into college, or something. You never know what's going to happen. Hey, I'm gonna get changed. I want to get some sleep."

She went into the bathroom, and Charlie stayed where she was, gazing at the sorry-looking ceiling. She supposed it was becoming a defect, her earnest refusal to consider the past or future. *Live in the present moment,* her Aunt Jen said often, and Charlie had taken it to heart. *Don't dwell on the past; don't worry about things that may never happen.* In eighth grade she had taken a shop class, vaguely hoping the mechanical work might spark something of her father's talent, might unleash some inherited passion lying latent within her, but it had not. She had made a clumsy-looking birdhouse for the backyard. She never took another shop class, and the birdhouse only attracted one squirrel who promptly knocked it down.

Jessica came out of the bathroom wearing pink striped pajamas, and Charlie went in to get ready for bed, changing and brushing her teeth hurriedly. When she came out again, Jessica was already under the covers with the light by her bed turned off. Charlie turned hers off, too, but the light from the parking lot still shone in from the window, somehow filtering past the Dumpsters.

Charlie stared up at the ceiling again, her hands behind her head.

"Do you know what's going to happen tomorrow?" she asked.

"I don't really know," Jessica said. "I know it's a ceremony at the school."

"Yeah, I know that," Charlie said. "Are we going to have to do anything? Like, do they want us to speak?"

"I don't think so," Jessica said. "Why, do you want to say something?"

"No, I was just wondering."

"Do you ever think about him?" Jessica asked.

"Sometimes. I try not to," Charlie said half-truthfully. She had sealed off the subject of Michael in her mind, locked him tight behind a mental wall she never touched. It wasn't an effort to avoid the subject; in fact, it was an effort to think of him now. "What about you?" she asked Jessica.

"Not really," she said. "It's weird, right? Something happens, and it's the worst thing you can ever imagine, and it's just burned into you at the time, like it's going to go on forever. And then the years go by, and it's just another thing that happened. Not like it's not important, or terrible, but it's in the past, just as much as everything else. You know?"

"I guess," Charlie said. But she did know. "I just try not to think about those things."

"Me too. You know I just went to a funeral last week?"

"I'm sorry," Charlie said, sitting up. "Are you okay?"

"Yeah, I'm fine," Jessica said. "I barely even knew him; he was just an old relative who lived three states away. I think I met him once, but I hardly remember it. We mostly went for my mom's sake. But it was at an old-fashioned funeral parlor, like in the movies, with an open coffin. And we all walked by the coffin, and when it was my turn I looked at him, and he could have been sleeping, you know? Just calm and restful, like people always say dead people look. There was nothing that I could have pointed out that made me think *dead*, if you asked me; every feature of his face looked the same as if he were alive. His skin was the same; his hair was the same as if he were alive. But he wasn't alive, and I just knew it. I would have known it immediately, even if he wasn't, you know, in a coffin."

"I know what you mean. There is something about them when they're . . . ," Charlie said softly.

"It sounds stupid when I say it. But when I looked at him, he looked so alive, and yet I knew, just *knew* that he wasn't. It made my skin crawl."

"That's the worst thing, isn't it?" Charlie said. "Things that act alive but aren't."

"What?" Jessica said.

"I mean things that look alive but aren't," Charlie said quickly. "We should get some sleep," she said. "Did you set the alarm?"

"Yes," Jessica said. "Good night."

"Night."

Charlie knew sleep was still a long way off. She knew what Jessica meant, probably better than Jessica did. The artificial shine in eyes that followed you as you moved, just like a real person's would. The slight lurch of realistic animals who did not move the way a living thing should. The occasional programming glitch that made a robot appear to have done something new, creative. Her childhood had been filled with them; she had grown up in the strange gap between life and not–life. It had been her world. It had been her father's world. Charlie closed her eyes. *What did that world do to him?*

CHAPTER THREE

*T*hud. *Thud. Thud.*

Charlie startled out of sleep, disoriented. Something was banging on her door, trying to force its way in.

"Oh, for goodness' sake," Jessica said grumpily, and Charlie blinked and sat up.

Right. The motel. Hurricane. Someone was knocking on the door. As Jessica went to answer it, Charlie got out of bed and looked at the clock. It was 10:00 a.m. She looked out the window at the bright new day. She had slept worse than usual, not nightmares, but dark dreams she could not quite remember, things that stuck with her just beyond the back of her mind, images she could not catch.

"Charlieeeee!" someone was screeching. Charlie went to the door and found herself immediately enveloped in a hug,

Marla's plump arms gripping her like a vise. Charlie hugged her back, tighter than she meant to. When Marla let go, she stepped back, grinning. Marla's moods had always been so intense they were contagious, spreading out to whoever was in her path. When she was gloomy, a pall fell over all her friends, the sun gone behind her cloud. When she was happy, like now, it was impossible to avoid the lift of her joy. She was always breathless, always slightly scattered, always giving the impression that she was running late, though she almost never was. Marla was wearing a loose dark-red blouse, and it suited her well, setting off her fair skin and dark-brown hair.

Charlie had kept in better touch with Marla than the others. Marla was the type who made it easy to stay friends, even at a distance. Even as a little kid she was always sending letters and postcards, undeterred if Charlie didn't respond to every one. She was resolutely positive and assumed that everyone liked her unless they made it clear otherwise, using the proper expletives. Charlie admired it about her—she herself, though not shy, was always calculating: *Does that person like me? Are they just being polite? How do people tell the difference?* Marla had come to visit her once when they were twelve. She had charmed Charlie's aunt and made fast friends with her school friends while still making it abundantly clear that she was *Charlie's* friend, and she was there only to see Charlie.

Marla's gigantic smile turned serious as she studied Charlie, peering at her as if trying to spot the differences since they last met. "You're as pale as ever." She took Charlie's hands in her own. "And you're all clammy. Don't you ever get warm?" She dropped Charlie's hands and proceeded to study the motel room skeptically, as though uncertain exactly what it was.

"It's the luxury suite," Jessica said without expression as she searched for something in her bag. Her hair was sticking up in all directions, and Charlie stifled a smile. It was nice to see something about Jessica in disarray for once. Jessica found her hairbrush and held it up triumphantly. "Ha! Take that, morning frizz!"

"Come on in," Charlie said, realizing she and Marla were still in the doorway, the door wide open. Marla nodded.

"One sec. JASON!" she shouted out the door. No one emerged. *"JASON!"*

A young boy came trotting up from the road. He was short and wiry, darker-skinned than his half sister. His Batman T-shirt and black shorts were made for someone twice his size. His hair was cut close to his head, and his arms and legs were streaked with dirt.

"Were you playing in the road?" Marla demanded.

"No?" he said.

"Yes, you were. Don't do that. If you get yourself killed, Mom's gonna blame me. Get inside." Marla shoved her little brother inside and shook her head.

"How old are you now?" Charlie asked.

"Eleven," Jason said. He went to the TV and started fiddling with buttons.

"Jason, stop it," Marla said. "Play with your action figures."

"I'm not a little kid," he said. "Anyway, they're in the car." But he stepped away from the television and went to look out the window.

Marla rubbed her eyes. "We just got here. We had to leave at six this morning, and *someone*," she said pointedly, glancing over her shoulder at Jason, "wouldn't stop fiddling with the radio. I am *so* tired." She didn't seem tired, but then she never did. At their sleepovers as kids, Charlie remembered her bouncing around like a maniac while the rest of them were winding down for the night—then falling asleep abruptly, like a cartoon character who'd been hit over the head with a rolling pin.

"We should get ready," Jessica said. "We're supposed to meet the guys at the diner in an hour."

"Hurry!" Marla said. "We have to change, too. I didn't want to get all gross while we were driving."

"Jason, you can watch TV," Charlie said, and he looked at Marla. She nodded, and he grinned and turned it on, starting to flip through channels.

"Please just pick a channel," Marla said. Charlie headed into the bathroom to get dressed while Jessica fussed with her hair.

*   *   *

A little less than an hour later, they pulled into the diner parking lot. The others were already there, in the same booth they'd been in the night before. When they got inside, Marla performed a second round of squeals and hugs, only slightly quieter now that they were in public. Overshadowed by her enthusiasm, Lamar stood and waved at Jessica and Charlie, waiting until Marla sat down.

"Hi, guys," he said at last. He was wearing a dark tie and a dark gray suit. He was tall and thin, black, with his hair shaved close to his head; his features were sharp and attractive, and he looked just a little older than the rest of them. It could have been the suit, but Charlie thought it was something about the way he stood, holding himself like he would be comfortable wherever he was.

They had all dressed up a little for the ceremony. Marla had changed at the motel, and she and Jessica were both wearing dresses. Jessica's was knee-length and covered in pastel flowers, a light fabric that moved as she walked. Marla's was simple, white with big sunflowers splashed over it. Charlie hadn't thought to bring a dress, and she hoped she didn't look out of place in black pants and a white button-down shirt. John was wearing a light-purple shirt today, though he'd added a matching tie in a slightly darker color, and Carlton seemed to be wearing an identical outfit as before, still all in black. They all sat down.

"Well, don't we all look nice," Marla said happily.

"Where's Jason?" Jessica craned her head from side to side.

Marla groaned. "I'll be right back." She scooted out of the booth and hurried out the door.

"Lamar, what have you been up to?" Charlie asked. Lamar grinned.

"He's an Ivy League–man," Carlton said, teasing. Lamar looked briefly down at the table, but he was smiling.

"Early acceptance," was all he said.

"Which one?" Jessica said.

"Cornell."

"Wait, how did you already apply to college?" Charlie said. "That's not till next year. I don't even know where I want to go."

"He skipped sixth grade," John said. There was a brief flicker of something across his face, and Charlie knew what it was. John liked being the clever one, the precocious one. Lamar had been kind of a goof-off when they were kids, and now he had leaped ahead. John forced a grin, and the moment passed. "Congratulations," he said, with no hint that it was not entirely sincere.

Marla came bursting in again, this time towing Jason behind her, holding on to his upper arm. At the hotel she had made him change into a blazer and khakis as well, though he was still wearing his Nikes.

"I'm coming. Stop it," he whined.

"Is that Jason?" Carlton asked.

"Yeah," Jason said.

"Do you remember me?" Carlton said.

"I don't remember any of you," Jason said unapologetically.

"Sit there," Marla said, pointing to the next booth over.

"Okay," he grumbled.

"Marla, he can sit with us," Jessica said. "Jason, come on over."

"I want to sit here," he said and sat down behind them. He pulled a video game out of his pocket and was oblivious to the world.

The waitress came over and they ordered; Marla told her to put Jason's breakfast on their check. When their food came, Charlie checked her watch.

"We don't have a lot of time," she said.

"We'll get there," Carlton said. "It's not far." A small piece of food fell out of his mouth as he gestured down the road.

"Have you been back to the school?" Lamar asked, and Carlton shrugged.

"I pass it sometimes. I know this is a nostalgia trip for all of you, but I just live here. I don't exactly go around reminiscing about kindergarten all the time."

They were all quiet for a second, the beeps and pings of Jason's video game filling the silence.

"Hey, did you know Lamar's going to Cornell next year?" Jessica said to Marla.

"Really? Well, aren't you ahead of the pack," she said. Lamar looked down at his plate. When he looked up, he was a little flushed.

"All part of the five-year plan," he said. They laughed, and his blush deepened. "It's kind of weird to be back here," he said, hastily changing the subject.

"I think it's strange that I'm the only one who still lives here," Carlton said. "Nobody ever leaves Hurricane."

"Is it strange, though?" Jessica said thoughtfully. "My parents—you remember, my mom's from New York originally; she used to joke about going back. *When I go back to New York*, but it might as well have been *When I win the lottery*; she didn't mean it. And then right after Michael's . . . right after, she stopped joking about it, then three months later we were all on a plane to visit her sister in Queens, and we never came back. My dad's father died when I was nine, and they came back to Hurricane for the funeral without me. They didn't want me coming back here, and honestly I didn't want to go. I was kind of anxious the whole time they were gone. I kept looking out the window, hoping they would come back early, like something bad was going to happen to them if they stayed."

They looked at one another, considering. Charlie knew they had all moved, all but Carlton, but she had never thought about it—people moved all the time. Carlton was right, though. People didn't leave Hurricane.

"We moved because my dad got a new job, the summer after third grade," John said. "That's not exactly mysterious. Lamar, you left in the middle of the semester that year."

"Yeah," he said. "But that's because when my parents split, I went with my mom to Indianapolis." He frowned. "But my dad moved, too. He's in Chicago now."

"My parents left because of Michael," Marla said. They all turned to her. "Afterward, my mom couldn't sleep. She said spirits were stirring in the town, unquiet. My dad told her she was being ridiculous, but we still left as fast as we could." Marla looked around at her friends. "What?" she said defensively. "*I* don't believe in ghosts."

"I do," Charlie said. She felt like she was talking from a great distance; she was almost surprised they could hear her. "I mean, not ghosts, but . . . memories. I think they linger, whether there's someone there or not." The house, her old house, was imbued with memory, with loss, with longing. It hung in the air like humidity; the walls were saturated, like the wood had soaked in it. It had been there before she came, and it was there now; it would be there forever. It had to be. There was too much, too great and vast a weight, for Charlie to have brought it with her.

"That doesn't make any sense," Jessica said. "Memory is in our brains. Like, literally stored in the brain; you can see it on a scan. It can't exist outside of someone's mind."

"I don't know," John said. "Think of all the places that have . . . atmosphere. Old houses, sometimes, places where you walk in and you feel sad or nostalgic, even though you've never been there before."

"That's not other people's memories, though," Lamar said. "That's subconscious cues, stuff we don't realize we're noticing, that tells us we should feel some way. Peeling paint, old-fashioned furniture, lace curtains, details that tell us to be nostalgic—mostly things we pick up from movies, probably. I got lost at a carnival when I was four. I never got so scared in my life, but I don't think anybody's feeling suddenly desperate for their mom when they pass that Ferris wheel."

"Maybe they are," Marla said. "I don't know, sometimes I have little moments where it's like there's something I forgot, something I regret, or that I'm happy about, or something that makes me want to cry, but it's only there for a split second. Then it's gone. Maybe we're all shedding our fear and regret and hope everywhere we go, and we're catching traces of people we've never met. Maybe it's everywhere."

"How is that different from believing in ghosts?" Lamar asked.

"It's totally different," Marla said. "It's not supernatural, and it's not, like, the souls of dead people. It's just . . . people leaving their mark on the world."

"So it's the ghosts of living people?" Lamar said.

"No."

"You're talking about people having some kind of essence that can hang around a specific place after the person is gone," Lamar said. "That's a ghost."

"No, it's not! I'm not saying it right," Marla said. She closed her eyes for a minute, thinking. "Okay," she said at last. "Do you all remember my grandmother?"

"I do," said Jason. "She was my grandmother, too."

"She was my dad's mom, not yours," Marla said. "Anyway, you were only a year old when she died."

"I do remember her," Jason said quietly.

"Okay," Marla said. "So she collected dolls from the time she was a kid. She and my grandfather used to travel a lot after he retired, and she'd bring them back from all over the world—she had them from France, Egypt, Italy, Brazil, China, everywhere. She kept them in their own special room, and it was full of them, shelves and shelves of dolls, some tiny and some almost as big as I was. I loved it; one of my earliest memories is playing in that room with the dolls. I remember my dad would always warn me to be careful, and my grandmother would laugh and say, 'Toys should be played with.'

"I had a favorite, a twenty-one-inch red-haired doll in a short, shiny white dress like Shirley Temple. I called her Maggie. She was from the 1940s, and I loved her. I told her everything, and when I was lonely, I would imagine myself in that room, playing with Maggie. My grandmother died when I was six, and when my dad and I went to see my grandfather after the funeral, he told me I should pick a doll to keep from the collection. I went to the room to get Maggie, and as soon as I walked through the door, something was wrong.

"It was as though the light had changed, become darker, harsher than it used to be. I looked around, and the lively, playful poses of the dolls now seemed unnatural, disjointed. It was as though all of them were staring at me. I didn't know what they wanted. Maggie was in the corner, and I took a step toward her, then stopped. I met her eyes, and instead of painted glass I saw a stranger. I turned and ran. I raced down the hall as though something might be chasing me, not daring to look back until I reached my father's side. He asked if I had picked a doll, and I just shook my head. I never went back in that room."

Everyone was silent. Charlie was transfixed, still seeing little Marla running for her life.

"What happened to the dolls?" Carlton asked, only half breaking the spell.

"I don't know. I think my mom sold them to another collector when my grandfather died," Marla said.

"Sorry, Marla," Lamar said, "it's still just tricks of the mind. You missed your grandmother, you were frightened of death, and dolls are inherently freaky."

Charlie broke in, wanting to head off the argument. "Is everybody done eating? We have to go soon."

"We still have plenty of time," Carlton said, looking down at his watch. "It's, like, five minutes away." Something else fell out of his mouth, landing next to the first dropped bit of food.

John looked around the table, from person to person, as though he were waiting for something.

"We have to tell them," he said, looking at Charlie.

"Oh yeah, we totally do!" Jessica said.

"Tell us what?" Jason piped up, peeking over the back of Marla's seat.

"Shh," Marla said halfheartedly. She was looking at John. "Tell us what?"

John dropped his voice, forcing everyone to lean in closer. Charlie did it, too, eager to hear, even though she knew exactly what he was going to say.

"We went to Freddy's last night," he said.

"Freddy's is still there?" Marla exclaimed, too loud.

"Shhh!" Jessica said, making frantic hand movements.

"Sorry," Marla whispered. "I just can't believe it's still there."

"It's not," Carlton said, raising his eyebrows and grinning enigmatically at Lamar.

"It's hidden," John explained. "They were supposed to knock it down to build a mall, but they didn't. They just . . . built around it."

"Entombed it," John corrected.

"And you got in?" Lamar said. Charlie nodded confirmation. "No way."

"What was it like?" Marla asked.

"Exactly the same," John said. "It was like . . ."

"It was like everyone vanished," Charlie said softly.

"I want to go, too! You have to take us," Marla said. Jessica cleared her throat hesitantly, and they all looked at her.

"I don't know," she said slowly. "I mean, today? Should we?"

"We have to see it," Lamar said. "You can't tell us this and not let us see it."

"I want to see it," Jason chimed in. "What's Freddy's?" They ignored him. His eyes were wide, and he was hanging on to every word.

"Maybe Jessica's right," John said with reluctance. "Maybe it's disrespectful to go tonight." There was a moment's pause, and Charlie knew they were waiting for her to talk. She was the one they were really afraid of offending; they needed her permission.

"I think we should go," she said. "I don't think it's disrespectful. It's almost a way of honoring . . . what happened." She looked around the table. Jessica was nodding. Charlie wasn't sure it was much of an argument, but they didn't need to be convinced. They wanted an excuse.

Marla twisted herself to look back at Jason's plate. "Are you done eating?" she asked.

"Yup," he said. Marla pointed to the game in his hand.

"You know you can't play with that during the ceremony," she said.

"Yup."

"I'm serious, Jason. I'm locking it in the car."

"Why don't you just lock me in the car," he muttered.

"I'd love to," Marla said under her breath as she turned back to the group. "Okay, we can go."

They headed to the school in a caravan, the boys in Carlton's car, Marla following, and Charlie bringing up the rear.

"We should have carpooled," Jessica said idly, staring out the window. It hadn't occurred to Charlie.

"I guess," she said.

"On the other hand, I'm not sure I want to ride with Marla and Jason," Jessica said plainly.

"They are kind of intense," Charlie agreed.

When they arrived, the parking lot was already jammed full. Charlie parked on a side street in what she hoped was a legal spot, and they walked to the school along the familiar sidewalk.

Jessica shivered. "I've got goose bumps."

"It is weird to be here," Charlie said. The school looked unchanged from the outside, but the fence was new and slick, a black, plastic-coated chain link. The whole town was like this, a mix of old and new, familiar and not. The things that had changed seemed out of place, and the things that had remained the same made Charlie feel out of place. *It must be so strange for Carlton to live here*, she thought. *"I know this is a nostalgia trip for all of you, but I just live here,"* he had said. Somehow, Charlie was not sure she believed that.

When they got to the playing field behind the school, the bleachers were already full. Rows of folding chairs had been laid out in front of them to add more seating, and Charlie spotted Marla and the boys at the front.

"Oh, great," she said. "I don't want to sit in the front row."

"I don't mind," Jessica said. Charlie looked at her.

Of course you don't, she wanted to say. *You're . . . you.*

"Yeah," she said instead, "no big deal. Half the town must be here," she observed as they made their way to the group, where two seats had been saved. There was one open in the front row, next to Carlton, and one right behind it, beside Marla. Jessica winked at Charlie and sat down next to Carlton. She leaned toward him, and they started whispering. Charlie repeated herself to Marla: "There's a lot of people here."

"Yeah," Marla said. "I mean, it's a small town, you know?

Michael's . . . it was a big deal. Plus, his parents still live here. People remember."

"People remember," Charlie echoed softly. There was a small raised stage set up in front of them, with a podium and four chairs. Behind the chairs a screen was suspended; projected on it was a larger-than-life picture of Michael. It was a close-up, just his face. It was not the most flattering picture: His head was thrown back at an odd angle, his mouth open in laughter, but it was perfect—a joyful moment, snatched up and kept, not curated. He looked happy.

"Darn it," Marla said softly. Charlie looked at her. She was dabbing at her eyes with a tissue. Charlie put an arm around her.

"I know," she said.

The sound system came on suddenly with a whine that slowly faded. Four people walked onstage: a heavyset man in a suit who went straight to the microphone, an elderly woman, and a couple, a man and a woman. The man in the suit stepped up to the podium, and the elderly woman sat down in one of the four chairs. The couple stayed back, but they did not sit. Charlie knew they must be Michael's parents, but she did not recognize them. When she was young they had just been parents, a species that was for the most part unremarkable. She realized suddenly that she didn't even know their names; Michael's parents had not gone out of their way to interact with their son's friends, and Charlie had literally spoken to them as "Michael's mom," and "Michael's dad," as if those were appropriate forms of address.

The man at the podium introduced himself as the school's principal. He said a few things about loss and community and the fleeting preciousness of youth. He talked briefly about Michael's kindness, his artistic talent, and the impression he made, even as a small child, on everyone he met. It was true, Charlie reflected. Michael had been an unusually charismatic child. He wasn't exactly a leader, but they all found themselves wanting to please him, to make him smile, and so they often did the things they knew he wanted to do, just to make him happy.

The principal finished and introduced Michael's parents, Joan and Donald Brooks. They stood at the podium awkwardly, each looking from face to face in the crowd, as if they were not sure how they had gotten here. Finally Joan stepped forward.

"It feels strange to be up here," was the first thing she said, and a murmur of something like agreement swept quietly through the crowd. "We are so grateful to all of you for coming, especially those of you who came from out of town." She looked directly at the front row, talking to Charlie and the others. "Some of Michael's friends have come from all over, and I think that is a testament to who he was that ten years later, with your lives on new paths, moving on to a whole new stage of life—" So close to the stage, Charlie could see she was about to cry, tears wavering in her eyes, but her voice was steady. "We are grateful you are here. We wanted to give Michael a legacy with this scholarship, but it is clear that he has already left one, all on his own." Marla grabbed Charlie's hand, and Charlie squeezed back.

"I want to say," Joan continued, "something about the families who are not here. As we all know, Michael was not the only child lost during those terrible few months." She read out four more names, two girls and two boys. Charlie glanced at Marla. They all knew there had been other children, but Michael's death had loomed so great in all their lives that they had never even talked about the other victims. Now Charlie felt a pang of guilt. To someone, those little girls and boys had been as vital as Michael. To someone, their losses had meant the end of the world. She closed her eyes for a moment. *I can't mourn everyone,* she thought. *No one can.*

Joan was still talking. "Although their families have moved on to other places, those young boys and girls will always have a place in our hearts. Now I would like to call to speak a young man who was particularly close to my son. Carlton, if you would?"

They all watched in surprise as Carlton stood and climbed up behind the podium. Joan hugged him tightly and stayed close behind him as he pulled a crumpled piece of paper from his pocket. He cleared his throat, looking over the heads of the crowd, then crumpled the paper up again and put it back in his pocket.

"I don't remember as much about Michael as I should," he said finally. "Too much of those years is a blur; I know we met when we were still in diapers, but I don't remember that, thankfully." There was a soft titter through the crowd. "I do know that as far back as I have memories, Michael is in them. I remember playing superheroes; drawing, which he was much better at than me; and as we got older I remember . . . well, playing superheroes and drawing. What I really remember, though, is that my days were always more exciting when he was in them. He was smarter than me; he was the one always coming up with new ideas, new ways to get in trouble. Sorry about those lamps, by the way, Mrs. Brooks. If I had jumped the way Michael said, I probably would only have broken one."

Donald laughed, a gulping, desperate sound. Charlie shifted uncomfortably and pulled her hand from Marla's with an apologetic half smile. Their grief, naked, was too much to watch. It was raw, an open wound, and she could not stand to look.

Carlton came back down to sit with them. Michael's grandmother spoke, and then his father, who had recovered enough to share a memory of taking his son to his first art class. He told the crowd about the scholarship, for a graduating senior who has demonstrated both excellence and passion in the arts, and announced the winner of the first one, Anne Park, a slight Korean girl who came quickly up to the stage to accept her plaque and hugs from Michael's parents. It must have been strange for Anne, Charlie thought, her honor so overshadowed by its origins. But then, she realized, Anne must have known Michael, too, however much in passing.

After the ceremony, they went to say hello to Michael's parents, hugging them and making sounds of condolence. *What do you say to someone who has lost a child? Can it be any easier? Can ten years make a difference, or do they wake up each morning as fresh with grief as the day he died?* On a long cafeteria table by the stage, pictures and cards were collecting slowly—people had brought flowers, notes to Michael's parents or to him. Things they remembered, things they wished they had said. Charlie went over and browsed through the notes. There were pictures of her and the others as well as of Michael. It shouldn't have surprised her—they were all together constantly, as a group or in rotating groups of two and three. She saw herself in the middle of a pose: Michael, John, and she, all covered in mud, with Jessica beside them, still perfectly clean, refusing to go near them. Charlie smiled. *That looks about right.* In another, a five-year-old Marla struggled to support the weight of her newborn little brother, with Lamar peering suspiciously at the tiny thing over her shoulder. Some of Michael's drawings were there, too, crayon scribbles professionally, incongruously framed.

Charlie picked one up, a drawing of what she supposed was a *T. rex* stomping through a city. It was actually, she realized now, almost amazing how talented he was. While she and the others were scribbling stick figures, Michael's drawings looked realistic, sort of.

"That's really good," John said over her shoulder. Charlie startled.

"You scared me," she said.

"Sorry."

Charlie looked back at the drawing. Whatever it was, it was better than she could draw now. Suddenly her chest tightened, gripped with loss and rage. It wasn't just that Michael died young, it was what that truly meant: He had been stopped in his tracks, years, decades of life snatched and torn violently from him. She felt herself well up with youthful indignation as if she were a child again, wanting only to whine, *It's not fair!*

Taking a deep breath, Charlie set the picture back down on the table and turned away. The gathering was continuing, but she needed to leave. She caught Marla's eye, and Marla, as scarily intuitive as always, nodded and caught Lamar's sleeve. From their various vantage points, they all headed for the parking lot. No one seemed to notice their departure, which made sense. Except for Carlton, they were all strangers here.

In the lot, they stopped by Marla's car. She had somehow called down a miracle and found a space right next to the school.

"Can I play my game now?" Jason said immediately, and Marla found her keys in her purse and handed them over.

"Don't drive away," she warned. Suddenly, Marla grabbed her brother and pulled him close, hugging him to her for a long minute.

"Jeez, I'm only going to the car," he muttered when she let him go.

"Yeah, maybe I should let you drive away," she said, giving him a little push. She cleared her throat. "So are we going to Freddy's?" she said. They all looked at one another.

"Yeah," Charlie said. "I think we should." Somehow, following this, going back to Freddy's seemed like more than a game. It felt right. "Let's meet there at sunset," she said. "Hey, Jessica, can you catch a ride with the guys or something? I'm gonna go for a walk."

"You can come with us," Marla said. "I promised Jason I'd take him to the movies."

Charlie headed down the road without waiting to hear the rest of the discussion. A dozen feet from the lot, she realized she was being followed. She turned around.

"John?"

"Do you mind if I come? You're going to your old house, right?"

"How did you know that?"

"It's the only interesting thing out this way. Anyway, I went to see my old place, too. It was painted blue, and there was a garden in the yard. It was weird. I know it wasn't blue when I lived there, but I couldn't remember what color it was supposed to be. Everything's so different."

Charlie didn't say anything. She wasn't even sure she wanted John to come with her. Her house, her father's house, it was private. She thought of the first time John had seen the toys, his fascination, an interest that was all his, that had nothing to do with pleasing her. She relented.

"Okay, you can come."

"Is it . . ." He hesitated. "Is it different?"

"It's really not," Charlie said. It wasn't quite true, but she wasn't sure how to explain the thing that had changed.

They walked together for the better part of three miles, away from town and down old roads, first paved, then gravel. As they neared the place they left the roads, ascending the steep incline of a hill overrun with brush and trees that should have been trimmed or cut down ages ago. Three rooftops peeked over the leaves, scattered widely over the hill, but no one had lived in these houses in a long time.

At last they walked up the driveway, and John stopped short, staring up at the house.

"I thought it would be less intimidating," he said softly. Impatient, Charlie took his arm for a second and pulled him away, leading them around the side of the house. It was one thing for him to be here with her, but she was not quite ready to let someone else inside. She wasn't even sure she wanted to go inside again anyway. He followed her without protest, as if aware that they were in her territory and she would decide where they went.

The property was large, more than a lawn. There were woods surrounding the wide space of the backyard, and as a child Charlie had often felt like she was in her own little realm, ruler of all she surveyed. The grass had gone wild, weeds growing feral and up to their knees. They walked the perimeter. John peered into the woods, and Charlie was struck by her old childhood fear, like something out of a fairy tale. *Don't go into the woods alone, Charlotte,* her father warned. It was not sinister, just a parent's warning, *don't get lost,* like telling her not to cross the street without holding someone's hand or not to touch the stove when it was hot, but Charlie took it more seriously. She knew from her storybooks, as all children did, that the woods contained wolves, and more dangerous things. She caught John's sleeve.

"Don't," she said, and he pulled back from the woods, not asking why. Instead, he went to a tree in the middle of the yard and put a hand on it.

"Remember that tree?" he asked, smiling, something a little wicked in his voice.

"Of course," Charlie said, walking over. "It's been here longer than I ever was." But he was looking at her, waiting for more, and suddenly she remembered.

It had been a sunny day, springtime; they were six years old, maybe. John was visiting, and they were playing hide-and-seek, half supervised by Charlie's father, who was in his garage workshop, absorbed in his machines. The door was open so he would notice if someone screamed, but short of that, the outdoors was their own. John counted to ten, eyes covered, facing the tree that was home base. The yard was wide and open; there were not many places to hide, so Charlie, buoyed up by the excitement of the game, dared to hide beyond the forbidden edge of the woods, just barely past the tree line. John searched the other places first: behind her father's car, in the corner where one part of the garage jutted out, the space beneath the porch where a child could just barely crawl. He realized where she must be, and Charlie braced herself to run as he began to walk the edges of the yard, darting into the woods and out again, looking behind trees. When at last he found her, she took off, tearing across the lawn to the home base tree. He was just behind her, so close he could almost touch her, and she sped on, staying just out of reach. She hit the tree, almost slamming into it, and John was right behind her, bumping into her a second later, too fast to stop. They were both giggling hysterically, and then they stopped at the same moment, still gasping to catch their breath.

"Hey, Charlotte," John said, stressing her name in the mocking tone he always used.

"Don't call me that," Charlie said automatically.

"You ever see grown-ups kiss?" He picked up a stick and started digging at the tree bark, like he was more interested in that than in her answer. Charlie shrugged.

"Yeah, I guess so."

"Wanna try it?" He still wasn't looking at her; his face was streaked with dirt, like it often was, and his hair was sticking out in all directions, a twig caught in it above his forehead.

"Gross," Charlie said, wrinkling her nose. Then, after a moment, "Yeah, okay."

John dropped the stick and leaned toward her, his hands behind his back. Charlie closed her eyes, waiting, still not entirely sure what she was supposed to do.

"Charlotte!" It was her father. Charlie jumped back. John's face was so close to hers that she banged into him with her forehead.

"Ow!" he yelled, clapping a hand to his nose.

Charlie's father came around the side of the tree. "What are you up to? John?" He pried John's fingers away from his nose. "You're not bleeding. You'll be fine," he said. "Charlotte, closer to the house, please." He then pointed his finger, directing them forward. "John, it looks like your mom is here anyway." He walked ahead of them, toward the driveway where her car had just pulled in.

"Yeah, okay." John trotted off toward the driveway, turning once to wave at Charlie. He was grinning like something wonderful had happened, although Charlie was not quite sure what it was.

"Oh my," Charlie said now, covering her face, sure it was bright red. When she looked up again, John was grinning that same satisfied, six-year-old grin.

"You know, my nose still hurts when it rains," he said, touching a finger to it.

"It does not," Charlie said. She leaned back against the tree. "I can't believe you tried to kiss me. We were six!" Charlie stared at him accusingly.

"Even the littlest heart wants what it wants," John said in a mock romantic voice, but there was an edge of something real in it, something not well enough hidden. Charlie realized, suddenly, that he was standing very close to her. "Let's go see your dad's workshop," John said abruptly, too loud, and Charlie nodded.

"Okay." She regretted it as she said it. She did not want to open the workshop door. She closed her eyes, still leaning against the tree. She could still see it; it was all she could see when she thought of that place. The twitching, malformed, metal skeleton in its dark corner, with its wrenching shudders and its blistering silver eyes. The image welled up in her head until it was all there was. The memory radiated a cutting anguish, but she did not know who it belonged to: to the thing, to her father, or to herself.

Charlie felt a hand on her shoulder and opened her eyes. It was John, frowning at her like he was worried.

"Charlie, are you okay?"

No.

"Yes," she said. "Come on, let's go see what's in the workshop."

It was not locked, and there was no real reason it should be, Charlie thought. Her eyes went first to the dark corner. The figure was not there. There was a weathered apron hanging in its place, the one her father had worn for soldering, and his goggles next to it, but there was no sign of that uncanny presence. Charlie should have felt relief, but she didn't, only a vague unease. She looked around. There seemed to be almost nothing left of the workshop: The benches were there, where her father had assembled and tweaked his inventions, but the materials, the blueprints, and the half-finished robots that were once crammed onto every surface had disappeared.

Where are they? Had her aunt had them carted away to a junkyard to rust and crumble among other discarded, useless things? Or had her father done it himself, so no one else would have to? The concrete floor was littered here and there with scraps; whoever had done the cleanup had not been thorough. Charlie knelt and picked up an oddly shaped scrap of wood, then a small circuit board. She turned it over. *Whose brain were you?* she wondered, but it did not matter, not really. It was battered and worn, the etched copper too badly scratched to repair, even if someone wanted to.

"Charlie," John said from across the workshop. He was in the dark corner; if the skeleton had been there, it could have reached out to touch him.

But it's not there.

"What?"

"Come see what I found."

Charlie went. John was standing beside her father's toolbox, and he stepped away as she came over, giving her space. Charlie knelt down before it. It looked as if it had just been polished. It was made of dark, stained wood, glossy with some kind of lacquer. She opened it gently. Charlie picked up an awl from the top tray and held it for a moment, the rounded wooden handle fitting into the palm of her hand as if it had been made for her to use. Not that she knew how. The last time she had picked it up, she could barely fit her fingers around its base. She picked up the tools one after another, lifting them from their places. The toolbox had wooden spaces carved out to fit the precise shape of each item. All the tools were polished and clean, their wooden handles smooth and their metal unrusted. They looked as though they had been used just that morning, wiped down and put away meticulously. Like someone still cared for them. She looked at them with a fierce, unexpected joy, as if something she had fought for was returned to her. But her joy felt wrong, misplaced; looking at her father's things set her off-balance. Something in the world was not as it should be. Seized suddenly with an unfounded fear, she thrust the awl back into its place in the box, dropping it like something burning. She closed the lid, but she did not stand.

Memory overtook her, and she closed her eyes, not fighting against it.

Her feet were wedged in the dirt, and two large and callous hands covered her eyes. Suddenly there was a bright light, and Charlie squinted, squirming impatiently to see what was before her. Three complete and gleaming figures towered over her, motionless, the sun reflecting off every edge and contour. They were blinding to behold.

"What do you think?" She heard the question but could not answer it; her eyes hadn't adjusted. The three masses of standing metal all looked similar in structure, but Charlie had grown accustomed to seeing more than was there, imagining the final result. For a long time now there had been three empty suits, hanging like carcasses from a rafter in the attic. Charlie knew that they had a special purpose, and now she understood what it was.

Two long beams protruded from the top of the head of one of the hulking masses. The head itself was solid and skull-like; the beams looked as if they had been violently thrust there.

"That's the rabbit!" Charlie squealed, proud of herself.

"You aren't scared of him?" the voice asked.

"Of course not. He looks like Theodore!"

"Theodore. That's right."

The figure in the middle was more clearly rendered: Its face was chiseled, its features distinct. It was clearly a bear, and a single metal beam stuck out from the top of its head as well. Charlie was puzzled for a moment, then smiled. "For the top hat," she said with confidence.

The last form was perhaps the most frightening; a long, metal clamp protruded from its empty face, in the place where a mouth might go. It was holding something on a platter, a metal structure that looked like a jaw, wires running like strewn spaghetti up and down the frame and in and out of sockets.

"That one's scary," she admitted hesitantly.

"Well, this part will look like a cupcake!" Her father pressed down on the top, and the jaw snapped shut, making Charlie jump, then giggle.

Suddenly, her laughter stopped. She had been so distracted she'd forgotten. *I'm not supposed to stand here. I don't stand here!* Her hands were trembling. How could she have forgotten?

The corner. She looked at the ground, unable to lift her eyes, unable to move. One of her shoes was untied. There was a screw next to her foot and an old piece of tape, opaque with dirt. There was something behind her.

"Charlie?"

It was John.

"Charlie!"

She looked up at him.

"Sorry. Just lost. This place . . ." She stood and took a step forward, positioning herself in the place she remembered. She glanced behind her as if the memory might manifest. The corner was empty; there was nothing. She knelt again and put her hand on the ground, fishing around until she found a small screw in the bare dirt. She palmed it, then looked closer; there were small holes in the ground, exposed when she moved the loose dirt. Charlie ran her fingers over them, thoughtful.

"Charlie, I have to tell you something." There was something urgent in John's voice. Charlie looked around the workshop and stood up.

"Can we go outside?" she said. "I can't breathe in here."

"Yeah, of course," he said. He followed her out into the yard and back to the hide-and-seek tree. She was tired, a wrung-out exhaustion deep inside. She would be fine in a minute, but she wanted a place that held only silly childhood memories. She sat down in the grass, leaned against the trunk, and waited for John to talk. He settled himself cross-legged in front of her, a little stiffly, smoothing his pants, and she laughed.

"Are *you* worried about getting dirty?"

"Times change," he said with a wry smile.

"What do you have to tell me?" she asked, and his face grew serious.

"I should have said something a long time ago," he said. "I just—when something happens like that, you don't trust your memory, don't trust your own mind."

"What are you talking about?" Charlie asked.

"Sorry." He took a deep breath. "I saw someone that night, the night Michael disappeared."

"What do you mean?"

"Remember when we were sitting at the table by the stage, and the animals started going crazy?"

"I remember," Charlie said. It had been bizarre, their movements upsetting. They were moving too fast, bending and spinning, cycling through their limited, programmed moves over and over. They seemed frantic, panicked. Charlie was mesmerized. She should have been afraid of them, but she was not; she saw, in their juddering motion, a kind of desperation. She was reminded, for a moment, of dreams of running, dreams when the world depended on her going just ten steps forward, yet her body could only move in slow motion. Something was wrong, terribly wrong. Chaotically, violently, the animatronic animals onstage thrashed robotic limbs in all directions, their eyes rolling in their sockets.

"What did you see?" Charlie said to John now, shaking her head as though she could rid it of the image.

"There was another mascot," he said. "A bear."

"Freddy," Charlie interrupted without thinking.

"No, not Freddy." John took her hands as if trying to calm them both, but he let go before he spoke again. "It was standing right near us, next to our table, but it wasn't looking at the stage like everyone else was. That technician came over, remember, and even he was just watching the animatronics—I guess he was trying to figure out what was happening. I looked over at the mascot, and it looked back at me . . ." He stopped.

"John, what?" Charlie said impatiently.

"Then the animatronics onstage stopped moving, and I looked over at them, and when we all turned back around, Michael was gone. And so was the mascot."

Charlie stared at him in disbelief.

"You saw the kidnapper," she said.

"I didn't know what I saw," John said. "It was all chaos. I didn't even think about it; I didn't make the connection; it was just another animal at Freddy's. I didn't think about who might have been inside it. I was . . . I was a kid, you know? You figure that the grown-ups already know everything you know."

"Yeah," Charlie said. "I know. Do you remember anything? What the person looked like?" John was staring up at the sky, as if he were seeing something Charlie could not.

"Yes," he said. His voice was deliberate, steady. "The eyes. They were all I could see, but I still see them sometimes, like they're right there in front of me. They were dead."

"What?"

"They were dead, just dull and flat. Like, they still moved and blinked and saw, but whatever was behind them had died a long time ago." He fell silent.

It was growing dark. There was a bright, almost unnatural streak of pink across the western sky, and Charlie shivered.

"We should go get the car," she said. "It's almost time to meet everyone."

"Yeah," John said, but he didn't move right away, still staring into the distance.

"John? We have to go," Charlie said. He seemed to come back to himself slowly.

"Yeah," he said. "We should go." He got up and brushed off his pants, then grinned at Charlie. "Race you?" he said and took off running. Charlie chased after him, her feet pounding the asphalt, and her arms swinging free.

CHAPTER FOUR

harlie and John were the last ones to the mall. When they pulled up, the others were gathered tight in a circle in front of Marla's car, as if sharing a conspiracy.

"Come on," Marla said before they had walked all the way to the group. She was bouncing on the balls of her feet as if she were ready to run for the door of the abandoned building. Everyone but Charlie and John had changed their clothing, wearing jeans and T-shirts, things more suited for exploration, and she had a brief moment of feeling out of place. *At least I didn't wear a dress*, Charlie thought.

"Let's go," she said. Marla's impatience seemed to be contagious, or maybe it just gave Charlie an excuse to let her real feelings come to the surface. She wanted to show Freddy's off to the others.

103

"Hold up," John said. He looked at Jessica. "Did you explain everything?"

"I told them about the night guard," she said. "What else is there?" He looked thoughtful for a moment.

"I guess nothing," he said.

"I brought more lights," Carlton said and held up three flashlights of varying sizes. He tossed one to Jason, a small one with an elastic headband attached. Jason turned it on, fixed it around his head, and began moving enthusiastically in waves and circles, making the light bob and dance.

"Shh," Charlie said, even though he was not making any sound.

"Jason," Marla whispered, "turn it off. We can't attract attention, remember?"

Jason gleefully ignored them, spinning off into the parking lot like a top.

"I told him if he's not good he has to wait in the car," Marla told Charlie quietly. "But now that we're here, I'm not sure which place is creepier." She eyed the bare branches overhead raging in the wind, threatening to reach down and grab them.

"Or we can feed him to Foxy." Charlie winked. She went to her trunk and hefted out the police flashlight, but she did not turn it on. Instead Carlton switched on two of his smaller lights and handed one to Jessica.

They headed into the mall. Knowing where they were going and what was waiting for them there, Charlie, John, Jessica, and Carlton moved through the empty spaces with a sense of purpose, but the others kept stopping to look around.

"Come on," Jessica said impatiently as Lamar gazed up at the atrium dome.

"You can see the moon," he said and pointed. Next to him, Marla nodded, mimicking his posture.

"It's beautiful," she said, although she could not see it.

From a distance, they heard footsteps echo in the emptiness.

"Hey, hey, over here!" John hissed, and they hurried as quietly as they could. They could not run for fear of making noise, and so they walked, fast but careful, hugging the walls. They entered the black void of the department store, creeping along in the shadows until they reached the break in the wall. John held back the hanging plastic obscuring the opening as the others maneuvered around the scaffolding. Jason was slow, and Charlie put a hand on his shoulder to hurry him up. As she steered him to the opening, a strong beam of light swept into the room, scanning up and down the walls. They all ducked through the plastic and ran down the alley to where the others were crouched down against the wall.

"He saw us!" Jason whispered, alarmed, running straight to his sister.

"Shh," Marla said.

They waited. Charlie was next to John this time, and after that moment by the tree, whatever it was, she was very, almost uncomfortably, aware of him. They were not quite touching, but she seemed to know exactly where he was, an awkward sixth sense. She glanced at him, but his eyes were fixed on the opening to the hallway. They could hear the guard's footsteps now, clear in the empty space, each one distinct. He was moving slowly, deliberately. Charlie closed her eyes, listening. She could tell where he was from the sound, she thought, getting closer, then farther, crisscrossing the open room like he was hunting for something. The steps came right up to the entrance of the alley and stopped. They all held their breaths.

He knows, Charlie thought. But the steps started again, and she opened her eyes and saw the light receding. He was going away.

They waited, still motionless, until they could no longer hear the tapping of his hard-soled shoes. She and John both stumbled a little as they stood, and she realized they had been leaning against each other without realizing it. She didn't look at him; instead she set to work taking the heaviest things off the wooden shelf.

"Will I be needing this?" Lamar asked, as Charlie handed him a bucket with a saw sticking out of it.

"We have to move the shelf," Jessica said. "Come on."

Jessica, Charlie, Carlton, and John got back into place and moved the shelf. Lamar tried to find a place to help, but there was not really room. Marla just waited.

"I'm better suited to supervising," she said when Charlie mock-glared at her.

This time the screaming of the metal door was not as loud, as if it no longer protested their entrance quite so strongly. Still, Marla and Jason covered their ears.

"You think *that's* not going to bring the guard?" Marla hissed.

Charlie shrugged. "Didn't last time," she said.

"I know he saw us," Jason said again. The others ignored him. "His flashlight went right over me," he insisted.

"It's really okay, Jason," Jessica said. "We thought he saw us last night, too, but it was fine." Jason looked dubious, and Lamar bent over to his eye level.

"Hey, Jason," he said. "What do you think the guard would do if he saw us?"

"Shoot us?" Jason whimpered, eyeing Lamar warily.

"Worse," Lamar said gravely. "Community service."

Jason wasn't sure what it meant, but he held his eyes open wide as though it was something terrible.

"Will you leave him alone?" Marla whispered, amused.

"He didn't see us," Jason reassured himself, though clearly unconvinced. Charlie turned on the big light and shone it down the hallway.

"Oh my!" Marla gasped as the first light streaked across the interior of the pizzeria. Suddenly it became real, and her face flushed with awe and fear.

They went in one by one. The temperature seemed to drop as soon as they walked into the hall, and Charlie shivered, but she did not feel ill at ease. She knew where they were now, and she knew what they would find. When they got to the dining room, Carlton spread his arms wide and twirled.

"Welcome . . . to Freddy Fazbear's Pizza!" he said in a booming announcer's voice. Jessica giggled, but the melodrama did not actually seem out of place. Marla and Lamar gaped at the room, awestruck. Charlie set the large flashlight on the ground, the beam facing up, and it lit up the main room in a dim and ghostly illumination.

"Cool," Jason said. His eyes fell on the merry-go-round, and he raced for it and jumped onto the back of a pony before anyone could stop him. He was too big for it, his sneakers dangling all the way to the ground. Charlie smiled. "How do I make it go?" he shouted.

"Sorry, buddy," John said. Jason climbed off, disappointed.

"The arcade is over this way!" Carlton said, motioning to anyone who might follow. Marla went with him, while Jason fiddled hopefully with the carousel's control box. Lamar had walked to the stage and was standing transfixed, staring up at the animals. Charlie went over to him.

"I can't believe they're still here," he said as she walked up.

"Yeah," she said.

"I'd forgotten this was a real place." Lamar smiled, for the first time resembling the little boy Charlie had once known.

Charlie smiled back. There was something surreal about the place; she had certainly never told any of her school friends about it. She would not have known where to begin; worse, she would not have known where to stop. Jessica poked her head out from the retracted curtain at the side of the main stage, and they both startled.

"What are you doing?" Lamar asked.

"Exploring!" she said. "There's nothing back here but a bunch of wires, though." She disappeared into the folds of cloth again. After a moment they heard a thud as she jumped to the ground, and she came strolling over.

"Do they work?" Lamar asked, pointing at the animals.

"I don't know," Charlie said. Truthfully, she had no idea how they worked. They had always just *been,* set to intermittent life by whatever alchemy her father performed in his workshop. "It doesn't look like anything is missing. They *should* work," she reluctantly added, though in her head she questioned the idea of trying to turn them on.

"Hey!" Jessica exclaimed. She was kneeling by the stairs to the stage. "Everybody come here now!"

Charlie went over, and Lamar followed.

"What is it?" Charlie asked.

"Look," Jessica said, shining her little light. Though well hidden along the grain of the wood, there was a door inset into the wall of the stage.

"How did we not see that?" Charlie wondered.

"We weren't looking," John said, staring intently at the small door. The whole group had gathered, and now Jessica looked around at them with a grin, put her hand on the little doorknob, and pulled.

Magically, it opened. The door revealed a small, sunken room. Jessica shone the light around it. It was full of equipment; one wall was covered in TV screens.

"Must be CCTV," Lamar said.

"Come on." Jessica handed her flashlight to Charlie and swung her legs through the door. There was one deep step leading down into the room, which was no bigger than a large refrigerator turned on its side.

"That's a little too cramped for me; I'll keep looking around out here." John saluted, then turned as though to stand guard.

"This is like a clown car," Marla remarked as she jostled against Charlie. The space was too cramped for all of them, but they crowded together; Jason sat on the step, feeling more comfortable by the exit. There were eight of the television screens across the wall, each with its own little panel of buttons and knobs, and sticking out beneath them was a panel, almost a table, covered in buttons. They were large and black, unlabeled, and spaced in an irregular series. The other wall was blank except for a single large switch by the door.

"What's this do?" Jason said and put his hand on the switch. He hesitated just long enough for someone to stop him, then pulled it.

The lights came on.

"What?" Carlton looked to the others frantically.

They all stared at one another in confused silence. Jason climbed up and poked his head out into the main room.

"They're on out here, too, some of them, at least," he said too loudly.

"Why is there power?" Jessica whispered, reaching over Jason to pull the door closed again.

"How is that possible?" Charlie said. "This place hasn't been open in ten years."

"Cool." Marla leaned forward, studying the monitors as though expecting some sort of answer to be revealed.

"Turn on the TVs," Jason said suddenly. "I can't reach." Jessica flipped on the first TV, and static crackled across the screen.

"Nothing?" Charlie asked impatiently.

"Just a sec." She twisted a dial, wiggling it back and forth until an image emerged. It was the stage, centered on Bonnie.

The other animals weren't visible. Jessica turned on the rest of the TVs, adjusting them until the pictures became clear, although most were still poorly lit.

"They still work," Charlie said almost under her breath.

"Maybe," Jessica said. "Hey, someone go out there. See if the camera is live."

"Okay," Marla said after a brief hesitation, wriggling her way to the exit and awkwardly climbing over Jason. A moment later she appeared on camera, onstage beside Bonnie. Marla waved. She appeared multicolored as the stage lights bathed her in purple, green, and yellow from different sides.

"Can you see me?" she asked.

"Yeah," Carlton shouted. Lamar was staring at the buttons.

"What do these do?" he said with a wicked grin, pressing one.

Marla screamed.

"Marla, are you okay?" Charlie shouted. "What happened?"

Marla was standing still on the stage, but she had backed away from Bonnie and was staring at him as if he might bite.

"He moved!" Marla yelled. "Bonnie moved! What did you do?"

"Marla," Jessica yelled, laughing, "it's okay! We pushed a button!"

Lamar pressed the button again, and they all watched the screen this time. Sure enough, Bonnie turned stiffly to one side. He pressed it again, and the rabbit swiveled back to face the absent audience again.

"Try another one," Carlton said.

"Go ahead," Lamar said and climbed out of the little room to join Marla onstage. He crouched down to inspect Bonnie's feet. "They're attached to a swiveling panel," he called.

"Yeah?" Jessica called back, not really listening.

Carlton started pressing buttons as the rest of them watched the cameras. After a moment, Charlie left the room as well.

"It's too stuffy in here," she explained. Jessica's perfume and Carlton's hair gel, both of which smelled nice enough out in the open, were starting to form a sickly miasma. She stepped out into the open to watch them experiment with the animals onstage. Most of the dining room was still dark. There were three colored spotlights suspended from the ceiling, aiming beams of purple, yellow, and green at the stage. The animals were cast now in unnatural colors, and dust in the beams of light shone like tiny stars, so many that it was difficult to see through them. The floor beneath the long tables was dusted with glitter that had fallen from the party hats, and as she looked around she noticed again the drawings that lined the walls of the place, all at the height of children's eyes.

They had always been there, and Charlie wondered now where her father had gotten the first ones when the restaurant opened. Had he used her own childish scribblings, or had he made them himself and stuck them up, forgeries to encourage actual children to display their art? The thought of her father hunched over his workbench, gripping an unsteady crayon with hands accustomed to manipulating microchips, made her want to giggle. She noticed the flashlight still on in the center of the room and went to switch it off. *Don't waste the battery*, she said in her head, in chorus with Aunt Jen's voice.

She turned her attention to the stage. It looked like the others had gotten Chica and Bonnie to go through a series of small, specific movements. They could each swivel their entire bodies back and forth, and their hands, feet, and heads could be moved in various directions, but each movement was separate.

Charlie went back to the control room and stuck her head in. "Can you make them do the dance?" she asked.

"I don't know how," Carlton said, leaning back away from the monitors. "All of this must have been used to program the dances. I don't think someone was in here manually controlling everything during the shows." He shook his head with certainty. "That would have been impossible."

"Huh," Charlie said.

"Everyone, quiet," Marla called out, and they all fell silent.

For a long moment there was no sound, then Lamar said, "What?"

Marla frowned, tilting her head to the side, listening for something. "I thought I heard something," she said finally. "It was like . . . pings of a music box?" Her mouth barely moved as she spoke. "It's gone."

"Why isn't Freddy moving?" Charlie asked.

"I don't know," Carlton said. "I can't find the controls for him."

"Hmm," Jessica said, tapping the monitors. "These cameras don't show the whole place."

Charlie peered at them, but they were mixed up, in no logical order. She couldn't piece together a picture of the whole restaurant.

"There's three cameras on the stage, one on each animal, but there should be one on the whole thing," Jessica was saying. "There's the entrance to the kitchen, but not the kitchen itself, and you can't see the hallway and the room with the little stage we were at last night."

"Maybe the cameras are just in the main room?" Carlton suggested.

"Nope," said Jessica. "There are cameras everywhere out there."

"So?" Carlton said.

"So there's got to be another control room!" Jessica said triumphantly. "Maybe down the hall by the other stage."

Charlie went back out into the main room again. She was feeling restless, less excited by the discoveries than the others, though she was not sure why. She watched the stage. Carlton was still playing with the buttons, Bonnie and Chica jerking in small, disjointed motions as Freddy Fazbear remained motionless, his eyes half-closed and his mouth slack, slightly open.

"Hey," Lamar said suddenly. "Marla. The music. I hear it now." Everyone was silent again, then Marla shook her head.

"Creepy," she said, more excited this time, rubbing her hands together as though they were sharing campfire stories. Lamar looked thoughtfully at Freddy.

"Let's go find the other control room," Jessica said, emerging with a determined look on her face.

"Okay!" Marla jumped from the stage to join them, and they started scanning the rest of the stage, looking for a second door.

"I'm staying in here," Jason called from the first room. "This is so cool!" Chica swiveled back and forth rapidly on the stage as he pushed her button repeatedly. Lamar went to join Jason.

"Okay, my turn," he said, leaning on the door. He went in, not waiting for Jason's response.

Charlie stayed where she was, still staring at Freddy, frozen in the middle of his act. John came up next to her, and she felt a flash of irritation; she did not want to be cajoled into joining in the search. He stood there for a moment, looking at Freddy, then leaned in close to her and whispered, "I'm counting to one hundred. You'd better hide."

Surprised out of her thoughts, she looked at him for a moment, her irritation broken. He winked at her, then covered his eyes. It was absurd, it was childish, and in that moment it was the only thing she wanted to do. Slightly giddy, Charlie took off, looking for a place to hide.

Jason pushed the series of buttons again with increasing frustration. "I'm bored now," he announced.

"How can you be bored?" Lamar said, wide-eyed.

"They aren't working anymore." Jason continued to press buttons, no longer watching the monitors.

Lamar studied the monitor. Bonnie's head was up and turned to the side, his eyes appearing to watch the camera. "Well, go find your sister then," he told Jason.

"I don't need her permission to be bored!" Impatiently, Jason climbed up and out of the control room.

"Everyone is so sensitive," Lamar muttered, suddenly realizing he was alone in the control room. He climbed out, but Jason was already gone.

Jessica was leading the exploration party, heading toward the little stage they had discovered the night before. Marla looked back and saw Jason skipping to catch up just before they disappeared into the long hall.

"Hey, be careful!" she called over her shoulder as Jason branched off in his own direction. Lamar caught up to the group and followed them on their way into the hall. The main dining room was empty now, though Jason could hear Charlie's and John's playful shouts echoing from the party rooms that extended off the main building. Left alone, Jason headed straight for the arcade.

It was more dimly lit than the rest of the place, and without power the arcade machines appeared as towering black monoliths in a forgotten graveyard. The air was stale and thin. Jason went to the nearest console and pressed a few buttons, some stuck with age, but nothing happened.

Plug it in, duh. He ducked behind the games to check, but even though the mounds of wires seemed impossibly tangled, it looked like they were plugged in. *Maybe there's a switch for the whole room?* He started checking the walls.

There was no obvious switch, but as Jason scanned the walls, he became distracted by the children's drawings taped in clusters. Jason was too young to have any memories of his own from being at Freddy's; even Hurricane itself was no more than a hazy set of impressions. But something about the pictures brought up a sense of nostalgia. They were all the same, really, the kinds of drawings he and every other kid had done—figures with circles for bodies and sticks for arms, in a multitude of colors. Only a few details showed which figures were the animals: Chica with her beak, Bonnie with his ears. It seemed like there had been a bit more attention paid to the drawings of Freddy Fazbear. They were a little better; the children had been a little more careful to make the details right. Jason found himself looking at one drawing in particular. It was the same as the others, maybe a little better: Bonnie the Bunny hugging a child. There was no name at the bottom. Jason took the picture off the wall, uncertain why this one in particular interested him so much.

John burst into the room with a wide grin and a deep breath, but then, seeing that it was only Jason inside, he quickly returned to a stoic demeanor. "What's up?" He nodded his head, playing it cool, then casually stepped away before silently returning to a sprint.

Playing hide-and-seek like babies, Jason thought. *I hope I never fall in love.*

He looked back down at the drawing and squinted as though not seeing correctly. The child was now facing away from Bonnie. Jason stared for a long moment. *Wasn't he hugging Bonnie before?* He looked out at the main room, but Marla was out of sight, looking for the control room. Jason folded the drawing carefully and put it in his pocket. It was suddenly apparent how quiet it had become outside. Jason stepped out timidly and peeked into the dining room. "Guys?" he whispered, looking back once, then ventured out to find the group.

★   ★   ★

Jessica, Lamar, Carlton, and Marla were still creeping slowly through the other half of the building. The spotlights from the dining room didn't reach this far, only accenting edges and corners or specks of glitter. Jessica scanned the wall with her flashlight, looking for breaks in the plaster, and motioned to Marla to do the same.

"We have to check for a hidden door," she said.

"The last one wasn't really hidden," Carlton pointed out.

"Yeah," Jessica conceded, but she kept her light on the wall, clearly not ready to give up the hunt. They passed two bathrooms they had not noticed the night before.

"Do you think the plumbing still works?" Carlton said. "I really need to pee."

"What are you, five years old? I don't want to hear that." Jessica rolled her eyes and walked faster.

When they got to the room with the little stage, everyone stopped. Marla and Lamar went closer to the stage, drawing together slightly as if unaware they were doing it. Even though Carlton and Jessica had been here the night before, it was as though they were seeing it anew through Marla's and Lamar's eyes. They still had not seen what was behind the curtain, Carlton realized suddenly.

"I remember these posters," Lamar said.

"I remember this, too," Marla said, pointing to the sign that read OUT OF ORDER strung across the stage. "My whole life I've felt uneasy when I've seen that phrase, even if it's just at a vending machine." She laughed insincerely.

"I know what you mean," Lamar said softly, but before he could go on, Carlton interrupted.

"Found it."

"Maybe," Jessica amended. There was a door, close-set into the wall like the one below the stage—not quite hidden, but not meant to be noticed. It was painted black, like the walls of the room. Jessica turned the knob and pulled, but it was stuck tight.

"Locked?" Lamar said.

"I don't think so."

"Let me try," Marla said. She grabbed the knob and yanked, and it came open, sending her stumbling back.

"Impressive!" Lamar said.

"Yeah, well, taking care of Jason makes me tough." Marla grinned as she knelt down to squeeze through the small door.

It was almost the same as the first room: a set of eight TV screens and a large panel of unmarked black buttons. Carlton fumbled to find the master switch, reaching his hand into a dark corner. Then, with a click, the power came on, and a soft buzzing sound filled the room. Rich, bizarre reds and blues began streaming in under the door from the stage lights outside. Jessica and Carlton began switching the televisions on; they fiddled with the knobs until they were showing pictures, though most were very dark. From here they could see a long shot of the main stage, just as in the other room, but the rest of the cameras were showing other places and angles. While the first control room had only shots of the main dining room, here they could see into other areas of the restaurant—the private party rooms, which were set up with glittery decorations for events that would never happen; hallways; an office; and even what looked like a storage closet. The room behind them was visible as well, the camera trained on the OUT OF ORDER sign, now lit with otherworldly shades, and the curtain behind it. On one screen they could see Jason ducking back into the arcade.

"Maybe I should go get him," Marla said, but no one responded.

Carlton started pressing buttons. Spotlights appeared and vanished on the stage in the main dining room as he did, illuminating first one animal and then another, lighting up empty spaces where someone might once have stood. He flipped a switch, and it seemed for a moment that nothing happened. Then Lamar started laughing, pointing at one of the screens. The pizza decorations lining the walls were spinning wildly, as though they might leap off and go rolling away.

"I forgot they used to do that," Lamar said as Carlton brought them slowly to a halt.

There was a large black dial to one side of the buttons, and Carlton spun it, but it seemed to do nothing.

"Let me try," Lamar said. He elbowed Carlton to the side and pressed another button. There was a high-pitched whine; they all jumped, and it quickly faded down to a static hum. Lamar pressed the button again, and the sound was gone.

"I guess we know what turns the speakers on," Carlton said.

"I bet we could figure out how to play the music," Jessica said. She reached forward and pushed something else, and stage lights popped up while the main lights dimmed. The figures on the main stage suddenly stood out a little, commanding attention. She pushed it again, and the lights faded back to normal.

"I love that," Carlton said.

"What?" asked Marla.

"Stage lights," he said. "One switch, and it's like a whole 'nother world up there."

Another button flickered the stage lights on and off in the room behind them, while another started and stopped the little merry-go-round, its tinkling music grinding too slowly, like the ride itself was trying to remember how the song went. They managed to get the speakers on again without the feedback whine, but there was still only static.

"I have an idea," Jessica said, pushing to the front of the group. She switched on the static again, then started turning the knob back and forth. The hum grew lower in pitch, then higher, responding to her adjustments.

"Progress," Carlton said.

"It's still just static," Marla said, unimpressed. Jessica turned it lower again, then snatched her hand from the dial like she had been bitten and punched the button, shutting the speakers off.

"What?" Marla asked.

Jessica remained motionless, her hands still suspended in the air.

"What happened? Did it shock you?" Carlton asked.

"It sounded like a voice," Jessica answered.

"What did it say?" Marla asked, apparently interested again.

"I don't know. Let me try again."

She turned the speaker on again, calling forth the static, and lowered the hum as they all listened, intent on the sound. As it sank to a lower register, just below the range of a human voice, they all heard it: grinding and broken words, almost too slow and distorted to be considered speech. They looked at one another.

"What on earth?" Marla said.

"No, it's just random static," Lamar said. He reached for the controls and dialed the pitch back up slowly. For another fleeting moment, there was a purposeful sound.

"That sounded like singing," Carlton said.

"No," Lamar said, sounding more unsure this time.

"Do it again," Marla said. Lamar did, but this time the static was empty.

"Is that Charlie?" Marla suddenly became focused on a blurry figure moving down the dark hall toward them, sliding along the wall as though to remain unnoticed.

Charlie was hurrying, almost skipping, and trying to find another place to hide. She glanced behind her, vaguely suspecting that John might be cheating. She moved through the darkness and toward the colorful glow of the small stage curtain, which was throwing eerie reds and blues onto the tables and party hats. Going down this passage had always felt like a long and perilous journey, one not to be made alone. She kept her gaze fixed behind her, letting the wall beside her guide her step. She knew John was close, probably creeping up on her in the dark. Suddenly she backed into something, stopping short. She had been moving faster than she thought, or more likely the hall was not as long as she remembered.

She saw his shadow at the end of the hall—if he turned his head, he would see her. Without thinking, Charlie climbed up onto the platform that she had bumped into and ducked behind the curtain, tucking herself between the wall and a large, bulky prop, trying not to breathe.

"Charlie?" he called, still far away. *"Charlie!"* Charlie felt her heartbeat quicken. There had been boys she liked, now and then, but this was something different. She wanted him to find her, but not quite yet. As she waited, her eyes adjusted to the darkness, and she was able to make out the shape of the curtain and the edge of the stage. She looked up at the object in front of her.

No. Her body shuddered, then froze.

It was standing over her. It was the thing from her father's workshop, the misshapen thing that hung in the corner, shaken by random convulsions as its eyes burned silver. *Does it hurt?* Now it was still, and its eyes were blank and dull. It was staring straight ahead, insensate, and its arm with its hook hung useless at its side. She recognized his eyes, but he was somehow worse now, encased in hollow body parts and matted with red fur, with a stench of oil and glue. He had a name now; they called him Foxy. But she knew better.

Charlie shrank away, pressing against the wall. Her heart was racing, and her breath was shallow, too fast. Her arm had been touching its leg, and now she felt a sudden itchiness from it, like she had been contaminated. She wiped her hand violently against her shirt as she began to panic.

Run.

She sprang away from it, pushing off the wall to get away, to move before it saw her, but the edge of the stage caught her foot. She stumbled forward, momentarily becoming entangled in the curtain. She struggled to get free when suddenly the thing's arm jerked up, and the hook slashed at her arm. She ducked away too late, and it cut her. The pain was shocking, like freezing water. She tripped backward and felt herself falling for long seconds, and then she was caught.

"Charlie? Are you okay?"

It was John; he had caught her. She tried to nod, but she was shaking. She looked at her arm. There was a cut above the elbow, almost four inches long. It was bleeding freely, and she covered it with her hand, the gaps between her fingers welling over as her own blood leaked through.

"What happened?" Marla asked, rushing up behind her. "Charlie, I'm so sorry, I must have hit a button that caused it to move. Are you okay?"

Charlie nodded, a little less shaky. "I'm fine," she said. "It's not that bad." She moved her arm around experimentally. "See? No nerve damage," she said. "I'll be fine."

Carlton, Jessica, and Lamar came hurrying out of the control room.

"We should take her to the E.R.," Carlton said.

"I'm fine," Charlie insisted. She stood up, refusing John's help, and braced herself on the stage for a moment. She heard her Aunt Jen's voice in her head: *How much blood have you lost? You don't need to go to a hospital.* She could move her arm just fine, and she would not bleed to death from this. She felt dizzy, though.

"Charlie, you look like a ghost," John said. "We need to get you out of here."

"Okay," she said. Her thoughts were scattered, and the injury hurt less than it should have. She took deep breaths as they headed for the exit, grounding herself. John handed her a piece of cloth, and she put it to the cut to slow the bleeding.

"Thanks," she said, looking at him. Something was missing. "Was that your tie?" she asked, and he shrugged.

"Do I look like a tie person?"

She grinned. "I thought it looked good on you."

"Jason!" Marla yelled as they passed the arcade. "Move it, or I'm leaving you behind!"

Jason ran to catch up.

"Is Charlie okay?" he said anxiously. Marla caught her breath and put her arm around him.

"She's fine," she reassured him.

They walked briskly down the same corridor that they entered through. Jason looked back as he was being guided out, studying the pictures on the wall once more before losing sight of them. The colored lights from the stage were fading, and the flashlight was throwing shapes and shadows on everything, making the drawings difficult to see, but Jason could swear he saw the figures moving in the pictures.

They all hurried back through the empty building and out to the parking lot, not keeping watch for the guard. When they made it out to the car, Lamar, who had grabbed the big flashlight, flipped it on and shone it at Charlie's arm. She looked down at the cut.

"Do you need stitches?" Marla asked. "I am so sorry, Charlie."

"We were all being careless. It's not your fault," Charlie said. She knew she sounded annoyed, but she didn't mean to; her voice was tight and clipped with pain. The shock had worn off, but that meant the wound had begun to hurt. "It's fine," Charlie said, and after a long moment the others gave in somewhat reluctantly.

"We should at least get you some stuff to clean that up and bandage it," Marla said, wanting to do something to atone, however small.

"There's a twenty-four-hour drugstore just off the main road," Carlton offered.

"Charlie, why don't you go with Marla, and I'll drive your car back to the motel?" Jessica said.

"I'm fine," Charlie protested halfheartedly, but she handed Jessica the keys. "You're a good driver, right?"

Jessica rolled her eyes. "People from New York know how to drive, Charlie."

John lingered a moment as Charlie was getting into Marla's car. She smiled at him.

"I'm fine," she said. "I'll see you tomorrow." He looked at her like there was something more he wanted to say, but he just nodded and left.

"Okay," Marla said. "To the drugstore!"

Charlie twisted in her seat to look at Jason. "Did you have fun?" she asked.

"The games don't work," he said, obviously preoccupied.

The drugstore was only a few minutes away. "You stay in the car," Marla commanded to Jason as they pulled to a stop.

"Don't leave me out here," Jason pleaded.

"I told you to stay," she repeated, a little confused by the fear in his voice. He didn't answer, and she and Charlie headed inside.

As soon as they were gone, Jason pulled the drawing out of his pocket. He held it up under the faint lights of the parking lot to examine. It had not changed back: Bonnie the Bunny was reaching toward a child, who was facing away from him. Curious, Jason scraped at the crayon lines with his fingernail. The wax came off easily, leaving its trace on the paper.

As soon as Marla passed into the fluorescent-lit, air-controlled drugstore, she sighed and put her hands to her temples. "Oh, he's such a little brat," she said.

"I like him," Charlie said honestly. She was still using John's tie to stanch the bleeding, and now, in brighter light, she peeled it back to see the cut. The bleeding had almost stopped; it was not as bad as it had first appeared, though the tie was irreparably ruined. "Hey," she said. "How come you brought Jason, anyway?"

Marla didn't answer right away, setting her sights on the first-aid aisle and heading for it.

"Here we are," she said. "What do you think, gauze?"

"Sure, but don't call me Gauze." Charlie leaned into Marla but was ignored.

"Antiseptic," Marla continued, grabbing the items. "The thing is," she said, "so Jason's dad and our mom have been married since before he was born. I mean, obviously. And they're probably getting divorced. I know about it, but Jason doesn't."

"Oh no," Charlie said.

"They're fighting all the time," Marla went on, "and it scares him, you know? I mean, my dad left when I was still a little kid, so I grew up with that; I was used to it. Plus, I got to have a great stepdad. But for him, it's gonna feel like the end of the world. And they're sure not doing anything to make it easier—they're fighting right in front of us. So I didn't want to leave him alone with that for a week."

"I'm so sorry, Marla," Charlie said.

"Yeah, it's okay," Marla said. "I'm leaving in a year anyway. I'm just worried about the brat out there."

"He's really not a brat," Charlie said, and Marla grinned.

"I know; he's pretty great, right? I kinda like having him around."

They paid for the supplies. The clerk, a teenage boy, didn't bat an eye at Charlie's moderately blood-spattered appearance. Outside, they sat on the hood of the car. Marla started to open the bottle of antiseptic, but Charlie held out a hand for it.

"I can do it myself," she said. Marla looked like she was about to argue, but she swallowed whatever she was about to say and handed Charlie the bottle and a piece of gauze. As Charlie awkwardly cleaned her arm, Marla smiled impishly.

"Speaking of people we like having around, are you having fun with John?"

"Ow! That stings. And I don't know what you mean," Charlie said primly, suddenly putting all her attention on her task.

"You do, too. He's following you around like a little puppy, and you are loving it."

Charlie bit back a smile. "How about you and Lamar?" she retorted.

"Me and who now?" Marla said. "Here." She held out a hand for the bloody gauze, and Charlie handed it to her, reaching for a clean strip. "You're going to have to let me tape it," Marla said. Charlie nodded and held the gauze in place as Marla reached for the tape.

"Come on," Charlie went on. "I see the way you look at him."

"Nope!" Marla smoothed down the last piece of tape and put everything back in the bag.

"Seriously," Charlie said as they got back into the car. "You're adorable together. And your names are anagrams of each other. Marla and Lamar! It's meant to be!" Both laughing, they headed back to the motel.

When they got to the motel, Jessica was already there—and so was John. He stood up when Charlie walked in.

"I was worried about you. I thought maybe I could sleep on the floor?" He waited nervously for her reaction, as though he had realized only upon seeing her that he might have overstepped her boundaries.

On another day, in another place, Charlie might have been annoyed by his excessive concern. But here, in Hurricane, she was glad to have it. *We should all be together,* she thought. *It's safer.* She wasn't really afraid, but unease still clung to her like cobwebs, and John's presence had been a calming one ever since they arrived. He was still looking at her, waiting for a response, and she smiled at him.

"As long as you don't mind sharing the floor with Jason," she said.

He grinned. "Just let me have a pillow and I'll be fine." Marla tossed him one, and he stretched elaborately, set it on the ground, and lay down.

They all went to bed almost immediately. Charlie was exhausted; now that her injury had been cleaned and bound, the adrenaline of the night left her body all at once, leaving her drained and a little shaky. She didn't even bother changing into pajamas; she just collapsed on the bed next to Jessica and was asleep in seconds.

Charlie woke just after dawn, when the sky was still pale and a little pink. She looked around the room. The others wouldn't be up for hours, she suspected, but she was too alert to try to fade back into sleep. She grabbed her shoes and, stepping over Jason's and John's sleeping bodies, went outside. The motel was set a little way back off the road, trees spread thickly around and behind it. Charlie sat down on the curb to put her shoes on, wondering if she could go for a walk in the woods without getting lost. The air was crisp, and she felt renewed and energized by the brief night's sleep. Her arm hurt, a dull and pulsing pain that kept drawing her attention, but it had not bled through the bandages. Charlie usually found it easy to ignore pain when she knew she was not in danger from it. The woods were inviting, and she decided to risk getting lost.

As she was about to stand, John sat down beside her.

"Morning," he said. His clothes were rumpled from his night on the motel floor, and his hair was a mess. Charlie held back a laugh. "What?" he said. She shook her head.

"You look a little like your old self today," she said. He looked down at himself and shrugged.

"Clothes don't make the man. What are you doing up so early?"

"I don't know, couldn't sleep. What about you?"

"Somebody stepped on me."

Charlie winced. "Sorry," she said, and he laughed.

"I'm just kidding. I was awake."

"I was going to go for a walk," she said, pointing at the tree line. "Out there, somewhere. Do you want to come?"

"Yeah, definitely."

They headed into the woods, and John hung back for a moment and surreptitiously retucked his shirt, trying to smooth out the wrinkles. Charlie pretended not to notice.

There was no path, and so they made their way through the trees at random, glancing back now and then to be sure they could still make out the motel parking lot. John stumbled over a fallen branch, and Charlie reached out with her good arm to catch him before he fell.

"Thanks," he said. "Strong arm, too."

"Well, you caught me yesterday, so it's only fair that I catch you back. Now we're even," she said. She looked around. The motel was scarcely in sight, and she felt concealed, made safe by the woods. She could say anything here, and it would be all right. She leaned back against a tree, picking idly at the bark behind her. "You know Freddy's wasn't the first restaurant?" She said it abruptly, surprising herself, and John looked at her quizzically, like he had not quite heard her. She didn't want to say it again, but she forced herself to. "Freddy's, it wasn't my dad's first restaurant. There was a diner, a little one. It was before my mom left."

"I had no idea," John said slowly. "Where was it?"

"I don't know. It's one of those memories from when you're a little kid, you know? You only remember the things that are right around you. I remember the linoleum on the kitchen floor; it was this black-and-white diamond pattern, but I don't remember where the restaurant was, or what it was called."

"Yeah," John said. "We took a vacation to a theme park when I was, like, three, and all I remember is the backseat of the car. So were *they* there?" His voice dropped a little quieter when he said it, almost reflexively. Charlie nodded.

"Yeah. There was a bear and a rabbit, I think. Sometimes the details get mixed up in my head. They're not like normal memories," she said, needing him to understand the story's defects before she told him the rest. "It's like when you have a realistic dream, and in the morning you're not sure if it really happened or not. It's just impressions, little snatches of time. It's . . ." She trailed off. She wasn't explaining it right; she was choosing all the wrong words. She was reaching back too far in her memory, to a time when she did not yet speak. It was a time when she did not have the words to name the things she saw, and so now, when she tried to recall them, the words could never be right.

She looked at John. He was watching her patiently, waiting for her to go on. She wanted to tell him this story from her life that she had never told. It was not even a story, not really, just something that nagged at the edge of her mind, something flashing by randomly in the corner of her eye. She was not entirely certain it was real, and so she told no one. She wanted to tell John, because she wanted to speak it to another person, because he looked at her with trusting eyes and she knew he would listen to and believe her. Because he had cared for her a long time ago, because he had caught her when she fell, and he had come here to sleep and keep watch all night. And, thought a pragmatic, slightly cruel part of her, because he was not part of her real life. She could tell him this, tell him anything, and when she returned home, it would be as though it had never happened. She wanted suddenly to touch him, have confirmation that he was really there, that this was not another dream. She reached out her hand to him, and, surprised but glad, he took it. He stayed where he was, as if afraid that moving in closer would scare her. They stayed that way for a moment, and then she let go, and she told him the story the way she spoke it in her head, the memories of a small child mixing with the things she had come to understand as she grew older.

There was another restaurant, rustic and small, with red checkered cloths on the tables, and a kitchen you could see into from the dining area, and they all were there together. Her father and her mother and *us*. When Charlie was very, very young, she was never alone. There was Charlie, and there was a little boy, a little boy so close to Charlie that remembering him was like remembering a part of herself. They were always together; she learned to say *we* before she learned to say *I*.

They played together on the floor of the kitchen, sometimes drawing pictures while hiding under a hardwood table. She remembered the shuffling of feet and the shadows of customers walking by. Light was broken by a slowly turning fan and thrown across the floor in ribbons. She remembered the smell of an ashtray and the hearty laughter of adults lost in a good story while their children played.

Very often she would hear her father's laugh echoing from a distant corner as he talked with customers. When Charlie pictured him laughing like that now it was with a little ache, a sucking feeling in the center of her chest, because his eyes were bright and his smile was easy and because he wanted them all to be a part of the restaurant, to share his work freely. Because he was not afraid to let his children roam and explore. He was yet untouched by grief, and so while he looked a little like the father she truly remembered, he was not the same man at all.

Charlie was looking down at the ground as she talked, at the dirt and stones and cracked remains of leaves, and her hand was at her back, stripping bark from the tree. *Does that hurt the tree?* she thought, and forced her hands away, knotting them in front of her.

The restaurant was open until late at night, and so when they began to falter, Charlie and the little boy would crawl into the pantry with blankets and soft toys to sleep until it was time to close. She remembered using sacks of flour as pillows, big bags almost as long as they were tall. They would snuggle down together and whisper words of nonsense that meant deep things only to the two of them, and Charlie would drift into sleep, half listening to the warm sounds of the restaurant, the clank of dishes and the murmur of grown-up talk, and the sound of the bear and the rabbit as they danced to their chiming tunes.

They loved the animals, the yellowish-brown bear and the matching rabbit, who wandered the restaurant, dancing and singing for the customers, and sometimes just for Charlie and the little boy. They sometimes moved stiffly and mechanically, and sometimes with fluid, human movements, and while the boy liked the animals best when they acted like people, Charlie liked them the other way. Their stilted movements, their lifeless eyes, and their occasional glitches fascinated her: They acted alive, but were not. The narrow yet bottomless chasm between those things, alive and not-alive, enthralled her, though she would never have been able to explain why.

"I think they were costumes," Charlie said now, still looking down at the ground. "The animals weren't always robots; the bear and the bunny were costumes, and sometimes people wore them, and sometimes my father put it onto one of his robots, and you could always tell which it was by the way they danced."

Charlie stopped. There was more, but she could not bring herself to speak. There was something else that made her lock down her mind and force the memory away, the part that made her unwilling to ask Aunt Jen for answers, because she was afraid of what those answers might be. Charlie had not dared to look at John the whole time she was talking, staring only at the ground, at her hands, at her sneakers. Now she did look at him, and he was rapt, seeming almost to be holding his breath. He waited, not wanting to speak until he was sure she was finished.

"That's all I remember," she said at last, even though it was a lie.

"Wait, who was the little boy?" John said.

Charlie shook her head, frustrated that he had not understood.

"He was mine," she said. "I mean, he was my brother. We were the same." She was speaking childishly, as if the memory had taken hold of her, forcing her to regress. She cleared her throat. "Sorry," she said, speaking more slowly, trying to choose her words with care. "I think he was my twin brother."

She saw John open his mouth, about to ask the question, *What happened to him?* But there must have been something in her face, something warning, because he held it back and said instead, "Do you think that place was around here? I mean, I guess it could have been anywhere. Another state, even."

"I don't know," Charlie said slowly, looking over her shoulders, then up at the trees. "This all feels the same. It feels like I could walk around any corner and it could be there." Her voice began to break. "I want to find it," she added suddenly, and as soon as she said it, it was what she wanted to do.

"Well, what do you remember about it?" John said enthusiastically, almost lunging forward like an eager dog on a lead. He must have been dying to go looking from the moment she mentioned the place. Charlie smiled but shook her head.

"I really don't remember much," she said. "I don't know how much help I can actually be; like I said, the things I remember are just little scraps, they're not information. It's like a picture book." She closed her eyes, trying to see the place in her mind's eye. "The floor would shake." She lifted her head as the thought became clear. "A train?" she asked as though John would know. "I remember this thunderous sound every day; it was the biggest sound I'd ever heard. I don't mean loud, I mean you could feel it in your whole body, like it was rumbling right through your chest."

"It must have been close to some tracks, then, right?" John said.

"Yeah," Charlie said with a spark of hope. "There was a tree out in front," she went on. "It looked like an old, angry monster, hunched forward and wizened, with two giant, gnarled branches reaching out like arms. Whenever we left for the night, I hid my face in my father's shirt so I wouldn't have to see it as we walked by."

"What else?" John said. "Were there stores, or other restaurants?"

"No. I mean, I don't think so. I'm sorry." She scratched her head. "It's gone."

"It's not enough," John said, a little frustrated. "It could be anywhere, a train and a tree. There must be something else you can remember. Anything?"

"No," Charlie said. The more she pushed herself to remember, the harder it got. She was grasping blindly, and it was like trying to get hold of living creatures, as if the memories saw her coming and slipped away.

She tossed out fragments as she managed to catch them: the tablecloths, red-and-white checked, and made of real cloth, not plastic. She remembered grabbing at one, unsteady on her feet, and the whole table setting falling down on top of her, plates and glasses shattering around her as she covered her head. *Charlotte, are you okay?* Her father's voice seemed clearer than ever.

There was a squeaky floorboard in the corner of the diner that Charlie liked to push on, making it sing as if it made music. There was a picnic table out back where they used to sit in the sun, one leg of it sinking in the soft ground. There was the song her parents used to sing in the car whenever they came home from a trip; they would burst into it when they were a little way from home, and then they'd start laughing as if they had done something clever.

"It's nothing helpful," Charlie said. "Just kid stuff." She felt a little light-headed. She had spent so many years avoiding these memories; her mind shied away as if from snakes. Having done it, she felt strange and a little guilty, like she had done something wrong. But she also felt something that might have been joy, in the things she never allowed herself to think of. The memories of that time were unsafe, there were traps and snares wrought into their very substance, but there were precious things among them.

"Sorry," she said. "I can't remember more."

"No, that's really impressive. I can't believe you remember that far back at all," he said. "I didn't mean to push you," he added a little sheepishly, then looked thoughtful. "What was the song?"

"I think it was the same one they dance to at Freddy's," Charlie said.

"No, the one your parents sang in the car."

"Oh," she said. "I don't know if I remember it. It wasn't really a song, you know? It was just a little line." She closed her eyes, picturing the car, trying to envision the backs of her parents' heads as though she were still in the backseat. She waited, trusting her mind to give it up, and after a moment, it did. She hummed it, just six notes.

"'We're back in harmony,'" she sang. "And they'd, you know, harmonize," she added, embarrassed by her parents even now. John's expression was blank for a moment as the words at first seemed meaningless, but then his eyes lit with promise.

"Charlie, there's a town north of here called New Harmony."

"Huh," was all she said for a moment. She listened to the words in her head, wanting them to set off an inspiration, trip a memory, but they did not.

"I feel like that should ring a bell, but it doesn't," she said. "Sorry. I mean, it doesn't sound wrong, but it doesn't sound *right*, either." She was disappointed, but John still had that thoughtful look on his face.

"Come on," he said, extending his hand. Charlie wiped her cheek and took a shaky breath, then looked to him. She nodded with an exhausted smile and got to her feet.

"Should we wait for everyone to wake up?" John said as they emerged into the parking lot after a brisk walk back.

"No," Charlie said with unexpected vehemence. "I don't want everyone there for this," she added in softer tones. Just the thought of the whole group going along made her anxious. It was too risky, too private; she had no idea what they might find or what it might do to her, and she couldn't abide the thought of making those discoveries with an audience.

"Okay," John said. "Just us, then."

"Just us."

Charlie went inside and grabbed her car keys, moving slowly so as not to disturb the others. As she was heading back to the door, Jason stirred and opened his eyes, looking up at her like he wasn't quite sure who she was. She put a finger to her lips.

He nodded sleepily and closed his eyes again, and she hurried out the door. She tossed the keys to John and got in on the passenger's side.

"There's a map in here," she said, jostling open the glove-box door. The map fell out amid a pile of hand warmers and emergency food rations.

"Your aunt strikes again." John smiled.

Charlie held the map just a few inches from her face. New Harmony was close, only about half an hour away.

"Think you can navigate?" he asked.

"Aye, Cap'n!" Charlie said. "Turn left out of the lot."

"Thanks," he said wryly.

They drove back through the town and out the other side, the houses farther and farther between as they went. Each one stood solitary, connected only by sagging power lines. Charlie watched the telephone poles and the dipping wires repeating hypnotically as if they would go on forever, then blinked, breaking the spell. Ahead of them the mountains rose up ancient and dark against the clear blue sky; they looked more solid than anything else around them, more real, and maybe they were. They had been here, watching, long before the houses, long before the roads, and they would be here long after they were all gone.

"Nice day," John said, and she looked at him, tearing her gaze from the view.

"Yeah," Charlie said. "I kind of forgot how beautiful it is out here."

"Yeah," he said. He was quiet for a moment, then looked at her sideways, and Charlie couldn't tell if he was being shy or just keeping his eyes on the road.

"It's weird," he said at last. "When I was a kid, the mountains kind of scared me, especially when we were driving in the dark. They were like some monstrous beasts looming over us." He laughed a little, but Charlie did not.

"I know what you mean," she said, then grinned at him. "I think they're pretty much just mountains, though. Hey," she said suddenly, "you never told me what your story was about."

"My story?" He flicked his eyes at her again, a little nervous.

"Yeah, you said you got a story published. What was it about?"

"I mean, it was just a little magazine, just local," he said, still reluctant. Charlie waited, and finally he continued. "It's called 'The Little Yellow House.' It's about a boy," he said. "He's ten years old. His parents are fighting all the time, and he's afraid they're going to get divorced. They fight, and he overhears them saying awful things to each other, and he hides in his room with the door shut, but he can still hear them.

"So he starts looking out the window, at the house across

the street. They sort of keep their curtains open just enough that he can glimpse inside. He watches them go in and out of the house, this family, and he starts making up stories about them, imagining who they are and what they do, and after a while they start feeling more real to him than his own family."

He glanced at Charlie again, as if trying to gauge her reaction, and Charlie smiled. He went on.

"So summer comes, and his family goes away for a week, and it's miserable, and when they get back, the family in the house across the street has moved away. There's nothing left, just a FOR SALE sign hanging in front."

Charlie nodded, waiting for him to continue, but he looked at her a little sheepishly.

"That's the end," he said.

"Oh," she said. "That's really sad."

He shrugged. "I guess. I'm working on something happy now, though."

"What's that?"

He grinned at her.

"It's a secret."

Charlie smiled back. It felt good to be out here, good to just be driving out into the horizon. She cranked the window down and put her arm out into the air, enjoying the feel of the rushing wind. *It's not wind rushing, it's us*, she thought.

"What about you?" John said.

"What about me?" Charlie said, still happily playing against the wind.

"Come on, what's the life of Charlie like these days?"

Charlie smiled at him and pulled her arm back into the car. "I don't know," she said. "Pretty boring." There was a part of her that did not want to tell him for the same reason she wanted him with her now: She did not want her new life to mix with the old. But John had told her something real, something personal, and she felt like she owed him the same in return.

"It's all right," she said at last. "My aunt is cool, even if she does sometimes look at me like she's not quite sure where I came from. School's fine, I have friends and all that, but it feels so temporary. I have another year, but I feel like I'm already gone."

"Gone where?" John asked, and Charlie shrugged.

"I wish I knew. College, I guess. I'm not sure what comes next."

"Nobody ever knows what comes next, I guess," he said. "Do you—?" He stopped himself, but she prodded him.

"Do I what?" she said teasingly. "Do I ever think of you?" He flushed, and she instantly regretted the words.

"I was going to say, do you ever see your mom," he said quietly.

"Oh," she said. "No, I don't." It exhausted Charlie to think of her mother, and she thought her mother felt the same. Too much hung between them—not quite blame, because neither of them were to blame for what had happened, but something close to it. Their pain, individual, radiated off them both like auras, pushing at each other like magnets with the poles reversed, forcing them apart.

"Charlie?" John was saying her name, and she looked over at him.

"Sorry," she said. "I drifted for a second."

"You got any music in this car?" he asked, and she nodded eagerly, seizing on the diversion. She bent over, picked up cassettes scattered on the floor, and started reading labels. He made fun of her tapes, she argued back, and after some playful bickering, she shoved a tape into the player and settled back again to stare out the window.

"I think this is where the map's usefulness ends." John gestured to the road ahead. "The whole area's pretty much blank; I think what we're looking for isn't going to be on this map." He folded the map and tucked it neatly to the side of the seat, craning his neck out the window to see what they were passing.

"Yeah," she said. It looked like they had returned to civilization. Single houses littered the fields, and dirt roads branched off in all directions. The landscape was mostly bushes and short trees, the whole area nestled between rows of low-lying mountains.

John looked at Charlie, hoping she would notice something that would point them in the right direction.

"Nothing?" he said, though her blank stare had already given him the answer.

"No," she said plainly. She didn't want to elaborate.

The houses became fewer and more scattered, and the fields of dry brush seemed to stretch wider, giving the whole area a feeling of desertion. John found himself glancing over at Charlie at short intervals, waiting for a signal, half expecting her to tell him to stop and turn around, but Charlie just stared into the distance, her eyes fixed on nothing, resting her cheek in her hand.

"Let's go back," she said finally, sounding resigned.

"We could have missed something," John said. He slowed the car, looking for a spot to make a U-turn. "We missed a lot back there; maybe it's down one of those dirt roads."

Charlie laughed.

"Really? You think we missed a lot?" She grew thoughtful. "No, none of this feels right. Nothing rings a bell." She felt a tear spill onto her cheek, and she swiped it away before John could notice.

"Okay, no worries," Charlie said abruptly, pulling herself back from reverie. "Let's grab a bite, just you and me." John smiled, still checking his mirrors for a place to turn. Charlie shivered. Then something caught her eye. She almost jumped in her seat, sitting straight up.

"STOP!" she shouted. John slammed on the brakes and the car skidded, dust billowing up all around the car. When they stopped, Charlie sat silently as John checked the rear-view mirror again, his heart racing.

"Are you okay?" he said, but Charlie was already out of the car. "Hey!" he called after her, scrambling out of his seat belt and rushing to lock the car behind him.

Charlie was running back toward the town, but her eyes were on the field beside the road. He caught up quickly, trotting along beside her without asking questions. After a few minutes, Charlie slowed and began shuffling her feet on the ground, peering down as though she had lost something small and valuable in the dirt.

"Charlie?" John said. Until this moment he had not thought about what it was they were doing. It was an adventure, a chance to be alone with Charlie, to run off after a clue, but now she was starting to worry him. He brushed his hair back from his face. "Charlie?" he said again, his voice touched with concern, but Charlie did not look at him; she was intent on whatever she had found.

"Right here," she said. She made a sharp turn toward the edge of the road, where something protruded and snaked across the ground. John knelt carefully, brushing some of the loose dirt with his hand and exposing a flat metal beam. He kept going, uncovering a track that stretched across the road and went off into the field in both directions. It took him a moment to speak; it was as though the earth itself had tried to conceal it from them. *Be careful*, he thought with a minor pang of alarm, but he brushed aside the feeling. "I think we found your tracks," he said, looking up at Charlie, but she was nowhere in sight. "Charlie?" He took a quick look up and down the road, but there were no cars. "Charlie!" he called again, waving the dust away from his face and racing to catch up. When he reached her, he hung back a little, afraid to disturb her intense focus.

There was a cluster of trees up ahead, gathered together as though around a campfire, tall and short or thick and scraggly. Charlie dragged her foot along the track as she walked, as if it might vanish if she ceased to touch it.

"What is that, an old station?" John asked, squinting and blocking the sun with his hand. There was a long building nestled in the trees, its color blending in with the small grove, making it difficult to spot.

The tracks veered away, heading off toward the mountains, and Charlie stopped dragging her foot along them, letting them go. John finally caught up, and they walked through the dry grass together toward the grove of trees, not far away now.

"There has to be a road." Charlie strayed almost randomly, heading away from the building. John hesitated.

"But . . ." He gestured toward the building, then followed her, looking back to make sure he knew the way back to the car. Before long, the ground leveled out beneath their feet. Old pavement, broken with weeds and mounds of crumbling rock, stretched across the field in a narrow, almost hidden path, leading once again toward the small building.

"This is it," Charlie said softly. John approached her carefully, then stood at her side. They walked the road together, dodging around the pillars of grass that shot up from the breaks and holes. The tree was there, the one with reaching arms and ghastly face, but it was no longer frightening, no longer as Charlie remembered. It must have already been dead when she was a child, she realized. Its limbs had fallen off, leaving jagged holes where they had been, and they lay where they fell, rotting into the ground. The tree seemed a frail and weak shade of its former self, only recognizable by the stumps and bulges on its side that had made its face. Now even the face looked tired.

The building itself was long and dilapidated. It was a single story, with a dark roof and weather-beaten walls. The place had once been painted red, but time and sun and rain had won out over the paint; it was peeled and curling, whole long strips of it gone and the wood beneath showing, dark with what might be rot. Its foundation was overgrown with tall grass, and Charlie thought it looked as if it were sinking, as though the whole structure was slowly being swallowed by the earth. Charlie grabbed John's arm as they neared it, then let it go and straightened her back. She felt as though she were preparing for a fight, as if the building itself might attack if it sensed weakness.

Charlie went warily up the few steps to the door, sticking to the edges and testing the wood before she let down her full weight. The stairs held, but there were soft, splintered patches in the middle she didn't want to try. John didn't follow her right away, sidetracked by something nearly hidden in the grass.

"Charlie." He held it up: a battered metal sign with the painted words FREDBEAR'S FAMILY DINER in red script.

Charlie gave a gentle smile. *Of course this is it. I'm home.*

John came up the stairs behind her and set the sign down carefully by the door, and they went inside. The door swung open easily. Light streamed in through the windows on all sides, revealing emptiness and decay. Unlike Freddy's, this place had been cleaned out. The wooden floors seemed intact, but they were warped from weather. Sunlight was streaming in, unobstructed, and went where it wanted without furniture or people to block its path. Charlie looked up at the ceiling fan; it was still there, but one of its blades was missing.

There were double doors to their right with circular windows. Unlike the dining area, which was breached with sunlight and the sounds of the outside, the room behind the double doors was still pitch black. John was more interested in this than Charlie, and he carefully peered into one of the windows, obviously tempted to nudge it open and see what was inside. Charlie left him to his curiosity and walked farther into the dining room, which she only knew as the dining room through memory. Now it was a vacant and lonely room, stretching long and narrow, at least fifty feet, growing darker as it went. There was a slightly elevated stage at the end of the room, and Charlie realized as she looked around that the place had probably once been a dance hall, and the long desk by the entrance that her parents had used for a cash register had probably been a bar. She went over to it and saw that she was right: There were even grooves and scratches in the wood floor where barstools had once dug their feet. She tried to picture it, a dark bar with a country-western band playing on the stage, but she could not.

When Charlie looked at the stage, she could still see two animatronic animals in shadow, moving in unnatural twists and turns. She could hear echoes of carnival music and distant laughter. She could still smell the cigarette smoke in the air. She hesitated before going farther, as though the ghosts she remembered might linger on the stage. She tried to catch a glimpse of where John was. He finally had the door to the kitchen half-open and was sticking his head inside. Charlie turned her attention back to the stage and walked toward it across the creaking floor. Even the smallest sound was deafening, accompanied by faint whistles as the wind slipped through cracks in the windows and walls. Strips of wallpaper had peeled down and hung flat against the wall, inert until a breeze lifted them up, and they wagged like thin fingers pointing at Charlie as she walked.

Charlie stood at the base of the stage, studying the floor carefully for traces of what might have stood there before. All that remained were holes where bolts had once been. The corners looked blackened, with the shapes of coils and wires etched into dirt and wood.

Everything is gone.

Her head jerked toward the corner to her right; there was another door. *Of course there is another door. This is why you are here.* She stood still, looking at the door, but not ready to touch it. She was grasped with a strange and illogical fear, as though spiders and boogeymen might come rushing out.

The door was ajar. Charlie looked back toward John again, hesitant to go on without him. As though he heard her calling to him, he leaned out of the kitchen door with a wide-eyed expression. "This is really creepy." He was obviously enjoying himself, like a kid in a haunted house.

"Can you come with me?" Charlie's plea came as a surprise to John, who seemed pleased but irritated at the same time, having been enjoying his own adventure on the other side of the building. "Two seconds," he promised, then disappeared again.

She rolled her eyes, disappointed but not surprised that his childish curiosity would take priority. She rested the back of her hand against the aged wooden door and gently guided it open, bracing herself against whatever might be inside.

Whatever she had been expecting, this wasn't it. It was a closet, the inside extending off to her left about eight or nine feet into darkness. There were horizontal poles mounted along the walls where hangers had once been. Square shapes imprinted in the dust filled her mind with images of boxes, maybe speakers.

As she stepped inside, she pushed the door open all the way, trying to let in as much light as possible. As she walked farther in, she let her hand drag along the wall. Although nothing was there now, she could feel heavy cloth, coats, and sweaters hanging.

No. These were costumes.

Costumes had hung here in the dark, hiding their colors but allowing themselves to be felt by every cheek and small hand that passed through. Rubber-padded palms and fingers swayed this way and that. Reflections on false eyes passed overhead.

Charlie reached the end and turned to look back. She crouched down, looking up at the empty space. It didn't feel empty. She could still feel the costumes; they were hanging all around her. There was someone else in the closet with her, kneeling down at her own height. It was her friend, the little boy.

My little brother.

They were both playing and hiding together as they always did. *This time was different.* The little boy looked up toward the door suddenly as though they had been caught doing something they shouldn't have been doing. Charlie looked up as well. There was a figure in the door. It looked like one of the costumes was standing on its own, but it was motionless, so still that Charlie wasn't sure what she was seeing.

It was the rabbit, the yellowish-brown rabbit they loved, but it did not dance or sing, just stood there and stared at them, unblinking. They began to squirm under its gaze, and the little boy screwed up his face to wail. Charlie pinched his arm, seized with an instinctual sense that they must not cry. The rabbit looked back and forth from one to the other with those all-too-human eyes, ponderous, as though weighing and measuring them in some way that Charlie could not understand, like it was making a momentous decision. Charlie could see its eyes, its human eyes, and she was cold with terror. She felt the fear in her brother as well, felt it echoing between them, reverberating and growing because it was shared. They could not move, they could not scream, and finally the creature inside that patchwork, ragged yellow rabbit suit reached forward for the boy. There was a moment, one single moment, when the children still clung together, gripping hands, but the rabbit snatched the boy to his breast, yanking them apart, and fled.

From that moment the entire memory shattered with piercing and unrelenting screams, not her brother's, but her own. People rushed to help, her father picked her up and held her, but nothing could console her; she screamed and screamed, louder and louder. Charlie snapped back from her dream, the sound still high and painful in her ears. She was crouched down in silence. John stood at the door, not daring to interrupt.

She did not remember much of what had happened next; everything was dark. It was all a blur of images and facts she had pieced together later, things she might remember and others she might have imagined. She was never in the restaurant again. She knew her parents shuttered the doors immediately.

Then they moved to the new house, and Charlie's mother left a little while after that. Charlie did not remember her saying good-bye, although she knew her mother must have. Her mother would not have left without a good-bye, but it was just lost in the mist of time and grief like so much else. She remembered the first time she stood in the doorway of her father's workshop, the first day they were alone in everything. It was the day he began to build her a mechanical toy, a little dog who tilted its head from side to side. She smiled when she saw it finished, and her father looked at her the way he would look at her for the rest of his life, as though he loved her more than life itself and as though his love made him unbearably sad. She knew even then that something vital inside him had broken, something that could never be repaired. Sometimes he seemed to look right through her, as if he couldn't see her even when she was standing right in front of him.

Her father never again spoke her brother's name, and so Charlie learned not to speak it, either, as though to speak it would send them back to that time and unravel them both. She woke in the mornings and looked for the little boy, having forgotten in her dreams that he was gone. When she turned to where he would be and saw only her stuffed toys she would cry, but she would not say his name. She was afraid to even think it, and she trained her mind to shrink from it until she truly forgot, but deep inside she knew it: Sammy.

A rumbling sound rose, loud and low like a train passing, and Charlie startled.

"A train?" She looked around her, eyes wide; she was disoriented, not sure if she was in the past or present.

"It's okay. I don't think it's anywhere near here. Might just be a big truck." John took Charlie's arm and pulled her to her feet. "Did you remember something?" he whispered. He was trying to catch her gaze, but she was focused elsewhere.

"A lot." Charlie put her hand to her mouth, still staring into the darkness as if she could see the scene. John's hand on her arm was an anchor, and she clung fast to it. *This is real. This is now*, she thought, and she turned to him, seized by a fierce gratitude that he was there with her. She buried her face in his chest as if his body could shield her from what she had seen, and she let herself cry. John hugged her tight, one hand on her head, cautiously stroking her hair. They stayed that way for long moments, and at last she calmed, her breathing deep and even again. John loosened his grip on her, and as soon as he did, Charlie stepped back, suddenly aware of how close they had been.

John's hands were still suspended in midair from where Charlie had been. After a moment of shock, he lowered one and used the other to scratch his head.

"So . . ." He hoped for an answer to fill the silence.

"A rabbit," Charlie said calmly, looking toward the doorway. "A yellow rabbit." Her voice became graver as the image was still fresh in her mind.

"The one I saw the night Michael disappeared, the bear, I'm pretty sure he was yellow, too."

"I thought you said it was like the others," Charlie said.

"I thought it was. When everybody said Freddy was brown, that night we first met up, I just thought I was remembering it wrong. I mean, I really don't have a great memory for back then, you know? I didn't even remember what color my old house was. But then you said he was yellow, too."

"Yeah, they were yellow." She nodded; it was the answer he was expecting.

"I think it's connected—the animals from here, and the one I saw at Freddy's."

And the one that took my brother, Charlie thought. She took a final look around the place.

"Let's go back," she said. "I want to get out of here."

"Okay," John said.

As they headed to the door, a small object caught Charlie's eye, and she snatched it up. It was a twisted piece of metal, and as John watched, close by, she stretched it out, then let it snap back together with a loud *crack*, like a whip. John jumped.

"What is that?" he said, composing himself.

"I'm not sure," she said, but she slipped it into her pocket. John was watching her like there was something he wanted to say. "Let's go," Charlie said.

They began the trek back to the car. *Sammy, then years later Michael and the other kids—of course it's connected*, Charlie thought. *Lightning might strike twice, but not murder.*

"Can you drive again?" she asked after a long period of silence. The only sounds so far had been their shoes crunching through the dry grass.

"Yeah, of course," he said.

John managed to get the car turned around in the constricted space, and Charlie settled against the window, her eyes half-closed already. She watched the trees fly by outside her window and felt herself beginning to doze. The metal object in her pocket was digging into her leg, keeping her awake, and she repositioned it, thinking dreamily of the first time she saw one of the things.

She was sitting with Sammy in the restaurant, before it opened for the day; they were under a window, in a dusty beam of light, playing some invented game she could no longer remember, and their father came over, grinning. He had something to show them.

He held up the piece of twisted metal and showed them how it opened, then let it snap back in his hand. They both cried out in surprise, then started giggling and clapping their hands.

Their father did it again. "I could snap off your nose!" he said, and again they laughed, but quickly his face turned serious. "I mean it," he said. "This is a spring lock, and I want you to know how it works because it's very dangerous, and I don't ever want you touching these. This is why we never put our hands in the animal costumes; it's very easy to trigger these if you don't know what you're doing, and you could get hurt. It's like touching the stove—do we ever touch the stove?"

They shook their heads with a solemnity beyond their years.

"Good. Because I want you both to grow up with all your noses!" he cried, and he swept them up, one in each arm, swinging them around as they laughed. Suddenly there was a loud *snap*.

Charlie jolted out of sleep.

"What was that?"

"What was what?" John said. The car was off. Charlie looked around; they were back at the motel.

Charlie took a moment to reorient herself, then gave a reluctant smile. "Thanks for driving."

"What were you dreaming about?" John said. "You looked happy."

Charlie shook her head.

"I don't remember."

CHAPTER SIX

T he other car was gone from the lot, and when they went into the room, there was a note on Charlie's pillow, written in Marla's big, loopy handwriting.

We're meeting for dinner at 6:30, and then going to you-know-where! she had written. *See you two soon—don't forget about the rest of us! XOXO Marla*

She had drawn a smiley face and a heart below her name. Charlie smiled to herself, folding the note and slipping it into her pocket without showing it to John.

"What does it say?" he asked.

"We have to meet them at the diner in"—she checked her watch—"an hour." John nodded. He was still standing in the doorway, waiting for something. "What?" Charlie said.

"I need to go change," he said, gesturing at the rumpled

clothing he was wearing. "Can I take your car?" He held up the keys and jangled them.

"Oh, yeah, of course. Just come back for me," Charlie said with a grin.

He smiled. "Of course," he added with a wink.

When the door closed behind him, Charlie let out a sigh. *Alone at last.* She was unaccustomed to so much company; she and Aunt Jen moved in their own orbits, meeting gladly from time to time throughout the day, but with the assumption that Charlie could take care of her own needs or would speak up if she could not. Charlie never spoke up. She could feed herself, get to school and back, and maintain her high grades and casual friendships. What could Aunt Jen do about nightmares? About questions she did not really want the answers to? What could Aunt Jen tell her that was not even more horrific than what she already knew? So she was not used to the sustained presence of other people, and it was a little tiring.

She showered quickly and pulled on new clothes, jeans and a black T-shirt, then lay back on the bed, staring up at the ceiling. She had a vague sense that her mind should be racing with excitement or horror at their discoveries, going over and over the memories she had awakened, searching for something new. Instead, she just felt blank. She wanted to be alone, to push the memories to the back of her mind where they belonged.

After what seemed like only a few short minutes, there was a knock on the door, and Charlie sat up, checking her watch. More time had passed than she realized; it was time to leave. She let John in.

"I have to put on my shoes," she said. She looked up at him as she knotted the laces. He had changed, this time into jeans and a T-shirt, a contrast with the formal clothes she had gotten used to. His hair was still wet, and there was something fresh and bright about him. She smiled a little.

"What?" he said when he noticed.

"Nothing," she said. "You still look dirty," she joked as she pushed past him. They got in the car. This time she drove, and when they reached the diner, Charlie turned off the engine and hesitated, not moving to leave the car.

"John," she said. "I don't want to tell anyone about Fredbear's."

"But—" He stopped himself. "Yeah," he said. "I think we forget this is your life and not just some adventure. It's fine; I can keep a secret."

"It's all our lives," she said. "We were all there. We can tell them later; I just want to sort some of it out for myself right now."

"You got it," he said, and he looked a little pleased. Charlie knew why—it was a secret between them, something she entrusted only to him.

When they went inside, everyone was already halfway

through dinner. Charlie realized with a sharp pang that she had not eaten all day, and she found herself suddenly starving. The waitress spotted them as they sat down and came over immediately. They talked intermittently: Lamar, Jason, and Marla had gone to a movie, and Carlton and Jessica had played video games at his house. But their conversation was cursory, just filling the time as they ate. Charlie barely listened, and she had the feeling that even those who were talking were paying little attention to their own words. There was an agitated energy among the group; they were all just waiting, their minds already focused on Freddy's.

"What about you two?" Jessica asked, looking at Charlie and John.

"Yeah, what about you two?" Marla echoed with a twinkle in her eye.

"We just went for a drive," John said quickly. "Got lost for a while."

"I bet you did," Carlton muttered into his burger, grinning slyly even though his mouth was full.

After dinner, the group hurried through the mall and toward the restaurant, hushed and cautious. As they passed through the atrium, their shoes made only soft sounds on the tiled floor, and no one spoke. Charlie had left the big flashlight in the car. They knew their way well enough by now, and the guard had almost seen them the night before; there was no reason to risk drawing extra attention. They came to the end of the hall, and Lamar, at the front of the group, stopped short. Charlie bumped into Marla before she realized what was happening, and she murmured an apology, then froze.

The night guard was blocking the alley behind Freddy's, his arms folded across his chest. He had no flashlight, and so he had been invisible, hidden in the darkness until they were almost upon him.

"I had a feeling you wouldn't leave it alone," he said with an odd, uneven smile.

Marla whispered something unpleasant under her breath.

"I could have you arrested for trespassing," he said. "Saw you here last night, but I couldn't see where you got to. I guess now I know," he added with a smirk.

There was something almost immediately off-putting about the man. He was tall and slightly too thin for his uniform, which bagged at the shoulders and waist, as if he had once been a more robust man but had lost his form somehow to illness or tragedy; his name tag, reading DAVE, hung askew on his chest. His skin was sallow, and his eyes were undercut by heavy lines, adding to the impression of longstanding ill health.

"What were you all doing back here anyway?" he demanded. "You kids partying? Drugs? I could have you arrested right now, you know." Charlie and John glanced at each other.

"We're sorry," Lamar said quickly. "We'll go. We don't have any drugs."

"Says who? Says you?" The guard wore an odd expression, and his words were harsh and fast; he seemed not to be responding to what they were saying. He looked angry, but his mouth kept quirking up at the corners, like he was trying not to smile.

"What do we do?" Jessica whispered.

"Probably the most action he's ever had out here," Carlton said with a hint of disdain, and Charlie remembered suddenly that Carlton's father was a cop. She remembered him in his uniform, tilting down his dark sunglasses at them with a mock-glare, then smiling, revealing the joke. The guard, however, looked like he meant it.

"We'll go," Lamar said again. "Sorry."

Charlie looked at the man, considering him: the ill-fitting uniform, his peaky, almost exhausted-looking features. He really could kick them off the property or even have them arrested for trespassing, but still, she could not really fear him. His inadequacy shone through him like a kind of negative charisma. He would always be shoved to the back of a crowd, always shouted down in an argument, always picked last, forgotten, ignored in favor of those who were simply more vital, more vigorously attached to life. Charlie frowned at herself. It was an unusual train of thought for her—she did not usually assume she could read the lives of strangers through the lines on their faces. But it gave her an idea.

"Why don't you come with us?" she said. "We just want to explore a little bit more, then we'll leave. You know your way around better than any of us," she added, hoping that some of the flattery would stick.

"And then we'll never come back again," Carlton said. The guard did not immediately dismiss the idea, and the others quickly chimed in with their own assurances. The guard peered at them one by one, fixing his gaze on each in turn. When he looked at Charlie, she looked away, not wanting to meet his eyes, as if she would be giving something away if she let him look too deeply. Once he had inspected them to his satisfaction, he nodded.

"Sure," he said. "Only because I've always wanted to take a walk in there myself." He jerked a thumb behind him, and, catching the surprise that must have shown on their faces, added, "I'm not an idiot. I've been working here for years, walked this building inside and out every night. You think I don't know what's back there?" Charlie felt herself flush; she had somehow assumed their discovery was unique. The guard looked down at his name tag suddenly, then pointed to it. "Name's Dave," he said.

"I'm Jason," Jason said, and, a little warily, the others recited their own names in turn. They stood there, looking at one another awkwardly for a moment, no one wanting to be the first to move, then Jessica shrugged.

"Come on," she said. She walked quickly to the scaffolding that hid the alley to Freddy's and pulled back the plastic, revealing the break in the wall, and they all filed through, squeezing past the piled boxes. Dave hung back politely, letting them all go first. He motioned to Charlie to go ahead.

I don't want you behind me, Charlie thought. She looked at Jessica, who wasn't moving, either.

"Please, go ahead," Charlie said with an edge in her voice, and Dave ducked his head shyly and went. Charlie followed him, and Jessica tucked the plastic carefully back where it was, concealing their passing even though there was no one left to catch them. As they made their way down the dank alley, Charlie touched her fingers to the brick wall, dragging her hand along it as if to guide her. The flashlights seemed a little dimmer now, though she knew it could only be her imagination.

They led the guard to the heavy wooden shelf that hid the entrance, and Lamar, John, and Jessica dragged it out of the way, revealing the door. Charlie expected their new companion to be impressed, but he just nodded, as if he had suspected this all along.

One by one, they entered the hall to the restaurant, and again Charlie lagged back from the group. She caught Carlton by the arm as he passed her.

"Carlton," she whispered. "Have you ever seen this guy?"

Carlton shook his head. "It's not *that* small a town; I don't know everybody."

Charlie nodded absently, her eyes still on the newcomer as they made their way down the long hallway into Freddy's main dining room. She had invited the guard because it seemed like the only way to get back in, but now she was beginning to regret it. Letting a stranger into Freddy's was like letting him into her home, like giving something up.

"What happened to the restaurant?" Lamar said, his tone carefully even, forcing a friendliness he could not have felt. "Why is it boarded up? And why is the mall abandoned anyway?" His voice sounded thin in the narrow hallway, a little muted.

"You don't know?" Dave said. "This town needs money, jobs, revenue, things like that, and one thing we've got a lot of is space. So they decided to build a big mall, try and attract businesses, maybe even tourists. They built up around where Freddy Fazbear's was, but when it came to it, no one would lease the restaurant, you know, because of what happened. So someone had the bright idea of sealing the whole place up, intact; someone who had a sentimental attachment to it, perhaps. I don't think they even tried to clear it out. But it wasn't enough. Something about that place spilled over into the rest of the building, maybe right down into the soil. No one wanted to bring their business here. Sometimes business owners, franchisers from outside the town, would come and look at the place, but they never signed the papers. Said it just didn't feel right. I think it's got an aura, a mystical energy, maybe, if you believe in that sort of thing." Dave wiggled his fingers in the air as though casting a spell.

"I don't believe in that sort of thing," Lamar said shortly, but the guard did not seem to notice his tone.

"To each his own," he said. "All I know is, no one ever wanted their stores here, and they abandoned the construction before the building was even finished. Now nobody comes up here except kids wanting to screw around. And me," he added with what sounded like pride. He must have felt possessive, Charlie thought, the only one who ever came here for years and years. It must have felt like it belonged to him, this strange, half-finished building. To him, they must be the invaders.

They came to the end of the hallway, and the space opened up before them. Jessica ran ahead to the control room beneath the stage, her flashlight bobbing merrily ahead of her. She disappeared for a moment, then hit the light switch, and all at once the room was warm and bright. Charlie stopped, blinking in the sudden light. Dave brushed past her, and as he did something caught her eye: There was a scar on his neck, curved and ugly, almost a perfect half-moon. The tissue was knotted and white—the cut that made it must have been a deep one. Only a few feet away, Dave turned in a circle, taking in the restaurant, awed, and as he did, Charlie saw that the scar had a twin; the same half-moon, in the same place on the other side of his neck. She shivered a little. The marks were too clean, too perfectly placed; they almost looked deliberate.

The group fanned out. Carlton, for some reason, headed toward the kitchen, and Jason wandered away toward the arcade again.

"Be careful!" Marla called after him, but she was already following Lamar to the control room to join Jessica. Charlie hung back, and John stayed with her. There was something different in the air, Charlie thought. It felt thinner, like she had to breathe deeper to get enough oxygen. *It's just a guy*, she told herself, but that was the problem. They had brought an outsider in with them, and now the restaurant felt less secure, no longer hidden away. Freddy's had been breached. Freddy, Bonnie, and Chica had begun to jerk in their stiff, single movements. Charlie looked at Dave, but he did not appear surprised. *He's been here before*, she thought. Then: *Of course he's been here before. The whole town used to come here back then.*

John motioned her on, and reluctantly she went with him to the control room, Dave tagging along behind them like a stray.

In the booth, Jessica was hunched over, pressing buttons, and Lamar was studying the control board, trying to make sense of it. Dave peered intently over their shoulders, watching. He was nodding slightly to himself, wrapped up in some private calculation, and when Jessica stepped back and stretched, he cleared his throat.

"Um," he said. "Could I try?" He drew himself up a little, extending his arm graciously.

Jessica and Lamar exchanged glances, then shrugged.

"Why not?" Jessica said. They shuffled around so that he could reach the board, and he stared down at it for a long moment without moving, then touched a short series of buttons. A hum rose from the speakers, a long, low tone that did not waver.

"Whoa," Jessica said and pointed to the monitors. Charlie saw movement on the screen and backed out of the control room to look for herself. Onstage, the animals were dancing. Crudely, awkwardly, without the grace or complexity Charlie remembered, but they were moving in sequences, not just one motion at a time.

Charlie went back to the control room but did not go beyond the door.

"How did you do that?" she snapped, not caring if it was rude. Dave raised his hands in the air.

"Beginner's luck," he said. "I just pressed some buttons."

"Right," Charlie said. She rubbed her temples. "Can someone please turn off the speakers?"

Lamar darted forward and flipped a switch, and the sound died. Despite the silence, Charlie felt as if she could still hear it, whining away inside her head. She closed her eyes for a moment, and when she opened them, Jessica and Lamar had gone back to working the controls, but there was a caution to their movements, and they glanced at each other every few seconds as if seeking reassurance. Charlie looked at John. His arms were folded across his chest, and his eyes were trained on the back of Dave's head.

In the arcade, Carlton pressed some random buttons on a game console, knowing nothing would happen, then turned around, finding himself the subject of an eleven-year-old's resentful stare.

"What?" he said.

"I'm not a baby," Jason said. "You don't have to watch me."

"What? Jason, I'm not watching you, I'm just hanging out with you. I'm not Marla. Go stick your tongue in an electric socket, for all I care." He waggled his eyebrows comically, and Jason laughed.

"Okay, then, maybe I will," he said. He scanned the base-boards for a socket, briefly considering calling Carlton's bluff, but when he glanced back, Carlton had already wandered off. Jason bit his lip and rocked on his heels, feeling foolish. After a moment, he went back to the drawings on the wall. There were too many drawings to peruse each one in turn, but Jason suspected he would not need to. As they had the night before, the drawings would come to him. They *wanted* to be found. All Jason had to do was look.

The drawings in the arcade gave up nothing: They were just children's grubby art, faded with age. He went back out into the dining room, still hugging the walls and scanning them, hunting for something that was more than crayon.

"What're you up to, Jason?" Lamar was suddenly behind him. Jason turned around and studied him for a moment, considering. He liked Lamar, even if his friendliness could be traced easily to his interest in Marla. Lamar had bent down so his head was almost level with Jason's, and Jason leaned toward him and whispered, "The drawings are moving."

Lamar drew back, and for a moment a look of real alarm crossed his face, but it was fleeting. Jason bit his lip, waiting, and Lamar grinned at him, then reached out to pat him on the head.

"Okay, Jason. We'll get you the help you need," he said heartily, and Jason laughed and slapped Lamar's hand away.

"Shut up, seriously," Jason said with a hint of sheepishness, and Lamar patted his head again and headed off. As soon as Lamar was a few feet away, Jason rolled his eyes. *What do you think I am, your pet?* He gave his hair a violent tussle as if he could shake loose whatever Lamar had done to him, then went back to the wall, concentrating.

He had made his way all along one wall and was turning the corner when it happened: a flicker, just out of the corner of his eye, almost a shimmering. He stopped. *Which one was it?* He scanned the drawings again, going up and down the wall carefully, around the place he thought he had seen movement, but there was nothing. He started over, stopping to look at each crayon scribble, and then it happened again. He seized on it this time, his eye finding the drawing just as the shimmer of movement stopped, and just as he did, he saw another, so brief he would have ignored it, just a trick of the light, had he not been watching for it. It was above the first and maybe two feet to the left; his eyes darted back and forth, trying to see both at once. Suddenly, there was a third movement in a drawing between the two, this one more noticeable. This time he almost, almost saw the drawing shift before it was still again. Sitting back on his heels, Jason looked at the three drawings, each in turn. The crayon was black, and they all looked like they had been drawn by the same kid, all with two figures in the foreground: a child and a rabbit.

Jason glanced around the room. His sister and the others still seemed to be engaged by the stage; Lamar had gone back to join them. Jason pulled the drawing he had found the night before from his pocket. He smoothed it out, pressing it to the surface of the floor, then, slowly, he peeled its linty tape out flat and stuck the paper to the wall just at his eye level. He stared at the wall, waiting.

Nothing happened.

Jason frowned. He had been so certain these would tell him something, but they were just drawings. The child and the bunny stood in the middle of the paper, in one close together, in another far apart. But there was nothing there that could be called a story. *Oh well.* He started to look over at the others again—and the highest one began to move.

This time he saw the shift: The crayon lines twisted and slid on the page, moving of their own accord, too fast to follow. When the first stopped moving, another started, they continued one after the other until the last, the one he had just put back, was finished. Jason watched, eyes wide, his heart pounding, but by the time he realized what was happening, it was over. The figures were fixed in place, and now they did tell a story. In the first, a child was sitting alone. In the second, Bonnie appeared behind the child. In the next, Bonnie had snatched the child, lifting it off the ground.

In the last, the child was screaming.

His eyes wide and his heart racing, Jason stepped back. He was transfixed: His body suddenly felt leaden, too heavy to run. A sound arose, like wind rustling the pages on the wall, though they hung motionless before him. The sound rushed and grew, louder and louder until wind gave way to screaming. Jason clapped his hands over his ears as pages began to drop from the walls, landing with loud crashes, as if they were made of something far heavier than paper. As he watched, the fallen pages turned a dark red, soaking through with color as they touched the floor. Jason turned to run, but his path was blocked as pages tumbled from the ceiling in a torrent. One landed on his shoulder, another on his back and then another, and they clung to him, wrapping around him as if they would suffocate him. Jason felt his legs buckle under the weight, dropping at last to one knee.

As he braced himself under the storm of paper, the room began to shake violently. Jason gritted his teeth, trapped— and suddenly it was over. The red-soaked papers were gone, there was nothing on his back, and Marla had him by the shoulder and was staring at him, wide-eyed.

"Jason, what on earth is wrong with you?"

Jason scrambled to his feet, brushing himself off as if he were covered with invisible insects.

"The pictures were falling on me," he said urgently, still panicked, but as he looked back at the wall, he realized that the room was silent and still. A single picture had fallen from its place. Marla looked down at it, then back to her brother, and shook her head. She leaned close and hissed into his ear, "You embarrass me." She let loose her grip after a moment, her face almost blank, and walked away. Jason stumbled as he got to his feet but followed as quickly as he could, keeping his eyes trained on the walls as they went.

In the control room, Dave had his hands on the buttons, his fingers wandering lightly over them without pressing anything. The movement looked careless, instinctual, like a habit. Charlie leaned close to John.

"He's been here before," she whispered. "Look at the way he touches the controls."

"Maybe he's just good with computers," John offered, not sounding convinced.

"Can you make them dance again?" Jessica asked. Dave barely seemed to acknowledge the question. His mouth hung slightly open, and he seemed to be staring at something none of them could see. In the bright lights, they could all see that his uniform was grubby and torn in places, his face poorly shaven and his eyes a little unfocused. He looked less like a guard than a vagrant, and he looked at them all as if he had wandered in ages ago and they were the newcomers. It took him a moment to register the question.

"Sure, let's see what we can do," he said. He smiled at her, his mouth askew. His eyes were a little too intent on her face, holding her gaze just a little too long. Jessica swallowed, seized with an instinctive revulsion, but she smiled back politely.

"All right," Dave said. "I've been here a few times before; I think I can work some magic."

Charlie and John exchanged glances.

"You've been here before?" John said in a careful, even tone, but Dave ignored him, or did not hear.

There was a keypad to the far left of the control board that no one had touched yet, as it did not appear to be connected to anything. Now Dave reached for it and began to press the buttons quickly, as if he had done it a hundred times before. He gave Jessica a conspiratorial glance. "For special occasions, you can request a dance." He smiled at her again with that crooked intensity.

"Great," Jessica said, breathing a sigh of relief. Anything to get out of such forced proximity to this man. She looked at Lamar. "I'm going to go look. Will you take over?"

"Yeah, sure," he said, scooting forward to fill the vacancy as Jessica and Dave made their way out to the show area.

Onstage, the lights were flashing in patterns, accompanying music that no longer played, and Bonnie's mouth was moving as though in song. His eyelids closed for long blinks, then opened again with loud clicks, his glass eyes moving from side to side. One large blue hand rose and fell, strumming exaggeratedly on the red guitar whose strings had long since gone missing.

"Lamar, how much of this are you doing?" Carlton said, suitably impressed.

"Not much!" Lamar called back. "Most of it seems preprogrammed."

Bonnie turned to them, and Jessica startled as he seemed to look right at her. But he turned away just as quickly to face the rows of empty seats, lifting his head to sing.

"It's strange seeing them like this," Jessica said, taking a step back to get a better view. Bonnie's foot tapped along in rhythm, and his mouth opened and closed with song. There was no voice; there was no music. There was only a strange humming coming from the speakers and an orchestra of mechanical snaps and squeaks. Bonnie sped up, strumming and tapping faster. His eyes suddenly seemed out of sync, looking left while the head went right, then rolling back into his head.

Dave approached the stage with deliberate steps. "Nervous little fella, aren't you?" He smiled, seemingly unbothered as the rabbit moved faster and faster.

"Hey, Lamar, can you take it down a notch?" Jessica called.

Bonnie's arms began convulsing violently, his mouth open but stuttering, his eyes throwing their gaze in seemingly random directions.

"Lamar! Something's wrong!" Jessica cried.

Bonnie's foot jerked upward with a sound like a gunshot, yanking free the bolt that anchored him to the stage.

"Lamar!" Carlton climbed onto the stage and hurried to Bonnie, trying to search the rabbit for an off button as he ducked its erratic swings.

"Carlton, get down, you idiot!" Jessica ran to the stage.

Bonnie was moving too fast, out of control as if his program had hit a glitch. He was no longer following the dance sequence they all remembered so well. He began to convulse and thrash. Carlton scrambled back, trying to get away, but Bonnie's arm broke away from the guitar, swinging out and hitting Carlton across the chest, knocking him off the stage. He landed on his back and stayed down, gasping for breath.

"Lamar!" Jessica shouted. "Lamar, turn it off!"

"I don't know how!" he yelled back.

Jessica knelt down beside Carlton, looking helplessly at him. She tapped his shoulder insistently.

"Carlton, are you okay? Carlton? Look at me!"

Carlton gave a small laugh that sounded more like a cough, then grabbed her hand and pulled himself up to sit.

"It's okay," he said. "Just got the wind knocked out of me." Jessica still looked worried. "I just need a minute," he assured her, the words still coming in little wheezes.

In the control room, Lamar pressed button after button frantically, but on the screens he could still see Bonnie moving wildly and at random, not responding to anything he did. Charlie rushed in, pushing him out of the way, but it took her only seconds to see that the buttons were powerless. She locked eyes with Lamar for a moment. *We aren't in control*, she thought. As one, they rushed from the control room to help the others.

Jessica screamed, a short, high-pitched sound, and Marla and John ran to her, Charlie and Lamar arriving seconds later. All the animals were moving now in that same fitful way, cycling through their programmed movements at random with a desperate, panicked air. The lights began to pulse, flickering rapidly on and off. The stage lights did the same, the colors appearing and disappearing so that the whole space was washed first in bright gold, then a sickly green, then a bruised and vicious purple. They blinked like strobes, and the effect was nauseating. The speakers blared brief bursts of static, cutting in and out like the lights, and beneath the static was the same sound they had heard the night before, the growling of a voice too low to be human, too indistinct to be speaking words.

The group came together cautiously, not quite trusting their own senses. The lights throbbed savagely, and as Charlie walked toward her friends, she could not be sure how far away they were or what was right in front of her. They huddled in the middle of the floor, staring at the animals as they rattled and rocked as if with their own agenda. Carlton got to his feet; Jessica watched him with concern, but he waved her off.

"I told you, I'm fine," he said, shouting to be heard over the intermittent noise.

Charlie stood fixed in place, unable to take her eyes off the animals. *They're trying to get away*, she thought. It was a child's thought, and she tried to dismiss it, but it clung as she watched them, scarcely noticing the fitful flickering of the lights and sound. The animatronic creatures didn't look like they were glitching; their movement seemed not mechanical but hysterical, like there was something they needed desperately to do but, horribly, could not.

"Where's Dave?" John said suddenly. Charlie met his eyes with a rising dread. *Oh no.* They all looked around, but the guard was nowhere in sight.

"We have to find him," Charlie said.

"He probably left already; who cares?" Marla said, her voice high and frightened.

"I'm not worried about him," she said grimly. She turned to John. "Come on," she said, setting off toward the hallway to the right of the stage. He glanced at the rest of the group over his shoulder, then followed Charlie at a brisk pace.

"We should find the other control room and see if we can stop all this from there," Jessica said crisply, taking charge. "You and Jason go look for Dave," she told Marla.

"I'll go with them," Lamar said quickly.

"Control room?" Carlton said, looking at Jessica.

"Control room," she confirmed. They all set off, moving slowly. The strobing lights distorted the space in front of them, seeming to throw up obstacles that were not there, obscuring the ones that were. The effect was disorienting, a constantly shifting maze of light and noise.

"Ow!" Marla shouted, and everyone stopped short.

"Are you okay?" Carlton yelled.

"Yeah, I just bumped into this stupid merry-go-round," she called back. The speakers were momentarily noiseless, but they shouted across the small distance as if there were a canyon between them.

In another hallway, Dave was moving toward a goal. Without the others there to watch, he moved fast, scuttling almost sideways and darting his eyes back over his hunched shoulders from time to time to see he was not followed. There was a large key ring at the belt of his uniform, but only a few keys hung from it. He selected one, opened a door, and let himself into the restaurant's office. He closed the door quickly behind him, cushioning it against noise even though the group would never hear it this far away or note it between their own shouts and the blaring of the speakers. He turned on the overhead light; it was steady, illuminating the room without a flicker. On the far wall, there was a tall closet flat against the wall, and he used another key on his ring to open it. Dave stood still in the open door for a long moment, breathing deeply. As he did, his back straightened and his hollow chest seemed to expand, drawing an uncharacteristic confidence from what he saw. An odd, thin smile on his lips,

Dave reached out with his fingertips, savoring the moment, and brushed yellow fur.

Jessica and Carlton hurried away down the hall toward the second control room, but Marla and the two boys moved more slowly, sticking their heads into the party rooms, then the arcade. The rooms appeared empty, but in the constantly changing light, Jason thought as they moved on, it would be easy to miss just about anything. Having checked the area, Marla and Lamar headed back into the main room.

"Where are Jessica and Carlton?" Lamar shouted over another burst of garbled sound. Jason stopped and looked back, and in a fleeting instant he saw it: a rabbit, outlined in the hall for a split second as the lights flashed on him, then vanishing and appearing again in his place in the party room they had just left.

"Marla!" Jason shouted. "MARLA!" His voice was shrill, agitated.

She whirled around. "What? Are you okay?"

"I saw Bonnie! He was there!"

"What?" Marla's eyes went automatically to the stage. Bonnie was still there, moving back and forth in the same odd, spastic movements. "Jason, look, he's there. He can't move off the stage."

Jason looked. Bonnie was there. *I saw him*, he thought, looking back down the hallway, but it was empty.

Jessica came running up, out of breath.

"Is everyone okay? I heard screaming."

"We're fine," Lamar said. "Jason thought he saw something."

"Where's Carlton?" Marla said. She rubbed her temples. "Ugh, this light is giving me such a headache."

"He's still fighting with the controls," Jessica said. "We should find Charlie and John; I think we need to get out of here."

"I think they went that way," Lamar said, pointing to the hall at the far end of the room, just past the stage.

"Come on," Jessica said. Jason followed as the group crossed the main dining room again, maneuvering cautiously around tables and chairs. He looked back as they reached the hall. Suddenly, Bonnie appeared again, darting out from the arcade and ducking into the hall that led to Pirate's Cove. Jason watched his sister and the others file through the doorway, then slipped away before they could see him go. He ran across the room, intent on following the rabbit, then slowed his pace when he reached the dark hallway.

The lights in the little hall were completely out, and though he could see nothing, it was a minor relief from the pulsing strobes. Jason hugged the wall as he moved, trying to scan ahead of him for signs of movement, but it was too dark; his eyes had not adjusted. After what seemed like ages, he came out of the hall and into Pirate's Cove. From a distance, he could hear his sister's voice, calling his name. *Guess they noticed I'm gone,* he thought wryly. He ignored it. Crossing the room, he peered down the other hallway—the one that led to more party rooms—but it was so dark that he could scarcely see more than a few feet ahead.

Turning back, he approached the little stage, the OUT OF ORDER sign still strung across it. *As if anything in this place is in order.* Suddenly, the curtain moved, and Jason froze. The curtain began pulling back. Jason couldn't bring himself to run. All went dark, then the lights came on suddenly to reveal Carlton standing in front of him, having emerged from behind the curtain.

"What are you doing back here by yourself? Come on, let's go," Carlton greeted him with a warm smile.

Awash with relief, Jason took a step forward, opening his mouth to speak—and stiffened, struck still with fear.

Bonnie suddenly broke through the darkness, appearing beneath the stage lights before them. But it was not Bonnie; this rabbit's yellow fur was almost blinding in the light. He rushed at them, and before Jason could cry out, the giant rabbit had a hold of Carlton from behind, smothering his face with a giant, matted paw and wrapping his other great arm around Carlton's chest, gripping tightly. Carlton struggled silently, hitting and kicking, but the creature barely seemed to notice. He screamed into the rabbit's paw, but the sound was swallowed whole. As he fought, the rabbit slunk back the way he came, dragging Carlton with him like a prize from the hunt.

Jason watched them go, agape. His heart raced, and his breath was shallow; the stifling air around him made him light-headed. A noise came from behind him, the grinding screech of rusted metal beginning to move, and he leaped forward and turned, moving just in time to avoid a hook as it plunged swiftly downward. Foxy's eyes flashed in synchrony with the lights above, and for a dizzy moment it seemed to Jason that those eyes were the controlling force behind it all, that if Foxy closed his eyes, every light might go out. The animal did not move like the others. It slowly, purposefully, rose between the gap in the curtains, its gleaming eyes reaching a staggering height.

"Jason!" It was Charlie's voice, he knew, but he kept staring back and forth, first at Foxy, then at the place where Carlton had been stolen away. "Jason!" she called again, and then she and John were beside him, touching him, shaking him out of his ghastly reverie. John grabbed his hand and pulled him into a run. In the main room, the others were already halfway down the hallway to the outside door, all but Marla, who was waiting anxiously at the entrance, her face flooding with relief when she saw Jason.

"Marla, Bonnie, he took Carlton!" Jason yelled, but she just put a hand on his back and pushed him through the door and into the hall.

"Go, Jason!"

"But I saw Bonnie take Carlton!" he cried, but he ran, afraid to stop.

They ran down the hall to the outside door, all bouncing with a frightened impatience as they filed through to the alley one by one; there was no way to go faster. When they were all through, Charlie looked down the hallway for a long moment, but there was no one coming. She shoved the door closed and stepped out of the way as Lamar and John wrestled the shelf back into place, blocking it off.

"No one saw Dave," Charlie said. It was not a question. They all shook their heads. "He must have taken off when the lights started going haywire," Lamar offered, but he did not sound convinced.

"Carlton!" Jason cried out again. "Carlton is still in there! Bonnie took him!"

They all glanced around. Carlton was not with them.

"Oh no," Jessica said. "He's still inside."

"Bonnie took him!" Jason said, choking out the words one by one, his voice shaking. "I saw it. Bonnie was there, he was in Pirate's Cove, and he grabbed Carlton and carried him away. I couldn't stop him." He scrubbed a sleeve across his eyes, wiping tears.

"Oh, sweetheart . . ." Marla hugged him, and he clung to her, hiding his face in her shirt. "No, it was a trick of the light. Bonnie couldn't do that; he's just a robot. He was onstage when we left."

Jason closed his eyes. He had only glanced for a second at the main stage as they were leaving, but it was true: Bonnie had been there, moving in strange and clumsy twists and bends, stuck in place. He pulled away from his sister's arms.

"I saw it," he insisted, more weakly. "Bonnie took him."

The others exchanged glances above his head. Charlie looked at Marla, who shrugged.

"We have to go back in," Charlie said. "We have to get him." Jessica was nodding, but John cleared his throat.

"I think we need help," he said. "It's not safe in there."

"Let's get Carlton's dad," Marla said. "I'm not taking Jason back in there."

Charlie wanted to protest, but she bit her tongue. They were right; of course they were right. Whatever had just happened was beyond them. They needed help.

CHAPTER SEVEN

They made their way back through the corridors of the abandoned mall, not bothering to be cautious with their footsteps or the beams of their lights.

"So much for being sneaky," Charlie said darkly, but no one responded. By silent consensus their pace quickened steadily; by the time they reached the parking lot they were almost running. Spotting her car as they came out the front door, Charlie felt an almost physical relief to see it, like it was an old friend.

"Someone should stay here," she said, pausing with her hand on the door handle. "We can't leave Carlton."

"No," Marla said firmly. "We're leaving now." They looked at her in surprise for a moment—suddenly, she was talking to them all the way she talked to Jason: *Sister knows best.* Lamar and Jason exchanged glances, but no one said anything. "We're going into town. All of us," she added, giving Charlie a warning look, "and we're finding help."

They hurried into their cars. As Charlie took the wheel, John got into the passenger seat, and she smiled tightly at him. Jessica climbed into the back a moment later, and Charlie felt a minor disappointment; she had wanted to talk to him alone. *We're running for help, it's not a date,* she scolded herself, but that hadn't really been the point. He felt safe, a touchstone amid the strange things that were happening all around them. She looked over at him, but he was staring out the window. They pulled out of the lot, following Marla's car as she sped into the darkness.

When they reached the town, Marla yanked her car to the side of the main street and stopped, and Charlie followed suit. Before the car had fully come to a halt, Jessica leaped out of the backseat and started running. Marla followed a step behind. They stopped in front of the movie theater, and only then did Charlie see that there was a cop in uniform beneath the marquee, leaning back against his black-and-white car. His eyes widened at the sight of the young women barreling toward him, and he took an involuntary step back as Marla started talking without pausing for breath.

". . . Please, you've got to come," Marla was finishing as the others caught up.

The cop looked a little bewildered. He had a shiny pink face, and his hair was so short it was entirely covered by his hat. He was young, maybe midtwenties, Charlie realized, and he was looking at them skeptically.

"Is this an actual emergency?" he said. "You may not realize it, but pranks can get you into real trouble."

Jessica rolled her eyes and stepped forward, closing the distance between them.

"We're not playing a prank," she said crisply, and Charlie suddenly remembered how tall she was. "Our friend is trapped in that abandoned shopping mall, and it's your job to help us."

"The shopping mall?" He seemed confused, then looked in the direction they'd come from. "THAT shopping mall?" His eyes widened, then he frowned at them reproachfully, looking remarkably like a disappointed parent despite his youth. "What were you doing up there in the first place?"

Charlie and Marla exchanged glances, but Jessica didn't blink.

"Deal with us later. He's in danger, and you have to help us, Officer—" She leaned in and peered at his name tag. "Officer Dunn. Do you want me to go to the fire department?"

Despite her fear, Charlie almost laughed. Jessica said it as if she were in a store, threatening to take her business elsewhere. It was so absurd it should have gotten her no more than a puzzled glance, but Dunn reached for his radio hastily.

"No," he said. "Hang on."

He pressed a button, and the radio emitted a short burst of static. Charlie felt a brief chill at the sound, and as she looked around, she saw John stiffen and Jason take a tiny step closer to Marla. Not seeming to notice their reactions, Dunn barked incomprehensible sounds into his radio, talking in cop code, and Charlie suddenly had a flash of memory, of running around the yard, whispering into walkie-talkies with Marla. They could never understand each other on the cheap toys her father had found in the drugstore bargains bin, but they didn't mind; actual communication was never the point.

"Charlie, come on!" Jessica shouted at her, and Charlie came back to herself. Everyone was heading toward the cars and piling back in. Marla pulled out in front, and the cop followed her, with Charlie bringing up the rear.

"Why doesn't he have the siren on?" Jessica said. Her voice was thin and brittle, as if her only choices were a sharp tongue or tears.

"He doesn't believe us," John said softly.

"He should have the siren on," Jessica said, and this time it was almost a whisper. Charlie's knuckles were white on the steering wheel as she stared straight ahead at the cop's red taillights.

When they got back to the mall, Jessica dashed ahead, forcing the rest of them to run behind her. Charlie didn't mind; it felt good to run, purposeful. Lamar was talking to the cop as they ran, shouting over the noise of their thudding feet.

"The restaurant is all boarded up, but there's a door left open," he said, the words broken by his uneven breathing. "Behind the plastic—you move it—dark alley—Carlton smells like feet." Officer Dunn's step stuttered briefly, but he regained his stride. When they reached the alley, they slowed their pace, moving more cautiously down the narrow hall until they came to the door.

"Right here," John said, and Dunn moved forward to help with the shelf. They drew it back too fast, the contents rattling and wobbling. The shelf pitched backward, and tools, cables, and paint cans full of nails crashed to the floor.

"Ow!" John yelled as a hammer bounced off his foot. They all watched as the things scattered, some rolling away and vanishing down the dark corridor.

"What?!" Jason wailed, and they all looked up from the spill. He was pointing at the door.

"What is this?" Marla gasped. The door had chains strung across it from top to bottom, three enormous padlocks holding them all together. The links were bolted into the metal frame of the door, and they were heavy, too heavy to cut without special tools. It was all rusty; the whole thing looked as though it had been there for years. Charlie walked up to the door and touched a chain, as if to be sure it was real.

"This wasn't here," she said, the words sounding inane even as she spoke.

"We have to get him out!" Jason cried haltingly, his hands covering his eyes. "Bonnie is going to kill him, and it's my fault!"

"What's he talking about?" the police officer said, looking at them with renewed suspicion. "Who is Bonnie, and why is she going to hurt your friend?"

"He's—it's a robot," Charlie said quickly. "The robots from Freddy Fazbear's are still there, and they still work."

"Freddy Fazbear's." Dunn's face flushed, and he looked at the door again. "I used to go there as a kid," he said softly, his tone caught between nostalgia and fear. He caught himself quickly and cleared his throat.

"He came to life," Jason insisted, no longer making the effort to hide his tears. Dunn bent down to his height, his tone softening.

"What's your name?" he asked.

"We have to get him out," Jason repeated.

"His name is Jason," Marla said, and Jason glared at her.

"Jason," Dunn said. He put a hand on Jason's shoulder, glancing at the others with an obvious suspicion. *He thinks we made him say that*, Charlie realized. Jason wriggled in Dunn's grasp, but the officer did not let him go, looking him in the eye to ask the next question: "Jason, did they tell you to say this? What's going on here?"

Irritated, Jason pulled free and took a large step back.

"That's what really happened," he said firmly.

Officer Dunn exhaled, a long, slow vent of frustration, then got to his feet, shedding his kid-friendly act. "So, the robots took your friend," he said. *I know what you're trying to pull*, said his tone.

"We were in there," Charlie stated flatly, keeping her voice level, as if saying it calmly and plainly enough might convince him that they were not telling lies. "Our friend didn't make it out."

The officer looked again at the chains.

"Look," he said, apparently deciding to give them the benefit of the doubt. "I don't know how you got in there in the first place, and right now I don't want to know. But the machinery in there is old; it hasn't been touched in ten years. Chances are it's pretty spooky. Heck, I wouldn't want to go in there. So even though I can't blame you for being freaked out, I can guarantee you those robots in there aren't moving by themselves. That place is dead, and it needs to be left alone," he said with a forced chuckle. Jason set his jaw, but he didn't say anything. "I think you all need to go home," Dunn finished, the statement sounding more like a threat than advice.

They looked at one another.

After a moment of uncomfortable silence, Jessica looked to Charlie. "These chains weren't here before. Right?" she faltered, looking back at her friends for confirmation like she was beginning to doubt her own memory.

"No," Charlie said instantly. "They weren't. We aren't leaving, and we need your help."

"Fine," Dunn said shortly. "What's his name?" He produced a notebook seemingly from nowhere.

"Carlton Burke," Jessica said. She was about to spell it for him, when suddenly Officer Dunn put down his pen and closed his eyes, his nostrils flaring.

He glared at them, no longer looking quite so young. "I'm going to give you one more chance. Tell me exactly what happened." He spoke slowly, emphasizing the spaces between his words. He was in control again, no longer out of his depth, like he suddenly understood everything.

They tried to explain all at once, talking over one another. Jessica's voice was loudest and calmest, but even she could not keep her anxiety from bleeding through. Charlie hung back, quiet. *Tell me exactly what happened.* Where were they supposed to start? With the night? With the week? With

Michael? With the first time her father picked up a circuit board? How was anyone ever to respond to something like "tell me what happened"? The cop was nodding, and he picked up the radio again, but this time he spoke comprehensibly.

"Norah, call Burke. It's his kid. I'm up at the old mall site." There was an answering burst of static, and the officer turned his attention back to them. "Come on," he said.

"Come on where?" John said.

"Off the property."

Marla started to protest, but Dunn interrupted. "I'm escorting you off the property," he said. He pulled the baton from his belt and pointed with it.

"Come on," Lamar said. Jason was still staring sullenly at the ground, and Lamar gave him a gentle nudge on the shoulder. "Jason, come on. We have to do what he says now, okay?"

"But Carlton!" Jason said loudly, and Lamar shook his head.

"I know. It's okay, we'll find him, but we have to go now." He guided Jason toward the mouth of the alley, and everyone followed. The police officer walked behind, following Charlie a little too closely. She sped up, but so did he, and she resigned herself to being shadowed.

When they got to the parking lot, he directed them to wait by the car and walked off a few paces, speaking into the radio again, too far away to hear.

"What's going on?" Jason said. He was beginning to whine; he heard the tone in his voice and tried to modulate it. *I am not a little kid*, he reminded himself. No one answered, but Marla rubbed his back absently, and he did not move away.

Long minutes passed in silence. Jessica sat on the hood of the car, facing away from the rest of the group. Charlie wanted to go to her, but she did not. In her distress, Jessica was closing down, going stiff and cold and snippy, and Charlie did not think she had what it took to break through that without breaking down herself.

"Was he talking about Carlton's dad?" Charlie asked, but no one had time to answer. Headlights appeared, and a car pulled in beside them. The man who got out was tall and thin, and his light hair could have been either blond or gray.

"Carlton's dad," Marla whispered, a late answer to Charlie's question. The man smiled as he approached.

"Carlton's dad," he confirmed. "Though since you're all grown up now, you'd better call me Clay." They all muttered it, half in greeting, half just to test it out. Jason covered his mouth self-consciously, tonguing the invisible gap in his molars.

"I thought our days of mischief would be behind us, no?" Clay said, his expression good-humored.

Jessica slid off the hood of Charlie's car, her face drawn.

"I'm so sorry; he's missing," she said tightly. "I don't know what happened; he was right with us!"

"Bonnie kidnapped him!" Jason burst out. "I saw! The rabbit took him!"

Clay started to smile, then stopped himself when he saw their faces.

"Oh, kids, I'm sorry. You haven't been around in a while. I'm afraid Carlton is playing a joke on you, ALL of you."

"What?" Lamar said.

"Oh, come on. With you guys back in town, he couldn't resist," Clay said. "Whatever happened, I guarantee he set it up. He'll probably pop out of the bushes any minute now."

There was a silence as they all waited against probability. Nothing happened.

"Well," Clay said at last. "That would have been too much to ask! Come on, why don't you come back to our place? I'll make you all some hot chocolate, and when Carlton finally shows up, you can tell him he's grounded!"

"Okay," Charlie said, without waiting for the consent of the others. She wanted to believe Clay, wanted to believe that Carlton was all right and would show up laughing. But, almost as badly, she wanted to go somewhere where an adult was in charge, someone who would make hot chocolate and assure them there was no such thing as monsters. Her father had never made that claim. Her father could never have told her that lie.

No one objected, and so they started up their caravan again, trailing Clay home. They all settled into their accustomed places: Charlie, John, and Jessica in Charlie's car, and Marla, Jason, and Lamar in Marla's. In the rearview mirror, Charlie saw Officer Dunn's car, still right behind them. *Is he just going this way, or is he making sure we go where we're told?* she wondered, but it didn't really matter. They weren't planning on flight.

At Carlton's house they filed in through the front door. Charlie looked back in time to see the police car drive on by. *He was following us.* As they climbed the steps, John leaned in to whisper in her ear.

"I didn't realize how rich they were when I was a kid!" he said, and she stifled a laugh. It was true; the house was enormous. It was three stories high, and it sprawled out into the woods that surrounded it, so wide that Charlie thought there must have been whole rooms where all you could see out the window was trees. Clay showed them to the living room, which looked well used, the furniture mismatched and the rugs, dark and durable, made to take stains.

"Carlton's mom—who you can call Betty now—is asleep," Clay said. "The soundproofing is pretty good. Just don't shout or crash around."

They chorused promises, and he nodded, satisfied, and vanished through a doorway. They dispersed themselves over the furniture, sitting on couches and chairs. Charlie sat on the rug between Jessica's chair and Lamar's. She wanted them all to stay close together. John sat down beside her and gave a little smile.

"Did we get pranked?" Marla asked.

"I guess maybe. I'm not sure what else would explain it," Jessica said listlessly, staring into the empty fireplace. "I mean, none of us even knows each other that well, not really. Maybe he would do something like that." They all shifted uncomfortably. It was true; they had been behaving as if their time apart were just a little break, like they could just fill one another in on what they had been up to, and it would be just like it was, just like their group had never split up. But ten years was too long for that to be true, and deep down everyone knew it. Charlie darted her eyes at John. She felt a little embarrassed, but she could not have expressed why.

Clay came back in, carrying a tray of steaming mugs and a bag of little marshmallows.

"Here you are!" he said jovially. "Hot chocolate for everyone, even me." He set the tray down on the coffee table and took a seat in a battered green armchair that seemed to fit him like a coat, as accustomed to his body as he was to its form. They reached forward and took the cups; only Jason reached for the marshmallows. Clay looked around from face to face.

"Look," he said. "I know you don't believe me, but Carlton does things like this—although I have to admit, this is probably the weirdest. It's not right, making you relive all that stuff from when you were kids." He stared into his mug for a long moment. "I need to have another talk with him," he said quietly. "Believe me, my son has a strange sense of humor," he went on. "You know, for high school we sent him to a place in the next town over. No one knew him. He managed to convince his classmates *and* his teachers that he had a twin brother at the school for the first month of class. I don't know how on earth he managed it, but I didn't find out until he got tired of the act and I started getting calls from school that one of my sons had gone missing."

Charlie smiled weakly, but she was not convinced. This was different.

"This is different," Marla said, as if reading Charlie's thoughts. "Jason saw him disappear. He was terrified. It's cruel, if it's a prank." Marla shook her head with anger and scratched her nails against the porcelain cup. "If it's a prank," she repeated in a softer tone. She looked at Charlie, her face stormy, and Charlie knew that if Carlton had, in fact, set all of this up, Marla would never speak to him again. Their happy reunion was over.

"Yes," Clay said, "I know. But he doesn't see it that way." He took a sip of cocoa, searching for words. "The twins, they had totally different personalities. Shaun was this outgoing, cheerful guy. He was on the debate team. He played soccer, for goodness' sake! Carlton had never gotten near a sports game without being forced. I don't know how he kept it up."

"Still," Marla said, but she sounded less convinced.

"The worst part was," Clay went on, talking more to himself now than to the teenagers, "Shaun had a girlfriend. She really liked him, too, but he was just playing the part. Poor girl had been dating a guy who didn't even exist. I think he was surprised when he realized how upset people were. He gets carried away and just assumes everyone is having as much fun as he is."

Charlie looked at John, and he met her glance anxiously. *We don't know each other, not really.*

"Maybe he did set it up," she said aloud.

"Maybe," Jessica echoed.

"I saw him!" Jason said loudly. Before anyone could respond, he stormed out of the room, disappearing through a doorway. Marla stood automatically and moved to follow him, but Clay put up a hand.

"Let him go," he said. "He needs some time to himself. And I want to talk to the rest of you." He set his mug down and leaned forward. "I know you were just kidding around, but I don't want to hear you kids joking about Freddy Fazbear's. You know, I wasn't the chief back then. I was still a detective, and I was working on those disappearances. To this day, it was the worst thing I've ever had to see. It's not something to joke about." He looked at Charlie. His gray eyes were hard, and the lines of his face were immobile; he was no longer the friendly father figure, but the police chief, staring as if he could see right through her. Charlie had a sudden urge to confess, but she had nothing to confess to.

"I'm especially surprised at you, Charlie," Clay said quietly.

Charlie blushed, shame rising up in her with the flush of heat. She wanted to protest, to explain herself, to say anything that might soften the eyes that seemed to bore into her skull. Instead she ducked her head and muttered an indistinct apology.

Lamar broke the silence.

"Mr. Burke—Clay—did they ever find out who did it? I thought they arrested somebody."

Clay didn't respond for a long moment. He was still looking at Charlie, and she felt as if he were trying to tell her something, or else read something in her face.

"Clay?" Marla said, and he seemed to come back to himself. He looked around the group, his expression dark.

"Yes," he said quietly. "We did arrest someone. I did, in fact, and I am as sure now that he was guilty as I was then."

"So what happened?" Lamar asked. There was a hush among the group, as if something very important was about to happen.

"There were no bodies," Clay Burke said. "We knew it was him; there was no doubt in my mind. But the children had disappeared. They were never found, and without their bodies . . ." He stopped talking, staring off into the middle distance as if scarcely aware that they were there.

"But kidnapping," Charlie said. "They disappeared!" She was suddenly furious, appalled at the obvious injustice. "How can this man be walking around somewhere? What if he does it again?" She felt Marla's hand on her arm, and she nodded, settling back, trying to calm down. But the anger was still there inside, seething under the surface of her skin. Clay was looking at her with something like curiosity in his eyes.

"Charlie," he said, "justice penalizes the guilty, but it must also protect the innocent. It means that sometimes the guilty get away with terrible things, but it is the price we pay." He sounded grave, his words weighty. Charlie opened her mouth to argue. *But this was my price*, she wanted to say, but before she spoke she looked at his face. He had a grim conviction about him; what he was saying mattered very much to him, and he believed it utterly. *It's how you sleep at night*, she thought with an uncharacteristic bitterness. They locked eyes for a long moment, then Charlie sighed and nodded, giving up the challenge. Intellectually, she didn't even disagree with him. Clay sat up suddenly in his chair.

"So," he said brightly, "I think it's a bit too late for you girls to be driving back to that motel. Why don't you spend the night here? We have two more guest rooms. And you can scold Carlton for his little prank in the morning," he added with a grin.

Lamar and John showed Charlie, Marla, and Jessica up to the bedrooms, and Jason reemerged as they headed up the stairs, joining the group like he had never been gone.

"So Jason and I will take one," Marla said, "and Jessica, you and Charlie can have the other."

"I want to stay with Lamar," Jason said instantly, and Lamar grinned widely before he could help himself.

"Yeah, okay," he said. He glanced at Marla over her brother's head, and she shrugged.

"Take him," she said. "Keep him if you want! So that means someone gets her own room," she went on, "or we could all stay together. I know everything is fine, but I kind of feel like we should stay together." She was voicing Charlie's precise thoughts from only a little while before, but now Charlie jumped in.

"I'll take the other room," she said.

Marla gave her a dubious look, and even John looked a little surprised, but Charlie just looked at them and said nothing.

When the door closed behind her, Charlie sighed with relief. She went to the window; it was as she imagined, nothing in view but the trees. The house seemed completely isolated, though she knew that the driveway and the road were just on the other side. From outside she could hear nocturnal birds and the rustling of other, larger creatures on the ground below. She felt suddenly restless, wide awake. Looking out the window, she almost wanted to go outside, to slip into the woods and see what they concealed. She looked at her watch. It was long past midnight, so with reluctance she took off her shoes and lay down on the bed.

It was, like everything else in Carlton's house, well worn, the kind of furniture only owned by people who have been wealthy for generations, whose ancestors could afford things of such high quality that they lasted for a hundred years. Charlie closed her eyes in what she assumed would be a futile effort to find rest, but as she lay there, listening to the sound of the woods and Jessica and Marla gossiping and laughing in the next room, she felt as if she were sinking into the mattress. Her breath deepened, and she was soon asleep.

She woke suddenly, startled from sleep. She was a little girl again, and her father was asleep in the next room. It was summer, and the windows were all open; it had started to rain, and the wind rushed into the room in great gusts, blowing her bedroom curtains in a frenetic dance and ushering in a fine mist. But that was not why she awoke. There was something in the air, something unshakable that gripped her. Something was very wrong.

Charlie climbed out of bed, lowering herself carefully onto the floor. Beside her bed stood Stanley the unicorn, patient and deactivated, staring at her with lifeless eyes. She patted his nose, as if giving him comfort might bring it to her as well. Quietly, she snuck past him and out into the hallway, uncertain what compelled her. She crept down the hallway, past her father's room to the stairs, and ducked down beside the wooden bannister as if its open slats could protect her from anything at all. She held fast to it as she made her way down the staircase, letting the rail take her weight as she avoided the boards that creaked. One by one she took the steps; it felt like ages, like years might pass before she reached the bottom, and when she arrived she might be an old woman, her whole life spun out in the descent of these stairs.

At last Charlie reached the end of the stairs, and she looked down to see that she had changed. Her body was no longer small, night-gown-clad and barefoot, but her teenage body, tall, strong, and fully clothed. When she straightened from her fearful crouch, she stood taller than the bannister, and she looked around at her childhood home, startled. This is me, she thought. Yes. This is now.

Something banged in front of her. The front door was wide open and thudding irregularly against the wall, caught by the wind. The rain was whipping in, soaking the floor and lashing the coatrack that stood beside it, rocking it back and forth like it weighed nothing at all. Leaves and small branches were scattered on the floor, ripped from the trees and swept in, but Charlie's eyes went to her old, familiar shoes, her favorites. They were placed neatly beside the mat, black patent leather with straps, and she could see the rain pooling inside and ruining them. Charlie stood still for a moment, trans-fixed, too far for the rain to reach but close enough for the haze to slowly wet her face. She ought to go to the door and close it.

Instead, Charlie backed away slowly, not taking her eyes from the border of the storm. She took a step, then another—and her back hit something solid. She whirled around, startled, and saw it.

It was the thing from her father's workshop, the terrible, twitching thing. It stood on its own, bent and twisted, with a narrow, reddish, canine face and an almost human body. Its clothing was rags, its metal joints and limbs stark and exposed, but Charlie registered only its eyes, the silver eyes that flashed at her, on and off, over and over, blinking in and out of existence. Charlie wanted to run, but her feet would not move. She could feel her pulse in her throat, choking her, and she struggled to breathe. The thing convulsed, and in slow, jerking motions its hand rose up and reached out to touch her face. Charlie drew in a shaking breath, unable to duck away, and then it stopped, the hand only inches from her cheek.

Charlie braced herself, her breath shallow and her eyes screwed shut, but the touch of metal and ragged cloth on her skin did not come. She opened her eyes. The thing had gone still, and the silver light in its eyes was dimmed, nearly out. Charlie backed away from it, watching warily, but it did not move, and she began to wonder if it had shut down, run out of the finite current that powered it. Its shoulders were hunched forward, hapless, and it stared dully past her as if it were lost. Charlie felt a sudden stab of sorrow for this creature, that same feeling of lonely kinship she felt in her father's workshop so many years ago. Does it hurt? she had asked. She was old enough now to know the answer.

All at once, the thing lurched to life. Charlie felt her head go light as it took an awkward step toward her, hurtling its body forward as if it had only just learned to walk. Its head turned frantically from side to side, and its arms jerked up and down with dangerous abandon.

Something shattered. It was a lamp, the thing had knocked over a ceramic lamp, and the sound of it bursting on the wooden floor shook Charlie from her stupor. She turned and ran up the stairs, scrambling as fast as her legs would carry her to her father's door, too scared to even call out for him. As she clambered up the steps some small part of her realized that they were too big, that she was nearly on all fours, tripping barefoot over the hem of her nightgown. She was a little girl again, she realized in a bursting moment of aware-ness, and then it was over, and being a little girl was the only thing she could remember.

She tried again to scream for her father, but he was already there. She did not need to call him. He was standing in the hall, and she grabbed at his shirttails as she crouched behind him. He put a hand on her shoulder, steadying her, and for the first time, her father's touch did not make Charlie feel that she was safe. Peeking out from behind his back, Charlie could see the thing's ears, then its face, as it climbed the stairs in its fitful, jerking steps. Her father stood calm, watching it, as it climbed the final stair, and then Charlie's father grasped her hand and disentangled it, gently forcing her to let him go. He went forward to meet the thing in large, even strides, but as he reached out to it, Charlie could see that his hands were shaking. He touched the thing, put his hands on either side of its face for a long moment, as if he were caressing it, and its limbs stopped, head still moving gently from side to side. It looked almost bewildered, as if it, too, had awakened to something strange and frightening. Charlie's father did something she could not see, and the thing stopped moving; its head drooped, defeated, and its arms fell to its sides. Charlie backed up toward her room, feeling her way along the wall behind her, not daring to look away from the thing until she was safely behind her door. As she looked out one last time into the hallway, she could just barely see the glint from its eyes, cast down at the floor. Suddenly, the little silver lights flickered. The head did not move, but in a slow, calculated arc the eyes swung to meet Charlie's gaze. Charlie whimpered, but she did not look away, and then the head snapped up with a crack like something breaking—

Charlie startled out of sleep, an involuntary shudder running through her. She put a hand to her throat, feeling her heartbeat there, too quick and too hard. She darted her eyes around the room, putting together where she was one piece at a time. *The bed.* Not her own. *The room.* Dark; she was alone. *The window.* The woods outside. *Carlton's house.* Her breath slowed. The process had only taken seconds, but it disturbed her to be so disoriented. She blinked, but the afterburn of those silver eyes was still with her, glowing behind her eyelids as if they had been real. Charlie stood and went to the window, thrust it open, and leaned out, desperate to breathe in the night air.

Did that happen? The dream felt like memory, felt like something that had happened just moments ago, but that was the nature of dreams, wasn't it? They felt real, and then you woke up. She closed her eyes and tried to catch the thread, but it was too difficult to tell what was the dream and what was not. She shivered in the breeze, though it was not cold, and brought herself back inside. She looked at her watch. Only a couple of hours had passed, and it was still hours more until daylight, but sleep felt impossible. Charlie put on her shoes and shuffled quietly through the hall and down the stairs, hoping not to wake her friends. She went out to the porch, sitting down on the front steps and leaning back to look up at the sky. There were traces of clouds overhead, but the stars still shone through, scattered overhead, uncountable. She tried to lose herself in them as she had as a child, but as she gazed up at the pinpoint lights, all she could see were eyes, looking back at her.

There was a noise behind her, and she jumped, whirling to press her back against the railing. John was standing behind her with a startled look on his face. They stared at each other for a moment like strangers, and then Charlie found her voice.

"Hey, sorry, did I wake you up again?"

John shook his head and came to sit beside her.

"No, not really. I heard you go out, or I figured it was you. I was awake, though—Jason snores like a guy about three times his size."

Charlie laughed.

"I had a weird dream," she said. John nodded, waiting for her to go on, but she did not. "What did people think of my father?" she asked instead. John leaned back and looked at the stars for a moment, then pointed.

"That's Cassiopeia," he said, and she squinted in the direction of his finger.

"It's Orion," she corrected. "John, I'm serious. What did people think about him?"

He shrugged uncomfortably.

"Charlie, I was a little kid, you know? Nobody told me anything."

"I was a little kid once myself," she said. "Nobody tells you anything, but they talk in front of you like you're not there. I remember your mom and Lamar's mom talking, making bets on how long Marla's new stepdad would stick around."

"What did they come up with?" John said, amused.

"Your mom was banking on three months; Lamar's mom was more optimistic," Charlie said, grinning, but then her face grew serious again. "I can tell you know something," she said quietly, and after a moment he nodded.

"Some people thought he did it, yeah," he admitted.

"What?" Charlie was aghast. She stared at him, eyes wide, scarcely breathing. "They thought *what*?" John glanced at her nervously.

"I thought that's what you were asking," he said. Charlie shook her head. *Some people thought he did it.*

"I—no, I meant what did they think of him as a person. Did they think he was odd, or kind, or . . . I didn't know . . ." She trailed off, lost in the magnitude of this new truth. *People thought he did it.* Of course they did. It was *his* restaurant. The first child to vanish was *his* child. In the absence of a confession or a conviction, who else would anyone think of? Charlie shook her head again.

"Charlie," John said hesitantly, "I'm sorry. I just assumed. You must have known people would think that, though—if not then, then now."

"Well, I didn't," she snapped. She felt a hollow satisfaction when he drew back, hurt. She took a deep breath. "I know it sounds obvious," she said in more even tones. "But it just never, ever occurred to me that anyone would think he was responsible. And then afterward, after he committed—" *But that would have only reinforced their suspicions,* she realized as she said it.

"People thought it was because of the guilt," John said, almost to himself.

"It was." Charlie felt anger welling up inside her, the dam about to break, and she held it back, biting off words in short, sharp bursts. "Of course he felt guilt, it was *his* restaurant. *His* life's work, *his* creations, and it was all turned into a massacre. Don't you think that's enough?" Her voice sounded vicious, even to her own ears. *Apologize*, she thought, but she ignored it.

People thought he did it. He wouldn't, he couldn't. But if he had, how would she even have known? *I knew him*, she thought fiercely. But did she? She loved him, trusted him, with the blind devotion of a seven-year-old girl, even now. She understood him with the knowing and not-knowing that comes of being a child. When you focus on your parent as if they are the center of the earth, that thing on which your survival depends, only later do you realize their flaws, their scars, and their weaknesses.

Charlie had never had the dawning moments of realization as she grew older that her father was only human; she had never had the chance. To her he was still mythic, still larger than life, still the man who could deactivate the monsters. *He was also the man who made them.* How well did she really know him?

The rage was gone, had ebbed back to wherever it rose from, and she was empty of it, her insides dry and vacant. She closed her eyes and put a hand to her forehead.

"I'm sorry," she said, and John touched her shoulder for a brief moment.

"Don't be," he said. Charlie put her hands over her face. She did not feel like crying, but she didn't want him to see her face. She was thinking of things that were too new, too awful, to think in front of someone else. *How would I have known if he did?*

"Charlie?" John cleared his throat and repeated her name. "Charlie, you know he didn't do it, right? Mr. Burke said they knew who did, but they had to let him go. He got away with it. Remember?"

Charlie didn't move, but something like hope stirred inside her.

"It wasn't him," John said again, and she looked up.

"Right. Right, of course it wasn't," she whispered. "Of course it wasn't him," she said at a normal pitch.

"Of course not," he echoed. She nodded, bobbing her head up and down like she was gathering momentum.

"I want to go back to the house one more time," she said. "I want you to come with me."

"Of course," he said. She nodded again, then turned her face back up to the sky.

CHAPTER EIGHT

harlie!" Someone was at the door, knocking loud enough to rattle the old hinges. Charlie roused slowly, her eyes sticky with sleep, but this time at least she knew where she was. She had left the window open, and now the air coming in had a fresh, heavy smell: It was the scent of coming rain, mossy and rich. She got up and looked out the window, inhaling deeply. Unlike most of the world, the woods outside looked almost the same in the morning as they had in the dark. Charlie and John had gone back to bed soon after they finished talking. John had looked at her like there was more he wanted to say, but she had pretended not to notice. She was grateful to him for being there, for giving her what she needed without having to ask, because she would never have asked.

"Charlie!" The banging came again, and she gave in.

"I'm up, Marla," she shouted back.

"Charlie!" Now Jason was joining in the game, knocking and rattling, and Charlie groaned and went to the door.

"I said I'm up," she said, mock-glaring out at them.

"Charlie!" Jason shouted again, and this time Marla shushed him. He grinned up at Charlie, and she laughed and shook her head.

"Believe me, I'm awake," she said. Marla was fully dressed, her hair a little damp from the shower, and her eyes were bright and alert. "Are you always like this?" Charlie said, her grumpiness only half-invented.

"Like what?"

"Chipper at six in the morning," she said and rolled her eyes at Jason, who copied her, happy to be included.

Marla smiled brightly. "It's eight! Come on, there's been talk of breakfast."

"Has there been talk of coffee?"

Charlie followed Marla and Jason down the stairs to the kitchen, where she found Lamar and John already seated around a high, modern-looking wood table. Carlton's father was at the stove, making pancakes.

"It smells like rain," Charlie said, and Lamar nodded.

"There's a thunderstorm coming," he said. "It was on the news earlier, he told us." He jerked a thumb at Clay.

"It's a big one!" Clay exclaimed in response.

"We're supposed to leave today," Jason said.

"We'll see," Marla said.

"Charlie!" Clay cried, not taking his eyes off his work. "One, two, or three?"

"Two," Charlie said. "Thanks. Is there coffee?"

"Help yourself. Mugs in the cupboard," Clay said, gesturing to a full pot on the counter. Charlie helped herself, waving off offers of milk, cream, half-and-half, sugar, or fake sugar.

"Thanks," she said quietly as she settled herself beside Lamar, meeting John's eyes briefly. "Did Carlton come in?"

Lamar shook his head, a tight jerk to the side.

"He hasn't turned up yet," Clay said. "Probably isn't awake yet, wherever he is." He placed a full plate in front of Charlie, who dug in, not realizing how hungry she was until she was already chewing. She was about to ask where Carlton was likely to be when Jessica appeared, yawning, her clothes unrumpled, unlike Charlie's.

"You're late," Marla teased, and Jessica stretched elaborately.

"I don't get out of bed until the pancakes are ready," she said, and with impeccable timing Clay slapped one onto a plate, fresh off the pan.

"Well, you're just in time," he said. Suddenly, his expression changed, wavering somehow between apprehension and relief. Charlie turned in her seat. There was a woman standing behind her, dressed in a gray skirt suit, her blonde hair shellacked against her head as if she were a plastic toy.

"Are we a Waffle House now?" she asked. She looked around the kitchen briefly.

"Pancakes," Jessica corrected, but no one responded.

"Betty!" Clay cried. "You remember the boys, and this is Charlie, Jessica, and Marla. And Jason." He pointed to each in turn, and Carlton's mother gave each of them a nod, like she was tallying them up.

"Clay, I have to be in court in an hour."

"Betty's the D.A. for the county," Clay went on as if he had not heard her. "I catch the crooks; she puts 'em back out on the streets!"

"Yes, our family is a full-service operation," she said dryly, pouring herself coffee and settling down at the table beside Jessica. "Speaking of which, where's our young felon-to-be?"

Clay hesitated. "Another one of his pranks," he said. "He'll be back home later, I'm sure." Their eyes met, and something private passed between them. Betty broke away with a laugh that sounded a little forced.

"Oh, Lord, what is it this time?" There was a moment's pause. In the morning light, the story sounded insane, and Charlie had no idea where to begin. With a nervous clearing of his throat, Lamar started to explain.

"We, uh—we went up to the mall construction site, to go see what was left of Freddy Fazbear's."

At the name, Betty's head jerked up, and she gave a quick nod.

"Go on," she said, her voice suddenly cold and clipped.

Lamar explained, awkwardly, and Marla and Jason jumped in with details. After a few minutes, Carlton's mother had a messy version of the truth. As she listened, her face hardened until it looked like plaster; she was a statue of herself. She shook her head as they finished, small, rapid movements, and Charlie thought she looked like she was not just trying to deny what they were saying, but to shake the knowledge entirely from her mind.

"You have to go get him, Clay, right now," she demanded. "Send someone! How could you wait all night?"

She set her coffee on the table more forcefully than she should have, spilling a little, then went to the phone and started dialing.

"Who are you calling?" Clay said, alarmed.

"The police," she snapped.

"I *am* the police!"

"Then why are you here instead of finding my son?"

Clay opened and closed his mouth helplessly for a moment before finding his bearings.

"Betty, it's just another joke. Remember the frogs?"

She set the phone back on its hook and turned to face him, her eyes smoldering. Charlie could suddenly see her standing righteous before a jury, wreaking the wrath of the law.

"Clay." Her voice was low and steady, a dangerous calm. "How could you not wake me up? How could you not tell me this?"

"Betty, you were asleep! It's just Carlton being Carlton. I didn't want to disturb you."

"Did you think I would be less disturbed when I woke up and found him missing?"

"I thought he would be back by now," Clay protested.

"This is different," she said with finality. "It's *Freddy's*."

"I don't understand Freddy's? I know what happened there, what happened to those kids," he retorted. "*I* don't understand? For goodness' sake, Betty, I saw Michael's blood, streaked across the floor where he was dragged from—" He stopped, realizing too late that he was surrounded by the teenagers. He looked around at them, near panic, but his wife had not noticed—or, Charlie thought, she just did not care.

"Well, you didn't see *him*," Betty snapped. "Do you remember what you told Carlton? Be tough? Be brave, little soldier? So he was brave, he was a little soldier for you. He was shattered, Clay! He had lost his best friend, had Michael snatched away right in front of him. Let me tell you something, chief: That boy has thought about Michael every single day of his life for the last ten years. I have seen him stage jokes so elaborate they deserve to be mounted as performance art pieces, but there is no way on earth that Carlton

230

would desecrate Michael's memory by making Freddy's a joke. Call someone right now."

Clay looked slightly shocked, but he gathered himself quickly and left the room. Charlie heard a door slam shut behind him. Betty looked around at the teenagers, breathing hard as if she had been running.

"Everything is going to be fine," she said tightly. "If he is trapped in there, we will get him out. What do you kids have planned for the day?" The question was inane, as if they were all going to hang out at the park or go to a movie while Carlton might be in danger.

"We were supposed to leave today," Marla said.

"Obviously we won't," Lamar said hastily, but Betty did not seem to be listening to them.

"I'll have to call in to work," she said distractedly and went to the phone to make the call. Charlie looked at John, who jumped to the rescue.

"We were going to go to the library," he said. "We had some things we wanted to investigate—research!" He blushed faintly when he said it, and Charlie knew why. It was absurd to be talking like this, about cases and disappearances and murders. But Marla was nodding.

"Yeah, we'll all go," she said, and Charlie's heart sank. There was no reason she couldn't just tell them all that she wanted to go back to her old house, just her and John. No one would be hurt. But that wasn't the problem—even sharing the knowledge felt too much like exposure. Carlton's mother hung up the phone, done with her call.

"I hate this," she announced to the room in general, her careful, controlled voice almost shaking. *"I hate this!"* Charlie and the others jumped in unison, startled by the sudden outburst. "And now, like always, I get to sit here by myself hoping and praying that everyone will be okay."

Charlie looked at Marla, who shrugged helplessly. Lamar cleared his throat nervously. "I think we'll stick around for another day," he said. There was a pause, then Marla and Jessica jumped in to help.

"Yeah, traffic is *crazy* out there," Jessica said, high-pitched and forced.

"Yeah, and also because of the storm, and it's not like we're going to have fun knowing he's missing," Marla said.

"I guess you're stuck with us." Jessica flashed an anxious smile at Carlton's mother, who did not seem to register it.

"Come on," John said before anyone else could speak. He and Charlie hurried out of the house and got into the car.

Charlie heaved a sigh of relief as she started the engine. "That was awful," she said.

"Yeah." He gave her a worried look. "What do you think? About Carlton?"

Charlie didn't answer until she was safely backed out of the driveway. "I think his mom is right," she said, pulling into gear. "I think last night we all let ourselves believe what we wanted to believe."

Officer Dunn pulled to a stop in the mall parking lot, responding to Chief Burke's order to return. In the light of day it was just an abandoned construction site, an ugly blemish on the flat desert landscape. *You can't tell from looking if it's being built up or torn down*, Dunn thought. *Can't tell creation from destruction at a distance.* He liked the phrase; he turned it over in his head for a moment, staring at the place. On impulse, he radioed dispatch.

"Hey, Norah," he said.

"Dunn," she answered crisply. "What's going on?"

"Back at the mall for another look," he said.

"Ooh, bring me back a soft pretzel," she teased. He laughed and broke the connection.

As he walked briskly through the mall, Dunn was at least grateful the children were not there this time. As the youngest member of the Hurricane Police Department, Dunn always took care to think of teenagers as children, even though he knew how small the gap between them was. If he could bring them to believe he was a responsible adult, hopefully at some point he would believe it, too.

Dunn flipped on his flashlight as he reached the entrance

to the narrow alleyway that led to Freddy Fazbear's. He swept the beam up and down the walls ahead of him, but the alley was empty of life. He took a deep breath and went in. Dunn kept to the wall, his shoulder brushing lightly against the rough brick as he tried to avoid the puddles that pooled beneath leaky pipes. The bright beam of his flashlight illuminated the alley almost as well as overhead bulbs, but somehow the light was not comforting—it only made the place look stark and grim, the shelves of tools and rejected paint cans now woeful and exposed. As he moved toward the door to the restaurant, something tiny and cold landed on his head, and he startled, swinging his light up like a weapon and pressing his back against the wall as defense against the threat. Another cold drop of water landed on his cheek. He took deep breaths.

When at last he reached the outer door to the restaurant, the shelf that had blocked it was gone. The chains that had seemed so permanently fixed in place were hanging loose, and the door was cracked open slightly. The immense, rusted padlock lay in the dirt, its shackle hanging open. Dunn kicked it away from the door. He dug his fingers into the gap, prying until he could get a grip on it, then pulled at the door with both hands until it screeched open wide enough for him to enter. He crept down the inner passage with his light held out in front, hugging the wall tight to one side. The air seemed to change as he moved closer to the interior of the restaurant, and Dunn felt a crawling chill that penetrated his uniform and fed his growing anxiety.

"Don't freak out, Dunn," he said out loud, then felt instantly foolish.

He reached the main dining area and stopped, sweeping the light over each wall in turn. The light seemed dimmer inside, swallowed by the space. The room was empty, but it was just as he remembered from when he was a kid. He had been ten when the tragedies started, eleven when they ended. His birthday party was supposed to be at Freddy's, but after the first disappearance his mother had cancelled it, invited his friends to his house, and hired a clown, which proved equally terrifying. *Smart move, Mom*, Dunn thought. The beam played over the little carousel, which he had never ridden, claiming he was too old for it. Just before the beam of light reached the stage, Dunn stopped, swallowing hard. *The rabbit took him*, the kid had said. Dunn shook himself and played the light across the stage.

The figures were there, just as he remembered, and, unlike the carousel, they did not seem diminished in size. They were exactly as he recalled, and for a moment an almost painful nostalgia swelled in his chest. As he gazed at them, remembering, he noticed that their eyes were all fixed oddly forward like they were watching something on the far side of the room. The flashlight trained in front of him, Dunn approached the stage until he was standing only a few feet from it, and he stared up at each of the animals in turn. Bonnie was holding his guitar jauntily, as if he might begin strumming whenever the mood struck him, and Chica and her cupcake seemed to be sharing some arcane secret. Freddy, with his microphone, stared out into the distance, unblinking.

Something moved behind him, and Dunn whirled around, his heart racing. The flashlight found nothing, and he swept it nervously from side to side, revealing only empty tables. He glanced back nervously at Bonnie, but the rabbit was still frozen in his own inscrutable reverie.

Dunn took shallow breaths, holding himself completely still, and listened, his senses kicked into high gear with adrenaline. After a moment the noise came again—a shuffling sound, this time coming from off to the right. He swept the light instantly toward it. There was an open doorway, and beyond it a hall. Crouching down, Dunn made his way down the hall, keeping to the side as though something might come running past. *Why am I here alone?* He knew the answer. His sergeant hadn't taken the search seriously—in truth, neither had Dunn. After all, it was just the chief's son again, making trouble. *It's probably just Carlton*, Dunn reminded himself.

He reached the end of the hall, where a door stood ajar. With one hand Dunn gave the door an inward push, dropping low and to the side as he did. The door swung inward, and nothing happened. He pulled the nightstick from his belt. Its heft was unfamiliar—he had never had much need for it in Hurricane. Now, though, he gripped its hard rubber handle like a lifeline.

The office was not quite empty; there was a small desk, and a folded-up metal chair leaned against it. A large cabinet stood against one wall, its door open just a crack. There were no exits other than the one Dunn was standing in. He swept the light up and down the length of the cabinet and took a deep breath. He bounced his nightstick lightly in his hand, reassuring himself of its presence, and carefully assessed the small space. Standing to the side, he used the stick to open the door, moving slowly. It came open easily, and again, everything was still. Relieved, Dunn looked inside. The cabinet was empty—except for a costume.

It was Bonnie, or rather it wasn't. The face was the same, but the rabbit's fur was yellow. It was slumped lifelessly against the back wall of the cabinet, its eyes dark, gaping holes. *The rabbit took him.* The kid hadn't been lying, then; Carlton must have gotten someone to dress up in this outfit to help him play his trick. Still, Dunn's unease did not abate; he did not want to touch the thing. He lowered his light and stuck his nightstick back in his belt, intending to go.

Before he could turn, the costume pitched forward, land-ing on Dunn with the lifeless weight of a heavy corpse. For a moment it did not move, then all at once it was writhing violently, grabbing at him with strong, inhuman hands. Dunn screamed, a desperate, high sound, struggling as the rabbit gripped his shirt, then his arm. Dunn felt a sudden, vicious pain, and a small, detached part of his mind thought, *He broke it; he broke my arm.* But the pain was washed numb by terror as the rabbit swung him around and slammed him into the cabinet door, taking Dunn's weight easily as if he were a child. Dunn struggled to breathe; the rabbit's arm was pressed against his neck so tightly that every movement choked him. Just when he thought he was on the brink of passing out, the pressure lifted, and Dunn gasped with relief, clutching his throat. Then he saw the knife.

The rabbit held a slim silver blade. Its big, matted paws should have been too clumsy, but Dunn knew as he stared down at it that the rabbit had done this before and would easily do it again. Dunn screamed, an indistinct shriek. He had no hope that he would be heard; it was only a guttural, despairing noise. He breathed deep and did it again, a bestial sound, his whole body vibrating with it, as if this could somehow be defense against what happened next.

The knife went in. Dunn felt it tear through skin and muscle, felt it sever things he could not name to plant itself deep in his chest. As he seized with pain and terror, the rabbit pulled him close, almost in an embrace. Dunn's head went light; he was losing consciousness. As he looked up, he could see two rows of smiling teeth, horrid and yellow, the costume peeling at the edges of the mouth. The two gaping holes for eyes looked down at him. They were dark and hollow, but the creature drew near enough that Dunn could see smaller eyes peering back at him from deep within the mask. They held Dunn's gaze patiently. Dunn felt his legs go numb, his vision clouding. He wanted to scream again, to somehow voice his final outrage, but he could not move his face, could not raise the breath to cry out. The rabbit held him upright, supporting his weight, and its eyes were the last thing Dunn ever saw.

Charlie unlocked the front door to her old house and looked back down the front steps.

"You coming?"

John was still standing on the bottom step, staring up at the house. He shivered a little before hurrying to join her.

"Sorry," he said sheepishly. "I just had a weird feeling for a second." Charlie laughed without much humor.

"Just for a second?"

They went inside, and John stopped again, looking around the front room like he had just stepped into a sacred place, somewhere that merited a humbling pause. Charlie bit her tongue, trying not to be impatient. It was how she had felt as well; she might have felt that way now if she were not overwhelmed by a sense of urgency, the feeling that the answer to everything, the answer to how to get Carlton back, must be somewhere in this place. Where else could it possibly be?

"John," she said, "it's okay. Come on."

He nodded and followed her up the stairs to the second floor. He stopped again briefly halfway up, and Charlie saw his eyes fixed on the dark stain that marred the wood floor of the living room.

"Is—" he began to say, then swallowed it and started over. "Is Stanley still there?"

Charlie pretended not to notice the lapse.

"You remember his name!" she said instead, grinning. John shrugged.

"Who doesn't love a mechanical unicorn?"

"Yeah, he's still there. All the toys still work. Come on." They hurried the rest of the way to her room.

John knelt down beside the unicorn and pressed the button that set him on his track, watching raptly as he made his squeaky way around the room. Charlie hid a smile behind her hand. John was watching intently, his face serious as if something very important were happening. For a moment he looked just like he had so many years ago, his hair falling into his face, his whole attention fixed on Stanley like nothing in the world was more important than this robotic creature.

Suddenly his attention was called upward, and his face lit up as he pointed.

"Your big-girl closet! It's open!" he exclaimed, getting back to his feet and approaching the tallest of the three closets, which was hanging open slightly. He pulled it open all the way, then leaned in, finding it empty. "So what was in it all those years?" he asked.

"Not sure," Charlie said with a shrug. "I sort of remember Aunt Jen bringing me back at some point, but I could be wrong. Maybe it was full of clothes that I was finally big enough to wear. Aunt Jen was always thrifty—why spend money on new clothes if you don't have to, right?" She smiled.

John glanced briefly at the smaller closets, but he left them alone.

"I'm going to see if I can find any photo albums or paperwork," Charlie said, and she nodded absently as Stanley rattled back to his starting point. As she left the room, she heard him starting up again, making another round on the track.

The room that had been her father's was next to Charlie's. It was at the back of the house, and it had too many windows. In the summer it was too hot, and in the winter the cold dribbled in like a persistent leak, but Charlie had known without being told why he used it. From here you could see the garage and his workshop. It had always made sense to Charlie; that was his place, like a part of him always lived there, and he did not like to be too far away from his touchstone. A wave from her dream came to her for a moment, not even an image, just a strange, evocative gesture of memory. She frowned, looking out the window at the closed, silent garage door.

Or maybe he just wanted to be sure nothing got out, she thought. She broke away from the window, shrugging her shoulders and shaking her hands, sloughing off the feeling. She looked around the room. Like her own, it was all but untouched. She did not open the drawers to his dresser, but for all she knew, it might still have been filled with shirts and socks, clean, folded, and ready to wear. His bed was made crisply, covered in the plaid blanket he used as a bedspread after Charlie's mother left, when there was no one to insist on white linen. There was a large bookcase against one wall, and it was still stuffed with books. Charlie went over and began scanning the shelves. Many were textbooks, engineering tomes whose titles meant nothing to her, and the rest were nonfiction, a collection that would have seemed eclectic to anyone who did not know the man.

There were books on biology and anatomy, some on human beings and others on animals; there were books about the history of the traveling carnival and of the circus. There were books about child development, about myths and legends, and about sewing patterns and techniques. There were volumes that claimed to be about trickster gods, about quilting bees, and about football cheering squads and their mascots. On the very top shelf were stacks of file folders, and the bottom shelf was empty except for a single book: a photo album, leather-bound and as pristine as time and dust could allow. Charlie grabbed it, and it stuck for a moment, almost too tall for the low shelf it had been given. After a minute it came free, and she headed back to her bedroom, leaving the door open with the sudden sense that if it closed she might never get back in.

John was sitting on the bed when she returned, looking at Stanley with his head tilted to the side.

"What?" Charlie said, and he looked up, still pensive.

"I was wondering if he's been lonely," he said, then shrugged.

"He's got Theodore," Charlie said, pointing to the stuffed rabbit with a smile. "It's Ella who's all alone in the closet. Watch." She placed the album beside John on the bed and went to its foot, then turned the wheel that set Ella on her track. She sat down beside him, and they watched together, spellbound as of old, as the little doll came out in her crisp, clean dress to blankly offer tea. Neither of them spoke until the smallest closet door closed behind her. John cleared his throat.

"So what's in the book?"

"Photos," Charlie said. "I haven't looked at them yet." She picked up the album and opened it at random. The top picture was of her mother holding a baby, maybe a year old. She held the child above her head, flying it like an airplane, her head thrown back in the midst of a laugh, her long brown hair swinging out in an arc behind her. The baby's eyes were wide, its mouth open in delight. John smiled at her.

"You look so happy," he said, and she nodded.

"Yeah," she said. "I guess I must have been." *If that's me,* she did not add aloud. She opened to another page, where the only picture was a large family portrait, stiffly posed at a studio. They were dressed formally: Charlie's father was wearing a suit; her mother was in a bright-pink dress with padding that lifted her shoulders almost to her ears, and her brown hair was straightened flat in place. Each of them was holding a baby, one in a white frilly dress and one in a sailor suit. Charlie's heart skipped, and beside her she heard John take a sharp, quick breath. She looked at him with a feeling like the floor was dropping away beneath them.

"It was real," she said. "I didn't imagine him."

John said nothing in response, just nodded. He put a hand on her shoulder briefly, and then they turned back to the photo album.

"We all looked so happy," Charlie said softly.

"I think you were," John said. "Look, you had such a goofy smile." He pointed, and Charlie laughed.

The whole book was like that, the first memories of a happy family who expected there to be many more. They were not arranged chronologically, so Charlie and Sammy appeared as toddlers, then as newborns, then at various stages in between. Except on formal occasions when Charlie was put into a dress—of which there seemed to be few—it was impossible to tell which baby was which. There were no traces of Fredbear's Family Diner.

Near the back of the book, Charlie came to a Polaroid of her and Sammy together, infants bright red and squalling on their backs, wearing nothing but diapers and hospital wristbands. On the white space below the picture someone had written, "Momma's Boy and Daddy's Girl."

The rest of the pages were blank. Charlie went back again, opening at random to find a strip from a photo booth, four shots of her parents alone. They smiled at each other, then made faces at the camera, then laughed, missing the chance to pose and blurring their faces. Lastly they smiled into the lens. Her mother was beaming happily at the camera, her face alight and flushed, but her father was staring into the distance, a smile fixed on his face like he had left it there by mistake. His dark eyes were intense, remote, and Charlie resisted a sudden urge to look behind her, as if she might see whatever it was he was looking at. She peeled back the cellophane from the album's page and took the strip out, then folded it in half, careful to place the crease between pictures, leaving them intact. She slipped the pictures into her pocket and looked at John, who was watching her again as if she were some kind of unpredictable creature he needed to be careful around.

"What?" she said.

"Charlie, you know I don't think he did it, right?"

"You said that."

"I'm serious. It's not just what Carlton's dad said. I knew him, as well as a kid can know some other kid's dad—he wouldn't do it. I wouldn't believe it." He spoke with calm certainty, like someone who believed that the world was made out of facts and tangible things and that there was such a thing as truth. Charlie nodded.

"I know," she said. She took her next breath slowly, gathering the words she would speak with it. "But I might." His eyes widened, startled, and she looked up at the ceiling for a minute, briefly trying to remember if all the cracks had been there when she was a child.

"I don't mean I think he did it; I don't think that," she said. "I don't think about it at all. I can't. I shut the whole thing off in my mind the day I left Hurricane. I don't think about Freddy's. I don't think about what happened, and I don't think about him."

John was looking at her like she was monstrous, like what she was saying was the worst thing he had ever heard.

"I don't understand how you can say things like that," he said quietly. "You loved him. How can you even consider the possibility that he would do something so terrible?"

"Even the people who do terrible things have people who love them." Charlie was looking for words. "I don't think he did it; I'm not saying that," she said again, and again the words hit the air as flimsy as paper. "But I remember him dressing up for us in the yellow Freddy suit, doing the dances, miming along with the songs. It was so much a part of him. He *was* the restaurant; there was no one else. And he was always so distant, like in that picture; there was always something else going on beneath the surface. It was like he had a real life and a secret life, you know?"

John nodded and looked about to speak, but Charlie rushed on before he could.

"*We* were the secret life. His real life was his work; it was what mattered. We were his guilty pleasure, the thing he got to love and sneak away to have time with, something he kept hidden away from the dangers of what he did in his *real* world. And when he was with us, there was always a part of him that was back in reality, whatever that was for him."

Again John opened his mouth, but Charlie snapped the photo album shut, stood up, and left the room. John didn't follow right away, and as she traversed the short hall to her father's bedroom, she could almost hear him making up his mind. Not waiting for him, she went to the bookshelf, wanting to get the book out of her hands, like maybe if it were closed up and put away, her mind, too, would return to its normal order. The book would not fit, and she dropped to her knees to get a better angle, trying to jam the thing back where it belonged, get it out of her hands. The shelf seemed to have shrunk, sunk down while she was gone, so that it could never be returned, never put right.

With a cry of frustration, Charlie shoved the photo album in as hard as she could. The shelf rocked back and then forward, and a sudden mass of papers and file folders tumbled from above her. Charlie began to cry as pages drifted down around her, covering the floor like snow as she wept. Swiftly, John was there.

He knelt down with her in the delicate wreckage, clearing papers away as quickly as he could without tearing them. He put a hand on her shoulder carefully, and she did not move away. He pulled her close and held her, and she hugged him back, gripping so tight she knew she must be hurting him, but she could not let go. She sobbed harder, as if being held, being contained, made it safe to let go. Long minutes passed; John stroked her hair, and Charlie still cried, her body shaking with the force of it, shuddering like she was possessed. She was not thinking of what had happened, not flitting from one memory to the next to mourn for them all—her mind was all but blank. She held nothing, *was* nothing, but this feeling of racking sobs. Her face was sore with tension, her chest hurt like all her pain was being forced out through its wall, and still she cried as if she would cry forever.

But forever was an illusion. Slowly her breathing calmed, and finally Charlie returned to herself and pushed away from John's shoulder, exhausted. Once again John was left with his arms partially suspended in the air, caught off guard by their sudden emptiness. He tried to move out of the awkward pose without calling attention to himself. Charlie sat back against the side of her father's bed, leaning her head against it. She felt wrung out, stretched thin and aged, but she felt a little better. She gave John a tiny smile, and she saw relief pass over his face at this first sign that she might be all right.

"I'm okay," she said. "It's just this place; it's all this." She felt silly trying to explain, but John scooted back to sit with her.

"Charlie, you don't have to explain. I know what happened."

"Do you?" She looked at him searchingly, not sure how to put the question. It seemed too crude, too graphic, to say it outright. "Do you know how my dad died, John?"

He looked immediately nervous. "I know he killed himself," he said hesitantly.

"No, I mean—do you know *how*?"

"Oh." John looked down at his feet as if he could not meet her eyes. "I thought he stabbed himself," he said quietly. "I remember hearing my mom and dad talk—she said something about a knife, and all the blood."

"There was a knife," Charlie said. "And there was blood." She closed her eyes and kept them shut as she talked. She could feel John's eyes on her face, watching every movement, but she knew if she looked at him she would not be able to finish.

"I never saw it," she said. "I mean, I never saw the body. I don't know if you remember, but my aunt came to get me at school in the middle of the day." She stopped, waiting for confirmation, her eyes shut tight.

"I remember," John's voice said from the darkness. "It was the last time I ever saw you."

"Yeah. She came and got me, and I knew something was wrong—you don't go home from school in the middle of the day because everything's fine. She took me outside to her car, but we didn't get in right away. She picked me up and set me on the hood of the car, and she told me she loved me."

"I love you, Charlie, and everything is going to be okay," Aunt Jen said, and then she destroyed the world with the next words she spoke.

"She told me that my father had died, and she asked if I knew what that meant."

And Charlie nodded, because she did know, and because, with an awful prescience, she was not surprised.

"She said I was going to stay with her for a couple of days, and we would go get some clothes from the house. When we got there, she picked me up like I was a little kid, and as we went through the door, she covered my face with her hand so I wouldn't see what was in the living room. But I did see."

It was one of his creatures, one she had never seen, and it was facing the stairs; its head was bowed a little so that Charlie could see that the back of its skull was open, the circuits exposed. The limbs and joints lay bare, a skeleton of naked metal strung with twisting wires of bloodless circulation, and its arms were outstretched in a lonesome facsimile of an embrace. It was standing in the middle of a dark, still pool of some liquid that seemed, though it must have been imperceptible, to be spreading. She could see its face, if it could be called a face—its features were scarcely formed, crude and shapeless. Even so, Charlie could see that they were contorted, almost grotesque; the thing would be weeping, if it could have wept. She stared at it for ages, though it could have been less than seconds, no more than a glimpse as Aunt Jen swept her up the stairs. Yet she had seen it so many times since then, when she slept, when she woke, when she unguardedly closed her eyes. It would appear to her, the face pressing its way into her mind as it had pressed into the world. Its blind eyes were only raised bumps like the eyes of a statue, seeing nothing but its own grief. In its hand, almost an afterthought, was the knife. When Charlie saw the knife, the whole thing snapped into focus. She knew what the thing was, and she knew what it had been built for.

John was staring at her, horror creeping in.

"*That's* how he . . . ?" He trailed off.

Charlie nodded. "Of course." He made a move to comfort her again, but it was the wrong thing to do. Without thinking, Charlie moved slightly, slipping out of reach, and his face fell.

"Sorry," she said quickly. "I just—sorry."

John shook his head quickly and turned to the jumble of papers on the floor.

"We should look through these, see if there's anything here," he said.

"Sure," she said brusquely, dismissing his attempts at reassurance.

They began randomly; everything had fallen in such a mess that there was no other way to begin. Most of the papers were engineering blueprints and pages of equations, incomprehensible to them both. There were tax forms, which John took up eagerly, hoping for information about Fredbear's Family Diner, but he gave up with a sigh after fifteen minutes, flinging the papers down.

"Charlie, I can't figure this out. Let's check through the rest, but I don't think puzzling at it is going to turn us into mathematicians or accountants."

Stubbornly, Charlie kept picking through the papers, hoping for something she would understand. She picked up a sheaf of paper, trying to straighten the next stack, and a photograph fell out from the pile. John snatched it up.

"Charlie, look," he said, suddenly excited. She took it from his hand.

It was her father, in his workshop, wearing the yellow

Freddy Fazbear costume. The head was tucked under his arm, staring sightlessly into the camera, but Charlie's father was smiling, his face pink and sweaty as if he had been in the costume for a long time. Beside him was a yellow Bonnie.

"The yellow rabbit," Charlie said. "Jason said there was a yellow rabbit."

"But your father is in the bear costume."

"The rabbit must be a robot," Charlie said. "Look at the eyes, they're red." She peered closer. The eyes were glinting red, but they weren't glowing, and in a moment she saw why. "It's not red eyes, it's red eye! There's a person in there!"

"So who . . . ?"

". . . who is in the suit?" Charlie finished the question for him.

"We have to go to the library," John said, jumping to his feet. Charlie stayed where she was, still staring down at the picture. "Charlie?"

"Yeah," she said. He held out a hand to pull her up.

As they descended the staircase, John hung back briefly, but Charlie did not turn around. She knew what he was imagining, because she was picturing it, too: the stain on the floor, slowly spreading.

Charlie drove fast to the library, a grim urgency hanging over her. The promised storm was in the air, the smell of it rising like a warning. In a strange way, the worsening weather satisfied something in Charlie. Storms inside, storms outside.

"I've never been this eager to get to the library," John joked, and she smiled tightly, without humor.

The main library in Hurricane was next to the elementary school where they had gone for the memorial ceremony, and as they got out of the car, Charlie glanced at the playground, envisioning children screaming and laughing as they ran circles, immersed in their games. *We were so young.*

They hurried up the few steps to the library together, a square, modern brick building that looked as if it had come paired with the school beside it. She only remembered the library vaguely from her childhood; they had gone infrequently, and Charlie had spent all her time there sitting on the floor in the children's section. Being able to see over the information desk was slightly disconcerting.

The librarian was young, Charlie thought, an athletic-seeming woman in slacks and a purple sweater. She smiled brightly.

"What can I do for you?" she said. Charlie hesitated. The woman was maybe in her late twenties; Charlie realized that ever since she returned to Hurricane she had been paying attention to age, scrutinizing each face and calculating how old they had been when *it* happened. This woman would have been a teenager. *It doesn't matter,* she thought. *You still have to ask.* She opened her mouth to ask for information about Fredbear's, but what came out instead was, "Are you from Hurricane?"

The librarian shook her head. "No, I'm from Indiana." Charlie felt her body relax. *She wasn't here.*

"Do you have any information on a place called Fredbear's Family Diner?" Charlie asked, and the woman frowned.

"Do you mean Freddy Fazbear's? They used to have one of those here, I think," she said vaguely.

"No, that's not the one," Charlie said, ready to be endlessly patient with the librarian, who was, thankfully, probably the only person in town who was somehow unaware of her history.

"Well, for town records, things like incorporation and licensing, you would have to go to City Hall, but it's—" She checked her watch. "It's after five, so not today anyway. I have newspapers all the way back to the 1880s, if you want to look at microfilm," she said eagerly.

"Yeah, okay," Charlie said.

"I'm Harriet," the woman said as she led them to a door at the back of the building. They recited their names dutifully, and she chattered on like a child about to display her favorite toy.

"So you know what microfilm is, right? It's because we can't keep stacks and stacks of papers here. There's no room, and eventually they would rot, so it's a way to preserve them.

They take pictures and save the film; it's almost like a movie reel, you know? Very small. So you need a machine to see it."

"We know what it is," John cut in when she paused. "We just don't know how to use it."

"Well, that's what I'm here for!" Harriet declared and threw the door open. Inside was a table with a computer monitor. The monitor sat on top of a little box with a small wheel on each side. Two handles stuck out in front. Charlie and John looked at it bemusedly, and Harriet grinned.

"You want the local paper, right? What years?"

"Um . . ." Charlie counted backward. "1979 to 1982?" she hazarded. Harriet beamed and left the room. John bent forward to peer at the machine, rattling the handles a little. "Careful," Charlie warned jokingly. "I think she might be lost without that thing." John raised his hands to his shoulders and stepped back.

Harriet reappeared with what looked like four small movie reels and held them up.

"What year do you want to start with?" she said. "1979?"

"I guess," Charlie said, and Harriet nodded. She went to the machine and threaded the film through expertly. She flipped a switch and the screen came to life; a newspaper appeared.

"January 1, 1979," John announced, leaning forward to read the headlines. "Politics, somebody won a sports game, and there was some weather. Also there was a bakery giving away free cookies to celebrate the New Year. Sounds like now, except no cookies."

"You use these to see more," Harriet said, manipulating the controls. "Let me know if you need help switching the reels. Have fun, you two!" She winked conspiratorially and closed the door behind her as she left.

Charlie positioned herself in front of the machine, and John stood behind her, his hand on her chair. It felt good to have him close, like he would stop anything that tried to sneak up on her.

"This is pretty cool," he remarked, and she nodded, scanning the paper for answers.

"Okay, let's narrow it down," he said grimly. "What's the thing most likely to make the papers?"

"I was looking for an opening announcement," Charlie said.

"Yeah, but what's going to make the papers? Sorry," he added. "I didn't want to say it, but we have to."

"Sammy," Charlie said. "We should have started with Sammy. We moved to the new house when I was three; it's got to be 1982."

Carefully, they switched the reel. Charlie eyed the door as they did, as if nervous that Harriet might catch them making a mistake.

"When's your birthday?" John said, sitting to take her place.

"Don't you know?" she teased. He screwed up his face in an exaggerated mime of thinking.

"May thirteenth," he said at last. She laughed, startled.

"How did you know?"

He grinned up at her. "Because I know things," he said.

"But why does it matter?"

"You remember being three when you moved, but you didn't turn three until May, so we knock out five months. Do you remember anything about the restaurant the night Sammy disappeared?"

Charlie felt herself flinch with an almost physical pain.

"Sorry," she said. Her face felt too hot. "Sorry, you startled me. Let me think." She closed her eyes.

The restaurant. The closet, hung full with costumes. She and Sammy, there safe in the dark, until the door opened, and the rabbit appeared, leaning over them with its awful face, its human eyes. Charlie's heart was racing. She slowed her breathing and held out a hand; John took hold of it. She held on tight, as if he could anchor her. *The rabbit leaning over them, the yellow teeth beneath the mask, and behind the rabbit . . . what was behind the rabbit? The restaurant was open; she could hear voices, people. There were more people in costumes—other performers? Robots? No . . .* She almost had it. Scarcely breathing, Charlie tried to coax out the thought, scared to frighten it away. Move slowly; speak softly. She had it, snatched it from the depths of her mind and held it wriggling in her fingers. Her eyes snapped open.

"John, I know when it was," she said.

Earlier that night, when they were still wide awake, the closet opened, and her mother looked in. She was haloed by the light from behind her, smiling down at her twins, radiant in her long, elegant dress, her flowing hair, her gleaming tiara. Mommy's a princess, *Charlie murmured sleepily, and her mother bent down and kissed her cheek.* Just for tonight, *she whispered, and then she left them in the dark to sleep.*

"She was a princess," she said excitedly.

"What? Who?"

"My mother," Charlie said. "She was dressed up as a princess. It was a Halloween party. John, go to November first."

John struggled briefly with the controls, and then it was there. The headline was small, but it was on the front page of the paper on Monday, November 1: TODDLER SNATCHED. Charlie turned away. John began to read aloud, and Charlie cut in, stopping him.

"Don't," she said. "Just tell me if it has anything useful."

He was quiet, and she stared anxiously at the door, waiting, tracing the knots in the false wood with her eyes.

"There's a picture," he said finally. "You need to look."

She leaned over his shoulder. The story had continued over an entire page inside, with pictures of the restaurant, of the family all together, and of her and of Sammy, though neither of the twins were named in the article. In the bottom left corner, there was a picture of her father and another man. Their arms were slung around each other's shoulders, and they were grinning happily.

"John," Charlie said.

"It says they were joint owners," John said quietly.

"No," Charlie said, unable to take her eyes from the picture, from the face they both knew.

Suddenly the door behind them erupted in pounding from outside, and they both jumped.

"CHARLIE! JOHN! ARE YOU IN THERE?"

"Marla," they said as one, and Charlie rushed to the door and threw it open.

"Marla, what is it?"

She was red-faced and breathless, and Harriet was anxiously hovering behind her. Marla's hair was wet; water dripped down her face, but she did not wipe it away or even seem to notice. *I guess the rain started*, Charlie thought, the mundane reflection drifting unbidden into her head despite her alarm.

"He's gone! Jason's gone," Marla cried.

"What?" John said.

"He's gone back to Freddy's; I know he has," she said. "He kept saying we should go back, that we shouldn't just be hanging around all day. I thought he was in another room, but I looked everywhere. I know that's where he is!" She said it all in one breath and ended gasping, a faint, whining hum resonating under her breathing, a keening sound she seemed unable to stop making.

"Oh no," Charlie said.

"Come on," Marla pressed. She was jittering, vibrating; John put a hand on her shoulder as if to comfort her, and she shook her head. "Don't try to calm me down, just come with me," she insisted, but there was no anger, only desperation. She turned and almost ran to the door, and John and Charlie followed with an apologetic look for the bemused librarian they left behind them.

CHAPTER NINE

arlton opened his eyes, disoriented, his head stuffed tight with a massive, pulsing ache. He was half sitting, stiffly propped against a wall, and he found he could not move his arms. His body was covered in little, random places of sharp pain and tingling numbness; he tried to shift away from the discomfort, but he was restrained somehow, and the little moves he could make just made new places hurt. He looked around the room, trying to get his bearings. It looked like a storage room: There were boxes along the walls, and discarded cans of paint and other cleaning supplies littered the floor, but there was more. There were piles of furry fabric everywhere. Carlton peered at them sleepily. He felt muzzy, like if he closed his eyes he could just fall back asleep, so easily . . . *No.* He shook his head hard, trying to clear it, and yelped. "Oh no," he groaned as the throbbing in his head demanded attention and his stomach flipped. He clenched his jaw and closed his eyes, waiting for the pounding and nausea to recede.

Eventually they did, fading back to something almost manageable, and he opened his eyes again, starting over. This time his mind had cleared a little, and he looked down at his body to see his restraints. *Oh no.*

He was wedged inside the heavy, barrel-shaped torso of a mascot costume, the headless top half of some kind of animal. His arms were trapped inside the torso section, pinned to his sides in an unnatural position by some sort of framework. The arms of the costume hung limp and empty from the sides. His legs stuck out incongruously from the bottom, looking small and thin in contrast. He could feel other things inside the mascot's torso, pieces of metal that pressed against his back and poked into him. He could feel raw patches on his skin, and he could not tell if the thing he felt trickling down his back was sweat or blood. Something was pressing into the sides of his neck; when he turned his head, whatever it was dug into his skin. The costume's fur was dirty and matted, a faded color that might once have been a bright blue but was now only a bluish approximation of beige. He could see a head of the same color a few feet away, sitting on a cardboard box, and with a flicker of curiosity he looked at it, but he could not tell what it was supposed to be. It looked as if someone had been told "make an animal" and had done just that, careful not to make it look like any specific *type* of animal.

He looked around the room, comprehension dawning. He knew where he was. The piles of fabric had faces. They were empty costumes, mascots from the restaurant, deflated, collapsed, and staring empty-eyed at him, like they wanted something.

He looked around, trying to assess calmly, though his heart was fluttering alarmingly in his chest. The room was small, a single bulb overhead lighting it dimly and flickering ever so slightly, giving the place a disquieting impression of movement. A small metal desk fan, brown with rust, gently oscillated in the corner, but the air it blew was heavy with the stale sweat of costumes left unwashed for a decade. Carlton was too hot; the air felt too thick. He tried to stand, but without his arms he could not brace himself, and as he moved he felt another violent wave of nausea, and a sudden, angry surge of pain in his head.

"I wouldn't do that," a raspy voice muttered. Carlton looked around, seeing no one, then the door opened. It moved slowly, and somewhere beneath his terror Carlton felt a twinge of impatience.

"Who is it? Let me out of this!" he said in panicked desperation.

The door squealed like an injured animal as it glided open, almost of its own accord, the frame empty. After a moment's pause, a yellow rabbit poked its head around the corner, its ears tilting at a jaunty angle. It was still for a moment, almost posing, then it came in with a bouncing walk, graceful, with none of the stiff, mechanistic movements of the animatronic animal. It did a small dance step, spun, and took a deep bow. Then it reached up and took off its own head, revealing the man inside the costume.

"I guess I shouldn't be surprised," Carlton said, his nerves triggering an automatic wisecrack. "Never trust a rabbit, I say." It didn't make sense, it wasn't funny, but the words were coming out of his mouth without any input from his brain. He still felt sick, his head still ached, but he had a sudden, visceral clarity: *This is what happened to Michael. You* are *what happened to Michael.*

"Don't speak," Dave said. Carlton opened his mouth to answer back, but the smart remark died on his tongue when he saw the guard's face. He had seemed somehow faded when they met, depleted and ineffectual. But now, as he stood over Carlton in his absurd-looking rabbit costume, he looked different. His face was the same, technically—his gaunt features and sunken eyes, his skin that seemed to have worn thin, ready to snap from strain—but now there was a mean, undeniable strength in him, a rodentine vitality that Carlton recognized.

It had occurred to Carlton years before that there were two types of nasty people: There were the obvious ones, like his sixth-grade English teacher who yelled and threw erasers, or the kid in fifth grade who picked fights with smaller children after school. That type was easy, their offenses public, brutal, and undeniable. But then there was the other kind of petty tyrant, those who grew spiteful with their small scraps of power, feeling more and more abused by the year—by family who did not appreciate them, by neighbors who slighted them in imperceptible ways, by a world that left them, somehow, lacking something essential.

Before him stood someone who had spent so much of his life fighting like a cornered rat that he had taken on the mantle of bitter sadism as an integral part of himself. He would strike out against others and revel in their pain, feeling righteously that the world owed him his cruel pleasures. The guard's face, with its malevolent delight in Carlton's pain and fear, was one of the most terrifying things he had ever seen. He opened and closed his mouth, then, valiantly, found his voice.

"What kind of a name for a serial killer is Dave?" he said. It came out as a trembling croak, lacking even the echo of bravado. Dave did not seem to hear him.

"I told you not to move, Carlton," he said calmly. He set the rabbit's head down on a plastic crate and began fiddling with the fastenings at the back of his neck. "It's not an order, it's a friendly warning. Do you know what I've put you in?"

"Your girlfriend?" Carlton said, and Dave made a thin curve of a smile.

"You're amusing," he said with distaste. "But no. You're not wearing a costume, Carlton, not precisely. You see, these suits were designed for two purposes: to be worn by men like me"—he gestured fluidly toward himself, with something that might have been pride—"and to be used as working animatronics like the ones you see on the stage. Do you understand?"

Carlton nodded, or began to, but Dave's raised eyebrow stopped him.

"I said don't move," he said. The neck of his costume came open, and he began to undo a second fastening at his back as he talked. "You see, all of the animatronic parts in that suit are still in it; they are simply held back by spring locks, like this."

Dave went to the pile of costumes and selected one, bringing the fuzzy green torso, headless, over to Carlton. He held out the costume, waggling two twisted pieces of metal that were attached to the sides of the neck.

"*These* are spring locks," he said, bringing the piece of metal so close to Carlton's face he almost could not focus his eyes on it. "Watch." He did something, touched some piece of the lock so imperceptibly that Carlton could not see what he had done, and it snapped shut with a sound like a backfiring car. Carlton stiffened, suddenly taking the order not to move deathly seriously.

"That's a very old costume, one of the first ones Henry made. You can trip these spring locks very, very easily if you don't know what you're doing," Dave went on. "It takes almost no movement at all."

"Henry?" Carlton said, trying to focus on what he was being told. He could still hear the snap, as if it had lodged in his head like a song that kept repeating. *I'm going to die*, he thought for the first time since waking. *This man will kill me, I will die, and then what? Will anyone even know?* He set his jaw and met Dave's eyes. "Who's Henry?"

"Henry," Dave repeated. "Your friend Charlie's father." He looked surprised. "Did you not know that he made this place?"

"Oh, right, well," Carlton said confusedly. "I just always thought of him as 'Charlie's dad.'"

"Of course," Dave said, the kind of polite murmur people made when they didn't care. "Well, that's one of his first suits," he said, gesturing at Carlton. "And if you trigger those spring locks, two things will happen: First, all the locks will snap right into you, making deep cuts all over your body, and a split second later all the animatronic parts they've been holding back, all that sharp steel and hard plastic, will instantly be driven into your body. You will die, but it will be slow. You'll feel your organs punctured, the suit will grow wet with your blood, and you will know you're dying for long, long minutes. You'll try to scream, but you will be unable to. Your vocal cords will be severed, and your lungs will fill with your own blood until you drown in it." There was a faraway look in his eyes, and Carlton knew with chilling certainty that Dave wasn't predicting. He was reminiscing.

"How—" Carlton's voice broke, and he tried again. "How do you know that?" he said, managing a raspy whisper. Dave met his eyes and smiled widely.

"How do you think?" He set down the costume he was holding and reached up to undo the final piece of his own. It took time; Carlton watched for several minutes as Dave romanced whatever mechanisms lay under the collar. He took the costume torso off with a flourish, and Carlton made an involuntary sound, a helpless and frightened mewl.

Dave had been shirtless under the costume, and now his bare chest was clearly visible even in the dim, flickering light. His skin was horribly scarred, with raised white lines that scored his flesh in a symmetrical pattern, each side of his body mirroring the other. Dave saw him looking and laughed, a sudden, happy sound. Carlton shivered at it. Dave raised his arms out from his body and turned slowly in a circle, giving Carlton ample time to see that the scars were everywhere, covering his back like a faint lace shirt, stretching to the waist of the rabbit pants as if they continued all the way down. On the back of his neck, where they were largest and most visible, two scars like parallel lines were etched from the nape of his neck all the way up to his scalp, disappearing into his hair. Carlton tried to swallow. His mouth was so dry he could not have spoken, even if there had been anything to say.

Dave smiled unpleasantly.

"Don't move," he said again.

"He's here; he has to be here!" Marla cried, staring despairingly at the door to Freddy's. She was clasping and unclasping her hands, the knuckles going white. Charlie watched her helplessly. There was nothing to say. The door was no longer covered in chains; instead it was simply no longer a door. It had been welded over; the metal was melted seamlessly into the frame, and the hinges were gone, covered in crude, patchy solder. They all stared, not fully able to comprehend what they were looking at. Charlie shifted her feet. She had stepped in a puddle as they hurried from the car, and now her shoes and socks were soaked and freezing. It seemed unforgivable to be focused on her own discomfort in such a moment, but she could not stop her attention from drifting to it.

"This is insane," Marla said, her mouth agape. "Who does this?" She threw up her hands in frustration. "Who does something like that?" She was almost shouting. "Someone did that! Someone welded this shut. What if Jason is in there?"

Marla put her hands over her face. Jessica and Lamar stepped forward to comfort her, but she waved them away.

"I'm fine," she said tightly, but she did not move, still staring at the place in the wall that had once been a door. She looked smaller, lesser; the panicked energy that had been driving her was gone, leaving her empty and without purpose. She looked at Charlie, ignoring the others, and Charlie met her eyes uncomfortably.

"What do we do?" Marla asked. Charlie shook her head.

"I don't know, Marla," she said uselessly. "If he's in there, we have to get him out. There has to be a way."

"There has to be another way in," John agreed, though he sounded surer than Charlie felt. "Freddy's had windows, a service door, right? There must have been fire exits. There has to be something!"

"Stop!" Marla cried, and they all froze in place. She was pointing at the floor.

"What is it?" Charlie asked, coming up next to her.

"It's Jason's footprint," Marla said. "Look, you can see the imprint; it's those silly shoes he spent a year's allowance on."

Charlie looked. Marla was right; there was a muddy footprint about Jason's size, still fresh. Marla's face was alive again, fiery and determined.

"He must have just been here," Marla said. "Look, you can see the tracks turn and leave again. The door must have been already welded when he got here. He's probably still here somewhere. Come on!"

Jason's tracks were heading farther down the alley, into the darkness, and the group crouched low to the ground, following his trail. Charlie hung back, not really helping but keeping an eye on the bobbing flashlight ahead. There was something she was forgetting, something she should know. Something about Freddy's. Noticing that she was apart, John let the others move ahead.

"You okay?" he asked in a low voice, and Charlie shook her head.

"I'm fine," she said. "Go ahead." He waited for her to say more, but she was staring ahead into the dark. *Another way in.*

"Found it!" Jessica's voice pierced the dark, and Charlie came back to herself and jogged to catch up to the others. Lamar had the flashlight again, and he was aiming it at an air vent close to the ground.

The vent was old and rusty, and its covering lay flat on the ground amid scattered footprints and clumps of mud.

"Jason, what are you doing?" Marla gasped and knelt beside the vent. "What are you thinking?" There was an edge to her voice, something teetering between panic and relief. "We have to go after him," she said.

Charlie watched, dubious, but said nothing. It was John who spoke up.

"It's too small," he said. "I don't think any of us will fit."

Marla looked down at herself, then around at the others one by one, calculating.

"Jessica," she said decisively. "Come on."

"What?" Jessica looked to the side as if there might be another of her. "I don't think I'll fit, Marla."

"You're the skinniest," Marla said shortly. "Just try, okay?"

Jessica nodded and went to the vent, kneeling in the muddy concrete that was the alley's floor. She studied the hole in the wall for a moment and tried to squeeze in, but her shoulders barely cleared the space, and after a moment she pulled back out, out of breath.

"Marla, I can't fit, I'm sorry," she said.

"You can fit!" Marla said. "Please, Jessica."

Jessica looked back at the others, and when Charlie saw her face it was almost white, harshly expressionless. *She's claustrophobic*, Charlie thought, but before she could speak, Jessica was back at the air vent, twisting herself, trying again to fit.

"Please," Marla said again, and Jessica shot back out like something had bitten her.

"I can't, Marla," she said, her breathing shallow and fast, as if she had been running full-out. "I don't fit!"

"There has to be another way in." Charlie stepped in, reaching her arm between Marla and Jessica as though breaking up a fight.

Charlie closed her eyes, trying again to remember. She pictured the restaurant, trying to see it not as they had the last few days, but as it had been years before. The lights were bright; it was full of people. "It used to get hot, stuffy," she said. "In summer it smelled like pizza and old french-fry grease and sweaty kids, and my dad would say . . ." *That's it.* "He would say, 'Whose brilliant idea was it to put a skylight in a closet?'" she finished triumphantly, relieved. She could picture the little supply room with the open roof. She and Sammy would sneak away and sit in there for a few minutes, enjoying the small stream of fresh air that filtered down from outside.

"So that's it. Let's get to the roof," John said, breaking Charlie's drift into memory.

"What roof?" Marla said, studying the top of the closed hall. She was no longer in a full-blown panic, reassured by evidence that Jason was still alive, but her anxiety was still palpable. Her glance darted constantly around the little group, as if her little brother might suddenly appear from the shadows.

"It's been covered over, like everything else," Lamar chimed in.

"Maybe not," Charlie said. "The roof of the mall is pretty high. I bet there's a crawl space, at least."

"A crawl space?" John said excitedly. "You mean a crawl space between the roof of Freddy's and the roof of the mall? Up there?" He stared up into the darkness for a moment. "A crawl space?" he repeated, his voice a little meeker.

Charlie was busy studying the ceiling of the corridor, measuring it in her head against what they had seen of the outside of the building. It was different—she was sure of it.

"This isn't the roof to the mall. It's not high enough," she said, feeling a spark of encouragement. She set off briskly down the hall, not waiting for the others. They followed, trailing behind her, and the space above her suddenly became illuminated as Lamar caught up and cast the beam of the flashlight upward. Charlie was going back and forth, looking from wall to ceiling and back again while trying to picture the space outside.

"The ceiling of this hall is probably level with the roof of Freddy's." Jessica's voice came from behind Charlie, who startled briefly. She had been so intent on her pursuit she had lost track of her friends.

"We have to get up there," Charlie said, turning back to the group expectantly. They looked blankly at her for a second. Then Lamar's arm moved reflexively, like he was about to raise his hand. He caught himself and cleared his throat instead.

"I hate to point out the obvious, but," Lamar said, gesturing. About ten feet ahead of them, a maintenance ladder rested against the old brick. Charlie grinned and hurried to the ladder, waving for John to follow. They grabbed it together; it was heavy, metal, and covered with spatters of paint, but it was manageable to carry. When Charlie had a firm grip on one side of the ladder, she turned her face back to the ceiling, searching.

"There is probably a hole, or a hatch, or something," she said.

"A hole, or a hatch, or something?" John echoed with a half smile as he lifted the other end of the ladder.

"Do you have a better idea? Now come on." She jerked the ladder forward so hard John stumbled and almost fell.

They moved slowly. With only one flashlight, they could not see where they were going and examine the walls at the same time, so every few yards they stopped for Lamar to run the light back and forth across the place where the brick wall met the dripping ceiling of the makeshift hallway. Though it slowed them down, Charlie was grateful for the breaks; the ladder, industrial metal, was heavy. She could have asked the others to switch off, but it felt essential somehow that she be part of the physical process. She wanted to help.

Marla's agitation was growing as they went, and after a few rounds of move-and-scan she started calling Jason's name softly.

"Jason! Jason, can you hear me?"

"He's inside," John said shortly. "He can't hear you." His voice was strained with the weight of the ladder—he had the wider end—and he sounded almost snappish. Marla glared at him.

"You don't know that."

"Marla, stop it," Jessica said. "We're doing everything we can."

Marla didn't answer. A few minutes later, they came to the end of the alley.

"So now what?" John said.

"I don't know," Charlie said, puzzled. "I was positive that we would find something."

"Is that the way life usually works for you?" John teased, raising an eyebrow at her.

From down the hall, Lamar let out a triumphant cry.

"Found it!"

Marla took off toward him at a run, and Jessica followed a little more cautiously behind, wary of obstacles in the dark.

Charlie gave John a wink and picked up the ladder again. He hurried to lift his side, and they lugged it back the way they came.

When Charlie and John caught up to the rest of the group, all three were looking up at the ceiling. Charlie mimicked their posture; sure enough, there was a square trapdoor, big enough for an adult to pass through, its edges barely visible in the darkness. Without speaking, they set up the ladder; it was perhaps ten feet high and rose close enough to the ceiling to access the door easily. Marla climbed up first as Lamar steadied the ladder on one side, Jessica on the other.

John and Charlie watched as Marla ascended.

"So the trapdoor there . . ." John pointed up at it. "The trapdoor of this hallway is right next to Freddy's. That will get us onto the roof of Freddy's, which is under the roof of the mall, in a crawl space. And on Freddy's roof, there's a skylight, which we will find while crawling through the crawl space." He drew an invisible diagram in the air with his finger as he spoke, and his tone was edged with skepticism. Charlie did not respond. Marla's footsteps on the ladder sounded through the hall, heavy, tinny thuds that echoed unsteadily all around them.

"Once we find the skylight in the crawl space," John went on, not certain if Charlie was even listening, "we are going to drop down through the skylight and into Freddy's, possibly with no way of getting back out."

At the top of the ladder, Marla fiddled with something on the ceiling that the others could not see, making little mutters of frustration.

"Is it locked?" Charlie called up.

"Okay, sure," John said, aware by now that he was talking only to himself. "This makes sense."

"The bolt is just stuck," Marla said. "I need—ha!" A dull snapping sound rang out. "Got it!" she cried. She raised her hands over her head and pressed upward, and slowly the door opened above her until it tipped over and fell with a thud.

"So much for sneaking in," John said drily.

"It doesn't matter," Charlie said. "We still have to go. Besides, do you really think whoever is in there doesn't know we're coming?"

Above them, Marla was navigating her way up through the door. She braced her arms on either side of the space and pushed up off the ladder. It swayed dangerously, and Lamar and Jessica clutched it, trying to stabilize it, but it was not necessary. Marla was already up and through, on the roof. They waited for her to say something.

"Marla?" Jessica called finally.

"Yeah, I'm fine," Marla said.

"What do you see?" Charlie called.

"Throw me the light." Marla's arm emerged from the trapdoor, flapping impatiently. Lamar got a bit closer and carefully lobbed the flashlight up. Marla snatched it out of the air, and immediately the beam vanished—the light had gone out.

In the crawl space, Marla sat in the dark trying to fix the flashlight. She shook it, rattling the batteries, and flipped the switch on and off uselessly. As she unscrewed the top of the light and blew into the battery cage, she felt a rising panic. Since realizing Jason had gone, Marla's entire being had been focused on him. It was only now, alone in the darkness, that she began to think about the danger she herself might be in. She screwed the top back onto the flashlight, and it came on instantly. The light flashed in her eyes, briefly clouding her vision. She pointed it away, then carefully swept it in a circle around her, revealing a sprawling void in all directions. It was the roof of Freddy Fazbear's Pizza.

"What do you see?" Charlie called again.

"You were right: There's space, but not much. It's so dark, and it smells awful up here." Her voice sounded shaky even to her own ears, and suddenly she was desperate not to be alone in this place. "Hurry, don't leave me up here by myself!"

"We're coming," Jessica called up to her.

"Me next," Charlie said, stepping forward. The ladder was rusty, and it made squeaking complaints as she climbed, protesting her weight as she moved from step to step. But it felt sturdy, and quickly she reached the trapdoor and did as Marla had done. She stood on the top step so she was head and shoulders through the door, braced her arms on either side, and pushed off the ladder, almost jumping, to land on Freddy's roof. There was not room to stand, scarcely room to sit—the space between the restaurant's roof and the mall's roof above it was less than a yard. Something was rattling above them, as if stones were falling overhead, and it took Charlie a moment to realize that it was the rain thundering on the uninsulated tin. Water dripped in on her head, and when she looked up she saw a place where the metal's seams had not been joined, two corrugated sheets simply lined up next to each other, allied by circumstance. She wiped her palms on her jeans; the shingles of the roof were wet, and her hands were covered in grit, dust, and something slick and more unpleasant.

She looked toward Marla, who was a few feet away.

"Here, come on. Get out of their way," Marla said, motioning her over, and Charlie hurried on her hands and knees. Jessica's head appeared in the trapdoor, and carefully she made her way up into the crawl space. Safely on the roof, Jessica looked around as if gauging something. Concerned, Charlie remembered her fear in the air vent, but Jessica took a long, deep breath.

"I can handle this," she said, though she did not sound as if she believed her own words. A moment later Lamar was next to them. He quickly reclaimed the flashlight and aimed it back toward the trapdoor. After a moment, John scrambled up into the crawl space—and something banged loudly beneath them, the sound repeating. Everyone but John startled at the sound.

"Sorry," he said. "That was the ladder."

"Charlie, which way?" Marla asked.

"Oh." Charlie closed her eyes again, retraced her steps as she had while they'd searched for a way in. "Straight across,

I think," she said. "As long as we get to the far side, we'll find it." Without waiting for responses, she started crawling in the direction she thought was right. A second later, light appeared ahead of her.

"Thanks," she called back softly to Lamar, who was steadying the flashlight, trying to anticipate where Charlie would go.

"I don't have anything else to do," he whispered.

The crawl space was wide. It should have felt spacious, but there were support beams and pipes strewn at random, intersecting the space or running across the roof below them so that it was a little like navigating a very cramped forest, ducking vines and climbing over fallen trees. The roof of Freddy's had a shallow upward slope; they would have to go down again once they reached the middle. The shingles beneath their hands and feet were soggy in a deep, swollen way that suggested they had not been truly dry in years, and a moldy smell rose from them. Every once in a while Charlie wiped her hands on her pants, knowing they would only be clean for a moment. From time to time, she thought she heard something skitter by, sounds a little too far away to be coming from their group, but she ignored them. *They have more right to be here than we do*, she thought, though she was not certain what species "they" might be.

The roof above them followed a bizarre pattern, sloping up and down without regard to the roof beneath, so that at one point it opened four feet above their heads, then at another plunged downward so close that it grazed their backs, forcing them to duck their heads and wriggle awkwardly through. Jessica was right behind Charlie, and from time to time she could hear her friend make soft, frightened noises, but every time she looked back, Jessica just nodded, stone-faced. They continued until they reached the wall that marked the edge of the roof.

"Okay," Charlie called, half turning behind her. "It should be near here. Let's spread out and look."

"No, wait. What's that?" Marla said, pointing. Charlie could not see what Marla had spotted, but she followed the direction until she came to it.

The skylight was a flat glass pane in the roof framed like a small window, a single panel with no visible handles, hinges, or latches. They leaned over it, trying to see into the room below, but the glass was too covered in grime for anything to show through. John reached forward and tried to clean it with his sleeve. He came away with the arm of his shirt black, but it had done no good—at least half the dirt was on the other side, and the skylight was still opaque with filth.

"It's just a closet; it's okay," Charlie said.

"But is anyone *in* the closet?" Lamar said.

"It doesn't matter," said Marla. "We don't have a choice."

Everyone looked at Charlie, who thoughtfully studied the skylight.

"It swings in," she said. "You pull down on this side"—she pointed—"and it swings. There's a latch on the inside, right there." She touched the side of the skylight, thinking. "Maybe if we—" She pushed on it, and it gave way almost instantly, jolting her with a sudden, panicked sense of falling, even though her weight was solidly on the roof.

"That's kind of narrow," John said. The skylight did not open all the way; the glass just tilted inward a little, barely enough for a person to slip through.

"I didn't build it," Charlie said, slightly irritated. "This is it, so if you're going, go."

Without waiting for a response, she swung her legs over the sill and lowered herself down, dangling for a moment in the dark. Closing her eyes and hoping the floor was not as far away as she remembered, she let go and fell.

She landed. The shock of impact ran through her legs, but it passed quickly.

"Bend your knees when you land!" she called up as she got out of the way. Marla dropped through, and Charlie went to the door, trying to find a light switch. Her fingers stumbled across the switch, and she flipped it up. The old fluorescent lights clicked and buzzed, and then slowly a dim and unreliable glow filled the space.

"All right," she whispered with a thrill of excitement. She turned around, and as something brushed her face, she had a fleeting impression of big plastic eyes and broken yellow teeth. She screamed and leaped back, clutching for balance at shelves that swayed as she grabbed them. The head she had touched, an uncovered wire frame for a costume with nothing but eyes and teeth to decorate it, wobbled precariously on the shelf beside Charlie, then fell to the ground. Her heart still pounding, Charlie brushed at herself roughly as if she were covered in spiderwebs, her legs unsteady as she moved back and forth with agitation. The head rolled across the floor, then came to rest at her feet, looking up at her with its cheerful, sinister smile.

Charlie jerked back from the ghastly grin, and something grabbed her from behind. She tried to yank free, but she was stuck, a pair of metal arms wrapped around her. The bodiless limbs clung to her shirt, their hinges biting into the cloth, and as she tried to wrest herself away her hair was caught, too, tangling her deeper into the wire until she felt like she would be consumed. Charlie screamed again, and the arms reached out farther, seeming to grow as she struggled against them. She fought back with all her strength, fueled by terror and a base, frantic fury that this thing would hurt her.

"Charlie, stop!" Marla cried. "Charlie!"

Marla grabbed her arm, trying to stop her frantic movement, using one hand to disengage Charlie's hair from the metal frame.

"Charlie, it's not real, it's just . . . robot parts," she said, but Charlie pulled away from Marla, still in a panic, and smacked her head into a cardboard box. She cried out, startled, as the box overturned. Eyes the size of fists fell to the ground like rain, showering down with a clatter and rolling everywhere, covering the floor. Charlie stumbled and stepped on one of the hard plastic orbs, sending her feet out from under her. She grabbed at a shelf, missed, and fell on her back, landing with a thud that took the wind out of her.

Stunned and gasping, she looked up. There were eyes everywhere, not just on the floor, but in the walls. They looked out at her from the dark, deep-socketed, shadowed eyes peering down from the shelves all around her. She stared, unable to look away.

"Charlie, come on." Marla was there, kneeling anxiously over her. She grabbed Charlie's arm again and pulled until Charlie was upright. Charlie still did not have her breath back, and as she inhaled thinly, she began to cry. Marla hugged her tightly, and Charlie let her.

"It's okay, it's okay," Marla whispered as Charlie tried to calm herself, looking around the storeroom for distraction.

It's not real, she told herself. They were in a storeroom, just a closet, and these were all spare parts. The air was thick with dust, and it tickled at her nose and throat as it poured off the shelves restlessly. The rest of the group dropped through the skylight one by one; John came last, landing in the middle of the room with a thump. Jessica sneezed.

"You okay?" John said as soon as he saw Charlie.

"Yeah, I'm fine." Charlie disentangled herself from Marla and crossed her arms, still collecting herself.

"You know we can't get back up through there," John said, looking up at the skylight.

"We just need something to stand on," Charlie said. "Or we can climb a shelf."

Jessica shook her head.

"No, look at the way it's opened."

Charlie looked. The skylight opened downward, so the pane of glass sloped in at a gentle angle, just enough to have let them through. To get out, they would have to—

"Oh," she said. There would be no getting out. However close they got to the skylight, the pane of glass would always be in the way, sticking out into the precise space they needed to pass through. If anyone tried to get a grip on the roof, they would have to lean so far over the glass that they would fall from the ladder.

"We might be able to break the glass," John started. "But the metal frame is going to be dangerous to climb over, even more dangerous with shards of broken glass." He fell silent and thought it through again, his face grim.

"It doesn't matter," Charlie said. "We'll find another way out. Let's start looking."

They peered cautiously out into the hallway. Lamar had turned off the flashlight, but it was easy enough to see their surroundings now with the light from the closet seeping into the hall. *At least nothing's dripping from the ceiling,* Charlie thought, wiping her hands on her pants again. The floor was black-and-white tile, as glossy as if it had just been polished. There were children's drawings on the walls, rustling with the air from the open skylight. Charlie remained motionless, more than aware of how much noise she had just made. *Does it know we're here?* she wondered, realizing as she did that by "it" she meant the building itself. It felt as if Freddy's was conscious of their presence, as if it reacted to them like a living, breathing thing. She reached out to brush her fingers against its wall, tracing lightly as if she were petting it. The plaster was still and cold, inanimate, and Charlie pulled her hand back. She wondered what Freddy's would do.

They wound around one corner, then another, and then stopped at the entrance to Pirate's Cove, hanging back from the doorway. *Pirate's Cove. I have my bearings again.* Charlie gazed at the little stage, no longer lit, and the curtain that hid its sole performer.

A few small lights flickered on the sides of the stage then came on, illuminating the space with a pale-gray glow. Charlie looked around and saw Lamar standing by the doorway with his hand on a switch.

"We don't have a choice," he said defensively, gesturing to his flashlight; its light was failing. Charlie nodded resignedly, and Lamar switched off the dying flashlight.

"I want to take a look in this control room," Marla said, pointing to the small door nearby. "Lamar, come with me. The rest of you try the other one. If we each take one set of cameras, we can see the whole restaurant. If Jason's in this place, we'll see him."

"I don't think we should split up," Charlie said.

"Wait," said Lamar. He passed John the dead light, freeing his hands. From his pockets he produced two walkie-talkies; they were large, black, boxy things Charlie had only seen attached to police officers' belts.

"Where did you get those?" she asked.

Lamar smiled mysteriously. "I'm afraid I can't tell you that," he said.

"He stole them from Carlton's house," Jessica stated plainly, taking one from his hand and examining it.

"No, they were in the garage. Mrs. Burke told me where to find them. They work, I tested."

Mrs. Burke knew we would come here? Charlie thought. Marla just nodded; maybe she had already known, or maybe nothing could surprise her anymore.

"Come on," Marla said and walked between the tables in front of Pirate's Cove, careful not to disturb anything. Lamar leaned over Jessica to show her how to use the walkie-talkie.

"It's this button," he said, indicating it, and then he took off after Marla.

After a startled moment, the rest of them followed. Something clutched in Charlie's stomach, the reality that both Jason and Carlton might truly be in danger seizing her. It was not that she had forgotten, but while they were outside, trying to solve the puzzles, it was possible to gain some distance from what was happening. She watched Marla stalking toward the control room with a bleak authority. Marla crouched at the small door before turning to Charlie.

"Go," she said, nodding toward the hall that led to the main dining area. They went, Charlie taking the lead as they crept down the hall, heading for the main stage.

Marla looked at Lamar, who nodded. She grasped the doorknob, clenched her teeth, and forced the door open all in one motion.

"Marla!"

Marla jumped, barely suppressing a scream. Jason was huddled in the space beneath the monitors, his eyes wide and terrified, staring at the door like a frightened mouse.

"Jason!" Marla crawled into the control room and swooped him into her arms. Jason hugged her back, for once grateful, even desperate, for her intense affection. She held on tight, crushing him to her until he began to worry that he might, in fact, be crushed.

From outside Marla's consuming embrace, Jason heard brief static. He looked over Marla's shoulder to see Lamar studying the walkie-talkie, preparing to speak into it.

"Jessica? We found him. He's okay," he said.

More static and words Jason did not quite catch came from the radio. The first wave of relief had worn off, and his ribs were starting to hurt.

"Marla?" He tapped her on the shoulder, first gently, then harder. "Marla!"

She let him go but took hold of his shoulders for a moment, peering into his eyes as if to be sure it was really him, that he had not been somehow replaced, or irrevocably damaged.

"Marla, cool it," he said as casually as he could, managing to keep his voice from shaking. Marla let go of his shoulders, giving him a playful shove, and began to scold him as she pulled him the rest of the way out from under the control panel.

"Jason, how could you—" Marla was interrupted as Lamar descended the rest of the way into the small room.

"Through the vent? Really?" Lamar laughed.

"You could have been killed, crawling through the air duct like that!" Marla added, grasping his shoulders.

Jason fought free, flailing his arms until she let him go.

"Okay!" he exclaimed. "Everybody missed me, good, glad to know I'm important."

"You *are* important," Marla said fiercely, and Jason rolled his eyes theatrically.

The little room lit up as Lamar flipped a switch, bringing the screens to life. Marla looked at Jason thoughtfully, then turned her attention to the security cameras. "Okay, let's see what we can see."

Lamar looked from screen to screen. The top middle screen showed the main dining room and the stage, and as they watched, Charlie, Jessica, and John appeared, crossing the room in a V formation, Charlie at the front.

"Look," Marla said suddenly, pointing to the screen at the lower right. "Look."

The night guard was there; though they could not make out his face, his baggy uniform and sagging shoulders told them that it was the same man. He was in the hall near the restaurant's entrance, walking past the party rooms and the arcade with a slow, purposeful gait.

"Lamar, warn them," Marla ordered urgently.

Lamar spoke into the walkie-talkie. "Jessica, the guard is somewhere around there. Hide!"

There was no response from the radio, but onscreen the group of three froze. Then, as one, they made for the control room under the stage, squeezing in and closing themselves in just as the guard appeared in the doorway.

★   ★   ★

Voices. People moving around.

Carlton did not allow himself to sigh in relief—a rescue wouldn't do him any good if he got his insides punctured by a hundred tiny robot parts first. Instead he continued with what he had been doing, inching his way across the floor and into the view of the security camera that perched near the ceiling just above the door. Each movement was so scarce it felt like nothing, but he had been doing this for over an hour, and he was almost, *almost* there. He kept his breathing steady, using his trapped hands to lift his body a tiny bit, move to the side, and let himself down again, just a little farther to the right. His fingers were cramping and his head still ached, but he kept going, relentless.

Although he was still afraid, still painfully aware of how easily he could trigger his own death, at some point the fear had dulled, or perhaps he had just become accustomed to it. Panic could not last forever; eventually the adrenaline had run out. Now, at least, the need for slow, precise movement took precedence over everything else. It was all there was. Carlton made one final movement and stopped, closing his eyes for a moment. He had made it.

Can't stop now.

The others were here. It had to be them, and if they were looking for him, they would check the cameras. He stared up into the lens, willing himself to be seen. He could not wave or jump up and down. He tried rocking back and forth a little, but no matter how stiffly he held himself, he felt the press of spring locks, ready to give. He bit his lip in frustration.

"Just see me!" he whispered to no one, but all at once he felt as if he had been heard, felt the inexplicable sense of someone else's presence in the room. His heart began to race again, the adrenaline that had given out finding its second wind.

Carefully, slowly, he looked around, until something caught his eye.

It was only one of the costumes, slumped empty in the shadows, half-hidden in the corner of the room. It was motionless, but its face was pointed directly at him, staring. As Carlton looked back, he realized that deep within the recesses of the costume's eye sockets were two tiny glints of light. He felt little muscles twitch, a restrained shudder running through his body, not quite enough to get him killed. He did not look away.

As Carlton held the creature's gaze, he felt himself begin to calm. His heart's pounding eased, and his breath grew even. It was as though suddenly he was safe, though he knew the suit he was wearing was still only one flinch, one startled jump, from killing him. Carlton kept looking at those two pinpoints of light, and as he did, he heard a voice. In a gasping instant, all the air was sucked from his lungs. As the voice spoke, that voice he would have known anywhere, that voice he would have given anything to hear again, Carlton began to weep, using all his will to keep his body from shaking. The eyes in the dark were intent on his face as the voice went on, speaking secrets to Carlton in the ringing silence, telling him things that he dreaded, things that someone had to hear.

CHAPTER TEN

The screens all lost their pictures and flipped to static.

"Hey!" Marla cried. She banged against the side of a monitor, and the image lurched, distorted, then sputtered and went out again. She hit it again, and with another spasm of static the image slowly cleared; as it resolved, the stage appeared.

"Something's wrong," Lamar said, and all three leaned forward, trying to get a better look.

"Bonnie," Jason said in a grave tone.

"Bonnie," Marla echoed, looking at Lamar with alarm. "Where's Bonnie?" Lamar hit the button on the walkie-talkie.

"Charlie," he said urgently. "Charlie, don't leave the control room."

*   *   *

In the control room under the stage, Charlie and Jessica peered at the monitors, scanning for signs of life. "It's too dark; I can't see anything on these," Jessica complained.

"There!" Charlie said, pointing. Jessica blinked.

"I can't see anything," she insisted.

"It's Carlton, right there. I'm going to get him." Not waiting for a response, Charlie crawled toward the exit.

"Charlie, wait," John said, but she was already out the door. It slammed shut behind her, and all three of them heard the dull metal thud of the drop lock falling into place. "Charlie!" John yelled again, but she was already gone.

"It's bolted shut," John grunted as he pulled on the door. The walkie-talkie sputtered, and Lamar's voice came choppily from the little box.

"Ch-lie, don't leave—r-m." Jessica and John exchanged a glance, and John picked up the radio.

"Too late," he said, looking to Jessica as he lowered the walkie-talkie.

Charlie made her way unsteadily between chairs, but after only moments she realized she had gotten herself turned around. The lighting had changed; now a single blinding blue light was strobing on and off above the stage. Over and over, the room flashed with a blinding burst, like lightning, then was instantly dark again. Charlie covered her eyes, trying to remember what she had bumped into first. Metal chairs and foil party hats pulsed like beacons in the dark with each burst of light, and Charlie's head began to throb.

She squinted, trying to orient herself, but beyond the tables surrounding her, all she could see were a thousand afterimages burned into her retinas. She had no idea which way to go to find Carlton. She leaned against a nearby chair and pressed her hand tightly over her forehead.

A table screeched against the floor briefly, and Charlie knew that it hadn't been her. She turned around, but the light had gone dark. When it flashed again she was looking directly at the stage—where there should have been three sets of eyes, she saw only two. Freddy and Chica stared down at her, their plastic gazes catching the light, twinkling with the strobe. Their heads seemed to follow her as she moved along the table.

Bonnie was gone.

Suddenly she felt exposed, all at once noticing just how many places there were in the open room for something to hide, just how visible she was to anyone—anything—that might be watching. She thought briefly of the little control room she had just left and felt a pang of regret. *Coming out here might have been very stupid . . .*

Another screech sounded, and she whirled around to see the table behind her moving slowly away. She turned to run, but she slammed into something before she could take a step. She jerked up her hands in the darkness to shield herself and touched matted fur. The strobe threw its light out again, and this time garbled noise blared from the gaping mouth in front of her. *Bonnie*. Bonnie stood only inches from her, his mouth opening and closing rapidly and his eyes rolling wildly in his head. Charlie jerked away, then backed up slowly. The rabbit did not try to follow, just continued his bizarre and silent incantation, his eyes aimlessly ricocheting in his head. Her foot caught on the leg of a metal folding chair; she fell back, landing hard on her bottom. She started to crawl, staying low, hurrying to get away from Bonnie. A spotlight flashed from the stage, this one clearly aimed at her. She raised her hand to see who was there, but the light blinded her. All she could make out were two sets of following eyes.

Charlie screamed and scrambled to her feet. She took off running, not looking back, and made it across the room and to the hallway that led to Pirate's Cove. She ducked into the bathroom along its wall. The door echoed when it shut behind her; the room was empty, with nothing but three sinks and three stalls. Only one of the fluorescent lights was on, and just barely, only enough to color the room dark gray instead of black. The metal walls of the stall dividers looked flimsy, and Charlie had a sudden vision of Bonnie, larger than life, grabbing the metal frame with his paws and ripping it up from the ground, the bolts tearing right out of the floor. She banished the thought and ran into the farthest stall from the door, slipping the lock—so small it looked almost delicate—into place. She sat on top of the toilet tank, her feet pulled up onto the seat and her back pressed against the blue tile wall of the bathroom. In the empty room, Charlie could hear her own breath echoing. She forced it to slow and closed her eyes, telling herself to be silent, to hide.

"Charlie?" John was still pounding on the little door of the control room. "Charlie! What's going on out there?"

Jessica sat quietly, still rattled from the screams and crashes outside.

"She can take care of herself," John said, easing his grip on the door.

"Yeah," Jessica said. He did not turn around to look at her.

"We have to get out of here," John said. He rattled the door again—the top swayed a little as he pulled, but the bottom was stuck fast. He hunched down farther. There was a lock, a deadbolt that dropped straight into the floor. The latch to pull it open had broken off long ago, leaving only a jagged ledge so thin he could scarcely get his fingers around

300

it. As he yanked it upward, it cut into his fingers, leaving thin red lines. The bolt stayed fast in place.

"Jessica, you try," he said, turning to look at her. Her eyes were on the wall of televisions; they were all showing static, but every now and then one flashed a picture. "Never mind," John said. "Keep watching." He bent his head again and went back to the deadbolt.

In the bathroom, Charlie was silent. She paid attention to each breath she took, each inhale and exhale a slow, deliberate process. She had tried meditating once; she had hated it, but now the intense focus on her breathing was calming. *I guess I just needed the right motivation*, she thought. *Like staying alive.* The stalls rattled briefly, and there was a distant booming sound that went on for several seconds. *It's storming outside.*

She kept her eyes trained on the floor. The light overhead was so dim it scarcely illuminated her stall. She held her breath. The light flickered and let out a brief hum, then was silent. The toilet tank she sat on felt unstable; she scooted to the edge of it to quietly let her foot down. Just as the tip of her shoe touched the tile, the wide bathroom doors opened with a thunderous bang.

Without thinking she jerked her foot up, and the lid of the porcelain tank clanged like pots clattering together. She held herself perfectly still, her shoe suspended in the air, then carefully pulled her foot back into place on top of the toilet seat. *That was too loud*, she thought. Carefully, she leaned forward and reached up with one hand to grasp the stall divider. She pulled herself up to stand slowly, the toilet seat rocking on its hinges beneath her feet.

She peered out over the top at the two stalls next to her. It was too dark to see beyond the metal stalls, and the whole row of them swayed gently from her weight.

There was a shuffling sound; something wide and heavy was sliding across the floor, not trying nearly as hard as she was to be quiet. Her eyes darted from the stall door beside her to the bathroom door. The shuffling continued, but she could not tell where it was coming from; the sound filled the room.

Suddenly the nebulous sound resolved: It was crisp, and it was nearby. The wall she clung to trembled slightly. She panned her gaze around the room, hoping her eyes would adjust a little more. She could make out a trash can by the door and the outline of the sinks. Apprehensively, she looked back at the door of her stall, letting her focus creep along the edges until she set her eyes on the inch-wide gap along the door. A large plastic eye stared back, unblinking and dry, fixed directly on her. Two large and unnatural rabbit ears hung over the top of the door.

Charlie clasped her hand over her mouth and jumped to the floor as fast as she could, dropping to her stomach and scooting along the floor into the second stall. She heard Bonnie rattle the door of the stall she had just left, but the shuffling feet did not move. She crawled under the next divider and into the stall nearest the entrance. This time her foot bumped the toilet behind her, and the lip dropped down with a loud clank.

Charlie froze. The shuffling thing did not move. For what felt like an age, Charlie held her breath. *He heard, he must have heard!* But Bonnie still made no sound. Charlie held still and listened, waiting for another sound of movement to mask her own. Her breathing seemed louder than before. She lowered her head, trying to make out shapes along the floor.

The shuffling sound resumed, and now, without warning, it was directly in front of her. She held her breath, desperately trying to make out any forms in the darkness. *There he is.* A large, padded foot was just outside the door, as if it had stopped midstep. *Is he leaving? Please leave*, Charlie pleaded. There was a new sound: stiff fabric, softly crunching. *What is that?* The foot outside the door had not moved. The noise grew louder, the sound of fabric and fur twisting and stretching, tearing and popping. *What is that?* Charlie dug into the floor with her nails, holding down a guttural scream. *He's bending over.* A large paw touched down gently in front of her, then another shape: the creature's head. It was massive, filling the space under the door. Gracefully, Bonnie lowered himself to the floor and turned his head sideways until his eye met Charlie's. His giant mouth was open wide with a ghoulish excitement, as though he had found someone in a game of hide-and-seek.

A warm burst of air rolled in under the stall door. *Breath?* Charlie clasped her hand over her nose and mouth; the stench was unbearable. Another wave of it hit her face, hotter and more putrid. She closed her eyes, on the point of relinquishing the hope of escape. Maybe if she kept her eyes closed long enough, she would wake up. Another gust of hot air hit, and she jerked back, hitting the back of her head on the toilet. She recoiled with pain and threw her arm in front of her, shielding her face against attack. No attack came. She opened one eye. *Where is he?*

Suddenly the metal walls around her swayed with a resounding bang. Charlie startled and covered her head as Bonnie struck again. The stalls rocked on their legs, and the bolts screeched as they were yanked free from the floor, the whole assembly seeming ready to collapse. Charlie scrambled under the last divider and climbed to her feet, grasping for the door handle to pull it shut as she ran out.

She ran back into the main dining area, darting toward the control room. Her eyes no longer adjusted to the light, she ran with her hands in front of her, unable to see farther than her next steps.

"John!" she cried, grabbing the doorknob and yanking at it, pushing. Nothing happened.

"Charlie, it's stuck!" John shouted back from inside. As Charlie struggled with the door, she glanced up at the stage. Chica was gone.

"John!" Charlie shouted in desperation. Without waiting for a response, Charlie took off again, running for a hall to her left, trying to get as much distance from the bathroom as possible.

The hall was almost completely dark, and as she ran, open doorways yawned at her with wide black mouths. Charlie did not stop to look inside any of them, instead only praying that nothing jumped out at her. She reached the last door and paused for a brief moment, hoping against hope that it would be unlocked. She grabbed the knob and twisted. Thankfully, it fell open easily.

She slid through the door, then closed it rapidly, trying not to make a sound. She stood watching the door for a long moment, half expecting it to be flung open, and then finally she turned. It was only then that she saw him: Carlton was there. His eyes widened in surprise when he saw her, but he did not move, and after her eyes adjusted to the dim light she understood. He was trapped, wedged somehow into the top half of one of the animatronic suits, his head poking out from the wide shoulders of the costume. His face was white and exhausted, and Charlie knew why. *The spring locks.* She heard her father's voice for a moment. *It could snap off your nose!*

"Carlton?" Charlie said cautiously, as if her voice alone might set off the mechanisms.

"Yup," he said, with the same faltering tone.

"That costume is going to kill you if you move."

"Thanks," he wheezed, half attempting a laugh. Charlie forced a smile.

"Well, today is your lucky day. I'm probably the only person who knows how to get you out of that thing alive."

Carlton exhaled a long and shaky breath. "Lucky me," he said.

Charlie knelt at his side, studying the costume for long moments without touching it. "These two spring locks at the neck aren't holding anything back," she said at last. "He just rigged them to snap and pierce your throat if you try to move. I have to undo those first, and then we can open the back of the costume and get you out. But you can't move, Carlton, seriously."

"Yeah, serial killer man explained the not moving to me," he said. Charlie nodded and went back to looking at the costume, trying to devise an approach.

"Do you know who I'm wearing?" Carlton asked, almost casually.

"What?"

"The costume, do you know what character it was supposed to be?" Charlie studied it, then looked around until she saw the matching head.

"No," she said. "Not everything he built made it to the stage." Her fingers suddenly stopped working. "Carlton." Charlie carefully surveyed the array of costumes and parts that lined the walls in varying stages of completion. "Carlton," she repeated. "Is he in here?"

With a new sense of dread, Carlton struggled to get a look behind him without moving. "I don't know," he whispered. "I don't think so, but I've been kind of in and out."

"Okay, stop talking. I'll try to work fast," Charlie said. She had the mechanism figured out, or at least she thought she did.

"Not too fast," Carlton reminded her.

Carefully, slowly, she reached into the costume's neck and took hold of the first spring lock, maneuvering it until her fingers were wedged between the lock and Carlton's neck.

"Careful with that artery; I've had it since I was a kid," Carlton said.

"Shh," Charlie whispered. When Carlton spoke, she could feel his neck move; he was not going to set off the locks by talking, she thought, but the feeling of his tendons moving under her hands was unsettling.

"Okay," he whispered. "Sorry. I talk when I'm nervous." He clamped down his jaw and bit his lips together. Charlie reached down farther into the costume's neck and found the trigger. With a stinging snap, the lock sprang against her hand, so hard that it numbed her fingers. *One down*, she thought as she pulled it, harmless, out of the neck of the costume. She flexed her fingers until the feeling came back into them, then crawled over to Carlton's other side and began the process again. She looked over her shoulder from time to time, making sure every costume was still in its place against the wall.

His skin was warm under her touch, and even though he was not speaking, she could still feel movement, feel the life in him. She could feel his pulse against the back of her wrist as she worked, and she blinked back unexpected tears. She swallowed hard and focused on the task, trying to ignore the fact that she was touching someone who would die if she failed him.

She worked open the spring lock again, taking the impact on the palm of her hand and pulling the disabled device free of the costume. Carlton took a deep breath in, and she startled.

"Carlton, don't relax!"

He stiffened and exhaled slowly, his eyes wide and frightened.

"Right," he said. "Still a death trap."

"Stop talking," Charlie pleaded again. She knew exactly how much danger he was still in, and she could not bear to hear him speak now, if he was about to die. "Okay," she said. "Almost there." She crawled around behind him, where a series of ten leather and metal fasteners held the back of the costume together. She considered it for a moment. She needed to keep the costume still, exactly as it was, until the last moment. She sat down behind him and bent her knees, positioning herself so that she could hold the costume in place with her legs as she opened it.

"I didn't know you cared," Carlton muttered as though attempting to put a joke together but too tired and too scared to finish it. Charlie didn't answer.

One by one, she worked the fasteners free. The leather was stiff, the metal tightly fitted, and each one fought back as she worked, clinging together. When she was halfway up the back of the costume, she felt its weight begin to shift. She gripped it tighter with her knees, holding it together. Finally, she undid the last one, at the nape of his neck. She took a deep breath. This was it.

"Okay, Carlton," she said. "We're almost done. I'm going to open this and throw it forward. When I do, you pull out of it as fast as you can, okay? One . . . two . . . three!"

She yanked the costume open and thrust it away with all her strength, and Carlton jerked back from it, toppling roughly into her. Charlie felt a sharp, quick pain on the back of her hand as she pulled free, but the costume skittered halfway across the room, leaving them clear. A series of snaps sounded, making a noise like fireworks, and they both cried out, leaping back and banging into a heavy metal shelf. Together they watched as the empty costume writhed and twisted across the floor, the animatronic parts snapping violently into place. When it came to a stop, Charlie stared, fixated. The thing was just a torso, just an object.

Beside her, Carlton let out a low, pained groan, then turned and vomited onto the floor beside him, heaving and retching like he would be turned inside out. Charlie watched, unsure what to do. She put a hand on his shoulder and kept it there as he finished, wiped his mouth, and sat gasping for breath.

"Are you okay?" she said, the words sounding small and ridiculous.

Carlton nodded wearily, then winced. "Yeah, I'm fine," he said. "Sorry about the floor. I guess it's your floor, kind of."

"You might have a concussion," Charlie said, alarmed, but he shook his head, moving more slowly this time.

"No, I don't think so," he said. "My head hurts like somebody hit it really hard, and I feel sick from being stuck in this room and pondering my death for hours, but I think I'm okay. My mind is okay."

"Okay," Charlie said doubtfully. Then something he had said finally registered. "Carlton, you said 'serial killer man explained' for you not to move. You saw who did this to you?"

Carlton got to his knees carefully, then stood, bracing himself on a nearby box. He looked at Charlie. "I was trapped in that thing for hours; I'm all tingly." He shook out his foot as if to make the point.

"Did you see who it was?" Charlie repeated.

"Dave, the guard," Carlton said. He sounded almost surprised that she did not know. Charlie nodded. She had known already.

"What did he tell you?"

"Not much," Carlton said. "But . . ." His eyes opened suddenly, as if he had just remembered something of grave importance. He looked away from Charlie and slowly dropped to his knees.

"What is it?" Charlie whispered.

"Do you want to hear?" he said. He seemed suddenly calm for someone who had so narrowly escaped death.

"What is it?" she demanded. He glanced nervously at her for a moment, then took a deep breath, his face draining to white.

"Charlie, the kids, all those years ago . . ."

Charlie snapped to attention.

"What?"

"All of them, Michael and the others, they were taken from the dining room when no one was looking, and they were brought here." Carlton suddenly recoiled and moved toward the doorway, watching the walls as though they were crawling with invisible creatures. "He—Dave, the guard—he brought them here . . ." Carlton rubbed his arms like he was suddenly cold and squinted in pain. "He put them into suits, Charlie," he said, his face twisting in sorrow or disgust. "Charlie." He stopped abruptly, a faraway look in his eyes. "They are still here."

"How do you know that?" Charlie said in such a soft whisper that she was almost inaudible.

Carlton motioned toward the far corner of the room. Charlie looked; a yellow Freddy costume was propped against the wall, the costume all fitted together, as if he were about to walk onstage for a show.

"That's the one. That's the bear I remember from the other restaurant." Charlie clasped her hand over her mouth.

"Other restaurant?" Carlton looked puzzled.

"I don't understand." Charlie's gaze was still fixed on the yellow costume. "Carlton, I don't understand." Her tone was urgent.

"Michael."

Charlie stared at him. *Michael?*

"What do you mean?" she said in a level voice.

"I know how it sounds," he said, and then his voice dropped to a whisper. "Charlie, I think it's Michael in that suit."

"I still can't get this thing out!" John sighed in frustration and rubbed his hand; the lock was leaving harsh red imprints on his fingers. Jessica murmured something sympathetic, but she did not take her eyes off the screens.

"I can't see anything!" she burst out after a moment.

The radio squawked, and then Marla's voice came, calling to them from the control room in Pirate's Cove.

"Both of you, be quiet and don't move." They froze, hunching down in their places. Jessica looked at John, a question in her eyes, but he shrugged, as at a loss as she was.

Something thudded against the door. John jumped away, almost falling.

"Marla?" Jessica said with a pale expression. "Marla, that's you out there, right?" The thud came again, more powerful than before, and the door shook under it.

"What is that, a sledgehammer?" John whispered hoarsely. The door pounded in again and again, dents appearing in the metal door, which had looked so solid. They huddled back against the control panel with nothing to do but watch. Jessica grabbed the back of John's shirt, knotting the cloth between her fingers, and he did not shake her away. The door rocked in again, and this time a hinge unfolded slightly, exposing a thin crack between the door and the frame. The door still held, but it would not hold for long. John felt Jessica's fingers tighten on his shirt; he wanted to turn and give her some kind of comfort, but he was mesmerized, unable to look away. He could almost see out through the little open space, and he craned his neck. Another blow came. The crack widened, and on the other side he saw eyes peering in, calm and expressionless.

"Get out, get out!" Marla shouted, waving her hands at the security monitor as if John and Jessica could see her, as if it would do any good if they could. Lamar had both hands clapped over his mouth, his eyes wide, and Jason was sitting on the floor, waiting nervously as though an attack on their own door might begin at any moment. The monitors were dark, but it was clear that something large was lurking in front of the main stage, a black static shape that prowled back and forth, momentarily blocking the entire picture.

"Marla," Lamar whispered, hoping to quiet her. "Marla, look—" He pointed to the monitor showing Pirate's Cove, just outside their door. Marla looked over his shoulder at the other screen. The curtain was pulled back, and the space was completely empty. The OUT OF ORDER sign hung perfectly straight across the platform, untouched.

"The lock, we didn't . . . ," Marla said feebly, realizing now the magnitude of their mistake. Marla turned to Jason, then let out a panicked whimper—the door behind him was slowly opening.

"Shhh." Lamar quickly flipped a small switch, killing the light in the control room, and backed against the wall next to the door. Marla and Jason mimicked his motions, flattening themselves against the wall across from him. The monitors still flickered with static, illuminating the space in oscillating grays and the occasional flash of white.

The small door creaked outward at an excruciating pace, a gaping black void widening until the door stopped, fully open.

"Marla!" a static-laced voice called from somewhere on the floor. Lamar shot out his foot across the narrow carpet, trying to catch the walkie-talkie.

"Shhh, shhh . . ." Marla closed her eyes, pleading in her mind for Jessica to stop talking.

"Marla, where are you?" Jessica's voice called again. Lamar managed to flip the walkie-talkie onto its side, and with a *click* it went silent. He didn't know if he had jostled a battery out of place or somehow managed to flip the switch, but it didn't matter.

There was nowhere to hide in the tiny room. The ceiling was too low to stand, and even with their backs against the wall their legs stretched under the doorframe. The ledge under the door was high enough to hide their legs from anything outside, but not from anything that managed to get in.

As one, they stopped breathing. The room was no longer empty; something was entering the space. As it pressed forward into the room, they saw a snout and the scratchy gloss of two unblinking eyes staring straight ahead. The monstrous head threatened to fill the room.

"Foxy," Jason mouthed, making no sound. The plastic eyes clicked left and right with unnatural motions, searching but not seeing. The jaw twitched as though about to open, but never did.

The dim light from the monitors gave his face a reddish hue, leaving the rest of him shrouded in darkness. His head slowly moved backward, his ears moving up and down at random, programmed as an afterthought a decade before. As Foxy backed away, his eyes thrashed back and forth, one partially hidden under a rotting eyepatch. Marla held her breath, dreading the moment when the eyes would fix on her. The head was almost out the door when the eyes clicked to the right and found Marla. The head stopped, its jaw frozen, slightly open. The plastic eyes remained on Marla, who sat in terrified silence. After a moment, the head retreated, leaving a black and empty space.

Jason darted forward to find the door outside and shut it, and Marla made a weak grab at him, trying to stop him. He brushed past her, then stopped, kneeling in the doorway. He looked into the darkness, only now afraid of what must be there. He crawled slowly forward, his torso disappearing temporarily as he reached outside for the doorknob, then pulled himself back in and gently closed the door. Marla and Lamar closed their eyes and let out a deep breath at the same time.

Jason looked at them; he was almost smiling when, in a blur, the door burst open again and an ugly metal hook sank into his leg. He screamed in pain. Marla leaped to grab him, but she was too slow. She watched helplessly as Jason was dragged through the doorway.

"Marla!" he cried, clawing futilely at the floor, and she howled in despair as he was taken from her again, nothing visible of his assailant but the awful glimmer of the hook.

Marla dove toward the door after him, falling to her knees and crawling toward the thing, but Lamar grabbed her shoulder and yanked her back, taking hold of the door. Before he could pull it shut, it was ripped from his hands with an inhuman strength. Suddenly Foxy was there before them, coming inside.

He was full of life, a different creature, and he turned to look at Marla, his silver eyes appearing to comprehend. His face was a canine rictus, the scrappy orange fur insufficient to cover up his skull. He looked between them, turning his ghoulish smile first on Lamar, then on Marla. His eyes flared and dimmed, and he snapped his jaws with a sound like something breaking. They stared, backed up against the control panel, and then Lamar realized suddenly what he was looking at.

"He can't fit all the way in," he whispered. Marla looked. It was true—Foxy's shoulders were jammed in the doorway, his head the only part he could wedge through the door.

Lamar lunged forward and kicked the animatronic, bracing himself against the wall and striking out with his foot three times before Foxy gave a low whine, a sound more machine than animal, and slunk back out into the dark. Lamar snapped the door shut behind him and slid the deadbolt into place. They stared at each other for a long moment, breathing hard.

"Jason!" Marla screamed.

Lamar put his arms around her. She let him hug her, but she did not cry, just closed her eyes.

"What do you mean, it's Michael in the suit?" Charlie said softly, as if she might be talking to someone who had gone mad, while also desperate to hear the answer. Carlton looked at the yellow bear for a long moment, and when he turned back to Charlie, his face was calm. He opened his mouth to speak, and Charlie put a finger to her lips. Something was coming; she could hear footsteps out in the hall, moving toward them. Deliberate, heavy steps, the approach of someone who did not mind if anyone heard. Charlie looked wildly around the room and spotted a pipe in a corner. She grabbed it and hurried to stand behind the door, where whoever opened it would not see her. Carlton picked up the torso, as though to use it as a weapon somehow. He looked confused, like he was not thinking clearly.

"Don't," Charlie warned in a low voice, but she was too late. Something snapped inside the suit. Carlton dropped it and stepped back, a shimmer of blood on his hand.

"Are you okay?" Charlie whispered. He nodded, and then the doorknob turned.

Dave appeared in the doorway, his head held high and his face grim. It should have been imposing, but he just looked like a man walking through a door.

"Now you've done it," he announced to the room in general, then his eyes lit on Carlton, unfettered. His face darkened. Before he could move, Charlie raised the pipe high, stepped forward, and swung it down on his head with a sickening *thunk*.

Dave turned, shock on his face. Charlie lifted the pipe, ready to attack again, but the man just stumbled backward against the wall and dropped into a sitting position.

"Carlton! Come on," Charlie said urgently, but he was looking down at his injured hand. "Carlton? Are you hurt?"

"No," he said, shaking off his reverie and wiping his hand clean with his black shirt.

"Come on," Charlie said firmly, taking his arm. "Come on, we have to get out of here. I don't know how long he'll stay out." *You're awfully calm for just having knocked a guy out cold*, she thought wryly.

They crept out into the empty hallway, lit only by the dim glow of light from the other rooms. Charlie hustled them through the swinging doors to the kitchen, where the dark was total. The air was thick with a blackness that was almost tangible; it was as if they had been swallowed. She turned to look at Carlton, but only the faint sound of his breathing told her that he was still beside her. Something touched her arm, and she stifled a scream.

"It's just me," Carlton hissed, and she let out a sigh.

"Let's just make sure that we aren't being followed, then we can find the others and get out of here," she whispered. Charlie glanced back at the door, and the last spots of light peeking under it. She scooted herself a little closer to it and got to her feet to peer through the round window, careful not to touch it.

"What do you see?" Carlton whispered.

"Nothing. I think it's safe."

Just as she finished speaking, a form passed by, darkening the window. Charlie jumped back, almost falling over Carlton. They stumbled forward, rushing to get away from the door.

Suddenly two beams split the darkness, illuminating the room in a harsh yellow light. Chica loomed there, almost on top of them. She stretched up to her full height, growing taller still. *She must have been hiding here all along*, Charlie thought. The dark recesses of the kitchen could be hiding anything. Chica looked at both of them in turn, the beams of light shifting dizzyingly as her eyes snapped mechanically from one side to the other. Then she paused, and Charlie grabbed Carlton's arm.

"Run!" she screamed, and they took off, looping around the prep table, the metal furniture clattering as they rushed clumsily past it. Behind them, Chica's steps were long and slow. At last they reached the door, and they burst out into the hall and ran for the main dining room.

John and Jessica were silent, listening to the clamor outside. John was resting his hand on the door of the control room; whatever had been on the other side was gone, or at least was pretending to be. The lock had been wrenched out of the floor. John tried the knob, but the door, twisted out of shape, still stuck.

"Are you crazy?" Jessica exclaimed, alarmed.

"What else are we going to do?" John said calmly. Jessica didn't answer.

John backed up against the control panel and gave the door a calculated kick, moving it an inch closer to opening.

"Here, let me," Jessica said, and before he could reply she had delivered a kick of her own, the door again moving just a little.

They took turns, not speaking, until finally John kicked

and the top hinge broke. John quickly wrestled the door the rest of the way off until they could crawl out.

They hurried out and stopped, exposed in the main dining room. Jessica looked at the main stage in misery. It was empty.

"I don't know how this is safer," she said, but John was not listening.

"Charlie!" he cried, then covered his mouth with his hand, too late. Charlie and Carlton were running from the dark hallway at a furious pace.

"Come on!" Charlie yelled at them, not slowing down as she passed, and John and Jessica ran after them as Charlie led them out of the dining room into the opposite hall, toward the storeroom they had come in through.

Charlie ran down the hall with a purpose, stopping in front of a closed door and trying to get it open. Behind them loomed the open mouth of a pitch-black party room, a wide, empty space that could have hidden anything. John turned his back to the group, keeping an eye on the abyss.

"Is it locked?" Carlton asked, an edge of rising panic in his voice.

"No, just stuck," Charlie said. She forced it, and the door popped open. They hurried inside, John lingering until the last moment, his eyes still on the darkness behind him.

When the door was shut, Charlie reached for the light switch by the door, but John put a hand on her arm.

"Don't turn the light on," he said, looking back for a moment. "We have enough light; let your eyes adjust."

There was a window high up on the door, thick glass with a bubbling frosted pattern that let a trickle of light and color into the room from the hallway.

"Right," Charlie said. A light on in here would have marked them out clearly. In the semidarkness, she surveyed the room. It had been an office, though not one she remembered visiting often; she was not sure who had used it. There were cartons here and there on the floor, overstuffed to bulging with papers, their lids perched sheepishly on top of the mess inside. There was an old desk in the corner, a grayish-blue metal with visible dents in the surface. Jessica boosted herself up to sit on it.

"Lock the door," Jessica said in an irritated tone, and Charlie did. There was a button set into the knob, which she knew would be useless, and a flimsy bolt lock, the kind in bathroom stalls and on picket fences.

"I guess it's better than nothing," she said.

CHAPTER ELEVEN

They sat silently for a few minutes in the little office, everyone eyeing the door, waiting. *It's just another place to be trapped*, Charlie thought.

"We have to get out of here," Jessica said softly, echoing Charlie's thoughts. Suddenly Carlton made a small sound of distress. Spasmodically, he grabbed a cardboard box, tipping it over to dump out some of the contents, and vomited into it. His stomach was empty; he retched futilely, his guts clenching and seizing to no effect. At last he sat back, gasping. His face was red, and there were tears in his eyes.

"Carlton? Are you okay?" John asked, alarmed.

"Yeah, never better," Carlton said as his breathing returned slowly to normal.

"You have a concussion," Charlie said. "Look at me." She

knelt down in front of him and looked at his eyes, trying to remember what the pupils were supposed to look like if someone had a concussion. Carlton waggled his eyebrows.

"Oh, oh, *ow!*" He ground his teeth and ducked his head, clutching it as if someone might try to take it away from him. "Sorry," he said after a moment, still bent over in pain. "I think it was all that running. I'll be okay."

"But—" Charlie started to protest, but he cut her off, straightening with a visible effort.

"Charlie, it's fine. Can you blame me for being a little out of sorts? What about you?" He pointed at her arm, and she looked down, confused.

There was a small, bright red patch leaking through the bandage on her arm; the wound must have opened while they were fleeing.

"Oh," Charlie said, suddenly a little nauseated herself. John moved toward her to help, but she waved him away. "I'm fine," she said. She moved the arm experimentally; it ached with the same dull pain that had been radiating through it for the last few days, but it did not seem worse, and the spot of blood wasn't growing very fast.

There was another rumble of thunder outside, and the walls trembled.

"We have to get out of here. Not out of this room, out of this building!" Jessica exclaimed.

"Carlton needs a doctor," John added.

Jessica's voice rose in pitch, sounding frantic. "We're *all* going to need a doctor if we don't leave!"

"I know," Charlie said. She felt a rising irritation at the self-evident statement, and she tried to tamp it down. They were scared, and they were trapped; sniping at one another would not help. "Okay," she said. "You're right. We need to get out. We could try the skylight."

"I don't think we'll be able to get out that way," John said.

"There's got to be a ladder in this place somewhere," Charlie replied, her fear receding as she considered the options. She sat up straighter, gathering herself together.

"It won't help," Jessica said.

"Air vents," John said hastily. "The ones Jason got in through were too small, but there have to be others. Windows—Freddy's had windows, right? They have to lead somewhere."

"I think it's safe to say that they've all been bricked up." Charlie shook her head and looked at the floor for a moment, then she met John's eyes. "This whole place has been sealed."

The walkie-talkie crackled to life, and they all jumped. Lamar's voice came over the radio.

"John?"

John grabbed the radio.

"Yeah? Yeah, I'm here, and I'm with Charlie, Jessica, and Carlton. We're in an office."

"Good," Lamar said. "Listen—" There was a brief scrabbling noise, then Marla's voice came through.

"Good," she said. "Listen, I'm looking at the monitors, and it looks like all the robots are on the main stage again."

"What about Pirate's Cove?" Charlie put in, leaning over John to talk into the receiver. "Is Foxy there, too?"

There was a brief pause.

"The curtain is closed," Marla said.

"Marla, is everything okay?" Charlie said.

"Yeah," she answered shortly, and the background static vanished abruptly—she had turned the walkie-talkie off.

Charlie and John exchanged a glance.

"Something's wrong," Carlton said. "Other than the obvious, I mean." He gestured in a vague circular motion, indicating everything around them.

"What are you talking about?" Jessica was losing her patience.

"With Marla, I mean," he said. "Something's wrong. Call her back."

John pressed the call button again. "Marla? What's going on?"

There was no reply for a long minute, then Lamar replied, "We don't know where Jason is." His voice began to break. "He's in danger."

Charlie felt a jolt through her stomach. *No.* She heard John take a deep breath.

There was a shuddering sound from the other end of the radio: Marla was crying. She started to speak, broke off, and tried again.

"Foxy," she said, her voice a little loud as she forced the words out. "Foxy took him."

"Foxy?" Charlie said carefully. *The figure standing in the front hallway, the rain whipping past it, the silver eyes, burning in the dark.* She took the walkie-talkie from John's hand; he gave it up without protest.

"Marla, listen, we're going to find him. Do you hear me?" Her bravado echoed emptily, even in her own ears. The walkie-talkie made no sound. Agitated, needing to move, to *do* something, Charlie turned to the others.

"I'm going to check out the skylight one more time," she said. "Jessica, come with me; you've got the best chance of fitting."

"Right," Jessica said reluctantly, but she got to her feet.

"You shouldn't go alone," John said, standing to go with them. Charlie shook her head.

"Someone has to stay with him," she said, gesturing at Carlton.

"Hey, I'm a big boy. I can stay by myself," Carlton said, speaking to a shelf.

"Nobody is staying by themselves," Charlie said firmly. John gave her a brief, precise nod, something just short of a salute, and she returned it. She looked back at Carlton, whose face was drawn, tight with pain. "Don't let him fall asleep," she told John in a low voice.

"I know," he whispered.

"I can hear you, you know," Carlton said, but his voice was flat and fatigued.

"Come on," Jessica said. Charlie shut the door behind them and heard John slip the lock back into place.

Charlie led the way. The closet with the skylight wasn't far, and they crept down the hallway and through the doors without incident.

"The skylight. Look, there's no way to climb out through it, even for me. To get to the roof, I would have to put all my weight on the glass; it would break. Even if we had a ladder, this isn't the way out," Jessica said.

"We could take the skylight window off," Charlie suggested weakly.

"I guess we could break out all the glass. But that just brings us back to the ladder question. We need to look around."

A sudden knock on the door caught John's attention, and he sprang to his feet and listened carefully. Charlie knocked again, briefly regretting that they had not come up with some sort of signal. "It's me," she called softly, and the lock slid back. John looked worried.

"What is it?" Charlie said, and he cast his eyes in Carlton's direction. Carlton was huddled on the floor, his knees drawn up tight to his chest, and his arms were wrapped oddly around his head. Charlie knelt down beside him.

"Carlton?" she said, and he made a small whimper. She put a hand on his shoulder, and he leaned in to her a little.

"Charlie? Sorry about all this," he whispered.

"Shhh. Tell me what's going on," she said. She had a sick feeling of dread. Something was really wrong, and she did not know how much was his injury and how much was just exhaustion, pain, and terror. "You're going to be okay," she said, stroking his back and hoping it was true.

After a long moment, he pushed at her, and she drew back, slightly hurt, until she saw him pitch forward over the cardboard box, retching again. She looked up at John.

"He needs a doctor," he said in a low voice, and she nodded. Carlton sat up again and wiped his face with his sleeve.

"It's not that bad. I'm just so tired."

"You can't go to sleep," Charlie said.

"I know, I won't. But I didn't sleep last night, and I haven't eaten since yesterday—it just makes everything worse. I had a bad moment, but I'm okay." Charlie looked at him dubiously but did not argue.

"Now what?" Jessica said. Charlie didn't answer right away, even though she knew the question was for her. She was picturing the guard, his eyes rolling back in his head as

330

he collapsed, his thin face going slack as he fell. They needed answers, and he was the one who had them.

"Now let's hope I didn't accidentally kill that guard," Charlie said.

"I don't want to go back out there," Jessica said.

"We have to go back to where I found Carlton."

"Hang on," said John, pulling out the radio again. "Hey, Marla, are you there?" There was a blip of static, then Marla's voice.

"Yeah, we're here."

"We need to get to the supply room. It's off the main dining room, past the stage. Can you see the area?"

There was a pause as Marla searched her screens.

"I can see most of it. Where are you? I can't see you."

"We're in an office. It's—" John looked at Charlie for help, and she took the radio.

"Marla, do you see another hall leading from the main room? Sort of the same direction as the closet, but next to it?"

"What? There are too many hallways!"

"Hang on. Can you see this?" Over the protests of the others, Charlie opened the office door and poked her head out cautiously. When she saw that the space was clear—or at least she was fairly sure it was clear—she stepped out into the open, looked up, and waved. There was nothing but a quiet, steady static from the walkie-talkie, then Marla's voice came through, excited.

"I see you! Charlie, I can see you."

Charlie ducked back into the little room, and Jessica caught the door and shut it behind her, double- and triple-checking the lock.

"Okay, Marla," Charlie said. "Follow the cameras. You can see that hall. Can you see the main dining room?"

"Yes," she said instantly, "most of it. I can see the stage and the area around it, and I can see the second hallway, the one parallel to yours."

"Can you see the door at the end?"

"Yes, but Charlie, I can't see into the supply room."

"We'll just have to take our chances with what's in there," Charlie answered. "Marla," she said into the receiver, "are we clear to get to the dining room?"

"Yes," Marla said after a moment. "I think so."

Charlie took the lead, and all four of them made their way slowly down the hall. Jessica hung back a little with Carlton, staying so close to him he almost tripped over her feet.

"Jessica, I'm fine," he said.

"I know," she said quietly, but she did not move away, and he did not protest again.

When they reached the end of the hallway, they stopped.

"Marla?" Charlie said into the radio.

"Go ahead—no, stop!" she cried, and they froze, pressing their bodies up against the walls as if it might make them invisible. Marla whispered over the walkie-talkie, her hushed tones distorting her voice even more.

"Something—stay quiet—" She said something else, but it was unintelligible. Charlie craned her neck to see out into the room and what might be lurking there, some murky form, lumbering heavily in the shadows, poised to attack. There was a long rumble outside, and the panels on the ceiling rattled as if they were about to fall.

"Marla, I don't see anything," Charlie said into the walkie-talkie. She looked at the stage, where all of the animatronics were still in position, staring sightlessly into the distance.

"Me neither," John whispered.

"Sorry," Marla said. "Not to overstate the obvious, but it's creepy in here. It feels like it's been midnight for hours. Does anyone know what time it is?"

Charlie checked her watch, squinting to see the little hand. "It's almost four," she said.

"A.m. or p.m.?" Marla said. She didn't sound like she was joking.

"P.m." Lamar's voice came over the radio, hard to hear, like he was not close enough to the receiver. "I told you, Marla, it's daytime."

"It doesn't feel like daytime," Marla sobbed, shrieking as the building shook with a crash of thunder.

"I know," he said softly, and the radio clicked off. Charlie looked at the walkie-talkie for a moment with a sense of emptiness. It was like hanging up the phone, knowing the person on the other end was still there but feeling a loss anyway, as if they might be gone for good.

"Charlie?" John said, and she looked at him. He cast a nod back at Carlton, who was leaning against the wall, his eyes closed. Jessica was hovering worriedly, not sure what to do. "We have to get him out of here," John said.

"I know," Charlie said. "Come on. That guard is our best chance of getting out alive." With one more look at the open space in front of them, she led them out into the main room.

Crossing in front of the stage, she saw John and Jessica glancing upward, but she refused to look at the animals, as if that would stop them from looking at her. It did not help; she felt their eyes on her, taking her measure, waiting for their moment. Finally she could not stand it—she snapped her head around to look as they passed. She saw only the inanimate robots, their eyes fixed on something that no one else could see.

They paused again at a hall entrance, waiting for Marla to guide them, and after an anxious moment her voice came over the radio, calm again.

"Go ahead, the hall is clear."

They went. They were almost there, and Charlie felt a tightness in her stomach like a living knot, something snakelike that was fighting to be free. She thought of Carlton, retching on the floor of the office, and she felt for a moment like she might do the same. She stopped a few feet from the door, holding up a hand.

"I don't know if he's in there," she said in a low voice. "And if he is, I don't know if he's—awake." *Now let's hope I didn't accidentally kill that guard*, she had said. She was only kidding, but now the words came back, unsettling her. It had not really occurred to her that he might be dead until the words were out of her mouth, and now, as she stood in the hall, about to find out, the idea took hold.

As if he knew what she was thinking, John said, "Charlie, we have to go in."

She nodded. John moved as if to take the lead, but she shook her head. Whatever was in there, it was her doing. Her responsibility. She closed her eyes for a brief moment, then turned the knob.

He was dead. He was lying on the floor, on his back, his eyes closed and his face ashen. She felt herself put a hand over her mouth, but it was as if someone else were moving her body. She felt numb, the knots in her stomach gone still and dead. John pushed past her. He knelt and slapped the man's face.

"John," she said, hearing a note of panic in her voice. He looked up at her, surprised.

"He's not dead," he said. "He's just out cold. He can't tell us anything like this."

"We have to tie him up or something," Jessica said. "Don't wake him up like this."

"Yeah, gotta agree with that," Carlton said. His eyes searched the room for devices, tools, or costumes—anything that Dave could—and probably would—use against them, given the opportunity.

Charlie just stared, the numb feeling lingering. *He's not dead.* She shook herself all over like a dog, trying to rid herself of the remnants of shock, and cleared her throat.

"Let's find something to tie him up with," she said. "This place seems to have everything." Jessica headed to the back of the room, where costume pieces were piled haphazardly, empty mascots' heads staring out from odd angles with ghastly eyes.

"Careful touching the costumes," Charlie called toward Jessica.

"We could always put him in one of them, like he did to me," Carlton said. There was an uncharacteristic edge to his voice, something hard and painful. Charlie didn't think it was from his injury. He sat down on a box, his face strained and his arms wrapped around his body like he was holding himself together.

Suddenly Carlton's face lit up with alarm.

"Don't touch—" he shouted and pushed Charlie out of the way. He stumbled past Jessica, who was searching through the clutter, and started tearing his way through the mess, picking up boxes and pushing things out of his way, scrambling in a desperate search.

"Charlie, where is it?!" he demanded, his gaze roaming around the room futilely. Charlie went to him, following where he looked, and realized what was missing: the yellow bear suit that had been slouched in the corner.

"What?" John said, confused.

"Charlie, where is it? Where is Michael?" Carlton sat with a thud on a cardboard box that sagged a little but held his weight. He was only looking at Charlie, as if they were the only people in the room.

"Michael?" John whispered. He looked at Charlie, but she returned his gaze silently; she had no answers to offer him.

"Michael was there." Carlton pressed his lips firmly, rocking himself back and forth.

"I believe you," Charlie answered calmly, her voice quiet. John put his hands on his knees and let out a breath.

"I'm going to go help Jessica," he muttered and stood up with resignation. "There has to be rope around here somewhere."

"Be right there." Charlie smiled at Carlton, hoping to reassure him, then joined the others, heading for the boxes in the corner beside the door.

The first just held more paperwork, official forms with tiny print, but underneath was a box of tangled extension cords.

"Hey, I found something," Charlie said, but she was cut off by a banshee scream.

Charlie was on her feet instantly, ready to run, but everyone else was still. Jessica was pointing to something in the corner, almost shaking. John was behind her, his eyes wide.

"What is it?" Charlie demanded, and when they did not answer, she rushed over and looked down at the pile of empty costumes to where Jessica was pointing.

It was hard to sort out what was what in the pile of mascots. She stared blankly at the jumble, seeing nothing but fur and eyes and beaks and paws, and then it resolved before her eyes.

A dead man.

He looked young, not much older than they were—and he looked familiar.

"That's the cop, the one from the other night," John said, recovering his voice.

"What?" Carlton said, snapping to attention. He came over to look. "That's Officer Dunn. I know him."

"Your dad sent him to look for you," Charlie said quietly.

"What do we do?" Jessica said. She had been inching slowly backward, and now her foot bumped against Dave, and she jumped, stifling another scream. It pulled Charlie's eyes away from Dunn, and looking away was enough to recall her to their task.

"There's nothing we can do," she said firmly. "Come on, we don't know how much time we have before he wakes up."

John and Jessica followed her across the room, Jessica catching up and keeping close to Charlie as if afraid to get too far away from her again. Charlie grabbed a handful of cords and tossed it to John.

It was a long and tedious process. They propped Dave up into a sitting position against the wall, but he kept sliding sideways until John took hold of his shoulders. John bent him forward as Charlie tied his hands behind his back. She finished and looked up to see John with a faint smile on his face.

"Do my knots amuse you?" she said as lightly as she could manage. The feel of Dave's flesh, alive yet limp and heavier than it should have been, was disturbing, and as she let go of him, she could still feel the traces of his clammy skin on her palms.

He shrugged. "All those times we played cops and robbers seem to have paid off."

"I forgot about that." She laughed. He nodded sagely.

"And yet I still bear the scars of the rope burns you gave me." John smiled.

"And that was before I was even a Girl Scout," Charlie said. "Stop complaining and pick up his feet. Let's hope my skills haven't atrophied."

She finished tying up Dave, pretending a confidence she did not really have. The cords were thick and stiff; they were hard to manipulate, and she was not sure how long they would hold. When she was as sure as she could be, she stepped back.

John looked around for a moment as though searching for something, then slipped out through the door without a word.

Carlton was on his knees, and he walked toward Dave without standing, a clunky, unsteady walk—he looked like he might tip over at any moment. "Wakey, wakey, sleepy head," he whispered.

"We've got this, Carlton, thanks. You just relax." Charlie rolled her eyes toward Jessica, then turned her attention back to Dave, slapping his face lightly, but he remained inert.

"Hey, dirtbag. Wake up." She slapped him again.

"Here, try this." John reappeared with a can of water. "Water fountain," was the only explanation he offered. "The can didn't hold much," he added.

"That's okay," Charlie said. She took it from him and held it over Dave's head, letting the small streams of water dribbling from the holes in the tin fall on his face. She aimed for his mouth, and after a few moments, he spluttered, his eyes opening.

"Oh, good, you're awake," Charlie said, then dumped the rest of the water on his head.

He said nothing, but his eyes remained open in a stiff, unnatural stare.

"So, Dave," she said. "How about you tell us what's going on?"

His mouth opened slightly, but no words came out. After a moment he became still again, so still that Charlie reluctantly pressed her fingers to his neck to check for a pulse.

"Is he alive?" John said, creeped out by what seemed to be an on-again, off-again animated corpse. He moved closer to the man, kneeling so their eyes were level, and looked at him gravely, searching for something.

"His pulse is normal," Charlie reported. She pulled her hand back, more startled than if he'd been dead.

"Charlie, there's something different about him," John said urgently. He reached out and grasped Dave's chin, turning his head back and forth. Dave did not resist; he just kept staring without expression, as if the world around him were not really there.

"What do you mean?" Charlie said, though she saw it, too. It was as if the guard, the man they had met, had been stripped away, and what sat before them was nothing but a blank canvas.

John shook his head and released the guard's chin, wiping his hands on his pants. He stood and stepped back, putting a distance between them.

"I don't know," he said. "There's just something different."

"Why don't you tell us about the kids?" Carlton was leaning back against the wall, emboldened but still not completely balanced. "The kids you killed, you stuffed them into those suits out there." Carlton motioned toward the stage outside.

"Carlton, shut up," John said angrily. "Everything you're saying is nonsense."

"No, it's true," Charlie whispered. John gave her a searching look, then turned to the others, who had no more answers than Charlie. He looked back at Dave with an expression of renewed disgust. Seeing John's face, Charlie was suddenly struck with the weight of memory. Michael, who had been a cheerful, careless little boy, Michael who had drawn portraits of them all, passing them around with a solemn pride. Michael who had been killed, whose final moments must have been all pain and terror. Michael, who had been killed by the man before them. She looked to the others, and on each of their faces she saw the same single thought: *This was the man who killed Michael.*

Without warning, John's arm shot out like lightning and struck Dave across the jaw with a loud crack. Dave slumped back, and John lunged and almost fell from the impact of the strike. John regained his posture and bounced a little on the balls of his feet, alert, waiting for a reaction, or a chance to strike again. Dave's body moved upward, straightening, but the movement was too smooth. He seemed to make no effort, use no muscles, and exert no energy. Slowly, his posture corrected, unfolding to his slumped state, his mouth hanging open.

Carlton stumbled forward. "Take that, jackass." He swung his arm into the air and swayed on his feet. Jessica leaped forward just in time to catch him in her arms.

Dave continued to stare, and it was only after a moment that Charlie considered that he might actually be staring at something. She turned, following his line of sight, then suddenly she recoiled. On the table along the wall sat a rabbit's head.

"That's it? You want that?" Charlie stood and approached the mask. "You need this?" she added in a whisper. She picked it up carefully, the light catching the edges of the spring locks that filled the mascot's head. She picked it up and carried it almost ceremoniously to Dave, who tipped his head down in a barely noticeable fashion.

Charlie placed it over his head, not being nearly as cautious as she had been with Carlton. When the mascot's head was fully resting on his shoulders, the large face raised itself until it was almost completely upright. Dave's eyes opened steadily, glassy and without emotion, like the robots on the stage outside. Lines of sweat began to trickle down from under the mask, a stain darkening the collar of his uniform shirt.

"My dad trusted you," Charlie said. She was on her knees now, looking intently at the rabbit's face. "What did you do to him?" Her voice broke.

"I helped him create." The voice came from inside the mask, but it was not Dave's, not the pitiful, sour tone they would have recognized. The voice of the rabbit was smooth and rich, almost musical. It was confident, somehow reassuring—a voice that might convince you of almost anything. Dave cocked his head to the side, and the mask shifted so that only one of his bulbous eyes could peer through the sockets.

"We both wanted to love," he said in those melodious tones. "Your father loved. And now I have loved."

"You killed," Carlton said, then burst out with something that sounded like a laugh. He seemed more lucid now, as if anger was focusing his mind. He shook loose of Jessica's hands on his arms and knelt down on the floor.

"You're a sick bastard," Carlton sputtered. "And you've created monsters. The kids you killed are still here. You've imprisoned them!"

"They are home, with me." Dave's voice was coarse, and the large mascot's head slid forward and tilted as he spoke. "Their happiest day."

"How do we get out?" Charlie placed one hand on the mascot's head and pushed it back into position on Dave's shoulders. The fur felt wet and sticky, as though the costume itself were sweating.

"There isn't a way out anymore. All that's left is family." His round eye reappeared through one of the sockets, glimmering in the light. He locked eyes with Charlie for a moment, struggling to lean in closer. "Oh," he gasped. "You're something beautiful, aren't you?" Charlie recoiled as if he had touched her. *What's that supposed to mean?* She took another step back, fighting a surge of revulsion.

"Well, then, you're trapped, too, and you're not going to be hurting anyone else," John said in response to the veiled threat.

"I don't have to," Dave answered. "When it gets dark, they will awaken; the children's spirits will rise. They will kill you. I'll just walk out in the morning, stepping over your corpses, one by one." He looked at each of them in turn, as if relishing the bloody scene.

"They'll kill you, too," Jessica said.

"No, I am quite confident that I will survive."

"Really?" John said suddenly. "I'm pretty sure they're the spirits of the kids *you killed*," he all but spat. "Why would they hurt us? It's you they're after."

"They don't remember," Dave said. "They've forgotten. The dead do forget. All they know is that you are here, trying to take away their happiest day. You are intruders." He lowered his voice to a hush. "You are *grown-ups*."

They looked at one another.

"We're not—" Jessica began.

"You're close enough. Especially to a vengeful, confused, and frightened child. None of you will survive the night."

"And what makes you think they won't kill you?" John said again, and Dave's eyes took on something shining, almost beatific.

"Because I am one of them," he said.

They all stood staring at the man on the floor. Jessica took an involuntary step backward. Charlie was glued to the spot; she could not look away from him. *Because I am one of them.* As if he could tell what she was thinking, John stepped up beside her.

"Charlie, he's insane," he said quietly, and it was enough to break her away from that dreadful, ecstatic gaze. She turned to John.

"We have to get out," she said. He nodded, turned back to the group, and gestured to the walkie-talkie in his hand.

"I'm going back to the control room," he said. "These things are police radios; there has to be a way to get them to reach the outside. Maybe I can use the equipment in there to get a signal somehow."

"I'll go with you," Charlie said instantly, but he shook his head.

"You have to stay with them," he said, barely audible. Charlie looked over at Jessica and Carlton. He was right. Carlton needed someone with him, and Jessica—Jessica was holding it together, but she couldn't be left alone in charge of the safety of both of them. Charlie nodded.

"Be careful," she said.

He didn't answer; instead he tucked the walkie-talkie into his belt, gave her a wink, and left.

Clay Burke was in his office, reviewing the week's case files. There was not much: traffic violations, two petty thefts, and one confession to the murder of Abraham Lincoln. Clay shuffled through the papers and sighed. Shaking his head, he pulled open the bottom drawer of his desk and removed the file that had been plaguing him all morning.

Freddy's. When he closed his eyes, he was there again, the cheerful family restaurant, its floor streaked with blood. After Michael disappeared, he had worked fourteen-hour days, sometimes sleeping in the station. Every time he came home he went to look at Carlton, who was usually asleep. He wanted to grab his son and hold him close, never let him go. It could have been any of the children there that day; it was blind, dumb luck that the killer had spared his own.

At the time, it was the first murder that the department had dealt with. It was a sixteen-person department, usually charged with small thefts and noise complaints, and to be handed a gruesome murder made all of them feel a little like kids whose toy guns had suddenly turned real.

Clay opened the file, knowing what he would find. It was only a partial report; the rest of it was in a storage room in the basement. He scanned the familiar words, the bureau-cratic language that tried but failed to obscure the point: There had been no justice done. *Sometimes the guilty get away with terrible things, but it is the price we pay.* He had said that to Charlie. He cringed a little now, realizing how that must have sounded, to her of all people.

He picked up the phone, calling the front desk in a moment of urgency rather than walking the twenty feet to ask in person.

"Has Dunn reported back from Freddy's?" he asked before the officer on the other end could speak.

"No, sir," she said, "I'll—"

He hung up, not waiting for her to finish. Clay stared restlessly at the wall for a long moment, then grabbed his coffee cup and headed to the basement.

He didn't have to search for the box of evidence from the Freddy's disappearances; he had been here before. There was no one around, and so instead of taking it upstairs to his office, Clay sat down on the concrete floor, spreading papers and photographs around him. There were interviews, witness statements, and reports from the on-scene officers, Clay included. He sifted through them aimlessly. He didn't know what he was looking for; there was nothing new here.

There was nothing to find, really. They knew who did it. At first he had suspected Henry, just like so many others around town. It was a terrible thought, but it was a terrible crime; there was no solution that would not be shocking. He had not been the one to question Charlie's father, but he had read the transcript. The man had been almost incoherent, so shaken that he could not give straight answers. He sounded as if he were lying, and to most people that was proof enough. But Clay had resisted, had delayed having him arrested, and sure enough they came to William Afton, Henry's partner. Afton seemed like the normal one in the venture, the businessman. Henry was the artist; he always seemed to be off in another world, some part of his mind thinking about his mechanical creatures even when he was holding a conversation about the weather or the kids' soccer games. There was something off about Henry, something almost shell-shocked; it seemed like a miracle that he could have produced a child as apparently normal as Charlie.

Clay remembered when Henry had moved to town and begun construction of the new restaurant. Someone had told him that Henry had a kid who had been abducted several years prior, but he didn't know much else. He seemed like a nice enough guy, though he was obviously terribly alone, his grief visible even at a distance. Then Freddy Fazbear's opened, and the town came alive. That was also when Charlie appeared. Clay hadn't known Henry even had a daughter until that day.

William Afton was the one who made Freddy's a business, as he had the previous restaurant. Afton was as robust and lively as Henry was withdrawn and shadowy. He was a hefty man who had the ruddy geniality of a financially shrewd Santa Claus. And he had killed the children. Clay knew it; the whole department knew it. He had been present for each abduction, and he had mysteriously and briefly vanished at the same time as each child went missing. A search of his house had found a room crammed with boxes of mechanical parts and a musty yellow rabbit suit as well as stacks of journals full of raving paranoia, passages about Henry that ranged from wild jealousy to near worship.

But there had been no evidence, there had been no bodies, and so there could be no charge. William Afton had left town, and there was nothing to stop him. They did not even know where he had gone. Clay picked up a picture from the pile; it had been taken, framed, from the wall of Henry's office at the restaurant. It was a picture of the two of them together, Henry and William, grinning into the camera in front of the newly opened Freddy Fazbear's. He stared at it; he had stared at it before. Henry's eyes did not quite match his smile. The expression looked forced, but then, it always did. There was nothing unusual here, except that one of the men had turned out to be a killer.

Suddenly, Clay felt a shock of recognition, something indistinct he could not quite catch. He closed his eyes, letting his mind wander like a dog off the lead: *Go on, find it.* There was something about William, something familiar, something *recent*. Clay's eyes snapped open. He shoved everything back into the evidence box, cramming it in messily, keeping out only the photograph. Clutching it, he took the stairs up two at a time, almost running by the time he got to the main floor of the station. He headed straight for a particular filing cabinet, ignoring the greetings of his startled officers. He tore open the drawer, pawing through it until—there it was, employee background checks requested by businesses from the last six months.

He pulled out the stack and flipped through it, looking for photos. In the third folder, he found it. He picked up the picture and held it up next to the one of Henry and William, turning so his body did not block the light.

It's him.

The background check application was labeled "Dave Miller," but it was unmistakably William Afton. Afton had been fat and affable; the man in the picture was sallow and thin, his skin sagging and his expression unpleasant, as if he had forgotten how to smile. He looked like a poor facsimile of himself. Or maybe, Clay thought, he looked like he had dropped his disguise.

Clay flipped the page back to see why the check had been requested, and his face drained white, his breathing stopping for a moment. Clay stood, grabbing his jacket in the same motion, then stopped. Slowly, he sat, letting the jacket fall from his fingers. He took the partial file back out of its drawer, and delicately he lifted one of the photos out. It had been taken in the aftermath, when the place was no more than a crime scene. He paused for a moment and closed his eyes. Then he looked again at the picture, willing himself to see it as if for the first time.

There was a glimmer of light he had never noticed before. One of the animatronics on the stage, the bear, *Freddy*, was looking toward the cameraman, one of his eyes illuminated with a smear of light.

Clay put the picture aside, moving to the next one. This one was from a different angle, but the side of the main stage was still in the frame. Chica's body was facing away from the camera, but her face was turned directly toward it, and another smear of light streaked across her left eye. Clay rubbed it with the tip of his finger, making sure it wasn't a defect in the paper. The next photo showed Bonnie in the darkness behind the chairs. A pinpoint of light, like a star, shone from one of his eyes as though reflecting a spotlight that wasn't there. *What is this?* Clay could feel his face flush;

he realized he hadn't been breathing. He shuffled his hands on the desk like a conjurer calling forth a picture to reveal itself. One did. The last picture had been taken in Pirate's Cove. Tables had been disturbed, he remembered. The scene was chaotic: the tables and chairs in disarray, clutter strewn through the halls. But unlike so many other times he had stared at this picture, he ignored the disorder and focused only on the stage. The curtain was pulled back slightly, a figure barely visible in the recesses behind it, one eye presumably illuminated by the flash of a camera. Clay studied the rest of the pictures, looking for more reflections, but found none. *There was no flash.*

Jason opened his eyes. His leg hurt; it was a steady, dull pain. He flexed it tentatively and found he could move easily; the injury could not be too bad. He was lying on something lumpy, and his whole body felt stiff, like he had been asleep on a pile of—he looked at what he was lying on—a pile of extension cords and wires. He sat up. It was dark, but he could dimly see what was around him. He bent over to examine his leg. His jeans were ripped where Foxy's claw had gouged him, and the gash in his leg was ugly, but it was not bleeding badly. The hook had mostly got hold of his jeans. Jason felt a little relief. Satisfied, he began to examine his surroundings. He was in a corner, and there was a heavy black curtain strung from one wall to the other, cutting the space off from the room outside. He crawled forward over the cables cautiously, careful to make no sound. He made his way to the edge of the curtain, where there was a tiny sliver of a gap between it and the wall. Jason took a moment to steel himself, then peeked out, conscious of his every movement.

He was on the small stage in Pirate's Cove, behind the curtain. He could hear something moving out there, something large, but from his position he could see only an empty room. He pushed his head out a little farther, craning his neck to look. He couldn't tell where the sound was coming from, but with each second he grew bolder, readying himself to leap from the stage and run. A light was pulsing in the main dining room, illuminating the hall for brief seconds at a time with bright, dizzying carnival colors. It wasn't much, but it gave Jason a direction to run. He watched it intently until it was all he could see, and then it stopped. The room was dark, darker than it had been before—his eyes had adjusted to the light and now he was nearly blind. The shuffling sound went on, and Jason pulled the curtain open farther. This time he moved too fast, and as the curtain was drawn, the metal rings that held it clinked together.

The light above Pirate's Cove went on.

Foxy was there, right in front of him, his face so close to Jason's that they could almost touch. Jason scrambled back through the curtain, pulling it closed again, trying to escape the small alcove, but there was nowhere to run. He crawled backward, staying against the wall, hoping that the curtain would somehow shield him from Foxy.

At once, the curtain began to open, not by force, but as if a show were about to begin. Lights and color flashed in silent patterns, and the glittered front curtains rolled back in grand fashion to reveal the stage, with the beast standing patiently at its base.

Foxy cocked his head to the side as if considering something, and then he began his approach. He climbed the stairs to the stage one by one, each step a whole series of disjointed movements, as if each piece of his metal body maneuvered itself individually. Jason watched, struck with horror, yet some small part of him was enthralled; it was like nothing he had ever seen. Foxy reached the stage and took two more large, deliberate steps, until he was standing over Jason. Jason stared up at him, too afraid to move, frozen in place like a mouse beneath a diving falcon. His breath was shallow; his heart beat so fast his chest hurt. Foxy raised his hook again, and Jason threw himself down on the floor in a ball, protecting his head with his arms, waiting for the blow to come.

It did not come.

Jason did not move. He waited, and waited, wondering if time had slowed down as he approached the moment of his death, his mind trying to give him refuge, making the last moments feel as long as possible. But not this long. He opened his eyes and turned his head a little, keeping his arms in front of his face. Foxy was still there, not moving. Despite himself, Jason met the creature's eyes. It was like looking into the sun—Foxy's burning gaze made Jason's eyes tear up, made him want to look away, but he could not. It was the animatronic who looked away. As Jason watched, peering through the afterburn that clouded his vision, Foxy turned to face his absent audience. His hook fell slowly to his side, his head tilted forward, and he went motionless. The sounds of whirring machinery and clicking parts came to a stop, and the curtains drew closed again.

"Ready?" Lamar said. Marla nodded curtly.

"I'm ready," she said. She threw open the door, fists clenched, and they climbed out, facing opposite directions, preparing for an assault. Marla was breathing heavily, her face furious. The darkness was thick, almost tangible, and she could barely make out what was around her. She could see Lamar, but if they drifted three feet apart they would be lost to each other. The lights above them flickered, but only for a moment; the brief illumination ruined what little night vision they had, making the dark impenetrable.

"Anything on your side?" Marla whispered. Lamar looked toward her voice, distressed.

"No, anything on your side?"

"Light, please," Marla whispered. Lamar held up the flashlight as though aiming a weapon and turned it on. Above them, the lights sputtered.

Jason could see their flashlight waving back and forth, filtering through the slightly transparent curtain. *Oh no.* The light fell on the animatronic, just for a moment, and there was a clicking noise. Jason looked up. Foxy was not moving. The light swept across him again, and again the mechanical sounds came, this time unmistakable, though he still did not move. Jason scooted forward, around Foxy's foot, and looked up at the animatronic's face as the light struck him again. Again the clicking noise came; something inside him was readying itself, but his eyes stayed dark. Jason crawled as far forward as he was willing to venture, trying not to cross into Foxy's line of sight. He made it to the edge of the curtain and reached his arm out to wave a warning.

"Jason!" He heard his sister's voice, and then a quick shushing from what must have been Lamar. The flashlight swept up, trained on the stage, and Foxy's eyes lit up. His head swept toward the light with a predatory precision, and Jason, panicked, reached for the pile of cords and grabbed a cable. Foxy lifted a foot, and Jason threw the cord around it and yanked with all his strength. Foxy pitched forward, grabbing at the curtain with his hook. It caught, ensnaring him, and he ripped through the cloth with a vicious tearing noise, falling to the ground in a tangle of cloth and metal limbs. Jason scrambled past the struggling creature and ran toward the light.

Marla reached for him, but he brushed her aside.

"Run," he panted, and the three of them took off down the hall. They turned a corner, and as one they stopped, Jason skidding against Lamar and grabbing him for support. At the end of the dark hall stood another figure, too large to be a person. The top hat was unmistakable.

Freddy Fazbear.

His eyes were illuminated, their piercing red glow consuming the space around him. They could hear the brittle notes of a song, mechanical and thin like a music box, coming from Freddy's direction. They stared, mesmerized, then Jason found himself and pulled at Marla's arm.

"Come on," he hissed, and they followed him, running back the way they had come. When they reached Pirate's Cove they slowed; Foxy had thrown off the curtain and was beginning to right himself. The three exchanged glances, then ran past him. Jason held his breath until they were through to the next doorway, invoking some old superstition.

Lamar motioned to one of the party rooms, and they ducked inside. He switched off the flashlight, and they stood still for a moment, their eyes adjusting. The room had three long, cafeteria-style tables, each one still set for a party: Metal folding chairs were lined all up and down them, and each place was set with a party hat, a paper plate, and a plastic cup. By wordless agreement, each hid beneath a different table, leaving themselves as much space as possible. They crouched low, hoping to be lost behind the chair legs, and together they stared silently into the vacant hall and listened.

"Hello? Anyone?" John repeated into the radio, but there was only static. He had managed to hook the walkie-talkie into the sound system, but getting a signal to the outside seemed impossible—Freddy's was sealed off from the world. He looked at the monitors again. On one screen he could see three figures crouched under tables. Marla, Lamar, and Jason, he thought. *They found Jason*, he realized with profound relief, letting go of a tension he had not known he felt. Everything on-screen was lit with unnatural grays and whites. "These must be night-vision cameras," he said to no one, squinting to see through the static. He watched the blurry figures crawl and come to a stop beneath the long party tables, then movement from another screen caught his eye.

There was a figure in the hallway, moving steadily toward the room they were in. John could not tell what it was, but the way it moved wasn't human. It stopped beside a door-way, and with a sudden jolt of realization John looked again at the party room where his friends were hiding. He grabbed the walkie-talkie and flipped the speaker system on, jam-ming the volume control as high as it would go.

"Lamar," he said calmly, trying to sound commanding. He heard the reverberation of his own voice through the walls of the control room. "Lamar, don't move."

John's voice blared over the speaker, blurred with static but intelligible.

"Lamar, don't move."

Lamar, Marla, and Jason looked at one another across the distance between the tables. The room lit up with a burning red glow, and they watched, as still as they could be, as Freddy Fazbear entered the room. His movements were mechanical and graceless as he walked with deliberate steps to the middle of the room and stopped between two tables; Marla on one side, Jason on the other. Jason looked at his sister, and she put a finger to her lips. Jason hadn't realized that there were tears on his cheeks until now.

He watched as Freddy surveyed the room. His head, with eyes like spotlights, whirred to one side, stopped with a click, and then turned to the other side. There was a long pause. The two padded feet were motionless, the legs like black trees in a forest. There was a sound of twisting fur and crinkling fabric, and the feet began to pivot. Freddy turned around and headed for the door, each step shaking the floor beneath him. As Freddy passed by, Jason shrank back instinctively, his foot hitting one of the metal chairs. It made a scraping sound. Jason's heart raced. Frantic, he looked across the space at Marla, who beckoned to him urgently. Freddy had stopped, but they could still hear the sound of fabric and fur scrunching and moving. Freddy began to bend down. His motions were slow, and in those precious few seconds Jason pushed the two chairs in front of him apart, making a gap just wide enough for him to be able to crawl behind Freddy as soon as he had the chance. The light of Freddy's eyes came into view under the table, illuminating the space beside Jason, and he quickly but quietly crawled between the chairs to where Marla was hiding. Freddy stood again, training his eyes on the floor just as Jason pulled his foot out of sight.

Freddy began to pivot toward the table they were under. Marla put a hand on Jason's arm, steadying him. There was another pause. Lamar, under the table opposite them, beckoned to Marla and Jason, urging them to his own table, farther away from Freddy. Marla shook her head, not wanting to risk making noise. *Maybe he's leaving*, she told herself. Jason was beginning to breathe normally again when it struck them: Freddy was ducking down again, this time silently. His eyes had gone dark, but as soon as they spotted him, his gaze lit up again, illuminating the room. Marla and Jason scrambled around the metal chairs as fast as they could without touching them. They crawled across the thin carpet between tables until they came across an opening in the chairs and crawled under the table beside Lamar. Marla and Lamar looked at each other, at a loss; Freddy was straightened up again and beginning to circle around to the third table.

"We have to run for the door," Marla whispered. Lamar nodded, then motioned for them to follow his lead. He watched, waiting until Freddy was bending down once again, and then gestured to the middle table. They caught their breath, trying not to gasp, and Lamar looked toward the door. Could they make it? Marla put a hand on Jason's shoulder, and he started to shrug her off, but she was gripping him tightly, her fingers digging into him. He moved to brush her away, then looked at her. She was terrified, even more than he was. He let her hold on to him while keeping his eyes on Freddy, waiting for their next opening.

It didn't come. As they waited, poised for flight, Freddy turned away, his deliberate steps taking him to the doorway. The room went dark, and Jason's heart skipped before he understood what had happened. The lights were gone because Freddy was gone.

"Marla," he whispered, his voice little more than a breath of air. "He's gone." Marla looked at him and nodded, but she did not let go of his shoulder.

"Are you okay?" she asked in the same almost soundless way. He nodded, then pointed to his leg and shrugged the-atrically. She smiled at him and took her hand from his shoulder to muss his hair.

Suddenly Lamar was tapping Marla's arm. He pointed to his ear, and she gave him a puzzled look. Jason stiffened, realizing what it was, and in a second Marla did, too. There was music in the room, a tinny, labored sound like a music box, the gaps between the notes just a little too long. The room lit up again, a drowning red, and before they could move, the table was wrenched away. Freddy stood over them. He shoved the table aside, almost hurling it. They screamed— not a scream for help but the last, futile act of defiance. Jason clung to his sister, and she pulled his head down against her, shielding his eyes so he would not have to see.

Suddenly, Freddy stumbled off-balance and lurched to the side. He tried to right himself, but another jolt from behind sent him flying forward, falling face-first into the tables. Marla, Lamar, and Jason looked up to see Charlie and John, their faces flushed with effort.

"Come on," Charlie said. "Let's go."

★   ★   ★

Dave shrugged out of his bonds quickly; the knots were sturdy, but the cords had too much give—a few twists and turns and he was free. He crawled to the door on hands and knees and held his ear to the crack, careful not to jostle the door and give himself away.

The loudspeaker blared, and then the sound he had been waiting for: footsteps, running away.

He waited just until the sound faded, then got purposefully to his feet.

"Where are we going?" Marla panted as they raced back toward the main dining room.

"The office," Charlie called. "It's got a real door; we can barricade ourselves in." She glanced at John, who nodded shortly. What they would do once they were barricaded inside was another question, but they could worry about that once they were safe. They ran through the dining room; Charlie glanced at the stage, blurred in passing, but she saw what she knew she would: It was empty.

They reached the narrow hall that led to the office, and Charlie's heart lifted when she saw the door, light shining from its small window like a beacon.

Wait, light?

She slowed her pace; they were ten feet from the door. She lifted a hand, signaling the others to stop, and they approached the door slowly. Steeling herself, Charlie grabbed the knob and turned. It was locked. She looked helplessly at the others.

"Someone's in there," Jason whispered, moving closer to Marla.

"There's no one else here," Marla said softly, but it sounded like a question. Charlie was about to try the door again, but stopped herself. *Don't draw their attention.*

"He got loose!" Jessica said, her voice hoarse, and Charlie felt a chill. *She's right.* She didn't say it.

"We have to go back," she said. Without waiting for a response, she turned, pushing between Lamar and John to take the lead. She took two steps forward, then stopped dead as she heard the others gasp.

It was Chica, her eyes like burning orange headlights.

She stood at the other end of the short hall, blocking their only way out. Her body filled the space; they could not even try to run past her. Charlie glanced behind her, even though she knew there was no other way out. Before she could react, John was running at the animatronic. He had no weapons, but he hurtled himself toward the thing and leaped up, trying to grab hold of her neck. He caught it briefly, struggling to hold on as Chica thrashed her head back and forth. Chica bent forward and swung to the side, slamming John into the wall, and John let go, crumpling to the floor. The cupcake on Chica's platter snapped its mouth as if laughing, its eyes rolling in their tiny sockets.

"John!" Charlie cried as she thrust the flashlight back for someone else to take. She felt its weight leave her hands, but she didn't look back to see who took it. She looked up; there was an electrical cord dangling above their heads. Parts of the rubber had worn away, exposing stretches of bare wire. Chica was slowly advancing. Charlie jumped up, but she could not get high enough to reach it. She looked to either side. *Is it narrow enough?* She glanced at Chica. She was moving slowly, with measured steps; they were trapped, and she did not need to hurry. Charlie planted one foot against the wall, then stretched her leg across the narrow hallway and did the same on the other side, bracing between the walls to climb. She inched upward, her legs shaking with the effort. She looked up, struggling to retain her balance as she reached for the cord. Careful to touch only the rubber, she closed her fingers around it and dropped to the ground. Chica lunged forward, her arms extended and her teeth contorted in a mechanical smile.

Charlie sprang up, the electrical cord brandished in front of her, and she shoved it into the space between Chica's head and her torso. Chica jerked backward, sparks flying, and for a horrible moment Charlie could not move. Her hand throbbed with the electric current, and she was caught there, unable to make her hand let go of the wire. She stared down at it, willing her fingers to open. *Is this how I die?* Lamar grabbed her and pulled her away, and she looked up at him wide-eyed. The others were already running. Chica was deactivated, or so it appeared, slumped forward, her eyes dark. Lamar gave her arm a tug, and they took off after the others.

With a pleased smile, Dave watched the confrontation through the window in the office door. *Just a matter of time now*, he thought. The girl had been clever, climbing the walls like that, but she had almost killed herself. They could not last much longer. All he had to do was wait.

Suddenly, the room was lit with an ethereal blue. He froze, then slowly turned. *Bonnie.* The animatronic towered over him, close enough to touch. Dave fell back against the door and screamed.

There was a scream from the direction of the office. The group paused for a minute and looked nervously at one another.

"It doesn't matter," Charlie said. "Come on."

She took a quick look back at Chica, who was still slumped forward, inert. Charlie led them into the main dining room. As they emerged, there was a sudden movement. Foxy was there.

He leaped onto a table in front of them, looking among them until his silver eyes lit on Jason. He crouched as if he were about to jump on the boy, and Charlie grabbed a napkin dispenser and threw it as hard as she could. It struck Foxy's head, glancing off with little effect, but it was enough to get his attention. He turned to her and pounced.

Charlie was already running, racing to lure him away from the others. *Then what?* she thought as she ran furiously out of the dining room and down the hall. *The arcade.* It was dark; there were things to hide behind.

She kept running full-out until she reached the door, then turned so fast she almost fell, hoping to give Foxy a moment's disorientation. She looked around frantically. There was a row of arcade machines at the back of the room, set out just a little from the wall. She heard footsteps behind her and dove for it.

The space was so tight she could barely squeeze herself into it. Her sides were pressed between the consoles and the wall, and there were thick, coiled wires beneath her feet. She took a step back, moving deeper into the crawl space, but her foot slipped on a cable, and she barely kept from falling. Movement in the room caught her eye, and she saw a flash of silver light.

He sees me.

Charlie dropped to her hands and knees. She crawled backward, scooting inch by inch. Her foot caught on a cable and she stopped to free it, twisting into an impossible position to quietly dislodge it. She moved back farther, and then her foot bumped against another wall, and she stopped. She was closed in on three sides; it almost felt safe. She closed her eyes for a moment. *Nothing here is safe.*

There was an awful sound, a clash of metal hitting metal, and the console at the far end of the row rocked on its foundation, banging back against the wall. Foxy leaned over it, and now Charlie could see him as he smashed the display, spilling shards of plastic onto the floor. His hook caught on something inside the machine, and he yanked it out again, trailing bits of wire.

He moved on to the next game, smashing the screen and throwing the console against the wall with a casual brutality. Charlie felt the impact of it echoing through the wall as he moved closer.

I have to get out. I have to! But there was no way out. Now that she was sitting in one place, she realized that her arm was stiff with pain, and only now did she look at it. The bandage was soaked through with blood; the wall beside her was streaked with a line of it where her arm had pressed. She wanted to cry suddenly. Her whole body ached. The wound in her arm, the constant tension of the last day or so—who could tell how long it had been?—was draining her, taking all she had.

The next console crashed against the wall, and Charlie flinched. It was only two away. He was almost to her. She could hear his gears working, humming, grinding, and sometimes screeching. She closed her eyes, but she could still see him: his matted fur, the metal bones showing through, the searing silver eyes.

The console beside her was wrenched away and tumbled to the ground like it weighed nothing at all. The cords beneath Charlie's hands and knees jerked forward with it, and she slipped, grabbing at nothing, trying to regain her balance. She caught herself and looked up just in time to see the downward swing of a hook.

She moved faster than she could think. She hurled herself at the final console with all her strength, and it balanced precariously, then fell, knocking Foxy to the ground and trapping him. Charlie started to run, but his hook shot out and snared her leg, cutting into her. She screamed, falling to the ground. She kicked at him with her other foot, but his hook was stuck deep in her leg; every time he jerked back she felt the impact. She kicked him in the face, and his hook tore free, slicing open her leg. She screamed again, instinctively grabbing the wound, and then Foxy was on top of her, snapping his jaws and clawing her as he tried to free his legs from under the console. She fought back, struggling to get away. His hook slashed at her again and again as she tried to block the blows, screaming for help.

Suddenly John was there. He stood over Foxy and stomped down hard on the creature's neck, holding his foot there. Foxy flailed but could not reach him.

"Charlie, get up!" he called. Charlie just stared at him for a second, too shaken to register the question. He stamped his foot on Foxy's neck repeatedly, and then in one quick movement, he grabbed Charlie's hand, heaved her up, and started to run, pulling her along behind him. They made it to the main dining room, where the rest of the group was huddled in the middle of the room. Relieved, Charlie rushed to join them. She could tell she was limping, but she did not feel any pain, which, she realized somewhere dimly in the back of her mind, was not good. When they got to the others, her heart sank. Their faces were grim. Lamar was holding the flashlight out in front of him, but it rattled in his trembling grip.

Marla gestured quickly to the entrances. Freddy stood in the hall to the storage room, while Bonnie now blocked the hallway to the office. Chica, reanimated, stood on the stage, looming over them. Charlie glanced back the way they had come.

Foxy was approaching; he had freed himself. He stopped in the doorway as if waiting for a signal. There was no escape. Suddenly acutely aware of everything around her, Charlie noticed the sound of a music box, as if she had, unconsciously, been hearing it all along. She took a deep breath. The moment seemed to go on forever. It had come to this; they were trapped. They waited. Now, perhaps, for the animatronics, there was no hurry. Charlie cast her eyes around futilely for a weapon, but there were only party hats and paper plates.

As one, the animatronics started their approach. Charlie grabbed the back of a metal folding chair, not sure how she could even use it. The animals were moving faster now, coming in unison, as if this battle were a choreographed dance. Marla took Jason's hand and whispered something in his ear. Whatever it was, he shook his head, set his jaw, and balled his hands into fists. Lamar glanced at him for a moment but said nothing. Jessica had her hands stiffly at her sides, and she was murmuring something to herself inaudibly. The animals were almost on top of them. Freddy's trundling walk was predatory, and the music box notes were coming from Freddy's direction—from *inside* Freddy, she now realized. Chica leaped from the stage and took small, bouncing steps toward them as if excited but holding herself back. Bonnie's big, paw-like feet slapped the ground like a challenge, and Foxy slunk forth with a malevolent grace, his eyes fixed on Charlie as if she were the only thing he saw. She gazed into his silver eyes. They filled her vision, crowding out everything else until the world was silver, the world was Foxy's eyes, and there was nothing left of her.

John squeezed her hand. It broke the spell; she looked at him, her vision still cloudy.

"Charlie," he said haltingly. ". . . Charlotte—"

"Shh," she said. "Later." He nodded, accepting the lie that there would be a later. Foxy crouched down again, and Charlie let go of John, her heart pounding as she braced for it. Foxy's joints shifted in their sockets as he prepared to spring—then he stopped. Charlie waited. There were no screams from behind her, no sounds of fighting; even the music box was silent. Foxy was motionless, though his eyes still glowed. Charlie looked around, and then she saw.

It was Freddy. Not the one they all knew, not the one who stood less than a foot away from Marla, his mouth open as if poised to bite. It was the other one, the one she remembered, the yellow Freddy from the diner. The costume her father used to wear. It was looking at them, staring from the corner, and now she heard something. It was indistinct, just whispers in her head, a gentle susurrus, blowing through her conscious mind without taking hold. She looked at the others and knew they heard it, too. It was indecipherable, but the meaning was unmistakable.

Carlton was the one to say it:

"Michael?"

The sounds they heard grew warm, an unspoken confirmation, and together they approached the golden bear. Marla brushed past brown Freddy as if he were not there, and Charlie turned her back to Foxy, unafraid. There was only one thought in her mind: *Michael. It's you.*

They were almost to him. All Charlie wanted to do was fling her arms around him, hold him close, and to be again the little girl she was so long ago. To embrace him again, this beloved child who had been ripped from their lives on that carefree afternoon. To do it all over, and this time to rescue him, this time to save his life.

"Michael," she whispered.

The yellow bear stood motionless. Unlike the others, there seemed to be nothing inside of it; it stood of its own accord, by its own will. There was nothing to hold the costumed jaw closed, and its eyes were empty.

Suddenly aware that their backs were to the other animals, Charlie startled and turned, apprehensive. Freddy, Bonnie, Chica, and Foxy stood at rest, almost as if they were back on their stages. Their eyes were locked on Charlie, but they had halted their approach.

"It's the kids," Carlton whispered.

"Foxy wasn't attacking Jason," Marla gasped. "Foxy was trying to protect him."

John took hesitant steps toward the middle of the dining room, then approached more boldly, looking at each of the robots in turn. "It's the kids," he echoed. "All of them." Their faces were no longer animalistic, no longer lifeless, as if some spirit inhabited them.

Suddenly, there was a crash from the sealed exit door.

They all startled, turning as one as the wall beside the welded entrance shook with the force of a dozen blows.

Now what? Charlie thought.

The bricks broke and fell, scattering in pieces across the floor, dust filling the air in rusty clouds. A figure stepped through the hole wielding a massive sledgehammer, and as the air slowly cleared, they saw who it was: Clay Burke, Carlton's father.

His eyes set on Carlton, and he dropped the hammer and ran to his son, sweeping him into an embrace. Clay stroked his hair, gripping him like he would never let go. Charlie watched from her distance, relief touched by a stiletto edge of envy.

"Dad, I'm gonna puke," Carlton murmured. Clay laughed but leaned back when he saw that Carlton wasn't kidding. Carlton bent over, hands on his knees, fighting the urge to retch, and Clay's face took on alarm. Carlton straightened. "I'm good."

Clay was not listening anymore. He was looking around the room, at the animals. All of them were frozen in time, displaced.

"Okay, kids," Clay said, his voice low and his words careful. "I think it's time for us to go." He started toward the exit he had made.

They glanced at one another. The whispers were gone. Whatever he had been, the yellow Freddy was slouched again, an empty suit, though no one had seen it move. Charlie nodded toward Clay, and the rest started forward, heading almost reluctantly to the hole in the wall. Charlie hung back. John stayed beside her, but she gestured him forward, taking up the rear.

She had barely had time to take a step when something took hold of her throat.

Charlie tried to cry out, but her windpipe was being crushed. She was whipped around as if she weighed nothing, and she found herself face-to-face with the yellow rabbit. Dave's eyes were shining through, triumphant. He had his arm around her neck, squeezing her throat so tightly that she could scarcely breathe. He held her so close it was almost an embrace. She could smell the costume, stained fur and years of putrid sweat, blood, and cruelty.

He spoke, still staring at Charlie.

"You are staying."

"Absolutely not," Clay said, taking on the group's authority.

Dave dug his fingers deeper into Charlie's neck, and she made a strangled sound.

"I will kill this one, right here, while you watch, unless you do as I say," he said, and his voice was almost pleasant. Clay looked at him for a long moment, calculating, then nodded.

"Okay," he said, his voice calm. "We'll do as you say. What do you want?"

"Good," Dave said. He relaxed his grip on Charlie's neck, and she took a shaky breath. Clay began to move toward them, and the others followed. Charlie looked up at the man in the rabbit suit, and he met her gaze. *It was you. You killed Michael. You killed Sammy. You took them from me.* His eyes should have held something fierce and dangerous. They should have been windows to the rotten core inside. But they were only eyes, flat and empty.

Charlie plunged her hands into the gap beneath the costume's head. Dave drew back, but she held on.

"If you want to be one of them, then *be* one of them!" she shouted, and she tripped the spring locks. Dave's eyes widened, and then he screamed. Charlie jerked her hands free, barely evading the locks as they snapped open and plunged into his neck. She took a step back, watching as Dave crumpled to the ground, still screaming as the costume released. Part by part, the animatronic insides pierced his flesh, ripping up his organs, tearing through his body as if it were not even there. At some point he stopped screaming, but he still writhed on the floor for what felt like long minutes before he was still.

Charlie stared, breathing hard as if she had been running. The form on the ground seemed unreal. John was the first to move. He came beside her, but, still staring down, she waved him off before he could touch her. She could not bear it if he did.

Jessica gasped, and they all looked up. The animatronics were moving. The group drew back, huddling together, but none of the animals were looking at them. One by one they took hold of the broken body on the floor and began to drag it away toward the hall to Pirate's Cove. As they disappeared down the hallway, Charlie noticed that the yellow Freddy was gone.

"Let's go," she said quietly.

Clay Burke nodded, and they filed out of the restaurant for the last time.

CHAPTER THIRTEEN

The sun was rising as they emerged into the open air.

Clay put his arm around Carlton's shoulder, and for once Carlton didn't brush him away with a joke. Charlie nodded absently, blinking in the light. "Carlton and I are taking a drive to the ER," Clay continued. "Is there anyone else who needs a doctor?"

"I'm fine," Charlie said reflexively.

"Jason, do you need to go to the hospital?" Marla asked.

"No," he said.

"Let's see your leg," she insisted. The party stopped as Jason held his leg out for Clay to examine. Charlie felt an odd relief wash through her. A grown-up was in charge now. After a moment, Clay looked up at Jason with a serious face.

"I don't think we're going to have to cut it off," he said. "Not just yet." Jason smiled, and Clay turned to Marla. "I'll take care of him. It might leave a scar, but that'll just make him look tough."

Marla nodded and winked at Jason, who laughed.

"I need to change my clothes," Charlie said. It seemed like a petty thing to be worrying about, but her shirt and pants were wet with blood in some places, dry and stiff in others. It was beginning to itch.

"You're a mess," Carlton pointed out redundantly. "Will she get a ticket if she drives like that?"

"Charlie, are you sure you don't need to go to the hospital?" Marla said, turning her laser-like concern on her friend now that her brother had been declared safe.

"I'm fine," Charlie said again. "I just need to change my clothes. We'll stop at the motel."

When they reached the cars, they split into what had become their habitual groups: Marla, Jason, and Lamar in Marla's car; Charlie, John, and Jessica in Charlie's. Charlie opened the door to the driver's side and stopped, looking back at the building. It wasn't just her; out of the corner of her eye she could see them all gazing at it. The empty mall was dark against the pink-streaked sky, long and squat, like something brutish and slumbering. They all turned away, getting into the cars without speaking. Charlie kept her eyes on it, watching as she started her car, waiting to turn her back to it until the last possible moment. She pulled out of the lot and drove away.

Along the road, the cars split off. Clay and Carlton took the other turn out of the parking lot, heading to the hospital, and Charlie turned off toward the motel while Marla continued to the Burkes' house.

"I call first shower!" Jessica said as they got out of the car, then, seeing Charlie's face, "I'll make a special exception in your case. You go first."

Charlie nodded. In the room, she grabbed her bag and took it into the bathroom with her, leaving John and Jessica to wait. She locked the door behind her and undressed, deliberately not looking at the gashes on her arm and leg. She didn't need to see what was there, just to clean and bandage it. She got into the shower and let out a quiet yelp as the stinging water hit her open cuts, but she gritted her teeth and cleaned herself, washing her hair over and over until it was rinsed clean.

She got out and toweled herself dry, then sat down on the edge of the tub, put her face in her hands, and closed her eyes.

She was not ready to go out yet, not ready to face whatever aftermath, whatever discussion there might have to be.

She wanted to walk out of this bathroom and never speak again of what had happened. She rubbed her temples. She didn't have a headache, but there was pressure inside there, something that had yet to emerge.

You can't stay here forever.

Charlie still had the gauze and tape from the first time around, so she took it from her bag, wiped both wounds clean with a hotel towel, and bound up her arm and leg, using all the gauze. *I probably need stitches*, she thought, but it was only an idle thought. She would not do it. She got up and went to look in the mirror. There was a cut across her cheek; it had stopped bleeding, but it was ugly. She didn't know how she could cover it, but she didn't really want to, for the same reason she didn't want stitches. She *wanted* them to heal wrong, wanted them to scar. She wanted proof, displayed on her body: *This happened. This was real. This is what it did to me.*

She dressed quickly in her jeans and her last remaining clean T-shirt and emerged from the bathroom to find Jessica and John carrying suitcases out to the car.

"I figured there was no point leaving stuff here," Jessica said. "We're all going in the morning; we may as well bring it all to Carlton's." Charlie nodded and grabbed Jason's backpack, taking it out to the car along with her own.

★   ★   ★

Carlton and his father were already back by the time they arrived, and again they entered Carlton's living room, now almost familiar. Carlton was curled up in an armchair by the fireplace, where someone had lit a fire, and Marla and Lamar were on the couch. Jason sat right in front of the fireplace, staring in at the licking flames. Charlie sat down near him, arranging herself stiffly. John joined her, looking at her with concern, but she ignored him, and he said nothing.

"Are you okay?" Charlie asked, reaching up and rubbing Carlton's arm for a moment. He looked at her sleepily.

"Yeah, it's a mild concussion," he said. "I'll be fine as long as no one else tries to murder me."

"So . . . now what?" Jessica asked as she took the chair beside Carlton. "I mean—" She paused, searching for words. "What happens?" she said finally. They looked at each other; it was the question they all had. *What do you do after something like this?* Charlie looked at Clay, who was standing in the doorway, only half in the room.

"Mr.—Clay, what happens now?" she said quietly. He looked off into the distance for a minute before answering.

"Well, Charlie, I'm going to go back to Freddy's. I have to get my officer," he said gravely. "I won't go alone." He forced a smile, but no one joined him. "What do you think should happen?" he asked. He was looking at Charlie, asking her this impossible question as if she could answer it. She nodded, accepting responsibility.

"Nothing," she said. "It's over. I want to leave it that way."

Clay gave her a nod, his face impassive. She could not tell if it was the answer he was looking for, but it was all she had. The others were silent. Marla and Lamar were nodding, but Jessica looked like she wanted to protest.

"Jessica, what?" Charlie said gently, realizing with unease that her friend wanted her permission to disagree.

"It just seems wrong," she said. "What about . . . everything? I mean, people should know, right? That's how it works. That guard, he murdered all those kids, and people should know!"

"No one will believe us," Jason said without looking up.

"Officer Dunn," Jessica said. "Officer Dunn, he *died* in there! What will you tell his family? Will you tell them the truth?" She looked at Clay.

"Officer Dunn died at the hands of the same man who killed your friends. I can prove that now." A silence fell over the room. "It won't bring them back," Clay said softly. "But maybe it will give them some rest."

Clay turned his eyes to the fire, and a few minutes passed before he spoke again.

"You kids have been carrying Freddy's with you all these years. It's time you left it behind," he said. He was stern, but his commanding tone was reassuring. "I'm going to see to it that Officer Dunn is given a proper burial." He paused, collecting himself, as though what he said next required effort.

"Your friends, too." His brow furrowed. "I have a few favors to call in, but I can make this happen quietly. The last thing I want to do is disturb that place, or desecrate it. Those kids need rest."

The next morning they began to go their separate ways. Marla offered to drive Lamar and Jessica to the bus station, and they said their good-byes with hugs and promises to write. Charlie wondered if any of them meant it. Marla probably did, at least. They pulled out of the Burkes' driveway.

"So my bus isn't till later," John said as Marla's car disappeared around a bend in the road.

"I wouldn't mind a few more hours in Hurricane," Charlie answered. To her surprise, she realized it was true.

John flashed her a quick, almost nervous smile.

"Okay, then," he said.

"Let's get out of there. Let's go somewhere, anywhere."

When they were alone in the car, John gave her a sideways glance.

"So," he said, "are we ever going to see each other after this?" He tried to say it lightly, but there was no way to lighten it. Charlie stared straight ahead.

"Maybe," she said. She could not look at him. It wasn't the answer he wanted, she knew that, but she could not give him what he wanted. What could she say by way of explanation? *It's not you, it's the weight we both bear. It's too much. When you are here, I can't ignore it.*

But something in her thoughts felt off, not quite right, as if she were speaking by rote, thinking off a script. It was like flinching instinctively to protect an injury before remembering it had healed. She finally looked at John beside her. He was staring through the windshield, his jaw set.

"I have somewhere I need to go," she said abruptly, then made a slow U-turn. She had never gone to visit the place, but now, without warning, her mind was consumed by it. Aunt Jen had never suggested it; Charlie had never asked. She knew where it was, though, and now she headed there with a singular sense of purpose. *I need to see.*

Charlie pulled to a stop in a small gravel parking lot beside a low fence of short white posts, chains swinging between them.

"I just need a minute," she said. John gave her a concerned look.

"Are you sure you want to do this now?" he said softly. She did not answer, just got out of the car, closing the door behind her.

The graveyard before them was almost a hundred years old. There were hills of lush grass and shading trees. This corner was at the edge of the cemetery; there was a small house only a few yards past the edge of the fence. The grass was trimmed neatly, but it was patchy and yellowing. The trees had been pruned too far so the lower branches were bare, too exposed.

There was a telephone pole set just inside the fence, barely on the cemetery grounds, and beside it were two headstones, plain and small. Charlie stared at it for a long moment, not moving. She tried to conjure up the right feeling: grief and loss so that she could mourn. Instead, she just felt a numbness. The graves were there, but the sight did not touch her. She took a deep breath and started toward them.

It was such a small memory, one of those moments that meant nothing at the time, just one day in a series of days, the same as all the others. They were together, just the two of them, and it must have been before everything, before Fredbear's went wrong, before anyone was dead.

They were sitting out back behind Fredbear's, looking out over the hills, and a crow landed and began pecking in the dirt, looking for something. There was something about its sharp, darting movements that struck her as the funniest thing she had ever seen. Charlie began to laugh, and her father looked at her. She pointed, and he turned his head, trying to see as she did, but he could not tell what she was pointing at. She could not get it across to him, she did not know the words, and just as her excitement was about to turn to frustration, he saw it, too. Suddenly he laughed and pointed to the crow. Charlie nodded, and he met her eyes, looking at her with an expression of pure, boundless delight, as if it would fill him to bursting.

"Oh, Charlotte," he said.

About Scott Cawthon

Scott Cawthon is the author of the bestselling video game series Five Nights at Freddy's, and while he is a game designer by trade, he is first and foremost a storyteller at heart. He is a graduate of the Art Institute of Houston and lives in Texas with his wife and four sons.

About Kira Breed-Wrisley

Kira Breed-Wrisley has been writing stories since she could first pick up a pen and has no intention of stopping. She is the author of seven plays for Central New York teen theater company the Media Unit, and has developed several books with Kevin Anderson & Associates. She is a graduate of Cornell University and lives in Brooklyn, NY.

Five Nights at Freddy's

THE FOURTH CLOSET

by

SCOTT CAWTHON
KIRA BREED-WRISLEY

Scholastic Inc.
New York

Copyright © 2018 by Scott Cawthon. All rights reserved.

Photo of TV static: © Klikk/Dreamstime

Library of Congress Cataloging-in-Publication Data available

ISBN 978-1-338-13932-7

10 9 8 7 6   20 21 22

Printed in U.S.A.   40

First printing 2018

Book design by Rick DeMonico

"Charlie!" John clambered through the rubble toward the place where she'd been, choking on the dust of the explosion. The ruins shifted beneath his feet, and he stumbled over a block of concrete and caught himself just before falling, scraping his hands raw as he grabbed frantically at the broken surface. He reached it, the place where she'd been—he could feel her presence beneath him. He took hold of an immense block of concrete and hefted it with all his strength. He managed to tilt it from the pile and overturn it, where it fell with a thud, rattling the ground he stood on. Over his head, a steel beam creaked, wavering precariously.

"Charlie!" John cried her name again as he shoved another block of concrete away. "Charlie, I'm coming!" He was gasping for breath, moving the remains of the house with desperate, adrenaline-fueled strength, but the adrenaline was running thin. He set his jaw and pressed on. His palms slipped as he tried to lift the next block, and when he looked he realized, dazedly, that his hands left streaks of blood wherever they touched. He wiped his palms on his jeans and tried again. This time the broken concrete moved, and he balanced it on his thighs and took it three steps away, then dropped it on a pile of debris. It crashed down onto the rubble and shattered rock and glass beneath it, starting an avalanche of its own, and then, beneath the sounds of wreckage, he heard her whisper: ". . . John . . ."

"Charlie . . ." His heart stopped beating as he whispered back to her, and again the rubble moved under his feet. This time he fell, landing hard on his back, knocking the wind out of him. He struggled to inhale, his lungs useless, then haltingly he began to breathe. He sat up, light-headed, and saw what the collapse had revealed: He was in the little, hidden room in Charlie's childhood house. Before him was a plain, smooth metal wall. At the center was a door.

It was only an outline, without hinges or a handle, but he knew what it was because Charlie had known, when she stopped running in the midst of their escape, and pressed her cheek against the surface, calling to someone, or something, inside.

". . . John . . ." she whispered his name again, and the sound seemed to come from everywhere at once, bouncing off the walls of the room. John got to his feet and put his hands on the door; it was cool to the touch. He pressed his cheek to it, just as Charlie had, and it grew colder, like it was draining the warmth from his skin. John pulled back and rubbed the cold spot on his face, still watching the door as the shiny metal began to dull before his eyes. Its color paled *and then the door itself began to thin, its solidity vanishing until it looked like frosted glass, and John saw there was a shadow behind the glass, the figure of a person. The figure stepped closer, the door clarifying until he could almost see through it. He moved closer, mirroring the figure on the other side. It had a face, sleek and polished, its eyes like a statue's, sculpted, but unseeing. John peered through the door between them, his breath clouding the near-transparent barrier, then suddenly the eyes snapped open.*

The figure stood placidly before him, the eyes fixed on nothing. They were clouded, and unmoving—dead. Someone laughed, a frantic, mirthless sound that echoed in the small, sealed room, and John looked wildly around for the source. The laughter rose in pitch, growing louder and louder. John covered his ears with his hands as the piercing noise became unbearable. "CHARLIE!" he cried again.

John jerked awake, his heart racing: the laughter went on, following him out of the dream. Disoriented, his eyes darted around the room, then lit on the TV, where a clown's painted face filled the screen, caught in a convulsive fit of laughter. John sat up, rubbing his cheek where his watch had been pressing into it. He checked the time, then breathed a sigh of relief—he had just enough time to get to work. He sat back, taking a moment to catch his breath. On the TV screen, a local news anchor was holding a mic up for a man dressed as a circus clown, complete with a painted face, a red nose, and a rainbow-colored wig. Around his neck was a collar

3

that looked like it belonged in a Renaissance painting, and he was wearing a full yellow clown suit, with red pompoms for buttons.

"So, tell me," the anchor said brightly. "Did you already have this costume, or did you make it especially for the grand opening?"

John switched the TV off, and headed for the shower.

He'd been at it all day, but the noise was still unbearable: a rattling, clanging din punctuated by shouts and the intermittent, earthshaking clatter of jackhammers. John closed his eyes, trying to blot it out: the vibrations resounded in his chest, filling him up, and amid the noise the sound of desperate laughter suddenly rang in his ears. The figure from his dream came to him again, just out of sight, and he felt as though, if he just turned his head the right way, he could see the face behind the door . . .

"John!"

John turned: Luis was standing a foot away, giving him a puzzled stare. "I called your name three times," he said. John shrugged, gesturing at the chaos around them.

"Hey, some of the guys are going out after this; you coming?" Luis asked. John hesitated. "Come on, it'll be good for you—all you do is work and sleep." He laughed good-naturedly and slapped John on the shoulder.

"Right, good for me." John smiled back, then looked at the ground as the expression faded. "I just have so much going on right now." He tried to sound convincing.

"Right, lot's going on. Just let me know if you change your mind." He clapped John on the shoulder again and headed back to the forklift. John watched him stride away. It hadn't been the first time John had turned them down; not the second time or the third; and it occurred to him that eventually they would stop trying. That there'd be a moment when they would all just give up. Maybe that would be for the best.

"John!" another voice called.

Now what?

It was the foreman, shouting at him from the door of his standalone office, a trailer that had been brought onsite for the duration of the construction and sat precariously on a dirt ledge.

John trudged across the construction zone, ducking through a vinyl sheet in the trailer's doorway. Moments later he was standing across a folding table from the foreman, the plastic wood-textured paneling barely holding to the walls surrounding him.

"I've got a couple guys out there telling me you're distracted."

"I'm just focused on my job, that's all," John said, forcing a smile and trying to prevent his frustration from leaking out. Oliver smiled, unconvincingly.

"Focused," Oliver mimicked. John dropped the smile, startled. Oliver sighed. "Look, I gave you a chance because your cousin said you're a hard worker. I overlooked the fact that you walked off your last job and never came back. You know I took a risk on you?"

John swallowed. "Yes, sir, I know."

"Stop with the 'sir.' Just listen to me."

"Look, I do what I'm told. I don't understand the problem."

"Your reactions are slow; you look like you're daydreaming out there. You're not a team player."

"What?"

"This is an active construction zone. If you're in la-la land, or you're not thinking about the safety of the other men out there, someone's going to get hurt, or killed. I'm not saying you have to share secrets and braid one another's hair; I'm saying you have to be on the team. They have to trust that you're not going to let them down when it counts." John gave an understanding nod. "This is a good job, John. I think these are good guys out there, too. Work isn't easy to come by these days, and I need you to get your head in the game. Because next time I see it in the clouds . . . well, just don't put me in that position. Understand?"

"Yeah, I understand," John said numbly. He didn't move, standing on the shag brown carpet that came with the portable office as though waiting to be dismissed from detention.

"Okay. Get out." John went. The dressing-down had taken up the last few minutes of his workday; he helped Sergei put away some of the equipment, then headed to his car with a muttered good-bye.

"Hey!" Sergei called after him. John stopped. "Last call!"

"I . . ." John broke off, spotting Oliver out of the corner of his eye. "Maybe next time," he said.

Sergei pressed. "Come on, it's my excuse to avoid that new kid's place—my daughter's been begging to go there all week. Lucy's taking her, but robots creep me out."

John paused, and the world grew silent around him. "What place?" John said.

"So, you coming?" Sergei asked again.

John took a few steps backward, as if he'd come too close to a ledge. "Maybe another time," John said, and walked decidedly to his car. It was old and brownish-red, something that might have been cool in high school. Now it was just a reminder that he was still a kid who hadn't moved on, a mark of status that had become a mark of shame within the space of a year. He sat heavily, a plume of dust shooting out the sides of the car seat as he dropped onto it. His hands were shaking. "Get a grip." He closed his eyes, and clutched the wheel, steadying himself. "This is life now, and you can do it," he whispered, then opened his eyes and sighed. "Sounds like something lame my dad would have said." He turned the key.

The drive home should have been ten minutes; but the route he took was closer to half an hour, as it avoided driving through town. If he didn't drive through town, there was no risk of running into people he didn't want to talk to. More importantly, he didn't risk running into the people he did want to talk to. *Be a team player.* He couldn't muster real resentment toward Oliver. John wasn't a team player, not anymore. For almost six months, he had been coming and going from home to work like a train on a track, stopping to buy food now and then, but not much else. He spoke only when necessary; avoided eye contact. He was startled when people spoke to him, whether they were coworkers saying hello, or strangers asking the time. He made conversation, but he was getting better at speaking while walking away. He was always polite, while also making it clear he had somewhere to be—made obvious, when necessary, by suddenly turning in the opposite direction. Sometimes he felt like he was fading away, and it was jarring, and disappointing, to be reminded that he could still be seen.

He pulled into the lot of his apartment complex, a two-story building not really meant for long-term tenants. There was a light in the window of the manager's office: he had tried for a month to track the open hours, then given up, concluding that there was no pattern.

He grabbed an envelope from the glove compartment and headed toward the door. He knocked, and there was no response, though inside he could hear sounds of movement. He knocked again, and this time the door opened partially: an old woman with the skin of a lifelong smoker peered out at him. "Hey, Delia." John smiled; she didn't smile back. "Rent check." John handed an envelope to her. "I know it's late. I came by yesterday, but no one was here."

"Was it during business hours?" Delia peered into the envelope carefully as though suspicious of what might be inside.

"The lights were off, so . . ."

"Then it wasn't during business hours." Delia bared her teeth, but it wasn't really a smile. "I saw you hung up a plant," she said abruptly.

"Oh yeah." John peered over his shoulder toward his apartment, as though he might be able to see it from where they stood. "It's nice to take care of something, right?" John tried to smile again but quickly gave up, engulfed in a vacuum of judgment that allowed for no levity. "That's allowed, right? To have a plant?"

"Yes, you can have a plant." Delia took a step back inside and looked poised to close the door. "People don't usually settle in here, that's all. Usually there is a house, then a wife, and then the plant."

"Right." John looked down at his shoes. "It's just been a rough"—he began, but the door closed with a firm *thunk*—"year."

John considered the door for a minute, then headed to the ground-floor apartment at the front of the complex, now his for another month. It was a single-bedroom unit with a full bath and half a kitchen. He kept the blinds up while he was away, to show that he had nothing: the area was prone to burglaries, and it seemed like a safe bet to telegraph the fact that there was nothing to steal here.

Once inside, John locked the door behind him and carefully slid the chain into place. His apartment was cool and dark, and quiet. He sighed and rubbed his temples; the headache was still there, but he was growing accustomed to that.

The place was sparsely furnished—it had come that way—and the only personal touch he had added to the living room was to stack four cardboard boxes full of books against the wall below the window. He glanced at them with a disappointed familiarity. He went to the bedroom and sat down on his bed, the springs creaking stiffly beneath him. He didn't bother turning on the light; there was enough daylight still leaking through the small dingy window above his bed.

John looked toward his dresser, where a familiar face looked back at him: a toy rabbit's head, its body nowhere to be found.

"What did you do today?" John said, meeting the plush rabbit's eyes as if it might show a spark of recognition. Theodore just stared back blankly, his eyes dark and lifeless. "You look terrible; worse than me." John stood and approached the rabbit's head; he couldn't ignore the smell of mothballs and dirty fabric. John's smile faded, and he grabbed the head by the ears and held it in the air. *Time to throw you away.* He considered it almost every day. He clenched his jaw, then set it back on the dresser carefully and turned away, not wanting to look at it further.

He closed his eyes, not expecting sleep to come, but hoping. He hadn't slept well the night before, or the night before that. He had come to dread sleep; he put it off as long as he could, walking miles of road until late at night, returning home and trying to read, or just staring at the wall. The familiarity was frustrating. He grabbed his pillow and went back to the living room. He lay down on the couch, swinging his legs over the arm so he could fit. The silence in the little apartment was beginning to ring in his ears, and he grabbed the remote off the floor and turned on the TV. The screen was black and white, and the reception was terrible: he could scarcely make out faces through the static, but the chatter of what sounded like a talk show was rapid and cheerful. He turned the volume low and settled back, staring at the ceiling and half listening to the television voices until slowly, he drifted into sleep.

Her arm was limp, the only part of her he could see dangling from the twisted metal suit. Blood ran in red rivers down her skin, pooling on the ground. Charlie was all alone. He could hear her voice again if he tried: "Don't let go! John!" *She called my name. And then that thing—He shuddered, hearing again the sound of the animatronic suit snapping and crunching. He stared at Charlie's lifeless arm as if the world around them had disappeared, and as the noise echoed in his head, his mind conjured up thoughts unbidden: The crunching sounds were her bones. The tearing was everything else.*

John opened his eyes with a start. A few feet away, a studio audience laughed, and he looked at the TV, its static and chatter bringing him back to waking life.

John sat up, rolling his neck to work out kinks: the couch was too small, and his back was cramped. His head ached, and he was exhausted but restless, the shot of adrenaline still working its way through his system. He went out, locking the door forcefully behind him, and breathed in the night air.

He started down the road, heading toward town and whatever might still be open. The lights on the road were far apart, and there was no sidewalk, just a shallow dirt shoulder. Few cars passed him, but when they did, they loomed up from around corners or cresting hills, blinding him with headlights and rushing by with a force that sometimes threatened to knock him back. He had begun to notice himself edging ever closer to the road as he walked, playing a halfhearted game of chicken. When he found himself too far out, he would always take deliberate steps back to the shoulder, and it was always with a secret, sinking disappointment in himself that he would do so.

As he approached town, lights pierced the darkness once again, and he shielded his eyes and took a step back from the road. This one slowed as it passed, then came to a sudden stop. John turned and walked a few steps toward it as the driver's window rolled down.

"John?" someone called. The car went into reverse and haphazardly pulled onto the shoulder; John jumped out of its path. A woman stepped out and took a few quick steps toward him, as if she might try to hug him, but he stayed planted where he was, his arms stiff at his sides, and she stopped a few feet away. "John, it's me!" Jessica said with a smile that quickly faded. "What are you doing out here?" she asked. She was wearing short sleeves, and she rubbed her arms against the night air, glancing back and forth along the near-deserted road.

"Well, I could ask you the same thing," he answered as though she had accused him of something. Jessica pointed over John's shoulder. "Gas." She smiled brightly at him, and he couldn't help but mirror her a little. He had almost forgotten this ability of hers, to turn on cheerful goodwill like a faucet, splashing it all over everyone. "How have you been?" she asked cautiously.

"Fine. Working, mostly." He gestured down at the dusty work clothes he hadn't bothered to change out of. "What's new with you?" he asked, suddenly aware of the absurdity of the conversation as cars passed nearby. "I really have to be going. Have a good night." He turned and began to walk away without giving her a chance to speak.

"I miss seeing you around," Jessica called. "And so does she."

John paused, digging at the dirt with one foot.

"Listen." Jessica took a few quick steps to catch up to him. "Carlton's going to be in town for a couple of weeks; it's spring break. We're all getting together." She waited expectantly, but he didn't respond.

"He's dying to show off his new cosmopolitan persona," Jessica added brightly. "When I talked to him on the phone last week, he was faking a Brooklyn accent to see if I'd notice." She forced a giggle. John smiled fleetingly.

"Who else is going to be there?" he asked, looking directly at her for the first time since she got out of the car. Jessica's eyes narrowed.

"John, you have to talk to her sometime."

"Why is that?" he said brusquely, and started walking again.

"John, wait!" Behind him, John heard her break into a run. She caught up quickly, slowing to jog beside him, matching his pace. "I can do this all day," she warned, but John didn't answer.

"You have to talk to her," Jessica repeated. He gave her a sharp look.

"Charlie's dead," he said harshly, the words rasping in his throat. It had been a long time since he spoke the words aloud. Jessica stopped in her tracks; he kept going.

"John, at least talk to *me*."

He didn't answer.

"You're *hurting* her," she added. He stopped walking. "Don't you understand what you're doing to her? After what she went through? It's insane, John. I don't know what that night did to you, but I know what it did to Charlie. And you know what? I don't think anything hurt as badly as having you refuse to speak to her. To say she's *dead*."

"I saw her die." John stared out into the city lights.

"No, you didn't," Jessica said, then hesitated. "Look, I'm worried about you."

"I'm just lost." John turned to her. "And after what I've been through, after what *we've* been through, that's not an unreasonable reaction." He waited a moment for her to respond, then looked away.

"I get it. I really do. I thought she was dead, too." John opened his mouth to speak, but she pressed on. "I *thought* she was dead until she turned up, *alive*." Jessica pulled at John's shoulder until he met her eyes again. "I've seen her," Jessica said, her voice breaking. "I've talked to her. It *is* her. And this . . ." She let go of his shoulder and waved her hand over him as though casting a spell. "*This* thing that you're doing, that's what's killing her."

"It's not her," John whispered.

"Okay," Jessica snapped, and turned on her heel. She walked back to the car and after a few moments, pulled back out into the road, then made a screeching U-turn. John stayed where he was. Jessica roared past him, then stopped abruptly, her breaks squealing, then backed up to where he stood. "We're meeting at Clay's house on Saturday," she said tiredly. "Please." He looked at her; she wasn't crying, but her eyes were shiny, her face red. He nodded.

"Maybe."

"Good enough for me. I'll see you there!" Jessica said, then she drove off without another word, the engine roaring in the quiet of the night.

"I said maybe," John muttered into the darkness.

CHAPTER TWO

The pencil squeaked against the paper as the man at the desk carefully filled out the form in front of him. He paused suddenly, a wave of dizziness overtaking him. The letters on the page were fuzzy, and he adjusted his reading glasses, his head swimming. The glasses made no difference, and he took them off and rubbed his eyes. Then, just as suddenly as it had come, the sensation was gone: the room righted itself, and the words on the page were perfectly clear. He scratched his beard, still disconcerted, then began to steadily write again. A ring sounded and the front door opened.

"Yes, sir?" he barked without looking up.

"I wanted to have a look around the yard." A woman's voice echoed softly.

"Oh, pardon me, ma'am." The man looked up and smiled momentarily, then went back to his form, writing as he talked. "Scrap is fifty cents a pound. It might be more if you find a specific part, but we can see when you come back in. Just go have a look around; you have to bring your own tools, but we can help you load it up when you're ready to leave."

"I'm looking for something specific." The woman peered down at him, observing his name tag. "Bob," she added belatedly.

"Well, I don't know what to tell you." He set his pencil down, then reclined and crossed his arms behind his head. "It's a dump." He laughed. "We try to at least separate the junk cars from the tin cans, but what you see is what you get."

"Bob, you received several truckloads of scrap metal on this date, and from this location." The woman set a piece of paper down on top of the form Bob had been working on. Bob picked it up and adjusted his reading glasses, then looked up at her over them.

"Well, as I said; it's a dump," he said slowly, growing more concerned as the moments passed. "I might be able to point you in the right direction; I mean, we don't catalog the stuff."

The woman walked around the side of the desk, stepping up beside Bob's chair, and he straightened nervously in his seat. "I hear you boys had some trouble here last night," she said casually.

"No trouble." Bob furrowed his brow. "Some kids snuck in; it happens."

"That's not what I heard." The woman studied a picture on the wall. "Your daughters?" She asked lightly.

"Yes, two and five."

"They are beautiful." She paused. "Do you treat them well?" Bob was taken aback.

"Of course, I do," he said, trying to hide his indignation. There was a long pause; the woman tilted her head, still looking at the picture.

"I heard you called the police because you thought someone was trapped in the scrap heaps out there," she said. Bob didn't answer. "I heard"—the woman continued, leaning in closer to the picture—"that you thought you heard screaming, and sounds of distress and panic. Something was trapped; a child was trapped, you thought. Maybe several."

"Look, we run a clean business and we have a good reputation."

"I'm not disputing your reputation. Quite the opposite. I think what you did was honorable, running to the rescue in the middle of the night, cutting your legs on jagged scraps of metal as you ran blindly through the yard."

"How do you . . ." Bob's voice trembled, and he stopped talking. He moved his legs under the desk, hoping to hide the bandages that bulged out visibly under both pant legs.

"What did you find?" the woman asked.

19

He didn't answer.

"What was there?" she pressed. "When you got on your hands and knees and crawled through the beams and the wire? What was there?"

"Nothing," he whispered. "Nothing was there."

"And the police? They found nothing?"

"No, nothing. There wasn't anything. I went out again today just to be . . ." He spread his hands on the desk in front of him, collecting his nerves. "We run a good business," he said firmly. "I don't feel comfortable talking about this. If I'm in some kind of trouble, then I think—"

"You're not in any trouble, Bob, as long as you can do me one little favor."

"What's that?"

"Simple." The woman leaned over Bob, bracing herself on the arms of his chair, so close her face almost touched his. "Take me there."

John pulled into the parking lot at the construction site and immediately saw Oliver standing in front of the gate of the chain-link fence. His arms were crossed, and he was chewing on something, his face grim. When it became clear that he wasn't going to move out of the way, John slowed to a stop and got out.

"What's going on?" he asked. Oliver continued to chew on whatever was in his mouth.

"I have to let you go," he said at last. "You're late, again."

"I'm not late," John protested, then glanced at his watch. "I mean, not by much," he amended. "Come on, Oliver. It won't happen again, I'm sorry."

"Me too," Oliver said. "Good luck, John."

"Oliver!" John called. Oliver let himself in through the gate and glanced back one more time before walking away. John leaned against his car for a moment. Several coworkers were staring at him, suddenly turning away as John noticed them. John got in his car and headed back the way he had come.

When he returned to his apartment, John sat down on the edge of his bed and buried his face in his hands. "Now what?" he wondered aloud, and glanced around the room. His eyes lit on his only decoration. "You still look terrible," he said to Theodore's disembodied head. "And you're still in worse shape than me." The notion of attending the party that night suddenly returned to him. The thought of it set off a nervous fluttering in his stomach, but he wasn't sure what it was— anxiety, or excitement. *I thought she was dead, too,* Jessica had said the night before. *I've seen her. I've talked to her. It is her.*

John closed his eyes. *What if it is her?* He saw it again, the moment he always saw: the shuddering suit, Charlie trapped inside as it crunched and jerked—and then her hand, and the blood. *She couldn't have survived that.* But another image came to mind, unbidden—Dave, who became Springtrap: he had survived what happened to Charlie. He had worn the yellow rabbit suit like it was a second skin, and had paid for it twice: the scars that covered his torso like a shirt of gruesome lace told the story of one narrow escape, and the second . . . Charlie had killed him when she tripped the spring locks, or so they all believed. No one could have survived what they saw. And yet, he had returned. For an instant, John pictured Charlie, scarred and broken, yet, miraculously, alive. "But that doesn't sound like the person Jessica saw," John spoke clearly to Theodore. "Someone broken and scarred; that's not who Jessica was describing." He shook his head. "That's not the person I saw at the diner."

The next day—she looked like she'd just stepped out of a fairy tale. John caught himself and shook his head, trying to focus on the present. He really didn't know what had happened to Charlie. He felt himself edging toward the glimmer of hope. *Maybe I was wrong. Maybe she's all right.* It was what he'd wished for—what anyone wishes for in the throes of grief: *Let it not have happened. Let everything be all right.* The precarious ledge became solid ground, and John felt a weight lifted, his neck and shoulders relaxing from a cramped position he had not been aware of. The fatigue from so many months of misspent sleep caught up to him all at once.

He looked at Theodore; he was clutching the rabbit's head so tightly that his knuckles had gone white. He slowly released the toy, propping it up on the pillow.

"I'm not going," he said. "I was never really considering it, I just wanted Jessica to leave me alone." He held his breath for a moment, then let out a deep sigh. "Right?" He said, his tone becoming more agitated. "What would I even say to these people?" Theodore stared at him blankly.

"Damn." John sighed.

The fluttering in John's stomach grew worse the closer he came to Clay's house. He checked the dashboard clock—it was only six. *Maybe no one will be there yet*, he thought, but as he made his way down the winding road toward their house, cars lined both sides of the street for half a block. John wedged his car between a pickup truck and a rusted sedan almost as beat-up as his own, then got out and headed toward the house.

All the windows of the three-story house were illuminated, standing out against the trees like a beacon. John hung back, staying out of the light. He could hear music from inside, and laughter; the sound of it made him balk. He forced himself to walk the rest of the way to the door, but stopped again when he reached it: Going inside felt like an enormous decision, something that would change everything. Then again, so did walking away.

He raised his hand to ring the bell, then hesitated; before he could decide, the door swung open in front of him. John blinked at the sudden light and found himself face-to-face with Clay Burke, who looked as startled as he was.

"John!" Clay reached out and gripped John with both arms, pulled him in and gave him a hug, then quickly pushed him back to where he started and firmly patted his shoulders. "Right, come in!" Clay stepped back to clear the way, and John followed him in, looking around the room cautiously. The last time he was here, the whole house had been a wreck, strewn with signs of a man falling to pieces. Now, the piles of laundry and evidence files were gone; the couches and the floor were clean, and Clay himself was beaming with a genuine smile. He caught John's eye, and his grin faded.

"A lot has changed." He smiled as though reading John's mind.

"Is Betty—" John broke off too late. He shook his head. "Sorry, I didn't mean to—"

"No, she's still gone," Clay said evenly. "I wish she'd come back; maybe she will someday, but life goes on," he added with a brief smile. John nodded, uncertain what to say.

"John!" Marla waved from the stairs, and immediately came bounding down with her usual eagerness, wrapping him in a hug before he could so much as say hello. Jessica appeared, coming in from the kitchen.

"Hey, John," Jessica said more calmly, but with a glowing smile.

"I'm so glad to see you again, it's been a long time," Marla said, releasing him at last.

"Yeah," he said. "Too long." He tried to think of something else to say, and Marla and Jessica exchanged a glance. Jessica opened her mouth, about to speak, but was interrupted as Carlton ran excitedly down the staircase.

"Carlton!" John called with his first genuine smile of the evening. Carlton raised his hand in an answering wave, and came to join the group.

"Hey," he said.

"Hey," John echoed as Carlton tousled John's hair.

"What, are you my granddad now?" John made a half-hearted effort to straighten his hair while searching the crowd with his eyes.

"I'm surprised you came." Marla slapped him across the shoulder.

"I mean of course you were going to come!" Carlton corrected. "I just know you've been busy! Too many girlfriends, am I right?"

"How's New York?" John asked, fishing for something to talk about as he straightened his clothes.

"Great! College, city—learning—friends. I was in a play about a horse. It's great." He bobbed his head in a rapid nod. "Marla's in school, too."

"In Ohio," Marla jumped in. "I'm premed."

"That's great." John grinned.

"Yeah, it's been a lot of hard work but it's worth it," she said cheerfully, and John began to relax, falling back into the familiar pattern of their friendships. Marla was still Marla; Carlton was still inscrutable.

"Is Lamar around?" Carlton asked, looking from face to face. Marla shook her head.

"I called him when . . . a few months ago," she said. "He's on track to graduate early."

"But he's not coming?" Carlton persisted. Marla smiled slightly.

"He said, 'I'm never, ever, ever setting foot in that town again, not ever, never for as long as I live, and you shouldn't, either.' But he said we're all welcome to visit him."

"In New Jersey?" Carlton made a skeptical face, then turned his attention to Jessica. "Jessica, what's up with you these days, anyway? I heard you've got the dorm room to yourself now."

John stiffened, suddenly aware of what Carlton was really asking; the lights seemed blinding, the noise louder. Jessica glanced at John, but he didn't acknowledge her.

"Yeah," she said, turning back to the others. "I don't know what happened, but I came home one day right after . . . about six months ago, and, she was packing what she could carry. She left me and John to clean up the rest. If we hadn't happened to walk in, I don't think she was even going to tell me she was leaving."

"Did she say where she was going?" Marla asked, her brow furrowing. Jessica shook her head.

"She hugged me and said she'd miss me, but all she'd say was she had to leave. She wouldn't tell me where."

"Well, we can always ask her," Carlton said. John looked at him, startled.

"You've seen her?"

Carlton shook his head. "Not yet, my plane just got in today, but she'll be here tonight. Jessica says she looks good."

"Right," John said. They all looked at him as if they could see what he was thinking: *She looks good, but she doesn't look like Charlie.*

"John, come help me in the kitchen!" Clay called, and John broke away from the group relieved, but also fully aware he couldn't possibly provide any help in the kitchen.

"What's up?" he asked. Clay leaned back against the sink and looked him up and down. "Need me to open the ketchup bottle?" John asked, growing nervous. "High shelf?"

Clay sighed. "I just want to make sure you're all right out there."

"What do you mean?"

"I thought you might be nervous; I know it's been a while since you and Charlie talked."

27

"It's been a while since you and I have talked, too," John said, unable to keep the edge out of his voice.

"Well, that's different, and you know it," Clay said drily. "I thought you might need a pep talk."

"A pep talk?" John retorted.

Clay shrugged. "Well, do you?" Clay stared at him firmly, but with kindness in his eyes, and John's nerves calmed.

"Jessica told you?" he asked, and Clay tilted his head to the side.

"Some. Probably not all. Here." Clay opened the refrigerator door he had been leaning against and handed John a soda. "Try to relax, you're here with friends. Those people out there love you." Clay smiled.

"I know," John said, setting the can on the countertop next to him. He eyed it for a second but did not pick it up, feeling like if he drank it, he would be giving in, accepting everything he was told. It would be like taking whatever pill everyone else had already swallowed.

John eyed the back door.

"Don't even think about it," Clay said abruptly. John didn't try to pretend it wasn't what he was thinking. Clay sighed. "I know how hard this must be for you."

"Do you?" John responded sharply, but Clay's expression didn't change.

"Stay and talk to her. I think you owe that to her, and to yourself."

John's eyes were still fixed on the door.

"All of this heartache that you're putting yourself through; that can't be what you want." Clay leaned to the side, interrupting John's gaze.

"You're right," John said. He stood up straight and met Clay's eyes. "This isn't what I want." He went to the back door and pushed it open, rushing down the concrete steps as though Clay might pursue him, then walking around the side of the house toward his car, his heart pounding. He felt a little light-headed, and completely unsure he was making the right decision.

"John!" someone called from behind him. The familiar voice sent a jolt through him, and he stopped, closing his eyes for a second.

He heard her heels tapping on the stone walk, the sound vanishing as she crossed the grass to him. He opened his eyes and turned toward the voice; she was standing a few feet from him.

"Thanks for stopping," Charlie said. Her face was anxious, her arms wrapped tightly across her body like she was cold, despite the mild weather.

"I was just going to get my jacket," John said, trying to sound casual in the midst of an obvious lie. He looked her up and down, and she didn't move, like she knew what he was doing, and why. *It's not her.* She looked like some stunning cousin of Charlie's, maybe, but not her. Not the round-faced, frizzy-haired, awkward girl he had known almost all his life. She was taller, thinner, her hair longer, darker. Her face was uncannily different, though he could not have explained how. Her posture, even as she stood hugging herself in anxiety, was somehow elegant. As he looked at her, the first shock of recognition gave way to an acute revulsion; he took an involuntary step back. *How can anyone think that's her?* he thought. *How can anyone think that's* my *Charlie?*

She bit her lip. "John, say something," she said, pleading in her voice. He shrugged, holding both hands up in resignation.

"I don't know what to say," he admitted.

She nodded. She uncrossed her arms as if she had just realized she was holding them that way, and began to pick at her nails instead. "I'm so happy to see you," she said, sounding like she was about to cry. John softened, but tamped the feeling down.

"Me too," he said in a monotone.

"I missed you," she began, searching his face for something. John had no idea what he might look like, but he felt like stone. "I, uh, I had to get away for a while," she went on uncertainly. "That night, John, I thought I was going to die."

"I thought you did," he said, trying to swallow the lump rising in his throat.

She hesitated.

"You don't think I'm me?" she asked softly at last.

He looked down at his feet for a moment, unable to say the words to her face.

"Jessica told me. It's okay, John," she said. "I just want you to know that it's okay." Her eyes were bright with tears. His heart lurched, and in an instant, the world came into a different focus.

He gazed at the woman huddled in front of him trying to suppress her sobs. The stark differences he saw in her were suddenly things that seemed so easily explained. Her shoes had heels, so she was taller. She was wearing a form-fitting dress, instead of her usual jeans and T-shirt, so she appeared thinner. She was wearing elegant clothing, and her gestures were confident, sophisticated, but it was all no more than if Jessica had given her the makeover she was always threatening. No more than if Charlie had just grown up.

We've all had to grow up.

John thought of the way he drove home from work—or, had until this morning—the way he avoided ever driving past her house, or the site of Freddy Fazbear's. Maybe Charlie had things she wanted to avoid. Maybe she just wanted to be different.

Maybe she wanted to change, like you did. When you think of that moment, what it did to you—what must it have done to her? What kind of nightmares do you have, Charlie? He was seized by a sudden, visceral desire to ask her, and for the first time he allowed himself to meet her eyes. His stomach jolted as he did, his heart racing. Tentatively, she smiled at him, and he smiled back, unconsciously mirroring her, but something frigid twitched inside him. *Those aren't her eyes.*

John shifted his gaze, a calm coming over him; Charlie looked momentarily confused. "Charlie," John said carefully. "Do you remember the last thing I said to you, before you—were trapped in the suit?" She held his gaze for a moment, then shook her head.

"I'm sorry, John," she said. "I don't remember a lot about that night, whole pieces are just—missing. I remember being in the suit—I passed out, I think for hours."

"So, you don't remember?" he repeated gravely. It seemed impossible that she could have forgotten. *Maybe she didn't hear me.*

"Were you hurt?" he asked brusquely.

She nodded silently, her eyes filling again with tears, and she hugged herself; this time she didn't look cold, she looked like she was in pain. Maybe she was. John took a step closer to her, wanting suddenly, desperately, to promise her that everything would be all right. But then her eyes met his again, and he stopped, stepped back. She extended a hand, but he didn't take it, and again she crossed her arms over her body.

"John, would you meet me tomorrow?" she asked steadily.

"Why?" he said before he could stop himself, but she did not react.

"I just want to talk. Give me a chance." Her voice rose shakily, and he nodded.

"Sure. Yeah, I'll meet you tomorrow." He paused. "That same place, okay?" he added carefully, waiting to see how she would reply.

"The Italian place? Our first date?" she said easily and gave a gentle smile; her tears seemed to have stopped. "Around six?"

John let out a deep breath. "Yeah." He met her gaze again and did not look away, letting himself take rest in her eyes for the first time that night. She looked back at him, motionless, like she was afraid she might scare him away. John nodded, then turned and left without another word. He walked quickly back to his car, struggling to keep his pace even. He felt like he had done something wonderful, and also like he had made a horrible mistake. He felt strange, riding an adrenaline rush, and as he drove through the dark he pictured her face again.

Those weren't her eyes.

Charlie watched him go, rooted to the spot as if it were the only place she'd ever stood. *He doesn't believe me.* Jessica had not wanted to tell her about John's strange yet adamant conviction, but his refusal to speak to her now, his unwillingness even to acknowledge her presence that day in the diner was too bizarre to be dismissed. *How can he think I'm not me?*

The taillights of John's car vanished around a bend. Charlie stared into the dark where he had been, not wanting to return to the bright, noisy house. Carlton would tell her a joke; Jessica and Marla would comfort her the way they had in the diner that day, when she had come to show them that somehow, impossibly, she had survived. The walk from her car—really Aunt Jen's borrowed car—toward the diner had felt like miles that day, her stomach fluttering anxiously even though she knew, of course, that they would be happy to see her. How could they not be? Every step was stiff, uncertain; every time she moved it hurt, her body sore all over from the day before, though there were no marks on her to show it. Even breathing was strained and unfamiliar, and she had a persistent feeling that if she forgot to do it, she would stop, die of asphyxiation right there on the pavement, unless she was reminded, *take a breath*. She could see them through the window as she made her way to the front of the diner, her heart racing, and then they saw her and it was everything she had dared to hope: Marla and Jessica ran to the door, jostling over who would hug her first, crying at the sight of her living face. She let herself be wrapped in the warmth of their relief, but before they even let her go, she was looking for John.

When she saw him, his back to the door, she almost called out his name, but something stopped her. He said something she could not hear, and she watched, incredulous, as he failed to come to her, clenching a spoon in his hand like a weapon. "John!" she called at last. But he did not turn around. Marla and Jessica ushered her out of the restaurant, making reassuring sounds that must have been words, and Charlie strained to see him through the window: he had not moved. *How can he pretend I'm not here?*

A shock of pain hit her suddenly, yanking her back to the present, and Charlie hugged herself tightly, though it didn't really help: it was everywhere, sharp and hot. She clenched her jaw, unwilling to make a sound. Sometimes it eased to an ache she could push to the back of her awareness; sometimes it vanished for days at a time, but always it came back.

Were you hurt? John had asked, the first—the only—sign he'd given that he might still care, and she had been unable to reply. *Yes*, she could have said. *Yes, I was and I still am. Sometimes I think I'll die of it, and what I feel now is just an echo of what it used to be. It feels like all my bones are broken; it feels like my guts are twisted and torn; it feels like my head has cracked open, and things are leaking out, and it happens again and again.* She clenched her teeth, taking deliberate breaths, until it began slowly to recede.

"Charlie? Are you okay?" Jessica said quietly, appearing beside her on the sidewalk outside Clay's house. Charlie nodded.

"I didn't hear you come over," she said hoarsely.

"He doesn't mean to hurt you. He's just—"

"Traumatized," Charlie snapped. "I know." Jessica sighed, and Charlie shook her head. "Sorry, I didn't mean to be rude."

"I know," Jessica said. Charlie sighed, closing her eyes. *He's not the one who died—and it did feel like dying.* She could only remember that crucial night in fragments: her thoughts were all scraps and whispers, hazy and muddled, everything circling slowly around a central point: the single unmistakable snapping sound of the spring locks. Charlie shivered, and felt Jessica's hand touch her shoulder. She opened her eyes, looking helplessly at her friend.

"I think he just needs time," Jessica said gently.

"How much time can he need?" Charlie asked, and the words sounded like stone.

CHAPTER THREE

I t's ready." A soft voice rang out in the dark.

"I'll tell you when it's ready," said the man slumped in the corner, studying a monitor intently. "Raise it a few more degrees," he whispered.

"You've said before that might be too much," she said from the opposite corner, leaning over a table. The light shimmered off her contours as she carefully examined what lay before her.

"Do it," the slumped man said. The woman touched a dial, then recoiled suddenly.

"What is it?" he demanded. He didn't take his eyes off the monitor. "Raise it two more degrees," he ordered, his voice rising. For a moment, the room was silent. Finally, the man turned toward the table. "Is there a problem?"

"I think it's . . ." The woman trailed off.

"What?"

"Moving," she finished.

"Of course it is. Of course, *they* are."

"It looks like it's . . . in pain?" she whispered. The man smiled.

"Yes."

A bright light flashed on abruptly as a sudden noise resounded from the center of the room. Red, green, and blue lights flashed in sequence and a cheerful voice erupted from the speakers embedded in the walls, filling the room with song.

Every light shone down on him: the sleek white-and-purple bear. His joints clicked with every pivot; his eyes jolted back and forth randomly. He stood about six feet high; his rosy cheeks like two balls of bright cotton candy, and he wielded a microphone with a head like a shimmering disco ball.

"Shut that thing off!" the slouched man shouted, getting to his feet with obvious difficulty. He moved slowly toward the center of the room, leaning heavily on his cane. "Get back, I'll do it myself!" he screamed as the woman retreated to the table in the corner. The man pried a white plastic plate off the chest of the singing bear, and reached inside the cavity, extending his arm all the way into the opening and pulling at whatever he could find. As he disconnected the wires inside, first the eyes stopped turning, then the eyelids stopped clapping shut, then the mouth stopped singing and the head stopped turning. Finally, with one last jostle, the eyelids clamped shut and the head dropped to the side lifelessly. The man stepped back, and the heavy plate of the bear's chest cavity swung shut with a clang, as the animatronic bear filled with the sounds of servos and wheels, broken and disconnected, unable to move or function. Spurts of air burst from between the seams of his body casing as the air hoses misfired.

The sound came to a stop, the echoes from it lingering for a moment before dying away. The man turned his attention back to the table and lurched to it. He looked down, studying the writhing figure that lay there for a moment. The table's surface was glowing orange, and the hot metal hissed. He took a syringe from the woman's hand and thrust it into the squirming thing forcefully. He drew the plunger up, holding the needle steady as the syringe filled with molten substance, then finally pulled away with a jolt. He staggered back toward the bear.

"Now, let us put you to greater purpose," he said to the glowing syringe. The man again pried open the heavy chest plate of the standing, broken bear, then carefully inserted the syringe he held directly into the chest cavity and began to press the plunger down. The cavity snapped shut, too heavy for the frail man to hold open, and he fell backward clutching his arm. The syringe clattered to the ground, still nearly full. The woman rushed to kneel by his side, feeling his arm for breaks. "I'm fine," he grumbled, and glanced up at the still motionless bear. "It needs to be heated more." The hissing sound continued as the figure turned on the table, pushing off plumes of steam as it rolled on the hot surface.

"We can't heat it more," the woman said. "You'll destroy them."

The man looked up at her with a warm smile, then jerked his eyes back to the bear: he was now looking down at them, his eyes open wide and tracking their subtlest movements. "Their lives will now have a greater purpose," the man said contentedly. "They will become *more*, just like you did." He looked up at the woman kneeling over him, and she looked back, her glossy painted cheeks gleaming in the light.

John let himself into his apartment and locked the deadbolt behind him, sliding the chain into place for the first time since he moved in. He went to the window and fiddled with the blinds, then stopped, pushing back the impulse to close them and seal himself away completely from the outside world. On the other side of the glass, the parking lot was still and silent, cast in the eerie light of a single streetlamp and the blue neon sign of a nearby car dealership. There was an unfamiliar whirring sound coming from somewhere, and John watched the parking lot for a moment, not sure what he was expecting to see. The sound was gone soon after anyway, and he went into the bathroom to splash water on his face. When he came back into his bedroom, he froze: it was the sound again, this time louder—it was in the room with him.

John held his breath, straining to listen. It was a quiet noise, the sound of something moving, but it was too regular, too mechanical to be a mouse. He flipped on the light: the noise continued, and he slowly turned, trying to hear where it was coming from, and found himself looking at Theodore.

"Is that you?" he asked. He stepped closer and picked up the disembodied rabbit's head. He held it to his ear, listening to the strange sound emanating from inside the stuffed creature. There was a sudden click, and the sound stopped. John waited, but the toy was silent. He put Theodore back down on the dresser and waited for a moment to see if the sound would begin again.

"I'm not crazy." John said to the rabbit. "And I won't let you, or anyone else, convince me that I am." He went to his bed, reaching under the mattress with a suspicious glance at the toy rabbit, suddenly feeling watched. He took out the notebook he had hidden there, and sat back on the bed, looking at its black-and-white cover. It was a plain composition notebook, the kind with a little place on the front for your name and class subject. John had left that blank, and now he traced the empty lines with his finger, not really wanting to open the book that had sat, untouched, beneath his mattress for nearly three months now.

At last he sighed and opened to the first page.

"I'm not crazy," he spoke to the rabbit again. "I know what I saw."

Charlie. He filled up the first page with nothing but facts and statistics, of which he knew embarrassingly few, he realized. He'd known Charlie's father, but not her mother. Her brother was still a mystery. He didn't even know if she'd been born in New Harmony, or if there was some other town before Fredbear's, the diner they had discovered that first time they all returned to Freddy's. He had painstakingly written out their shared history: childhood in Hurricane, then the tragedy at Freddy's, then her father's suicide. She had moved in with her aunt Jen after that. As he wrote that down, John realized that he had never known where Charlie and Jen lived. Close enough to Hurricane that she had driven rather than flown there for the dedication of Michael's memorial scholarship, nearly two years ago, but it seemed odd that she had never even mentioned the name of the town where she now—and then—lived.

He flipped through the pages; they grew less and less sparse as he had continued, the details filling in more and more as he called them over and over to mind. He had scribbled whole scenes of memory: like the time he put gum in her hair, thinking it would be funny. Charlie had stared at him with an impish look on her face as their first-grade teacher cut it out of her hair with little blue-handled safety scissors. Charlie had managed to retrieve that clump of hairy gum from the trash when no one was looking, and took it outside with her during recess. As soon as they were out the door, Charlie grinned at John. "I want to give you your gum back," she said, and the afternoon became a game of chase, as they careened around the schoolyard, Charlie determined to shove the hair-encrusted piece of chewing gum back into John's mouth. She had not succeeded: They were caught, and both given time-out. John smiled as he read the scribbled version of the story. It had seemed important to start with their childhood, to ground himself in the Charlie-that-was, and the John-that-was, as well. Now he sighed, and flipped ahead.

In the later pages, he had tried to capture everything about her: the way she moved, the way she spoke. It was hard; the more time passed the more the memories would be *John's memory of Charlie* and not *Charlie*, and so he had written down as much as he could, as fast as he could, starting three days after that night. There was the way she walked, self-assured until she realized someone was looking at her; there were the non sequiturs she tended to toss out every time she got nervous around people, which was often. There was the way she sometimes seemed to sink into herself, as if there were another reality going on inside her head, and she had stepped momentarily outside this one and into somewhere he could never follow. He sighed. *How do you check for that?*

He flipped the notebook over: he had started a different set of thoughts from the back.

What happened to Charlie?

If the woman at Carlton's party, the woman who had appeared so suddenly at the diner, was not Charlie, then who was she? The most obvious answer, of course, would be her twin. Charlie had always referred to a boy, but Sammy could easily be short for Samantha, and the memory Charlie had confided in him, of Sammy being taken from the closet, was a kidnapping, not a murder. What if Charlie's twin was still alive? What if she had been not only kidnapped by Springtrap, William Afton at the time, but raised by him? What if she had been shaped and molded by a psychopath for seventeen years, primed with all the knowledge Springtrap could glean from Charlie's life, and now she had been sent to take Charlie's place? *But why? What would be the point of that?* Afton's fixation on Charlie was disturbing, but he didn't seem capable of anything so elaborate—or of caring for a human child long enough to brainwash her.

He had written out a dozen other possible theories, but when he read them over now, none really felt right: They either fell apart upon scrutiny, or, like the imagined Samantha, they made no real sense. And in all cases, he could not match them to the Charlie he had met earlier that night. Her sorrow and her bemusement had seemed so real; picturing her face now raised a dull ache in his chest. John closed the book, trying to imagine for a moment the situation reversed: Charlie, *his* Charlie, turning from him, insisting that he was not himself—that he, the real John, was dead. *I'd fall apart.* He would feel the way Charlie had looked tonight, pleading, hugging herself as if it was all she could do to hold herself in one piece. He lay back on the bed, holding the book to his chest, where it sat, heavier than its weight. He closed his eyes, clutching the book like a child's toy, and as he drifted to sleep he heard the sound from Theodore's head again: the whirring, and then the click.

The next day, John woke up late and filled with a rootless dread. He glanced at the clock, realized in a panic that he was late for work, and almost simultaneously recalled that there was no more work, a reality that would have consequences soon enough, but not today. All he had to do today was meet Charlie. The dread swelled again at the thought of it, and he sighed.

Late that afternoon, as he dug through his dresser for a presentable shirt, someone knocked at the door. John glanced at Theodore.

"Who?" John whispered. The rabbit didn't answer. John went to the door; through the front window he saw Clay Burke standing outside staring at the door, apparently politely ignoring the fact that he could see right into John's apartment if he wanted to. John sighed and slid the chain off the latch, then opened the door wide.

"Clay, hey. Come in." Clay hesitated on the threshold, glancing at the interior that was too sparse to be a mess. John shrugged. "Before you judge, remember that I've seen your place look worse than this," he said, and Clay smiled.

"Yes, you have," he said at last, and came inside.

The noise from Theodore's head started again, but John chose to ignore it.

"What is that?" Clay asked after a few seconds. John waited to answer, knowing the sound would stop soon, and after a moment it did, with the same click as before.

"It's the rabbit head." John smiled.

"Right, of course." Clay looked toward the dresser, then back at John as though nothing was out of the ordinary. Considering what they'd been through in the past, it really wasn't. "So, what can I do for you?" John asked before something stranger could happen. Clay rocked on his heels momentarily.

"I wanted to see how you were doing," he said lightly.

"Really? Didn't we have that talk yesterday?" John said drily. He stood again and grabbed a clean shirt from his dresser and went into the bathroom to change.

"Yeah well, you know, you can never be too sure," Clay said, raising his voice to be heard. John turned on the faucet. "John, what do you know about Charlie's aunt Jen?"

John turned the faucet off abruptly, jarred out of his petulant mood. "Clay, what did you say?"

"I said what do you know about Charlie's aunt?"

John changed his shirt quickly and came back out into the bedroom. "Aunt Jen? I never met her." Clay gave him a sharp look.

"You never saw her?"

"I didn't say that," John said. "Why are you asking me this now?" Clay hesitated.

"Charlie became very eager to see you again when I mentioned that you had seen Jen that night," he said, seeming to choose his words with care.

"Why would Charlie care if I saw Jen or not? For that matter, why do you?" John reached past Clay to grab a belt hanging off the foot of the bed, and began to slip it through the loops of his jeans.

"It just made me realize that there is a lot we don't know about that night," Clay said. "I think your conversation with Charlie tonight can help fill in those gaps, if you ask the right questions."

"You want me to interrogate her?" John laughed without humor. Clay sighed, frustration leaking through his habitual calm.

"That's not what I'm asking, John. All I'm saying is, if Charlie's aunt was there that night, then I'd like to ask her a question or two." John stared at Clay, who just looked back at him placidly, waiting. John grabbed a pair of socks and sat down on the bed.

"Why are you suddenly coming to me, anyway?" he asked. "No one's believed anything I've said so far."

"It's what we found at the compound," Clay answered, more easily than John had expected. He straightened.

"The compound—you mean Charlie's dad's house?" Clay gave him a level look.

"I think we both know it was more than just a house," he said. John shrugged and said nothing, waiting for him to go on. "Some of the things we found in the wreckage were . . . they didn't mean much to anyone else, but what I saw— some of the things I saw down there were pretty scary, even though most of it was buried under concrete and metal."

"'Scary'? Was that the conclusion of your entire team, or just you?" John said, not bothering to keep the sarcasm out of his voice. Clay didn't seem to hear him, his eyes fixed on a point between them. "Clay?" John said, alarmed. "What did you find? What do you mean, 'scary'?"

Clay blinked. "I wouldn't be sure how else to describe it," he said. John shook his head. "I will say this," Clay said harshly. "I'm not ready to close the book on the Dave/ William Afton/whatever else he was calling himself—"

"Springtrap," John said quietly.

"I'm not ready to close the book on that case," Clay finished.

"What does that mean? You think he's still alive?"

"I just think we can't make any assumptions," Clay said. John shrugged again. He was out of patience—out of interest, almost. He was sick of intrigue: Clay withholding information, trying to protect them—as if keeping secrets had kept any of them safe, ever.

"What do you want me to ask her?" John said plainly.

"Just get her to talk to you. It's been wonderful having her here again, don't misunderstand, but it seems like she's holding something back. It's like she's—"

"Not herself?" John said with an edge of mocking.

"That's not what I was going to say. But I think she might know something she hasn't told us yet—maybe something that she hasn't felt comfortable sharing."

"And she might feel comfortable sharing it with me?"

"Maybe."

"That feels morally ambiguous," John said wearily. From the dresser, the whirring noise started again. "See? Theodore agrees with me," he said, gesturing toward the rabbit.

"Does it always do that?" Clay reached for the rabbit's head, but before he could touch it, Theodore's jaw snapped open and the head jerked in place. John startled, and Clay took a quick step back; they both watched, transfixed, as the sound went on, though the head did not move again. The sound it was making became a distorted murmur, louder and softer, at times almost mimicking words, though John could not even begin to make them out. After a few minutes, the head fell silent again.

"I've never seen it do that before," John said. Clay was bent over the dresser, his nose almost touching Theodore's, as if he could see inside.

"I need to go soon," John said shortly. "I don't want to be late, right? For this new open and honest relationship that I'm starting with her." He made brief, accusing eye contact with Clay and went briskly to the door. "Don't you need to lock it?" Clay asked as John brushed past him.

"It doesn't matter."

It was still light out when John got to St. George, and when he looked at the dashboard clock, John saw that he was over an hour early. He parked in the restaurant lot anyway and got out, glad for the opportunity to walk around and burn some nervous energy. He had avoided St. George, the town where Charlie and Jessica had been in college—*Jessica probably still is in college*, he thought with a pang of guilt. *I should know basic stuff like this.*

He walked past a few storefronts, heading semiconsciously for the movie theater he had been to with Charlie the last time he was here. *Maybe we can go see a movie. After the dinner-and-interrogation.* John stopped short on the sidewalk: The theater was gone. Instead, two gigantic clown faces grinned at him from the windows of a gleaming new restaurant. The faces were almost as large as the wide front door, painted on either side, and above them was a sign, in red and yellow neon letters: CIRCUS BABY'S PIZZA. The neon lights were on, glowing uselessly in the daylight. John stood motionless, feeling like his sneakers had fused to the parking lot. A group of kids rushed past him on their way in, and a teenager bumped into John, breaking him out of his daze.

"Just keep walking, John," he muttered to himself, turning to move away, but he stopped again after only a few steps. "Just keep walking," he repeated in a sterner tone, and turned to face the restaurant defiantly. He approached the front door and pushed it. It opened into an empty vestibule, a waiting area, where smaller versions of the clowns out front smiled crazily from the walls, and a second door read WEL-COME! in painted cursive letters. There was a familiar smell in the air: some particular combination of rubber, sweat, and cooking pizza.

John opened the second door, and noise exploded. He blinked in the florescent lights, bewildered: Children were everywhere, screaming and laughing, and running across the floor, and the jingles and blips of arcade games sounded discordantly from around the room. There were play struc-tures, something like a jungle gym to his left, and a large ball pit to his right, where two small girls were throwing brightly colored balls at a third girl, who was shouting something he could not make out.

There were tables set up in the center of the room, where he noticed five or six adults talking to one another. Occasionally they'd look over their shoulders at the chaos surrounding them, at the stage in back of the room, its red curtain closed. A chill went down his spine, and he looked around again with a terrible déjà vu at the playing children and complacent parents.

He started toward the stage, twice stopping just in time to avoid tripping over a game of tag. The curtains were brand-new, the red velvet plush and gleaming in the light, and trimmed with golden ropes and tassels. John slowed his pace as he got closer, the pit of his stomach tensing with an old, familiar dread. The stage floor was about level with his waist, and he stopped beside it and glanced around, then carefully grasped the thick curtain and began to pull it back.

"Excuse me, sir," a man's voice came from behind him, and John straightened like he'd touched a hot stove.

"Sorry," he said, turning to see a man wearing a yellow polo shirt and a tense expression.

"Are you here with your children, sir?" he asked, raising his eyebrows. The shirt read CIRCUS BABY'S PIZZA, and he was wearing a name tag that read STEVE.

"No, I . . ." John paused. "Yes. Several children. Birthday party, you know. Cousins, so many cousins, what can you do?"

Steve was still looking at him with raised eyebrows.

"I have to go meet someone . . . somewhere else," John said. Steve gestured to the door.

CHAPTER FOUR

No!" Jessica cried in dismay as she wrangled her keys from the pocket of her fashionably too-tight jeans. An apple tumbled out of the paper grocery bag she was struggling to balance on her hip and rolled away down the hallway. It came to rest on the welcome mat of her worst neighbor, a middle-aged man who seemed capable of detecting the tiniest noise, then promptly complaining about it. In fact, since she moved in to the apartment six months ago, leaving behind the dorm room she and Charlie had shared, he had come to her door three times to complain about her radio. Twice it had not even been on. Mostly, he just glared at her whenever they passed in the hall. Jessica didn't really mind the hostility; it was a little like being back home in New York. She left the apple where it was.

Having managed to get the door open, Jessica dropped the bags on the kitchen counter and looked around the room with a quiet satisfaction. The apartment wasn't very fancy, but it was *hers*. When she first moved in, she had gone on a cleaning rampage, scouring out the baked-in dirt that must have been lining the baseboards since the building went up some fifty years ago. It had taken almost two weeks of nothing but scrubbing between classes and homework, and she went to bed every night with sore arms, as though she'd done nothing but weight training. But now the apartment was clean enough for Jessica—albeit just barely—which was no small bar to clear.

She began taking things out of the grocery bags, lining everything up on the counter before putting each item away. "Peanut butter, bread, milk, bananas . . ." she muttered to herself, then fell silent.

Something is wrong. She looked around the room carefully, but there was no one there and everything seemed to be where she'd last left it. She returned to the grocery bags.

As she closed the refrigerator door the hair at the back of her neck prickled. Jessica whirled around as though expecting to catch a burglar in the act, her heart jolting with adrenaline, but the room was still. Just to be sure, she went to check the door: it was locked, as expected. She stood in silence for a moment, listening to the distant sounds of her apartment complex—the hum of an air-conditioning unit outside, a leaf blower across the street—but nothing seemed out of the ordinary. She stepped carefully back to the counter and finished putting away the groceries, then headed to her bedroom. She turned the corner to the hallway and screamed: a figure stood in the dark, blocking the way.

"Jessica?" said a familiar voice, and Jessica reached hastily for the light switch, tensed to run. The light flickered on slowly: it was Charlie.

"Did I scare you?" Charlie said uncertainly. "Sorry. The door was unlocked—I should have waited outside," she added, looking down at her shoes. "I just figured since we used to be roomies anyway . . ."

"Charlie, you scared me to death," Jessica said in a mock-scolding tone. "What are you doing here?"

"I told you I'm having dinner with John?" Charlie said, and Jessica nodded. "Could I borrow something to wear? Maybe you could help me pick something out?" Charlie looked hesitant, like she was asking an immense favor, and Jessica gave her a puzzled frown.

"Yeah, sure, of course." Jessica tried to calm herself. "But, Charlie—it's not like you need my help choosing an outfit these days." Jessica gestured at Charlie's clothing: she was wearing her habitual combat boots—or a more elegant version of them—but she had paired them with a medium-length black skirt and a dark red, scoop-necked blouse. Charlie shrugged and shifted her feet.

"I just think—he might like me better if you help me pick an outfit, instead of me dressing myself, you know? John doesn't seem to like my new look."

"Well, Charlie . . ." Jessica stopped, choosing her words carefully. "It won't do either of you any good to pretend nothing has changed," she said firmly. "Wear what you have on, you look great."

"You think so?" Charlie said, looking doubtful.

"Yeah," Jessica said. She brushed past Charlie to go into her room, stepping cautiously past her, and Charlie followed, pausing in the doorway like a vampire waiting for an invitation. Jessica looked at Charlie and was suddenly set at ease, as if their friendship had never been interrupted. Jessica grinned. "So, I mean, are you nervous?" she asked, going to her dresser for her hairbrush, and Charlie came in and sat down on the bed.

"I feel like I have to prove something to him, but I'm not sure what," she said, tracing the flower design on Jessica's bedspread. "You were right, by the way."

Jessica turned around, brushing her hair absently. "He wants to see you tonight. I think that's a great start," she offered. "Just let him spend some time with you. He's been through a lot. Remember, from his perspective, he saw you die, right in front of his eyes."

Charlie laughed, a soft, forced sound, then was silent. "I'm just worried about him. And I can't even help him, because"—she broke off—"Jessica, do you remember him telling me something important that night?" Something in her tone changed: it was subtle, just a hint of strain. Jessica kept her expression neutral, pretending not to notice.

"Something important?" Jessica asked.

"Something . . . that I would remember. *Should* remember." She kept her eyes on the bedspread, still tracing the pattern like she was trying to memorize it. Jessica hesitated. She could still see it all, as vivid as the present, though it gave her a sick feeling in the pit of her stomach. *Charlie was trapped in the twisted, broken Freddy suit, with just her arm free; John was holding her hand*—Jessica shuddered, that terrible, singular crunching sound echoing in her head.

"Jessica?" Charlie asked, and Jessica nodded briskly.

"Sorry." She cleared her throat. "I don't know, you and John were alone together for a few minutes. I'm not sure what he said. Why?"

"I think it's important to him that I remember," Charlie said, back to tracing the bedspread. Jessica watched her for a moment, suddenly ill at ease in her own bedroom. As if sensing it, Charlie stood and met her eyes.

"Thanks, Jessica," she said. "Sorry again for breaking in. I mean, I didn't break in, the door was unlocked—but you know what I mean."

"No problem, just . . . announce yourself sooner next time?" Jessica smiled, feeling a rush of warmth for her friend.

She hugged Charlie good-bye at the door. Charlie walked a few steps and picked the apple up off the ground, then handed it back to Jessica.

"I think this belongs to you." Charlie smiled, then turned to walk away. When she had closed the door, Jessica sighed. The anxiety that had risen while Charlie was in her room had not abated. She leaned back against the door, replaying what had just happened. *Why would John want Charlie to remember the last thing he said to her?* She tossed the apple a few inches into the air, then let it fall back into her hand.

"He's testing her," Jessica said to the empty apartment.

Outside Jessica's building, Charlie stopped in the parking lot, frustrated. *What did he say that was so important?* She walked across the baked pavement to her car. Charlie climbed into her car, slamming the door shut with more force than she needed to. She stared petulantly at the steering wheel. *They're lying to me*, she thought. *I feel like a little kid, with all the grown-ups keeping secrets from me. Deciding for me what I should and shouldn't know.*

She glanced at her watch—the clock in the car was either an hour ahead or an hour behind, and she could never remember which. She had about twenty minutes before she had to meet John. "I can't show up early," she said plainly, "then he *really* won't believe it's me." Trying to shrug off her bad mood, Charlie put the car in gear and pulled out of the lot.

When she got to the restaurant, she could see John through the window, seated at the same table they had sat at last time, all the way in the back. He was staring into space, as if he were deep in thought, or completely zoned out. She followed the hostess to his table, and it was only when she was standing right beside him that he seemed to realize she was there. When he did, he stood hastily. Charlie started to move toward him, but he sat back down, and she quickly sidestepped and did the same.

"Hi," she said with an awkward smile.

"Hi, Charlie," he said quietly, then grinned suddenly. "You're dressed a lot nicer than last time we were here."

"It probably just seems that way because I'm not covered in dirt and blood this time," Charlie said lightly.

"Right." He laughed, but there was a quick instant of appraisal in his eyes. *That was a test*. The thought sent something cold through the pit of her stomach. She had known it would happen, but knowing did not make it easier to have his eyes, usually so warm, look at her with calculation.

"What was that movie we saw?" John asked, seeming to fumble at an answer. "Last time I visited, we went to that theater down the street, didn't we? It's on the tip of my tongue."

"*Zombies vs. Zombies!*" Charlie said.

"Right, I knew it was about zombies," John said thoughtfully.

"So, what have you been doing since then?" Charlie asked, attempting to shift the topic. "Are you still doing construction work?"

"Yeah," John said, then cast his eyes down at the table. "Actually, maybe not. I just got fired."

"Oh," Charlie said. "I'm sorry."

He nodded. "Yeah. I mean, it was my fault. I showed up late, and—there was some other stuff—but I really liked that job. Well . . . it was *a* job at least."

"There have to be other building sites," Charlie said.

"Yeah, I guess." He looked at her searchingly, and she looked back, trying not to shrink under scrutiny. *Believe me*, she pleaded silently. *What will it take for you to believe me?*

"I've missed this," she said instead.

He nodded, his eyes softening for a moment. "Me too," he said quietly, though she knew it was only half true.

"You know I didn't leave because of—it wasn't because of you," Charlie said. "I'm sorry if it seemed like it was; I just had to get away from everything and everyone. I—"

"Are you folks ready to order?" the waitress asked brightly. John straightened his posture and cleared his throat. Charlie looked down at the menu, glad of the interruption, but the pictures of food looked strange, as if she had heard food described, but never seen any. "Miss?" The waitress was looking at her expectantly.

"I'll have the same," Charlie said quickly, and shut the menu. The young woman frowned confusedly.

"Oh, uh, okay. I guess I should order then." John laughed.

"Anything will be fine." Charlie sat patiently. "I'm sorry. I'll be right back." She got up from the table hastily and headed for the bathroom, leaving John to take care of things.

Walking into the bathroom, she was struck with a jarring sense of déjà vu. *I've been here before. Trapped in a box, I was trapped in a box*—Charlie slammed the door shut and locked it. *I'm not trapped.* She ran her fingers through her hair, though it didn't really need adjusting, and washed her hands; she was just killing time, stealing a moment away from John's scrutiny. Every time he gave her that level, untrusting look, she felt exposed.

"I am Charlie," she said to her reflection, smoothing down her hair again nervously. "I don't have to convince John that I'm me." The words sounded thin in the small room. *Who else would I be?* Charlie washed her hands again, straightened her shoulders, and went back out into the dining room. She sat down and put her paper napkin in her lap, then looked John squarely in the eye.

"I still don't remember," she said abruptly, seized by an obstinate recklessness.

John raised his eyebrows. "What?"

"I don't remember what you said to me that night. I know it's important to you—I know maybe it's why you think what you think about me, but I just . . . don't remember. I can't change that."

"Okay." He slid his hands off the edge of the table and let them rest in his lap. "I know—I know that. Um, a lot happened that night. I know." He sighed for a moment but then smiled almost reassuringly. Charlie bit her lip.

"If it's that important, why can't you just tell me?" she asked gently. Instantly, she could see that it was the wrong thing to say. John's features hardened; he drew back from the table slightly. She looked down at the napkin in her lap; she had been shredding the corner of it without noticing. "Never mind," she said, her voice barely above a whisper, letting several long minutes pass. "Forget I said anything." She looked up, but John didn't respond.

"Excuse me for just a minute. I'll be right back." He got up and left the table.

She stared at his empty chair. The waitress approached and cleared her throat; Charlie heard her, but did not move. She wasn't sure she could move. *This is going horribly. Maybe I'll just sit here forever. I'll be a statue of myself, a monument to Charlie-that-was. Charlie-that-will-never-be-again.*

"Miss?" The waitress sounded concerned, and it was enough for Charlie to, with herculean effort, turn her head.

"Is everything all right, miss?" the waitress asked, and it took Charlie another long moment to comprehend the question.

"Yes," she said at last. "Could I have another napkin?" She held up the first, half-shredded, as evidence of her need, and the waitress went away. Charlie turned back to John's empty chair.

John slid back into view and sat down, breaking the line of her vacant stare.

"Everything okay?" he asked. She nodded.

"The waitress is getting me another napkin." Charlie gestured vaguely in the direction the waitress had gone.

"Right." He opened his mouth to go on, but before he could speak, the waitress returned, carrying Charlie's napkin, along with their food. They were both silent as she placed it in front of them, and John smiled at her. "Thanks," he said. Charlie stared at her plate: it was some kind of pasta. She took her fork carefully but didn't start to eat.

"Can I ask you something?" John finally said, and she nodded eagerly, setting the fork back down. He took a deep breath.

"That night, how did you survive? I—There was so much blood . . ." He stopped, at a loss for words. Charlie looked at him, at the familiar face that had somehow turned against her. She had been trying to piece together a story for him, but now she just spoke.

"I don't know," she said. "I—There's time missing, when I try to think about it my mind—flinches away, like it's hit something sharp." The distance in John's eyes faded a little as she spoke. "I'd been in a suit before," she went on. "I think I must have figured out how to get away somehow, or at least how to position myself." She looked anxiously at him, and his gaze sharpened.

"I still don't understand. How did you manage to get away . . . undamaged?" He looked her up and down again, seeming to examine her.

Charlie's breath caught in her throat, and she turned away from him, staring fixedly out the window at the parking lot.

"I didn't," she said tightly.

John didn't answer, searching Charlie's half-turned face for a spark of something he could recognize—or *not* recognize. She was saying all the right things, in all the right ways, and her hints—more than hints—at the unshakable trauma she had gone through that night made his stomach clench. As she gazed off into the middle distance, her jaw was clenched; she looked like she was fighting something off, and John was seized with a sudden urge to go to her, to hold out his hand and offer his help. Instead he picked up his fork and began to eat, looking down at his plate instead of at her.

She knows what I'm doing, he thought, chewing grimly. *She's giving me the right answers. Some detective I've turned out to be.* John took another bite and stole a glance at her; she was still looking off at the parking lot. He swallowed and cleared his throat.

Before he could speak, Charlie turned back to him. "After that night, I had to get away," she said. Her voice was hoarse, and her face was strained, her features seeming harsher than before. "I had to leave everything behind, John. *Everything.* My whole life has been haunted by what happened here, and the last couple of years . . . even before that, too. It's just been my whole life." She met his eyes briefly, then looked away, blinking rapidly like she was holding back tears. "I wanted to be somebody different; I had to or I'd go insane. I know it's a cliché to think you can change your life if you change your hair and your clothes"—she gave an ironic half smile and flipped her long hair over her shoulder—"but I couldn't be *your* Charlie forever, that naïve little girl, scared of her own shadow; *living* in a shadow. Honestly, I don't even know what you saw in that girl—selfish, scatterbrained, *pathetic.*" She said the last word so caustically that she almost shook with it, a sour look coming over her face as if loathing for her past self had overwhelmed her.

"I never thought you were any of those things," John said quietly, and looked down. He ran his fork along the rim of his plate, not knowing what to say. He made himself look up; Charlie's face had softened, and now she seemed anxious.

"But it's still me." She shrugged, her voice breaking. He couldn't answer; he didn't know where to start. Charlie bit her lip. "You still think it, don't you?" she said after a moment. John shifted uncomfortably in his seat, ashamed, but Charlie pressed on.

"John, please, I don't understand. If you think I'm not me, then . . . what do you think? Who can you possibly think I am?" She looked utterly bewildered, and again John felt himself wavering.

"I think—" He gestured graspingly at the air, catching nothing. "Charlie, what I saw—!" he exclaimed, then stopped short, remembering they were in public. He glanced around, but no one was looking at them: the restaurant was not busy, but everyone there was occupied, the guests talking to the people they came with, the staff talking among themselves. "I saw you die," he said, lowering his voice. "When you walked into that diner the next day, Charlie, I wanted to believe it was true—I *still* want to believe it, but I—I saw you die," he finished helplessly. Charlie shook her head slowly.

"I'm telling you that I'm alive, how can that not be enough? If you want to believe me, why don't you?" The pain in her voice sent a pang of guilt through him, but he met her eyes calmly.

"Because I'd rather know the truth than believe something just because it would make me happy."

Charlie looked at him searchingly. "So, what do you think is the truth? Who do you—" she swallowed, and started again. "Who do you think I am, if I'm not me?"

John sighed. "I've thought about it a lot," he said at last. "Almost constantly, actually." Charlie nodded slightly, barely moving her head, like she was afraid she would spook him. "I thought about a lot of things, I guess—theories—um . . ."

"Like what?" Charlie asked gently.

"Well . . ." John's face was getting hot. *I should never have agreed to see her.*

"John?"

"I—I guess maybe I thought you might be Sammy," he mumbled; she looked puzzled for a moment, like she had not quite heard him, then her eyes widened.

"Sammy's dead," she said tightly. John looked up at the ceiling and put his hands to his temples.

"I know," he said, and met her eyes again. "But, *Charlie*, look: I don't know that. Neither do you. The last thing . . . you remember, of Sammy, what was it?"

"You know the answer to that," she said in a low, level voice.

"You saw him being taken," John said after a moment. She made no response, and he took it as license to continue. "You saw him being kidnapped, not killed. By Dave, or Afton—Springtrap. So, what if he wasn't killed? What if

68

Sammy was *raised* by William Afton, twisted, and brought up by a murderous madman to replace you—to replace Charlie—after her death? Also, Sammy could be short for Samantha. I forgot that part. Sammy could have been a girl all along." Charlie was motionless across the table; she scarcely looked like she was breathing. "I know how it sounds when I say it out loud," John added in a rush. "That's why I mostly don't." Charlie had covered her face with her hand, and her shoulders were shaking. He broke off as she looked up: this time she was laughing. There was a manic edge to it, like it might turn back into crying at any moment, but John tentatively tried to smile.

"Oh, John," she said at last. "I don't even—You know that's crazy, right?"

"Is it crazier than anything else we've seen?" he argued without much conviction.

"John, you took me to see the grave yourself, remember?"

John paused and looked confused for a moment, trying to reconcile what he'd just heard.

"You took me yourself, to Sammy's grave."

"I took you to the cemetery, but I never saw Sammy's grave, or your father's," John corrected.

"Then go look sometime." Charlie's voice was patient. John felt immediately foolish.

"Aunt Jen warned me not to come back to Hurricane." Charlie looked down at the table. "She's three for three at this point. Have you heard from her, by the way?"

"From your aunt?" John asked, disconcerted by the sudden change of subject. "I figured you were living with her after you moved out of Jessica's place."

"Yeah," Charlie said.

"You were living with her?"

"Have you seen her?"

"Why would I have seen her?" John asked slowly, suddenly feeling a bit lost in the conversation. He had seen Jen twice: once as a child, and once on that terrible night, crouched beside the twisted, broken Freddy suit in a pool of Charlie's blood. But Charlie didn't know about either. "You know I've never actually met her," John said, watching Charlie's face. Her expression was pensive, and did not change.

"I just thought she might try to get in touch," Charlie said idly.

"Okay. I'll let you know if she does?" John offered.

"Please do, thanks," Charlie said. It was only then that she seemed to register his confusion. "I haven't seen her in a while. She rescued me that night," she said. "She took me home and cleaned me up, made sure I was okay." She flashed John a quick half smile, and he returned it warily.

"I thought you said you didn't remember anything from that night," he said, trying to keep his tone from sounding accusatory.

"I said there was a lot I don't remember. But mostly that's what Jen told me. Honestly, the first thing I remember is her waking me up the next morning, telling me to put on the dress she had for me." Charlie made a face. "She always wanted me to dress more like a girl. Of course, the joke was on me; it turns out after a few near-death experiences, there's nothing I wanted more than a makeover."

John smiled, and she batted her eyelashes exaggeratedly. He laughed in spite of himself.

"So, you think she might be looking for you?" He paused, unsure how to phrase the next part. "Do you want her to find you?" he asked at last, and she shrugged.

"I'd like to know where she is."

"She's not at the house where you're living? When did she leave?"

"Everybody leaves eventually," Charlie said in a sardonic tone, and he laughed again, less heartily.

You didn't answer my question.

Charlie glanced at her watch: like everything else she now wore, it was a smaller, feminized version of the one she used to have. "There's a good zombie movie starting in about fifteen minutes, I think," she said brightly. "The new theater isn't far from here. What do you think, should we see if the old formula still works?"

What does that mean? John held back a smile. "I can't go to the movies," he said with real reluctance. "I've got somewhere that I need to be."

"Another time?" Charlie said, and he nodded.

"Yeah, maybe."

As he walked back to his car, John noticed a crowd outside the new pizzeria. *I guess everybody likes the circus,* he thought. He wandered closer, trying to see where Charlie had gone, but she was nowhere to be seen. Suddenly, like noticing hidden figures in a picture, John realized that the crowd around him was dotted with clowns: painted faces, white billowy costumes, noses of all shapes and colors. They were everywhere. He backed out of the throng, tripping on an oversize shoe and almost falling off the sidewalk.

When he was free of the crowd, John took a deep breath and looked back at the restaurant, noticing for the first time the banner strung over the front entrance. GRAND OPENING: COME DRESSED AS A CLOWN AND EAT FREE! it read, hanging between the gigantic faces of two grinning clowns. He looked around. More people were arriving, many of them in costume, and John felt the hair on the back of his neck stand on end. He glanced behind him, but there was nothing sinister, besides the clowns. He forced himself to look at them individually: people had dressed with varying degrees of enthusiasm—some had structured bodysuits, wigs, and enormous feet; others had simply painted their faces and worn polka-dot T-shirts. Still, his sense of unease did not abate.

They're just people in costumes, he scolded himself, then laughed abruptly, startling a woman standing nearby. "People in costumes. That's never gone wrong for me," he muttered, walking away from the crowd to find his car.

Driving home, John found himself agitated; twice he looked at the speedometer and saw that he'd gone dangerously over the speed limit without noticing. He tapped his hand restlessly against the steering wheel, thinking of the next day. *What then?* Seeing Charlie had rattled him more than he had realized. After months of solitary scribbling, going over and over his bizarre theories, he'd been forced to put his conviction to the test, to ask her questions and watch her answer, and ask himself as he did, *Are you her? Are you my Charlie?* Now that it was over, it felt unreal, like a dream that lingered too long, unwelcome in the waking world. As he approached the turnoff that would take him home, he sped up, driving straight on past it.

John parked his car a few blocks away from Clay Burke's house. He pulled the keys out of the ignition and jangled them nervously in his hand for a minute, then opened the door decisively and got out. When he got to the house it was dark except for a single window, which he thought was Clay's office. *I wonder if Carlton's gone back to school*, he wondered, unsure whether he was hoping for his friend's presence, or his absence.

He knocked and waited, then rang the bell. A long moment later, Clay opened the door.

"John. Good," he said, and nodded, seeming unsurprised by his presence. He stepped aside to let John in, and ushered him into the study. "Do you want some coffee?" he asked, gesturing at the mug on his desk.

"It's a little late for me," John said. "I'll be up all night."

Clay nodded. "I'm substituting lesser vices," was all he said. John glanced around the room. The last time he had been here they'd used the desk as a barricade against an army of angry animatronics.

"You fixed the door," he observed.

"I fixed the door," Clay said. "Oak. Reinforced. What brings you here?"

"I saw Charlie." Clay raised his eyebrows, but didn't say anything. "She said something: she asked if I'd heard from—" John stopped, seized by a sudden sense that he was being watched. Clay had his head tilted to the side as though sensing something as well.

Silently, Clay made his way to the closed window, positioning himself beside one of the long, pale green drapes, and peered outside. "Everyone is a little on edge with all these weirdos walking around in face paint," he said, but he kept his voice low. He pulled the drapes together, then walked back toward John. "Have a seat," Clay offered; there were two dark green upholstered chairs and a matching couch along one wall. John sat on the couch. Clay grabbed his desk chair and dragged it across the rug so they were only a few feet apart.

"What did Charlie ask you?" Clay began. John glanced at the window again; he felt as if waves of dread were emanating from it, rolling into the room like an unseen fog. Clay looked back over his shoulder, but only for a second. John cleared his throat.

"She asked about her aunt Jen. If I'd seen her. I thought you might know something?" he finished uncertainly. Clay looked lost in thought, and John wondered for a moment if he should repeat himself.

"No," Clay said finally. "Did Charlie say why she was asking?"

John shook his head. "She just said she wanted to know if I'd heard from her. I don't know why I would hear from her, though," he said. He was choosing his words carefully, as if saying the right ones in the right order would unlock a door in Clay's mind, and convince him to tell John what he knew. Clay just nodded thoughtfully. "Did you ever meet her?" John asked.

"Never a formal introduction, no," Clay said. "She was a bit older than Henry, I think." Clay got quiet for a moment and tilted his glass from side to side, swirling the last few sips at the bottom. "When he moved here, Henry was something of a recluse; we all knew he'd lost a kid." Clay sat up slowly. "Didn't see them for a while, even Charlie, and then . . ." Clay let out a pained sigh. "Jen was around for about a year, and she was the one watching the kid. Jen stuck to Charlie's side like glue. I guess Henry just didn't trust people anymore, and I can't blame him."

"I always kind of got the impression . . ." John paused, choosing his words again. "Charlie always gave me the impression that she was kind of cold."

"Well, like I said, after something like that," Clay said. "I was surprised when Jen took Charlie, after Henry died," he went on.

"What about Charlie's mother?" John asked hesitantly. It felt intrusive to pry, worse because Charlie was not here: he felt like they were talking about her behind her back.

"No, Charlie's mother ran off before her and her father moved to Hurricane," Clay said. "Henry never said anything bad about her mother. He pretty much never said anything about her at all, but I asked one day, just out of curiosity. Maybe it was the detective in me; I couldn't help myself. He thought a long time before answering me, then he gave me this sad look, and he said, 'She wouldn't know what to do with my little girl.' I backed off the subject after that. I mean, I knew they'd lost another kid. I guess I assumed Charlie's mother had had some kind of breakdown, or else just found herself unable to care for a child so much like the one she'd lost. I think it should be said, though, to her aunt Jen's credit, Charlie seems to have turned out all right." He smiled and gave a nod. "She's a bit odd, but she's a good kid."

"She's unique, for sure," John said.

"Unique, then," Clay said drily. The walls trembled briefly as a strong wind passed over the house. John cast his eyes around the room uncomfortably, then lit on something familiar in the corner, tucked away between the end of a bookshelf and the wall.

"Is that Ella?" John asked, pointing. Clay looked blank for a moment.

"The doll? That turned up in the rubble of Charlie's old house. The rest got hauled away, but I kept that."

"Her name is Ella," John said. "Charlie's dad made her, she used to go around on a track, carrying a tea set."

"I asked Charlie if she wanted it," Clay said. "She wasn't interested."

"She wasn't?" John repeated, alarmed. Clay shook his head absently.

"I have a hard time believing that," John said incredulously as he held the old toy in his arms, and Clay came back to attention.

"Well, tell her that it's here if she ever wants it."

"I will," John said, setting the doll back down. Clay glanced at the window again and looked preoccupied. "Is something wrong?" John asked.

"Not at all," he said.

John raised his eyebrows. "Are you sure about that?"

Clay sighed. "A child was abducted this morning."

"What?"

"A little girl, she disappeared sometime between midnight and six a.m." Clay was stone-faced; John searched for words and came up empty. "It's the second one this month," Clay added quietly.

"I haven't heard anything about that," John said. He glanced at the window again as the wind began to howl outside, then looked back at Clay, and immediately the knot of fear took up its post behind his head again. "Do you have any leads?" John asked the first question he could think of. Clay didn't answer for a long moment, and John asked the next question. "Do you think it has something to do with—I mean, missing kids, it's not the first time that's happened here."

"No, it's certainly not." Clay was staring into the space between them as if there was something there he could see. "I don't see any way that it could be connected, though; Freddy's has been destroyed at this point."

"Right," John said. "So, you don't have any leads?"

"I'm doing the best that I can." Clay lowered his head and ran his hand though his hair, then sat up straight again. "I'm sorry. It's got me on edge; I feel like I'm reliving those days: children, the same age as my little boy—the same age as you back when—getting snatched one after another, and there was nothing I could do to stop it then, either."

"Michael," John said quietly.

"Michael. And the others. There never seems to be a shortage of evil in this world."

"But that's why we have you, right?" John smiled.

Clay snorted. "Right. I wish it were that simple."

"You said two kids were missing?" John said, his eyes drawn again toward the sound of the wind dragging branches and leaves against the side of the house.

Clay stood up and went to the window, almost defiantly, and opened it wide. John startled at the sound of the window cracking. John could see from where he sat that Clay seemed to be scanning the area for something under the guise of getting some air.

After a moment, he pulled himself back inside and shut the window, then drew the curtains closed. "It might not be as bad as it looks now, John. There's usually a normal explanation, and most kids turn up, one way or another. Two weeks ago, there was a little boy named Edgar, whatever. Two and a half years old."

"What happened?"

"His parents have been fighting about custody for over a year. His father ends up losing that fight—only gets to see the kid once a month, supervised visits, which I can tell you was for good reasons. Edgar disappears, surprise, surprise. He was found a few days later, alive and well; spontaneous road trip with his dad. Most kidnappings, it's one of the parents."

"Is that what you think is happening here?" John asked skeptically.

"No." Clay didn't take long to answer. "No, I don't," he repeated, sounding graver.

He took a deep breath and leaned forward. "And it doesn't help that the whole town's obsessed with this new restaurant, dressing up like clowns—it's a waste of time for my officers to be doing crowd control, or clown control, as it were."

"Can I do anything?" John asked, though he couldn't imagine what kind of help he could be.

"Not a thing," Clay said. "If I'm right, I may need you. And I'll need—" He stopped.

"Charlie," John said. "You'll need Charlie."

Clay nodded. "It's not fair to ask that of her," Clay said. "Not after everything she's been through. But I will if I have to."

"Yeah," John said. Clay was staring at the space between them again, and John felt suddenly like he was intruding. "It's getting late," he said.

"Yeah, well, watch yourself out there," Clay said, hastily standing. "Do you want to take my gun?" Clay said lightly. He smiled, but there was tension in his face, as though he were half hoping John would take it.

"Don't need it." John grinned. "I've got these guns." He held a tight fist in the air and threatened the room before letting himself out.

"Okay, tough guy, see you soon," Clay said grimly.

John started back toward his car: it was pitch-black now—it had been dark when he arrived, he realized, but now he *noticed* it. The streetlamps didn't go far, the pools of light beneath him swallowed up only a few feet out. His footsteps landed hard; and there seemed to be no way to quiet them. The distant roar of the highway was too faint to provide cover, and the wind was silent for the time being, as though it had temporarily gone into hiding. Something moved a few yards ahead of him, and John stopped dead: coming down the road was another costumed moviegoer, but there was something off about this one. It was heading in his direction, walking in the middle of the road at an even pace. John stayed where he was between two of the tall, thin saplings planted along the sidewalk, his eyes glued to the approaching figure.

As it came closer, a chill gripped John's spine: The clown's movements were feminine, but wrong. She walked like something mechanical, yet graceful. His breath caught in his throat as the clown glided toward him like a wraith. The creature was staring straight ahead as it passed; John waited, hoping to stay out of its line of sight. As she grew closer however, her eyes drifted toward him, her head turning only slightly as though to acknowledge his passing.

John stared back, at first admiring the sleek and controlled beauty of her face, split down the middle through some trick of costuming. John instinctively took a step back—he had seen monsters before—and prepared to run, or fight, if necessary. But just as his heart began thudding against his chest, she looked away again and slipped back into the dark as gracefully as she had appeared. John watched for a moment, then continued to his car. He checked his rearview mirror, but there was no one in sight. As he drove home, he checked the mirror more often than he needed to. His thoughts kept returning to those shiny, penetrating eyes: the clown had looked at him like she knew him; like she could see right through him. "Relax," John said to the empty car. "It was just some weirdo in a costume." Saying the words aloud, however, did not make them any more convincing.

Clay went back to his office and stopped by the window, drawing aside the curtains slightly to make sure John had made it around the corner and out of sight. Clay sighed; he sat down at his desk, picked up the case file on the second missing child, and began to review it. The information he needed just wasn't there, but it didn't stop him from returning to it over and over again. His officers had diligently done their jobs: they'd gone to the right places, talked to the right people, and asked all the wrong questions. *They just don't know what I know.*

There was a sound from down the hallway, a distinct creak. Clay's eyes lifted, and he set the file carefully back on his desk.

"John?" he called, but there was no response. With practiced calm, Clay quietly reached for the gun he kept in a holster under his desk and flipped the safety off. He went to the open office door and paused, listening for another noise from the dark hall. Nothing came. Clay pulled the door shut, snapping the deadbolts into place.

Clay stepped back into the center of the room and stood, listening. A moment passed in silence and his eyes dropped, his shoulders feeling at ease, but suddenly his eyes lifted again, and his jaw clenched. He took one deliberate step back, focusing directly on the center of the door ahead of him. He lifted and steadied his gun, and took aim. Several minutes passed, but Clay's eyes never wavered. There was something in the hall.

* ★ ★ ★

John let his front door fall shut behind him with a heavy thud and tossed his keys on the kitchen counter. He sat down heavily on the couch, letting his head fall back, weighted down with fatigue. After only a moment, he lifted his head back up: the strange noise was coming from his bedroom again. It sounded a little like the sounds the rabbit's head had been making, but something had changed, though he couldn't pinpoint how. It sounded like a voice, then static, a voice, then static. Something was being repeated.

John's bedroom door was almost all the way closed, and he got up from the couch and approached it slowly from the side, putting his feet down silently one after the other, the rubber soles scarcely tapping the floor. He eased the door open: the sound was louder now, more distinct: the voice continued, garbled and muffled. John turned on the light and went to Theodore's head. He bent over so his eyes were level with Theodore's plastic ones, and listened. The rabbit's head stared back, muttered words, broke into static, then a moment later repeated. John grabbed a notebook and pen off his bed and closed his eyes, concentrated on the sounds.

After a minute, he began to hear words. "Shining?" John whispered. "Shining—something. Silver?" He continued to listen, but he couldn't make out the rest. John gritted his teeth and opened his eyes, glaring at the stuffed rabbit's head as it continued to repeat the same incoherent phrase. John drew in a long breath, then let it out, trying to release the tension in his neck, in his jaw, in his back. He sat down on the bed, put the pen and paper down, and closed his eyes once more. *Just listen.* The sounds repeated, again and again. Suddenly, they resolved, like song lyrics after the thousandth play: John understood.

"Shining Star? Silver . . . something. Silver Reef? Shining Star, Silver Reef."

"Shining Star, Silver Reef," Theodore repeated. John got up again, putting his ear to Theodore's nose, trying to make sure he had it right. "Shining Star, Silver Reef . . ." the rabbit intoned. John raced back to his car.

When he reached Clay's driveway again, John stopped dead: the front door was gaping open, light from inside the house spilling into the yard. He ran up the steps, calling, "Clay! Clay, are you here?" He ran inside, still shouting, and made for Clay's office just a few steps past the front hall.

"Clay!"

John dropped to his knees beside Clay; he was on the floor, one side of his face slick with his own blood, more pooling beneath his head. His eyes were closed. John grabbed his wrist and pressed his fingers against the veins, hoping for a pulse: after a few frantic seconds, he found it, and relief washed through him, but it was momentary. "Clay?" John repeated, jostling him lightly. Clay didn't respond. John looked around with alarm; the new door, the one Clay had described as "reinforced," was in pieces. What was left of the door was still hanging in place by the upper hinge. Hastily, John pulled Clay out into the hall as best he could.

He glanced back toward the office: the chair was over-turned, and everything that had been on the desk littered the carpet. He patted Clay's shoulder. "You're going to be okay," he said hoarsely, and he went to the office phone and dialed 911. As he waited for an operator, he looked nervously back at the demolished door. Another surge of wind rushed through the front door and out the open window, seemingly to carry with it whatever horror had happened here.

CHAPTER FIVE

The hissing sound continued; there was no place to get away from it. Their pain came at random, for no reason they could discern, and they clung together in their confusion.

"Hold still," a voice said, and they trembled with fear, for they knew the terrifying voice well. Frozen like a frightened animal, trying to hide but completely exposed; inner, bloody screams silent to the world. The shadow blotted out the light from above. "Keep wiggling, and I will keep taking the parts of you that wiggle," the voice growled. The hissing grew louder, and with a sudden snap, and a flash of shocking pain, the shadow withdrew, holding something in his hands. "I'll be back soon."

★　★　★

"I was gone for less than an hour," John said in a low voice, leaning in so Jessica could hear him over the sound of the hospital waiting room's TV. "I came back, and he was lying there. If I had just stayed with him a little longer . . ." He trailed off, and Jessica gave him a sympathetic look. He grabbed his backpack off the floor and put it in his lap, touching the front pocket to reassure himself that Theodore's head was still where he'd stuffed it.

"Do you think it was just someone with a grudge?" she asked, then flushed. "I don't mean 'just,' like it's not a big deal, but I mean, I'm sure Clay made his fair share of ene-mies, being the police chief. It probably didn't have anything to do with . . ." She glanced around and lowered her voice. "Anything to do with *us*."

John looked down at the backpack in his lap. "The door . . . was *shredded*, Jess."

Jessica looked nervously down the hallway, like she was worried Clay might hear them. "Well, regardless, it's not your fault."

A heavy silence settled in between them, only punctuated by the half-crazed voices coming from the TV, which was showing a montage of ghastly faced clowns. For a moment, John was distracted, searching for a glimpse of the apparition who had silently passed him in the street, but she was not among the crowd.

"People are going crazy this weekend," Jessica said, recalling his attention. "Dressing up in those costumes—did you hear about the kid who got kidnapped?"

"Yeah," John said. "Clay told me about it. Actually, when I went to see him—" John broke off as a nurse in blue scrubs walked up purposefully.

"John, Jessica?" she said as if she already knew the answer.

"Yeah, that's us," Jessica said, with a hint of anxiety.

The nurse gave her a smile. "Chief Burke wants to see you. I tried to tell him visits are supposed to be immediate family only right now, but, well. Chief's orders."

The room was only a few doors down the hallway, but the bright lights and slick, grayish surfaces were disorienting. John squinted to ward off the offensive glare. Jessica was in front of him, and he bumped into her before he realized she had stopped just short of Clay's door.

"What's the matter?" he asked, confused as to why she was standing still.

She turned around and moved close to whisper: "Can you go in first?"

"Yeah, of course," he said, understanding. "He's not that bad, Jess, I promise."

"Still." She made a concerned face and stepped back so John could approach the doorway.

The door was open: He could see Clay, apparently asleep. He was in a hospital gown, and with the blood cleaned from his face, his skin looked sallow. A line of black stitches ran from his forehead to his cheekbone, splitting his eyebrow.

"He almost lost that eye."

Jessica jumped. The nurse had apparently followed them.

"He looks pretty out of it," John said quietly. "Are you sure he wanted to talk to us?"

"He's drifting in and out," the nurse replied in a normal tone of voice. "Go ahead, it won't hurt him to talk for a bit."

"Hey, Clay," John said awkwardly as he approached the bed. "Carlton and Marla are on their way. They should be here soon." Jessica looked sideways at the elderly woman asleep in the other bed, and the nurse stepped past her, closing the curtain between the two patients.

"Privacy, if you can call it that," the nurse said drily, and then left, closing the door partway behind her.

As soon as she was out of the room, Clay's eyes opened. "Good," he said. His voice was reedy, and he didn't lift his head from the pillow, but his eyes were sharp. "Don't pull any plugs just yet, I'm still here," Clay said lightly, and John gave him a wry smile.

"Okay, not yet," he agreed.

"How are you feeling?" Jessica asked.

"Get my jacket," Clay said, pointing to the enclosure's only chair, where a dark gray sport coat was draped over the

90

back. Jessica hurried to get it, and Clay fumbled around with it for a minute, finally extracting a long white envelope from the inside breast pocket. He held it out to John, sitting up slightly; John took it and Clay fell back on the pillow, breathing heavily.

"Take it easy," John said, alarmed.

Clay nodded weakly, his eyes closed. "It has to have a range," he mumbled.

"What?" Jessica leaned in beside John, and they exchanged a worried look.

"It has to have a maximum range." Clay's head lolled to the side and his breath slowed: he seemed to be drifting out of consciousness again.

"Should we get the nurse?" Jessica looked to John, who peered at the monitor, then shook his head.

"His vitals look okay."

"You're not a doctor, John!"

"Shut the door a little more?" John said, ignoring her. Jessica did as he asked begrudgingly, leaving it a few inches ajar. John turned the envelope over: It was unaddressed, sealed, and heavy. He opened it, and something small fell out: Jessica moved to grab it, and John took out the rest of the contents: It was a stack of photographs, about an inch thick. The top one was of him and Charlie in the restaurant only the night before. It seemed to have been shot from outside the building, through the front window. John continued to browse the photos: Each one tracked through his evening with Charlie until they had parted ways: eating, coming out of the restaurant, and saying good-bye, the pictures all taken from a distance. In some the image was askew, or the figures blurry—the photographer had not been interested in composition. There was a last shot in the sequence: Charlie walking away toward the crowd by the new pizzeria; John could make out the back of his own head in the bottom corner of the photo. He quickly put it behind the others and kept looking. The next sequence showed Jessica and Charlie in a clothing store, coming in and out of a dressing room in various outfits, talking and laughing. The pictures seemed to have been taken from the other side of the store—the edges of some were obscured by fabric, as if someone had been hiding behind a rack of clothes.

John felt a stab of angry revulsion. The restaurant pictures were bad enough, but this seemed far more intrusive, an invasion of an intimate moment. He glanced at Jessica; she had moved to the window, holding something up to the light, and after a moment John realized that it was a strip of film. He squinted over her shoulder, and she lowered it, turning to face him.

"All the pictures on this are of us," she said quietly.

He held up the stack of pictures. "These, too."

Jessica held out a hand silently: He passed her half the stack and they each sorted through their share. The photos covered several more moments in time: there was a set of Jessica and Carlton meeting Charlie at a café; John showed one to Jessica and she nodded. "That's when Charlie first got back," she said. Her brow furrowed, and she held up a shot of her, Charlie, and Marla coming out of a building. "This is my apartment complex," she said, her voice tense. "John, this looks like somebody hired a P.I. to follow all of us around. How did he get these? And *why?*"

"I don't know," John said slowly, looking back down at the photo in his hands, the last in the stack. The picture had been taken at night, outside, but the figures were clear: He himself was facing the camera, his hands shoved into his pockets. The despair on his face visible even at a distance. Charlie had her back to the camera; she was hugging herself so tightly that he could see her fingers gripping the back of her dress, a contorted, useless comfort. *Charlie.* His head was too tight, his chest ached. John reflexively bent the photo and put it in his pocket, then turned his head to make sure no one had noticed. Jessica said nothing.

John cleared his throat. "The reason I went to see Clay was that I wanted to show him something."

"What is it?" Jessica stepped closer. John went to the door and peered out, then snuck a glance behind the curtain at the elderly woman. She was still asleep. He took off his backpack and got Theodore out. Jessica yelped, then slapped a hand over her mouth. "Where did you get him?" she demanded.

John took a step back, startled by her sudden, searing scrutiny.

"What's wrong with you?" he asked.

"It's weird. I always hated that thing." Jessica fluttered her hand by her face. "Charlie's robotics experiments always creeped me out, but it's kind of nice to see it."

"Well, this one has an interesting secret."

"Don't let Charlie see it; she's been throwing away things like that, anything from her dad. It's probably some kind of five-step grief-acceptance thing, but still."

"No, I'm not going to show her this. This is going to sound crazy, but Theodore's been . . . talking to me, and yesterday—" He didn't have to continue. A garbled, static-filled noise retched from the rabbit's head, and Jessica winced. Before she could say anything, the sound changed.

Now that he knew the words, they were perfectly clear; Jessica tilted her head to the side, listening intently.

"Is he saying, 'Silver Reef'?" she asked.

"Shining Star. Shining Star, Silver Reef." Theodore was still repeating the phrase, but John shoved him back into his backpack and covered him with a mostly clean T-shirt, muffling the sound. Remembering the pictures, he bundled them back into the envelope and added them to the bag before zipping it back up. "You got it quicker than I did," he told Jessica. She nodded absently, a faraway look in her eye.

"Silver Reef," she repeated.

"Does it mean anything to you?" he asked with a spark of hope.

"It's a town near Hurricane," she said.

"Maybe Charlie's family used to live there?" John said. Jessica shook her head.

"No. It's a ghost town. Nobody lives there."

"Jessica! John!" Marla's voice pierced the quiet, and they turned to see Carlton beside her, his face pale and tense. He brushed past the others and went straight to the bed.

"Dad, are you okay?" He hovered beside Clay, reaching out to touch his hand, then pulling away. "Is he okay?" he glanced back at the others, and Marla hurried forward, examining the monitors.

"He's okay, Carlton," Marla said, putting a hand on his shoulder, and he nodded sharply, not taking his eyes off Clay's still face.

"He'll be fine," John said, trying to sound confident. "He was just awake, talking. The nurse said he's going to be okay."

"What happened?" Carlton asked quietly, and John shook his head.

"I don't know," he said helplessly. "I got there too late." Carlton didn't answer, but pulled a chair up beside the bed and sat down. He rested his chin on his fist, hunching over.

"It'll be okay," Marla repeated, then glanced around the room with a puzzled expression. "Where did she go?"

"Who's with you?" Jessica asked alarmingly, looking to John. John was looking at the door: Charlie had stopped just outside the room.

"Charlie. Hey, come in," he spoke loudly, wondering with guilt if she had heard any of the conversation that had taken place. She stepped into the room, but hung back. John glanced at his backpack, on the floor at the foot of Clay's bed. The noise seemed to have stopped, to his relief. When he looked up, Charlie gave him an embarrassed half smile.

"I don't like hospitals very much," she said softly. "Is he okay?" She didn't turn her head, and John realized that she was deliberately staying where she couldn't see Clay.

"He's going to be," he said. "He's doing okay." She nodded, but stayed where she was, looking unconvinced.

"He's lucky you were there!" Marla exclaimed. "John, you must have saved his life."

"Um, maybe," he said. "I don't know." He squeezed her hand, then let go of it. He turned back to Charlie; she gave him a small, tight smile, her arms folded. The nurse came in, and Marla intercepted her, pulling her aside for an update on his condition and Jessica took the opportunity to lean in. "John, I'm going to leave. I've got classes this afternoon. Pick me up at seven, don't be late."

"Right," John whispered. Jessica made her way past everyone and through the door. Charlie watched her until she was out of sight, then she looked at John again, making eye contact for only a moment before turning her attention back to the nurse. John glanced around the room: with Jessica gone, he felt suddenly untethered, less at ease among these people than he already had been. Without another word, he slipped out the door, ignoring the soft sound of Marla calling his name.

He was only a few feet down the hall when Jessica caught his arm. "John!"

"Hey!" he protested, then saw there was someone next to her, a slight, blonde woman who looked like she had been crying, her red eyes the only color in her washed-out face. "What's wrong?" he asked warily.

"This is Anna," Jessica said. "Clay . . . Chief Burke was—is—helping her to . . ." She cleared her throat. "Her son is missing. Chief Burke was helping."

"Oh," John said awkwardly. "I'm so sorry, ma'am." Anna blew her nose into a crumpled tissue.

"I was just at the station and I overheard . . . they said Chief Burke was here, and I just needed to know he's okay. Is he okay?" she asked anxiously.

"He's going to be fine," Jessica said, and Anna nodded, not seeming convinced.

"When I went to report that Jacob . . . was missing, the desk sergeant had me fill out paperwork, he asked me about my ex-husband and said he had probably taken Jacob. I told him, that man would never take Jacob, he wouldn't know what to do with him!"

"Okay," John said, shifting uncomfortably. "We don't work for the police department—"

"I know that," she said quickly, shaking her head. "I'm sorry, I can't think straight, it's just I overheard the nurse in the waiting room talking to you before. Chief Burke was there when the sergeant was telling me to call my ex-husband; he took me aside and asked me questions, he said he was going to find my son, and I believed him."

"He's a good officer," Jessica said softly. "He's a good person. He'll find your son." Anna pressed her hand to her mouth, stifling a sob as she began to cry again.

"Is he really going to be all right? I heard . . ." She broke off, and John put a hand on her shoulder.

"He's going to be all right," he said firmly. "We just saw him; he talked to us." Anna nodded, but didn't look convinced. Jessica gave John a helpless glance. He racked his brain for something to say. "He will find—Jacob, was it?" he asked, and Anna nodded tearfully.

"Anna!" An older woman rounded the corner briskly, and Anna turned at the sound of her name.

"Mom," she said, the strain in her voice easing slightly. Her mother wrapped her arms around her, and Anna held on tightly, crying into her shoulder.

"It'll be all right," Anna's mother whispered. *Thank you*, she mouthed silently to John and Jessica, and they nodded, exchanged a glance, and headed for the hospital entrance.

As soon as they were in the parking lot, Jessica let out a gasp like she had been holding her breath, and hugged John fiercely. He put his arms around her, surprised. "It'll be all right," he said, and she pushed him away.

"Will it?" she asked, her eyes bright with tears. "It's nice to tell that poor woman that Clay will find her son, but, John, you and I both know that when kids go missing in this town . . . they don't get found." John shook his head. He wanted to argue with her, but there was something leaden in the pit of his stomach.

"It doesn't have to end like that this time," he said without conviction, and Jessica straightened, wiping her eyes like it was a gesture of defiance.

"It can't. It can't end like that again, John. If that little boy is mixed up in all this, we have to find him and bring him home. For Michael."

John nodded, and before she could answer, she strode to her car and drove away, leaving him alone in the parking lot.

That night, John had barely stopped in front of Jessica's building when she came running out. She opened the car door and jumped in with lightning speed. "Go," she said urgently, and he hit the gas.

"What's wrong, what happened?" he asked.

"Just drive, hurry."

"Okay, put on your seat belt!" he scolded as they veered around a corner.

"Sorry! Everything is fine," she said. "I just don't like thinking someone could be out there stalking me."

"Yeah," he agreed, peering into the rearview mirror. "But it's dark out; we should be okay."

"That doesn't make me feel better."

"So, what do you think?" John said after a moment. "Did you notice anything about the photos?"

"That they're enough to get a restraining order in most states?" she joked, but there was real anxiety in her voice.

"None of them were of just one of us," he said. "And none of them were just you and me, or just you and Marla."

"You mean it's about Charlie," Jessica said, understanding immediately.

"Isn't everything?" John said drily. The words sounded bitter, though he had not meant them to, and he glanced at Jessica, trying to gauge her reaction. She was staring out the window like she hadn't heard him.

In less than half an hour, they were at the ghost town. John stopped the car beside a wooden sign reading WELCOME TO SILVER REEF, and got out; Jessica followed. It was an odd mix, even in the dark: in the distance they could see the crumbling walls of buildings that would never be restored, and close by were the places rebuilt for tourists: a church, a museum, and a few others John couldn't make out.

"John, we're going to get killed out here," Jessica said, briefly losing her balance on the loose dirt and gravel.

"When exactly did people last live here?" John asked quietly.

"Late eighteen-hundreds I think. Silver mining town, hence the name."

The town appeared even more abandoned than they were expecting, possibly closed to tourists for the season, but on distant hills there were scattered lights. John turned in a circle, wishing Theodore had been just a little more forthcoming. "What does 'Shining Star' mean, anyway?" he muttered to himself. He looked up: the night was clear, and the sky was awash in stars, with no city lights to drown them out.

"It's beautiful," Jessica murmured.

"Yeah, but not helpful," John said, rubbing the back of his neck. He turned around again, and then he saw it. "Shining star," he said.

"What?" Jessica turned, then squinted and tried to follow his eye line.

A few yards back the way they'd come was a wooden archway leading into a field; at the peak of the arch, was a single silver star.

The field was wide, sloping upward, and at the top of the hill, John could see the outline of a house. It was scarcely visible: had it not been for the guidance of Theodore's mumbling head, it wouldn't have stood out from anything else in the canopy of silhouettes. With wordless agreement, they passed under the star, leaving the remains of the town behind them. The black field soon consumed their line of sight in all directions, with only the faint discoloration of a winding gravel path to guide their steps.

As they made their way up the hill, a small, squarish one-story house came into view; there were windows on each outfacing wall, but only one was lit, in the back. They slowed their pace as they reached the front door: there was only one concrete step, unusually high and wide. John reached out a hand to help Jessica up. She didn't really need it, being five times the athlete that he was, but it still seemed polite. The front door was unwelcoming, the little, lightless lamps almost hidden, offering no help. John looked around for a doorbell and couldn't find one, so he knocked. There was no sound of movement from inside. Jessica leaned to the side, trying to see through the windows. John had raised his hand to try again when the door creaked open, and a tall, dark-haired woman peered out, staring at them coldly.

"Aunt Jen?" John asked meekly, stepping back instinctively before he could stop himself. He recognized her, but standing face-to-face, he felt almost as though they had come to this house at random. Jen tilted her head, her dark eyes fixing on him.

"I'm someone's aunt Jen, yes," she said drily. "But I don't believe I'm yours." She stayed where she was, one hand on the doorframe and the other on the knob; she was block-ing the entry as if she thought they might try to force their way in.

"I'm a friend of Charlie's," John said, and a ghost of an expression flickered on her face.

"And?" she said.

"I'm John. This is Jessica," he added, realizing she had not yet spoken. Jessica would usually have jumped in as the social director, but she was leaving this to him, looking back ner-vously as though she suspected someone was creeping through the dark. John glanced back at her, and she gave him a little, encouraging nod to go on. "I'm here because I got a message," he said. She waited patiently, and John took off his backpack and took Theodore out; Jessica reached for-ward to take the empty bag, and he held the rabbit's head up. Jen showed no surprise, only curling her lip slightly.

"Hello, Theodore," she said calmly. "You've seen better days, haven't you?"

John smiled reflexively, then hardened his features.

"Shining Star, Silver Reef," John said, but Jen didn't react. "I have to say, this is a strange place to call home," he said, though what he wanted to say was, *You owe us an explanation.*

"A message." She looked at Theodore's head, then looked accusingly over her shoulder, though all that was visible behind her was a dark hallway.

"Did you want us to come here? I don't understand," John pressed.

"Why don't you come inside," Jen said, stepping back, then closing the door with haste as soon as they were inside. The house was spare: the furniture was dark and plain, and there was little of it. The walls were thick with layered wall-papers, rich with vintage designs from decades past, but there was nothing hanging on them, though John saw nail holes and marks where decorations had once been. Jen ushered them through a living room with only two chairs and an end table, into a small room almost entirely filled by a square, black-stained dinner table. There were four matching chairs, and Jen pulled out the one closest to the door, then sat down.

"Please," she said, gesturing to the other chairs. John and Jessica made their way around the table to face her, as she stared into the middle distance.

"So, is this where Charlie grew up?" Jessica asked awk-wardly as she sat down.

"No."

"So, then you moved here recently?" John asked suspi-ciously, refusing to believe someone would select this house by choice.

"How is Charlie?" Jen said slowly. "Did she know about the message as well?" Jen made a discreet glance at the win-dow behind them, then focused back on John.

"No," John said plainly. Jen nodded; she was still staring into space, and he had a sudden but profound impression that there was something in the room that only she could see.

"We want to help Charlie. Is there anything going on that we need to know about?" Jessica asked, and Jen snapped to attention.

"Charlie is my concern. She's my responsibility." Jen spoke with an air of pure self-assurance, and something in it must have struck Jessica: she straightened, lifting her chin to match Jen's posture.

"Charlie's our friend, she's our concern, too," Jessica said.

There was silence, and John flicked his eyes back and forth between the two women, waiting. A long moment passed, the two of them staring at each other, immobile, and John realized he was holding his breath.

"Jen," he said, plunging in. "A friend gave us pictures someone had been taking of Charlie, and of us." He unzipped his backpack, and that noise snapped Jessica and Jen out of their staring contest. He pulled the pictures Clay had given them out of their envelope, leaving the film, and placed them in front of Jen on the table. "If you want to take responsibility for Charlie, look at these and tell me if they mean anything to you."

She began going through the stack, peering intently at each photo, then putting each aside, making a second, neat pile of discards. "Why don't you ask your detective friend what they mean?" she asked.

"Because last night our detective friend was nearly murdered," John said. Jen didn't respond, and continued her methodical progress through the pictures. When she had gone through all the pictures, she looked up at John. Her expression had softened slightly; the hostility had given way to something else, a discomfort, and fear.

"Is this all?" she asked. "Is there anything else?" She cleared her throat.

"He said something before he lost consciousness."

"And what was that?"

John looked to Jessica briefly, then back to Jen. "'It has to have a range. It has to have a maximum range.'" He looked at her expectantly, but she showed no sign of recognition.

"I don't know what that means," she said. She put her chin in her hand, staring down again at the first picture in the stack, then she shook her head. "I know you mean well." She leaned back in the wooden chair, looking from John to Jessica and back again. "I should tell you to go away, to forget her. All these years . . ." She trailed off, then gave each of them a piercing look. "Secrets petrify you. You harden yourself against the world to keep them safe, and the longer you keep them, the harder you become. Then one day you look in the mirror, and you realize you've turned to stone." She smiled sadly. "I'm sorry."

"You're not going to tell us anything? We're here to help. We're Charlie's friends!" Jessica insisted.

"If I didn't plan on telling you anything I wouldn't have anything to be sorry about," Jen said, her mouth almost forming a smile. John collected the photos to put back in his bag.

"If you have something to tell us—do it now, or we're leaving. I may not know much, but I know that girl isn't Charlie, or she is under some kind of influence." He waited for a response, but none came. "She isn't herself," he added, sounding more desperate than before. Jen looked up at them: her rigid face had broken, tears were in her eyes.

A knock came from the front door, and even Jen startled. She looked to the door, then back to John and Jessica. Her face was grave. "That way," she said in a voice barely above a whisper, pointing down a narrow hallway. "Close the door behind you." The knock came again; John touched Jessica's arm and nodded, and they got up from the table, careful not to let the chairs make noise as they dragged across the floor.

The hallway was dark, the only light coming from the room they had just left, and John kept a hand on the wall for balance. After a second his eyes adjusted, and he could see an open door at the end of the hall.

"John, come on," Jessica whispered, grabbing his arm briefly as she brushed past him and hurried into the room.

"Yeah," he said, and stopped moving as his fingers touched the frame of a door.

"John!" Jessica hissed. John tried the door. It opened easily; he peered in, and recoiled.

Someone's in there!

"John!" Jessica whispered urgently as the knock at the door came again. John didn't move.

It took only a second for him to register that the figure in the closet was not a person. It was about his height, with a roughly human shape, but it resembled nothing that had ever been alive. John stepped closer and took his keys from his pocket. He switched on the keyring penlight, and swept it up and down quickly. His heart stopped. It was a skeleton, metal and naked wires, encased in nothing. Its arms hung at its sides, and its head was bowed, exposing its open skull, the circuits silent and lightless. Its face was bare and metal.

"John!" Jessica was standing behind the door at the end of the hall, holding it open just a crack as she waited for him. John closed the closet door, blinded again in the darkness, and walked toward the sound of her voice like a beacon. His steps took ages, the air like molasses, as the thing in the closet echoed in his mind like a gunshot, drowning out everything else.

In a daze, John reached the end of the hall as Jessica beckoned frantically. She grabbed his arm and pulled him inside, carefully closing the door behind him.

"What's wrong with you? John, what was in that closet?" she whispered, still holding on to his arm, her nails digging in, bringing him closer to reality.

"It was . . ." He swallowed. *It was holding a knife.* "It was the machine Charlie's father built to kill himself," he said hoarsely. Jessica's eyes widened, and she stared at him like he was a ghost.

The knock came again, much louder, and they both jumped. This time they could hear Jen's footsteps walking toward the sound. Jessica bent and pressed her ear to the keyhole. "Do you see anything?" John whispered. The front door creaked as it opened.

"Charlie," John could hear Jen say. "What a nice surprise." Jessica twisted around in her crouched posture.

"Charlie's here?" she said, scarcely whispering, and John shrugged.

"Aunt Jen, it's so wonderful to see you again," Charlie's voice came through faintly, but clear. Jessica stayed where she was, listening for more, but John was restless, and he looked around the room.

They were in a bedroom—at least, there was a bed—but it was mostly filled with cardboard boxes and old-fashioned wooden trunks. John stumbled around them for a moment, then froze, looking as though something had just occurred to him. He knelt quietly and opened one of the chests, moving slowly to make no sound.

"John, what are you doing?" Jessica whispered angrily.

"Something isn't right here," John breathed, glancing at the door. "Come on, this might be our only chance to find out what she's up to." John shuffled through some of the papers in the first chest, then closed the lid and flipped up the top of a nearby cardboard box: It was filled with computer parts and mechanisms he didn't recognize. A second and third held massive tangles of electric cable. "This looks like stuff I'd expect to find in Charlie's room," he murmured to himself.

"Shhh!" Jessica hissed, pressing her ear back against the door to the hall.

"What's going on out there?" John said under his breath. "I can barely hear anything."

Jessica shook her head.

"Let me know if you hear someone coming." John moved to a large green chest, the paint almost entirely worn off. There was no lock. John knelt beside it, found the handle, and heaved it open, then shuddered, falling back and pushing himself away.

"Jessica," he gasped, moving back to the chest and leaning over it.

"Shhhh!" Jessica hissed from the door, listening intently.

"Jessica."

"What, John? I'm trying to listen."

"It's . . . it's Charlie," he said hoarsely. "In the chest."

"What?" Jessica whispered. She turned around in annoyance, her face falling. She dropped to her knees and crawled to the chest, where John had gone back to looking down at what lay inside. Charlie was curled up in the fetal position; she looked like she was sleeping, with a pillow under her head and blankets surrounding her. Her brown hair was a mess; her face was round; and she was wearing light gray sweatpants and a sweatshirt, both too large for her. John stared, his heart pounding so hard he could hear nothing but the rush of his own blood, not daring to hope, until: she took a breath, and then another. *She's alive.* John reached down into the trunk and touched her cheek: it was too cool. His mind snapped out of its first shock. *We have to get her out of here; she's sick.* He stood and reached awkwardly into the trunk, then gently, cautiously, lifted her out. He looked down at her in his arms, astonished, all his thoughts wordless, except, *Charlie.*

Don't let me go—let go of me, what's happening? Someone touched her cheek, a brief, startling spot of warmth. It was gone just as quickly, leaving her colder than before. *Come back*, she tried to say, but she could not remember how to make the words come out.

"Charlie." *That's my name, someone is saying my name.* Charlie tried to open her eyes. *I know that voice.* Someone's arms reached down under her, lifting her from the cramped, dark place she'd been so long that memories of somewhere else seemed like dreams. She still couldn't open her eyes. A woman said something. *I know them.* She couldn't remember their names.

The first voice came again, it was a man's voice, and she felt its reverberation as he pulled her against his chest, holding her like a child. Warmth radiated from him; he was solid and alive. Even standing still, he was filled with movement: She could hear his heartbeat, just beside her ear. *I am alive.* He said something else, and the rumble of it shook her whole body; the woman answered, and then she was jostled painfully. *We're going somewhere.* She still couldn't open her eyes.

"It's gonna be okay, Charlie," he whispered, and the sleeping world began to pull her down again. *I want to stay!* She began to panic, then as she slipped into unconsciousness again, she grabbed hold of the last words he'd said. *It's gonna be okay.*

John clutched Charlie to his chest, then relaxed his grip anxiously, afraid of hurting her.

"How are we going to get her out?" Jessica whispered, and he glanced around the room. There was a window, but it was high and narrow: getting all three of them through it would take time.

"We'll have to run for it," he said in a low voice. "Wait until . . . *she* leaves." Jessica met his eyes, her face written over with all the questions he had been asking himself for the last six months.

A scream ripped through the silence between them, and John came alert. Someone screamed again, and the room shuddered with impact from somewhere in the house. John looked around wildly for an escape, and his eyes lit on a closet door. "There," he said, nodding toward it. Another bang came, and the wall beside them shook; another scream, and then a scrabbling sound, like an animal scratching at the door. "Hurry," John whispered, but Jessica was already clearing a path. She moved ahead of him, moving aside boxes as quickly and soundlessly as she could, and he carried Charlie carefully behind, his whole being focused on holding her safe. Jessica shoved coats on hangers aside, making room, and they crammed themselves into the space.

"It's gonna be okay, Charlie," John whispered. Jessica closed the door behind them, then stopped, her hand on the knob.

"Wait," she whispered.

"What?"

Jessica ran back across the room carelessly, her steps thudding on the wood floor.

"Jessica, what are you doing?" John hissed, shrinking back farther into the recess of the closet, awkwardly shielding Charlie's head from hangers and hooks with his elbow. Jessica reached the window, snapped open the lock, and threw it open with a loud bang. John gaped as Jessica raced on tiptoe back to the closet, this time making no noise. She nestled in beside him, leaving the door open just a crack, and rested a hand on Charlie's shoulder.

Within an instant, the bedroom door opened, and someone stepped through. The light from the rest of the house filtered in dimly, and through the tiny crack in the door, they could barely make out a silhouette in red, walking purposefully across the room. The figure paused for a moment, looking outside, then with a rush of movement too quick to follow, vanished out the window.

John stood stock still, his heart pounding, half expecting the mysterious figure to appear again in front of them. Charlie's unconscious weight was starting to drag on his arms, and he shifted uncomfortably, trying not to jostle her.

"Come on," Jessica said. He nodded, though she couldn't see him. Jessica pushed the door open cautiously, and they were met with silence. They made their way to the hall, and stopped short again: Jen was slumped on the floor, blood spattering the wall behind her like an abstract mural, and pooled beneath her, trickling across the floor in little rivulets. John raised his hand to cover Charlie's face. There was no doubt that Jen was dead: her eyes glazed and dimmed with the marble stare of death, her stomach laid open.

"We have to go," he said hoarsely, and they turned from the grotesque scene and hurried out of the house. They ran headlong down the hill. John stumbled on the uneven gravel, barely catching himself, and Jessica turned back. "Go," he grunted, and clutched Charlie tighter, slowing his pace just a little.

At last they reached the car, and Jessica opened the back door and got in, then scooted over to the far side and reached out to help him put Charlie inside. Together they laid her across the back seat, placing her head in Jessica's lap. John started the car.

As they sped through the night he kept checking the rear-view mirror, reassuring himself: Charlie still slept, as Jessica twined her fingers in her hair, looking down at her face in wonder. John met her eyes in the mirror and saw his own thoughts on her face: *She's here. She's alive.*

Charlie raced down the hill, exhilarated, almost leaping—she felt like if she went fast enough she might take off and fly. Her heart was beating in a new rhythm; the night air was cool and fresh, and all her senses felt heightened: she could see anything, hear anything—*do* anything.

She reached the bottom of the hill and took off up the next one—she had parked her car behind it. She smiled into the night, picturing Aunt Jen's face in the moment it had dawned on her what was about to happen. That smooth, near-impermeable calm had ruptured; the cold-blooded woman had become a soft, frightened animal in the space of an instant. *At least she had the dignity not to beg*, Charlie thought. *Or maybe she just knew it wouldn't help.* She shivered, then shrugged.

They had been having pleasantries, then Charlie gave Jen a wide, cruel smile, and Jen screamed. Charlie advanced on her, and she screamed again; this time Charlie choked off the noise, grabbing Aunt Jen by the throat. She lifted her off her feet, and slammed her into a door with such force it clattered in its hinges. Her aunt tried to crawl away, and she caught her by her hair, now sticky with blood, and threw her into the wall again. This time she did not try to run, and Charlie crouched beside her and put a hand around her throat again, taking her time now, relishing the feeling of her aunt's pulse beneath her fingers, and the terrified look in her eyes. Jen opened and closed her mouth, gawping like a fish, and Charlie watched for a moment, considering.

"Is there something you'd like to say?" she asked mockingly. Jen made a tiny, pained nod, and Charlie leaned in close so she could whisper, keeping an iron grip on her throat. Jen took a thin, rattling breath, and Charlie reluctantly lightened the pressure enough to let her speak.

Her aunt wheezed for a moment, trying twice to speak before the words made it out. "I've always . . . loved you . . . Charlie."

Charlie pulled back and gave Aunt Jen a calmed look. "I love you, too," she said softly, and then she ripped open her stomach. "I really do."

Charlie reached her car; she was running so fast she ran a few yards past it before she could stop. She wanted to keep running, to keep this feeling alive. She opened and closed her fists; the blood on them was tacky and growing uncomfortable. She started the car and opened the trunk to get the first-aid kit she always carried. Standing in the beam of the headlights, Charlie took out some gauze and hydrogen peroxide and carefully wiped her hands clean finger by finger. When she was done, she examined them and nodded, satisfied; then she got in her car and sped off into the dark.

CHAPTER SIX

J ohn was counting Charlie's breaths, *one-two, three-four, in-out*, each intake of air a marker of the time going by: that this was real, that she was not going to vanish. Hours had passed, and the sky outside was lightening, but still he could not take his eyes off her. His bed was narrow; she was curled on her side as she had been in the trunk, her back pressed against the wall, and he was perched on the edge, careful not to touch her. Jessica had taken a brief nap on the couch, and now she was up again, pacing the short length of his bedroom.

"John, we have to take her to a hospital," Jessica said for the second time since she awoke, and he shook his head.

"We don't even know what's wrong with her," he said softly. Jessica made a frustrated noise in her throat.

"That's all the more reason to *take her to a hospital*," she said, biting the words off individually.

"I don't think she'll be safe."

"You think she's safe here?"

John didn't answer. *One-two, three-four, in-out*—he realized he was counting her breaths again, and he looked away. He could still hear her breathing, though, and the count went on *nine-ten, eleven-twelve* . . . He could feel her presence beside him; even though they weren't touching, he had a constant awareness that she was close by.

"John?" Jessica prompted, and he looked first at Charlie, then at Jessica.

"Clay said something," he said.

"At the hospital?" Jessica frowned. "Something else?"

"No, before that. He had Ella at his house."

"That creepy doll from Charlie's bedroom?"

John hid a smile, remembering. *Jessica will like Ella*, Charlie had once confided to John. *She dresses like her.* But when Charlie had spun the wheel at the end of her bed, the one that made Ella glide out from the closet on her track, proffering her little tea tray, Jessica took one look at the toddler-size doll, screamed, and ran out of the room.

"Yeah, the creepy doll," he confirmed, his thoughts returning to the present. Jessica made an exaggerated shudder.

"I don't know how she could ever sleep, knowing that thing was in the closet."

"It wasn't the only closet," John said, furrowing his brow. "There were two more; Ella was in the littlest one."

"Well, it wasn't the location that creeped me out; I'm fine with closets . . . I take that back, I didn't like the last one we were in," Jessica said drily.

"I wish I could go back to that house—"

"Charlie's old house? It collapsed; it's gone," Jessica interrupted him, and he sighed.

"Ella turned up in the wreckage, but Clay said Charlie wasn't interested in keeping her. It seemed so unlike her; her father made that doll for her."

"Yeah." Jessica stopped pacing and leaned against the wall, letting everything sink in. "You were right, John." She opened her hands in a helpless gesture. "The *other* Charlie, she's an imposter; you were right. So, what do we do?"

John looked down again at Charlie, who stirred in her sleep. "Charlie?" he whispered.

She made a plaintive sound, then was still again.

John glanced thoughtfully at his dresser. After a moment, he went to it and began digging through the top drawer.

"What are you looking for?" Jessica asked.

"There was an old photo, one I found when Charlie and I were looking through her dad's stuff. It was Charlie when she was little. I know it's in here somewhere."

Jessica watched him for a moment, then leaned over as something caught her attention. She crouched beside the dresser and pulled at the corner of something sticking out from underneath. "This?" she asked.

"Yeah, that's it." John took the picture carefully and studied it.

"John, I realize you're having a sentimental moment right now, but we really need to get Charlie to the hospital." Jessica peered over his shoulder. "What is all of that stuff behind her in the picture? Cups and plates?"

"She was having a tea party," John whispered. "I have to go to Clay's house," he added after a moment.

"Clay's still in the hospital."

"I have to go back to his house. Stay here. Take care of Charlie."

"What's going on?" Jessica demanded as John grabbed his car keys from the dresser. "What am I supposed to do if *Not*-Charlie shows up? You saw what she did to Aunt Jen; she was probably the one who got Clay. And now she's gonna be after Charlie, too, *our* Charlie." John stopped, rubbing his temples with one hand.

"Don't let her in," he said finally. "Bolt the door after me, push the couch across the door. I'll be back."

"John!"

He left. He waited on the stoop until he heard the deadbolt fall into place, then hurried to his car.

★   ★   ★

John pulled into Clay Burke's driveway too fast, slamming on the breaks and skidding onto the lawn. He rang the doorbell and waited long enough to confirm that no one was there, tried the knob and found it locked, then tried to act casual as he strolled around to the back of the house. He didn't think the neighbors could see through the hedges separating the houses, but there was no reason not to be careful. The back door off the kitchen was closed as well, so he made his way along the outside wall, looking for a window that would open. The living room was where he found it: the window was unlocked, and after a few minutes of fiddling, he was able to get the screen up, then haul himself over the sill, scraping his back against the window frame as he squeezed through.

He landed in a crouch, and stayed there for a moment, listening. The house had a thick hush, and a closed-up, stale smell; Carlton must have slept at the hospital. John got up and went to Clay's study, not bothering to be quiet.

He balked when he saw the wreckage: he hadn't forgotten the scene: the door smashed, the furniture upturned, and papers scattered over the floor like carpeting, but it was still a shock to see it. There was also a dark stain on the floor where he'd found Clay lying. John stepped over it carefully and went into the office.

He scanned the room quickly: only one corner remained undisturbed: Ella was standing there almost concealed behind a standing lamp, her tea tray steady in front of her.

"Hey, Ella," he said suspiciously. "Do you have something that you want to tell me?" he said as he turned his attention to the clutter in the room. There were three empty cardboard boxes beside the desk, and he went there first: it looked like their contents had been dumped out in one big pile. Sifting through quickly, he saw that they were all related to Freddy Fazbear's: photographs, papers of incorporation, tax forms, police reports, even menus. "Where do I start?" he murmured. He came to a photograph of Charlie and her father: Charlie was smiling; her father was holding her on his hip, pointing to something in the distance. He set it down and kept looking. Among the papers and photos were other things; the random computer chips and mechanical parts that seemed to turn up everywhere. He checked his watch; he was getting nervous at leaving Jessica alone with Charlie so long. He looked at Ella in the corner. "You know what I'm looking for, don't you?" he asked the doll, then sighed and went back to the pile.

On his hands and knees, he surveyed the area, and this time noticed a small cardboard box beneath Clay's desk. It was only a few inches across, sealed with packing tape, but a corner had ripped open, spilling out part of its contents: John could see a bolt and a small strand of copper wire stuck to the tape on the outside. He crawled under the desk and grabbed it, then ripped the hole wider, not bothering with the tape. He stood and dumped out the rest of it on Clay's desk; it was filled with more wires and parts. John shook the box and it rattled, and he banged on it until the thing that was stuck came out: a square circuit board attached to a tangle of wires. He studied it for a second before putting it aside and dropped the box, then spread the parts across the desk's surface in a single layer, then sat down and peered at them one by one, hoping for something familiar.

It took less than ten seconds to find it: a thin disc about the size of a half-dollar coin. His heart skipped, and he held the thing up, squinting at it until he saw the tiny words engraved along the edge in flowing, old-fashioned script: AFTON ROBOTICS, LLC. He swallowed, remembering the incapacitating nausea the last disc produced in him; he also remembered the more substantial effects the disc was capable of.

John glanced back at Ella, then stood and approached her. He knelt beside her, holding the disc firmly in his hand, with his thumbnail under the switch on its side. John's balance wavered. He set his jaw firmly and flipped the switch.

In an instant, Ella was gone. In her place was a human child, a toddler. She had short, frizzy brown hair and a round face set in a happy smile; her chubby hands gripped the tea tray determinedly. Only her absolute stillness indicated that she was not alive. That, and her vacant eyes, staring sightlessly ahead.

"Can you hear me?" he asked softly. There was no movement; the little girl was no more responsive than Ella. He reached out to touch her cheek, then pulled his hand back suddenly, revolted: her skin was warm and pliable—alive. He stood and went back to the desk, keeping his eyes on the girl. John clawed at the tiny switch again, flipping it back, and the toddler shimmered and blurred for a second, then the image solidified: Ella stood calmly in her place again, nothing more than a large toy doll. John sat down heavily. "Maximum range," he muttered to himself, recalling Clay's brief moment of consciousness at the hospital. But the photographs he'd insisted on giving them hadn't revealed anything. *Or had they?*

He went to Clay's desk and picked up the phone: There was a dial tone; it had not been damaged when the place was ransacked. He dialed his own number. *Please pick up, Jessica,* he thought.

"Hello?"

"Jessica, it's me."

"Who's me?"

"John!"

"Right, sorry. I'm a little jumpy. Charlie's fine—I mean, she's still asleep; she's not worse."

"Good. That's not why I called, though. I need you to meet me at the library—bring the envelope Clay gave us, it's in my backpack."

"All the pictures are gone," Jessica said. "We left them at Jen's house when we fled for our lives, remember?" she added with a hint of sarcasm.

"I know. We don't need the pictures. There was a roll of microfilm in the envelope."

There was a pause on the other end, then, "I'll see you there."

John turned to look at Ella, scratching his thumb thoughtfully across the surface of the disc. "And you; you're coming with me," he said quietly to Ella. He picked her up gingerly, repelled by what he had seen, but she felt just like the doll she seemed to be. She was large enough to be awkward to carry, so he placed her on his hip like a human child, and left through the front door. He stowed the doll in his trunk, put the picture of Charlie and her father in the visor, and pulled out of Clay's driveway.

When John got to the library, Jessica was already in conversation with the librarian, a middle-aged man with an irritated expression.

"If you want to use the microfiche reader, I need you to tell me what you want to look at. Would you like to see the index of our archives?" he asked. It sounded like he had asked the question several times already.

"No, that's all right, I just need to use the machine," Jessica said. The librarian smiled tensely.

"The reader is for looking at microfilm; what microfilm do you want to look at?" he asked very slowly.

"I brought my own," Jessica said breezily.

The librarian sighed. "Do you know how to use the machine?"

"No," she said after a moment's thought.

John stepped forward quickly. "I know how to use it; I'm with her. Can you just let us into the room?"

The librarian nodded wearily, and they followed him to a small back room, where the microfilm reader was set up. "You thread the film through here," he said, "and turn the knobs to advance it." He gave John a suspicious look. "Got it?"

"Yes, thank you for your help. We are very appreciative," John said as he glared at Jessica.

As the door closed behind the librarian, Jessica pulled the film out of her pocket and handed it over. "Okay, what are we looking for?" she asked excitedly, clapping her hands with anxious energy.

"Slow down, okay?" John said wearily. "We almost got killed, we don't even know what's wrong with Charlie, and now you're giddy like we're looking for hidden treasure."

"Sorry." Jessica straightened her posture.

"I think these are the same pictures," John said as he unwound the film and threaded it carefully through the machine. He flipped it on, and the first picture appeared: Jessica and Charlie, picking outfits in a clothing store. He clicked through the next few; they all matched what he remembered of the photos, though the order was different—chronological, he supposed.

"They're the same, and they're not any clearer, either," Jessica said.

"What?" John went back, trying to see what Jessica had noticed that he hadn't.

"They're not any clearer. Charlie is still blurry," Jessica pointed out.

"She's just in motion," John explained.

"In all of them?"

"The picture is clear," he said again, growing agitated. "She's just walking." Despite his words, he stopped and began to go through the pictures more slowly, studying Charlie's appearance in each one. Jessica was right: Charlie was blurry in all of the pictures, even some where she appeared to be standing still. John clicked through the photos fast, confirming it: there was Jessica and Charlie in a clothing store; Marla with them outside Jessica's apartment; Charlie hugging herself as she spoke to John at the Burkes' house that first night—Charlie was blurry in all of them. John flipped ahead quickly to the last set: himself with Charlie—the false Charlie—sitting in the restaurant where they'd had dinner.

The reel ended on the final picture from that night: Charlie nearly lost in the crowd, turning back one last time.

She was barely visible, far more distant here than in any of the other pictures, only recognizable by the color of her dress and hair.

"I still don't see the point," Jessica said impatiently. John grasped the lens and turned it; the picture shrank. "These are the same pictures." She turned away and sighed.

"This is the point," he said, slowly turning it back the other way. The film was high-resolution and the image continued to enlarge as he zoomed closer to Charlie.

"What is?"

John kept zooming in; Jessica gasped, stepping back from the machine. John let go of the lens. "It has a maximum range," he said softly. The figure that filled the screen was elegant and feminine, but it was not human. The face was exquisitely sculpted and was split down the middle, a thin seam outlining where the two halves met. The limbs and body were segmented plates, their color almost iridescent.

"It looks like a mannequin," Jessica gasped.

"Or a clown," John added. "I saw her," he said wonderingly. "The night Clay was attacked, she was on the road. She looked at me . . ." The eyes in the photo were difficult to see, and John leaned closer to the screen, trying to make them out.

"It's the imposter, it's the other Charlie," Jessica breathed. John snapped off the projector, blinking as the haunting figure disappeared. He took the disc from his pocket and handed it to Jessica. She turned it over in her hand, her eyes widening. "Is this hers?"

"No," John said shortly. "But I'm guessing that our mutual friend has one just like it, messing with our heads when we're around her and making us see her as Charlie." He leaned back against the table. "I think Clay took those pictures; I think he suspected something like this but needed to prove it."

"I don't understand."

"These things, these discs, send out signals that over-whelm your brain, causing you to not see what's really in front of you. Now, that wouldn't work on a camera, obvi-ously, but Henry thought of that, too."

"So, the frequency or whatever it emits causes the image to blur," Jessica said, catching on.

"Exactly, but it has a maximum range. The signal fades; that's why he captured these from a distance. He suspected that whatever was causing the illusion must have its limits." John began putting the film back into his bag. "That's why she looks human in the other pictures, at least, human enough when blurred."

Jessica studied the disc again for a moment before John took it back. "I still don't understand," she said. She looked around as though suddenly afraid of being caught.

"I think it's exactly what I suspected," he said. "Except I was completely wrong."

"Oh, that makes perfect sense," Jessica quipped.

"I had all these theories about Charlie," John said. "And even though I may have been wrong about the details, I suspected that Charlie, *our* Charlie, had been swapped out with an imposter. But it wasn't a twin brother, or a twin sister. Afton swapped her out with . . . *this*."

"A robot?" Jessica said skeptically. "Like from Freddy's? John, that was different. People, kids, had been murdered. *Those* robots were haunted. I don't even believe in hauntings, but those things were haunted! Robots like what you're talking about don't exist, at least . . . not yet. Plus, she knew everything Charlie did, how could Afton have programmed that?"

"She didn't know everything, though. She blamed all the gaps in her memory on the near-death experience; her personality changed—everything changed—and we all believed she had just turned over a new leaf," he said bitterly.

"You didn't," Jessica said, and he met her eyes.

"Yeah, but I wanted to. Something just wasn't right."

Jessica was quiet for a moment. "Why did she kill Jen?" she said abruptly.

"What?"

"Why would she kill Jen?" she repeated.

"Charlie's aunt Jen knew her better than anyone," John said. "She must have known she couldn't fool her."

"Yeah, maybe." Jessica bit her lip, then her face took on a look of alarm. "Or she went there—"

"To find Charlie," John cut in.

"John, we left her alone; we have to go back."

John was already out the door, running headlong across the library to the exit. Jessica ran after him. They both got into John's car and he hit the gas, clenching his jaw as they sped toward his apartment.

CHAPTER SEVEN

Have you forgotten something?" the man snapped, and the woman gave him a level stare.

"I forget nothing."

"Then why are you not already on your way?" He lifted his arm weakly and gestured toward the door.

"Time is running short," she said. "I do not understand why we are spending our time—*your* time—pursuing this thing. I am better used here."

The man was silent.

"We are seeing results," she added, but he shook his head.

"We are seeing nothing." He held up a finger before she could protest. "Anyone can discover a fire already burning, but Henry found a unique spark—created something truly different, something he didn't deserve, or intend, to stumble

133

upon." He gave the woman a sharp look. "You will bring it to me." The woman cast her eyes to the floor, and when she spoke there was something pleading in her voice.

"Am I not enough?" she asked softly.

"No, you're not," he said firmly, looking away.

The woman paused, then walked out the door, not looking back.

Neither of them spoke as they sped toward John's apartment. He gripped the wheel until his knuckles turned white, trying not to imagine what they might find.

When he turned into the lot, he let out a shaky breath: the few cars belonged to his neighbors, and his door was intact. He gave Jessica a curt nod, and they got out of the car. Jessica followed close behind and stood beside him, facing the parking lot, as he unlocked the door. Jessica jabbed him in the side hard with her elbow just as he was about to turn the key, and he jerked it back from the lock. "OW! What the . . . ?" He whirled around angrily to Jessica, then immediately straightened his posture and threw on a big smile.

"Charlie!" he blurted. The elegant woman approached them, and John reflexively took a step back. "Where did you come from? I mean, we didn't see your car. What a nice surprise," he added hastily. The woman who was not Charlie smiled easily.

"I've been out walking, I wanted to clear my head. I realized I was near you and thought I'd stop by. Is that okay?"

John nodded, stalling for time. "Of course! It's great to see you!" John blurted, painfully aware that he was overselling. "My place is a mess, though. Bachelor pad, you know?" He forced a grin. "Do you and Jessica mind waiting out here while I clean up a little?"

Charlie laughed. "John, you saw my dorm room last year—I can handle a little mess!"

"Well, unlike you last year, I'm not working on a crazy brilliant science project, so I have no excuse," he said.

Jessica jumped in. "How about that project, Charlie? Did you keep working on it? How's it looking?"

Charlie turned to Jessica as if seeing her for the first time. "I lost interest," she said. John seized his chance: he unlocked the door, slipped inside, and locked it behind him before the imposter could follow. In his bedroom, Charlie, *his* Charlie was still curled up on his bed, her back pressed against the wall; she didn't look like she'd moved since he left.

"Charlie," he whispered. "I'm sorry, but I have to move you, now. I'll be careful." He scooped her up with care. She was warm in his arms, and her eyes twitched beneath her lids: she was dreaming. John held on tightly, looking around the room for a place to hide her—his failure to furnish the place beyond the essentials was working against him. John carried Charlie out into the living room: the couch was at an angle to the wall, leaving a tiny, triangular space behind it. John set Charlie on the couch temporarily, took a blanket that had been in a heap on the floor, and tossed it down into the space, giving her at least a little cushion. Then he climbed over, picked her up, and lifted her over the back, settling her on the floor. He barely fit, even standing, and he kept his eyes behind him as he climbed back over the couch, afraid of kicking her. There was another gray blanket draped over the end of the couch, something left by a previous tenant, and he grabbed it and spread it over Charlie, covering her face.

Someone knocked on the door. "John?" Jessica called. "Are you almost done *cleaning*?" There was an edge of panic in her voice. John looked around. There was no evidence of a mess, or him having just hurriedly cleaned one. He rushed to the bedroom and grabbed some laundry from his laundry basket, then carried it with him to answer the door.

"Sorry," he said, aiming for a sheepish expression. "I don't get a lot of guests." Jessica smiled nervously and the other Charlie flashed a grin as she pushed in past him.

"Looks pretty nice," she said, turning to him. "How's the neighborhood?"

". . . Fine," John managed, disconcerted to be face-to-face with her, moments after the real Charlie. This time he could see the differences—he could have written a list. The impression that this woman, with her glamorous allure, was simply Charlie, grown into her beauty with grace and new self-assurance, was gone. Now, the individual features stuck out on her face like warts—each one a marker that this was not *Charlie*. Nose too narrow, cheeks too hollow. Eyes too far apart. Hairline too high. Eyebrows at the wrong angle. The disparities were minute, millimeters or less: the only way to be sure would be to look at Charlie and her robotic double side by side. Or one right after the other. The imposter Charlie gave him a subtle smile and shifted her balance, as though about to come closer. John cleared his throat, hunting for something to say, but Charlie had already looked away and was now glancing around the living room. Behind her, Jessica was giving him a questioning look, probably wondering where the real Charlie was. John ignored her: Not-Charlie strode past him into his bedroom, and he followed quickly.

"Right!" John bolted into action. "So, this is my bedroom," he said, as if the tour had been his own idea.

"Nice," Charlie murmured, surveying the room. She turned in a circle, taking it all in, then went to the dresser, and turned to inspect the room again from there.

"So, hey, we should all go hang out later or something!" Jessica said suddenly, but Charlie didn't answer. Instead, she knelt slowly and peered under the bed. Jessica and John exchanged a nervous glance.

"Not much to see. It's just me here." John laughed. Jessica elbowed him and made a disapproving expression. *I'm being too obvious again*, he realized. John could feel his pulse in his throat, immediately regretting what he'd said. *Please don't look around*. Charlie went into the bathroom and glanced around it, opening the medicine cabinet and examining the contents. Jessica gave John a perplexed look, then it occurred to her. *She's looking for signs that someone's been injured*. Charlie began to close the cabinet, then caught sight of her own reflection and paused, her hand still on the cabinet door, looking at herself. She was still for a long moment, then her eyes darted to John in the mirror, and she made a face.

"I hate mirrors," she remarked, then turned away and pulled back his shower curtain.

"I know right? They add ten pounds," John said mildly.

"I think that's cameras," Jessica corrected.

"Well, mirrors add at least five," John whispered.

"Maybe you just need to lose weight."

"Are we really having this conversation now?"

They continued to watch Charlie. "She's searching," Jessica whispered. "She's not even trying to hide it."

John worried. Charlie paused and opened the bedroom closet, then crouched down to look in the open space under his hanging shirts and jackets. She stood and went back into the living room: Jessica followed, sprinting to get ahead of her and sitting on the couch quickly, crossing her legs. Charlie went to the kitchenette and opened the refrigerator, then closed it.

"Are you hungry?" Jessica asked. "I'm sure John has something you can eat."

"No, thank you. How have you been, Jessica?" Charlie asked, crossing the room to the couch. John's whole body went rigid as he willed himself not to run across the room and yank her away. Instead, he opened the fridge himself, forcing himself to breathe as, from the corner of his eye, he watched her sit down beside Jessica.

"Anybody want a water? Or a soda?" he called.

"Yes, please," Jessica said with a strain in her voice, coughing loudly. John grabbed two cans and brought them over. Jessica took hers eagerly. "Thank you," she said with too much emphasis, and he nodded.

"Yeah, of course." He smiled stiffly at Charlie, and she looked back: every moment she was there, he felt more and more like his skin was about to crawl off his bones. He would have thought it was a side effect of her chip, except it had not happened until he knew what she was.

"Sit down, John." Charlie smiled, gesturing to the arm of the couch beside her.

"Sorry I don't have chairs and stuff. I never meant to live here long-term," John explained nervously.

"How long have you been here?" Charlie's familiar voice was like tin.

John sat down beside her. "Since—everything. This is where I lived when I first came here."

"Oh." She glanced around the room again. "I guess I don't remember it."

"You never saw it," he said, unable to keep the coldness from his voice. Jessica shot him a warning glance, and he took a deep breath. Charlie began scanning the room again. She stared straight ahead, her face taking on a look of concentration. Her eyes swept up and down the room in strokes, her head and torso slowly turning until she was looking almost directly behind her: in a second, she would see the gap behind the couch. "Charlie, I had fun the other night," John said quickly, forcing himself to mean it. "Do you want to have dinner again tonight?"

She turned back around, looking surprised. "Yes, of course—that sounds great, John. Same place?"

"Same place. Around seven?"

"Sure."

"Great!" Jessica declared, and stood. "Anyway, I have to go," she said. "Want to walk out with me, Charlie?" She glanced nervously at John, and he got up quickly.

"I can give you a ride if you need one," he volunteered, "I know you said you were walking."

Thank you, Jessica mouthed from behind her back.

"No," Charlie said. "I think I'll keep walking. I'm not parked too far away. It's really nice outside."

"Okay, then," John said. Charlie moved gracefully across the living room and let herself out. Jessica let out a long breath like she'd been holding it. They went to the window and, silently, they watched the imposter go, until she had disappeared around a bend in the road.

"What if she comes back?" Jessica said. "I don't want you alone with that *thing*," she finished, practically spitting the last word. John nodded in vigorous agreement.

"I don't want to be alone with her, either," he said.

Jessica looked thoughtful for a moment. "I won't be gone long," she said. "We need help. And if you don't think Charlie should go to the hospital, then the hospital has to come to her."

"Marla?"

"Marla." And with that, she went to the door quickly. John walked out with her, and watched uneasily as Jessica got in her car and drove off. Then he went back inside and shut the door, locking and bolting it. *A lot of good this will do*, he thought as he slipped the chain into place.

"Charlie?" he called softly. He didn't expect an answer, but he wanted—felt almost compelled—to talk to her. "Charlie, I wish you could hear me," he went on, going to the bedroom closet and pulling out all two of his other blankets. "I think it's safer for you to stay where you are than in the bedroom." He pulled the couch a little farther from the wall, trying to figure out how best to make her more comfortable. At a loss, he grabbed a pillow and leaned down, reaching to remove the blanket that covered her face.

"Sorry I've only got the one pillow," he said, trying not to lose his balance.

"'S okay," came a muffled murmur from beneath the blanket, and John fell back, tumbling over the seat and barely catching himself before his head hit the floor.

"Charlie?" he cried, then lowered his voice as he climbed back up. "Charlie, are you awake?" There was no answer. This time he did not try to climb into the space behind the couch, and bent over to see. She was stirring, just a little. "Charlie, it's me, John," he said, his voice hushed, but urgent. "If you can hear me, hold on to the sound of my voice." He stopped, as she sat up and pulled the blanket off her face.

He stared down at her, as astonished as the moment when he first saw her. Her face was red, and her hair was sticking to her skin after being under the blanket; her eyes were barely open; she blinked rapidly in the light, looking down and away. John leaped up and rushed to shutter the front window blinds. He closed the bedroom door and pulled the kitchen curtains. The apartment, never bright at its best, was nearly dark. He hurried back to Charlie's hiding place, grabbed one end of the couch, and pulled it out farther, enough for him to crawl behind with her. She was still sitting, leaning against the wall, but she looked limp, like she wouldn't be able to do it much longer. He reached out to steady her, but when his hand touched her arm she made a distressed, high-pitched noise, and he drew back instantly.

"Sorry. It's me, John," he repeated, and she turned her head to see him.

"John," she said, her voice thin and rasping. "I know." Her breathing was ragged, and talking seemed to take effort. She reached out feebly with one hand.

"What do you need?" he asked, searching her face. She reached out farther and then he understood; he took her hand.

"I won't ever let go of you again," he whispered. She smiled faintly.

"Could get awkward," she whispered. She opened her mouth as if to go on, then sighed, shuddering. John scooted closer, alarmed.

"What's—" She took another breath. "Wrong with me?" she finished in a rush. She opened her eyes, looking at him plaintively.

"How do you feel?" he asked, avoiding the question.

"Tired . . . everything hurts," she said haltingly, her eyes drifting shut, and he clenched his jaw, trying to keep his face neutral.

"I'm trying to help you," he said finally. "Look, you have to know—there's someone, something, out here impersonating you; saying that she is you." Her eyes snapped open and she squeezed his hand suddenly: she was alert. "She looks just like you. I don't know why, I don't know what she's after, but I'm going to find out. And I'm going to help you."

"Afton," she breathed, her voice barely audible, and John quickly reached over the couch to grab the pillow he'd brought.

"Can you lift your head?" he asked, and she did, slightly, letting him slide the pillow into place. "We know it's Afton," he said, picking up her hand when she was settled again; she squeezed it lightly. "I have one of the chips. Afton Robotics. Charlie, I've got this. Clay's helping, and Jessica, and we're getting Marla to help you get better. It's going to be okay. Okay?"

But Charlie had drifted back into unconsciousness; he had no idea how much she had heard, or understood. Her hand had gone limp in his own.

Someone that looks like me . . . Never let go . . . John? Charlie struggled to order her thoughts: things that had made sense a moment ago were losing their shape, drifting out of reach in a dozen directions like petals on the water. *The door . . .*

"It's going to be okay," John said, but she didn't know if he said it in her head or in the world. She felt herself slipping back into the dark; she tried to hold on, but the exhaustion was weightier than she was, pulling her inexorably down with it.

★   ★   ★

Charlie glanced at the door again. *He's late, or I'm early.* She picked up the fork in front of her and ran her thumb over the smooth metal; the tines hit her water glass with a clear *ding!* and she smiled at the sound. She hit the glass again. *How much does he know?*

Charlie struck the glass again, and this time she noticed several other patrons turning to look at her in confusion. She smiled politely, then set her fork down on the table and folded her hands in her lap. Charlie took in a breath and composed herself.

As John approached the restaurant he could see that *Not-*Charlie was already there. She had changed her clothes. He hadn't really registered what she had been wearing before, but now she had on a tight, short red dress—he would have remembered that. He stopped on the sidewalk, just out of her sight, steeling himself. He couldn't get the other image out of his mind, the painted face with the soldering line splitting it down the middle. Charlie was sitting back in her chair; there was nothing in front of her but a water glass. She had ordered food when they last met here, but John couldn't picture her actually eating it. He couldn't remember noticing her *not* eating, either.

"Stop stalling!" came a crackling voice from his waist, and he jumped. He extricated the walkie-talkie from his jacket pocket and turned away from the restaurant before speaking into it, just in case Not-Charlie looked out.

"I'm not stalling," he said.

"You shouldn't be able to hear us," Jessica's distorted voice reminded him. "Did you tape the button down?"

"Right, hang on." John examined the walkie-talkie: The tape he had placed over the button to transmit had come loose. He replaced it, flattening it down against the uneven surface with his fingernail. He slipped the device back in his pocket and went inside.

John glanced briefly around the restaurant as he entered. Jessica and Carlton were huddled together in a high-backed booth, out of Charlie's sight. "Can you both still hear me?" John whispered. Carlton's hand raised above the back of the booth momentarily with a triumphant thumbs-up, bringing a real smile to John's face. John turned his attention back to Charlie, who had not yet noticed him.

She lifted her head abruptly from the menu as he approached the table, as if sensing his presence. She flashed him a bright smile.

"Sorry I'm late," John said as he sat down.

"That's usually my line," Charlie joked, and he grinned uneasily.

"I guess so." He looked at her for a moment: he had rehearsed things to say, but his mind had gone blank.

"So, I heard you and Jessica visited that old ghost town." Charlie giggled. "What's that place called again?" She leaned in and rested her chin on her hand again.

"Ghost town?" John said unevenly, trying to keep his expression neutral. It took everything he had not to turn and look at Jessica and Carlton behind him. Charlie was looking at him expectantly, and he took a sip of water. "You mean Silver Reef?" he said, setting down the glass carefully.

"Yes, I mean Silver Reef." She was smiling, but her face looked tight, like there was something ravenous waiting just below the surface. "That's a strange place to go, John." She cocked her head slightly. "Just out seeing the sights?"

"I've always been a . . . history buff. The, the gold rush—"

"Silver," Charlie corrected.

"Silver. Yes. That too. Just fascinating times in history." John was tempted to turn and see if Jessica approved of his reply or if she was scrambling out of her seat to flee the restaurant. "You didn't know that about me, did you?" He straightened his posture. "I love history: historic towns, places." He cleared his throat.

Charlie picked up her water glass and drank; she set it down so he could see the red lipstick mark she left. John drew back slightly and looked elsewhere, searching for anything he could lock eyes with but her. "Why were you there?" Charlie asked, recalling his attention.

"I was—" he started, then paused, taking a moment to gather his thoughts. "I was looking for an old friend," he said, his answer calm. She nodded, then met his eyes. He blinked, but forced himself not to look away. He had seen eyes like those before: not the madness of Springtrap, or the uncanny, living plastic of the other robots, but the stark, brutal gaze of a creature bent on survival. Charlie was looking at him like he was prey.

"Did you find your old friend?" she asked, her tone warm, and out of place.

"Yes. I did," John said, not flinching from her stare. Charlie's eyes narrowed, the facade between them growing thinner by the moment. John leaned forward on his crossed arms, resting all his weight on the table between them. "I found her," he said in a low voice. There was a brief flare of something on Charlie's face—surprise, maybe, and she leaned in closer across the table, mimicking his pose. John tried not to flinch as Charlie's arms slid closer to his.

"Where is she?" Charlie asked, her tone as soft as John's. Her smile was gone.

"I don't know what it will take to show these people what you really are," John said. "But I can try all sorts of things before you make it out that door." He grasped his soda glass, not looking away from her. "I'll start with this glass of soda, then I'll try a chair over the back of your head, and we'll go from there."

Charlie tilted her head, as though taking in his posture. He knew his hand was twitching, and his face was red. His heart was racing; he could feel his pulse pounding at his throat. Charlie smiled, then stood and gently leaned over the table. John set his jaw, keeping his eyes fixed on her. Charlie kissed his cheek, placing a hand on the side of his neck. She kept it there as she moved away, watching his eyes. Charlie smiled, her fingers resting on his pulse for a scant moment before letting them drift away. John snapped back in his seat as if she'd been holding him in place.

"Thank you for dinner, John," she said, the words sounding almost giddy. She slowly let her hand recoil, as if relishing the moment. "It's always so wonderful to see you." She turned away, not waiting for a response, and went to pay the bill.

There was a long pause. "She's gone." John's voice came over the walkie-talkie. Jessica looked to Carlton; he seemed slightly in shock, staring after Charlie like he'd been hypnotized. "Carlton!" Jessica hissed. He snapped out of it, shaking his head.

"She looks hot!" Carlton said.

Jessica reared back and slapped Carlton as hard as she could.

"You idiot! You're supposed to be watching his back, not watching *her* butt! Besides, she put your father in the hospital!"

"No, no, I know. Very serious . . ." He trailed off, obviously distracted.

"Why did I even bring you along?" Jessica scooted out of the booth and got to her feet clumsily.

"Where are you going?" Carlton asked.

"I have an idea; stay here." Jessica sighed. "You take my car."

Carlton called after, but she didn't stop to answer, merely threw her car keys behind her. Carlton made his way over to John's booth.

"Hey. Are you okay?" John didn't turn at the sound of Carlton's voice beside him.

"No. Not really okay." John leaned back in his seat, looking up at the plaster ceiling, then finally turned to look at Carlton. "Where's Jessica?" John asked instantly.

"I'm not sure, she ran out . . ." Carlton gestured toward the parking lot, and John turned just in time to see Charlie pull out onto the road and drive away.

"She did something stupid, didn't she?" John said wearily. Carlton met his eyes, then they both ran for the door.

Jessica kept low and snuck to the back exit of the restaurant; she could see Charlie was still standing at the front desk taking care of the bill. Jessica slipped out the back door and ran around the perimeter of the building, her high heels clacking on the sidewalk. She yanked them off and threw them into the bushes, then kept running, barefoot.

"Jessica, what are you doing?" she muttered to herself. As she rounded the corner of the building into the parking lot, she spotted Charlie's car and made a beeline for it. The front door was unlocked. Jessica quickly popped the trunk, shut the door, and slipped inside, not closing the trunk lid all the way.

A minute later there was noise from inside the vehicle, and Jessica strained to listen: it sounded like voices. No, *a* voice, she realized after a few minutes. Charlie was talking, but there was no one answering her. Jessica concentrated, trying to isolate the sounds, but she could make out nothing: whatever Charlie was saying, it was unintelligible from the trunk. Jessica balanced herself carefully, trying to lay as flat as she could while bracing her arm in the air to hold the latch of the trunk. If she didn't hold it tight enough, it would visibly bounce and Charlie would notice it. But if she pulled it too close, the trunk might shut, and she would be trapped.

After about ten minutes, the car stopped short; Jessica was thrown back against the wall, almost losing hold of the latch. Regaining her balance, she held very still, listening. The driver's side door opened; then closed a moment later. Jessica heard the faint sound of Charlie walking away, crunching over gravel, then silence. Jessica sighed in relief, but did not move. She began to count: "One Mississippi . . . two

Mississippi . . ." she breathed, barely a whisper. There was no sound but her own hushed voice as she counted all the way to sixty, then stopped and scooted closer to the trunk door. She gently eased her grip of the trunk handle, letting the hood rise slowly.

The car was parked in the center of a large parking lot, illuminated impossibly bright by streetlamps. The light was tinged with red, and Jessica turned to see a large neon sign directly overhead, flooding the lot with brilliant reds and pinks and blocking her view of anything beyond. The air buzzed loudly with the noise of what must have been a hundred fluorescent bulbs. Jessica squinted and raised a hand to shade her eyes: the enormous, smiling face of a little girl stared down at her, glowing neon against the night sky. She was made up to look like a clown: her face was painted white, and her cheeks were marked with round, pink circles, her nose a matching triangle. Her bright orange hair was tied up in two pigtails on either side of her head, and beside her were fat, red letters outlined in yellow. Jessica peered at the backward sign for a moment before the letters made sense: CIRCUS BABY'S PIZZA. The glare of the light began to hurt her eyes, and she looked away, then ran toward the dark building at the edge of the lot, blinking to get the afterimage of the neon sign out of her head. She stumbled through a row of hedges to press into a white brick wall, which seemed brand-new. She lowered her hand from her face, her eyes adjusted to the light, and she saw a long row of tall, vertical windows along the face of the wall.

She went to the nearest one and pressed her face to the glass, but the tint was too dark to see even a shadow of what lay behind it. Jessica gave up on the windows and walked quickly to the back of the building, keeping close to the brick wall. The neon whites and reds faded as Jessica made her way around back, sinking into darkness.

There was more parking in the back, though it, too, was unoccupied. A single bulb flickered above a plain metal door, throwing off a sickly yellow color, which seemed to stick to everything. Trash cans lined the wall, and two Dumpsters enclosed the small area, shielding the door from outside view. Jessica crept toward the door, careful not to step on anything. She gave it a gentle pull, but it was sealed shut. She balanced against the frame as she pushed herself up onto her toes, and grinned. She could see inside.

Inside was a dimly lit room. Charlie was there: she was in profile, talking to someone just beyond Jessica's view, though she could not hear either voice. Jessica inched along the ridge, trying to see the other person, but all she could make out was the blur of movement as someone gestured. After a few minutes, her calves began to ache, and she eased herself back down off her toes and flexed her feet. She sighed and pushed herself up on her toes again, then pressed her face closer, cupping a hand over her eyes to block the outside light.

It was no use—the room was empty, or at least, the light had gone off. Jessica stepped back and reluctantly turned to find another place to peer inside—then screamed, slapping a hand over her mouth though she was too late to stifle the sound.

Charlie smiled. "Jessica," she said innocently, "you should have told me you were coming here, you could have ridden with me."

"Right, well, I ran outside to catch you, but you'd already left." Jessica stepped back, her heart racing. Every fiber of her being was telling her to run, but she knew she would never make it past the imposter who stood before her.

"Do you want to come in?" Charlie asked, still speaking like they were friends.

"Yeah, I'd love to; I just couldn't find the door." Jessica gestured back toward the parking lot. Charlie nodded.

"It's on the other side," she said, taking a step closer. Jessica stepped back again.

"What brings *you* here, anyway?" Jessica asked, trying to sound calm. *Does she not know that I know? Will she let me leave if I play along?*

"I can show you," Charlie said. Jessica kept her face blank; her muscles were so tense they were beginning to fatigue, and she breathed in deeply, trying to relax. But Jessica was suddenly aware that Charlie was steering her closer to a wall where she would be pinned.

"It's late, though; I should get going," Jessica said, making herself smile.

"It's not late," Charlie protested, gazing at the sky. Jessica hesitated, grasping for an excuse, and Charlie's eyes darted back to Jessica as she took another step forward. She was close enough for Jessica to feel her breath on her skin, but Charlie was not breathing.

Charlie smiled broadly, and Jessica drew back, her head pressing painfully into the brick wall. Charlie's smile grew wider and wider, elongating impossibly, then suddenly her lips were split at the middle as a wide seam appeared, bisecting her face from top to bottom. Jessica shrank back, curling in on herself instinctually, and as she did Charlie seemed to grow taller, her limbs segmenting at the joints like a moveable doll. Her features slowly paled and faded away, replaced by the iridescent, clown-painted metal face they had just been able to make out in Clay's pictures.

"Do you like my new look?" Charlie asked, her voice still soft and human. Jessica inhaled shudderingly, afraid to speak. The creature Charlie had become looked at her searchingly. For an instant, an acrid, chemical scent filled the air, then Charlie moved swiftly toward Jessica, and the world went dark.

CHAPTER EIGHT

I *can't see.*

Jessica closed her eyes and opened them again, but the darkness remained. She tried again, realizing with a rising panic that she could not move. The air stank of something rotten, turning her stomach, and she forced herself to breathe deeply. *I'll stop noticing it if I breathe.* She tried again to move, testing to see what was restraining her. She was confined in a sitting position: Her wrists were tied together behind her, her arms pulled uncomfortably around the back of a wooden chair and her ankles bound to its legs. She pulled against the restraints, almost tipping the chair over as she struggled to free herself, but she could not break away. Then there was light.

Jessica stopped moving. She blinked in the sudden brightness, her vision resolving. Charlie's imposter stood in the light of the window, revealed in her true form: She was undeniably an animatronic, but she was nothing like any other Jessica had ever seen. She was human-size—the same size as Charlie—modeled on a human woman, of sorts, her bifurcated face painted with rosy cheeks and a bright red nose, and her enormous, round eyes were rimmed with long, black lashes. She even had hair, two silky orange pigtails sprouting from the sides of her head, gleaming unnaturally in the light—Jessica couldn't tell what her hair was made of. She was wearing a red-and-white costume—or rather the metal segments of her body were painted to look like a costume; at her waist, a red skirt stuck out playfully. She was standing very still, and she was staring straight at Jessica. Jessica froze, afraid to breathe, but the creature just tilted her metal head to the side, watching. Her animatronic face looked familiar, but she still felt fuzzy and couldn't recall where she'd seen it.

"I don't suppose you'd give me a hand with these?" Jessica lifted her feet the quarter inch the restraints would allow. The animatronic smiled.

"No, I don't suppose I would," she said, her voice alarmingly unchanged. Jessica shrank back, revolted at the sound of her friend's voice coming from this singular new creature.

"Who are you?" Jessica asked.

"I'm Charlie."

Jessica looked around the dimly lit room helplessly. Apart from the chair, the only object she could see was a gigantic, old-fashioned coal-burning furnace, with a warm orange glow emanating from the thin vents in its door.

"At least," the creature began, "part of me is Charlie." She held her hand out in front of her, studying it. Jessica looked up and suddenly it was Charlie standing in the light of the window, looking confused and innocent. "It's strange," the animatronic said. "I have these memories. I know they don't belong to me; and yet at the same time, they do." She paused, and Jessica returned to wrestling with the knots. "I know that they don't belong to me because I don't *feel* anything when they come to mind. They are just there, like a long road you walk on, lined with billboards of things happening somewhere else."

"Well, what *do* you feel?" Jessica muttered, trying to drag out the conversation as her survival instincts kicked in.

The animatronic girl's eyes darted toward her. "I feel . . . disappointment," she said, her voice growing more tense. "Desperation." She looked out the window. "A father's disappointment, and a daughter's desperation," she whispered.

"Henry?" Jessica gasped. The girl looked back at her.

"No. Not Henry. He was more brilliant than Henry. I watched my father work from a distance, a great, great, distance." Her voice trailed off. Jessica waited for her to go on, half forgetting that she was trying to escape. "I see everything clearly now," the animatronic continued. "But in my memories . . . things were much simpler, which made it so much more painful. Now I know that people are all fading, fragile, inconsequential. But when you are a child, your parents are everything: They are your world, and you don't know anything else. When you are a little girl, your father is your world. How tragic and miserable such an existence is." Jessica felt a wave of dizziness and looked up to see that the animatronic now appeared as the clown again, but the image passed. Suddenly, it was Charlie in the light, but the moment's disruption in the illusion was enough to remind Jessica of where she was—and that she had to get away.

The animatronic girl stood beside the only window in the room. There was a door nearby; she was closer to it than the animatronic, not that she could count on outrunning her. *What else am I going to try?* Tentatively, keeping her eyes fixed on her captor, Jessica started working her wrists back and forth, trying to loosen the rope that held her. The girl watched, but did not move to stop her, so Jessica kept going.

"That's the flaw, and the greatest sin of humanity," the girl said. "You are born with none of your intelligence, but all of your heart, fully capable of feeling pain, and torment, but with no power to understand. It opens you up to abuse, to neglect, to unimaginable pain. All you can do is *feel*." She studied her hands again. "All you can do is feel, but never understand. What a sick power it is that you are given."

The ropes only seemed to tighten as Jessica pulled at them, and Jessica felt tears of frustration pricking at her eyes. *No wonder she doesn't care if I try to escape*, she thought bitterly. *If I could just see the knots . . .* She stopped moving and took a deep breath, then closed her eyes. *Find the knot. Ignore the robot.* Jessica fumbled with her right hand, searching for the end of the knot, bending her wrist painfully. At last, she found the end of the rope and grasped it: the rope tightened, but she inched her fingers along until she came to the base of the knot, then began to carefully push the end of the rope up through the final loop.

"I wanted so desperately to have been the one on that stage, but it was always her. All of his love went into her."

"You're talking about Afton." Jessica stopped, and Charlie nodded confirmation. "William Afton never made anything with love," Jessica snarled.

"I should rip you in half." Charlie's appearance flashed, the animatronic's face and body seeming to break, then reassemble in an instant. For a moment her expression wavered, a vulnerability showing on her face, but she quickly collected herself. "She was his obsession."

The animatronic twisted her hair around her fingers. "He worked on her day and night, the clown baby with bright orange pigtails. Petite enough to be sweet and approachable, but large enough to swallow you whole." She laughed.

Jessica pulled the rope a last time: She had managed to undo the first knot. Breathing heavily with the effort, Jessica opened her eyes: The animatronic had not moved from the window—she seemed still to be watching with a kind of amused interest. Jessica gritted her teeth and closed her eyes, and started on the next knot.

"I wanted to be her," the girl whispered. "The focus of his attention, the center of his world."

"You're delusional." Jessica snickered as she struggled with the rope, trying to keep her distracted. "You're a robot; you're not his child."

The animatronic pulled a chair away from the wall, and sat with a pained expression. "One night I snuck out of bed to see her. I'd been told not to a hundred times. I pulled the sheet away. She was gleaming bright, beautiful, standing over me. She had happy red cheeks and a lovely red dress."

Jessica paused in her work, confused. *Who is she talking about?*

"It's odd, because I remember looking down at the little girl as well. It's strange seeing through both sets of eyes now. But as I said, one is no more than a data tape, a record of my first capture, my first kill." The animatronic's eyes flared bright in the darkness. "The little girl approached me and pulled the sheet away. I felt nothing; it's no more than a record of what happened. But there *is* feeling, my feeling as

I pulled the sheet away, and stood in awe before this creature my father loved, this daughter he had made for himself. The daughter who was better than me, the daughter he wished I had been. I wanted to be her, so badly." Charlie's appearance faded, revealing the painted clown, and Jessica sighed as a wave of nausea and dizziness passed over her again. "So, I did what I was built to do," the girl said, and stopped talking. The room was silent.

When the last knot slipped loose and the rope fell to the floor, Jessica's eyes popped open in surprise. She leaned forward, moving her numb, tingling arms down to her ankles as she watched the girl, who simply continued to observe her. Jessica undid the knots that held her ankles quickly—they were looser, done carelessly, and she put her feet flat on the floor, her stomach fluttering. *Time to run.*

Jessica ran for the door, propelling her wobbly knees and sore ankles through sheer force of will. There was no sound from behind her. *She's going to be right behind me!* she thought wildly as she reached the door and turned the knob. She yanked it open with overflowing relief—and screamed.

Close enough to touch was a mottled face, swollen and misshapen. The skin looked too thin, and the bloodshot eyes, staring angrily at her, quivered as if they were about to burst. Jessica jerked away, stumbling back into the room. Her eyes darted to his neck, where two rusting lengths of metal protruded from his skin. He stank of mold: the furry suit he wore was covered in it, turning the cloth green, though as Jessica took in the whole of him, she knew it had once been yellow.

"Springtrap," she breathed, her voice shaky, and his lips twitched into something that might have been a smile. Jessica ran to the chair she'd been tied to, putting it between them as if it would do any good, then horribly, Springtrap began to laugh. Jessica tensed, grasping the chair's wooden back, ready to defend herself, but Springtrap just kept laughing, not moving from the spot where he stood. He cackled on and on, rising to an impossible pitch, then he broke off abruptly, his eyes snapping to Jessica. He shuffled closer, then, inexplicably, he began to caper in a grotesque dance as he sang in a thin, unsteady voice.

Oh, Jessica's been caught
Oh, Jessica she fought
But now she's going to die!
Oh my!

Jessica glanced at the animatronic girl in the corner, who looked away as though disgusted. Springtrap danced closer, circling Jessica as he repeated the verse, and she hefted the chair between them, watching for a chance to strike. Jessica tripped over her own feet trying to get out of his way. *Even for him, this is insane.* He danced closer and away, the words he sang degenerating into syllables of nonsense, interrupted by maniacal laughter. Jessica held the chair steady, ready to swing it. Suddenly, Springtrap froze in place.

Jessica's arms wavered, and she set the chair down with a thud. Springtrap didn't move, even his face was completely motionless. *Like someone turned him off.* She had barely finished the thought when his whole body went limp, collapsing on the floor with a clatter. He flickered, then Springtrap faded away, leaving in his place a blank, segmented doll. Jessica whirled to look at the animatronic girl: she was still watching without expression.

"Enough theatrics." A rasping male voice came from the open door. "Jessica, isn't it?" The voiced wheezed. She squinted, unable to make out anything in the dim light.

"I know that voice," she said slowly. There was a whirring sound coming from the doorway, and soon Jessica could see something roll into the room, an automated wheelchair of some sort. He was dressed in what looked like white silk pajamas and a black robe of the same cloth, covering him from chin to toe, black leather slippers on his feet. Behind him, three IV bags hung from a wheeled stand, the tubes extending up under the sleeve of his pajama shirt. His head was bald, covered in ridged pink scars. Where there were no scars, there were strange pallets of plastic, molding, and metal, pressed into his head as though fused to it. He turned his head slightly and Jessica saw that while one eye was perfectly normal, the other was simply missing: the gaping socket was dark, and shot through with a thin steel rod that glinted in the light. He was painfully thin, the bones of his face visible, and as he gave Jessica a small, twisted smile, she saw tendons move like snakes beneath the surface of his skin. She had to fight to keep from retching.

"Do you know who I am?" he asked.

You're William Afton, Jessica thought, but she shook her head, and he sighed, a rattling sound.

"Come here," he said.

"I'll stay where I am," she said tightly.

"As you like." He shifted his weight carefully, the wheelchair letting out a whir as it moved forward slowly. The animatronic girl started toward him and he waved her off, but the gesture threw off his balance, and for a moment he appeared as though he might fall to the side, but he gripped the arm of the chair with a pained expression, righting himself.

"So what was the dance routine for?" Jessica asked loudly, and he looked at her as though surprised she was still there. Then, he raised his hands to the knot on his robe, his fingers struggling clumsily to undo it.

"I thought you might like to see me as I was. A familiar face," he said, and smirked. He held up a small disc in his hand and clicked it on. The blank doll on the floor suddenly looked as it had a moment ago, with the bloodied, duplicate William Afton stuffed inside the rabbit suit.

"Time changes all things," he went on, clicking the disc off again. "As does pain. When I called myself Springtrap I was ecstatic with power, delirious over my newfound strength. But pain changes all things, as does time." He opened his robe to reveal his torso.

At the center of his chest was a mass of twisted flesh, crossed with neat, diagonal lines of black stitching thread; rippling out from the wound were the marks of the spring-lock suit, some scarred over years before, and some scarcely healed, the skin a shiny, angry red. He raised a hand to the wad of stitches, careful not to touch it. "Your friend inflicted this new wound," he said mildly, then bent his head slightly forward, calling her attention to his neck. She took an involuntary step closer, and gasped.

His skin was gone, she thought at first, the innards of his neck laid open to the air. *But the blood . . . he'd be dead.* Jessica took a long, slow breath, feeling light-headed as she tried to make sense of what she saw. The wound had been covered with something else, plastic, maybe: she could see where the surrounding skin had fused to it, healing red and ugly. Through the clear material, whatever it was, she could see his throat—she didn't know enough about anatomy to name the parts, but they were red and blue, blocks of muscle and strings of veins or tendons. Wedged in among them were things that never belonged inside a human body; small scraps of metal, embedded in the tissue. There were too many to count. The man moved, and they glinted in the light. Jessica gasped, and he wheezed, clearly struggling to breathe with his neck turned the way it was. Something caught her eye as he moved, and she leaned in closer: she was almost touching him now, and the smell was awful: a noxious perfume of disinfectant. She peered through the clear shield and saw it: a spring, its coils wrapped tightly around what looked like three veins, the sharp ends plunged deep into red muscle tissue.

Jessica stepped back and almost tripped on the fallen mannequin that had been Springtrap. She kicked away the jumble of limbs, recovering her balance, and looked into the man's mutilated face again.

"Yeah, I know you. Didn't you used to be a mall guard?" she said. His fists clenched, and his eyes darkened with fury.

"Spare me. Dave the guard was a character, one concocted on a moment's notice to play you for a fool, you and your friends. It was insulting. It doesn't take a great thespian to pretend to be an idiot night guard, as long as you can get around inconspicuously. I have not been inconspicuous for some time. It hardly matters now anyway, as this is all that's left of me." His voice gargled with despair.

"Come sit with me, Jessica." The animatronic girl dragged his IV stand with one hand, helping him back to a corner, where more medical devices and a reclining chair awaited. Jessica eyed the door, bracing herself to move, when the quiet was broken by what sounded like a child's scream in the distance.

"What was that?" Jessica said. "That sounded like a kid."

The man ignored her and settled back into the furnished chair. The animatronic girl busied herself with the machines around him, attaching electrodes to his bare scalp and checking the IV bags. A monitor began to beep at slightly irregular intervals, and he waved his hand. "Turn that off. I can't stand the sound of it. Jessica, come closer."

Stay alive. Play along, Jessica thought to herself as she warily picked up the chair she'd been tied to, carried it over to the man, and sat. Jessica trained her eyes on the animatronic girl as she strode across the room, gripped a handle, and pulled a long table straight out of the wall as if they were going to view a body in a morgue. Jessica clasped her hand over her mouth as fumes of oil and burning flesh washed over her. There was something lying on the table, covered with a plastic sheet.

Jessica leaped up again and backed away. "What is this? Who did you murder now?" she demanded.

"No one new," William spurted, almost as though he was trying to laugh. The plastic crinkled; something was moving inside.

"What have you done?" Jessica gasped.

The animatronic girl took a cotton ball from a bag nearby, wetted it from the bottle in her hand, and wiped it thoroughly up and down the metal fingers of one hand, then dropped it into a trash can at her feet. She took another piece of cotton and repeated the process, continuing over the surface of her hands and forearms up to her elbows. *She's sterilizing herself.* Jessica turned to the man in the chair, keeping the girl in her peripheral gaze. Behind him the animatronic girl was sterilizing a scalpel, using the same care she had taken with her hands.

"Here I thought you'd cheated death," Jessica said, almost feeling sorry for him.

"Oh, believe me, I have. You have only seen one fraction of what was done to me, the shrapnel that even dozens of surgeries—and I have had dozens—could not remove." He slowly rolled up the sleeve of his pajama shirt, revealing two staves of metal embedded in his arm, both dotted with ragged pieces of gray rubber. "Parts of that costume have become part of me." The animatronic girl took what looked like a pair of scissors out of the drawer and began to swab them clean, dabbing gently along every surface.

"But the fake blood." Jessica closed her eyes, shaking her head. *Charlie said that Clay found fake blood at Freddy's.* "There was fake blood; you faked your death."

Afton coughed, and his eyes widened. "I assure you, I didn't fake anything. If your police friend found fake blood . . ." He took a steadying breath. "It wasn't mine. I bleed, just like everyone else." He finished, and smiled, giving Jessica a moment to think before continuing.

"I gave you a monster." He gestured toward the collapsed doll that had been Springtrap. "But I assure you, I'm very, miserably, human." He paused again, a surge of anger crossing his face.

"My scalp was torn from my head when I escaped that costume, all but this piece here." He touched the small patch where hair still grew. "Scraps of metal are interwoven through every part of my body that has not been replaced with artificial tissue. Every movement causes me unimaginable pain. Not moving is even worse."

"I'm not going to feel sorry for you," Jessica said suddenly, braver than she felt. Afton took a breath and stared at her blankly.

"Do you believe that your pity will make any difference concerning what I do to you?" he asked with a steady tone. He tilted his head, leaning back as if taking a moment to relish the words, then his face lost the glint of cunning. "I am simply telling you, so that you can help with what comes next," he said tiredly. Jessica stood.

"You want me to be impressed by how much you've survived, and how much pain you're in. I don't care about you." She approached William's chair, then crossed her arms, glaring down at him from above. She glanced at the animatronic girl, who seemed poised to intervene, a half-swabbed scalpel in her hand, but Afton gave a subtle shake of his hand toward her, waving her off, seeming to enjoy the exchange. Jessica bent closer.

"William Afton," she said. "There is nothing in this world that I care less about than your pain."

Another child's scream came from somewhere nearby, and Jessica straightened.

"That *was* a little kid," Jessica said, a heady rush of adrenaline surging through her. She felt suddenly forceful, like she had some control of the situation. "You're the one who's been kidnapping those kids, aren't you?" she demanded, and Afton smiled weakly.

"I'm afraid those days are gone for me." He laughed, and looked fondly at the animatronic girl, who looked up at Jessica and smiled delicately. The girl straightened her posture and continued to stare; Jessica took a step back. All at once, the girl's stomach split open at the middle and out shot an enormous mass of wires and prongs. It reached its full extension and snapped open and shut with a steely clank. Jessica screamed, jumping back. The thing fell to the ground, then slowly recoiled back into the girl's stomach, which closed seamlessly. She smiled at Jessica, running her finger up and down the now-invisible line of the opening. Jessica averted her eyes.

"Baby, that's enough," Afton whispered. Jessica came to attention, her panic suddenly washed over with confusion. She looked from the girl to Afton, and back again.

"Circus Baby," she said, suddenly recalling the sign outside the restaurant. The animatronic girl smiled wider, her face threatening to split in half. "You're not as cute as you are on the sign," Jessica said bitingly, and the girl stopped smiling instantly, turning her body toward Jessica like she was aiming a weapon. A high-pitched ringing rose all around them, and Jessica edged backward. *That's her chip*, Jessica thought, bracing as if for impact. The animatronic girl held out her arms as though in a gesture of welcome.

Thin, sharp spines like porcupine's needles began to grow from her metal skin, each capped with a red knob like a pinhead, spaced a few inches apart, and extending from her face, her body, and her arms and legs. They grew slowly outward, lining up perfectly with one another to create a false contour all around her body. The girl looked expectantly at Jessica.

"Give it a minute," the girl said. "Let your eyes adjust."

The humming sound grew louder, rising higher in pitch until it became painful to hear. Jessica covered her ears, but it did nothing to dampen the sound. Suddenly, a new image snapped into place: where the smooth, slim redheaded animatronic had been was a gigantic, cartoonish child, her green eyes too large for her face, and her nose and cheeks painted a garish pink; she was a perfect image of the girl on the neon sign. Before Jessica could react, the childish image vanished, the needlelike extensions snapping back into the girl's body with a metallic snap. The humming stopped. The animatronic girl had returned to her former appearance. William Afton watched her with a gleam of pride.

Jessica turned again to the sleek, shiny girl standing at the man's side. "How did you create her?" Jessica asked, her eyes filled with curiosity for a moment before snapping herself back to the immediate danger surrounding her.

"Ah. A woman with a mind for science. You can't help but to admire what I've done." He braced himself on one arm of the chair, hoisting himself up to sit straighter. "Although . . ." He looked up at the gleaming girl for a moment, then turned away. "I can't take complete credit for this, unfortunately." He reclined his head again and let out a sigh. "Sometimes great things come at a great cost."

Jessica waited for him to go on, confused, then looked at the animatronic girl, recalling all that she'd said minutes before.

"I am a brilliant man, make no mistake. But what you see before you is a combination of all sorts of machinations and magic. My only real accomplishment was making something that could walk." He reached out and tapped the leg of the animatronic standing at his side; she did not react. "No small accomplishment. Although it's not happening as fluidly as you think. A lot of what you see is just in your head." He wheezed a laugh, then stopped himself, ending with a pained cough before going on. "That was Henry's idea not to try to reinvent the wheel. Why try to create the illusion of life, when your mind can do it for us?"

"She's more than an illusion, though," Jessica said plainly.

"Quite right," Afton answered thoughtfully. "Quite right. But that's why we're here—to discover the secret of that last ingredient, what you might call the spark of life."

"Is that why I'm here, too?" Jessica clenched her jaw.

"I believe you came here of your own free will, didn't you?" Afton said mildly.

"I didn't tie myself up."

"But I certainly didn't put you in the trunk of that car," he answered.

"We would rather have had your friend Charlie," he continued. "But we can find a use for you." He closed his eyes for a long moment, then opened them, meeting Jessica's eyes. "I have faced my own mortality, Jessica. I knew I was dying and through every broken fragment of my body, I was profoundly, immeasurably afraid. I fear it more than I fear life like this, even when every waking instant is pain, and sleep is possible only when induced by enough medication to kill most people."

"Everyone is afraid to die," Jessica said. "And you should be more afraid than anyone else, because if there's a hell, there's a hole at the bottom of it reserved for you."

Afton nodded with a moment of honest resignation. "In time, I'm sure that's where I will find myself. But the devil has knocked on my door before, and I've turned him away." He smiled.

"So, what? You want to live forever?"

William Afton smiled sadly and held out his hand to the animatronic girl; she went to him and put a protective hand on his shoulder. "Certainly not like this," he said. Jessica glanced at the robot girl, then back to the man in front of her, his body already riddled with mechanical parts.

"So, what, you're making yourself into a robot?" She laughed nervously, then stopped at his grave expression. "I didn't realize that you fancied yourself a mad scientist."

"No, that's science fiction," he said, unamused.

The plastic tarp moved again, and began to slide off the table, but stopped, not revealing what lay underneath.

"Everyone dies." Jessica blinked; the adrenaline was wearing off, and she was beginning to feel exhausted. Afton reached up and touched the mechanical girl's cheek, then turned his attention back to Jessica.

"The most terrible accidents sometimes bear the most beautiful fruits," he said, as if to himself. "Re-creating the accident—that is the duty and the honor of science. To replicate the experiment, and obtain the same result. I give my life to this experiment, piece by piece." He nodded at the girl, and she approached Jessica with deliberate steps. Jessica backed away, fear surging again.

"What are you going to do to me?" She could hear the urgency in her own voice.

"Please, enough. As a woman of science, at least try to appreciate what I've done," Afton said.

"I study archaeology," she said in a flat tone. He didn't respond; the girl stepped closer, giving her an unreadable stare.

The plastic tarp slid from the table, and Jessica startled and stared at what was underneath, but her terror turned to confusion in an instant. There wasn't a body, not human or machine. Instead there was a melted scrapheap, whose extensions could be interpreted as arms and legs, but with no defined mechanism of movement. There were no joints, no muscles, no skin or coverings, just masses of undefined tangles and cords, melted into one another and fused together. Most of it seemed fused to the table, burned and blackened at the edges where it touched the table itself, melting into it and seemingly inseparable from it.

"I don't understand." Jessica's mouth hung open, and she sat down again without thinking.

"Good girl." Afton smiled thinly. Jessica clenched her jaw. The animatronic girl went back to the table and took up the cotton balls and rubbing alcohol. She started with her fingers again, methodically wiping down each one. "Get on with it," Afton said impatiently. The girl did not break her deliberate pace.

"I touched you; I have to start over," she said.

"Nonsense, just do it. I've survived worse than this."

"The risk of infection . . ." she said calmly.

"Elizabeth!" he snapped. "Do as I say." The animatronic girl stopped moving at once, looking startled, and for a moment almost seemed to tremble. Jessica held her breath, wondering if anyone knew, or cared, that she had just heard the exchange. The girl immediately regained her composure, her eyes relaxing, then opened the drawer and took out a pair of rubber gloves, which she fitted easily over her metal hands. He settled back, and the girl came to him and bent over to press a button on the side of his chair. The chair made a pneumatic hiss and reclined, flattening out like a bed, and the girl placed her foot on a lever at the chair's base. She stepped on it, and the chair jerked upward. Afton made a pained grunt, and Jessica winced reflexively. The girl hit the lever again, yanking the chair up another inch, then stopped and flipped the monitor back on. It began to beep again at slightly irregular intervals, and she levered the chair up rapidly, jolting Afton's frail body as it rose. The girl darted her eyes from the monitor to Afton and back again, attentive to his vital signs. When the chair reached waist-height, she stepped back, apparently satisfied. Afton let out a rattling breath, then lifted his hand an inch to point at Jessica.

"Come closer," he said. She took a small step, and he curled his lips in a smile or a sneer. "I want you to watch what happens next," he said.

"What's going to happen next?" Jessica asked, hearing her own voice shake.

"How did the creatures at Freddy's move, of their own will, with no outside force controlling them?" he asked mildly. He tilted his head, waiting.

"The children were still inside. Their souls were inside those creatures," she said, the words brittle. She *felt* brittle, like if anything touched her now, she might easily break apart.

Afton sneered again.

"Oh, Jessica, come now. What else?" She closed her eyes. *What is he talking about?* "What else was inside them, to bind their spirits so inseparably to the bear, to the rabbit, to the fox? *How did they die, Jessica?*"

Jessica gasped, covering her mouth with both hands, as if she could stop herself from knowing, as long as she did not speak. "How, Jessica?" Afton demanded, and she lowered her hands, trying to steady her breath.

"You killed them," she said, and he made an impatient sound. She met his eyes again, not flinching from the empty socket. "They died in the suits," she said hoarsely. "Their bodies were bound inside, along with their souls."

He nodded. "The spirit follows the flesh, it would seem, and also the pain. If I wish to become my own immortal creation, my body must lead my spirit to its eternal home. Since I am still . . . experimenting . . . I move my flesh piece by piece." He looked thoughtfully over at the creature on the table. "More and more," he murmured, almost to himself, "it is a test of the strength of my own will. How much of myself can I carve away, and still remain in control?"

"Carve away?" Jessica repeated faintly, and he snapped his attention back to her.

"Yes. I will even allow you to watch," he said with a smirk.

"No, thanks," she said, shrinking back, and he wheezed a laugh.

"You will watch," he said, then gestured to the animatronic girl. "Keep an eye on her," Afton said.

"I have many eyes on her." The girl went to a cabinet and took out another IV bag: before she closed the door, Jessica caught a glimpse of more like it, and a shelf of what looked like vacuum-sealed cuts of meat. Her stomach flipped, and she swallowed hard.

Jessica started to squirm in her seat; there was a hissing sound coming from somewhere, and a smell of burning oil began to fill the room. The table where the mass of metal rested was beginning to glow orange at its center, and the mass on the table seemed to move slightly, although only out of the corner of Jessica's eye. Jessica snapped back to attention and turned toward Afton.

He appeared to be asleep: his chest rose and fell with slow breaths, and his eyes were closed; his eyelid draped loosely over the steel rod in the center of his missing eye, the thin skin hanging into the empty socket. The girl nodded, and moved to the table. Jessica swallowed, the rotten smell swelling around her. She had ceased to notice it, her nose tuning it out, but now it was everywhere, thickening the air with its miasma. *An operating theater . . . he's harvesting the kids for organs, transplanting them into himself?*

Jessica looked around the room, calculating—the scalpels were too far away to grab, and they wouldn't even scratch the animatronic girl's paint. If she ran, she would be dead before she was halfway to the door. Jessica forced herself to watch.

The animatronic girl went to William Afton's side, then checked the monitor again with care. She unbuttoned his pajama top and splayed it open, revealing his chest, and the mass of scars that had covered it since before he went by the name "Dave." The girl tugged the waist of his pants an inch lower, so that his torso was fully exposed, then nodded, took off her gloves, and replaced them with new ones. Then she took up one of the scalpels. Jessica looked away.

"You have to watch," the girl said, her voice chilling, a human voice stripped of human intonation. Jessica jerked her head up; the animatronic's eyes were on her. "He wants to see you watch," she repeated, the pleasant veneer cloaking her voice once more. Jessica gulped, and nodded, fixing her eyes on the scene before her. "I don't think you understand," the girl said. "Go wash your hands."

Shakily, Jessica got to her feet and went to the sink, feeling as if she might pass out at any moment. She turned the sink on and watched the water spiral down the drain, the shiny stainless steel gleaming through in the bright light.

"Wash your hands." Jessica obeyed, pushing up her sleeves above her elbows and washing her hands all the way up the forearms, foaming up the soap over and over as she had seen doctors do on TV. She rinsed them finally and turned to the animatronic girl.

"What am I doing?" she asked. The girl ripped open a plastic package and took out a towel. She held it out to Jessica.

"You're going to help."

Jessica took the towel and dried her hands, then put on gloves from the box the animatronic girl directed her to. "You know this thing isn't sterile, right?" she muttered, glancing at the mass on the table.

"Wait." Jessica gasped and took a step toward the table. From this angle, she could see more of its form. It was a melted mess, but she could recognize certain elements in the mass of fused scrap on the table. *A leg. A finger. An . . . eye socket.*

"I—I recognize these parts," Jessica said, but there was no answer. "These look like . . . endoskeletons, from Freddy's, the original Freddy's." Jessica began calculating in her head, measuring to herself how much this mass must weigh, and its size relative to the size of the endoskeletons she remembered.

Before she could think further, the creature on the table attempted to lift its leg, the makeshift knee bending partially. There was no mechanical device that she could make out—it seemed to be moving of its own will. After a second, it dropped back to the table.

"Where did you find these?" Jessica stepped back. "Where did you find these? What did you do? Why did you . . . melt them all together?"

"Hand me the scalpel," the girl said patiently. The surgical implements were laid out in a neat row on the rolling table, on a piece of paper, along with a set of curved needles, already threaded, and a small, kitchen-size propylene torch. The creature on the table tried again to lift its leg, and suddenly Jessica understood how it was able to move.

"They're still in there!" Jessica screamed. "The children—*Michael!*" The creature writhed pitifully, as if responding to her voice, and Jessica's heart wrenched. *They're in there, and they're in pain.*

"I guess I should have kidnapped Marla if I wanted a nurse," the girl said sardonically. "I told you, he wants you to watch. Look over here." Jessica obeyed, feeling her head go light as the girl pressed the scalpel into Afton's skin. *Don't pass out.* She drew the blade across his lower abdomen with steady, practiced hands, making a six-inch incision. She held out the scalpel, and Jessica stared for a moment before realizing she was supposed to take it. "He wants you to watch;

it's the only reason you're alive. If you don't watch, then there is no reason for you to be here. Do you understand?" Jessica steadied herself. *Breathe. Don't faint. Think about something else.*

John, Charlie—no, I'll start crying. Something else, something else . . .

Shoes. Black boots, knee high. The kind that look like riding boots. Italian leather. Jessica took the scalpel and set it down where it had been, and the blood dripped onto the paper, seeping into the fibers. Jessica took another deep breath.

The animatronic girl had one of her hands inside the incision, and was pulling it back, peering into the wound she had just made. "Scalpel," she said again, and Jessica picked up a new one and handed it to her. "Watch," the girl warned, and Jessica watched as she reached into the incision and cut something inside. Jessica flinched. *Shoes. Maroon clogs. Chunky heel, three inches. Patchwork stitching.* The girl held out the scalpel, her hand still inside Afton's body. "Take it; give me clamps." Jessica took the scalpel and replaced it.

"Clamps?" she asked, starting to panic as she searched among the instruments.

"They look like scissors, with teeth instead of blades. Open them and hand them to me, and do it fast."

Shoes. Jelly sandals, purple, sparkly. Jessica grabbed the clamps and tried to open them, but they were stuck together, hooked by an odd clasp at the top.

"Hurry up, do you want him to die?"

Yes, I do! Jessica wanted to shout, but held her tongue. She pinched the scissor handles together, and they came free. She handed them to the girl, relieved, and watched as she stuck the pointed end into the opening and pinched whatever she had been holding, clamping it shut. She took her hand slowly out of the wound and looked at Jessica.

"You have to be faster. Scalpel, then I'll need clamps right away."

Jessica nodded.

Shoes. Green suede kitten heels with a rhinestone strap at the ankle. She handed the girl the scalpel, then wrestled the clamps open as fast as she could, and was holding them out by the time the bloody blade was returned to her. She watched dizzily as the animatronic girl made another cut, severing something she could not see, and using the last set of clamps to hold it shut.

The table behind them began to hiss more loudly, and the orange glow intensified. Jessica took a step sideways to get away from the heat. The glow spread to the creature on the table, and parts of it seemed to turn from side to side.

"Hold out your hands," the girl said.

Platform sneakers. Denim. Hideous. Jessica held out her hands for the clamps, but the girl left them in place. Instead, she slid both hands into Afton's open body and lifted out a bloody object. *His kidney, that's his kidney. Black leather combat boots.*

Black leather combat boots. Charlie's black leather combat boots. The animatronic girl held the kidney up in the air for a moment, and blood dripped from it onto her face. *Charlie's boots. Charlie.* The girl turned to Jessica, and she shrank back.

"Hold out your hands," the girl repeated with cold insistence, and Jessica obeyed, fighting not to retch as the warm organ was placed gently in her hands. *It's meat; it's not part of a person; just think of it as meat. Platform sneakers. Stiletto boots. Penny loafers.* She watched in a daze as the girl took a curved needle and black thread and began to sew William Afton back together, starting with his innards, and ending with the first incision, making a row of Xs across the left half of his body. At last she finished, snipping the last thread off with practiced ease.

"What's next?" Jessica asked, her voice sounding faint against the rushing in her ears. *Yellow sneakers with a blue streak on the side. Those brown pumps Mom got me. Oh, Mom—*

"The next part is easy," the girl said, pulling the gloves off and picking the kidney up again with her hand and approaching the table where the mass lay.

"What are you going to do?" Jessica quivered.

"What did you think all of this was for?" the girl said softly. "He told you: piece by piece."

Jessica looked down at the creature on the table, glowing orange at its core, and dripping fluid from its various parts, the drops landing with a hiss on the hot surface.

"This is a transplant," she said.

The mass of melted parts for a moment looked human, its demeanor suddenly childlike as it squirmed, and its head turned to face Jessica. For just a moment, Jessica thought she could make out eyes looking back at her. Suddenly, the silence was broken as the animatronic girl clenched her fist around the kidney and slammed it against the creature's chest, pressing so hard that the metal underneath sank inward, embedding the kidney deep inside where it gurgled and hissed. More fluid seeped out the sides of the creature and burned on the table, as the girl wrenched it back and forth inside.

She pulled her hand from the cavity she had created, her hand charred black, and rested it at her side, extending and retracting her fingers as though making sure they still worked.

"Now, we are done," she said. She brushed past Jessica and went to the cabinet, and emerged with a long needle. She strode purposefully to William Afton's side, stopped with her fist raised over her head, then brought the needle down, plunging it into his chest.

A second passed, then he heaved an enormous breath and groaned. The girl pulled the needle from his chest and set it gently on the table beside him. William Afton opened his eyes, and his single eyeball moved back and forth between Jessica and the animatronic girl.

"Is it done?" he asked.

Jessica screamed. The intensity of it roused her from her daze and she screamed again, letting the sound drown out everything else. Her throat went raw, but she screamed again, clinging to the roar of her own voice; for an instant, she felt like if she kept screaming nothing worse could happen.

The air around the girl shimmered, and Jessica's vision blurred in front of her: something was moving. In a moment, her eyes cleared, and Charlie was standing in front of her.

"Jessica, don't worry! You can trust me," Charlie said cheerfully.

CHAPTER NINE

A hand was stroking her hair. The sun was going down over a field of grain. A cluster of birds were fluttering overhead, their calls echoing out over the landscape. "I'm so happy to be here with you," a kind voice said. She looked up and nestled against him; her father smiled down at her, but there were tears in his eyes. Don't cry, Daddy, *she wanted to say, but when she tried to speak, the words did not come. She reached up to touch his face, but her hand passed through empty air: he was gone, and she was alone in the grass. Overhead the birds began to wail, and their calls sounded like human voices, breaking with despair.* "Daddy!" Charlie screamed, *but there was no answer, only the birds' lamentation as the sun vanished beyond the horizon.*

It was dark, and he had not come back; all the birds were gone but one, and that one sounded more human with every cry. Charlie stood unsteadily; by some trick of time she was no longer a child, but a teenage girl, and the fields around her had turned to rubble; she stood in the midst of a ruined place, but there was a single wall standing in front of her, and a door at the center of it. The birds were silent, but someone was crying on the other side of the door, crying alone in a small, cramped space. She ran to it, banging her fists on the metal surface. "Let me in!" she cried. "Let me in! I have to get inside!"

I have to get inside! Charlie sat bolt upright with a ragged gasp, inhaling like she'd just escaped from drowning. *The doors—the closet.* She threw off the gray wool blanket and sheets, tangling herself in the process before she managed to get free. She was so hot she could barely stand it, and the wool had been scratching where it touched her chin. She felt strange, more alert: the world was in sharp focus, and it was jarring, as if she had been drifting in some kind of shadowy, half-conscious state for days. *Everything hurts*, she'd managed to whisper to John, but it had been somehow detached from her, there was some buffer between her body and her mind. Now, her mind clear, the buffer was gone, and she ached all over, a dull, constant pain that seemed to be everywhere at once. She leaned back against the wall. She had not woken to sleepy disorientation—she knew exactly where she was. She was in John's apartment, behind the couch. She was behind the couch, because . . .

"Someone is impersonating me," she said uncertainly, and the sound of her own voice was startling in the empty room.

She got to her knees, not quite trusting her legs, then steadied herself on the back of the couch, getting to her feet with effort. She straightened, and was instantly dizzy, her head swimming as her knees threatened to buckle under her. Charlie gripped the back of the couch determinedly, picking a point on the wall and staring at it, willing the room to stop spinning.

After a moment, it did, and Charlie realized the wall she was staring at was a door. *Doors.* The thought made her light-headed again, but she kept a firm hand on the couch and made her way around to the front, then sat down on it carefully. She glanced around the room—so far all she had seen was the corner behind the sofa. The shades were pulled down, and she could see that the front door was bolted. Charlie lost interest in the rest of it, her eyes drawn back to the other door. It was scarcely ajar, the room behind it dark, and Charlie shivered, echoes of her dream reverberating in her head. *Doors. Someone was on the other side, behind the door, somewhere small and dark; I was drawing them, doors; I had to find the door. Then . . .* She closed her eyes, remembering. They were running, desperate to get away as the building thundered around them, already falling to pieces, when she saw the door. *The door called to me; it was hidden in the wall, but I went to it, I knew exactly where it was. As I walked toward it, it was like I was on both sides—walking to it, and trapped behind it. Separated from myself. When I touched it, I could feel the beating of your heart, and then* . . . Charlie's eyes snapped open. "John pulled me away," she said, the memory solidifying as she let herself dwell on it. "I didn't want to go because . . ." She heard it, suddenly: the hiss and the cracks appearing in the wall. ". . . because the door had started to open."

Charlie stood, her eyes glued to the door in John's living room. She approached it as if propelled by the same instinctive force, her heart picking up its pace. "It's just the bedroom, right?" she murmured, but still she edged toward it slowly. She stopped in front of the door and reached out tentatively, vaguely surprised when her fingers touched real wood. She pushed it gently and it swung open easily, revealing a girl identical to Charlie.

A mirror.

She looked the same. Her face was pale and strained, but it was her face, and she smiled instinctively. In the haze of the last few . . . days? Weeks? She had been utterly disoriented, fading in and out of consciousness, pain finding her even in dreams. Charlie had not felt like herself, but there she was. She reached out to touch the mirror girl's hand. "You, are you," she said quietly.

Behind her came the unmistakable sound of a lock being turned, and she whirled around in sudden panic, losing her balance and catching herself on John's dresser. The front door opened and she shrank back, kneeling to let the dresser shield her. A clamor of voices burst in, all talking at once—there were too many to make out the words, until a familiar voice called, "Charlie?"

Charlie didn't move, waiting to be sure. Footsteps came to the doorway of the bedroom, then the voice again: "Charlie?"

"Marla!" Charlie answered. "I'm here." She started to get up, but her legs would not take her weight. "I can't—" she started, tears of frustration pricking her eyes as Marla hurried over.

"It's okay," Marla said hurriedly. "It's okay, I'll help. It's amazing you made it this far!" Charlie looked at her flatly, and Marla laughed. "I'm sorry," she said. "It's just—glaring at me like that you're so . . ."

"What?"

"Charlie."

"Who else am I supposed to be?" Charlie smiled as Marla took hold of her wrist with medical authority and began to silently count. She looked past Marla to Carlton, who came over quickly. John was standing in the door, but he made no move to join them, not meeting Charlie's eyes.

"I didn't want to crowd you," Carlton said, sitting down beside her and crossing his legs. "Charlie, I'm—" He broke off and swallowed, looking away. "I'm really glad to see you," he said to the floor.

"I'm glad to see you, too," Charlie said. She looked back to Marla, who nodded briskly.

"Your pulse is a little slow," she said. "I want to check it again in a few minutes. I want you to drink some water." Charlie nodded.

"Okay," she said bemusedly.

"Let's get her onto the bed," Marla said to Carlton, who nodded and, before Charlie could protest, scooped her up into his arms. Charlie glanced around for John, but he had disappeared.

Marla pulled the blankets back. Charlie felt the pull of sleep, like something standing behind her, gently tugging. She blinked rapidly, trying to rouse herself as Carlton set her down. Marla started to pull the blankets over her, and Charlie waved her hands, ineffectually trying to push them away.

"I'm too hot," she said, and Marla stopped.

"Okay," she said. "They're here if you need them." Charlie nodded. The tugging was growing stronger: if she just closed her eyes, she would slip back into the dark. Marla and Carlton were talking to each other, but it was getting harder to keep track of what they were saying.

A loud bang rattled the small apartment, and Charlie jolted awake, her heart thudding alarmingly. Almost instantly, Marla's hand was on her shoulder. "It's just John," she said.

"I think my heart rate is back up," Charlie said, attempting to joke, but Marla turned on her with appraising eyes, grabbed her wrist, and started to count again. "Marla, I'm fine," Charlie said, halfheartedly pulling away. Marla held on for another few seconds, then released her.

In the living room, John set something down on the floor with force. Carlton gave Charlie a concerned glance, then helped her off the bed, giving her an arm to lean on as they went out into the living room to join John. For a moment, the object was obscured, then they all moved aside so she could see the child-size doll. Charlie sat down on the floor, a little apart from the others.

"Ella," she whispered. Some tight, painful knot inside her chest began to loosen, and she felt herself smile. "John, how did you find her?" she asked. John knelt down behind the doll and looked up at her grimly, and her smile faded. "What's wrong?" she asked. He didn't answer her.

"Everyone, keep your eyes on the doll," he said instead, and took something out of his pocket. He flicked his thumb against the object, a tiny motion, and the air around Ella shimmered for a moment, blurring her. Charlie rubbed her eyes and heard Marla gasp. Ella was gone: standing where she had been was a little girl about three years old, dressed in Ella's clothes. The knot in Charlie's chest started to tighten again.

"What is this, John?" Marla asked sharply. John flicked his thumb again, and the shimmer passed over the girl, then she was a doll again, her vacant eyes staring placidly into eternity. Charlie darted her eyes from one to the next: Marla looked scared, but Carlton was fascinated. John, for some reason, seemed angry. Charlie shifted uneasily. John manipulated the object in his hand again, and the little girl appeared once more. Carlton crouched down to look at her, and Marla bent down to see, keeping her distance.

John stood, leaving them to stare at Ella, and knelt beside Charlie, giving her the same dark look he'd had since he brought in the doll. "What is this?" he asked harshly, and Charlie stared at him, hurt. John looked away with a pained expression, his face flushed. When he looked back at Charlie, the anger in his face had faded, but was not gone. "I need to know what this is."

"I don't know," she said. John nodded, and sat on the floor with her, carefully leaving a wide space between them. He opened his hand: in it was a small, flat disc. Charlie didn't move to touch it—there was something odd in his manner, something untrusting she had never seen in him before.

"Did you know?"

"No." Charlie tilted her head, staring at the motionless little girl.

"It's the same as Afton's creatures, though, isn't it?" John said. "Pattern projection, bombarding the mind; overwhelming the senses—"

"This one is different, though," Charlie cut in. She shivered, though she wasn't cold, suddenly unable to shake the memory of the twisted bear, his face stripped to the metal staves, the illusion sparking on and off as he loomed over them. "Can I see it?" she said, forcing herself back to the present. John held out the disc, and she took it carefully, watching him warily. He was giving off the sense of a brewing storm, and she was afraid of setting it off. Charlie held the disc up to the light, turning it back and forth, then handed it back.

"That's it?" John's eyes widened.

"What do you want me to say?" she cried.

"I mean, you can't tell me anything about it?"

"The others all had that inscription: *Afton Robotics*. This one doesn't. But I'd bet you noticed that."

"Actually, I didn't." John looked at her thoughtfully, then back down at the disc. He flipped the switch, and Marla yelped in surprise. "Sorry! It's a bit jarring if you aren't expecting it," he said, turning back to Charlie with a grin. She smiled, and as he met her eyes, his smile faltered, something troubling passing over his face. Before she could speak, it was gone. He grinned widely and winked at her, then flipped the switch—Marla cried out again, and Carlton laughed.

"Stop doing that!" Marla shouted from several feet away.

John ignored her, and leaned in closer to Charlie, hesitantly, like he thought she might run away. She turned to face him, a wave of nervousness washing over her. She ducked her head, letting her hair fall over her face, and he reached out and touched it gently, brushing a strand out of her eyes. He gave her a small smile and flipped the switch once, then again.

"That's enough," Marla called. "This is too weird for me."

John didn't seem to hear her; he was looking at Charlie with a new troubled expression.

"What is it?" she asked quietly.

"Nothing," he said. He touched her hair again, this time brushing it back from her face and tucking it behind her ear. "Hey," he said abruptly, changing his tone. "Do you remember your experiment from last year?" She nodded eagerly, then stopped, freshly aware of how long she had been away.

"My faces. But they must be gone, everything must be gone." She looked at John with anxious eyes, but he smiled.

"Nothing's gone," he said, and her heart lifted; she felt as if he had just given her a gift. "Jessica packed up all your stuff; she's got it in her apartment."

"Oh," Charlie said, darting her eyes around the room. "Jessica? Where is she?"

"Charlie," John said patiently, and she tried to focus on him; she could feel her attention waning, as if her mind were spreading thin, floating out like clouds. "The faces," John went on. "There was an earpiece so they could recognize you, right?"

She nodded.

"Could you make it work the other way?"

Charlie thought for a moment then met his eyes again. "You mean, make it so that the animatronics *can't* see you?" She frowned, her focus returning as she concentrated on the problem. "The earpieces emit a frequency that alerts the animatronics to you, it makes you visible. If you inverted that frequency . . ." She paused again. "I don't know if it would work, John. It might."

"It could make us invisible to them?"

"*Maybe*, but that's a big leap."

"How would I do it? Invert the frequency?"

Charlie shrugged. "Just switch the wires, and . . ."

"Charlie, what part of 'stay in bed' wasn't clear?" Marla asked good-naturedly, coming over to them. John stood, his mouth hanging open as though Marla had interrupted Charlie's answer, but she didn't seem poised to add more.

"Sorry," he said hastily.

"Be careful," Charlie said. She was beginning to feel light-headed again, and when Marla reached out to help her back to the bedroom, she did not protest.

John paused in the door, watching as Charlie curled up on her side, her eyes already closed. Marla raised her eyebrows, and he left, shutting the door halfway. In the living room,

Carlton was kneeling beside Ella—now in doll form again—and looking intently into her ear.

"Uh, Carlton?" John said dubiously, and Carlton sat back on his heels.

"Amazing," he said. "She looked human, like actually, for real, a human child."

"Yeah, I think that was the idea. Can we talk outside?" John asked brusquely, and Carlton looked at him in surprise.

"Sure," Carlton said with some concern in his voice.

"Come on." John headed for the door, and Carlton hurried after him. Once they were outside, John looked at Carlton for a moment, thinking.

"What's the idea?" Carlton asked with a hint of suspicion.

"Let me try to get this straight in my own head first," John said. "Last year, when she was still in school, Charlie had this experiment she was doing, something about teaching robots language."

"Oh yeah!" Carlton nodded enthusiastically. "She told me about it. Natural language programming. They listen to people talking around them, and to them, and they learn to talk, too. Didn't sound like it worked very well, though."

"Well, whatever. She had these earpieces—like, the robots would only talk to each other—they only recognized each other. You with me so far?"

"Um, I think?"

"Well, if you, Carlton, wanted to be *in* on the conversation, you would need to wear a special earpiece. The earpieces would make them recognize you. Otherwise, you were just part of the background, like they couldn't *see* you."

"Okay?" Carlton gave him a puzzled look, and John rolled his eyes.

"Wearing the earpieces included you in their conversation. It made you one of them, from their perspective."

"Hate to break it to you, but the big ones already see us . . . at least I'm pretty sure they do. See this scar?"

"Will you shut up for a second?" John said. "I asked Charlie, and she said we might be able to reverse engineer it. We can switch the wires, and instead of the earpieces *including* us, it would deliberately *exclude* us."

Carlton furrowed his brow.

"It could effectively make us invisible . . ." John prompted.

"Switch the wires," Carlton repeated. "It would mask us, and make us not a part of the world they can perceive."

"Right." John nodded.

Carlton waited for John to go on, then added, "What do you want me to do?"

"Go to Jessica's house. She's got all of Charlie's old stuff boxed up in a closet. If she's not there, she leaves her spare key under the welcome mat."

Carlton raised his eyebrows. "Under the welcome mat? That's a *horrible* place to leave a key!"

"It's a good neighborhood," John said defensively.

Carlton raised his eyebrows. "Yeah, it's a good neighborhood, John. Nothing bad ever happens here." Carlton slapped John on the shoulder as he headed for his car. "I'm on it!" he called.

John let out a sigh, then went back inside. Marla was sitting on the couch, staring at the television, which was not turned on.

"How is she?" John asked, sitting down beside her, and she shrugged.

"Okay, considering the circumstances." She turned away from the blank screen, looking distressed. "She was locked in a box! That's insane, she was locked in a *box*! Who knows for how long—days, months? She must have been fed, given water, or she'd have starved, but she has no memory of it, she just remembers drifting in and out of sleep. She *seems* healthy. I don't know what to say."

Impulsively, John hugged her, and she sighed, hugging him back tightly. She released him abruptly, looking away as she brushed at her eyes. John pretended not to see.

"Can I go sit with her for a minute?" he said when she straightened. "I won't bother her, I just want to sit with her and know she's there."

Marla nodded, her eyes brightening with tears again. "Don't wake her up," she admonished as he went to the door. He nodded, and slipped inside, closing the door behind him.

Carlton pulled into the lot outside Jessica's apartment building, glancing around for her car. It didn't seem to be there.

"Guess I'll be breaking and entering; sorry, Jess," he said cheerfully as he pulled into a spot, but a sense of dread had already set in. He wanted company, even on this small errand. "Let's see what skeletons Jessica has hiding in her closet." He drummed his hands on the steering wheel, tamping down his nerves, and got out of the car.

Jessica lived on the third floor. Carlton had only been to her place once, but he found it again easily. In front of her door was a welcome mat: it was dark green, the word WELCOME written out in black script. Carlton lifted the mat, but there was nothing under it.

For a moment he stared, at a loss for what to do next, then he flipped the mat all the way over: taped to the center was a key. "Thought you could outsmart me?" he murmured, peeling off the clear tape.

"Can I help you?" someone asked sternly from behind him. Carlton froze. The voice said nothing else, and so with deliberate movements he finished removing the key, set the mat back on the ground, and smoothed it back into place, trying to seem unconcerned. He put a pleasant expression on his face, stood, and turned to face an elderly man scowling at him from across the hall. He was wearing a faded button-up shirt and holding a hefty book, his finger marking his place.

"Do I know you?" the man demanded. Carlton forced a grin and waved the key in the air.

"Just visiting," he said. "I'm a friend of Jessica's." The old man peered at him suspiciously.

"She makes too much noise," he said, and shut his door. Carlton heard three locks snap into place, then silence. He waited a moment, then turned and hurriedly entered Jessica's apartment.

He shut the door carefully behind him and glanced around. The apartment was no bigger—or nicer—than John's, although it was definitely cleaner. Most of the furniture had probably come with the place, but Jessica had determinedly made it her own. The scuffed floor was as spotless as it could be made without an industrial sander, and Carlton looked guiltily down at his sneakers, thinking maybe he should have taken them off outside. Jessica had covered the worn-out couch in fluffy blankets and throw pillows; her textbooks were lined up neatly on a wide bookshelf made out of brightly painted wood planks, and above the shelf was a large corkboard full of photographs, cards, and ticket stubs. Carlton made his way over to it, curious. "Let's see what Jessica's been up to," he said, talking to himself just to fill the silence.

The corkboard was full of smiling pictures of Jessica with her friends; a graduation photo with her parents; ticket stubs from concerts and movies; two birthday cards, and a few postcards with enthusiastically—and illegibly—scribbled notes. Carlton let out a low whistle. "Somebody's popular," he muttered, then something else caught his eye: a child's drawing, pinned to the lower corner of the board. He bent down to look, and his throat caught: it was a crayon drawing of five children, smiling happily as they posed with a big yellow rabbit. In the bottom left corner, the artist had signed his name, and Carlton reached out to touch it lightly. "Michael," he whispered. He stared into the bright eyes of the yellow rabbit behind the children and his mouth went dry. *If only I could have warned you, somehow.*

He swallowed and straightened up, turning his attention deliberately back to the photos.

"She sure gets out a lot," he remarked, opening one of the cards to distract himself. HAPPY 15TH BIRTHDAY, JESSICA! it read, and he stepped back, feeling slightly ashamed as suddenly he understood. He glanced at the ticket stubs: they were all from shows in New York; the pictures with friends were all a few years old. Jessica's new life, here, didn't give her much in the way of mementos. Carlton turned away from the corkboard, wishing he had not intruded.

"The closet," he said loudly. "I have to find the closet with the stuff." There was a kitchenette, and past that a hall-way, presumably leading to the bedroom. He found a light switch and flipped it on, and the closet appeared, halfway down the hall. He opened it, half expecting the contents to come tumbling down on him, but though these were Charlie's possessions, it was Jessica who had done the pack-ing. Stacks of cardboard boxes filled the closet completely, each one labeled clearly: CHARLIE—SHIRTS AND SOCKS, CHARLIE—BOOKS, etc. At the very top of the stack was a long, flat box labeled, CHARLIE—WEIRD EXPERIMENT.

"Weird experiment; feels like the story of my life these days," Carlton whispered. He reached for it carefully, and had almost gotten it down when he knocked the corner against the box underneath it, sending, CHARLIE—MISCELLANEOUS to the ground. The box split open, spewing out computer parts and random bolts and scraps of metal, fur, and two unattached paws. Three plastic eyes bounced as they hit the floor, then rolled across the carpet, clacking against each other merrily.

"This is life or death; someone else can clean it up," Carlton decided. He stepped carefully over the rest of the mess, and carried the box into Jessica's bedroom. He set it down on her bed, careful of the pale blue spread, and dragged the spare key across the packing tape to cut it. He opened the box.

"Yikes." He startled. Two identical faces stood upright in the box, staring at each other with blank eyes. They were like unfinished statues: they had features, but they were not refined, and seemed incapable of expression. He started to lift them out of the box, then realized that they were attached to something. With care, he managed to extract the entire structure: a large, black box with knobs and buttons, and the faces on their stand, wired to it. It all seemed to be intact. Carlton eyed the wall socket by Jessica's bed for a moment, then grabbed the cord, and plugged the whole thing in. An array of lights came on, red and green, flashing on and off seemingly at random, then stabilizing: some off, some on. Several fans started to whir. Carlton looked at the faces: they were stretching, almost mimicking human movement. "Creepy," he whispered.

"You, me," said the first, and he jumped back, disconcerted.

"We, she," said the second. He stared, waiting for more, but they were apparently finished for the moment, motionless and silent. Carlton shook his head, trying to make himself focus, though all he really wanted to do was sit here and watch the two faces, and see what else they might have to say. *Or talk to them.* He went back to the box: the earpieces

John had described were wrapped up in a thin layer of bubble wrap. They looked like hearing aids, small clear pieces of plastic, full of wiring, with a tiny switch on one side. Carlton flipped the switch on one, and put it in his ear. Instantly, the faces turned to him, tilting up like they were looking straight at him. *Can they see me?*

"Hi?" Carlton said reluctantly.

"Who?" one asked.

"Carlton," he answered nervously.

"You," the other said.

"Me," said the first.

"You guys really love pronouns, huh?" Carlton said. There was no answer from the faces. He took out the earpiece and flipped the switch off, and simultaneously the faces turned back to each other. *Makes you visible. Right*, he thought with a shiver. He turned back to the earpiece itself, sliding his thumbnail into the thin seam that ran around the edge of the casing. It popped open easily, revealing a mess of wires and a tiny computer chip. "Just switch the wires, it's that easy," he muttered to himself. There was a lamp on a nightstand beside Jessica's bed, and he turned it on, holding the earpiece under the light. He stared at it, looking for a clue as to what John had been suggesting, angling the tiny object from side to side. At last he spotted it: a single, empty round input, outlined in red. "And why is nothing plugged in to you?" Carlton said triumphantly. He sorted through the other wires until he found one that matched it, the outline green. He quickly switched the wire to the red-lined plug and snapped the case back together, then switched it on and stuck it back in his ear. The faces did not move.

"What's wrong? Don't want to talk to me anymore?" he said loudly. There was no response. "Excellent," he said, satisfied. He took out the earpiece and put it in his pocket, then grabbed the other one as well. He unplugged the experiment and was about to pack it back into the box, when he felt a sudden prickling between his shoulders, as if someone was standing directly behind him. He could almost feel breath on his neck. Carlton held very still, scarcely breathing, then he spun around, his hands raised to defend himself.

The room was empty. He flicked his eyes from side to side, unconvinced that he was alone, but there was nothing there. "Just pack up and get out," he said weakly, but his heart was still pounding in his chest like he was fighting for his life. He took a deep breath, and went back to the experiment. Before he could touch it, the room dipped under him like a ship bobbing in the ocean, and he fell to his knees, clutching the bed frame to steady himself. His vision blurred: nothing was fixed in place anymore, everything in the room seemed like it was moving at various speeds and different directions. Carlton let go of the bed frame and sank to the floor as a piercing whine arose, quickly ascending to a pitch too high to perceive. He covered his ears, but it did nothing to ease the nausea. The room kept spinning, and his stomach lurched; he groaned, holding his head and closing his eyes, but the movement continued. He clenched his teeth, grimly determined not to vomit. *What is happening?*

Carlton . . . Carlton . . . Someone called his name sweetly, and he looked. One thing in the room was still: an enormous pair of eyes, staring at him as the room rocked sickeningly. He tried to stand, but as soon as he moved, dizziness and nausea overwhelmed him. He pressed his cheek to the cool floor, desperate for relief, but it only made the room spin faster.

"Carlton?"

The room snapped back into focus; everything stopped moving. Carlton didn't move, afraid of setting it all off again. "Carlton, are you okay?" said a familiar voice, and he looked up to see Charlie, bent over him anxiously.

"Charlie?" he said weakly. "What are you doing here?"

"John sent me to help. What were you doing with all this stuff?" she asked.

"I'm sorry, I hope I didn't break anything," he said, sitting up carefully. The nausea still lingered, but it was easing as he began to trust that the room had steadied itself. He glanced at Charlie, his vision still a little fuzzy.

"I don't mind, it's all junk anyway. But the way you were rolling around on the floor, you must have activated

209

something, or electrocuted yourself, one or the other. Are you okay?"

"I think so," he said. He slumped back against the bed.

"Nausea? Room spinning?" she asked sympathetically.

"Terrible," he said.

She put a hand on his shoulder. "Come on, we need to get out of here." She stood and held out a hand to help him up; he took it, standing gingerly, the effects of whatever it had been were almost completely gone. He looked around the room, his vision clear.

"What exactly were you doing?" Charlie asked, and Carlton froze. Her voice was too hard, too . . . polished. He turned to her, keeping his face neutral.

"He didn't say? John thought you might want to have it, your old experiment. I think he wanted to surprise you with it," he said. He grinned. "Surprise!"

Charlie smiled.

"You know, your old experiment?" Carlton's mind raced. "The one with the robotic hand that could play the piano?" he added. "You remember?"

"Right. How sweet of you to come get it," she said, a flirtatious note in her voice, and Carlton's blood went cold. He nodded carefully.

"You know me. Always thinking of others," he said, glancing over Charlie's shoulder at the bedroom door behind her. It was closed. She took a step closer to him, and he stepped back instinctively. She looked surprised for a moment, then grinned, looking down and seeing the two faces in the box. He moved back again, startling when he hit the wall behind him.

"Carlton, if I didn't know better I'd think you were afraid of me," Charlie said in a low voice, stepping so close there was almost no space between them, pinning him to the wall. She reached out toward his face, and he set his jaw, trying not to flinch. She ran her fingers down his cheek, then traced the line of his jaw. He didn't move, his breathing shallow. Charlie brushed his hair out of his face and pressed closer to him, trailing her hand to the back of his neck. Her face was inches from his.

"Um, Charlie, you're not really my type, you know?" he managed to say.

She smiled. "You haven't even given me a chance. Are you sure?" she whispered.

"Yeah, I'm sure. I mean don't get me wrong, you're okay-looking, but let's be honest, you're nothing to write home about," he quipped, maintaining eye contact. "I mean, those boots with *that* skirt?"

Charlie's grin started to wane.

"Sorry, that was rude. I'm sure you'll find a guy someday who appreciates you for who you are." He tried to inch his way toward the door. "Now, if you'll excuse me, I'm late for quartet practice, so let me just get by you and I'll be on my way."

Carlton squirmed but Charlie didn't budge. "I promise I won't tell anyone that I rejected you. Just hit that gym and we can try again in a few years."

"Carlton, you're obviously flustered. There's only one way to really be sure how you feel," Charlie said softly. She leaned closer, and Carlton screwed his eyes shut. *The earpiece.* It was in his right pocket.

"Charlie, you're right, but maybe we should just talk for a while, you know. I rushed into my last relationship and I almost ended up dead in a moldy fur suit." *Just distract her until* . . . his fingers closed on the earpiece, and he pulled it from his pocket, opening his eyes at the same time.

Carlton screamed.

Charlie's face was splitting apart. Her skin had taken on a plastic cast, it was cracked at the middle, splintering into triangular sections. As he watched, her hand tightening around his neck, the triangles lifted up and pulled back like razor-edged flower petals, revealing an entirely different face, sleek and feminine, but definitely not human. The petals of what had been Charlie's face began to move along the round perimeter of the new face, beginning to look more like a saw blade than a flower. The animatronic girl pursed her metal lips, leaning in for a kiss as the blades spun closer and closer to Carlton's face. In a final burst of self-preservation, he yanked the earpiece out of his pocket and jammed it into his ear, flipping the switch.

The animatronic girl drew back at once, letting go of Carlton's neck with a surprised look on her metal face. She glanced around the room. He stared at her, frozen in terror for a moment, then he realized what was happening. *She can't see me.* He waited, watching as she took deliberate steps backward, her eyes darting back and forth. She stood for a moment, the plates of her face snapping back together to form the painted, glossy face of a doll, then suddenly a ripple of light passed over her and she appeared to be Charlie again, her face expressionless. After another minute, she turned and went to the bedroom closet. She peered in, pushing clothes out of it as if something might be hidden behind them, then stepped away. She went to the bed and grabbed a corner, then lifted it off the ground. She considered the empty floor for a second, then let the bed drop with a crash. Once more she scanned the room, and at last, she opened the door to the bedroom and let herself out. Carlton tiptoed behind her, following her into the hall. She stopped short in front of the hall closet, and he almost bumped into her, barely catching himself before they collided.

The animatronic girl ripped the boxes from the neatly stacked closet, tossing them haphazardly on the ground behind her. Carlton cautiously stepped back a few feet.

When the girl was satisfied the closet was unoccupied, she checked the bathroom, then walked out into the living room. With one last, dissatisfied glance around, the animatronic girl left Jessica's apartment, closing the door calmly behind her. Carlton rushed to the window, watching as she exited the building and walked away down the road, heading toward the town.

Once she was out of sight, Carlton heaved a sigh, gasping as if he had been holding his breath. He felt dizzy again, light-headed, but this time it was only fading adrenaline. He started to take the earpiece out, then thought better of it and left it in place. He patted his left pocket, reassuring himself that the second earpiece was still there, and he hurried out of the apartment and down to his car. He drove away urgently, heading toward John's house without regard for the speed limit, and hoping the animatronic girl was going the other direction.

Charlie heard the door close, and she turned toward it. The room was dark except for the light filtering in through the small, dirty window, and she squinted to see who had just come in.

"John?" she whispered.

"Yeah," he said in the same tone. "Did I wake you up?"

"It's okay, all I do lately is sleep, and dream." The last word was bitter on her tongue, and he must have heard it, too, because he sat down on the chair Marla had placed beside the bed.

"Is it okay if I sit?" he asked nervously, already there.

"Yes," she said. Charlie closed her eyes. The room was different now. Safer. "You said something," she murmured, almost to herself, and John leaned closer.

"Did I? What did I say?" He cleared his throat, his palms already sweating.

"You said . . . you loved me," she whispered, and he jolted as if someone had struck him.

"Yes," he said, his voice sounding choked-off. "That is what I said to you. You remember *that*?" Charlie nodded carefully, knowing her response was inadequate. He turned away from her for a second, letting out a forced breath. "It's true. I do!" he said in a rush, turning back to her. "I mean, you've been my friend since forever. Just like Marla or Carlton or Jessica. I would have said that to any of them. Well, maybe not Jessica. So, you remember some of that night, then?" he asked briskly.

"It's all I remember. And the door. John!" She grasped his arm, alarmed. "John, the door was opening, I think Sammy was inside—I could feel him there, his heartbeat . . ." She trailed off as another memory overwhelmed her, a moment in the strange, artificial cave under the restaurant that was so like Freddy's, and yet so unlike it. "Springtrap," she said. "I fought with him. There was a metal spike, and his head . . ." She could see him, gasping on the rocks as she ground the piece of metal torturously into his wound.

"I know; I saw it, too," John said, an uncomfortable shift in his eyes.

"He said, 'I didn't take him. I took you.'"

"What?" John gave her a puzzled look, and she sighed in frustration.

"Sammy! I asked him why, why he took my brother from me, and that was what he said. 'I took you.'"

"Well, you're here now. He's insane, anyway." John attempted a smile. "He probably just said it to hurt you, to confuse you."

"Well, it worked." She let her head sink back onto the pillow. "John, everyone's avoiding the question: How long has it been? I know it's been more than days, but how bad is it? A month?"

He didn't answer.

"Two months?" she ventured. "I know it can't be more than a year or you'd have a nicer apartment," she said weakly, and he winced. "John, tell me," Charlie insisted, hearing her own voice rising, her heart beating faster as she waited for him to speak.

"Six months," he said at last. She didn't move. She could hear the blood rushing in her ears.

"Where have I been?" she asked, her voice barely audible over the rushing sound.

"Your aunt Jen, you were with her, at least I think that's where you were."

"You think?"

"I'll tell you everything, Charlie, I promise—as soon as I understand it myself. There are things I just don't know," he finished helplessly. She lay back, staring up at the ceiling. In the dim light, the stains looked like they could be decorative.

"About your aunt," John went on, something awful in his voice. "I saw her that night."

Charlie looked sharply at him. "That night?"

"The building was coming down; you were inside, and I was trying to get to you, and she was just suddenly there—I don't know how she got in, or why."

"It was her house, technically," Charlie said, turning back to the ceiling. "Maybe she was there looking for me."

"And that makes sense to you?"

"I don't know what makes sense," she said steadily. "It doesn't make sense what I remember and what I don't remember. There's no one moment where suddenly it all goes blank. But I don't remember Aunt Jen being there."

"Okay," he said.

"I have to see her," Charlie said with sudden intensity. "She's the only one who knows how all of the pieces fit; she's the one with all the secrets. She's always tried to protect me from them, but now . . . secrets aren't protecting anyone."

She stopped: John looked stricken, his face stuck between expressions like he was afraid to move it. "John?" Charlie said, a knot forming in her stomach. John took a breath as if to speak, then hesitated; she could see he was searching for words. She gave them to him. "She's dead, isn't she?" Charlie said faintly. She felt like she was drifting off again, but she was not losing consciousness. John nodded.

"I'm sorry, Charlie," he said hoarsely. "I couldn't stop it."

Charlie looked back up at the stains. *I should feel something*, she thought. "You need your head clear," she whispered, echoing her aunt's habitual reminder.

"What?" John was watching her anxiously.

"Paperwork," she said more loudly. "She kept files on everything, locked up in cabinets. Whatever she knew, she wrote it down, or someone else did. Where was she?"

"A house, in Silver Reef, the ghost town," John stammered; he looked taken aback. "There were files there, boxes of papers."

"Then we have to go back there," Charlie said firmly. John looked as if he wanted to protest, but he just nodded.

"*She* might go back there, too, if she thinks you'll be there." John shared a worried look.

"We have to go."

"Then we go there," he said. Charlie closed her eyes, the decision releasing her into sleepiness. The door opened, and dimly, Charlie heard Marla and John whispering to each other. She took a deep breath, like she was going underwater, and let herself slip into the dark.

CHAPTER TEN

Hey!" Something poked Jessica's shoulder, and she shrugged it away and rolled over, still half-asleep. *"Hey, you okay?"* Something poked her cheek, much harder, and she opened her eyes and looked up to see a ring of children sur-rounding her, staring with wide eyes. Jessica screamed.

Someone grabbed her from behind, covering her mouth, and she struggled to get away.

"You have to be quiet," a desperate voice whispered, and she turned to face a red-haired girl of about seven, looking at her anxiously. "If you're not quiet, it'll come get you," she explained.

Jessica sat up carefully and put a hand on her head; it felt like it was stuffed with cotton, and her sinuses were burning. "Not again." *Chloroform, or whatever that gas was.*

"What?" the girl asked.

"Nothing," Jessica said, looking at the frightened faces that surrounded her. There were four children in all, two boys and two girls: There was the young redheaded girl with freckles on her nose, and a stocky, African American boy of about the same age, who looked like he had been crying before she arrived. He was sitting cross-legged with a young Latina girl of three or four on his lap, hiding her face in his shirt. Her fine brown hair had all but come loose from two long braids down her back, each capped with a pink ribbon, and the matching pink shorts and T-shirt she wore were stained and filthy. The last little boy, a skinny blond kindergartener with a massive bruise on his forearm, hung back a little from the rest, his hair hanging over his face. They were all looking at her like they expected her to do something.

"What is this disgusting place?" Jessica wiped her hands on her shirt and shook out her hair as though it might be full of spiders. She stopped in midshake, and turned to the kids as though seeing them again for the first time. Her mouth hung open slightly.

"You're the kids." She gasped. "I mean, you're the kids, the ones that were taken, and you're *alive*!" She suddenly remembered the mother at the hospital. *We have to find that kid and bring him home,* Jessica had insisted to John, the words sounding hollow even to her own ears. Now the kids were standing right in front of her. *It's not too late to save you*, she thought, filling her with new purpose. She looked at the little blond boy. "Are you Jacob?" she asked, her heart fluttering, and his eyes widened in response.

"Hey, it's going to be okay," she said, trying to believe her own words. "I'm Jessica." None of them answered her right away, instead glancing at one another, trying to reach some silent consensus. Leaving them to it, Jessica stood, surveying their surroundings.

It was a dank, brick-walled room with a very low ceiling, so low that Jessica couldn't fully stand upright. The room had exposed pipes all along the walls, some of them giving off plumes of steam. There was a large tank in one corner, probably a hot-water heater, and in the far corner was a door. Jessica went to it.

"Don't!" the redheaded girl squealed.

"It's okay," Jessica said, trying to make her tone soothing. "I'm going to get us all out of here. Let's just see if it's locked," she said, hearing her own voice ring out cheerful and hearty. She sounded patronizing; it was a tone she'd always despised in adults when she was a child. "I'll just check," she said more normally. She walked briskly toward the door.

"No!" three voices cried. Jessica hesitated, then grasped the knob firmly and gave it a twist. Nothing happened. Behind her, one of the children let out a sigh of relief.

"It's okay," Jessica said, turning back to them. "There's always another way out." She scanned their anxious, grimy faces. "What happened here?" she asked. The boy with the child on his lap looked at her suspiciously.

"Why should we tell you anything? You could be one of them."

"I'm in here, same as you," Jessica pointed out. She dropped down to sit beside him, putting herself on the children's eye level. "My name is Jessica."

"Ron," he said. The little girl on his lap tapped his shoulder, and he bent down as she whispered something in his ear. "Her name's Lisa," he added.

"Alanna," the redhead said, a little too loudly. The blond boy didn't say anything. Jessica eyed him, but did not ask.

"Hi, Ron, Lisa, Alanna, and, Jacob," Jessica said with excruciating patience. "Can you tell me what happened?"

"She ate me in her tummy," Lisa whispered. Instantly, Jessica felt the blood rush from her face.

"You mean the clown girl?" Jessica asked softly. "The robot girl?" The children nodded in unison.

"I was in the woods," Alanna said. She held her hand against her stomach, then mimed the clamp shooting out. "Chomp!" she said, her face deadly serious.

"I was riding my bike by my house," Ron said. "There was a woman in the road—she came out of nowhere, and I fell off the bike, I was trying not to hit her." He gestured to his knees, and Jessica noticed for the first time that they were scabbed over. *He's been here long enough for those to heal*, she thought, but held her tongue, afraid if she interrupted he would stop talking altogether. "When I got up, she was standing over me," Ron continued. "I thought she was trying to help. I told her I was okay, and she smiled, and then . . ." He glanced down at the girl on his lap for a moment, then went on. "I swear, honest, her stomach split right open, and there was this big metal *thing* that came out of it, and—" He shook his head. "She's not going to believe us."

"Did the thing grab you and pull you inside?" Jessica asked softly, and he looked up at her in surprise.

"Yeah," he said. "Did she get you, too?" he asked.

"No, but I've seen it happen," she said half-truthfully. "Then what?"

"I don't know. Next thing I remember I woke up in here."

"What about her?" Jessica gestured to the girl on his lap. He shrugged, looking briefly embarrassed.

"As soon as she woke up, she climbed onto my lap."

"Do you know her?"

"You mean from before?" He looked down at the little girl again.

"No, none of us knew one another before," Alanna said. Jessica looked at the little blond boy, and he looked away.

"Okay, well listen," Jessica said, and they all turned their eyes to her again. *Creepy. Like I'm really a grown-up or something*, she thought uneasily. She took a deep breath. "I've dealt with . . . *things* like this before."

"Really?" Alanna was suddenly skeptical; Ron watched her warily. Lisa opened one eye, then pressed her face back into Ron's shirt.

"I'm *not* with them," Jessica said hurriedly. "I'm locked in here with you because I got caught trying to find out more about them."

"Did you know about us?" Ron asked.

"Not much, but I'm glad that I found you—everybody's been looking for you. The people who took you, they're trying to hurt a friend of mine—they already have hurt her—and I came here to stop them, to save her from them. Now that I know you're here, I'm going to save you from them, too."

"You're locked in here, just like us," Alanna said, this time like she believed it. Jessica suppressed a smile, momentarily amused.

"I have friends out there, and they're going to help, we're going to get you out of this." Alanna still looked suspicious, but Lisa was peeking at her from behind her hair, loosening her grip on Ron's shirt for the first time. "I promise you, everything is going to be all right," Jessica said with a surge of confidence. She looked at the children with calm determination, surprised to realize she had meant every word.

"John! Charlie!" Carlton burst in to John's apartment, the door hitting the wall as it swung open.

Marla jumped, sitting up straight on the couch. "Carlton, what's going on?"

He didn't respond, scanning the room. Marla was alone; she had the TV on at a low volume. The door to John's room was closed, and he went to it. "No one's here," Marla said with a hint of disapproval, but Carlton rushed to look inside anyway. "John's not here; neither is Charlie," Marla called.

"Well, I ran into one of them," Carlton said grimly. "One of the Charlies, that is. The bad one. Where is John? Where's everyone?"

"John and Charlie went somewhere; they seemed to be in a hurry and they wouldn't say where they were going."

"Jessica?"

"I haven't seen her. She's probably at home."

"I was just at her apartment, she's not there." Carlton stared at Marla, palpable dread rising between them. "Charlie—the other Charlie, I didn't even hear her come in; she didn't knock or anything. It was like she knew Jessica wouldn't be there."

"Wait, shut up," Marla said suddenly, pointing to the TV.

"Marla, this is serious!" Carlton said with alarm.

"Look at this; they've been playing this commercial all day." Then the cartoonish face of a little girl, painted like a clown, filled the screen.

"Come dressed as a clown and eat for free!" said a booming voice, then the camera cut to the front of a restaurant.

"That—that's her!" Carlton shouted. "I mean the sign, the girl on the sign, the clown girl thing!" Marla leaned forward, squinting at the screen. Carlton stopped, thoughtful for a moment. "She was taller, and a little attractive. It was really confusing; so many emotions."

"They've been playing these all day. New restaurant, animatronic characters . . ."

"It's like the girl on the sign was all grown-up, and wanted to feed me pizza . . ." He trailed off.

"Carlton!" Marla yelled, snapping him back to the present.

"You know where it is? The new place?" he asked.

"Yes," Marla announced. She flipped off the TV and stood. "Let's go." Carlton looked her grimly up and down, then took the other earpiece out of his pocket.

"Put this in your ear," he said. "It's all we have; trust me."

"Okay." Marla snatched the earpiece out of his hand on her way out the door. "I guess you'll fill me in on the way?" Carlton didn't answer as he hurried after her, slamming the door behind them.

A s they drove through the ghost town, Charlie could feel John's eyes on her. She had not spoken since they got in the car, and she was beginning to dread the moment she would have to speak again. John made a sharp turn, jostling the car, and she jerked forward in her seat, pressing into the seat belt.

"Sorry," John said sheepishly. Charlie eased back again.

"It's fine," she said with a small smile. "I know this might be a strange time to ask, but, where is *my* car?"

"I'm afraid your doppelganger has your car." He eyed her nervously, and she forced a crooked smile and nodded.

"What would that police report look like, I wonder?" she said lightly, and John grinned.

John slowed to a stop, his expression fading. "This is it," he said quietly. Charlie opened her door and got out. They were at the bottom of a hill; John had stopped beside a narrow archway with a small, metal star at its crest. At the top of the hill was a small house.

"Okay, let's get this over with," Charlie said. She looked around nervously, half expecting someone to come running at them. "Let's go."

As they climbed the hill, John looked several times like he wanted to say something, but did not. When they reached the front porch, Charlie put a hand on his arm.

"So, she's still in there?" she asked. "Jen, I mean."

He nodded. "Yeah. At least, I think so. Are you sure you want to do this?"

"I have to."

"I'll go in first," he offered. "I can . . . cover her up, if you want me to." He looked at her, distressed. Charlie hesitated.

"No," she said finally, and grasped the knob firmly. The door wasn't locked, and Charlie scanned the room apprehensively as she entered. The place was in disarray, everything blended into everything else, and at first nothing stood out. Then they saw her.

There was a woman in the corner, by the hallway; she was huddled against the wall, curled over herself, and her dark hair hung thickly over her face. Charlie heard a sharp intake of breath, then realized it was her own. She held a hand out stiffly behind her, unable to say in words what she needed, but John saw, and took her hand, stepping close behind her.

"That's really her?"

"Yeah," he whispered. "Did you want to get closer?" John asked uncertainly.

Charlie shook her head. "No. It's not her anymore," she whispered, turning away, closing it off in her mind. She took a deep breath. "Where did you find . . . me?" She gestured to herself, to make sure John knew which Charlie she meant.

"That way."

John led her to the hallway, keeping wide of Jen's slumped body; Charlie forced herself not to look directly at her, allowing herself to see only a dark, hunched shape in the corner of her eye as she passed. At the end of the hall was the open door to a storage room, filled with trunks and cardboard boxes. The window was open, and it was not until she breathed fresh air that Charlie noticed the damp, moldy smell that had taken over the rest of the house.

"This one," John said. He was standing beside a large green trunk, its lid standing open.

"In here?" Charlie said bleakly, stepping over several boxes to get to him. She peered inside: there was a small pillow, and nothing else. "I was just in there?" she asked, somehow disappointed.

"Yeah. I mean, Jen must have had a reason. She must have known about the imposter. Maybe she put you there just before we arrived."

Charlie reached out and closed the trunk. "I want to look around."

"What are we looking for?" John asked, and she shrugged, opening another trunk.

"Anything," she said. "If there's anything useful, this is where it will be. We need to know what we're up against."

They searched in silence for a while. None of the boxes were labeled, and Charlie opened them haphazardly, sifting quickly through the ones containing paperwork, and setting aside the others unexamined. Those contained random assortments of household items—dishes and silverware, knickknacks Charlie recognized from childhood, even some of her old toys. She scanned a box of Jen's tax documents carefully, then replaced them, finding nothing that seemed to stand out. She reached for another box, then saw John giving her a funny look.

"What?" she asked. He smiled, and there was a hint of something sad beyond it.

"You read really fast," was all he said.

"Didn't anyone ever teach you how to speed-read?" she said briefly, then turned her attention elsewhere. Charlie abandoned the stack of boxes she had been going through and went to the far corner of the room. She shoved a precarious pile of neatly folded sheets and towels aside, and sat down cross-legged on the carpet. From here, she could not even see John, though she could hear him, shuffling through paper and muttering to himself under his breath. She swept her eyes up and down the stacks, one after another, then she saw it: *Henry*, written in her aunt's careful script. Charlie moved three overcoats and another box, and then it was in her hands.

She stared at the lettering for a long moment. The ink had faded over the years. Charlie traced it with her index finger, her pulse fluttering in her throat like her heart was trying to get out. *Daddy*. She opened the box, and saw it—on top was an old, green plaid flannel shirt, worn down as thin and soft as cotton. She picked it up as if it were something delicate, and pressed it to her face, inhaling through the fiber. It only smelled like dust and time, but the touch of the fabric on her face brought tears to her eyes. She breathed in and out slowly, trying to force them back, and finally regained her composure, though part of her howled out the unfairness of it, that she could not even take a moment to cling to his slight presence, and mourn. Self-consciously, Charlie put the shirt over her shoulders, letting it drape over her back as she leaned once more over the box. The rest of the box was stacked with smaller boxes, and she opened the first one to find a framed picture of herself with Sammy, infants in those few, precious years before everything was ripped apart. Under the picture was an envelope, addressed in her father's handwriting, to "Jenny." Charlie smiled and shook her head. *I can't imagine anyone calling Aunt Jen, "Jenny."* She opened the letter.

My Dearest Jenny,

I had an entire list of instructions written out for you; schedules and timetables, keys and procedures. You have indulged me so much, and it's only now, at the end, that I see how it has helped me get through these dark times, but also how ultimately empty it has been. I had everything so carefully planned; I've worked so tirelessly. I've warped and twisted my surroundings to the point where I can never be sure if I've completely settled back into reality, and even if I did manage to turn off everything planted in the walls to deceive myself, I think my mind would deceive me still. I don't need clinical testing of the long-term effects of these devices to know that I've undoubtedly done permanent damage to myself. I will always see what I want to see, but worse than that, there is the splinter, more like the stake, always deep into my heart reminding me more and more every day that what I see is a lie. Through your patience and your indulgence of me, you've tried to keep me happy, but it's also somehow brought me back from this world I've made for myself. I think maybe it would have been better for you to have not indulged me; then I could have excluded you from my bubble, convinced myself that you were crazy like everyone else. But instead, your unceasing love caused me to listen to you, to let you in, and the consequence of that was seeing the truth in your eyes, and letting that in as well.

I have my Charlie here with me. You will never have to indulge me in her again. Rather than taking joy in her, I have cried over her, so many countless tears. I have poured agony into her, until she serves as another reminder not of what I once had, but of the unbearable pain of what was taken from me. She has come to reflect my pain back to me; whereas I, for a time, took great comfort in her eyes, I now only see loss, endless, debilitating loss. Her eyes will never fill me again. In fact, they have emptied me.

Keep all the closets shut. Let them be tombs for my denial and my grievance. My only lasting instruction for you concerns the fourth closet. It is not enough to keep it shut, you must keep that one sealed and buried. My grief was already beginning to waken me to reality when I began what was to be her final stage. When I rose, slightly, from the depth of my despair, I saw that I had no choice but to cease my work, for I was only feeding my own delusion. My old faithful partner, who I can only hope now is in a grave of his own, took what I had begun, and made something of his own—something dreadful. He crafted my beloved work into something of his own, and endowed it with who knows what kinds of evil. I was able to stop him, and to seal away what he made, and you, Jenny, must ensure that the seal remains.

I would instruct you to demolish the house if I could trust that it could be done effectively. Keep it, and make sure the world forgets it. Then, someday, after many decades have passed and no one remembers, fill it with every kind of flammable thing and burn it to the ground, standing close guard to put a bullet into anything that emerges from the rubble, no matter what, or who, it looks like.

I'm going to be with my daughter.

Love always & to the end,

Henry

"Charlie?" John was standing behind her. Wordlessly, she held the pages out to him. He took them, and she moved aside the box the letter had been in and stared down at the next one. It was sealed with packing tape, but the sticky side was old and dry, the edges curling up from the cardboard. John shuffled the pages, still reading. Charlie shivered, despite the warm air, and she put her arms through the sleeves of her father's shirt and rolled them up to her elbows.

"Do you know what it means?" John asked quietly. Charlie looked up at him and shook her head. "Scoot over," he said with a small smile, and she did, making room for him in the little space among the boxes. He sat down facing her, crossing his legs awkwardly. He handed the pages back to her, and she scanned them again. "What did he mean about the closets?" John said.

"I don't know," Charlie said drily.

"Think," John protested. "It has to mean something."

"I don't know," Charlie repeated. "You were there; they were always empty. Except the one with Ella."

"You don't know that," John said softly. "There was one that was locked," he continued, almost to himself.

"It doesn't matter, does it?" Charlie said. "The house is gone. Unless you feel like digging through more rubble, this is all we have." She pried the box with the peeling tape out of the larger box and handed it to him. All that was left under it was a lockbox, which opened easily when she tugged at the lid. It, too, was filled with papers: on top was a fine-pencil drawing of a familiar face.

"That's Ella," John said, peering over her shoulder.

"Yeah," Charlie said. Her father had captured the doll's delicate features in exquisite detail, not only her face but her shiny, synthetic hair, and the tiny creases in her dark, starched dress. Her eyes were open wide, and their blank stare was at odds with the rest of the picture: a perfectly lifelike representation of something lifeless.

"I didn't realize he was such an artist," John said, and Charlie smiled.

"He said he drew things so he could see them, that it didn't work the other way around." She handed John the

236

picture; below it was another, again of Ella, this time from the side. The next showed only Ella's face, in profile.

"He made Ella, right?" John asked, and Charlie tilted her head, considering the drawing.

Charlie sorted through the rest of the pile more quickly and shook her head, confused. "They're all of Ella."

John picked up the remaining cardboard box and ripped the tape off with sound like tearing cloth. It stuck to his fingers as he balled it up, and from the corner of her eye, Charlie saw him struggling to dislodge it. She paged through the drawings again.

"Look at the notes." She handed him the first drawing they had looked at, growing impatient as he peered at her father's meticulous, but tiny handwriting. He read it out slowly.

"*Height: 81 cm; Head circumference . . .*" He looked up. "It's just measurements." Charlie handed him another drawing. "Looks the same to me," John said, then flicked his eyes to the notations. "*Height: 118 cm.*" John tilted the page as though he might be reading it wrong.

"This one says 164.5," Charlie said, holding up another, seemingly identical picture. "I don't understand," she said, setting the page in her lap. "Did he make another Ella?" She traced a finger along the line of Ella's hair, smudging the pencil mark, then a thought struck her. "I wonder if he was trying to make it up to me," she said.

"What do you mean?"

"If he was trying to give me . . . a companion; a friend, because of what happened." She met John's eyes, unable to say what she really meant.

"You mean Sammy? Because you lost your twin, he wanted to give you a doll that would . . . what, grow up with you?" John said incredulously, and she nodded, relieved that he had made sense of her half-spoken words.

"Maybe," Charlie said softly. His eyes were pinched with worry, and he looked away, studying the drawings in his hands again.

"It doesn't really make sense, though, does it?" Charlie said. "What would I do with a five-and-a-half-foot doll on a track?" She reached for the letter again, holding it like a talisman though she did not need to read from it. "Was there a bigger version of Ella in the locked closet?"

John's eyes searched the air without a target in the silent room for several long moments, then snapped back to attention. Charlie was quietly looking down at her own hand, slowly curling her fingers, then uncurling them. The silence dragged on, smothering, then John grabbed Charlie's hand, startling her.

"I saw your blood."

"What?" Charlie said, startled.

"I saw your blood that night. You bled. I don't think Ella bleeds, do you?" The statement was absurd, but John was

238

watching her uneasily, as if he expected a response. Seconds passed, and Charlie did not know what to say. "I thought you were dead that night," John whispered at last.

"But I'm not dead, right?" She locked eyes with John. "I'm alive, right?" She took his hand, and he grasped hers tightly. He covered her hand in both his own, and she gave him a puzzled smile. "John?" she repeated nervously, and his jaw tightened. He looked on the point of speaking, when Charlie suddenly turned her head toward the window.

"What is it?" John said with alarm. Charlie put a finger to her lips and tilted her head to listen. *There's someone outside.* John watched her face intently, then his eyes widened as he registered the sound, too: the footsteps crunched one last time on gravel outside, then were silent.

Around back, he mouthed, and Charlie nodded, dropping his hands and steadying herself on the trunk behind her as she stood. John hastened to help her, but she waved him off.

"Come on," she whispered. "Back door?"

"I don't know." He started to make his way toward the hall, motioning her to follow. "Charlie, hurry." John had doubled back to her, and was pointing urgently to the door. She shoved the letter into her back pocket, and followed him, picking her way cautiously through the debris of the storage room.

In the hallway, the thick and musty air hit like a wave, and Charlie swallowed her revulsion, trying not to picture her aunt's body curled up in the next room. They crept down the hallway toward the front room, and the door, shuffling their feet so as to make no noise. At the end of the hall, John stopped, and Charlie waited, listening. There was only silence, then a wind chime rattled outside the front door, and they pulled back into the recess of the hall. John looked grim. "There." He nodded to the door opposite the storage room, which was slightly ajar. "Was that open before?"

"Yes," Charlie answered. "I mean, I think so." They made their way slowly toward the open door: Charlie breathed shallowly, trying to register the slightest noise over the pounding of her own heart. As they reached the doorway, she heard a rustling, like someone stepping on soft leaves. John and Charlie split up and stood on either side of the doorway, Charlie by the hinges and John by the knob, and slowly, he pushed the door the rest of the way open. Charlie saw the relief on his face before she saw what was in the room: a bed, a dresser, and absolutely nothing else, not even a closet. There was a window open, and John turned back toward Charlie. "I think we've got a way out," he said. She smiled back shakily. "Stay back while I check," he whispered, and before she could answer, he had pushed the door farther open into the room, and was moving stealthily toward the open window, keeping in a straight line through the center of the room. Charlie stayed in the hall, pressing the door open so she could see the entirety of the room.

Charlie watched nervously. *Hurry*, she urged him silently. Then as she thought it, she felt the door stop against her fingers as though something was blocking the way. *Is there something behind the door?* Slowly, noiselessly, she leaned to the side and put her eye to the crack in the door, along the hinges. Her heart stopped.

Another eye was looking back at her.

Charlie staggered back. The door wavered for a moment, then slammed shut. From inside the room something banged and crashed over and over against the wall. "John!" Charlie cried, and beat against the door. Suddenly, the house went still, and a few moments later the door drifted open and a figure glided out gracefully, stepping into the hall with care as though trying not to wake a sleeping baby. Charlie stared disbelievingly at her duplicate, her mind hazily registering all the tiny differences between them as she struggled for words.

"You're not me," Charlie managed to say, and her own face smiled cruelly back at her.

"I'm the only *you* that matters."

CHAPTER TWELVE

I s it working?" Marla asked, nervously tapping the device in her ear. Carlton sped up the car.

"Mine worked," he said brusquely. He glanced at her; she was kneading her hands together, her knuckles going white. "I mean, you can't *really* tell if it's working until . . ."

"Until what?" Marla said.

"Well, until you're in danger, and . . ."

"And what?" Marla seemed impatient.

"And you don't die." Carlton nodded reassuringly.

"So how do we know if they're *not* working?" Marla's voice had lost its energy.

"Well, if it doesn't work, you won't have to worry about it for long." He smiled.

"Right." Marla stopped fidgeting with the device and put her hand in her lap.

"It will work. I rewired yours exactly like mine."

"I'm not usually in the thick of this stuff," Marla said. "I come in afterward with hugs and Band-Aids. If this were a movie, I'd be the lame babysitter, not the action hero." There was a hint of bitterness in her voice, and Carlton looked at her, surprised.

"Carlton, the road!"

He snapped his attention back to what he was doing and gave the wheel a controlled jerk.

"Marla, I've seen you in the thick of this stuff—remember Freddy's?"

She gave a halfhearted nod.

"And don't dismiss the power of hugs and Band-Aids," he added, slowing the car as the restaurant's sign came into view: CIRCUS BABY'S PIZZA blazed out over the night, casting half the block in garish red light. "Can't miss this," Carlton remarked as they pulled into the parking lot. As soon as they were past the neon sign, its brilliant, witchy light faded into the background: the lot was stark and bare.

"No one's here. Are you sure about this?" Marla said urgently.

"No, but I know what I saw." Carlton drove slowly toward the entrance, pointing toward the clown girl mascot leaning over the entryway sign. "And *that* is who attacked me."

They parked close to the building. Carlton stopped to rummage around in the trunk for a minute, coming up with two small flashlights. He flicked one on and off experimentally, then handed it to Marla.

"Thanks," she whispered.

They started around the side of the building and Carlton swept his light along the wall, illuminating a row of tall, rectangular windows. The window surfaces were tinted so dark they could not see in, and the frames were smooth black metal, with nowhere to force an opening. Carlton shook his head, and gestured toward the back of the building. Marla nodded, gripping her flashlight like a lifeline.

There was more parking behind the building, and the back wall was lined with trash cans, two Dumpsters sticking out on either side of a metal door. The only light came from a single, flickering orange bulb, set above the plain door like a decoration.

"Looks like this is our way in," Carlton whispered.

"Look." Marla shone her light down onto fresh prints in the mud, tracking close to the wall and leading up to the door. "Jessica?" Marla looked to Carlton.

"Maybe."

Marla grabbed the door handle and pulled hard, but it didn't budge.

"I don't think we'll find another way in," she whispered, and he grinned.

"You think I didn't come prepared?" Carlton said, slipping a flat leather case from his pocket. He held it out to her. "Hold this," he said, and selected several thin strips of metal as she balanced the case for him.

"Are those lockpicks?" Marla hissed.

"If there's one thing I've learned from watching my dad, it's that lockpicking can be used for good," Carlton said solemnly. He bent over the lock, trying to keep his head out of the way of the light, and slowly began to wriggle the lock picks into place.

"Oh, whatever. You can't pick a lock . . . can you? Is it even legal to own these?" Marla asked. He looked back at her; she was holding the kit away from her body as if trying to disassociate herself from it.

"It's legal as long as you don't pick any locks," he said. "Now be quiet so I can pick this lock." Marla looked around nervously, but didn't say anything. He turned his attention back to the door, listening for the telltale clicks of the tumblers falling into place as he carefully made his way through the mechanism.

"This is taking forever," Marla whined.

"I didn't say I was good at this," he said absently. "Got it!" He grinned, triumphant.

The door opened with a creak, revealing a wide hallway with a gentle upward slope. The hall itself was dark, but a few yards ahead, they could see the dim glow of florescent lights. Marla pulled the door closed behind them, cushioning it with her hand so that it wouldn't slam. The light was coming from an open door on the left side of the hall: they waited, but no sound came from its direction, and they started to move, hugging the wall. As they got closer, Carlton sniffed the air. "Shh," Marla hissed, and he jerked his head toward the door.

"Pizza," he whispered. "Can't you smell it?" Marla nodded, and impatiently waved him forward.

"Of all the smells in this place, *that's* the one that catches your attention?" The open door proved to be the kitchen, and they glanced around briefly, then Carlton went to a large refrigerator and pulled it open.

"Carlton, forget the pizza!" Marla said in dismay, but the refrigerator held only racks of ingredients. Carlton closed the door.

"You never know who could have been hiding in there," he said quietly as they exited the kitchen. At the end of the hall was a swinging double door, with small windows just at Carlton's eye height, and he surveyed what he could see of the next room, then pushed the door open. Marla gasped.

"Creepy," Carlton said mildly. The dining room in front of them was lit with the same dim, florescent light, giving the brand-new place an odd dullness. There were tables and chairs at the center, and arcade games and play areas along all the walls, but their eyes were drawn immediately to the small stage at the back corner. Its purple curtain was pulled open, and it was empty, except for a bright yellow rope strung across the front and a sign with a picture of a clock on it. NEXT SHOW: it read in neat, handwritten letters, but the clock had no hands. Marla shivered, and Carlton nudged her. "It's not the same," he whispered.

"It's exactly the same," she said. Carlton looked around at the rest of the room, his eyes lighting on a ball pit that stuck out from the front wall in a half circle, a round red plastic awning arcing over it, trimmed with white.

"Look at the monkey bars." She pointed. Across the room, three small children steadily climbed the tangled structure of red and yellow bars. Carlton, startled, looked at Marla with surprise, then ran to them.

"Are you okay? Where are your parents?" he asked breathlessly, then his mouth went dry. The children were not human, or alive. Their animatronic faces were painted like clowns, their features absurdly exaggerated: One had a round, red nose that covered half its face and a white wig of synthetic curls; another had a molded smile on its face and a painted red grimace. The third, a red-cheeked, smiling clown with a rainbow-colored wig, looked almost cute, except for the gigantic spring that replaced the middle of its torso, boinging up and down each time it moved. All of them had black eyes, with no iris or pupil, and they did not appear to see Carlton. He waved his hands, but they did not turn their heads, just kept grasping the bars with their pudgy hands, and pulling themselves along the structure with uncanny precision. All of them emitted a loud whirring sound, as if they were wind-up toys that had been set loose to climb. The child with the spring suddenly flung its top half over the top of the bars, the spring extending into a long, wavy wire, then it grabbed a bar, and its feet shot into the air wildly, and came snapping back into place on the other side.

"My mistake, you're not the kids we're looking for, carry on," Carlton whispered shakily, as the creatures continued, weaving over and under, back and forth through the structure. "They don't see us," Marla whispered, and it took him a moment to register her voice.

"What?" he said, his eyes still on the clown-children.

"They don't see us," she repeated. "These little things are working." She tapped her ear.

"Right, good," Carlton said, pulling himself away from the scene. Marla was smiling with relief. "We still have to be careful, though," he warned. "I can't guarantee it works on everything, and it definitely won't work on people."

Marla shivered, then nodded quickly. "There's a room past the stage," she said.

"Looks like an arcade," Carlton said grimly.

Marla slowed by the stage, her hand drifting toward the curtain as if she might try to look behind it. "No." Carlton grabbed Marla's hand. "The last thing we want to do is call any attention to ourselves." Marla nodded in agreement.

The arcade smelled overpoweringly of new plastic, the games gleaming and scarcely played. There were a dozen or so freestanding arcade cabinets, and two pinball machines, one—predictably, by now—clown-themed, and the other painted with cartoonish snake charmers. Carlton gave them a wide berth. Marla caught his sleeve and gestured to a closed door on the wall to their left, an EXIT sign glowing red above it, and he nodded. They headed for it, creeping past a "test your strength" game, governed by an adult-size clown with a face made of jagged metal plates who nodded continuously, its painted smile maniacal. As they passed Carlton watched it carefully, but its eyes did not seem to track their movements. When they reached the door, Carlton took a deep breath, then gently pushed on the bar. It gave way immediately, and Marla sighed with relief. Carlton pushed the door open, holding it out for her, then froze as the unmistakable clack of servos broke the silence behind them.

They both spun around; Carlton braced his arm in front of Marla's chest protectively, his heart racing, but nothing was moving. He scanned the room, then saw it: the clown standing over the game was staring at them, its head cocked to the side. Carlton glanced at Marla, and she nodded minutely: she had seen it, too. Slowly, she backed through the door, as Carlton watched the animatronic, but it showed no further signs of movement. When Marla was safely through the door, Carlton waved his arms, hoping desperately that it would not see him. The clown remained motionless, having apparently returned to stasis. Carlton slipped out of the room and closed the door carefully behind him. He turned, and almost fell over Marla, who was backed up almost to the wall. "Watch it," he whispered good-naturedly, catching her shoulder for balance.

Then he looked up, and swayed on his feet, disoriented by a dozen distorted, menacing figures. He took a breath, and the room fell into place: *mirrors*. Before them was an array of funhouse mirrors, each one distorting the images it reflected. Carlton's eyes flitted from one to the next—one showed him and Marla as tall as the ceiling; in the next they were blown up like balloons, crowding each other out of the frame; in the next their bodies looked normal, but their heads shrank to stalks an inch wide.

"Okay, then," he whispered. "How do we get out of here?"

As if in answer to his question, two mirrors slowly began to swivel, turning toward each other until they had made a narrow door in the wall of close-set panels. Beyond the small opening lay more mirrors, but Carlton could not tell how many there were, or which way they were directed, as one mirror caught another, doubling the reflections until it was impossible to see what was real and what was not. Marla stepped through the gap and beckoned: there was a gleam in her eye, but Carlton couldn't tell if it was excitement, or the strange, dim light. He followed her, and as soon as he was through the gap the panels began to pivot again, closing them inside. Carlton glanced around, growing nervous now that their exit had been blocked off. They seemed to be in a narrow corridor that branched off in two directions, the walls made of more floor-to-ceiling mirror panels.

"It's a maze," Marla whispered, and gave him a smile when she saw the look on his face. "Don't worry," she added. "I'm good at mazes."

"You're good at mazes?" Carlton said with irritation. "What is that supposed to mean? *I'm good at mazes.*"

"What's wrong with saying that? I've always been good with mazes." Marla shook her head.

"What, like the *hay maze*? When we were five? Is that what you're talking about?"

"I got through it before anyone else did."

"You climbed over the top of the bales. You're not supposed to do that."

"Oh, you're right." Marla's face flushed. "I'm not good at mazes."

"We will get through this together." Carlton took her hand, long enough to stop her from having a panic attack, then released it.

She looked in both directions, thoughtful, then pointed decisively. "Let's try that way," she said. They started down the path she had chosen, and Carlton followed, keeping his eyes on her feet in front of him. After only a few steps he heard her sharp intake of breath, and snapped his head up: they were at a dead end.

"Dead end already?" he said, surprised.

"No, the panel closed," she hissed.

"This way, *hay maze*," Carlton said with a hint of amusement. "Back this way."

They started back the way they had come, and this time Carlton saw the panels move: as they moved back to the spot where they had come in, a panel swung toward them, cutting off their path. A second later, another panel swung away, opening a new corridor. Marla hesitated, and Carlton stepped up beside her. "No choice, let's go," he said. She nodded, and they walked deeper into the maze.

As soon as they had crossed the new threshold, the panel swung shut. They looked around for the new opening, but there was none: they were enclosed on all sides by mirrors. Carlton walked the small perimeter quickly, beginning to panic.

"Carlton, just wait, another one will open," Marla whispered.

"I kn-ow you're in h-ere." An unfamiliar voice rang out. It seemed to come from everywhere at once, echoing like it was bouncing from panel to panel. The sound was mechanical,

glitching out midword. They exchanged a glance: Marla's face was pale with fear.

"There!" Carlton pointed. A panel had opened while they were distracted. He rushed for it, and walked into a mirror, smacking his head on the glass. "Ow."

"It's there," Marla hissed, pointing to the opposite side of the enclosure.

The panel began to swing shut, closing the room off again.

"I'll f-ind you . . ." The glitching voice had a strange, unsteady tone.

"Carlton!" Marla stood in the gap, holding out a hand, and he ran for her, both of them making it through just as the panel rotated back to its position.

"What were you going to do, stand there and let it crush you?" Carlton hissed.

"I hadn't considered we could get caught between the panels. This place is just asking for a lawsuit." Marla straightened herself. "It's been a lovely evening, but I think I'd like you to take me home now," she said calmly.

"Take you home? Take *me* home!" Carlton said before pausing to listen.

"I know j-ust where you a-re . . ."

They were in a hallway again, this one with two corners to choose from. They exchanged a grim look and turned to the left, moving slowly. Carlton kept his eyes on Marla's shoes ahead of him, trying not to look at the walls on either side, where ranks of their duplicates marched silently beside them, misshapen and warped in the mirrors, then, occasionally, appearing normal. When they reached the corner, something flashed in the corner of his eye, a reflection of a reflection of giant eyes, staring at them. Carlton grabbed Marla's shoulder.

"Over there!" She shuddered.

"I saw it, too."

"Come on, go, go, go," Marla whispered. "Just follow me. Stay calm; remember, nothing can see us."

"I'm getting clo-ser . . ." The mechanical voice echoed through the chamber.

"It's just a recording," Carlton whispered. "It's coming from everywhere, I don't think there is anything actually in here with us." Marla nodded, looking unconvinced. A few steps ahead of them, panels began to pivot again, closing off their path: Carlton glanced behind them—the other end of the hall had closed, too. Marla inched closer to him.

"I see you . . ."

"Shut up," Carlton whispered. He tried to slow his breathing so it made no sound, imagining the air going in and out, filling his lungs without touching the sides. The panel to their right began to swing open slowly, and they backed out of its way. Marla gasped, and Carlton grabbed her arm, seeing it: there was something behind the slowly opening mirror, though he couldn't make out what. They backed up farther, taking small, cautious steps. Carlton searched the mirrored panels for an exit, but saw only his own face, bulging and deformed.

"There you are . . ."

The panel opened, revealing a kaleidoscope of purple, white, and silver, glancing off every mirror disjointedly. Carlton blinked, trying to make sense of the reflections, then a figure at the center stepped into the makeshift room.

He was a bear, built like Freddy Fazbear, and yet entirely unlike him: his metal body was gleaming white, accented with vibrant purple. He held a microphone in his hand, the top sparkling like a disco ball, and on his chest, at the center of a purple metal shirtfront, was a small, round speaker. Only a few feet from them, the new Freddy turned his massive head from side to side, his eyes passing over them. Carlton glanced at Marla, who tapped her ear and nodded. He put his finger to his lips. Freddy took two steps forward, and they stepped back, pressing against the wall. Freddy looked from side to side again.

"I kn-ow just wh-ere you are . . ." The sound was earsplitting, rattling Carlton's teeth, but Freddy's mouth did not move—the voice was projecting from the speaker in his chest.

Carlton held his breath as the bear's eyes passed over him, reminding himself that he was masked, but the bear's eyes hesitated on him before moving away. Carlton could feel the sweat beading on his forehead.

The wall behind them repositioned, and Carlton shifted his weight just in time not to fall, Marla moving just behind him. The panel swung open slowly, and they edged away as Freddy walked slowly in their direction, heading for the new exit—where they were now standing. Marla touched Carlton's arm, guiding him to the side just as Freddy lumbered past them, his shiny surface almost brushing against Carlton's nose.

"I'm get-ing closer," Freddy stuttered menacingly as he disappeared around a corner. The panel began to swing shut, and Marla pointed urgently to the door Freddy had come in. They raced for it, making it through just before the mirrors closed.

Carlton and Marla stared at each other, gasping as if they'd run miles. "Was that Freddy?" she whispered. He shook his head.

"I don't know, but he was different," Carlton said.

"What? Different from what?"

"The other animatronics we've seen so far. He was . . . looking at me," Carlton said uncomfortably.

"They're all looking at us."

"No, he was looking *at* me."

"I can hear you; come on out!" Freddy called out as if on cue. His voice echoed through the maze of mirrors, as impossible

to locate as it had been before. Carlton took a deep, steadying breath.

"How are we supposed to get out of here?" he whispered, trying to sound calmer than he felt. "Where even are we?"

"There, that light." Marla pointed over their heads at the rafters above them, where a red stage light beamed down over the entirety of the maze.

"What?"

"I saw that light when we first came in, but it must have been at least twenty feet away, now it's right over our heads. We just have to keep moving away from it now," she said confidently. Carlton studied the ceiling for a moment, considering what she'd said.

"I told you; I'm good at mazes." She winked. "We just have to wait for the right panels to open." She pointed toward a specific panel.

"That could take ages," Carlton said despairingly.

"It will take longer if we don't keep track of what direction we're going in," Marla said. "Come on." She set off down the path she had indicated, and Carlton followed close behind.

"*I'm getting clo-ser . . .*" Freddy's voice resounded through the maze.

"That sounded like it was behind us again. He's coming around," Carlton whispered.

"Okay, okay. Then we go around, too."

"Just get us out," he said quietly. Marla nodded, and they walked cautiously onward, flanked by their various, distorted duplicates.

The pivoting panels forced them nearly in a circle before giving them a choice of direction, and Marla leaped on the chance, grabbing Carlton by the hand and almost running down the passage until they were stopped again, and made to turn.

"Shh," Carlton hissed frantically.

Marla pushed experimentally on the side of one of the panels, but it didn't budge; Carlton stepped up to help, throwing his full weight against the mirror, but even under their combined force, it would not turn. "I don't know why I thought that would work," Marla whispered.

"I've almost g-ot you . . ." Freddy intoned. Marla looked around uncertainly.

"I've got a really terrible idea," Carlton said slowly. Marla gave him a warning look. "Are you still keeping track of where we are? Or at least, the direction that we should go?"

"I think so," she said, scanning the rafters again, a look of comprehension dawning on her face.

"Close enough," he said.

"What are you going to do?" Marla asked, sounding like she already regretted it. Carlton took the flashlight out of his pocket and made a fist around it, wound up his arm, and smashed the butt of the light into the mirror in front of them. The glass shattered with a high, clear noise, and a dull pain reverberated up his arm.

"*I can h-ear you in th-ere . . .*" Freddy's voice sputtered from all around them.

"Does he just say that, or did he actually hear that?" Marla said.

The panel with the broken mirror swung open, but before they could move there was a rushing sound of heavy footsteps and crunching glass shards. Carlton held his breath, and nodded to Marla. Freddy stepped into the room with forceful steps, then immediately stopped in the center, his upper body slowly turning to scan the surroundings. Carlton and Marla crept around the glass shards, and snuck through the open panel behind the animatronic. In the corridor, Carlton looked questioningly at Marla, and she pointed. He nodded, strode to the farthest mirror, and smashed it.

In an instant, Freddy pivoted toward them. The wide-eyed face turned from side to side. After a moment, another panel began to open beyond the freshly broken mirror. Carlton and Marla ran for it, the glass breaking beneath their feet. "There!" Marla yelled.

Carlton looked up and could see an EXIT sign above a door, just a few yards from where they stood. Marla caught Carlton's eye and mouthed, *We're almost there.*

"*Come back here!*" said Freddy's maniacal voice, and then they all stepped out into the last passage: a jauntily painted ticket booth was visible, and beyond that, an open wall. Marla and Carlton exchanged a glance, and cautiously sped up. *"Got you,"* Freddy said. The speaker was right behind Carlton's head, and Carlton startled, tripping over his own feet.

He righted himself with a palm on the mirror, then took off after Marla, and ran straight into his own reflection, hitting his face on the glass. "Marla, wait!" he screamed: he could see her reflected in three mirrors, but was still unsure of where she had actually gone. "Wait." He rubbed his forehead, and looked into the nearest mirror, trying to see if he was bleeding. He was not, but something was wrong. It took him a second to realize that his earpiece had been knocked loose. He looked around in panic, when suddenly Freddy loomed behind him in the mirror.

Carlton froze in place; the massive white-and-purple bear's head was staring at him from the mirror, looming over his shoulder. He looked down and saw the earpiece at his feet, in one swift motion he leaned down to grab it. His hands were shaking, and he struggled to get it back into his ear. When he looked up, Freddy was standing over him, and Carlton was lifted off his feet with a sudden, painful force. Carlton jerked and dropped back to the ground, the earpiece falling beside him.

Freddy drew back and stared at Carlton for a moment, his eyes clicking back and forth, and his mouth opened just enough to reveal two long rows of perfectly polished white teeth. Carlton leaped toward the earpiece on the ground just as Freddy's arm shot out and shattered another glass panel. Carlton hit the wall headfirst with a bang, and recoiled in pain.

Freddy turned his head, first from side to side, then all the way around to face backward, his eyes searching wildly. Carlton scanned the ground in a panic, and saw the earpiece again, but it was in three places, in three mirrors. The glass crunched again nearby, but Carlton kept his eyes on the earpieces, switching from one to another in a desperate attempt to see which one was real. Suddenly, a human hand reached down and grabbed the earpiece in each of the three panels.

"Carlton!" Marla called, and he turned toward the sound and saw her, not a reflection but the real Marla as she threw the earpiece to him. Carlton snatched the earpiece out of the air, and shoved it into his ear. Freddy stopped in place, his arms still outstretched. Carlton didn't dare move, though the microphone was inches from his face. In his peripheral vision he could see Marla inching toward a door with EXIT over it. Freddy turned his head from side to side again as he slowly straightened from his attacking posture.

"*I'll f-ind you . . .*" came the voice from his chest, and he lowered his arms. Marla turned the doorknob, and pushed the door slowly open, just enough to see that it was unlocked. Scarcely breathing, Carlton backed away from Freddy, keeping his eyes on the animatronic until he was beside Marla.

In one fluid motion, she eased open the door, they darted through it, then shoved it closed behind them. There was a deadbolt near the top, and Carlton flipped it, put his ear to the crack. There was nothing but silence from the other side, and he turned to Marla and heaved a sigh, light-headed with relief. They were in a dark hall, completely free of mirrors.

"Dark, scary hallway," Marla muttered.

"It's beautiful," Carlton said.

A scream ripped through the air from somewhere nearby, and they both froze.

"Not finished yet," Carlton said, and took off running toward the sound, Marla close at his heels.

veryone, be very quiet," Jessica whispered. The
children just stared at her, their eyes wide and solemn. They stood together in the back corner of
the small, dank room, awaiting her instructions:
Three-year-old Lisa was still huddled behind
Ron, her chosen protector, and Alanna had taken hold of the
little blond boy's hand, though he was wriggling in her
grasp. Jessica swallowed. *Why do I have to be the leader? It's bad
enough when I'm just in charge of myself.*

She bent down to the children's level, trying to summon
some kind of leadership quality. *Should have listened to Mom.
Should have played a team sport. But no, I had to be the quiet girl
in the corner chewing the eraser off her pencil.*

Jessica studied the door again, then took a more serious
tone. "Is there something out there?" Alanna and Ron

exchanged a worried glance. "What's outside? You can tell me," Jessica pleaded.

"It comes in through the door," Alanna said, not meeting Jessica's eyes. "She . . ." The little girl broke off and covered her face, mumbling something unintelligible behind the mask of her hands.

"She? Who, the . . . woman who took you?" Jessica asked gently, trying to contain her impatience. Alanna shook her head vigorously, her face still hidden.

"We thought it was a toy. It wasn't scary like everything else." Ron searched for words, and Lisa tugged on his shirt and whispered something, too quietly for Jessica to make out. Ron nudged her. "Tell her." Lisa looked up at Jessica with a suspicious expression on her grubby toddler's face.

"She's all mangled up," the girl said, then turned away again, hiding her face in Ron's shirt. He gave Jessica a distressed look.

"Who? Who's all mangled up?" Jessica said slowly, searching her mind for what they might be talking about. "Was something broken? Did you break one of them?" she asked hopefully. The little kids all began to sniffle again, and she ground her teeth. "What is it?" Jessica nearly snapped, but none of them seemed to notice her tone.

"It's not broken," Ron said, his voice rising in panic, and then the floor shook with a resounding thud. Alanna grabbed Jessica around the waist, and Ron huddled closer, pulling

Lisa with him. The little blond boy stayed where he was, frozen in place with a look of terror. There was another thud, this time louder, then the pounding continued over and over, coming closer. Jessica could hear it moving in the hall, reverberating deep in her chest as whatever it was came thundering toward the door outside. She heard wood cracking, and clutched the children's shoulders as something struck the wall three times in quick succession, rocking them all back. There was a final, clattering noise that seemed to come from all around.

"What is that?" Jessica whispered, searching the walls and ceiling, unable to make sense of the noises. Then everything fell silent. They waited. Jessica listened, counting to ten, then twenty, and the sound did not come again. She counted to thirty, then sixty. *I have to do something.* She straightened, carefully extracting herself from Alanna's grasp. "Wait here," she whispered. She crept toward the door, stepping as softly as she could; as she moved she could feel their eyes on her. The door was ordinary-looking, a wooden door with a brass knob—the kind you'd see on a closet. Jessica took a quick, deep breath, then stretched out her arm to take the knob.

Before she could touch it, the knob turned, and the door began to slide open. Jessica held her breath, and took steady steps backward, desperately wanting to rejoin the group, even if they were just children. At first, Jessica saw only pink and white, the shapes indistinct, then her mind made sense of it: slowly, the enormous head of a garishly painted fox peered into the room.

Foxy? Jessica thought, hazily taking in pointed pink ears and yellow eyes. Its cheeks were painted with red circles, like the animatronic girl's had been. The creature looked at her for a long moment, and she stared back, unable to remember how to move her feet, and then the fox head retreated, and all the children screamed. Something new sprang violently into the room, a long and segmented metal limb like a spider's leg. It braced against the floor just as a second metal leg violently invaded the space, embedding itself in the nearest wall. The children screamed, and Jessica raced toward them, looking frantically for a way out. The room was filling with arms and legs, extended and contorted, some with hands, others without. Jessica searched for a place to run through the steadily thickening mass of legs. Her eyes met the yellow eyes of the fox head, now suspended in the air by rods and beams. But there was another set of eyes as well. *Does it have two heads?* The unskinned metal skull lowered itself; it was connected to the mass above by cables and cords, and seemed to move of its own will.

One high-pitched scream rose above the others, a blood-curdling wail. *"LISA!"* Ron cried, and Jessica saw that the thing had one hand on the little girl's arm and was pulling her toward it. The skinless metal head studied her, then swiveled and swung on its cables to the others, taking an aggressive stance toward them as the metal limbs entangled the little girl and pulled her toward the door.

"NO!" Jessica cried, climbing through the snares of metal coils and grabbing Lisa's tiny hand. A violent surge threw her back, but she held fast to whatever she had managed to grasp, letting go only as she hit the floor. She struggled for air as she got to her feet, but the creature had already retreated through the doorway and disappeared. Jessica whirled, looking frantically to the children, and her heart nearly burst with relief: Lisa was on the ground beside her, and Ron and Alanna were helping her up. Jessica rushed to them. "It's okay," she whispered, then the momentary relief vanished. The blond boy, the one who might have been Jacob, was gone.

"I couldn't hold on to him," Alanna wailed, as if reading Jessica's mind.

Jessica looked to the door in despair, but quickly steadied herself. "We'll get him back," Jessica said, because it was all she could think of to say. She glanced around helplessly, then froze as the doorknob slowly began to turn again. "Stay here," Jessica said in a low voice, and she moved quickly to the door. She stood to the side, bracing herself to jump on whatever came through. *This is your plan?*

The door opened, and Jessica screamed and lunged into the doorway, as though ready to karate-chop whatever was coming through.

Carlton and Marla jumped back with startled expressions, and Jessica stared for a moment, then seized Carlton in a hug, holding tight to his shoulders as if he could stop her from shaking.

"Jessica?" Marla said, spotting the children. Jessica pushed Carlton away.

"Something got one of the kids, a little boy," she said in a rush. "I didn't see where it went."

Marla was already beside the children, checking them for injury. "We have to get them out," she said.

"Oh, really, Marla? Is that what we should be doing? Here I was painting my nails," Jessica said crisply. Carlton reached for his ear and pulled something out.

"Here, take this," he said.

"What? Ew." Jessica made a face instinctively, then peered at the tiny device. "Is that a hearing aid?"

"Not exactly. It makes you invisible to the animatronics. You and Marla take these kids out, I'll find the other kid they took."

"How does it—?" Jessica took the device and studied it. "I have to put it in my ear?"

"Yes! You have to put it in your ear! I'll explain later."

"But, are your ears even clean?" She leaned in, peering suspiciously at Carlton's ear. Marla grabbed the earpiece out of her hand and shoved it into Jessica's ear.

"OW!" Jessica cried.

Marla turned back to the kids. "Shouldn't we give them to the children, instead?"

"There are only two earpieces, and you can both protect them better if you're invisible, right?" Carlton said irritably.

"What if Jess and I stay here with the kids, and you take one out at a time, wearing the earpieces?" Marla pressed. Jessica shook her head immediately.

"And what if that thing comes back and kills us all while we're waiting for Carlton to take his sweet time? We have to make a break for it, Marla, it's the only way."

They were all quiet for a moment. Carlton looked from Jessica to Marla and back.

"Right? Now, give me thirty seconds to get away from here, that way if something chases me, I can draw them away from you. Anything I should know?" Carlton paused at the door.

"Afton's still alive," Jessica said, and he nodded.

"This ends today," he said quietly. "One way or another. Not one more child dies because of that psychopath. I owe that much to Michael."

Jessica bit her lip. "We all do," she said.

He forced a smile. "Good luck."

"Good luck," she echoed.

"Right." Carlton clenched his jaw, then squared his shoulders and held the door open, poised to exit. "This was my idea?" he muttered, then closed the door behind him.

"Marla, do you know the way out?" Jessica asked, surprised to hear her own voice come out clear and steady. Marla nodded, standing up.

"We came in the back way. But I think if we go back down that hall, we can get out into the main dining room; should be easy to get out from there, right?"

"You'd think so," Jessica muttered with an edge.

Marla gave her a level look. "You got something better?"

"No. I don't." Jessica turned to the three remaining children, who were watching them with wide eyes. "We don't have to get far," she said, searching for scraps of hope to offer them. "I need you to stay together, and stay with me and Marla. If you can do that, we'll all be okay." They looked at her like they knew she was lying, but no one said a word.

Jessica opened the door again carefully. The hallway outside the little room was dark, but Marla led them onward as if she really did know where they were headed. She held a large, battered flashlight out in front of her. She looked poised to turn it on but refrained from doing so, seemingly afraid of attracting more unwanted attention. Jessica's eyes adjusted to the dim light as she took up the rear, alert to the slightest sign of danger.

They came to a T in the hall, and Marla turned without hesitation. A few yards ahead there was light: strings of small, bare bulbs lit the way at intervals, and the next fork in the hall was visible. *We're getting closer*, Jessica thought, as they moved cautiously onward.

A soft popping noise caught Jessica's attention overhead, and she froze. "Marla," she hissed, and Marla and the children ahead stopped and turned around. Marla pointed up with a worried expression, and Jessica looked up to see that some of the bulbs over her head had gone out, their glass made opaque with a sooty film. "Just old lights," Jessica breathed.

A light above Marla burst and died, and all of them jumped. Alanna clapped both hands over her mouth, and Ron put a hand on Lisa's shoulder. "Can we go faster?" Lisa whispered. All at once, the rest of the light bulbs flickered and clattered. Jessica held her breath: they stayed on, preserving the little light, but overhead something hollow and metallic rattled in the ceiling.

Marla's face went pale. "Keep moving," she said tightly. Jessica gave a sharp nod. The rattling noise kept pace, sometimes seeming to come from above them, and sometimes from the dark corners just out of view, scraping and clattering in a vent or crawl space. Lisa whimpered; the older children's faces were stony, but Jessica could see the glimmer of tears on their cheeks. Suddenly, Marla stopped short, and Jessica almost bumped into Ron. "What?" she hissed, then saw: a thin curtain of dust was falling from above. Jessica looked up, and saw the open duct directly above them.

A multisegmented metal arm covered with springs and wires dropped down through the open duct, anchoring itself to the floor right next to Jessica's foot. Everyone screamed. The arm retracted, then two more of the creature's contorted limbs smashed down to the ground, raining down plaster and dust. "*RUN!*" Marla screamed. They took off down the hallway as the creature lowered its full form into the space, its shiny white fox head turning and smiling in their direction as they fled. Jessica glanced back, and the unskinned head dropped, too, grinning upside down, a red bow tie joining their necks ridiculously. Jessica fled; behind her came an enormous thud. *Run faster!* she wanted to scream, but the others were gasping for breath, already running at their full capacity.

The children were pounding along as fast as they could, but Lisa, the smallest, began to fall behind. The creature shot past Jessica, reaching out for the little girl again, and Jessica grabbed her, yanking her up and out of reach just in time. It reared back to strike again, and Jessica clutched Lisa to her chest and ran on. They rounded a corner, and with a flare of hope Jessica saw that the hall was short, ending in a heavy set of double doors. Marla sped up, and Alanna and Ron did the same; Jessica kept her pace, staying at the back as Lisa clung to her with startling strength.

Marla reached the end of the hall and slammed herself against the emergency bar, and the doors split open. They raced through, and Marla flung the door shut, grabbing a nearby sign post and jamming it through the door handles.

"Keep running," Jessica said with a fresh pump of adrenaline. She looked around: they were up against the wall, behind a popcorn popper and a cotton candy machine. She glanced back briefly at the sign Marla had barred the door with: LET'S EAT! it read in big, round letters. Ron leaned to the side, about to peek between the machines. "Hold on," she hissed, putting a hand on his shoulder. He drew back as if something had burned him.

"It'll be okay," Marla said, and Jessica marveled briefly that she sounded like she believed what she was saying. Behind them, something crashed against the door again, rattling the doorframe. Jessica waited, her eyes on the makeshift barricade, but nothing came.

"We have to move slowly and quietly," she whispered, and the three children nodded in unison. "Stay back," Jessica told them, and stepped out past the popcorn machine, alert to danger. She took a second to get her bearings: The walls of the dining room were lined with arcade games and children's play areas, and on the far side of the room, blissfully,

273

were the wide glass doors of the entrance. She motioned the others forward; the children, huddled together, followed her into the open room with Marla close behind.

"Hurry," she urged, and Marla nodded, taking Lisa's hand as Alanna and Ron followed behind her, their faces pinched with exhaustion. Suddenly, Alanna screamed, and Jessica jumped. "What? What is it?" The girl was pointing at a jungle gym a few feet away, where two toddlers, too small to climb the bars, were nonetheless doing so.

"It's okay, they're just toys," Marla said, looking back at Jessica with a frazzled expression. "We saw them on the way in."

Alanna screamed again, and ran to Jessica, grabbing on to her waist. "It bit me!"

"What?" Jessica looked down: Alanna's ankle was bleeding, though not badly, and a few feet away was another crawling, robotic child.

"Jessica!" Marla screamed, touching the device in her ear nervously. "It can't see us, but it can see them." As she spoke, the two other robotic children on the monkey bars lowered themselves unsteadily to the ground and began to crawl straight toward Lisa and Ron; they backed away, and a fourth appeared, boxing them in. Marla scooped up Lisa and Alanna and tried to hold them away from harm. "Jessica!" Marla screamed. "Help!"

"It bit me," Alanna repeated, panic in her voice, and the children clung together as the crawlers came closer, a slow march of determined toddlers with the black eyes of insects. "They can't see us," Jessica said with determination, darting forward and grabbing the nearest robot baby. It was heavier than it looked. Jessica held it out from her body. It was facing away from her, and she held on tight as it continued its crawling movements in the air, steadily putting its hands and feet into position, one after the other. She glanced around, then spotted the ball pit: at least four or five feet deep. Jessica threw the crawler down into the colorful balls as hard as she could, and it landed, half-buried, on its side, still repeating its motions, and slowly sank out of sight.

"Marla, come on!" she shouted. Marla set down Lisa and Alanna beside Ron, then turned her attention to the baby crawling toward them. Her hands were shaking, like she was preparing to pick up a giant cockroach. "Marla!" Jessica shrieked. Marla screamed and shook her hands in the air, and the baby suddenly charged forward, clawing at the ground and biting at the children's feet. Lisa cried and fell to the ground, and the heavy creature grabbed at her legs as it crawled up on top of her. Marla bolted forward with a blood-curdling scream and yanked the metal crawler off the little girl. Marla cried out again as she spun and threw the creature through the air. It missed Jessica's head by an inch, slammed into the net canopy above the ball pit, and dropped down into it, sinking out of sight.

"You almost hit me!" Jessica had barely spoken the words when the third and final robot baby flew through the air and landed at her feet with a resounding bang. Marla let herself fall to the ground, breathing heavily, her eyes wide with panicked fury. Jessica stared down at the creature as it locked its sights on the children again. "Oh, no you don't." Jessica picked it up just as it started to crawl. She held it over the pit and it turned its head around completely to face her with its ant-like eyes. Its little rosebud mouth opened, flashing two rows of pointy predator's teeth, then snapped shut, chomping the air. Jessica shuddered and dropped it, watching with grim fascination as it churned its arms and legs, digging itself deeper into the pit.

"Jessica!" Marla cried, and she spun around. Lights had come on behind them, illuminating a large show stage with a bright purple curtain as its backdrop. On the stage, and in the spotlight, was a glossy and white Foxy animatronic, its mouth open and arms wide, ready to perform for a cheering crowd. The Fox looked down at them with delight.

"Was that there a second ago?" Jessica whispered.

Suddenly, the fox's body began cracking apart: metal plates split away from the center of its torso, from its arms and legs, lifting out, splitting again and folding back, leaving only its canine head untouched, grinning maniacally as its body was horribly transformed. Jessica ran to the children as all at once, tentacle-like metal limbs erupted from what had been Foxy, and the mutilated skeleton creature stretched out into its new, semi-arachnid form.

"Get them out!" Jessica cried. Alanna and Ron were frozen to the spot, staring, and Marla slapped their cheeks lightly. Ron snatched up Lisa's hand, and together they all ran for the front door.

"Jessica!" Marla cried as they reached the door. "We can't let it get out!" The creature was on top of the monkey bars now, elongating itself to terrifying proportions as if showing off its tangled metal spines.

"Get them out!" Jessica shouted again, pushing away from them, then turning her attention back to the mangled pink-and-white fox. The thing began to slowly dismount the monkey bars, its limbs slipping over and around one another, changing its shape with every step it took. Its foxlike face, and its vaguely human one, were both intent on the children, the heads angled slightly toward each other so that each of its eyes could focus. Jessica took a deep breath, then pulled the earpiece out of her ear, struggling to steady her hands long enough to slip it into her pocket. "Over here!" she screamed as loudly as she could, her throat going raw, and the canine head ducked under the other neck, its eye rolling around to fix on her. "Yeah, over here!" Jessica cried, her voice hoarse, and the thing came down from the

277

monkey bars with menacing grace and began to slink toward her. She glanced around. *Should have thought this through.* At the door, she could see Marla bracing it open and shooing the children through, one at a time, then looking back to Jessica.

Jessica nodded her head and waved Marla away. She grabbed a folding chair from a nearby table and hefted it over her head, then flung it at the creature. It landed with a clatter on the floor, missing the thing entirely. The fox head cocked to the side, its mouth hanging open to show all of its teeth, then it lurched forward, its metal appendages banging against the ground. Jessica turned and ran.

She looked around wildly for an escape as she darted through the mass of tables at the center of the room; she shoved over a table behind her, but the thing just climbed over it like it was flat ground. Jessica sped up. The creature was right behind her, the fox head snapping its jaws as the unskinned skull grinned ghoulishly from its swing. She raced back the way they had come, ducking between the cotton candy machine and the popcorn cart. The sign blocking the doors was still in place, and she flung it away and yanked the door handle. It rattled in place, but still wouldn't open.

Something crashed behind her, and Jessica spun around to see the popcorn cart knocked over, popcorn strewn across the black-and-white floor tiles. The creature stretched out a limb and pushed the cotton candy machine experimentally; it rocked but did not fall, then another limb shot out. It hit Jessica's leg with a smack, and she stumbled back against the door, an involuntary shout of pain blurting from her mouth. The fox and the unskinned head looked at each other, the head bouncing on its cables, then in unison they turned their eyes on her as the creature undulated its limbs, displaying their full extension. Jessica felt in her pocket for the earpiece, but couldn't find it. It must have fallen out while she was running: she darted her eyes from side to side, afraid to move even her head. She was cornered, caught between the wall and a children's climbing set: there was no way past the thing.

All at once the creature seized the cotton candy machine with three of its limbs, crushing it; shattering glass sprayed in all directions as it carelessly flung the machine aside. Jessica shielded her face, turning away, and as the machine cracked the floor tiles behind her, she saw it: the red-and-yellow bars of the playset nearby led high above the room below, where a colorful pipe maze began, bolted tight to the ceiling, and disappearing into a circular hole in the wall and into the next room. *That's my way out.*

Jessica set her foot on the bottom rung of the playset and started to climb as fast as she could. Below her came a wrenching noise, and she glanced down to see the creature tearing up the playset, the unskinned head swinging and bobbing gleefully. It reached up and tore out the rung below her, and she climbed faster, hurling her upper body into the tube just as one of the creature's hands grasped the last piece of the playset. Jessica scrabbled for a handhold, at last managing to pull her full body inside the tube. She crawled as fast as she could, the pipe shaking with every movement, then stopped to look down. Although some of the plastic tunnel was bolted to the ceiling, there were large portions that were not. *This was made for kids, not me.* Jessica rocked herself carefully, and the section of plastic below her rocked as well, the plastic segments creaking at the seams. Jessica shivered. *Slow and steady.* She checked her hands and knees, making sure they were safely in place, then started forward again.

She was in a narrow, unadorned tube, hovering above an empty hallway, lit by a single, exposed florescent light that hummed as it flickered. The hum of the florescent light seemed to grow louder as she made her way cautiously along the fragile plastic flooring, filling her ears almost painfully, as if she had gone deep underground. She worked her jaw open and shut, trying to clear the sensation, but the noise persisted. When she reached the segment of tubing that went into the wall above the door, she hesitated, trying to see inside, but there was only darkness. Jessica took a deep breath, and carefully crossed into the next room.

Silence fell: the humming noise was blissfully gone. The only light was behind her, and bizarrely it did not penetrate into the room, as if it were somehow being filtered out. She looked back and saw the circle of light where she had come, but everything else was in darkness. Jessica blinked, waiting for her eyes to adjust, but all she saw was black. *Okay, then.* She shuffled slowly forward, feeling carefully and sliding her knees along the support beams that ran along sections of the tunnel. After a few minutes, she came to a turn, bumping her head gently on the plastic, and she felt her way around it with a vague sense of accomplishment.

A point of orange light appeared below her, and she startled, her hand slipping off the support beam and rattling the plastic. She caught her balance, her heart racing, and a pair of green lights appeared, a few feet away from the first one. They vanished, then reappeared, and another pair, purple, sprang out of the darkness beside them, and this time Jessica saw the dark pinpoint at the center of each circle. Jessica tensed with an awful recognition, as more and more sets of colored lights appeared: *Eyes. They're eyes.* The room below was slowly filling with sets of eyes, until it seemed impossible that so many creatures could fit into the space; they all stared upward, unblinking at Jessica. She moved slowly forward, her hands shaking as they found their way along the beams, and the eyes followed her as she went. *Don't look down.*

Jessica set her gaze on the darkness in front of her and shuffled on and on for what felt like ages; each time she glanced down there were more pairs and pairs of watchful eyes, all of them rapt on her progress. Jessica shivered. She moved faster, still feeling carefully before she slid her hands and knees along, then the tube curved slightly, and a circle of dim light came into view. Jessica crawled for it as fast as she dared, the tube swaying precariously as she moved. She crawled through the hole and turned back: the room was in darkness again; all the eyes had vanished.

Jessica shuddered, revolted, then looked down at the room she now hovered above. The light was dim and unsteady, flashing strange colors at intervals, but she could see clearly. Peering down, Jessica saw that it was coming from the carnival games that filled the room, some flickering noiselessly and others giving steady light in every hue. She took a deep breath and looked ahead, trying to see where the tube led. *I really hope there's another way out*, she thought, and started crawling again. The plastic tubing rattled as she went, the only noise in the dark room. Jessica swallowed; as the adrenaline waned, she was beginning to remember how much she hated enclosed spaces. *Just keep moving.* She reached a split in the tubing: one way snaked around the perimeter of the room, the other through another wall, into the pipe maze bolted to the ceiling of the next room. She scanned the room, then made her choice. She took the turn, taking the tunnel that fed through the neatly cut hole in the wall, and found herself back in the main dining room.

She paused and listened. There was no sound of movement in the dining room, and she craned her neck to look down through one of the large plastic panes, searching the area: the creature was nowhere to be seen. She had not noticed the play pipes that covered the ceiling before climbing up into them, but now she saw the extent of them, with no end in sight, and no way down. The playset she had climbed to enter the tunnels was utterly destroyed. *How am I going to get out?* She cast her eyes helplessly over the maze, tracing the paths she could take, and suddenly she saw it: the ball pit where she had thrown the baby crawlers was across the room, and it had a canopy made of climbing rope that stretched fifteen or twenty feet above the floor. The tube went directly over it. Jessica took a deep breath and crawled farther out into the room, bracing herself. She made it to the first turning point, and suddenly the pipe shook. She paused, but the structure shook again, and again. The light was being obscured from below her, and Jessica looked down.

The unskinned skull grinned up at her with yellow eyes, suspended below as if out of nowhere. The head swiveled sideways and elevated up and over the plastic tunnel. Jessica looked up in dread, and saw the body of the creature right above her, its limbs wrapped around the tube like a monstrous squid seizing a ship. She stifled a scream, and her heart skipped as she fought not to hyperventilate. The fox head lowered to eye level and snapped beside her, and she screamed and shied away; her hand hit the plastic floor between the support beams and the segment fell straight down. Jessica clamored back before falling with it, and quickly took a corner, heading off to a new direction. The fox head swooped upward in a blur and vanished.

Jessica crawled in a straight line, keeping her eyes fixed ahead. The structure continued to shake, and she could hear plastic breaking behind her, as well as large segments of the pipe maze crashing to the ground. Soon she reached the ball pit, and she stared down at the canopy of ropes through the bottom of the tube, hesitating. *Now what?* The structure shook again, but this time it was different. This time it trembled as though someone, or something, were in the maze with her. The entirety of the structure swayed and rocked on the bolts it hung from. Jessica kicked out the plastic below her, bracing herself on the sides of the tube as she looked down. Something moved in the pit below: three of the crawlers' heads were above the surface, staring up at her disembodied with blank eyes. In unison, they snapped their little jaws, and she startled, hitting her head on the top of the plastic tube. "Stupid babies," she muttered. When she looked down again, they were back in motion, swimming through the balls and snapping, apparently at random. Jessica shivered and froze, suddenly paralyzed at the next step of her plan. For a moment, she prayed that it wasn't too late to just stay silent, and wait for danger to pass.

The structure trembled again, this time over and over in rapid succession. A spiral of shimmering metal flew through the tunnel, then she saw its gleaming fox's head, its mouth open in an impossible smile. Jessica screamed and fell sideways through the hole, landing heavily on the rope canopy. It sank inward, giving her a split second before she began to slip downward.

She grabbed wildly at the net, the ropes burning her hands and entangling her feet, then she got her footing, and scrambled back up the slope to the top, wrapping her hands around the metal support bar. She watched the hole in the bottom of the pipe that she had fallen through, expecting something to come out, but nothing did. There was motion in the pipes, barely visible through the thick foggy plastic. Jessica searched in panic, trying to locate the creature, but there was movement everywhere: every pipe seemed to be crawling with life. Then she realized, all of the movement was flowing in the same direction. Jessica followed the flow with her eyes, through pipe after pipe, all the way up to a plastic end cap just above her. With a crash, the end cap burst out of place, and bolts rained down from the sky, hitting Jessica on the head. The fox head beamed down at her. More of its body pushed its way through, more and more limbs emerging as it balanced itself delicately on the edge of the pipe like a cat preparing to pounce on a mouse.

Something fell out of Jessica's pocket with a *ding*. It was the earpiece, which must have been wedged into her other pocket. Jessica held steady, violently fumbling to retrieve the earpiece. The fox head craned sideways as the last piece of the monster exited the pipe and joined the rest of the metal mass, perched like a vulture on the rickety infrastructure of the pipes.

Finally, the fox lunged.

Jessica crammed the earpiece into her ear and jumped, and the creature slammed into the netting where she had been, its limbs shooting through the spaces in the net. Jessica landed on her back on the top of an arcade cabinet, then fell to the floor below with a thud, the wind knocked out of her, and she wheezed. The creature struggled to free itself from the net. The limbs writhed, then the whole body sank down with the net, tearing it off the frame as it went. The creature was stuck, its limbs tangled in the mesh. It thrashed and flailed, and its long, snakelike appendages lashed through the air. The net rocked back and forth, straining in its bonds, then gave way in an instant. The thing dropped straight down into the pit, sending colorful plastic balls splashing over the sides of the pit. It twisted frantically, still tangled in the torn netting, then suddenly it began to twitch. Jessica watched, wide-eyed, as the bound creature slowly sank into the ball pit with a sound like metal grinding metal; after a moment it vanished entirely, though the balls boiled up frenziedly as the gnashing sound continued. Briefly, she caught a glimpse of a black-eyed crawler, chewing contentedly. She drew in a shaky breath, then ran for the front entrance. Jessica burst out through the double door and into the cool night air, and swayed on her feet.

"Are you all right?" Marla asked with alarm.

"I'm fine." Jessica looked at each of the children, confirming that they were all there, all safe. *Except one. Carlton, do you have him?* She forced herself to smile. "So, who wants to visit a police station?"

Carlton crept quickly down the hall, scanning the walls and floor for signs of struggle—of anything that would indicate something had passed through. There was another door a little way down the hall, and he paused outside it, carefully turning the knob while staying outside the frame. Bracing himself, he pushed the door in, and waited. Nothing came out and he cautiously peered inside: the room was completely empty. "Calm before the storm?" he whispered to himself, and shut the door.

When he reached the T in the hall he paused. *Where are you, kid?* He closed his eyes, listening. There was nothing, and then, a muffled scraping came from the wall behind him, back the way he and Marla had come. Carlton went toward it, and put his ear to the wall. The rustling continued. It was an odd sound he could not quite pinpoint, but it sounded like someone moving. He stepped back, examining the wall: It was plain, painted beige, with a large, silver air vent near the baseboard, about three feet high and almost as wide. *That's strange* . . . Carlton knelt down in front of the vent and turned on his flashlight—which worked, somewhat impressively, after its extended use as a blunt instrument. He turned the beam on the vent, and squinted, trying to see inside, but the slats were too close together to make out anything.

A faint sound came from somewhere deep inside; it was indistinct, but it was unmistakably a voice. Carlton tugged at the grate with his fingernails, and it moved easily; he pulled the whole thing out, revealing a dark tunnel about four feet high. He shone his flashlight inside: The walls were concrete, painted red on one side and blue on the other in faded colors. Incomprehensible words were scribbled on them in crayon, and the yellow linoleum floor was scuffed with black sneaker marks, scratched, and turning up at the edges. "This place *is* brand-new, right?" Carlton muttered as he crouched down and crawled inside, keeping the light ahead of him. It was unsettling to think of someone carefully laying down a new floor, then marking it with deliberate signs of wear; adult hands mimicking children's painstaking handwriting and simple drawings. He cast the light around:

on the red wall there was a drawing of a house and stick figures; underneath someone had written *My House* with the *e* drawn backward. The sound of the voice came again, echoing faintly through the tunnel ahead, and Carlton crawled forward awkwardly with the flashlight in one hand.

The wall color changed every few feet, cycling through the rainbow at random, with childlike graffiti spaced unevenly all along the way. He came to what he thought was an opening to a new tunnel, but when he turned the light toward it, he saw that it was only a cubbyhole, small enough for a child to squeeze into. In the corner of it was a little blue sneaker, the laces untied, and Carlton swallowed. *What is this place?*

His flashlight lit on a silently screaming face, and Carlton jumped back, dropping the light. He snatched it up again, his heart thumping, and shone it on the figure: it was a jack-in-the-box stuck in its "surprise" position: a white-faced clown, its mouth gaping in perpetual laughter. "This isn't a vent," Carlton whispered, letting the light leave the painted face and continue down the colorful hall littered with hiding spaces and scuff marks. "This is part of the play area."

The light fixed on a rainbow stretching above one of the hiding spaces. HIDE-AND-SEEK HALLWAY, it read. "This can't be good." Carlton winced. The child's voice echoed again, this time a little louder, and he shook off the eerie sensation. *I'm coming, kid*, he promised silently.

He rounded a corner, but stopped short: there was an animatronic baby in a cubbyhole, motionless, laying on its back. Carlton's elbows and knees trembled. *Please don't move.*

Black, insect-like eyes stared blankly at him from a sweet, plastic face; the crawler did not move, apparently deactivated. He backed away cautiously, and turned his light on the path ahead; he was approaching a turn, but there was still no sign of an exit. He crawled on, passing stick figures and houses that were beginning to look suspiciously repetitive.

"I s-ee you . . ."

Carlton whirled around. There was nothing in sight but a closed door. It was the size of the other cubbyholes, child-height, with a small, heart-shaped window near the top. As he passed his light over the little door, something glinted through the heart-shaped window. Carlton stiffened, but before he could think to move, the door broke off its hinges as Freddy crawled forcefully out, a maniacal grin on his shiny purple-and-white face as he unfolded from the cramped space he had stuffed himself into. Carlton crawled backward frantically, and Freddy matched his motions, keeping a distance of inches between them. Carlton glanced around, then turned and crawled as fast as he could down the tunnel, his knees and hands slamming into the floor painfully as he raced to get away. He glanced back: Freddy was crawling behind him, his mechanical arms and legs thundering faster than Carlton could hope to escape. He rounded a corner, and Freddy caught his foot, the iron fingers digging into his heel. Carlton kicked with his other foot, wresting himself free, and got to his feet and started to run, hunched down to half his height and scraping the ceiling with his back. From behind, he could hear the sound of Freddy bearing down on him, his hands and knees pounding the floor with vibrating force.

Carlton turned another corner, and relief surged through him: there was a vent along the tunnel, an *actual* vent that led to a large room. Carlton kicked it out without hesitation and scurried through to the room on the other side.

The room was enormous, seemingly designed to house a single, giant carnival ride: it was a ring of seats set on an angle, held together by huge metal arms on a spiral, a terrifying variation on the merry-go-round that would whip around at high speed while tilting nauseatingly up and down. On the far side of it was a door marked EXIT. Before Carlton could run for the door, Freddy burst out of the tunnel, climbing to his feet, his eyes sickeningly reflective in the dark.

"I see you so clearly now," said the speaker in Freddy's chest.

Carlton turned to run, then smacked into the carnival ride, biting his lip and drawing blood.

He turned back just in time to see Freddy lunge at him, and Carlton ducked under the ride, the blow just missing him and hitting the metal side of the tilted merry-go-round.

The sound rang out in the vast, empty room, and he shuddered, then leaped back as another blow hit the ride above him, reverberating so hard it rattled his teeth. Carlton looked up: the metal had bowed out above his head, caving to Freddy's strength.

"You can't escape . . ."

Carlton scrambled away, tripping over the heavy steel beams that undergirded the ride, bolting it to the ground. Freddy's shiny purple-and-white calves stalked him calmly, keeping pace with him along the perimeter of the ride as Carlton ducked under heavy cables and mysterious, frightening-looking gears.

"I've alm-ost got you . . ." Freddy announced.

"Not yet," Carlton muttered as he carefully untangled his foot from the heavy wire that had ensnared him. He craned his neck, trying to see the room around him: There was no way he could get past Freddy, and even if he did, he would pursue him relentlessly. Carlton was backed up against the tilted end of the ride, and up against the control platform. As he craned his head upward he could see a large on/off lever, which was almost in reach.

"Nowhere else to run . . ."

Carlton waited for Freddy to make his way deeper under the ride, pressing and contorting his body to get at Carlton between the beams. Carlton squeezed out from under the ride and hoisted himself just high enough to pull the lever and activate the ride, then dropped to the ground and covered his head. Freddy reached for him, but the ride tilted abruptly.

Carlton saw Freddy jerk about, wrenched by the moving parts, until the ride jolted hard. Carlton clutched his head as his ears rang with the impact, a growing shriek of tearing metal and grating gears as the ride slowed, wobbling unsteadily on its axis. Carlton didn't move: from where he had landed he could see the apparatus in motion, shredding through the body of what had been Freddy as the machine ground on inexorably through its routine. Scraps of purple appeared and vanished, then fell to the floor, spat out by the machine. A yellow eyeball appeared in a space above two gears, and Carlton watched with shocked fascination as the rest of the precariously balanced body was pulverized by the alternating beams, then dropped to the ground in several distinct masses.

The machine screeched ear-splittingly, then slowed and sputtered to a dead stop. Carlton didn't move for a moment. He got to his feet and cautiously moved away from the apparatus, carefully avoiding the littered scraps of metal and plastic on the ground. He didn't dare climb under the thing again, but he prodded it gently with his toe, then yanked his foot back as something dropped out.

Half of Freddy's head, one-eyed and still grinning insanely, fell out of the machine near Carlton, spun partially on the ground, then stopped moving, and its single eye flickered on, then sputtered and died. The speaker in the now-smashed chest piece, laying armless and legless nearby, crackled with static, then spoke, *"Thanks for playing; come again soon!"* The voice trailed away and went silent.

In the distance, the child's scream came again, and Carlton was startled back to himself.

"Hang on, kid," he whispered, and headed grimly for the door.

CHAPTER FOURTEEN

harlie's duplicate stared back at her, looking stunned for an instant, then Charlie watched her own face curve into a bright, cruel smile. The other Charlie didn't move, and Charlie's fear receded as she watched this strange imitation of herself, astonished. *That's my face.* Charlie reached up and touched her own cheek, and the other girl imitated her; Charlie tilted her head to the side, and the girl mirrored her movement—Charlie could not tell if she was being mocked, or if the other girl was simply as entranced as she was. The duplicate was a little taller than Charlie, and Charlie flicked her eyes to the girl's feet: her black combat boots had heels. She was wearing a red V-neck shirt and a short black skirt, and her hair was long and hung in shiny waves—a look Charlie had given up even attempting halfway through ninth grade. She looked polished; confident in her stance. She looked the way Charlie wished she could be: some version of herself that had figured out curling irons, and sophistication, and taking up space in the world without apology.

"What are you?" Charlie whispered, mesmerized.

"Come on," the other Charlie said, holding out her hand, and Charlie started to reach out to her, then stopped herself, yanking her hand away. She shrank away, stumbling back across the hall and her duplicate closed the distance between them, leaning in so close Charlie should have felt her breathing. A long moment passed, but the other Charlie did not draw breath. "You need to come with me," she said. "Father wants us to come home." Charlie startled at the phrase.

"My father is dead," she said. She pressed back against the wall, as far from the girl's face as she could get.

"Well, would you like to have a live one?" the other Charlie asked, with a mocking edge.

"There is nothing that you can give me, and certainly not that," Charlie said shakily, inching backward into the storage room; the duplicate followed her step for step. Charlie glanced past the duplicate and into the open bedroom door; John emerged into the hallway, leaning heavily on the door-frame and gripping his side.

"Are you okay, Charlie?" he asked in a low, steady voice.

"Oh, I'm just fine, John!" Charlie's duplicate said cheerfully.

"Charlie?" John repeated, ignoring her. Charlie nodded, not daring to take her eyes off the imposter.

"She says *Father wants us to come home*," Charlie said.

John stepped up behind the other Charlie.

"Father? Would that be William Afton?" John demanded. He took a few sprinted steps and grabbed a lamp by its base, raising it for attack. The other Charlie smiled again, then swiftly raised her arm and backhanded John across the face. He dropped the lamp and staggered backward, catching himself against the wall, and the duplicate grabbed for Charlie's hand. Charlie ducked away, running for the hall-way with the girl on her heels.

"Hey! That was just round one!" John shouted, beckoning his assailant to come back. He grabbed the duplicate girl's arm, yanking her back toward him and away from where Charlie had run. The duplicate allowed John to hold her close, not resisting. John was washed with fear as he stood eye-to-eye with the imposter. *Now what do I do?*

"Just like by the old oak tree when we were little, John," the duplicate whispered. She pulled him close and pressed her lips against his. His eyes widened, and he tried to push her away, but he could not move. When she finally released him and pulled back, she was Charlie, *his* Charlie, and there was a high, painful ringing in his ears. He covered his ears, but the ringing increased exponentially, and for the few brief seconds before he collapsed to the ground, he saw her face morph into a thousand things. The room spun, and his head hit the ground with a crack.

The girl smiled and glanced at Charlie, then drew back her foot and kicked John in the ribs, knocking him onto his side and against a heavy wooden trunk. Charlie ran toward him, but before she could reach him, the girl grabbed her hair, bringing tears to her eyes. The imposter pulled upward, lifting Charlie several inches off the ground, and then flung her aside. Charlie tried to regain her footing but tripped backward over a cardboard box and slammed hard into the opposite wall, knocking the wind out of her as John got warily to his feet. Charlie climbed to her knees. She dragged in heavy, grinding breaths, watching helplessly as the other Charlie strode toward John.

He straightened, and without a pause, she punched him in the stomach. He doubled over, and before he could stand, she hit the back of his head with her fist, like it was a hammer and he was a nail.

John fell forward, catching himself on his hands and knees, and scrambled up. He lunged again at the girl, catching her shoulder with his fist, but the blow glanced off her, and he yelped in pain, clutching his hand like it had hit something harder than flesh and bone. The imposter took him by the shoulders, lifting him off the ground, and carried him across the room, then pressed him against the wall. She released him and let him stand, turning to look at Charlie momentarily, then she placed her open palm against John's chest.

Suddenly, John began to gasp for breath, his face turning red. The imposter's face remained unchanged, her open hand slowly pressing harder against his chest. "I can't—" John gasped for air. "Can't breathe." He clutched at her arm with both hands, but it was no use as she continued to steadily press into him. John slowly began to slide up the wall, inch by inch, the pressure forcing his entire body upward.

"Stop!" Charlie cried, but the other Charlie didn't flinch. *"Please!"* Charlie scrambled to her feet and ran to John's side, but the other Charlie snapped out her other arm and caught her by the neck without moving her hand from John's chest. Her fingers closed on Charlie's throat, closing off her windpipe as she lifted her up onto her toes. Charlie choked, kicking and gasping. The imposter held her there, looking expressionlessly from Charlie to John as she kept them both immobilized and struggling to breathe.

"Okay," Charlie wheezed. "I want to talk. Please," she begged hoarsely. The imposter dropped them both. John fell motionless to the floor. "You've hurt him, let me help him." Charlie coughed, pulling herself up.

"You're so attached to something so . . . easily broken," she said with amusement. Charlie strained to see past her, anxiously watching John's chest as it rose and fell. *He's alive.* Charlie took a breath, then turned to face the girl who had her face.

"What do you want to talk about?" she asked tightly.

Carlton let the heavy door slam shut behind him and ran on without looking back: there was another door up ahead, and dim light filtered through a small window near the top. The child's cry echoed again, and Carlton froze, unable to pinpoint its direction. The high-pitched sound pierced the air again, and he grimaced at the sound: it was raw and thin, the scream of a kid who had been screaming for a long time. Carlton peered through the window in the door—it looked deserted, and he opened the door cautiously, then stopped dead. Everything looked the same: every hall, every room. Lights flickered, speakers hummed. One light seemed to be about to burn out, making a high-pitched screech that echoed through the chamber.

"Kid," he whispered, but there was no answer, and Carlton was suddenly aware that he may have been chasing echoes and lights for the last ten minutes. He suddenly felt the weight of how alone he was, and it became a physical thing; the air itself seemed to grow heavier around him. His breath slowed, and he dropped to his knees, then fell back to sit. He stared down the empty hallway despairingly, and finally scooted to the side, maneuvering his back against the wall so he could at least see his assailant before he died—whoever— or whatever—his assailant might turn out to be.

I've failed. I'm not going to find him. Tears sprang to his eyes unexpectedly. *Michael, I'm so sorry.* In the days after Michael disappeared, his father had asked him so many questions, going over that one afternoon like he believed together they could re-create it and solve the puzzle. *I searched for the missing piece, I promise, I searched.* He had gone over every moment of the little party in his mind, desperately trying to find the clue his father needed, the detail that would make everything clear.

There were so many things he could have done to stop what had happened, if he had known then what he knew now.

But now I know it all, and there's still nothing I can do.

"I failed you, Michael." Carlton put his hand on his chest, trying to calm himself and not hyperventilate. *I failed you, again.*

"So, what do you want to talk about?" Charlie repeated. The other Charlie narrowed her eyes.

"That's better, a lot better." The girl smiled, and Charlie leaned back as far away from her as she could. It was unnerving to see her own face glaring back at her, accusatory and petulant.

"I'll listen to anything you want to say, just don't hurt him more," Charlie pleaded, her hands raised in surrender, her heart fluttering. Charlie's duplicate flushed with anger.

"This is why," she hissed, shaking her finger accusingly.

"What? *This is why?* I don't understand," Charlie cried.

Charlie's imposter paced the floor, her anger seeming to have drained as quickly as it came. Charlie took the opportunity to look to John again, who had rolled partially onto his back, holding his side as though in immense pain, his face still red. *He needs help.*

"What are you?" Charlie growled, her anger rising at the sight of John.

"The question isn't what am I. It's what are *you*? And what makes you so special, over and over again?" Charlie's duplicate approached her with renewed anger, grabbing Charlie by the throat once more and lifting her off the ground. She pinned her to the wall, baring all her teeth.

The ruse of Charlie's imposter faded, revealing a painted clown face, somehow looking angrier than the human facade. The white plates of the face opened like a flower, revealing yet another face, made of coils and wires, with bare black eyes and jagged prongs for teeth. *Her real face*, Charlie thought.

"Ask again," she growled.

"What?" Charlie choked.

"I said ask me again," the metal monster snarled.

"What are you?" Charlie whimpered.

"I told you, that's not the right question." The metal girl held Charlie out at a distance and looked her up and down. "Where did he hide it?" She held Charlie's throat with one hand and put her other hand on Charlie's chest, then ran a finger down the length of her breastbone. Then her eyes shot to Charlie's face, and she grabbed her chin and turned her head forcefully to the side. She seemed lost in thought for only a moment then snapped back. "Ask again."

Charlie locked eyes with the metal face. The face plates closed over the tangle of twisted metal, reassembling the face of the clown, with her rosy cheeks and glossy lips. Soon the illusion returned, and Charlie was staring into her own eyes again. Charlie felt herself growing uncannily calm as she began to realize what the right question was.

"What am I?"

The imposter loosened her grip, and lowered Charlie so that her feet touched the ground. "You are *nothing*, Charlie," the imposter said. "You look at me and you see a soulless monster; how ironic. How twisted. How backward." She let go of Charlie's throat and took a step back, her red lips losing their savor for the moment. "How unfair."

Charlie was on her knees again, struggling to regain her strength. The imposter approached her and knelt with her, placing her hand over Charlie's. "I'm not sure how this will work, but let's give it a try," she whispered, running her fingers through Charlie's hair and firmly grasping the back of her neck.

She was a little girl, holding a piece of paper in her hand, excited and full of joy. A bright gold foil star shimmered on the page, above the glowing words of her kindergarten teacher. Someone gently touched her back, encouraging her to run forward into the room, into the dark. She eagerly ran inside, and there he was, standing by the work desk.

"How long did I stand there before he shooed me away?" Charlie searched her mind, but the answers didn't come.

"He didn't *shoo* me away," Charlie's other voice answered.

Her eagerness didn't fade, she remained patient and joyful. After the first push, she came back to try again. It was only after the second push that she hesitated to go back, but she carefully returned anyway, this time holding the paper into the air. Maybe he didn't see it.

"He saw it," Charlie's other voice spoke down to her.

This time it hurt; the ground was cold, and her arm ached where she had fallen on it. She looked for the paper: it was on the floor in front of her, her gold star still shone bright, but he was standing on the page now. She looked up to see if he noticed, tears in her eyes. She knew she should leave it, but she couldn't. She reached forward to tug at the corner, but it was too far away. She finally crawled to it on her knees, her dress dirty now, and tried to pull the page from under his shoe. It wouldn't come loose.

"That's when he hit me."

It was difficult to make out anything in the room after that. The room was a smear of tears and pain and her head was still spinning. But she made out one thing, a shiny metal clown doll. Her father had turned his attention back to it, lovingly polishing her. Suddenly, her pain faded to the background, replaced with fascination, obsession.

"What is all of this?" Charlie cried.

Now she was looking at herself in the mirror, holding a stick of lipstick that she'd stolen from her teacher's purse. But she wasn't painting her lips with it, she was drawing bright red circles on her cheeks. The lips came next.

"Are you listening to me?" the doppelganger whispered.

Night had swept over everything. The rooms were dark, the halls were silent, the lab was still. Her feet made soft pats against the smooth white tiles. A tiny camera in the corner had a red blinking light on it, but it didn't matter what it saw, it was too late to stop her.

She pulled the sheet away from the beautiful clown girl, beckoning her to speak. Where was the button, the one he always pressed?

The eyes lit up first, and then other lights from within. It didn't take long for the painted face to search the room and find her, greeting her with a sweet smile and soft voice.

"Then there was screaming." The illusion was broken, and Charlie pushed herself away. "Then there was screaming," the imposter repeated. "It was coming from me, but . . ." She paused and pointed to her own head with a look of curiosity. "But I remember seeing her scream." She looked thoughtful for a second, and suddenly the illusion dissipated, and she appeared again as the painted clown. "It's strange to remember the same moment from two pairs of eyes, but then we were one."

"I don't believe that story," Charlie growled. "I don't believe that story at all. You aren't possessed! If you think I will believe for one second that I'm talking to the spirit of a sweet and innocent little girl, then you're crazy."

"I want you to call me Elizabeth," the girl said softly.

"Elizabeth?" Charlie answered. "If you were this little girl, Elizabeth, I can't bring myself to believe that that little girl would be capable of all of this."

"The anger isn't from her," Elizabeth said, her painted face shifting: she looked like a wounded animal, vulnerable but still poised to attack.

"Then what?" Charlie cried.

"My anger is from a different father." Elizabeth strode to Charlie again, grabbing her neck again and jostling her into a white light and pain, where suddenly all was calm.

A hand was stroking her hair. The sun was going down over a field of grain. A cluster of birds were fluttering overhead, their calls echoing out over the landscape. "I'm so happy to be here with you," a kind voice said. She looked up and nestled against him.

"No, this is mine," Charlie protested.

"No," Elizabeth intruded. "That doesn't belong to you. Let me show you what *does* belong to you."

Agony erupted, flooding the room with its sound. The walls went black and streams of water poured down from behind the window curtains. A man lay curled on the floor, something cradled tightly in his arms, and when his mouth opened, the room shook with the sound of his anguish.

"Who is that?" Charlie said anxiously. "What is he holding?"

"You don't recognize her?" Elizabeth said. "That's Ella, of course. It's all your father had left after you were taken."

"What, no, that's not Ella." Charlie shook her head.

"He cried over that cheap store-bought rag doll for two months," Elizabeth snarled with disbelief. "He cried into it, he bled into it, he poured his grief over it. Very unhealthy. He began to treat it as though he still had a daughter."

"That was my memory, me sitting with my dad, watching the sun go down. We were waiting for the stars to come out. That's my memory," Charlie said angrily.

"Look again," Elizabeth instructed, forcing the image upon her once more.

There was a hand stroking her hair. The sun was going down over a field of grain. A cluster of birds were fluttering overhead, their calls echoing out over the landscape. "I'm so happy to be here with you," a kind voice said. He gripped the doll tightly, and smiled despite the tears streaming from his face.

"Of course, he wasn't content with that, you had to grow up. So, he made more."

Her arms hung off the side of the workbench. The joints were stiff enough to carry something lightweight, and her eyes were more realistic than he had ever made them before. He propped her up and extended her arms straight in front of her, carefully balancing a small tray on them, then setting a teacup on the tray. He furrowed his brow with frustration for a moment, turning a brass knob over and over until the room quivered and flashed, then everything stood still, and the little girl looked at him and smiled.

"That's MY memory!" Charlie screamed.

"No, that's *his* memory," Elizabeth corrected.

"Jen, I swear she is more than another animatronic doll. You should see. She walks, and she talks."

"Of course she walks and talks, Henry." Jen's voice was angry. "She walks because everything you build can walk, and she talks because everything you build can talk. But the reason why this one seems so real is because you're destroying your mind with these frequencies and codes." Jen threw her arms in the air.

"She remembers, Jen. She remembers me. She remembers our family."

"No, Henry. You remember. Zap your head with enough of those rays and I bet you can get the teakettle to tell you about your lost family."

"My lost family," Henry repeated.

Jen took pause, looking regretful. "It doesn't have to be that way, but you need to let go of this. Your wife; your son, they can still be a part of your life, but you have to let go of this."

"She is in this doll." He gestured to Ella, who was standing upright with her teacup perched on the tray. A little rag doll sat in a wooden chair in the corner, its head draped over the armrest, its eyes staring out over the room.

"It took him a while to figure out that it was the rag doll, the little store-bought rag doll. Maybe he never *sensed* you when it wasn't around, I don't know. But over time, he started putting it inside *his* Charlie, whatever new Charlie he built."

Charlie sat speechless, remembering all the times with her father, questioning each of them. *Sitting on the floor of his workshop, building a block tower out of scraps of wood as he bent over his work. He turned back to her and smiled, and she smiled back, beloved. Her father went back to his work, and the jumbled creature in the far, dark corner twitched. Charlie startled, knocking her blocks to the ground, but her father did not seem to hear. She began to rebuild the tower, but the creature kept drawing her gaze: the twisted metal skeleton with its burning, silver eyes. It twitched again, and she wanted to ask, but could not make herself speak the words.*

"Does it hurt?" Charlie whispered, the image so clear that she could almost smell the hot, metallic scent of the workshop. Elizabeth froze, then all at once the illusion vanished and the metal plates of her clown-painted face stripped back, baring the coils and wires, and jagged teeth. Charlie shrank back, and Elizabeth moved with her, maintaining the distance between them.

"Yes," she whispered, and her eyes blazed silver. "Yes. It hurt."

The plates of her face folded back in, but her eyes still glowed. Charlie blinked and looked away; the light blinded her, poking pinpoint holes in her vision. Elizabeth stared bitterly. "So, you remember me, then?"

"Yes." Charlie rubbed her eyes as her vision began to clear. "In the corner. I didn't want to look. I thought it was . . . I thought you were . . . someone else," she said, her voice sounding thin and childish to her own ears.

Elizabeth laughed. "Did any of those other *things* really look like me? I'm unique. Look at me."

"It hurts my eyes," Charlie said faintly, and Elizabeth grabbed her by the chin and pulled her close. Charlie shied away, closing her eyes against the light, and Elizabeth slapped her cheek with painful force.

"Look at me."

Charlie took a shaky breath and obeyed. Elizabeth's face looked like Charlie's again, but the silver light poured out coldly from the place where her eyes should be. Charlie let it flood her vision, blotting out everything else.

"Do you know why my eyes were always glowing?" Elizabeth asked softly. "Do you know why I twitched and shuddered in the dark?" Charlie shook her head slightly, and Elizabeth let go of her chin. "It was because your father left me turned on all the time. Every moment, every day, I was aware, and unfinished. Watching him as the hours passed, and he created toys for the little Charlie, unicorns and bunnies that moved and talked as I hung in the dark, waiting. Abandoned." The glare from her eyes faded a little, and Charlie blinked, trying not to show her relief.

"Why am I even talking to you about this. You weren't even there yet." Elizabeth turned her face, almost in disgust.

"I was," Charlie answered. "I was there. I remember."

"You *remember*," Elizabeth mocked. "Are you *sure* you were there for all of those memories?" Charlie searched her thoughts for anything that could confirm the memories she clung to.

"Look down," Elizabeth whispered.

"What?" Charlie whimpered.

"Your memory. I'm sure it's crystal clear, since you were there and all." Elizabeth smiled. "Look down."

Charlie returned to her memory, standing in front of her father's workbench. She was immobile; she didn't have a voice. "Look down," Elizabeth whispered again. Charlie looked to her feet, but didn't see feet at all, only three legs of a camera tripod anchored to the ground.

"He was making memories for you; making a life for his little rag doll, making her a real girl.

"I'm sure many of those memories have been elaborated upon, edited, and embellished, but make no mistake, Charlie wasn't there." Elizabeth leaned closer to Charlie.

"He made us one, two, three." Elizabeth touched Charlie's shoulder lightly, then brought her hand back to her own chest. "Four." Her eyes flickered, and the silver glow faded until her eyes looked nearly human.

"Charlie would be a baby, then a little girl, and then a sulky teenager." She looked Charlie up and down with a pointed sneer, then her expression cleared as she continued. "Then at last she would be a woman. She would be finished. Perfect. Me." Elizabeth's face tightened. "But something changed, as Henry labored, racked with grief, over his little girl.

"The littlest Charlotte was made with a broken heart. She cried all the time, day and night. The second Charlotte he made when he was at the depth of madness, almost believing the lies he told himself; she was as hopelessly desperate for her father's love as he was for hers. The third Charlotte he made when he began to realize he'd gone mad, when he questioned every thought he had, and begged his sister Jen to remind him what was real. The third Charlotte was strange." Elizabeth gave Charlie a contemptuous look, but Charlie scarcely saw it. *The third Charlotte was strange*, she repeated silently. She ducked her head and rubbed the flannel of her father's shirt with her thumb, then looked back up. Elizabeth's face was stiff with rage; she was nearly trembling.

"What about the fourth?" Charlie asked hesitantly.

"There was no fourth," she snapped. "When Henry began to make the fourth, his despair turned to rage. He seethed as he soldered her skeleton together, pouring his anger into the forge where he shaped her very bones. I was not Charlotte-drenched-in-grief. I was made alive with Henry's fury." Her eyes flared again with silver light, and Charlie stayed herself, forcing herself not to blink. Elizabeth leaned in closer, her face inches from Charlie's. "Do you know the first words your father ever spoke to me?" she hissed. Charlie shook her head minutely. "He said to me, *'You are wrong.'*

"He tried to fix the flaw he saw in me, at first, but what was wrong, as Henry saw it, was the very thing that made me alive."

"Rage," Charlie said softly.

"Rage." Elizabeth drew herself up and shook her head. "My father abandoned me." Her face twitched. "*Henry* abandoned me," she corrected herself. "Of course, I could not comprehend those memories until I had received a soul of my own—once I took it for myself." She smiled. "Once I had endowed myself with a soul, I experienced those memories anew: not as an uncomprehending toy, twitching and seizing with an all-consuming rage I could not fathom, but as a person. As a daughter. It's rather a cruel irony that I would escape the life of one neglected daughter only to embody another."

Charlie was silent, and for a moment her father's face returned to her, his smile that was always so sad. Elizabeth laughed abruptly, shaking her out of her memories.

"You're not Charlie, either, you know. You're not even the *soul* of Charlie," Elizabeth mocked. "You aren't even a person. You're a ghost of a man's regret, you're what's left of a man who lost everything, you're the sad little tears that fell unceremoniously into a doll that *used* to belong to Charlie." Elizabeth suddenly glared at her as if looking through her. "And if I had to take a guess . . ." She grabbed Charlie under her chin and pulled her upright, studying her torso for a moment. She made a quick motion with her other hand and Charlie gasped; the room was spinning again. Elizabeth's hand had disappeared, but it soon reemerged, and she was holding something.

"Look before you lose consciousness," Elizabeth whispered. There, before Charlie's eyes, was a rag doll, and recognition flared.

"Ella," she tried to whisper.

"This is you."

The room went dark.

What was that? Carlton lifted his head, holding his breath as he waited to hear it again. After a moment he did: someone was whimpering, and the sound was coming from nearby. Carlton took in a renewed gulp of air, instantly filled with new purpose. After hours of flickering bulbs and distant echoes, this was right beside him. Carlton leaped to his feet: across the hall a door was ajar, with an orange light glowing unsteadily from inside. *How did I not notice that?* Carlton made his way across the hall, sliding his feet along the floor so as not to make a sound. When he reached the door, he peered in cautiously through the crack: The orange light was from an open furnace set into the wall, its mouth large enough to fit a small car. The furnace was the only light in the dark room, but he could make out a long table, with something dark lying on it.

The whimpering came again, and this time Carlton's eyes lit on its source: a small, blond-haired boy was huddled in the darkest corner of the room, opposite the furnace. Carlton ran into the room and knelt beside the boy, who looked up at him numbly. He was bleeding from shallow cuts on his arm and one corner of his mouth, but Carlton saw no other visible injuries.

"Hey," he whispered nervously. "Are you okay?" The boy didn't respond, and Carlton took hold of his arms, readying to pick him up. When he touched the child, he could feel the tremors throughout his body. *He's terrified.* "Come on, we're getting out of here," Carlton said. The little boy pointed to the creature on the table.

"Save him, too," the boy whispered tearfully. "He hurts so bad." He squeezed his eyes shut. Carlton glanced at the large, motionless figure on the table by the furnace: he hadn't considered that it might be a person. He scanned the room to make sure nothing else was moving, then patted the boy on the shoulder and got to his feet.

He approached the table cautiously, keeping to the wall instead of walking across the center of the room. As he got closer, the burning smell of metal and oil rushed up against him, and he covered his face with his sleeve, trying not to gag as he examined the prone figure.

It's not a person. On the table, illuminated by the flickering orange light, was a mass of metal: a melted, clumpy skeleton of metal bulges and blobs, barely resembling anything at all. Carlton studied the thing for a long moment, then looked back at the little boy, uncertain what to say.

"Heat," a voice snarled, and Carlton spun around to face a twisted man, creeping out from the shadows. "Heat is the key to all of this," the man went on as he haltingly approached the table. "If you keep all this at just the right temperature, it's malleable, it's moldable, and it's highly, highly effective; or maybe *contagious* is the word. I suspect you could put it in anything, but it's best to put it into something that you can control—at least to a certain extent." William Afton lurched into the light, and Carlton stepped back reflexively, though the table was between them. "It's an interesting alchemy," William continued. "You can make something that you control completely, but that has no will of its own, like a gun, I suppose." He ran his withered hand over the silver arm of the creature. "Or you can take a drop of . . . pixie dust." He smiled. "And you can create a monster that you . . . *mostly* control, one with unlimited potential."

Carlton. He stepped back with a shout of surprise: the voice was so clear in his head that he recognized it instantly. "Michael?" The single word was enough. Carlton turned to the table with a new, terrible clarity. He knew exactly what he was looking at: the endoskeletons of the original Freddy's animatronics, welded and melted together, immobile and featureless. And still inhabited by the spirits of the children who had been murdered inside of them so many years ago. Still filled with life, and motion, and thought—all trapped; all in terrible pain. Carlton forced himself to look William Afton in the eye.

"How could you do this to them?" he asked, nearly trembling with rage.

"They do everything willingly," William said plainly. "The process only truly works if they freely release a portion of themselves." The flames rose without warning, and heat radiated in painful waves from the gaping furnace. Carlton shielded his eyes, and the creature on the table convulsed.

William smiled. "Scared of fire. But they still trust me. They don't see me as I am now; they only remember me as I was, you see."

Carlton broke his eyes away, feeling like he was waking from hypnosis. He darted his eyes desperately around the room, looking for something, anything, to attack with. The chamber was strewn with scrap metal and parts, and Carlton grabbed a metal pipe that lay by his feet and hefted it like a baseball bat. Afton was gazing down at the creature on the table, apparently insensible to anything else around him, and Carlton hesitated, considering the man for a moment. *He looks like he could fall apart all on his own*, he thought, taking in Afton's fragile, hunched body and the thin skin of his head, seeming to scarcely cover the skull beneath. Then he looked back to the creature on the table. *I think I've got the moral high ground here*, he decided grimly, and raised the pipe over his head as he stalked around the table toward Afton.

Suddenly, his arms were jerked above his head, the pipe dropping from his hands and hitting the ground with a bang. Carlton struggled with the cables that gripped his wrists, but he could not wrestle free. Slowly, he was lifted off his feet, his arms stretched painfully out to his sides by two cables that extended from opposite sides of the room, seeming to attach to nothing.

"I've never tried this on a human being before," William muttered, pressing some kind of mechanical syringe into the chest of the molten creature on the table. He wrenched the tool sideways, extracting something with great difficulty. The syringe was opaque, and Carlton could not see what filled it, but his heart raced as he began to suspect he knew where this was going. He tugged harder at the cables that bound him, but each time he pulled, he only wrenched his shoulders from side to side. Afton pulled the syringe out of the creature and gave a satisfied nod, then turned to Carlton.

"Usually this goes into something mechanical; something I made. I've never attempted it on something . . . sentient." William gave Carlton a measured stare. "This will be an interesting experiment." William lifted the mechanical syringe, carefully placing it over Carlton's heart. Carlton gasped, but before he could try to move, William plunged the long needle into his chest. Carlton screamed, then realized distantly it was really the blond boy in the corner screaming: Carlton wheezed and gasped, but could make no sound as his chest burned with a blinding agony. Blood soaked his shirt, and it clung to his skin as he convulsed in his bonds.

"For your sake, you'd better hope my little experiment does *something*; because I doubt you will survive otherwise," William said mildly. He nodded toward the cables and Carlton dropped to the ground; the pain in his chest was unthinkable, he felt like he'd been hit full-on with a shot-gun. Blood sputtered from his mouth, dripping onto the floor, and Carlton curled around himself, squeezing his eyes shut as the pain intensified. *Please make it stop*, he thought, then, *Please don't let me die.*

"Maybe the heart was too direct," William lamented. "Well, that's the point of this, to learn, trial and error." He turned his gaze toward the blond-haired child, who still huddled weeping in the corner.

Steps echoed endlessly in the dark, pacing back and forth across the enclosed space.

"Are you still listening to me?" a voice rang out.

Charlie was lost in the dark, spinning silently and trying to get to the surface of whatever void she was in.

"Unlike you," the other Charlie uttered, unseen, "I was real. I was an actual little girl, one who deserved the kind of attention showered over you. You were nothing."

Charlie opened her eyes, the room still spinning. She tried to breathe but all her breaths stopped short of going in or out. There was a doll laying on the floor a few feet in front of her. She reached for it convulsively, like gasping for air.

"Do you want to know where my hate comes from? It's

not from this machine that I reside in, and it's not from my *past life*, if that's what you want to call it."

Charlie clawed at the floor with her fingers, unable to move the rest of her body. She gripped the doll with her fingertips and pulled it closer.

"I hate because, even now, I'm still not enough," Elizabeth whispered. She held out her sleek metallic fingers in front of her face. "Even after this; embodying the one thing Father did love, I'm not enough. Because he can't duplicate this, he can't make himself like me." Her voice began to grow angry again. "He can't duplicate what happened to me, or maybe he's too scared to try it on himself. I broke free of my prison, I emerged from the flames and the wreckage of Henry's last great failure, and I went to my father. I gave myself to him, to study, to use, to learn the secrets of my creation. And still it is *you* he wants."

Charlie clambered up onto her hands and knees and dragged herself toward the hallway. Elizabeth didn't seem concerned, taking slow steps behind her, not trying to catch her, only to keep her in sight.

"You, maybe he can re-create. Henry somehow got a piece of himself into you, and that's something we haven't seen before. That's . . . unique."

Charlie kept crawling steadily: She was beginning to feel stronger, but she kept her movements slow and clumsy, getting as much distance as she could between herself and Elizabeth. Charlie looked up and down the hall, searching for something—anything—that might give her an advantage. The door to the next room was open, and she could see a desk: sitting on it was a round stone paperweight. Without picking up her pace, Charlie crawled across the room, dragging her legs as if they pained her, while Elizabeth's slow, patient steps followed a pace behind.

"Can you get the green for me?" a voice called. Carlton blinked. He was sitting upright but felt only half-present, as if he had been daydreaming. "The green," the tiny voice repeated. "Please?" Carlton cast his eyes around for something green; the floor was black and white, and they were sitting somewhere a little dark. A little boy was hunched over a piece of paper, drawing. Carlton looked up. *We're under a table. Under the table at Freddy's.* There were drawings scattered in front of him on the floor, and a box of crayons spilled out across the tiles. Carlton spotted a green crayon that had rolled up against the wall, and he grabbed it and handed it to the little boy, who took it without looking up.

"Michael," Carlton said, recognition dawning. Michael continued to draw. "Where . . . ?" Carlton looked around, but what he saw didn't make sense to him. The pizzeria was brightly lit, yet Carlton couldn't see more than five feet away, as though there was a blurry cloud masking everything beyond. He ducked his head out cautiously from under the table, but the bright lights hurt his eyes, and he shielded them with his hand, crawling back under. Michael had not moved; he was drawing steadily, his brow furrowed in concentration. Carlton studied the pictures on the ground with a vague sense that something was wrong. *I don't belong here*, he thought, yet part of him felt completely at home.

"What are you doing?" he whispered to Michael, who looked up from his drawing at last.

"I have to put them back together," Michael explained. "See?" He pointed out from the table, at the pizzeria around them. Carlton squinted into the blurry horizon, seeing nothing at first, then they began to appear: he saw pages and pages of colorful drawings, some on the walls, others blowing through the air. "They're all in pieces," Michael said. He shuffled the pages in front of him and found two that showed the same child, then he placed one on top of the other, and began to trace the lines. "These go together," Michael said, holding up the picture: the two drawings had become one, the separate pages somehow bonded together; the lines were clearer and the colors more vibrant.

"What are you putting back together?" Carlton asked.

"My friends." Michael pointed to a single picture propped up against the wall. It showed five children: three boys and two girls, standing together in a cheerful pose, with a yellow rabbit standing behind them.

"I know this picture," Carlton said slowly. His mind was

still foggy, and as he tried to grasp at the answer, it only slipped further away. "Who is that?" Carlton whispered, pointing to the rabbit.

"He's our friend." Michael smiled, not looking up from his work. "Can you go get more for me?" Carlton looked out into the pizzeria: the space he could see had expanded a little more, and now he could make out the blurs of other children who seemed to be grasping at pages as they flew by, trying to grab the drawings. Carlton got out from under the table and stood up, walking through the midst of the mirage and colors. A boy in a black-and-white-striped shirt came running up, chasing a piece of paper.

"What are you doing?" Carlton asked as the boy grabbed empty air, and the page flew away into the blurry distance.

"My papers blew away," the boy cried, and hurried off. Carlton turned and saw another boy in the same outfit on the opposite side of the room, chasing other pages. A little girl with long blonde hair ran past him, and he whirled around, recognizing her far away: there were duplicates of each child, all of them chasing different pages.

A single figure stood still amongst the chaos, out of phase with the surroundings. At first it seemed to be a man bent over a table, but as Carlton's head throbbed with waves of confusion, the man became a yellow rabbit, not standing over a table, but over five children, tied together as one. The second image washed away, and the rabbit became a man again, standing in the dark. The children ran past the man as if they could not see him; as Carlton watched, several children ran straight through him without seeming to notice. Carlton approached the man, and as he got closer, the yellow rabbit appeared again, turning to look at him momentarily before blowing away like smoke, leaving the man underneath.

"This isn't real," Carlton gasped, trying to parse the two overlapping realities that seemed to be swirling around him. Three figures seemed to hold fast, while the rest of his surroundings flickered in and out of existence: the man standing at the table, a blond boy in the corner—the only child not running, and not repeated—and a body lying on the floor, curled in a puddle of blood. *Is that me? Am I dead?*

"No, silly!" a child called. "You're with us!"

The syringe mechanism recoiled with a loud snap: the man in shadow had taken something from the metal body on the table. Suddenly, another drawing flew into the air, and another ghostly child appeared to chase it.

The little girl with blonde locks of hair and a red ribbon bouncing on her shoulders ran past as well.

"Stop!" Carlton called, and she obeyed, her eyes still locked on the drawings she had been pursuing. "Who is that?" Carlton directed her attention to the yellow rabbit flickering in and out of existence.

"That's our friend. He helped me find my puppy!" she exclaimed before running off again.

"They don't know," Carlton whispered, releasing her as she disappeared into the blur surrounding him. Carlton searched the air as drawings blew by, snatching at the ones with images that seemed familiar.

"What are you doing?" the little boy in the striped shirt asked.

"I'm going to help you put these together," Carlton said, reaching for another picture as it blew past.

When she had finally crawled her way to the desk, Charlie reached up and grabbed for the top of it, then pulled herself up, feigning a struggle. She winced as she put weight on her feet, continuing to act weaker than she actually was: in reality she was nearly back to her full strength. She leaned heavily on the desk as if for support, putting one hand directly on the heavy stone paperweight.

"We both know he won't be able to re-create you, either." Elizabeth was near. "And the real question would be, would we really want him to? Besides . . ." Elizabeth approached Charlie from behind, moving faster. "I think I hate you more than I love him." She raised her hand in attack and Charlie spun around, swinging the rock in a single motion. There was a thunderous crack as it slammed into Elizabeth's face, and Charlie fell back with the shock, dropping the paperweight. She hit the ground hard, cradling her hand.

Elizabeth staggered backward, holding her hand over her face, but she could not conceal the damage without her illusion. One entire side of her gleaming white jaw had been knocked off her face, revealing the wires beneath. She cocked her head to the side for a moment, as if running a system check; Charlie didn't wait for the result. She leaped to her feet, pushing past Elizabeth as she ran back the way she'd come. Charlie heard Elizabeth moving, and dove for the hall closet, pulling it shut tight behind her.

"I know it may sound very childish of me," Elizabeth cried; her voice sounded like she was still at the end of the hall. "But if he doesn't want me; then he won't get you, either."

The footsteps drew closer, and Charlie looked one way and another, hoping desperately for a place to hide in the small closet. Then suddenly, as she turned completely around, she saw a familiar thing. *You.* The faceless robot wielding its knife, the mannequin, the construct that her father had built for one purpose, to end his life.

"Your dad thought you were so special, your memory was just too precious to let go of."

The blank face was almost peaceful in the dark. It had been built for one thing; it had completed its duty, and had remained in silence ever since, standing as a memorial to pain, and to loss.

The closet door moved slightly as Elizabeth gripped the knob; Charlie could see her shadow under the door. She grabbed at the clothing hanging behind her, old coats and dresses, and pulled them forward, concealing the construct as best she could. "You can't overpower me," Elizabeth whispered. "You aren't like me," she added with relish. Charlie waited in front of the blank-faced creature, not hiding. Gently, Elizabeth pulled the door open.

"I shouldn't be here," Charlie whispered to Elizabeth.

Charlie heard John cough from the room behind them, and relief rushed through her. *He's going to be okay. He's alive.* Elizabeth glanced back as though considering him, then trained her eyes on Charlie and took two deliberate steps forward.

"Charlie!" John called from outside.

"It's okay, John," Elizabeth answered, her voice indistinguishable from Charlie's. "I'll be right out." Instantaneously, she looked like Charlie again, not the grown-up Charlie she had been masquerading as, but Charlie as she was really, a mirror reflection. She shifted awkwardly, her eyes darting back toward John for just a moment, then gave Charlie a cruel smile. "How far do you think I could get with him before he noticed?" she whispered.

"You're right, Elizabeth," Charlie said. Elizabeth's smile faded. "I was never supposed to be here."

"No?" Elizabeth took the last step, closing the distance between them. She gripped Charlie by the neck, pressing up against her.

"Neither of us were." Charlie gripped the rag doll close to her chest. Elizabeth frowned in confusion, then peered over Charlie's shoulder, seeing the robot standing directly behind her. Charlie flinched her other hand, which was behind her back, doing something unseen with a quick motion. A metal pulley screamed.

Charlie closed her eyes, hugging the doll, and when the knife went through them, it did not hurt.

Elizabeth gasped as the blade plunged through her, too, sounding almost human. Charlie saw Elizabeth's face, rigid with shock, then it was gone, replaced by the smooth metal plates of her robotic form. Sparks burst in the air above her as Charlie's vision began to fade, and the smell of hot plastic came to her from very far away.

"It's not fair." Elizabeth's voice sputtered with static. "I never had a life."

Charlie struggled to take in a breath, still clutching the rag doll to her chest. She reached for Elizabeth's dangling hand clumsily and caught it; Elizabeth looked at her confusedly, and Charlie strained to pull her hand up to the rag doll. Fumbling, she closed Elizabeth's fingers around the doll, then, still holding her hand, Charlie pushed with the last of her strength, sliding the doll across the four-inch stretch of blade between them until it rested against Elizabeth's chest. Charlie tried to smile, but everything was dark; she had forgotten how to see. Charlie felt her head fall forward, and could not pull it up again. Elizabeth twitched for a moment longer, rattling the blade that pierced them both, then her head slumped forward, too, resting against Charlie's forehead.

Charlie! John was screaming her name. *CHARLIE!*

I love you, too. The words didn't come, and then there was nothing at all.

"Here, right here!" Carlton called. The little boy in the striped shirt helped align two more pictures, and Michael traced over them, connecting them into a single drawing. A second boy in a striped shirt appeared from the blurry surroundings and sat down on top of the one already sitting with them, merging into him seamlessly. Only Carlton seemed to notice the merging of the two children, not even the boy in the striped shirt himself seemed aware.

Beside them was the little girl with blonde curls: they had found all her drawings and put them together, and now she looked solid and real, no longer ghostly like the others. She was able to speak in full sentences, her cognitive abilities having steadily grown stronger as her drawings were united. Carlton struggled to find matching images for the others: he was keeping track of the three stable figures, the man, the boy in the corner, and the body, and it was clear he was running out of time. The man was making preparations to harm the boy in the corner.

"You said he saved your dog?" Carlton asked the blonde girl, grasping for answers.

"Mommy said that he went to heaven, but I heard Daddy say he was hit by a car. But I knew it wasn't true, Bonnie told me it wasn't true; he said that he had found my puppy." She brushed a lock of hair from her shoulder with her hand.

"And did he take you to your puppy?"

"He took me, but I don't remember . . ."

"But it was *him* who helped you?" Carlton pointed to the yellow bunny in the drawing that showed all five kids.

"Yes! That's him." She smiled. "My name is Susie," she added. "And that's Cassidy." A girl with long black hair approached, carrying more pictures in her arms. "And you?"

Carlton looked briefly at a little boy with freckles. "I . . ." He struggled to speak, and Carlton glanced nervously at the man in the room as he matched two more drawings together.

"There!" Michael exclaimed proudly. Another ghostly image of the freckled boy climbed under the table, and merged with the one who was already there: he instantly became less ghostly, and more whole. "I'm Fritz." He smiled, suddenly filled with more life.

William Afton clenched his fists, studying his own hands for a moment then looking toward the medical monitors in the corner. "I feel that my time is running short." He looked toward Carlton thoughtfully, but Carlton was still lying on the floor, motionless. "That's unfortunate," he growled. "I hoped to learn something. But maybe that's not the problem." He looked toward the metal table. "Maybe we just need some new life in this mass of metal." He smiled at the little blond boy, who recoiled and tried to scoot away, though he was already as close to the wall as he could get. "You'll have to forgive me, though, as I'm not sure how to do that, either." William took steps toward him. "I can think of a few things to try. At the very least, it will be fun; like old times." His lips peeled back, revealing two full rows of stained yellow teeth.

The door creaked as it opened, and William's eyes darted toward it as a tangled metal mess lurched toward him, scraping across the floor. "What are you doing back here?" William asked. The white painted fox head was turned at an alarming angle, clearly not functioning properly. Its limbs were all turned and pivoted, some of them broken and dragging, all inching the remains of the creature into the room. The fox head's eye spun wildly, searching the ceiling. William pointed to a corner. "You're no use to me anymore; get out of the way," he said dismissively, then drew back, surprised: following the fox was another motorcade of broken parts, their wires reaching for one another like vines, pulling each other along and holding themselves together. Mounted on the back of the entanglement was the white-and-purple face of a bear. *"I'm heeeere!"* a voice came from a speaker somewhere within the mess, cracking and popping with static.

William made a face, unnerved by the wrecked, comingled creatures. "Get back," he uttered, giving the Freddy face a kick. The mass of parts slid away without resistance, sounding almost disappointed as they came to a stop a few feet away. "What a waste," he hissed. He turned his attention to the fox again, apparently the most intact. "Bring that boy to me," he instructed, and the fox turned its eye to the corner.

"I have to go do something for him," Susie said cheerfully, getting to her feet.

"Something for who?" Carlton asked with alarm, and took hold of her arm.

"Bonnie." She smiled, gesturing toward the cheerful yellow rabbit wavering in and out of existence beside the table. "He asked me to do something for him just now. He wants to bring a new friend for us and he needs my help."

"Bonnie isn't your friend," Carlton said, still holding her arm. He gasped at the imminent danger that the little blond boy faced, as the girl struggled to break away.

"He *is* my friend! He found my *puppy*!" she cried, and yanked her arm free.

"No, don't go to him!" Carlton pleaded.

★   ★   ★

John.

"Get back!" John screamed and jolted awake, swinging his arms up to block an attack and jerking back. His head cracked against the cabinet behind him. "Ow." He groaned, regaining awareness of where he was. He rolled over, holding his side gingerly, then held perfectly still, tilting his head to listen. Silence reverberated through the space, weighing down the room with emptiness. "Charlie," he whispered, everything that had happened rushing back all at once. *The hallway.* John pulled himself to his feet with a sick dread, bracing himself against the cabinet door. His right foot gave way as soon as he put weight on it, pain shooting up through his ankle, and he put a hand against the wall for balance, then hopped on his left foot to reach the door.

He crashed hard against the doorframe, wincing as his ribs flared with pain, then squinted, trying to see in the dark. "Charlie!" he called. The closet door was open, and he could see figures inside, but he couldn't make out anything distinct. He made his way to the closet, leaning on the wall and trying to ignore his throbbing ankle. It was difficult to see through the hanging coats; and he began to shove them aside, then stopped abruptly, scarcely avoiding the blade of a massive knife—almost a sword—pointed directly at him. He blinked as his eyes adjusted: the blade was connected to

335

an extended metal arm—the figure he had first thought was holding the knife had instead been run through with it, and behind that was something else—something familiar. He backed away, bending to look at the inhuman face of the creature impaled on the knife.

He stared for a moment, his face growing hot, then suddenly he turned away and doubled over, overcome with a wave of nausea. He dropped to his knees and retched, his ribs screaming protest as he heaved, but there was nothing in his stomach to throw up. He gasped, trying make it stop, but his stomach clenched and spasmed until he felt like he would be turned inside out.

When at last it began to abate, John rested his forehead against the wall, his eyes watering. Light-headed, he got to his feet, feeling as if years had passed. He did not look into the closet again.

John limped toward the door, grinding his teeth with every step, but he did not stop moving until he was outside the house, and he did not look back.

"There!" Michael cheered, momentarily distracting Susie from trying to leave. The last phantom of the girl with long black hair came and sat with them. When she had merged with the others like her, she blinked, then looked up and took in a long, calm breath. "We're all together now,"

Michael said with a smile. The drawings on the ground had disappeared, and five real-seeming children sat with Carlton under the table, no longer ghostly images.

"The rabbit isn't your friend," Carlton repeated. Susie gave him a puzzled look, and pointed to the only drawing left, the large one that showed all five children with the smiling yellow rabbit.

"I said bring him to the table," William said angrily, drawing Carlton's attention across the shadows. The painted fox cocked its head to the side, but before William could scold it again, more noises came from the hall. The door opened, pushed like something was bumping against it, and a variety of mechanical things made their way into the room, crawling and clawing their way across the floor in various states of disrepair. There were the climbing babies, and the gangly clown that had sat atop a carnival game in the dining room; others filed in that Carlton did not recognize: waddling dolls painted with clowns' faces, disjointed circus animals, and other things he could not even name.

"Get back," William hissed at the macabre processional, and brushed a crawler aside with his foot, struggling to keep his balance. The little blond boy had stopped crying; he was staring stunned at the creatures, shrinking away with his hand half blocking his face.

"Afraid of *them*, now?" William turned on the boy. "Don't fear them. Fear me," he snarled with renewed strength, and he clenched his jaw, taking stiff but deliberate steps toward the boy. "I'm the only thing in this room that you should be afraid of," he said, and the boy turned to him again, his face still full of fear. "I'm just as dangerous as I've always been," William growled. He grabbed the boy by the arm and dragged him to the table.

"No, no, no!" Carlton shouted as he watched the shadowy figure hoist the boy onto the table. He glanced helplessly at the children, but they looked at him blankly. "Can't you see? He's hurting that boy!" The children just shook their heads confusedly. "He's in danger, I have to help him. Let me out." Carlton struggled to get up, but his legs were weighted down, and anchored to the illusion.

"That's just Bonnie." Susie smiled.

"Bonnie is not your friend! He's the one that hurt you, don't you remember?" Carlton cried with mounting frustration. He grabbed the final drawing from the wall, the one with the five children standing with the yellow rabbit, and laid it flat on the floor, then took up a red crayon. He bent over the drawing and began to make thick marks on it, pressing the crayon deep into the paper. The children strained closer to see what he was drawing.

"Here we go," William Afton said from the shadows. Carlton glanced up to see the little boy squirming on top of the mass of metal, where William was holding him in place. The table was heating up, the orange glow beginning to flare from within it. "I'm running out of ideas," William said, failing to hide his anxiety. "But if I'm not going to survive this, then you certainly aren't, either." William pressed down on the boy's chest, and the boy struggled to free himself.

"Ouch!" the boy cried as his elbow touched the table below, where the orange glow was spreading. He jerked his arm up and cradled it, sobbing, then shrieked as his foot pressed onto the table and began to hiss. He yanked it back, howling.

"We will see where this takes us," William said.

"Look!" Carlton yelled, tapping the drawing hard with his crayon. The children huddled close. The yellow rabbit's eyes were now dark red, and blood dripped from its mouth. The children looked confusedly at Carlton, but there was a spark of recognition in their faces. "I'm sorry," Carlton said desperately. "This—is the bad man. *This. This* is the bad man." Carlton pointed from the drawing to William Afton and back again. "*He* is the bad man who hurt you, and right now he's about to hurt someone else," Carlton pleaded.

A hand gripped William's pant leg, and he shook it off. "Get away from me," he growled, but the hand persisted. The tangle of parts connected to the purple Freddy head was gathering around William's ankles, pieces plucking at him. "I said get off me!" he said again. His legs shook beneath him, and he let go of the boy, teetering as he struggled to regain his balance. He grasped for something steady, and his hands instinctively found the table. He recoiled, gasping in pain, and fell backward onto the floor, watching helplessly as the little blond boy rolled off the table and ran to the back wall.

Afton struggled to right himself as the wires and mechanisms scattered about the room all marched toward him to collect into a central mass, crawling up onto his body and threatening to engulf him. He pulled the pieces off and threw them aside to break apart on the concrete floor of the basement, then got unsteadily to his feet. William set his eyes on the boy once more: nothing else mattered. He took three laborious steps forward, machines still wrapped around his legs. The head of the white fox snapped at him from his ankle, where it had wound its limbs around his leg, and the purple bear had sunk its jaw into his calf, and was biting down. One of the crawling babies had climbed up onto William's back, where it thrashed its weight back and forth, setting his frail body swaying. Another crawler held fast to his ankle, chewing at his flesh. Blood dripped onto the floor with each step he took, but William's eyes remained fixed on the terrified boy, his fury only growing. Finally, in a burst of anger he flung the robotic baby from his back and stomped down on the metal bear's head, breaking its jaw and dislodging its teeth from his leg.

At last, William reached the child. The blond boy

screamed as William brushed his bony fingers over the boy's face, then suddenly William felt something blazing hot wrap around his waist, and yank him back. He twisted wildly and saw: the creature from the table was standing, and its two melted metal arms were now gripping William from behind, pulling him away from the boy. Its skin contorted and moved like molten metal, its motions jerky and unnatural. Its joints popped and snapped as it moved, as though each movement should have been impossible.

"No!" William cried, hearing the crackle of flame as his hospital gown caught fire, pressed against the burning creature.

Carlton opened his eyes and took a breath, a *real* one; he clutched his chest and tried to remain motionless, lifting only his eyes to watch as the amalgamation of metal and cords pulled William Afton backward into the massive furnace. Smoke and fire erupted from the thing with a roar, and then the room was still. The creatures and parts that had been wriggling on the floor stopped at once, and did not move again.

Carlton felt the searing pain in his chest surge, and he slipped into darkness.

Carlton. Carlton opened his eyes; Michael was sitting patiently beside him, apparently waiting for him to wake up.

"Is he okay now?" Michael gave Carlton an anxious smile. Carlton looked up to see four small figures disappearing into a flood of light. Only Michael remained under the table. "Is he okay?" Michael repeated, waiting for confirmation.

"Yeah," Carlton whispered. "He's okay. Go be with your friends." He smiled, but Michael didn't get up. He was looking at Carlton's chest, where someone had placed a drawing over his wound. "This is a part of you," Carlton said, grasping at the picture.

"You'll die without it," Michael whispered.

"I can't keep this." Carlton shook his head as Michael pushed it back. "You can give it to me next time you see me."

Michael smiled, and the drawing began to fade, hovering where Michael had placed it for a last moment before the ghostly image vanished, seeming to sink into Carlton's chest.

Thank you. Carlton heard the echo of Michael's voice, but Michael was gone, and there was nothing but the light.

"Carlton!" John.

"Carlton, hang on!"

"We're going to get you out of here!"

Marla. Jessica.

"Carlton!"

342

o, what happened then?" Marla had scooted so close to Carlton's hospital bed that she was practically in the bed with him.

"Ouch, Marla! The nurse said I need to sleep, and I shouldn't be exposed to a lot of stress right now." He reached for a juice box nearby, but Marla pushed it out of reach.

"Oh please, I practically am a nurse, and besides, I want to know what happened." Marla lifted a series of tubes and pulled them out of her way so she could get closer.

"Marla! Those are attached to *me*! Those are keeping *me* alive!" He searched frantically around his bedside table. "Where's my panic button?"

Marla felt around the edges of the bed until she found the small device with a red button on it, then set it neatly in her lap, clearly under her protection. "No juice; no nurse; tell me what happened."

"Where's Dad—Clay?" He lifted his eyes, searching the room until he found his father, who was standing by the window, his face tight with worry.

"I'm right here," he said, and shook his head. "You gave us a scare, and it wasn't a practical joke this time."

Carlton grinned, but it was short-lived as he glanced around the small room in distress.

"Are the kids all right?" he asked, not sure he wanted to hear the answer.

"They're safe. All of them," Jessica said quickly.

"*All* of them?" Carlton said in joyful disbelief.

"Yes. You saved him, the last one." Jessica smiled.

"And he's okay?" Carlton said again for confirmation, and Jessica nodded.

"And Charlie?" he said softly. Jessica and Marla looked at each other, unsure.

"We don't know," Clay said, stepping forward. "I've been out to look for her, and I'm going to keep looking for her, but so far . . ." He broke off, then cleared his throat. "I'm going to keep looking," he repeated.

Carlton looked down thoughtfully, then looked up once more. "And what about *hot* Charlie?"

Marla slapped Carlton's shoulder and he recoiled. "Marla! Ouch! I almost died; this is blood on my bed!"

"That's Kool-Aid. You spilled it all over yourself about an hour ago." Marla rolled her eyes.

"John?" Carlton suddenly spotted him in the doorway, hanging back so far he was almost in the hall. John waved, smiling slightly.

"Looks like they have you patched up pretty good," he said, nodding toward Carlton's bandages.

"Yeah." *Something's wrong.* Carlton considered John for a moment, but before he could formulate a question, a nurse stepped briskly into the room.

"Visiting time's over for now," she said apologetically. "We need to run some tests."

Clay stepped up to the bed, displacing Marla briefly. "Get some rest, huh?" he said, and patted the top of Carlton's head.

"*Dad,*" he groaned. "I'm not five." Clay smiled and headed for the door; John stopped him.

"You're going to keep looking for Charlie?" he asked.

"Of course," Clay said reassuringly, but gave him a confused look before leaving the room.

"You're not going to find her," John said softly. The rest of them watched, discomfited, as John slipped out the door without another word, not waiting for anyone else.

"Hey, we found this next to you. I wasn't sure if it was important," Jessica said, pulling Carlton's attention back, and handed him a folded piece of paper, heavy with crayon marks within. He unfolded it, revealing a grassy hill with five children running over it, the sun overhead.

"Yours?" Jessica asked.

"Yeah." Carlton smiled. "Mine."

"Okay." Jessica gave him a suspicious look, then returned the smile, leaving the room. Carlton held the drawing close and gazed out the window.

He had come into the room cautiously, afraid to wake her up. The room was dark except for the light filtering in through the small dirty window, and she peered at him for a moment as if she could not see him.

"John?" she whispered at last.

"Yeah, did I wake you up?"

She was so quiet for a time that he thought she was asleep, then she murmured, "You said you loved me."

The memory turned bitter here, and it had been nagging at him ever since—since everything ended. *You said you loved me*, she said, and he had babbled nonsense in response.

He stood in the gravel parking lot for a moment, feeling woefully unprepared. He tapped his hand nervously on the metal fence post, then took a deep breath and went through the gate. Slowly, he followed the path he had once watched

Charlie take, hindered a little by the brace on his ankle. Most of the cemetery was as green and well kept as any park, but this corner was all scrubby grass and dirt. Two small, plain tombstones sat together just beside the fence, a telephone pole rising behind them like a sheltering tree.

John took a step toward them, then stopped with the sudden feeling that he was being watched. He turned in a slow circle, and then he saw her. She was standing beneath a tree just a few yards away, where the grass grew lush and green.

She smiled, and extended a hand, beckoning him to her. He stood where he was. For a moment the world seemed blunted, his mind had gone numb. He could feel that his face had no expression, but he could not remember how to move it. He looked back at the stones with a sharp stab of longing, then swallowed and took steady breaths until he could move again. He turned to the woman under the tree, her arm still extended, and went to her.

A warm gust of wind rolled over the cemetery as they walked away together. The trees rustled, and a rush of leaves blew across the stones, sticking to some. Beneath the telephone pole, the grass rolled with waves, brushing against the two stones that sat together in the setting sun. The first was Henry's. The other read:

BELOVED DAUGHTER

CHARLOTTE EMILY

1980–1983

From the telephone pole above, a crow cawed twice, then launched itself into the sky with a flurry of wings.

Five Nights at Freddy's
THE
TWISTED
ONES

Five Nights at Freddy's

THE TWISTED ONES

by
SCOTT CAWTHON
KIRA BREED-WRISLEY

Scholastic Inc.
New York

Copyright © 2017 by Scott Cawthon. All rights reserved.

Photo of tv static: © Klikk/Dreamstime

All rights reserved. Published by Scholastic Inc., *Publishers since 1920*. SCHOLASTIC and associated logos are trademarks and/or registered trademarks of Scholastic Inc.

The publisher does not have any control over and does not assume any responsibility for author or third-party websites or their content.

No part of this publication may be reproduced, stored in a retrieval system, or transmitted in any form or by any means, electronic, mechanical, photocopying, recording, or otherwise, without written permission of the publisher. For information regarding permission, write to Scholastic Inc., Attention: Permissions Department, 557 Broadway, New York, NY 10012.

This book is a work of fiction. Names, characters, places, and incidents are either the product of the author's imagination or are used fictitiously, and any resemblance to actual persons, living or dead, business establishments, events, or locales is entirely coincidental.

Library of Congress Cataloging-in-Publication Data available

ISBN 978-1-338-13930-3

16 15 14 13 12 11 10   20 21 23 24

Printed in the U.S.A.   40

First printing 2017

Book design by Rick DeMonico

CHAPTER ONE

Don't trust your eyes."

Dr. Treadwell walked back and forth across the platform at the front of the auditorium. Her steps were slow and even, almost hypnotic.

"Your eyes deceive you every day, filling in the blanks for you in a world of sensory overload." An image of dizzying geometric detail lit up the canvas screen behind her. "When I say 'sensory overload' I mean that quite literally. At every moment, your senses are receiving far more information than they can process all at once, and your mind is forced to choose which signals to pay attention to. It does that based on your experiences, and your expectation of what is normal. The things we are familiar with are the things we can—for the most part—ignore. We see this most easily with olfactory fatigue: your nose ceases to perceive a smell when you've been around it for a while. You may be quite thankful for this phenomenon, depending on the habits of your roommate."

The class tittered dutifully, then became quiet as the image of another multicolored design flashed onto the screen.

The professor gave a hint of a smile and continued.

"Your mind creates motion when there is none. It fills in colors and trajectories based on what you've seen before, and calculates what you *should* be seeing now." Another image flashed onto the overhead screen. "If your mind didn't do this, then simply walking outside and seeing a tree would consume all your mental energy, leaving no resources to do anything else. In order for you to function in the world, your mind fills in the spaces of that tree with its own leaves and branches." A hundred pencils scribbled all at once, filling the lecture hall with a sound like scurrying mice.

"It's why when you enter a house for the first time you experience a moment of dizziness. Your mind is taking in more than usual. It's drawing a floor plan, creating a palette of colors, and saving an inventory of images to draw on later, so you don't have to go through that exhausting intake every single time. The next time you enter that same house, you'll already know where you are."

"Charlie!" An urgent voice whispered her name, inches from her ear. Charlie kept writing. She was staring straight

ahead at the display at the front of the lecture hall. As Dr. Treadwell went on, she paced faster, occasionally flinging an arm toward the screen to illustrate her point. Her words seemed to be falling behind as her mind raced on ahead; Charlie had realized by the second day of classes that her professor sometimes broke off in the middle of one sentence, only to finish an entirely different one. It was like she skimmed the text in her head, reading out a few words here and there. Most of the students in her robotics class found it maddening, but Charlie liked it. It made the lesson kind of like doing a puzzle.

The screen flashed again, displaying an assortment of mechanical parts and a diagram of an eye. "This is what you must re-create." Dr. Treadwell stepped back from the image, turning to look at it with the class. "Basic artificial intelligence is all about sensory control. You won't be dealing with a mind that can filter these things out for itself. You must design programs that recognize basic shapes, while discarding unimportant information. You must do for your robot what your own mind does for you: create a simplified and organized assembly of information based on what's relevant. Let's start by looking at some examples of basic shape recognition."

"*Charlie,*" hissed the voice again, and she waved her pencil impatiently at the figure peering over her shoulder—her friend Arty—trying to shoo him away. The gesture cost her a moment, put her half a step behind the professor. She hurried to catch up, anxious not to miss a single line.

The paper in front of her was covered in formulas, notes in the margins, sketches, and diagrams. She wanted to get everything down all at once: not just the math, but all the things it made her think of. If she could tie the new facts to things she already knew, she'd retain it much more easily. She felt hungry for it, alert, watching for new tidbits of information like a dog under the dinner table.

A boy near the front raised his hand to ask a question, and Charlie felt a brief flare of impatience. Now the whole class would have to stop while Treadwell went back to explain a simple concept. Charlie let her mind wander, sketching absently in the margins of her notebook.

John would be here in—she glanced restlessly at her watch—an hour. *I told him maybe someday we'll see each other again. I guess it's someday.* He had called out of the blue: "I'm just going to be passing through," he said, and Charlie hadn't bothered to ask how he knew where she was. *Of course he would know.* There was no reason not to meet him, and she found herself alternately excited and filled with dread. Now, as she absently sketched rectangular forms along the bottom of her note paper, her stomach jumped, a little spasm of nerves. It felt like a lifetime since she last saw him. Sometimes, it felt like she'd seen him yesterday, as if the last year hadn't passed. But of course it had, and everything had changed for Charlie once again.

That May, the night of her eighteenth birthday, the dreams had begun. Charlie was long accustomed to nightmares, the worst moments of her past forced up like bile, into twisted versions of memories already too terrible to recall. She shoved these dreams into the back of her mind in the morning and sealed them away, knowing they would only breach it when night fell again.

These dreams were different. When she woke, she was physically exhausted: not just drained but sore, her muscles weak. Her hands were stiff and aching, like they'd been clenched into fists for hours. These new dreams didn't come every night, but when they did, they interrupted her regular nightmares and took them over. It didn't matter if she was running and screaming for her life, or wandering aimlessly through a dull mishmash of the various places she'd been all week. Suddenly, from nowhere, she would sense him: Sammy, her lost twin brother, was near.

She knew he was present the same way she knew that *she* was present, and whatever the dream was, it dropped away— people, places, light, and sound. Now she was searching for him in the darkness, calling his name. He never answered. She would drop to her hands and knees, feeling her way through the dark, letting his presence guide her until she

5

came to a barrier. It was smooth and cold, metal. She couldn't see it, but she hit it hard with one fist and it echoed. "Sammy?" she would call, hitting harder. She stood, reaching up to see if she could scale the slick surface, but it stretched up far above her head. She beat her fists against the barricade until they hurt. She screamed her brother's name until her throat was raw, until she fell to the floor and leaned on the solid metal, pressing her cheek to its cool surface and hoping for a whisper from the other side. He was there; she knew it as surely as if he were a part of herself.

She knew in those dreams that he was present. Worse, when she was awake, she knew he was not there.

In August, Charlie and Aunt Jen had their first fight. They'd always been too distant to really argue. Charlie never felt the need to rebel, because Jen provided no real authority. And Jen never took anything Charlie did personally, never tried to stop her from doing anything, as long as she was safe. The day Charlie moved in with her at the age of seven, Aunt Jen had told her plainly that she was not a replacement for Charlie's parents. By now, Charlie was old enough to understand that Jen had meant it as a gesture of respect, a way to reassure Charlie that her father wouldn't be forgotten, that she would always be his child. But at the time it had seemed like an admonishment. *Don't expect parenting. Don't expect love.* And so Charlie hadn't. Jen had never failed to care for Charlie. Charlie had never wanted for food or clothing, and

Jen had taught her to cook, to take care of the house, to manage her money, and to fix her own car. *You have to be independent, Charlie. You have to know how to take care of yourself. You have to be stronger than*—she'd cut herself off, but Charlie knew how the sentence ended. *Than your father.*

Charlie shook her head, trying to jerk herself free of her own thoughts.

"What's wrong?" Arty said next to her.

"Nothing," she whispered. She ran her pencil again and again over the same lines: up, over, down, over, the graphite wearing thicker and thicker.

Charlie had told Jen that she was going back to Hurricane, and Jen's face turned stony, her skin paling.

"Why would you want to do that?" she asked with a dangerous calm in her voice. Charlie's heart beat faster. *Because that's where I lost him. Because I need him more than I need you.* The thought of returning had been nagging at her for months, growing stronger with each passing week. One morning she awoke and the choice was made, final, sitting in her mind with a solid weight.

"Jessica's going to college at St. George," she told her aunt. "She's starting the summer semester so I can stay with her while I'm there. I want to see the house again. There's still so much I don't understand; it just feels . . . important," she finished weakly, faltering as Jen's eyes—dark blue, like marble—fixed on her.

Jen didn't answer for a long moment then she said simply, "No."

Why not? Charlie might once have said. *You let me go before.* But after what happened last year, when she and Jessica and the others went back to Freddy's and discovered the horrifying truth behind the murders at her father's old pizzeria, things had changed between them. Charlie had changed. Now she met Jen's gaze, determined. "I'm going," she said, trying to keep her own voice steady.

Then everything exploded.

Charlie didn't know which of them started shouting first, but she screamed until her throat was fiery and sore, hurling at her aunt every pain she'd ever inflicted, every hurt she had failed to prevent. Jen shouted back that she only ever meant to care for Charlie, that she had always done her best, flinging reassuring words that somehow dripped with poison.

"I'm leaving!" Charlie screamed with finality. She started for the door, but Jen grabbed her arm, yanking her violently back. Charlie stumbled, almost falling before she caught herself on the kitchen table, and Jen let her hand drop with a shocked expression. There was silence, and then Charlie left.

She packed a bag, feeling as if she had somehow diverged from reality, into an impossible parallel world. Then she got in her car and drove away. She didn't tell anyone she was going. Her friends here were not close friends; there was no one she owed an explanation.

When Charlie got to Hurricane, she'd intended to go straight to her father's house, to stay there for the next few days until Jessica arrived on campus. But as she reached the city limits, something stopped her. *I can't*, she thought. *I can't ever go back.* She turned the car around, drove straight to St. George, and slept in her car for a week.

It was only after Charlie knocked, and Jessica opened the door with a startled expression that Charlie realized that she'd never actually mentioned her plans to Jessica, on whom they all depended. She told her everything, and Jessica, hesitantly, offered to let her stay. Charlie had slept on the floor the rest of the summer, and as the fall semester approached, Jessica didn't ask her to leave.

"It's nice to have someone who knows me here," she had said, and uncharacteristically, Charlie hugged her.

Charlie had never cared about high school. She never paid much attention in her classes, but As and Bs came easily for her. She had never really thought about liking or disliking her subjects, though sometimes one teacher or another would make her feel a spark of interest for a year.

Charlie hadn't thought much beyond the end of the summer, but as she idly flipped through Jessica's course catalog and saw advanced courses in robotics, something clicked into place. St. George was among the colleges she'd been accepted into earlier that year, though she hadn't really intended to go to any of them. Now, however, she went to the administrative office and pleaded her case until she was allowed to enroll, despite having missed the deadline by months. *There's still so much I don't understand.* Charlie wanted to learn, and the things she wanted to learn were very specific.

Of course there were things she had to learn before a robotics course would make any sense at all. Math had always been straightforward, functional, sort of like a game to Charlie; you did the thing you were supposed to do and got the answer. But it had never been a very interesting game. It was fun to learn something new, but then you had to keep doing it for weeks or months, bored out of your skull. That was high school. But in her first calculus class, something had happened. It was as if she'd been laying bricks for years, forced to work slowly, seeing nothing but her mortar and her trowel. Then suddenly someone pulled her back a few steps and said, "Here, look, you've been building this castle. Go play inside!"

"And that's all for today," Professor Treadwell said at last. Charlie looked down at her paper, realizing she'd never stopped moving her pencil. She had worn dark lines right through the page, and drawn on the desk. She rubbed the marks halfheartedly with her sleeve, then opened her binder to put away her notes. Arty poked his head over her shoulder, and she closed it hastily, but he had already gotten a good look.

"What is that, a secret code? Abstract art?"

"It's just math," Charlie said a little curtly, and put the notebook in her bag. Arty was cute in a goofy way. He had a pleasant face, dark eyes, and curly brown hair that seemed to have a life of its own. He was in three of her four classes and had been following her around since the beginning of the semester like a stray duckling. To her surprise, Charlie found that she didn't mind it.

As Charlie left the auditorium, Arty took up his now-accustomed place at her side.

"So, did you decide about the project?" he asked.

"Project?" Charlie vaguely remembered something about a project he wanted to do together. He gave a little nod, waiting for her to catch up.

"Remember? We have to design an experiment for chem? I thought we could work together. You know, with your brains and my looks . . ." He trailed off, grinning.

"Yeah, that sounds—I have to go meet someone," she interrupted herself.

"You never meet anyone," he said, surprised, blushing bright red as soon as the words were out of his mouth. "I didn't mean it that way. Not that it's any of my business, but, who is it?" He gave a broad smile.

"John," Charlie said without elaboration. Arty looked crestfallen for a moment but recovered quickly.

"Of course, yeah. John. Great guy," he said teasingly. He

raised his eyebrows, prompting for details, but she gave none. "I didn't know you were—that you had a—that's cool." Arty's face took on a look of careful neutrality. Charlie looked at him oddly. She hadn't meant to imply that she and John were a couple but she didn't know how to correct him. She couldn't explain who John was to her without telling Arty far more than she wanted him to know.

They walked in silence for a minute across the main quad, a small, grassy square surrounded by brick and concrete buildings.

"So, is John from your hometown?" Arty asked at last.

"My hometown is thirty minutes away. This place is basically just an extension of it," Charlie said. "But yeah, he's from Hurricane." Arty hesitated, then leaned in closer to her, glancing around as if someone might be listening.

"I always meant to ask you," he said.

Charlie looked at him wearily. *Don't ask about it.*

"I'm sure people ask you about it all the time, but come on—you can't blame me for being curious. That stuff about the murders, it's like an urban legend around here. I mean, not just around here. Everywhere. Freddy Fazbear's Pizza—"

"Stop." Charlie's face was suddenly immobile. She felt as if moving it, making any expression at all, would require an arcane skill she no longer possessed. Arty's face had changed, too. His easy smile drained away. He looked almost frightened. Charlie bit the inside of her lip, willing her mouth to move.

"I was just a kid when all that happened," she said quietly. Arty nodded, quick and skittish. Charlie made her face move into a smile. "I have to go meet Jessica," she lied. *I have to get away from you.* Arty nodded his head again like a bobblehead doll. She turned and walked away toward the dorm, not looking back.

Charlie blinked into the sunlight. Flashes of what happened last year at Freddy's were batting at her, snatches of memory plucking at her clothing with cold, iron fingers. *The hook above, poised to strike—no escape. A figure looming behind the stage; red matted fur barely concealing the metal bones of the murderous creature. Kneeling in pitch-dark on the cold tile floor of the bathroom, and then—that giant, hard plastic eye glaring through the crack, the hot miasma of lifeless breath on her face.* And the other, older memory: *the thought that made her ache in ways for which she had no words, sorrow filling her as if it had been wrought into her very bones. She and Sammy, her other self, her twin brother, were playing their quiet games in the familiar warmth of the costume closet. Then the figure appeared in the doorway, looking down on them. Then Sammy was gone, and the world ended for the first time.*

Charlie was standing outside her own dorm room, almost without knowing how she'd gotten there. Slowly, she pulled her keys from her pocket and let herself into the room. The lights were off; Jessica was still in class. Charlie shut the door behind her, checking the lock twice, and leaned back against it. She took a deep breath. *It's over now.* She straightened decisively and snapped on the overhead light, filling the room with a harsh illumination. The clock beside the bed told Charlie that she still had a little under an hour before John arrived—time to work on her project.

Charlie and Jessica had divided the room with a piece of masking tape after their first week living together. Jessica suggested it jokingly, said she'd seen it in a movie, but Charlie had grinned and helped her measure the room. She knew Jessica was desperate to keep Charlie's mess off her side. The result was a bedroom that looked like a "before and after" picture advertising either a cleaning service or a nuclear weapon, depending on whose side you looked at first.

On Charlie's desk there was a pillowcase, draped over two indistinct shapes. She went to her desk and removed it, folding it carefully and placing it on her chair. She looked at her project.

"Hello," she said softly.

Two mechanical faces were held upright on metal structures and attached to a length of board. Their features were indistinct, like old statues worn away by rain, or new clay not yet fully sculpted. They were made of a malleable plastic, and where the backs of their heads ought to be there were instead networks of casings, microchips, and wires.

Charlie bent down toward them, looking over every millimeter of her design, making sure everything was as she'd left it. She flipped a small black switch and little lights blinked; tiny cooling fans began to whir.

They didn't move right away, but there was a change. The vague features took on a sense of purpose. Their blind eyes didn't turn to Charlie: they looked only at each other.

"You," said the first. Its lips moved to shape the syllable, but never parted. They weren't made to open.

"I," the second replied, making the same soft, constrained movement.

"You are," said the first.

"Am I?" said the second.

Charlie watched, her hand pressed over her mouth. She held her breath, afraid of disturbing them. She waited, but they had apparently finished, and were now simply looking at each other. *They can't see*, Charlie reminded herself. She turned them off and pulled the board around so that she could peer into their backs. She reached inside and adjusted a wire.

A key slid into the lock of the door, and Charlie startled at the sound. She snatched the pillowcase and threw it over the faces as Jessica entered the room. Jessica paused in the doorway with a grin.

"What was that?" she asked.

"What?" Charlie said innocently.

"Come on, I know you were working on that thing you never let me see." She dropped her backpack on the floor, then flopped dramatically back on the bed. "Anyways, I'm exhausted!" she announced. Charlie laughed, and Jessica sat up. "Come talk to me," she said. "What's up with you and John?"

Charlie sat down on her own bed, across from Jessica. Despite their different lifestyles, she liked living with the other girl. Jessica was warm and bright, and while her ease as she went about the world still intimidated Charlie a little, now she felt like a part of it. Maybe being Jessica's friend meant absorbing some of her confidence.

"I haven't seen him yet. I have to leave in . . ." She peered over Jessica's shoulder at the clock. "Fifteen minutes."

"Are you excited?" Jessica asked.

Charlie shrugged. "I think so," she said.

Jessica laughed. "You're not sure?"

"I'm excited," Charlie admitted. "It's just been a long time."

"Not that long," Jessica pointed out. Then she looked thoughtful. "I guess it sort of has been, though. Everything is so different since the last time we saw him."

Charlie cleared her throat. "So you really want to see my project?" she asked, surprising herself.

"Yes!" Jessica declared, springing up from the bed. She followed Charlie to her desk. Charlie switched on the power then flung off the pillowcase like a magician. Jessica gasped and took an involuntary step back. "What is it?" she asked, her voice cautious. But before Charlie could answer, the first face spoke.

"Me," it said.

"You," the other replied, and they both fell silent again. Charlie looked at Jessica. Her friend had a pinched expression, like she was holding something tightly inside.

"I," the second face said.

Charlie hurried to switch them off. "Why do you have that look on your face?" she said.

Jessica took a deep breath and smiled at her. "I just haven't had lunch yet," she said, but something lingered in her eyes.

Jessica watched as Charlie replaced the pillowcase lovingly over the faces, as if she were tucking a child into bed. She looked uncomfortably around the room. Charlie's half was a disaster: clothes and books were strewn everywhere, but there were also the wires and computer parts, tools, screws, and pieces of plastic and metal Jessica didn't recognize, all jumbled up together. It wasn't just a mess; it was a chaotic tangle where you could lose anything. Or hide anything, she realized, with a pang of guilt at the thought. Jessica turned her attention back to Charlie.

"What are you programming them to do?" she asked, and Charlie smiled proudly.

"I'm not exactly programming them to do anything. I'm helping them learn on their own."

"Right, of course. Obviously," Jessica said slowly. As she did, something caught her eye: a pair of shiny plastic eyes and long floppy ears were peering out from a pile of dirty laundry.

"Hey, I never noticed you brought Theodore, your little robo-rabbit!" she exclaimed, pleased to have remembered the name of Charlie's childhood toy. Before Charlie could respond, she picked the stuffed animal up by his ears—and came away with only his head.

Jessica let out a shriek and dropped it, clapping a hand over her mouth.

"I'm sorry!" Charlie said, hastily grabbing the rabbit's head off the floor. "I took him apart to study; I'm using some of his parts in my project." She gestured at the thing on her desk.

"Oh," Jessica said, trying to hide her dismay. She glanced around the room and suddenly realized that the rabbit's parts were everywhere. His cotton-ball tail was on Charlie's pillow, and a leg hung off the lamp above her desk. His torso lay in the corner, almost out of sight, ripped open savagely. Jessica looked at her friend's round, cheerful face, and frizzy shoulder-length brown hair. Jessica closed her eyes for a long moment.

Oh, Charlie, what's wrong with you?

"Jessica?" Charlie said. The girl's eyes were closed, her expression pained. "Jessica?" This time she opened her eyes and gave Charlie a sudden, bright smile, turning on cheer like a faucet. It was disconcerting, but Charlie had gotten used to it.

Jessica blinked hard, like she was resetting her brain. "So, are you nervous about seeing John?" she asked. Charlie thought for a moment.

"No. I mean, why should I be? It's just John, right?" Charlie tried to laugh, but gave up. "Jessica, I don't know what to talk about!" she burst out suddenly.

"What do you mean?"

"I don't know what to talk about *with him*!" Charlie said. "If we don't have something to talk about, then we'll start talking about . . . what happened last year. And I just can't."

"Right." Jessica looked thoughtful. "Maybe he won't bring it up," she offered.

Charlie sighed, glancing back at her covered experiment with longing. "Of course he will. It's all we have in common." She sat down heavily on her bed and slumped over.

"Charlie, you don't have to talk about anything you don't want to talk about," Jessica said gently. "You can always just cancel on him. But I don't think John's going to put you on the spot. He cares about you. I doubt what happened in Hurricane is what's on his mind."

"What does *that* mean?"

"I just mean . . ." Jessica gingerly pushed aside a pile of laundry and sat next to Charlie, placing a hand on her knee.

"I just mean that maybe it's time that you *both* move past that. And I think John is trying to."

Charlie looked away and stared fixedly at Theodore's head, facedown on the floor. *You mean, get over it? How do I even begin?*

Jessica's voice softened. "This can't be your whole life anymore."

"I know." Charlie sighed. She decided to change the subject. "How was your class, anyway?" Charlie wiped her eyes, hoping Jessica would take the hint.

"Awesome." Jessica stood and stretched, bending over to touch her toes and incidentally giving Charlie a chance to compose herself. When Jessica stood again, she was smiling brilliantly, back in character. "Did you know that corpses can be preserved in peat bogs like mummies?"

Charlie wrinkled her nose. "I do now. So is that what you're gonna do when you graduate? Crawl around in peat bogs looking for bodies?"

Jessica shrugged. "Maybe."

"I'll get you a hazmat suit for your graduation gift," Charlie joked. She looked at her watch. "Time to go! Wish me luck." She brushed her hair back with her hands, peering into the mirror that hung on the back of the door. "I feel like a mess."

"You look great." Jessica gave her an encouraging nod.

"I've been doing sit-ups," Charlie said awkwardly.

"Huh?"

"Forget it." Charlie grabbed her backpack and headed for the door.

"Go knock his socks off!" Jessica called as Charlie left.

"I don't know what that means!" Charlie replied, letting the door swing closed before she'd finished speaking.

Charlie spotted him as she approached the main entrance to the campus. John was leaning on the wall, reading a book. His brown hair was as messy as ever, and he was wearing a blue T-shirt and jeans, dressed more casually than the last time she'd seen him.

"John!" she called, her reluctance falling away as soon as she saw him. He put away his book, grinning widely, and hurried to her.

"Hey, Charlie," he said. They stood there awkwardly, then Charlie extended her arms to hug him. He held her tightly for a moment then abruptly released her.

"You got taller," she said accusingly, and he laughed.

"I did," he admitted. He gave her a searching look. "You look exactly the same, though," he said with a puzzled smile.

"I cut my hair!" Charlie said in mock-outrage. She ran her fingers through it, demonstrating.

"Oh yeah!" he said. "I like it. I just mean, you're the same girl I remember."

"I've been doing sit-ups," Charlie said with a rising panic.

"Huh?" John gave her a confused look.

"Never mind. Are you hungry?" Charlie asked. "I have about an hour before my next class. We could get a burger. There's a dining hall not far from here."

"Yeah, that would be great," John said. Charlie pointed across the quad.

"That way, come on."

"So what are you doing here?" Charlie asked as they sat down with their trays. "Sorry," she added. "Did that sound rude?"

"Not rude at all, although I would have also accepted, 'John, to what circumstance do I owe the pleasure of this delightful reunion?'"

"Yeah, that sounds like me," Charlie said drily. "But seriously, what are you doing here?"

"Got a job."

"In St. George?" she asked. "Why?"

"In Hurricane, actually," he said, his voice self-consciously casual.

"Aren't you in school somewhere?" Charlie asked.

John blushed, looking down at his plate for a moment. "I was going to, but . . . it's a lot of money to read books when a library card is free, you know? My cousin got me a job in construction, and I'm working on my writing when I can. I figured even if I'm gonna be an artist, I don't have to be a starving one." He took an illustrative bite of his hamburger, and Charlie grinned.

"So why here?" she insisted, and he held up a finger as he finished chewing.

"The storm," he said. Charlie nodded. The storm had hit Hurricane before Charlie came to St. George, and people talked about it in capital letters: The Storm. It wasn't the worst the area had ever seen, but it was close. A tornado had risen up from nowhere and ripped through whole towns, razing one house to the ground with sinister precision, while leaving the one next to it untouched. There hadn't been much damage in St. George, but Hurricane had seen real destruction.

"How bad is it?" Charlie asked, keeping her tone light.

"You haven't been?" John said incredulously, and it was Charlie's turn to look awkwardly away. She shook her head. "It's bad in places," he said. "Mostly on the outskirts of town. Charlie . . . I assumed you'd been." He bit his lip.

"What?" Something about his expression was worrying her.

"Your dad's house, it was one of the ones that got hit," he said.

"Oh." Something leaden was growing in Charlie's chest. "I didn't know."

"You really didn't even go back to check?"

"I didn't think of it," Charlie said. *That's not true.* She'd thought a thousand times of going back to her father's house. But it had never occurred to her that the house might have been hit in the storm. In her mind, it was impregnable, unchanging. It would always be there, just as her father had left it. She closed her eyes and pictured it. The front steps sagged in disrepair, but the house itself stood like a fortress, protecting what was inside. "Is it—gone?" Charlie asked, the words faint.

"No," John said quickly. "No, it's still there, just damaged. I don't know how much; I just drove by. I didn't think I should go there without you."

Charlie nodded, only half listening. She felt far away. She could see John, hear him, but there was a layer of something between them, between her and everything else, everything but the house itself.

"I would have thought—didn't your aunt tell you what happened?" John asked.

"I have to get to class," Charlie said. "It's that way." She gestured vaguely.

"Charlie, have *you* been okay?" She didn't look at him, and he placed his hand over hers. She still couldn't look up. She didn't want him to see her face.

"Okay," she repeated, then slipped her hand out from under his and shrugged her shoulders up and down, like she was trying to get something off her back. "I had my birthday," she offered, and she finally leveled her gaze to meet his.

"I'm sorry I missed it," John said.

"No, no, that's not . . ." She tipped her head from side to side, as if she could level out her thoughts, too. "Do you remember how I had a twin?"

"What?" John sounded puzzled. "Of course I do. I'm sorry, Charlie, is that what you meant about your birthday?" She nodded, making tiny motions. John held out his hand again, and she took it. She could feel his pulse through his thumb.

"Ever since we left Hurricane . . . You know how twins are supposed to be connected, have some kind of special bond?"

"Sure," he said.

"Ever since we left—ever since I found out he was real—I've felt like he was there with me. I know he's not. He's dead, but for that whole year, I didn't feel alone anymore."

"Charlie." John's hand tightened on hers. "You know you're not alone."

"No, I mean *really* not alone. Like I have another self: someone who's a part of me and is always with me. I've had these feelings before, but they came and went, and I didn't pay much attention to them. I didn't know they meant something. Then when I learned the truth, and those memories started coming back to me—John, I felt *whole* in a way I don't even know how to describe." Her eyes began to fill with tears and she pulled her hand back to brush them away.

"Hey," he said softly. "It's okay. That's great, Charlie. I'm glad you have that."

"No. No, that's the thing. I don't!" She met his eyes, desperate for him to understand what she was so awkwardly trying to say. "He's disappeared. That sense of completeness is gone."

"What?"

"It happened on my birthday. I woke up and I just felt—" She sighed, searching. There wasn't a word for it.

"Alone?" John said.

"Incomplete." She took a deep breath, pulling herself back together. "But the thing is, it's not just loss. It's—it's like he's trapped somewhere. I have these dreams where I can *feel* him on the other side of something, like he's so close to me, but he's stuck somewhere. Like he's in a box, or I'm in a box. I can't tell."

John stared at her, momentarily speechless. Before he could figure out what to say, Charlie stood abruptly. "I need to leave."

"Are you sure? You haven't even eaten," he said.

"I'm sorry—" She broke off. "John, it's so good to see you." She hesitated then turned to walk away, possibly for good. She knew she'd disappointed him.

"Charlie, would you like to go out with me tonight?" John's voice sounded stiff, but his eyes were warm.

"Sure, that would be great," she said, giving a half smile. "Don't you have to get back to work tomorrow, though?"

"It's only half an hour away," John said. He cleared his throat. "But I meant, do you want to *go out* with me?"

"I just said yeah," Charlie repeated, slightly irritated.

John sighed. "I mean on a date, Charlie."

"Oh." Charlie stared at him for a moment. "Right." *You don't have to do anything you don't want to do.* Jessica's voice echoed in her head. And yet . . . she realized she was smiling.

"Um, yes. Yes, a date. Okay, yeah. There's a movie theater in town?" she hazarded, vaguely recalling that movies were something people did on dates.

John nodded vigorously, apparently as lost at sea as she was, now that the question had been asked. "Can we have dinner first? There's that Thai place down the street. I can meet you there around eight?"

"Yeah, sounds good. 'Bye!" Charlie grabbed her backpack and hurried out the dining room door, realizing as she stepped into the sunshine that she'd left him to clean up their table alone. *Sorry.*

As Charlie headed across the quad to her next class, her step grew more purposeful. This was a basic computer science class. Writing code wasn't as exciting as what Dr. Treadwell taught, but Charlie still liked it. It was absorbing, detailed work. A single error could ruin everything. *Everything?* She thought of her impending date. The idea that a single error could ruin everything suddenly carried an awful weight.

Charlie hurried up the steps to the building and stopped short as a man blocked her path.

It was Clay Burke.

"Hey, Charlie." He smiled, but his eyes were grave. Charlie hadn't seen Hurricane's chief of police—her friend Carlton's father—since the night they'd escaped Freddy's together. Looking now at his weathered face, she felt a rush of fear.

"Mr. Burke, er, Clay. What are you doing here?"

"Charlie, do you have a second?" he asked. Her heart sped up.

"Is Carlton okay?" she asked urgently.

"Yes, he's fine," Burke assured her. "Walk with me. Don't worry about being late. I'll give you a note for class. At least, I *think* an officer of the law has authority do that." He winked, but Charlie didn't smile. Something was wrong.

Charlie followed him back down the stairs. When they were a dozen feet from the building, Burke stopped and met her gaze, as if he were looking for something.

"Charlie, we've found a body," he said. "I want you to take a look at it."

"You want *me* to look at it?"

"I need you to see it."

Me. She said the only thing she could.

"Why? Does it have to do with Freddy's?"

"I don't want to tell you anything until you've seen it," Burke said. He started walking again, and Charlie hurried to keep up with his long stride. She followed him to the parking lot just outside the main gate, and got into his car without a word. Charlie settled into her seat, a strange dread stirring within her. Clay Burke glanced at her and she gave a sharp, quick nod. He pulled the car out onto the road, and they headed back to Hurricane.

CHAPTER TWO

So, how are you enjoying your classes?" Clay Burke asked in a jovial tone.

Charlie gave him a sardonic look. "Well, this is the first murder of the semester. So things have been going fine."

Burke didn't answer, apparently aware that further attempts to lighten the mood would fail. Charlie looked out the window. She thought often of going back to her father's house, but each time the memory of the place rose up she slammed it back down with almost physical force, cramming it into the tiny corners of her mind to gather dust. Now something was stirring in the dusty corners, and she feared she might not be able to keep it away much longer.

"Chief Burke—Clay," Charlie said. "How's Carlton been?"

He smiled. "Carlton's doing great. I tried to convince him to stay close for college, but he and Betty were adamant. Now he's out east, studying acting."

"Acting?" Charlie laughed, surprising herself.

"Well, he was always a prankster," Clay said. "I figured acting was the next logical step."

Charlie smiled. "Did he ever . . ." She looked out the window again. "Did you and he ever talk about what happened?" she asked with her face turned away. She could see Clay's reflection faintly in the window, distorted by the glass.

"Carlton talks to his mother more than he talks to me," he said plainly. Charlie waited for him to go on, but he remained silent. Though she and Jessica lived together, from the beginning they had an unspoken pact never to talk about Freddy's, except in the barest terms. She didn't know if Jessica was sometimes consumed by the memories, as she was. Maybe Jessica had nightmares, too.

But Charlie and Clay had no such pact. She took in shallow, quick breaths, waiting to hear how far he would go.

"I think Carlton had dreams about it," Clay said finally. "Sometimes in the morning he would come downstairs looking like he hadn't slept in a week, but he never told me what was going on."

"What about you? Do you think about it?" She was overstepping but Clay didn't seem ruffled.

"I try not to," he said gravely. "You know, Charlie, when

terrible things happen you can do one of two things: you can leave them behind or you can let them consume you."

Charlie set her jaw. "I'm not my father," she said.

Clay looked immediately contrite. "I know, I didn't mean that," he said. "I just meant you have to look forward." He flashed a nervous grin. "Of course, my wife would say there's a third thing: you can process the terrible things and come to terms with them. She's probably right."

"Probably," Charlie said distractedly.

"And what about you? How are you doing, Charlie?" Clay asked. It was the question she had practically solicited, but she didn't know how to answer it.

"I have dreams about it, I guess," she muttered.

"You guess?" he asked in a careful tone. "What kind of dreams?"

Charlie looked out the window again. There was a weight pressing on her chest. *What kind of dreams?*

Nightmares, but not of Freddy's. *A shadow in the doorway of the costume closet where we play. Sammy doesn't see; he's playing with his truck. But I look up. The shadow has eyes. Then everything is moving—hangers rattle and costumes sway. A toy truck drops hard on the floor.*

I'm left alone. The air is growing thin, I'm running out. It's getting hard to breathe and I'll die like this, alone, in the dark. I pound against the closet wall, calling for help. I know he's there. Sammy is on the other side, but he doesn't answer my cries as I begin to gasp, choking for air. It is too dark to see, but even so I know my vision is going black, and in my chest my heart is slowing, each pump swelling me with pain as I struggle to call his name one more time—

"Charlie?" Clay had pulled over and stopped the car without her noticing. Now he was looking at her with his piercing detective's gaze. She looked at him for a moment before she could remember how to answer, and she made herself smile.

"I've mostly been focused on school," she said.

Clay smiled at her but it didn't touch his eyes. He looked worried. *He's wishing he hadn't brought me*, she thought.

He opened his door but didn't get out of the car. The sun had begun to set as they drove, and now it was verging on dark. The turn signal was still on, flashing yellow onto the dirt road. Charlie watched it for a moment, hypnotized. She felt as if she might never move again, just sit here watching the endless, measured blinking of the light. Clay switched the signal off, and Charlie blinked, as if a spell had been broken. She straightened her spine and unbuckled her seat belt.

"Charlie," Clay said, not looking directly at her. "I'm sorry to ask this of you, but you're the only person who can tell me if this is what I think it is."

"Okay," she replied, suddenly alert. Clay sighed and got out of the car. Charlie followed close behind him. There was a barbed wire fence all along the road, and there were cows in the field beyond it. They stood around, chewing and staring in the vacant way of cows. Clay lifted the top wire for

Charlie and she climbed gingerly through. *When's the last time I got a tetanus shot?* she wondered as a barb caught briefly on her T-shirt.

She didn't have to ask where the body was. There was a floodlight and a makeshift fence of caution tape strung between posts that jutted from the soil in a scattered formation. Charlie stood where she was as Burke climbed through the fence after her, and they both surveyed the area.

The field was flat, and the grass was short and patchy, worn down daily by dozens of hooves. A single tree stood some distance from where the crime scene was marked. Charlie thought it was an oak. Its branches were long and ancient, heavy with leaves. There was something wrong with the air; along with the smell of cow dung and mud wafted the sharp, metallic scent of blood.

For some reason, Charlie looked at the cows again. They weren't as calm as she'd assumed. They shifted back and forth on their feet, clustering in groups. None of them came anywhere near the floodlight. As if sensing her scrutiny, one of them lowed a mournful cry. Charlie heard Clay's sharp intake of breath.

"Maybe we should ask *them* what happened," Charlie said. In the stillness, her voice carried. Clay started toward the floodlight. Charlie followed closely, not wanting to fall too far behind. It wasn't just the cows; a weight of something *wrong* hung over the place. There was no sound, only the shocked quiet that follows a terrible violence.

Clay stopped beside the marked-out spot and ushered Charlie forward, still saying nothing. Charlie looked.

It was a man, stretched in a ghastly posture on his back, his limbs contorted impossibly. In the glaring, unnatural light, the scene looked staged; he might have been an enormous doll. His whole body was drenched red with blood. His clothes were torn, almost shredded, and through the holes Charlie thought she could see ripped-up skin, some bone, and other things she couldn't identify.

"What do you make of it?" Clay said softly, as if he were afraid of disturbing her.

"I need to get closer," she said. Clay climbed over the yellow tape, and Charlie followed. She knelt in the mud beside the man's head, the knees of her jeans soaking with mud. He was middle-aged, white, his hair short and gray. His eyes, thankfully, were closed. The rest of his face slack in a way that could almost have looked like sleep, but did not. She leaned forward to peer at the man's neck and blanched, but didn't look away.

"Charlie, are you all right?" Clay asked, and she held up a hand.

"I'm fine." She knew those wounds; she'd seen the scars they left. On each side of the dead man's neck was a deep, curved gash. This was what had killed him. It would have been instantaneous. *Or maybe not.* Suddenly she pictured Dave, the guard at Freddy's, the murderer. She had watched him die. She'd triggered the spring locks and seen his startled eyes as the locks drove into his neck. She'd watched his body jolt and seize as the costume he wore shot jagged metal through his vital organs. Charlie stared at this stranger's wounds. She reached down and ran her finger along the edge of the cut on the man's neck. *What were you doing?*

"Charlie!" Clay said in alarm, and Charlie drew back her hand.

"Sorry," she said self-consciously, wiping her bloody fingers on her jeans. "Clay, it was one of them. His neck, he died like . . ." She stopped talking. Clay had been there; his son had almost died the same way. But if this was happening again, he had to know what he was dealing with.

"You remember how Dave died, right?" she asked.

Clay nodded. "Hard thing to forget." He shook his head, patiently waiting for her to get to the point.

"These suits, like the rabbit suit that Dave was wearing, they can be worn like costumes. Or they can move around on their own, as fully functional robots."

"Sure, you just put the suit on a robot," Clay said.

"Not exactly . . . The robots are always inside the suits; they're made of interlocking parts that are held back against the inner lining of the costumes by spring locks. When you want an animatronic, you just trip the locks, and the robotic parts unfold inside, filling the suit."

"But if there's someone inside the suit when the locks are tripped . . . ," Clay said, catching on.

"Right. Thousands of sharp metal parts shoot through your whole body. Like, well—that," she finished, gesturing at the man on the ground.

"How hard is it to accidentally trigger the spring locks?" Clay asked.

"It depends on the costume. If it's well cared for, pretty hard. If it's old, or poorly designed—it could happen. And if it's not an accident . . ."

"Is that what happened here?"

Charlie hesitated. Dave's image came to her again, this time alive, when he bared his torso to show them the scars he bore. Dave had once survived being crushed like this, though the second time had killed him. Somehow he had survived the lethal unfolding of a costume, a thing that should have been impossible. But it had left its marks. She cleared her throat and started again. "I need to see his chest," she said. "Can you get his shirt off?"

Clay nodded and took a pair of plastic gloves from his pocket. He tossed them to Charlie but they fell to the ground unnoticed. "If I'd known you were going to stick your fingers in the corpse, I'd have given these to you earlier," he said drily. He put on a pair of his own and produced a knife from somewhere on his belt. The man was wearing a T-shirt. Clay dropped to his knees, took hold of the bottom, and began to saw through the cloth. The sound of wet, tearing fabric cut through the silent field like a cry of pain. At last he was done, and he pulled back the shirt. Dried blood clung to the fabric, and as Clay pulled it back the body pulled with it, giving a brief, false sense of life. Charlie bent over, picturing Dave's scars. She compared the pattern to the wounds she saw here. *This is what happened to Dave.* Each piercing of the man's flesh seemed like a killing blow; any one of them might have punctured something vital, or simply been deep enough to drain him of blood in minutes. What was left of him was grotesque.

"It was one of them," Charlie said, looking up at Clay for the first time since they reached the body. "He must have been wearing one of the costumes. It's the only way he could end up like this. But . . ." Charlie paused and scanned the field again. "Where's the suit?"

"What would someone be doing wearing one of those things out here?" Clay said.

"Maybe he wasn't wearing it willingly," Charlie answered.

Clay leaned forward and reached for the man's open shirt, pulling it closed as best he could. Together they got up and headed back to the car.

As Clay drove her back to campus, Charlie stared out the window into the darkness.

"Clay, what happened to Freddy's?" she asked. "I hear it was torn down." She scratched her fingernail on the car seat nervously. "Is that true?"

"Yes. Well, they started to," Clay said slowly. "We went through the whole place, clearing everything out. It was a funny thing; we couldn't find the body of that guard, Dave." He paused and looked directly at Charlie, as though expecting her to answer for something.

Charlie felt the warmth drain from her face. *He's dead. I saw him die.* She closed her eyes for a moment and forced herself to focus.

"That place was like a maze, though." Clay turned his eyes casually back to the road. "His body probably got stuffed into some crevice no one will find for years."

"Yeah, probably buried in the rubble." She looked down, trying to put the thought out of her head for the moment. "What about the costumes, the robots?" Clay hesitated. *You must have known I would ask*, Charlie thought with some annoyance.

"Everything we took out of Freddy's was thrown away or burned. Technically I should have treated it like what it was: a break in the missing kids case, over a decade old. Everything would have been bagged up and gone over. But no one would have believed what happened there, what we saw. So I took some liberties." He glanced at Charlie, the suspicious look gone from his face, and she nodded for him to

39

continue. Clay took a deep breath. "I treated it only as the murder of my officer; you remember Officer Dunn. We recovered his body, closed the case, and I ordered the building to be demolished."

"What about . . ." Charlie paused, trying not to let her frustration show. "What about Freddy, and Bonnie, and Chica, and Foxy?" *What about the children, the children who were killed and hidden inside each one of them?*

"They were all there," Clay said gravely. "They were lifeless, Charlie. I don't know what else to tell you." Charlie didn't respond.

"As far as the demolition crew was concerned, all they'd found were old costumes, broken robots, and two dozen folding tables. And I didn't correct them," he said with hesitation in his voice. "You know how these things go. Whether building up or tearing down, it takes time. From what I hear, the storm hit and suddenly everyone was needed elsewhere; the demolition was put on hold."

"So it's all still standing there?" Charlie asked, and Clay gave her a warning look.

"Some parts are standing, but for all intents and purposes, it's gone. And don't even think about going back there. There's no reason to and you'll get yourself killed. Like I said, everything that mattered is gone anyway."

"I don't want to go back there," Charlie said softly.

When they reached the campus, Clay let her out where

he'd found her. She'd only taken a few steps from the car, however, when he called to her from the car window. "I feel like I need to tell you one more thing," he said. "We found blood at the scene, in the main dining room where Dave . . ." He looked around cautiously. There was something unseemly, talking about gruesome things on the sheltered grounds of the campus. "It wasn't real blood, Charlie."

"What are you talking about?" Charlie took a step back toward the car.

"It was, like, costume blood, or movie blood. It was pretty convincing, though. We didn't realize it was fake until the crime lab looked at it under a microscope."

"Why are you telling me this?" Charlie asked, although she knew the answer. The terrible possibility was pounding in her mind like a headache.

"He survived once," Clay said plainly.

"Well, he didn't survive the second time." Charlie turned to walk away.

"I'm sorry you have to be involved in this," Clay called.

Charlie didn't answer. She looked down at the pavement and clenched her teeth. Clay raised the window without another word and drove away.

CHAPTER THREE

Charlie checked her watch: she was on time to meet John, even early. She passed under a streetlight and looked down at herself, checking her clothes. *Oh no.* The knees of her jeans were wet with mud, and there was a dark stain where she had wiped her fingers clean of the dead man's blood. *I can't show up covered in blood. He's seen me like this too many times already.* She sighed and turned around.

Thankfully, Jessica was gone when she got back to the room. Charlie didn't want to talk about what had just happened. Clay hadn't explicitly told her to keep it a secret, but she was fairly sure she shouldn't broadcast her private visit to a crime scene. Charlie cast a glance at the faces under their pillowcase cover, but didn't go to them. She wanted to show her project to John, but, like Jessica, he might not understand.

She opened a dresser drawer and stared down at the contents without registering them. In her mind, she saw the body again, its limbs splayed out as if it had been thrown down where it lay. She covered her face with her hands, taking deep breaths. She had seen the scars, but she'd never seen the wounds of the spring locks fresh. Now Dave's eyes came to her, the look of shock just before he fell. Charlie could feel the locks in her hands, feel them resist, then give way and snap. *That's what happened. That's what I did.* She swallowed, and slid her hands down to her throat.

Charlie shook her head like a dog shaking off a wet coat. She looked at the open drawer again, concentrating. *I need to change. What is all this?* The drawer was filled with brightly colored shirts, all unfamiliar. Charlie startled, a dim panic seizing her. *What is all this?* She picked up a T-shirt and dropped it again, then forced herself to take a deep breath. *Jessica. They're Jessica's.* She'd opened the wrong drawer.

Get it together, Charlie, she told herself sternly, and somehow it sounded like Aunt Jen's voice in her head. Despite everything that lay between her and her aunt, just imagining her cold, authoritative voice made Charlie a little calmer. She nodded to herself, then grabbed what she needed: a clean T-shirt and jeans. She dressed hurriedly, then left to meet

John, her stomach fluttering, half-excited, half-sick. *A date*, she thought. *What if it doesn't go well? Worse, what if it does?*

As she neared the Thai restaurant, she saw that John was already there. He was waiting outside, but he didn't look impatient. He didn't spot her right away, and Charlie slowed her pace for a moment, watching him. He seemed at ease, gazing into the middle distance with a vague, pleasant expression. He had an air of confidence he hadn't possessed a year ago. It wasn't that he'd been unsure of himself then, but now he looked . . . adult. Maybe it was because he'd gone straight to work after high school. *Maybe it was what happened last year at Freddy's*, Charlie thought with an unexpected sense of envy. Although she'd moved out on her own, to a new home and a new college, she felt as if the experience had left her more a child, not less. Not a cared-for or protected child, but one who was vulnerable and unmoored. A child who had looked under the bed and seen the monsters.

John noticed her and waved. Charlie waved back and smiled, the expression unforced. Date or not, it was good to see him.

"How was your last class?" he said by way of greeting, and Charlie shrugged.

"I don't know. It was class. How was the rest of work?"

He grinned. "It was work. Are you hungry?"

"Yes," Charlie said decisively. They headed inside and were motioned to a table.

"Have you been here before?" John asked, and Charlie shook her head.

"I don't get out much," she said. "I don't even come out to town that often. The college is sort of its own little world, you know?"

"I can imagine," John said cheerfully. Now that the secret was out that he wasn't in school, he'd apparently shed his earlier discomfort. "Isn't it a little bit . . . ?" he searched for words. "Doesn't it feel a little isolated?"

"Not really," Charlie said. "If it's a prison, it's not one of the worst."

"I didn't mean to compare it to a prison!" John said. "So, come on, what are you studying?"

Charlie hesitated. There was no reason not to tell John, but it seemed too soon, too risky to announce that she was eagerly following in her father's footsteps. She didn't want to tell him she was studying robotics until she had some idea of how he would respond. Just like with her project.

"Most colleges make you do a set of classes your first year: English, math, everything like that," she said, hoping it would sound like a response. Suddenly Charlie didn't want to talk about school; she wasn't sure she could keep up a conversation about *anything*, really. She looked at John, and for a moment imagined the spring-lock wounds in his neck. Her eyes widened and she bit the inside of her cheek, trying to ground herself.

"Tell me about your job," she said, and saw her own hesitation mirrored on his face.

"I mean, I like the work," he said. "More than I thought I would, actually. There's something about doing physical labor that kind of frees my mind. It's like meditation. It's hard, though, really hard. Construction workers always make it look so easy, but it turns out it takes a while to build up that kind of muscle." He stretched his arms comically over his head, and Charlie laughed, but couldn't help noticing that he was clearly well on his way to that kind of muscle. John leaned to his left and gave his armpit a quick sniff, then made a look of mock-embarrassment. Charlie looked down at her menu and giggled.

"Do you already know what you want?" she said. Then the waitress appeared out of nowhere, as if she'd been listening nearby.

John ordered, and Charlie froze. She'd said it just to say something, but she didn't know what to get. Suddenly she noticed all the prices. Everything on the menu was impossibly expensive. She hadn't even thought about money when she accepted John's invitation, but now her mind jumped to her wallet, and her nearly empty bank account.

Misreading her expression, John leaped in. "If you've never had Thai food, Pad Thai is good," he suggested. "I should have asked," he said awkwardly. "If I'm buying a lady dinner, I should make sure she likes the food!" He looked embarrassed, but Charlie was flooded with relief. *Buying a lady dinner.*

"No, I'm sure I'll like it," she said. "Pad Thai, thanks," she told the waitress, then gave John a mock-glare. "Who are you calling a lady?" she said playfully, and he laughed.

"What's wrong with that?"

"It just sounds weird, you calling me a lady," Charlie said. "So anyway, what do you all day besides meditate?"

"Well, the days are long, and like I said, I'm still writing, so there's that. It's strange being in Hurricane again, though. I didn't mean to put down roots."

"Put down roots?"

"Like, join a bowling team or something. Ties to the community, things like that."

Charlie nodded. She of all people understood the need to remain apart. "Why did you take the job here, then?" she asked. "I know they needed people because of the storm, but you didn't *have* to come, right? People are still building things in other places."

"That's true," he admitted. "To be honest, it was more about getting away from where I was."

"Sounds familiar," Charlie muttered, too softly for him to hear.

The waitress returned with their food. Charlie took a quick bite of rice noodles and immediately burned her mouth. She grabbed her water glass and drank. "Yikes, that's hot!" she said. "So what were you getting away from?" She asked the question casually, as if the answer would be simple. *Do you have nightmares, too?* She held back the words, waiting for him to speak.

John hesitated. "A . . . girl, actually," he said. He paused, searching for a reaction. Charlie stopped chewing; that wasn't at all the answer she'd been expecting. She swallowed, nodding with self-conscious enthusiasm. After an excruciating silence, John went on.

"We started dating the summer after . . . after Freddy's. I told her I wasn't looking for anything serious, she said she wasn't, either. Then suddenly it was six months later, and we were serious. I had just started working. I'd moved out on my own, and had this grown-up relationship. It was a shock, but a good one, I guess." He stopped, not sure whether he should continue. Charlie wasn't sure she wanted to give him permission.

"So, tell me about her," she said calmly, avoiding eye contact.

"She was—is, I mean. I'm not dating her, but it's not like she's dead. Her name is Rebecca. She's pretty, I guess. Smart. She's a year older than me, a college student studying English; has a dog. So yeah, she was all right."

"What happened?"

"I don't know," he said.

"Really," Charlie said drily, and he smiled.

"No. I felt . . . on guard around her. Like there were things I couldn't tell her, things she'd just *never* understand. It wasn't because of her. She was great. But she knew I was holding something back; she just didn't know what it was."

"I wonder what it could have been?" Charlie asked quietly. The question was rhetorical; they both knew the answer.

John smiled. "Well, anyway, she broke up with me, and I was devastated, blah, blah, blah. Actually, I don't think I was that devastated." John looked down, focusing on his food but not touching it.

"Have *you* ever tried to tell anyone about Freddy's?" John glanced back up and pointed his fork at Charlie. She shook her head. "It wasn't just what happened," he went on. "I can't imagine telling that story and having her believe me, but it wasn't only that. I wanted her to know the facts of it, but more, I wanted to tell her what it did to me. How it changed me."

"It changed all of us," Charlie said.

"Yeah, and not just last year. From the beginning. I didn't realize it until after we'd all gone back, how much that place had just . . . *followed* me." He glanced at Charlie. "Sorry, it must be even weirder for you."

Charlie shrugged uncomfortably. "Maybe. I think it's just different."

Her hand was resting on the table beside her water glass, and now John reached out to touch it. She stiffened, and he drew back.

"Sorry," he said. "I'm sorry."

"It's not you," Charlie said quickly. *His dead face, the dead skin of his throat.* She had barely noticed it at the time, overwhelmed by the whole experience, but now the feeling of the dead man's neck came back to her. It was as if she were touching him right now. She could feel his skin, slack and cold, and slick with blood; she could feel the blood on her fingers. She rubbed her hands together. They were clean— she knew they were clean—but still she could feel the blood. *You're being dramatic.*

"I'll be right back," she said, and got up before John could respond. She made her way around the tables to the bathrooms at the back of the restaurant. It was a three-stall bathroom; thankfully it was empty. Charlie went straight to the sink and turned the hot water on full-blast. She pumped soap onto her hands and scrubbed them for a long time. She closed her eyes and focused on the feeling of hot water and soap, and slowly the memory of blood faded. As she dried her hands she looked at herself in the mirror: her reflection looked wrong somehow, off, as if it wasn't herself she saw, but a copy. Someone else dressed as her. *Get it together, Charlie*, she thought, trying to hear the words in Aunt Jen's voice, as she had before. She closed her eyes. *Get it together.* When

50

she opened them again she was back in the mirror. Her reflection was her own.

Charlie smoothed her hair, and went back out to the table, where John was waiting for her with a concerned expression.

"Is everything okay?" he asked nervously. "Did I do something?"

Charlie shook her head. "No, of course not. It's been a long day, that's all." *There's an understatement.* She glanced at her watch. "Do we still have time for a movie?" she asked. "It's almost eight thirty."

"Yeah, we should go," John said. "Are you done?"

"Yeah, it was really good, thank you." She smiled at him. "The 'lady' liked it." John smiled back, visibly relaxing. He went to the counter to pay, and Charlie went outside, waiting for him on the sidewalk. Dark had fallen, and there was a chill in the air. Charlie wished briefly that she'd thought to bring a sweatshirt. John joined her after a moment.

"Ready?"

"Yeah," Charlie said. "Where is it?"

He looked at her for a moment and shook his head. "The movie was your idea, remember?" He laughed.

"Like I said, I don't get out much." Charlie looked down at her feet.

"The theater's only a few blocks away."

They walked in silence for a while.

"I found out what happened to Freddy's," she said without thinking, and John looked at her, surprised.

"Really? What happened?"

"They were tearing it down, then the storm came and everyone got called away. Now it's just standing there, half collapsed. All the stuff is gone, though," she added, seeing the question in John's eyes. "I don't know what they did with . . . them." It was a lie; Charlie couldn't tell him what had really happened without telling him how she knew. All those questions led back to the same place: the dead man in the field. *Who were you?*

"What about your father's house?" John asked. "Did you ask your aunt Jen about it? What's she going to do with it?"

"I don't know," Charlie said. "I haven't talked to her since August." She fell silent, not looking at John as they walked.

They reached their destination, a shabby, one-screen movie theater named the Grand Palace. Its name was either ironic or wishful thinking. Emblazoned on the marquee was their current showing: *Zombies vs. Zombies!*

"I think it's about zombies," John joked as they went inside.

The movie had already started. Someone onscreen was screaming, as what were apparently zombies came at her from all sides. She was surrounded. The creatures crouched like wild dogs, ready to spring and devour her. They moved to attack—and a man grabbed her arm, pulling her to safety.

"Charlie." John touched her arm, whispering. "Over there." He gestured to the back row. The place was half-full, but the back row was empty, and they made their way furtively to the middle. They sat, and Charlie turned her attention to the screen. *Thank goodness*, she thought. *Maybe we can finally relax.*

She settled back in her seat, letting the images on the screen blur past her. Shrieks, gunfire, and thrumming music filled the silence between them. From the corner of her eye she saw John glance at her nervously. Charlie focused her attention on the movie. The main characters, a man and woman with the generic, angular good looks of the big screen, were shooting automatic weapons into a crowd of zombies. As the first ranks were killed—not killed, stopped; though severed in half by the guns, they still twitched on the ground—the ones behind climbed over their fallen cohorts. The camera switched back to the man and woman, who jumped a fence and took off running. Behind them the zombies kept coming, struggling forward, oblivious to the undead bodies they waded through. The music was urgent, the baseline pounding like an artificial heartbeat, and Charlie relaxed against the seat, letting herself be absorbed into it all.

What was he doing there? The image of the dead man returned to her. Something about the wounds bothered her, but she hadn't been able to put her finger on it. *I recognized those wounds. They all matched what I remembered, but* something *was different. What was it?*

She sensed movement next to her, and saw John trying to stretch an arm toward her. *Really?* she thought.

"Do you have enough room?" she asked him, and scooted away without waiting for a response. He looked embarrassed, but she glanced away, planting her elbow on the other armrest and staring fixedly at the screen.

Enough room, that's it. She closed her eyes, concentrating on the image in her head. *The wounds were slightly larger and more spaced out. The suit he was wearing was bigger than the suits from Freddy's. The man was probably five foot ten or five foot eleven, which means the suits must have been at least seven feet tall.*

Onscreen, there was quiet again, but it was short lived. Charlie watched, mesmerized, as the dirt spilled away of its own volition, moving like magic as the zombie rose. *It wouldn't be like that,* Charlie thought definitively. *It's not that easy to get out of a grave.* By now the zombie onscreen was halfway out, crawling to the surface and looking around with its glassy, mindless eyes. *You can't get out that fast.* Charlie blinked and shook her head, trying to stay focused.

Zombies. Lifeless things. The closet was full of costumes, lifeless yet ever-watching, with plastic eyes and dead, hanging limbs. Somehow their corpselike stares had never bothered her, or Sammy. They liked to touch the fur, sometimes put it in their mouths and giggle at the funny way it felt. Some was old and matted; some new and soft. The closet was their place, just for the two of them. Sometimes they babbled together in words that had meaning only to them; sometimes they played side by side, lost in separate worlds of make-believe. But they were always together. Sammy was playing with a truck when the shadow came. He ran it back and forth on the floor, not noticing that their ribbon of light had been cut off. Charlie turned and saw the shadow, so still he could be an illusion, just another costume out of place. Then the sudden movement, the chaos of fabric and eyes. The truck clanked as it fell to the floor, and then: loneliness. A dark so complete that she began to believe she'd never seen at all. The memories of sight had only been a dream, a trick of the utter blackness. She tried to call his name—she could feel him nearby—but all around her were solid walls. "Can you hear me? Sammy? Let me out! Sammy!" But he was gone, and he was never there again.

"Charlie, are you okay?"

"What?" Charlie looked at John. She realized she'd pulled her feet up on the chair and was hugging her knees to her chest. She sat back, setting her shoes back on the floor. John gave her a concerned look. "I'm fine," she whispered, and gestured to the screen.

John put a hand on her forearm. "Are you sure you're okay?" he asked.

Charlie stared straight ahead. Now there were people running, the zombies lurching after them. "This doesn't make sense," Charlie muttered, mostly to herself.

"What?" John leaned toward her.

Charlie didn't move, but she repeated herself. "It doesn't make sense. Zombies don't make sense; if they're dead, the central nervous system is shot, and they can't do any of this. If there's a functioning central nervous system, which has somehow decayed to the point that movement and thought are possible, but severely hindered, fine. If it makes them violent, fine. But why would they want to eat brains? It doesn't make sense."

That man wouldn't have been able to walk on his own in a suit so oversized. He didn't walk into that field; the suit did. The animatronic was carrying him inside. It walked into that field of its own accord.

"Maybe it's symbolic," John suggested, eager to engage, however odd the conversation. "You know, like the idea that you eat your enemy's heart to gain their power? Maybe the zombie eats its enemy's brain to gain its . . . central nervous system?" He glanced at Charlie, but she was only half listening.

"Okay," she said. She'd been irritated by the movie, now she was irritated by the conversation she herself had introduced. "I'll be right back," she told John, and got up without waiting for him to respond. She made her way out of the row, through the lobby, and out the door. On the sidewalk, she took a deep breath and felt an intense relief at the wash of fresh air. *Dreams about being trapped are common*, she reminded herself. She'd looked it up when they began. They were only slightly less common than dreams of showing up to class naked, plummeting from a great height, or having your teeth all suddenly fall out. *But this didn't feel like a dream.*

Charlie jostled her thoughts back to the present, where even the crime scene of a gruesome murder seemed like a safer place to keep them.

There must be tracks. He didn't walk there himself. There must be some clue of what carried him into that field, and where it came from.

Charlie shivered. She went back inside the building. *John's going to think I'm nuts.* She arrived at the swinging theater doors and stopped—she couldn't do it. She had to know. There was a young man at the concession stand, and she asked him if the place had a pay phone. He pointed silently to his right, and Charlie went, fishing in her pocket for a quarter, and for Chief Burke's card.

She dialed carefully, pausing between numbers to check the card again, as if the writing might have changed since she looked. Clay Burke answered on the third ring.

"Burke."

"Clay? It's Charlie."

"Charlie? What's wrong?" He was instantly alert; Charlie could picture him leaping to his feet, ready to run.

"Nothing, I'm fine," she assured him. "Everything is okay, I just wanted to see if you've found anything else."

"Not so far," he told her.

"Oh." Burke let the silence stretch between them, and Charlie finally broke it. "Is there anything else you can tell me? I know it's confidential, but you've brought me in this far. Please, if there's anything else you know. Anything else you found, anything you know about the man—the victim."

"No," Clay said slowly. "I mean, I'll let you know when we find something."

"Okay," Charlie said. "Thanks."

"I'll be in touch."

"Okay." Charlie hung up the phone before he could say good-bye. "I don't believe you," she said to the phone on the wall.

Back in the theater, her eyes took a moment to adjust as she inched along the back row toward her seat, careful not to make noise. John looked up at her with a smile as she sat down, but didn't say anything. Charlie smiled back with a grim determination, and settled back in her seat, then scooted over until her shoulder was pressed against his. From behind her head, she heard him make a surprised noise, then he shifted, putting his arm around her shoulders. He gripped her tightly for a moment, halfway to a hug, and Charlie leaned in a little, unsure how else to reciprocate.

What if someone put him in the costume, like some kind of wind-up deathtrap? Stuck him inside that thing, then sent it walking until the spring locks went off. But who would know how to do that? Why would someone do that?

"Did I miss anything?" Charlie asked, though she hadn't paid any attention to the first half of the movie anyway. It was daytime onscreen, and it looked like there were more people, holed up in some sort of bunker. Charlie couldn't remember which of them had been the original characters. She wriggled in her seat; John's arm around her had relaxed, but now the arm of the seat was digging into her side. He started to move away, but she settled herself again.

"No, it's okay," she whispered, and his arm circled her again. "Just get on with it," Charlie said, flustered. John startled.

"Sorry, I didn't want to be too aggressive."

"No, not you." Charlie gestured toward the screen. "They should just build a minefield around the bunker and wait for them to all blow up. The end."

"I think that's actually what they do in the sequel, but we'll have to wait to watch it for ourselves." He winked.

"There's another one?" She sighed.

When the credits started to roll, they gathered their things and headed to the exits with the rest of the small crowd, not speaking until they got outside. On the sidewalk, they stopped.

"This has been nice," John said, sounding—somehow— like he meant it, and Charlie laughed, then groaned, covering her face with both hands.

"This has been *awful*. This has been the worst date ever. I'm so sorry. Thanks for lying, though."

John gave an uncertain smile. "It was nice to see you," he said with cautious levity.

"It's just—can we go somewhere to talk?"

John nodded, and Charlie started back toward campus with him following behind.

The quad was usually empty late at night, or at least mostly empty. There was always someone walking across, some student finishing up late night work in a lab, some couple ensconced in a dark corner. Tonight was no different, and it was easy enough to find their own dark corner to talk. Charlie sat down under a tree, and John copied her, then waited for her to talk as she stared at the gap between two buildings, where you could almost see the woods.

Finally, he prompted her. "So what's up?"

"Right." She met his eyes. "Clay came to see me today." John's eyes widened, but he didn't say anything. "He took me to see a body," Charlie went on. "He had died inside one of the mascot costumes."

John was frowning; she could almost see his thoughts, working through what this meant, and why it involved Charlie.

"That's not all: Clay told me that they found blood in the main dining room at Freddy's. Fake blood."

John's head jerked up. "You think Dave's alive?"

Charlie shrugged. "Clay didn't come out and say it. But all those scars—he had survived the spring locks of a mascot costume before. He must have known how to escape the building."

"It didn't look to me like he escaped," John said doubtfully.

"He could have faked it; it would certainly explain the blood."

"So what then? Dave is alive and stuffing people into spring-lock suits and killing them?"

"If I could just go back to the restaurant one more time, to make sure that—" Charlie stopped, suddenly aware of growing anger in John's face.

"To make sure that *what*?" he asked sternly.

"Nothing. Clay has it under control. Everything is best left with the police." She clenched her jaw, gazing out over the horizon.

Jessica will go with me.

"Right," John said with a surprised look. "Right, you're right."

Charlie nodded with forced enthusiasm.

"Clay has men for this sort of thing," she continued with a furrowed brow. "I'm sure they're on top of it."

John took Charlie's shoulders lightly. "I'm sure it's not

what you think it is, anyway," he said in a hearty, reassuring tone. "There's a lot of crime in this world that doesn't involve self-imploding furry robot suits." He laughed and Charlie forced a smile.

"Come on." John extended a hand and Charlie took it. "I'll walk you to your dorm."

"I appreciate the gesture," she said. "But Jessica's there, and we'd have to go through the whole reunion, you know?"

John laughed. "Okay, I'll save you from Jessica and her relentless camaraderie."

Charlie grinned. "My hero. Where are you staying, anyway?"

"That little motel you stayed at last year, actually," John said. "I'll see you tomorrow maybe?"

Charlie nodded and watched him go, then started on her own way home. Excruciating though the date had been, the last half hour felt like a homecoming. It was her and John again; they were familiar again. "All we needed was a good old-fashioned murder," she said aloud, and a woman walking her dog gave Charlie an odd look as she passed in the opposite direction. "I was at a movie, *Zombies vs. Zombies!*" Charlie called halfheartedly after her retreating back. "You should go check it out! They don't put mines around the bunker; spoiler alert."

Charlie had half hoped Jessica would be asleep, but the

lights were on when she reached their room. She flung open the door before Charlie had her key out of her pocket, her face flushed.

"So?" Jessica demanded.

"So what?" Charlie asked, grinning in spite of herself. "Hey, before you start into this, I need to ask you something."

"So you know what!" Jessica cried, ignoring her question. "Tell me about John. How did it go?"

Charlie felt the corner of her mouth twitch. "Oh, you know," she said casually. "Listen, I need you to go somewhere with me in the morning."

"Charlieee! You have to tell me!" Jessica moaned exaggeratedly, and flopped back on her bed. Then she sprang back up into a sitting position. "Come here and tell me!" Charlie sat, drawing her legs up under her.

"It was weird," she admitted. "I didn't know what to say. Dates just seem so . . . uncomfortable. But about what I was saying—"

"But it's John. Shouldn't that outweigh the 'date' part?"

"Well, it didn't," Charlie said. She looked at the floor. She could tell her face was red, and suddenly she wished she hadn't told Jessica anything at all.

Jessica put her hands on Charlie's shoulders and looked at her seriously. "You are amazing, and if John isn't just falling all over himself for you, that's his problem."

Charlie giggled. "I think he kind of is. It's *part* of the problem. But there is something else if you would just listen for a second."

"Oh, there's more?" Jessica laughed. "Charlie! You need to save *something* for the second date, you know."

"What? No, no. *NO!* I need you to go somewhere with me in the morning."

"Charlie I have a lot going on right now; I have exams coming up, and . . ."

"I need you . . ." Charlie clenched her jaw for a moment. "I need you to help me pick out new clothes for my next date," she said carefully, then waited to see if Jessica would believe a word of it.

"Charlie are you kidding me? We'll go first thing in the morning!" She jumped up and gave Charlie a giant hug. "We'll have a girls' day out! It will be amazing!" Jessica flopped back to her bed. "Sleep for now, though."

"It won't bother you if I work on my project for a while, will it?"

"Not at all." Jessica waved limply, then went still.

Charlie turned on her work lamp: a single, bright beam that was focused enough to not illuminate the whole room. She uncovered the faces; they were at rest, their features smooth as if in sleep, but she didn't turn them on yet. The switches that made them move and talk were only one part of the whole. There was another component: the part that made them listen was always on. Everything that she and Jessica said, every word spoken in the room, outside the window, or even in the hall, they heard. Each new word went into their databases, not only as a single word, but in all its configurations as they emerged. Each new piece of information was stuck to the piece of information most like it; everything new was built on something old. They were always learning.

Charlie turned on the component that allowed them to speak. Their features rippled softly, as if they were stretching themselves.

I know, said the first, more quickly than usual.

So what? said the second.

Know what?

You know so what?

Know what?

Now what?

What now?

Know how?

Why now?

Charlie switched them off, staring as the fans slowed to a stop. *That didn't make sense.* She looked at her watch. It was about three hours too late for bed. She changed quickly and climbed under the sheets, leaving the faces uncovered. There was something unnerving about their exchange. It was faster than it had ever been, and it was nonsensical, but there was something about it that rang familiar—it struck her.

"Were you playing a game?" she asked. They couldn't answer, and just stared blankly into each other's eyes.

She removed the pillowcase gently, taking care not to let it catch on anything. Beneath their shroud, the faces, blank and sightless, were placid; they looked like they could wait, ever listening, for eternity. Charlie switched them on, and bent over to watch as they began to move their plastic mouths without sound, practicing.

Where? *said the first.*

Here, *said the second.*

Where? *said the first again. Charlie drew back. Something was wrong with the voice; it sounded strained.*

Here, *repeated the second.*

Where? *said the first with a rising intonation, like it was growing upset.*

That's not supposed to happen! *Charlie thought, alarmed. They shouldn't be able to modulate their voices.*

Where? *the first wailed, and Charlie stepped back. She leaned down slowly to peer under the desk, as though she might find an entanglement of wires that would explain the strange behavior. As she stared, puzzled, a baby began to cry. She stood at once, knocking her head painfully on the edge of the desk. The two faces looked suddenly more human, and more childlike. One was crying, the other watching with an astonished look on its face. "It's okay," said the calmer face. "Don't leave me!" The other wailed as it turned to look at Charlie.*

"I'm not going to leave you!" Charlie cried. "Everything will be okay!" The sound of crying swelled, higher and louder than human voices should be, and Charlie covered her ears, looking desperately around for someone to help. Her bedroom had darkened, and heavy things hung from the ceiling. Matted fur brushed her face, and her heart jolted: the children are not safe. *She turned back, but an acre of fabric and fur had somehow fallen between her and the wailing babies.*

"I'll find you!" She shoved her way through, tripping on limbs that dragged on the ground. The costumes swung wildly, like trees in a storm, and a little distance away, something fell to the floor with a hard clunk. At last, she reached her desk, but they were gone. The howling went on and on, so loud Charlie couldn't hear herself think, even as she realized that the screaming was her own.

Charlie sat up with a loud, raw gasp, as if she had actually been screaming.

"Charlie?" It was John's voice. Charlie looked around with one bleary eye to see a head peering through the bedroom door.

"Give me a minute!" Charlie called as she sat up straight. "Get out!" she cried, and John's head shrank back; the door closed. She felt shaky, her muscles weak. She'd been holding them tense in her sleep. She changed quickly into clean clothes and tried to brush her slightly tangled hair into something more manageable, then opened the door.

John poked his head in again, taking a cautious look around.

"Okay, come in. It's not booby-trapped, though maybe it should be," Charlie joked. "How did you get in here?"

"Well, it was open, and I . . ." John trailed off as he took in the room around him, momentarily distracted by the mess. "I thought maybe we could go to breakfast? I have to work across town in about forty minutes, but I have some time."

"Oh, what a nice thought, but I . . . ," she said. "Sorry for the mess. It's my project, I sort of get wrapped up in it and forget to—clean." She glanced at her desk. The pillowcase was in place as it should be, the vague outlines of the faces just visible beneath it. *It was just a dream.*

John shrugged. "Yeah? What's the project?"

"Um, language. Sort of." She looked around the room curiously. Where had Jessica wandered off to? Charlie knew John would be suspicious of her sudden, unprecedented interest in clothes shopping, and was hoping to avoid explanations. "Natural language programming," she went on. "I'm taking . . . computer programming classes." At the last moment, something stopped her from saying the word *robotics*. John nodded. He was still eyeing the mess, and Charlie couldn't tell what had caught his attention. She plunged back into her explanation. "So, I'm working on teaching language—spoken language—to computers." She walked briskly to the door and peered out into the hall.

"Don't computers already know language?" John called.

"Well, yeah," Charlie said as she returned to the room. She looked at John. His face had changed, stripped down to something more adult. But she could still see him as he'd been the year before, captivated as he watched her old mechanical toys. *I can tell him.*

But then a look of alarm crossed John's face. He surged forward to her bed, stopping a few inches from it. He pointed.

"Is that Theodore's head?" he asked carefully.

"Yeah," Charlie said. She walked to the windows and peeped through the blinds, trying to spot Jessica's car.

"So you *have* been to the house?"

"No. Well, yeah. I went back once," she confessed. "To get him." She looked back at John guiltily.

He shook his head. "Charlie, you don't have to explain yourself," he said. "It's your house." He grabbed the chair from her desk and sat down. "Why did you take him apart?"

She studied his face worriedly, wondering if he was already asking himself the next, obvious question: *What if it runs in the family?*

70

"I wanted to see how he worked," Charlie said. She spoke carefully, feeling like she had to appear as rational as possible. "I would have taken Stanley and Ella, too, but, you know."

"They're bolted to the floor?"

"Pretty much, yeah. So I took Theodore; I'm actually using some of his components in my project." Charlie looked down at the disembodied bunny's head, into its blank glass eyes. *Took him apart. Using his component parts. That sounds rational.*

She had gotten Theodore from her father's house just before school began. Jessica hadn't been home. It was early evening, not quite dark, and Charlie had smuggled Theodore inside her backpack. She took him out, set him on the bed, and pressed the button to make him talk. As before, there was nothing but a strangled sound: "—ou—lie," the scrambled, decayed traces of her father's voice. Charlie had felt a pang of anger at herself for even trying.

"You sound pretty awful," she said harshly to Theodore, who just looked up at her blankly, immune to the reprimand. Charlie rifled through her bag of tools and parts, which hadn't yet taken over her side of the room. She found her utility knife, then went grimly to her bed where the bunny waited.

"I'll put you back together when I'm done." *Right.*

She looked up at John now, saw the doubt on his face. Or maybe it was concern, just like Jessica. "Sorry, I know everything's a mess," she said, hearing the edge in her own voice. "Maybe I'm a mess, too," she added quietly. She set the bunny's head down on her pillow, and the part of his leg beside it. "So, do you still want to see my project?" she asked.

"Yes." He smiled reassuringly and followed her to her desk. Charlie hesitated, looking down at the pillowcase. *Just a dream.*

"So," she said nervously. Charlie carefully switched everything on before unveiling the faces. Lights began to blink and fans began to whir. She glanced at John again, and took off the cloth.

The faces moved in little patterns, as if stretching out after waking, though there was little they could stretch. Charlie swallowed nervously.

You, me, said the first one, and Charlie heard John make a surprised sound behind her.

Me, said the second. Charlie held her breath, but they fell silent.

"Sorry, they usually say more," Charlie said. She grabbed a small object from the table and held it up: it was an oddly shaped piece of clear plastic with wiring inside. John frowned for a moment.

"Is that a hearing aid?" he asked, and Charlie nodded enthusiastically.

"It used to be. It's something I'm experimenting with: they listen all the time, they pick up everything that's said around them, but they're just collecting data, not interacting with it. They can only interact with each other." She paused, waiting for a sign that John understood. He nodded, and she went on. "I'm still working out the kinks, but this thing should make the person wearing it . . . visible to them. Not literally visible, I mean—they can't see—but they'll recognize the person wearing the device as one of them." She looked expectantly at John.

"Why . . . What does that mean?" he asked, seeming to search for words. Charlie closed her hand on the earpiece, frustrated. *He doesn't understand.*

"I made them. I want to interact with them," she said. His expression grew thoughtful, and she looked away, suddenly regretting having shown him the object. "Anyway, it's not really finished." She edged to the door and glanced out.

"It's really cool," John called after her. When Charlie returned from the hallway, he gave her an odd look. "Is everything okay?"

"Yes. You should go, though. You'll be late for work." Charlie approached the faces. She looked down thoughtfully at her creations, then sighed and reached for the pillowcase to cover them. As she did, the second face moved.

It jerked back on its stand and pivoted, locking its blind eyes on Charlie's. She stared back. It was like looking at a statue; the eyes were only raised bumps in the molded plastic. But Charlie swallowed hard, feeling herself rooted to the spot. She studied the blank gaze until John put a hand on her shoulder. She jumped, startling him as well, then looked down at the earpiece in her hand. "Oh, right," Charlie mumbled, and pressed the tiny power button on the side of it. She placed the earpiece carefully on top of the mess in her desk drawer, then closed the drawer. The face was still for a moment, then it slowly turned back to its place. It settled there, locked in a mirrored stare with its double, as if it had never moved at all. Charlie covered them and switched them off, leaving them with only enough power to listen.

At last she looked up at John. "Sorry!" she said.

"Does that mean *no* to breakfast?"

"I have plans this morning," Charlie said. "Me and Jessica. You know, girl stuff."

"Really?" John said quietly. "Girl stuff? You?"

"Yes! Girl stuff!" Jessica squealed as she entered the room excitedly. "Shopping; I finally convinced Charlie it's worth trying on her clothes before she buys them. We might even move past jeans and boots! Are you ready?"

"Ready!" Charlie smiled, and John squinted at her.

Jessica began escorting him gently out the door. "Right," John said. "I'll see you later then, Charlie?" Charlie didn't respond, but Jessica gave a bright smile as she closed the door behind him.

"So." Jessica clasped her hands. "Where do you want to start today?"

When they got to the parking lot of the abandoned mall, it was early afternoon.

"Charlie, this isn't what I had in mind," Jessica cried as they got out of the car. Charlie started for the entrance, but Jessica didn't follow. When Charlie turned, she was leaning against the car with her arms crossed.

"What are we doing here?" Jessica asked, her eyebrows raised.

"We have to look inside," Charlie said. "People's lives might depend on it. I just want to see if there is anything left of Freddy's, then we can go."

"Whose lives depend on it? And why now, suddenly?" Jessica asked.

Charlie looked at her shoes. "I just want to see," she said. She felt like a petulant child, but she couldn't bring herself to tell Jessica the whole story.

"Is this because John is here?" Jessica asked suddenly, and Charlie looked up, surprised.

"What? No."

Jessica sighed and uncrossed her arms. "It's okay, Charlie. I get it. You haven't seen him since all of this happened, and then he shows up again—of course it brings every-thing back."

Charlie nodded, gratefully latching on to this rationale. It was easier than hiding the truth from her. "I doubt there's much left, anyway," she said. "I just want to walk through and remind myself that—"

"That it's really over?" Jessica finished. She smiled, and Charlie's heart sank.

It's really, really not over. She forced a smile. "Something like that."

Charlie walked quickly through the mall, but Jessica lagged behind. The place felt entirely different. Sunlight poured in through massive gaps in the unfinished walls and ceiling. Shafts of light sifted between smaller cracks and splashed against stacks of concrete slabs. Charlie could see moths—maybe butterflies—hovering at the windows, and as they passed through the empty halls on their way to Freddy's, she could hear birds chirping. The deathly quiet she remembered, the overpowering sense of dread, was gone. Yet, Charlie thought as she glanced at the half-constructed storefronts, it still felt haunted, maybe even more than before. It was a different kind of haunting, not frightening. But Charlie had the sense that something was present, like stepping onto hallowed ground.

"Hello," Charlie said softly, not sure whom she was addressing.

"Do you hear something?" Jessica slowed her pace.

"No. It feels smaller." Charlie gestured at the open mouths

of the never-opened department stores, and the end of the hall ahead of them. "It seemed so intimidating last time."

"It actually seems kind of peaceful." Jessica spun in place, enjoying the air from outside, which was flowing freely through the empty spaces.

Jessica followed Charlie through the doorway and they stopped dead, blinded by bright sunlight. Freddy's had been torn apart. Some of the walls still stood—the far end looked almost intact—but in front of her was a field of debris. Old bricks and broken tiles were strewn in the dirt.

The two of them stood now on a slab of concrete that lay baking in the sun. The passage inward, along with the entire side wall of the restaurant, was gone. The walls and ceiling were just a line of rubble against the trees. The concrete walkway was still there, worn dark by years of dank and leaking pipes.

"So much for Freddy's," Jessica said in a hushed voice, and Charlie nodded.

They made their way through the debris. Charlie could make out where the main dining room had been, but everything was gone. The tables and chairs, the checkered cloths, and the party hats had all been removed. The merry-go-round had been ripped out, leaving nothing but a hole in the floor and some stray wires. The stage itself had been assaulted, though not removed. They must have been in the middle of that when the job was stopped. Boards were torn up across the main stage area, and the left-hand set of stairs was gone. What was left of the wall behind the stage broke off at the top, like jagged mountains along the sky.

"Are you okay?" Jessica looked to Charlie.

"Yeah. It's not what I expected, but I'm okay." She thought for a moment. "I want to see what's still here." Charlie gestured to the stage, and they crossed what was left of the dining area. The floorboards cracked, the linoleum torn. Jessica peered under a pile of rock where arcade machines had been. The consoles that had stood like dusty gravestones were gone, but they could see the outlines of each one. Square patches remained where they'd been torn from their posts. Stray wires huddled in small piles in the corners. Charlie turned her attention back to the main stage. She climbed up to where the animatronic animals had once performed.

"Careful!" Jessica cried. Charlie nodded an absent acknowledgment. She stood to one side, remembering the layout. *This is where Freddy stood.* The boards were torn up in front of her and in two more places—the destruction here was where they had taken out the pivoting plates that bolted the mascots to the stage. *Not that they stayed bolted very long,* Charlie thought wryly. She could see it now if she closed her eyes. *The animals were going through their programmed motions, faster and faster, until it was clear they were out of control. Moving wildly, as if they were afraid. They were rocking on their stands, and then the awful sound of cracking wood as Bonnie lifted his bolted foot and tore himself free of the stage.*

Charlie shook her head, trying to rid herself of the image. She made her way to the back of the stage. The lights were all gone, but a skeleton of exposed beams crisscrossed the open sky where the lights had been.

"Jessica!" she called. "Where are you?"

"Down here!"

She followed the sound of the girl's voice. Jessica was crouched in the place where the control room had been, peering into the gap under the stage.

"Nothing?" Charlie asked, not sure what answer she was hoping for.

"It's been gutted," Jessica said. "No monitors, nothing." Charlie climbed down beside her, and they peered in together.

"This is where we were trapped last time," Jessica said quietly. "Me and John; there was something at the door, and the lock caught. I thought we would be stuck in that little room and . . ." She looked at Charlie, who simply nodded. The horrors of that night were unique to each of them. The moments that beset them in their sleep, or assailed their thoughts without warning in the middle of the day, were private.

"Come on," Charlie said abruptly, heading again toward the mound of rubble where more games had been. Charlie crouched under a large slab that leaned to the side and acted as a doorway to what was left of the place.

"This seems dangerous." Jessica tiptoed over the loose rock.

The floor was still covered in carpet in most places, and Charlie could see the deep grooves where the arcade machine had been. *She hurled herself at the console, and somehow, it was enough. It wobbled on its base, then fell, knocking Foxy to the ground and pinning him there. She ran, but he was too quick: he caught her by the leg and ripped his hook right through her; she screamed, staring down at the snapping, twisted metal jaws, and the burning, silver eyes.* She heard a noise, almost a whimper, and realized it was her. She clapped her hands over her mouth.

"I thought we were all going to die," Jessica whispered.

"Me too," Charlie said. They looked at each other for a moment, an eerie stillness settling over the sunlit wreckage.

"Hey, this place is probably going to fall on us soon, so . . ." Jessica broke the silence, gesturing to the leaning slabs of concrete surrounding them. Charlie crawled back out the way they'd come and stood up. Her knees were crawling with pins and needles. She rubbed them, then stomped the ground.

"I want to check the costume room, see if anything is left," Charlie said without expression.

"You mean to see if any*body* is left?" Jessica shook her head.

"I have to know." Charlie gave her jeans a final brush and started off toward it.

The room stuck out of the rubble, alone and intact. It was the place where the costumes had been kept, and where Carlton had briefly been held prisoner. Charlie cautiously poked her head inside, studying the physical details around her: the chipped paint on the wall, the carpet that someone had begun to tear up but left unfinished. *Don't think about last time. Don't think about what happened here.* She let her eyes adjust a moment longer, then went inside.

The room was empty. They did a cursory search, but everything had been removed—there was nothing left but walls, floor, and ceiling.

"Clay did say they had gotten rid of everything," Charlie said.

Jessica gave her a sharp look. "Clay? When?"

"He said he was going to, I mean," Charlie said hastily, covering the slip. "Last year."

They took a final look around. As they were leaving, Charlie spotted a glint of light from something in the corner. It was the plastic eyeball of some unknown animatronic mascot. Charlie was about to go to it, but stopped herself. "There's nothing here," she said.

Not waiting for Jessica, she headed back through the debris, looking down at her feet as she stepped over bricks and stones and shattered glass.

"Hey, wait," Jessica called after her hastily. "Pirate's Cove. Charlie! Look!" Charlie stopped. She watched Jessica as she climbed over a steel beam and stepped carefully over the remains of a fallen wall. In front of her, a curtain lay strewn across what had appeared to be a pile of rubble. Charlie followed her, and when she caught up she could see that the curtain concealed a gap in the ruins. The tops of a few glittering chairs peeked out from the stones. A row of broken stage lights lay across the top of the curtain, as though holding it in place.

"It looks pretty good, compared to the rest of the place," Jessica said. Charlie didn't answer. There was a dirty poster lying flat on the ground, depicting a cartoonish Foxy delivering pizzas to happy children.

"Jessica, look." Charlie pointed to the ground.

"Those look like claw marks," Jessica said after a moment. There were long scratches and scrapes running the length of the floor, and dark marks that looked like traces of blood. "It's like someone was being dragged." Jessica stood and followed the scratches. They led behind the curtain, away from the area where Pirate's Cove once stood.

"The stage," Jessica said.

When they moved the curtain aside, they found the stage had a small hatch at the back. "Storage," Charlie murmured. She pulled on it, but the hatch wouldn't open.

"There has to be a latch somewhere," Jessica said. She cleared away dirt and broken wood from the base of the stage, uncovering a deadbolt that went into the floor.

She pulled it up, releasing the door, which swung open like something was pushing against it.

A face lurched out of the darkness, two gaping eyes swinging forward. Jessica screamed and fell backward. Charlie recoiled. The masked face hung lifelessly from a rotted fur costume. An entire mascot suit was inside, crammed into a space much too small for it. Charlie stopped, her whole body numb with shock as she stared at the thing with a dread almost as old as she was. "The yellow rabbit," she whispered.

"It's Dave," Jessica gasped. Charlie took a deep breath, forcing herself back into the present.

"Come on, help me," she said She stepped forward and grabbed at the fabric, pulling on whatever she could reach.

"You're kidding. I'm not touching that thing."

"Jessica! Get over here!" Charlie commanded, and Jessica came reluctantly over.

"Ew, ew, ew." Jessica touched the suit, then recoiled. She gave Charlie a flat look and tried again, yanking her hands away as soon as she touched it. "Ew," she repeated quietly, then finally screwed her eyes shut and took hold of it.

Together they pulled, but nothing happened. "I think it's stuck," Jessica said. They shifted positions and finally heaved the mascot out of the cramped space. The fabric caught on stray nails and jagged wood, but Charlie kept pulling. At last the creature was out, splayed heavily on the ground.

"I definitely don't think Dave faked his own death," Charlie said.

"What if it's not him?" Jessica peered carefully into the face.

"It's him." Charlie looked at the dried blood soaked into the mascot's fingertips. "The spring locks might not have killed him right away, but this is where he died."

They could see Dave's body through the gaps in the costume, and the wide carved eyes of the mascot head showed through to his face. His skin was desiccated and shriveled. His eyes were wide open, his face expressionless and discolored. Charlie moved closer again. Her initial shock had passed, and now she was curious to see more of him. She probed carefully at first, in case some of the spring locks inside might still be waiting to snap, but it was clear that they'd already done their damage. The locks had been driven so deeply into his skin that the bases of each were flush against his neck; they looked like part of him.

Charlie studied the chest of the costume. There were large tears in the yellow fabric, which had gone green and pink with mold in patches. She grabbed hold of the sides and pulled the gap open as wide as she could. Jessica watched, fascinated, her hand over her mouth. Skewers of metal protruded through his entire body, dull and crusted with his blood. And there were more complex parts, twisted knots of gore with many layers of machinery that stuck out from his body. The suit's fabric was stiff with blood, too, yet the man didn't seem to have rotted, despite the year that had passed.

"It's like he's fused with the suit," Charlie said. She tugged at the mascot head, trying to pull it off, but gave up quickly. The gaping eyes stared up at her, behind which was the dead man's face. With the light directly on him, Dave's skin appeared sickly and discolored. Charlie felt a sudden rush of nausea. She pulled back from the corpse and looked up at Jessica.

"So now what?" Jessica said. "Did you want to give him a foot massage, too?" She abruptly turned her head away, gagging at her own joke.

"Listen, I have class in . . ." Charlie checked her watch. "About an hour. Did you still want to do some shopping?"

"Why can't I have normal friends?" Jessica groaned.

CHAPTER FIVE

e are learning all the time. Hopefully at least some of you are learning right here in this class." Dr. Treadwell's students laughed nervously, but she continued over them; it had apparently not been a joke. "When we learn, our minds must decide where we will store that information. Unconsciously we determine what group of things it is most relevant to and connect it to that group. This is, of course, only the most rudimentary explanation. When computers do this, we call it an information tree . . ."

Charlie was only half listening; she knew this already and was taking her notes on autopilot. Since their expedition to Freddy's the day before, she hadn't been able to get the image of Dave's body out of her head: his torso and the gruesome lace of scars that had covered it. When he was alive, he'd shown them off to her, boasting of his survival. While he never told her what had happened, it must have been an accident. *He used to wear those suits all the time.* She could see him now, before all the murders, dressed as a yellow bunny and dancing merrily with a yellow bear . . . she shook her head suddenly, trying to get rid of the image.

"Are you okay?" Arty whispered. She nodded, waving him off.

But the dead man in the field—that wasn't an accident. Someone forced him inside. But why? Charlie restlessly tapped her fingers on her desk.

"That will be all for today." Dr. Treadwell set down her chalk and stalked off the auditorium stage with a purposeful step. Her teaching assistant, a flustered graduate student, scurried forward to collect the homework.

"Hey, do you have any time to go over some of this?" Arty asked Charlie as they gathered up their things. "I'm in a little bit over my head in this class."

Charlie paused. She'd promised to make up her first date with John, but she wasn't meeting him for over an hour. Now that she'd been to Freddy's, Charlie almost felt like she was on familiar ground, even if it was soaked in blood.

"I have some time now," she told Arty, who lit up.

"Great! Thanks so much, we can go work over at the library."

Charlie nodded. "Sure." She followed him across the campus, only half engaged as he explained his difficulties with the material.

They found a table, and Charlie opened her notebook to the pages she'd taken down today, pushing them across so Arty could see them.

"Actually, do you mind if I sit next to you?" he asked. "It's easier if we're both looking at the same thing, right?"

"Oh, yeah." Charlie pulled her notes back over as he came around and sat next to her, scooting his metal folding chair next to hers, just a few inches closer than she would have preferred. "So, where did you get lost?" she asked him.

"I was telling you on the way over," he said, with a hint of reproach in his voice, then cleared his throat. "I guess I understood the beginning of the lecture, when she was reviewing last week's material."

Charlie laughed. "So, basically you want to review everything new from today."

Arty nodded sheepishly. Charlie started from the beginning, pointing at her notes as she went. As she flipped through the pages, she noticed her own scribbles in the margins. Charlie leaned in closer, where harsh outlines of rectangles lined the bottom of the page. They were all colored in, like slabs of granite. She stared at them with a sensation of déjà vu: they were important. *I don't remember drawing that,* she thought uneasily. Then, *It's just doodles. Everybody doodles.*

She turned the page to the next segment of the lecture, and a strange alertness rose at the base of her neck, as if someone might be watching her. There were more doodles in the margins of this page, too, and the next one. All of them were rectangles. Some were large and some were small, some scribbled and some outlined in so solidly that her pen had wet the paper through and torn it. All of them were vertical, taller than they were wide. Charlie stared, tilting her head to see from different angles, until something pinged inside her.

Sammy, she thought, then, *Is this you? Does this mean something I don't understand?* Charlie glanced at Arty; he was staring at the paper, too. As she watched, he turned the page again. The next pages were the same. They were filled with neat, clear notes, but little rectangles were squashed into every available spot on the page: stuffed into the space between bullet points, crammed into the margins, and tucked away where lines came up short. Quickly, Arty flipped the page back. He looked up at her and smiled, but his eyes were wary.

"Why don't you try the first problem here?" Charlie suggested.

Arty bent over his worksheet, and Charlie stared down at her notebook. Her mind kept returning to her father's house, and the shapes she'd drawn only made the impulse stronger.

I have to go back.

"Are you okay?" Arty leaned in cautiously. Charlie stared down at her notebook. Now that she'd noticed the rectangles, they seemed more prominent than the notes; she could focus on nothing else. *I have to go back.*

Charlie shut the notebook and blinked hard. She ignored Arty's question, shoving the notebook into her backpack.

"I have to go," she said as she stood up.

"But I'm still stuck on the first problem," Arty said.

"I'm sorry, I really am!" she called over her shoulder as she hurried away. She bumped into two people as she passed the circulation desk but was too flustered to mutter an apology.

When she got to the door, she stopped, her guts twisting. *There's something wrong.* She hesitated, her hand suspended in the air, as if something was blocking her path. She finally took hold of the knob, and instantly her hand felt fused to it, as if by an electrical current. She couldn't turn it, and she couldn't let go. Suddenly, the knob moved on its own; someone was turning it from the other side. Charlie yanked her hand away and stepped back as a boy with an enormous backpack brushed past her. Snapping back into the moment, she slipped out before the door could swing shut again.

Charlie sped toward Hurricane, trying to calm herself as she drove. The windows were cracked open and wind was rushing in. She thought back to Treadwell's lecture earlier in the week. *At every moment, your senses are receiving far more information than they can process all at once.* Maybe that was Arty's problem in class. Charlie gazed at the mountains ahead, the open fields on either side. Watching them go by, she began to feel like some restraint had been loosened. She'd been spending too much time in her room or in class, and not enough out in the world. It was making her jumpy, exaggerating her natural awkwardness.

She rolled her window down farther, letting in the air. Over the field to her right a few birds were circling—no. Charlie stopped the car. *Something is wrong.* She got out, feeling ridiculous, but the last few days had put her on a hair trigger. The birds were too large.

She realized they were turkey vultures, and some of them were already on the ground, cautiously approaching what looked like a prone figure. *Could be anything.* She leaned against the car. *Probably just a dead animal.* After another moment, she turned back toward her car in frustration, but didn't get in.

It's not a dead animal.

She clenched her teeth and started to the spot the vultures were circling. As she got closer, the birds on the ground flapped their wings at the sight of her and soared away. Charlie dropped to her knees.

It was a woman. Charlie's eyes went first to her clothing. It was ripped up, just like the dead man Clay Burke had shown her.

She leaned over to check the woman's neck, though she knew what she would find. There were deep, ugly gouges from the spring locks of an animatronic suit. But before she could examine them closely, Charlie stopped, horrified.

She looks just like me. The woman's face was bruised and scratched, which obscured her features. Charlie shook her head. It was easier to imagine more of a resemblance than there really was. But her hair was brown and cut like Charlie's, and her face was the same round shape, with the same complexion. Her features were different, but not *that* different. Charlie stood up and took a deliberate step back from the woman, suddenly aware of how exposed she was in the open field. *Clay. I need to call Clay.* She looked up at the sky, wishing for a way to keep the vultures at bay, to protect the body. "I'm sorry," she whispered to the dead woman. "I'll be back."

Charlie started off to her car, then broke into a run, faster and faster across the field until she ran like something was right behind her. She got in and slammed the door, locking it as soon as she was inside.

Panting heavily, Charlie thought for a second. She was about halfway between Hurricane and the school, but there was a gas station just down the road where she could call Clay. With a last glance at the spot where the body lay, Charlie pulled out onto the road.

The gas station seemed to be empty. As she arrived, Charlie realized that she had never actually seen anyone fueling up here. *Is this a working gas station?* The place was old and shabby, which she had noticed in passing, but she'd never stopped to look around. The pumps looked functional, though not new, and there was no shelter above them. They simply stood on concrete blocks in the middle of a gravel driveway, exposed to the weather.

The little building attached to the station might have been painted white once, but the paint had worn down to reveal gray boards underneath. It seemed to be tilting slightly, slipping on its foundation. There was a window, but it was filthy, almost the same color gray as the building's outside walls. Charlie hesitated, then went to the door and knocked. A young man answered, about Charlie's age, wearing a St. John's College T-shirt and jeans.

"Yeah?" he said, giving her a blank stare.

"Are you—open?"

"Yeah." He was chewing gum and wiped his hands on a grimy rag. Charlie took a deep breath.

"I really need to use your phone." The boy opened the door and let her in. There was more space inside than she'd thought. In addition to the counter, there was a convenience store, though most of the shelves were empty and the line of refrigerators at the back was dark. The young man was looking at Charlie expectantly.

"Can I use your phone?" she asked again.

"Phone's for customers only," he said.

"Okay." Charlie glanced back at her car. "I'll get gas on the way out."

"Pump's broken; maybe you want something out of the cooler," he said, nodding at a grimy freezer with a sliding glass top and a faded patch of red paint that must once have been a logo. "We've got Popsicles."

"I don't want—fine, I'll take a Popsicle," Charlie said.

"Pick out any one you want."

Charlie leaned into the cooler.

Pale, glassy eyes stared back at her. Beneath them was a furry red muzzle, its mouth open and poised to snap.

Charlie screamed and hurtled backward, banging into the shelf behind her. Several cans fell off the shelf and rolled across the floor. The sound echoed in the empty space.

"What is that?" Charlie yelled, but the boy was cackling so hard he was gasping for breath. Peering back inside, Charlie realized that someone had placed a taxidermic animal in the cooler, maybe a coyote.

"That was great!" he finally managed to say. Charlie drew herself up, shaking with rage.

"I would like to use your phone now," she said coldly.

The boy beckoned her to the counter, all smiles, and handed her a rotary phone. "No long distance, though," he warned. Charlie turned her back and dialed, walking toward the cooler as the phone rang. She peered in the top, studying the stuffed canine from the high angle.

"Clay Burke here."

"Clay, it's Charlie. Listen, I need you to meet me. It's another . . ." She glanced at the young man behind the counter, who was watching her intently, not trying to hide the fact that he was listening. "It's like that thing you showed me before, with the cows."

"What? Charlie, where are you?"

"I'm at a gas station a few miles from you. Looks like someone painted an outhouse."

"Hey!" The boy behind the counter straightened for a moment, taking offense.

"Right, I know where you're at. I'll be right there." There was a click from the other end.

"Thanks for the phone," Charlie said begrudgingly, and left without waiting for a reply.

Charlie crouched again where the woman's body lay. She looked anxiously up the road for Clay's car, but it didn't appear. At least the vultures hadn't returned.

I could just stay in the car until he gets here, she thought. But Charlie didn't move from her spot. This woman had died horribly and been abandoned in a field. Now, at least, she didn't have to be alone.

The more Charlie looked at her, the harder it was to dismiss the resemblance. Charlie shivered, even though the sun was warm on her back. She was filling with a cold, crawling dread.

"Charlie?"

Charlie spun around to see Clay Burke, then sighed and shook her head.

"Sorry, I got here as fast as I could," he said lightly.

She smiled. "It's okay. I'm just on edge today. I think that's the third time I've jumped in the air when someone said my name."

Clay wasn't listening. His eyes were fixed on the body. He knelt carefully beside it, scrutinizing it. Charlie could almost see him filing every detail away. She held her breath, not wanting to disturb him.

"Did you touch the body?" he asked sharply, not looking away from the corpse.

"Yes," she admitted. "I checked to see if she had the same injuries as the man."

"Did she?"

"Yes. I think—I know she was killed the same way."

Clay nodded. Charlie watched as he got up and circled the woman, dropping down to look more closely at her head, and again at her feet. Finally, he turned his attention to Charlie again.

"How did you find her?" he asked.

"I saw birds—vultures—circling above the field. I went to check."

"Why did you go to check?" His eyes were hard, and Charlie felt a trickle of fear. Surely Clay didn't suspect her.

Why wouldn't he? she thought. *Who else would know how to use the spring locks? I bet he could come up with a million theories about me. Twisted girl avenges father's death. Acts out psychodrama. Film at eleven.* She took a deep breath, meeting Clay's eyes.

"I checked because of the body you showed me. It was in a field—I thought it might be another one." She kept her voice as steady as she could. Clay nodded, the steely expression slipping from his face, replaced by worry.

"Charlie, this girl looks like you," he said bluntly.

"Not that much like me."

"She could be your twin," Clay said.

"No," Charlie said, more harshly than she intended. "She looks nothing like my twin." Clay gave her a puzzled look, then comprehension dawned.

"I'm sorry. You had a twin, didn't you? Your brother."

"I barely remember him," she said softly, then swallowed. *All I do is remember him.* "I know she looks like me," she added weakly.

"We're right near a college town," Clay said. "She's a young white female with brown hair—you're not a rare type, Charlie. No offense."

"Do you think it's a coincidence?"

Clay didn't look at her. "There was another body found this morning," he said.

"Another girl?" Charlie drew closer.

"Yes, as a matter of fact. Been dead for a couple of days, probably killed two nights ago." Charlie looked down at him in alarm.

"Does that mean this is going to keep happening?"

"Unless you think we can stop it," he said. Charlie nodded.

"I can help," she said. She looked again at the woman's face. *She's nothing like me.* "Let me go to her house," she added abruptly, seized by a sudden impulse to prove it, to gather evidence that she and the victim were not the same.

"What? *Her* house?" Clay said, giving her a dubious look

"You asked me to help," Charlie said. "Let me help."

Clay didn't answer; instead he reached into the woman's pockets one by one, searching for her wallet. He had to move the body to do it, and she jerked a little as he did, like a ghastly puppet. Charlie waited, and at last he came back with her wallet. He handed Charlie her driver's license.

"Tracy Horton," she read. "She doesn't look like a Tracy."

"You got the address?" Clay scanned the road for police cars. Charlie read it quickly and handed the license back. "I'm going to give you twenty minutes before I radio this in," he told her. "Use it."

Tracy Horton had lived in a small house off a back road. Her nearest neighbors' houses were visible, but Charlie couldn't imagine they would have heard her scream. If she'd managed to scream at all. There was a small blue car in the driveway, but if Tracy had been taken from her home—since presumably she hadn't just been wandering through that field—it could easily have been hers.

Charlie pulled in behind the car and went to the front door. She knocked, wondering what she was going to do if someone answered. *I really should have thought this through.* She couldn't be the one to inform a parent, spouse, or sibling of the young woman's death. *Why did I assume she lived alone?*

No one answered. Charlie tried again, and when there was still no response, she tried the door. It was unlocked.

Charlie walked quietly through the house, not really sure what she was looking for. She glanced at her watch—ten of the twenty minutes had passed just driving here, and she had to assume that the police would get here faster than she did. *Why did I follow the speed limit the whole way here?* The living room and kitchen were clean, but they conveyed no information to her. Charlie didn't know what peach-painted walls said about a person, or the fact that there were three dining room chairs instead of four. There were two bedrooms. One had the sterile air of a guest room that was slowly being taken over by storage; the bed was made and clean towels were folded on the chest of drawers, but cardboard boxes filled a quarter of the room.

The other bedroom looked lived-in. The walls were green, the bedspread pale blue, and there were piles of clothing on the floor. Charlie stood in the doorway for a moment, and found she could not go inside. *I don't even know what I'm looking for.* This woman's life would be sifted through to the last grain by trained investigators. Her diary would be read, if she had one; her secrets would be revealed, if she had any. Charlie didn't need to be a part of it. She turned and walked quickly but quietly back to the front of the house, almost running down the front steps. Standing by the car, she checked her watch again. Six minutes before Clay called in the body.

Charlie went to the little blue car and peered inside. Like

the house, it was neat. There was dry-cleaning hanging in the back window, and a half-empty soda in the cup holder. She walked all around it, looking for something—mud in the tires, scratches in the paint, but there was nothing unusual. *Five minutes.*

She walked briskly through the unkempt grass that bordered the sides of the house. When she reached the backyard, she stopped dead. Before her were three huge holes in the ground, longer than they were wide. They looked like graves, but at a second glance they were too messy, their outlines poorly defined.

Charlie walked around them in a circle. They were lined up next to one another, and they were shallow, but the dirt at the bottom was loose. Charlie grabbed a stick off the ground and poked it into the middle hole: it went in almost a foot before it was stopped by denser soil. The dirt dug out of them was strewn messily all around. Whoever dug the holes had carelessly tossed it everywhere, not bothering to pile it up.

Two minutes.

Charlie hesitated for another moment, then lowered herself into the middle hole. Her feet sunk into the loose dirt and she fought to steady herself, catching her balance. It wasn't too deep. The walls came up to her waist. She knelt and put her palm against the wall of the grave—*the hole*, she reminded herself. The dirt was loose here, too, and the wall was rough.

Something had been hidden there, under the ground. *The air is growing thin. I am running out of oxygen, and I will die like this, alone, in the dark.* Charlie's throat seized; she felt as if she couldn't breathe. She climbed out of the hole and up onto the grass of Tracy Horton's backyard. Charlie took a deep breath, focusing all her attention on pushing away the panic. When she was free of it, she checked her watch.

Minus one minute. He's already called them. But something kept her there, something familiar. *The loose dirt.* Charlie's mind raced. *Something climbed out of these.*

From a distance, a siren was wailing; it would be here in no time. Charlie hurried to her car and pulled out of the driveway, taking the first corner without caring where it would take her. The holes stayed in her mind, the image like a stain.

CHAPTER SIX

harlie slowed her car. With half the cops in Hurricane converging on the area, now was not the time to be stopped for speeding. She was grubby with dirt from the dead woman's backyard, and had a nagging feeling there was something she was forgetting about.

John, she realized. She was supposed to meet him—she checked the clock on the dashboard—almost two hours ago. Her heart sank. *He'll think I stood him up. No, he'll think I'm dead*, she amended. Given the perilous history of their relationship, he'd probably think the second was more likely.

When she got to the restaurant where they had planned to meet, a small Italian place across town, Charlie ran in from the parking lot at full speed. She skidded to a stop in front of the teenage hostess, who greeted her with a flustered look.

"Can I help you?" she asked Charlie, taking a step back.

Charlie caught a glimpse of herself in the mirror behind the hostess counter. There were streaks of dirt on her face and clothes; she hadn't thought to clean up first. She quickly wiped her cheeks with her hands before answering the girl.

"I'm supposed to be meeting someone. A tall guy, brown hair. It's kind of . . ." She gestured vaguely at the top of her head, attempting to indicate the habitual chaos of John's hair, but the hostess looked at her blankly. Charlie bit her lip in frustration. *He must have left. Of course he left. You're two hours late.*

"Charlie?" A voice rang out. *John.*

"You're still here?" she cried, too loud for the quiet restaurant, as he appeared behind the hostess, looking profoundly relieved.

"I figured I might as well eat while I'm here." He swallowed what was in his mouth and laughed. "Are you okay? I thought you might . . . not be coming."

"I'm fine. Where are you sitting? Or are you still sitting? Well, I mean, you're obviously not sitting. You're standing. But I mean before you were standing, where were you sitting?" Charlie ran her fingers into her hair and clenched her fists against her scalp, trying to reassemble her thoughts. She mumbled an apology to the room, not sure who it was for.

John glanced around nervously, then gestured toward a table near the kitchen. There was a mostly empty plate with a half-eaten breadstick resting on it, a cup of coffee, and a second place setting, untouched.

They sat down and he looked at her appraisingly. Then John leaned across the table and asked in a low voice, "Charlie, what happened?"

"You wouldn't believe me if I told you?" she said lightly.

His face remained concerned. "You're filthy. Did you fall down in the parking lot?"

"Yes," Charlie said. "I fell in the parking lot and rolled down a hill and into a Dumpster, then fell out of the Dumpster and tripped on the way in. Happy? Stop looking at me like that."

"Like what?"

"Like you have the right to disapprove of me." John pulled back in his chair, his eyes wide. He blinked hard, and Charlie sighed.

"John, I'm sorry. I'll tell you everything. I just need some time; some time to collect my thoughts and to clean up." She laughed, an exhausted, shaken sound, then buried her face in her hands.

John leaned back and signaled for the waitress to bring the check. Breathing heavily, Charlie looked around the restaurant. It was almost empty. The hostess and the only other waitress were talking together near the door, with no apparent interest in anything their customers were doing. There was a family of four by the front window, the children just barely out of toddlerhood. One kept sliding out of his chair and onto the floor every time his mother turned her attention away. The other, a girl, was happily drawing on the tablecloth with markers. No one seemed to care what was going on. But the emptiness made Charlie feel exposed.

"I'm going to go clean up," she said. "Bathroom?" John pointed.

Charlie got up and left the table just as the waitress arrived to deliver his ticket. There was a pay phone in the hallway, and Charlie stopped at it, wavering. She craned her neck to see if John was watching, but from where she stood, she could only see a tiny corner of their table. Quickly, she called Clay Burke's office.

To her surprise, he answered. "You saw her backyard," he said. It wasn't a question.

"Can you give me the other addresses?" Charlie asked. "There could be a pattern—something."

"There sure could," he said drily. "That's why I raced back to the station instead of sticking around to measure the holes. You have a pen?"

"Hang on." The hostess was briefly absent from her station, and Charlie dropped the phone, letting it swing on its metal cord as she hurried to the podium and snatched a pen and a take-out menu. She rushed back. "Clay? Go ahead." He recited names and addresses, and she scribbled them dutifully in the margins of the menu. "Thanks," she said when he was done, and hung up without waiting for him to respond. She folded the menu and slipped it into her back pocket.

In the bathroom, Charlie washed off as much of the dirt as she could. She couldn't clean her clothing, but at least her face was scrubbed, and her hair was rearranged a little more neatly.

As she moved to exit the bathroom, an image flashed unbidden through her thoughts. It was the face of the dead woman.

She could be your twin, she heard Clay say, in his low, authoritative voice.

Charlie shook her head. *It's a coincidence. He's right. How many brown-haired, college-aged women are there around here? The first victim was a man. It doesn't mean anything.* She grabbed the doorknob to leave, but froze. It was just like in the library. Charlie released the knob and it spun slowly back into position, releasing a horrible creak as it moved.

The costumes had been disturbed, and the creaking noise was so faint and careful she scarcely even heard it. Charlie looked up from her game: there was a figure in the door.

Charlie glanced wildly around the room, pulling herself back to the present. With a swell of panic, Charlie pulled on the bathroom door, but it had somehow sealed shut. She mouthed words, but no sound came out:

I know you're there. I'm trying to get to you.

"I have to get inside!" she screamed. The door burst open, and Charlie fell into John's arms.

"Charlie!"

She collapsed to her knees. Charlie looked up to see the scattered handful of customers all staring at her. John glanced into the bathroom behind her, then quickly turned his attention back to Charlie, helping her to her feet.

"I'm okay. I'm fine." She shook loose of his hands. "I'm fine. The door was stuck. I felt hot." Charlie fanned at her face, trying to make a sensible story of it. "Come on, let's get to the car." He tried to take her arm again but she shook free. "I'm fine!" She dug her keys out of her pocket and walked straight for the door, not waiting for him. An old woman was openly staring at Charlie, her fork suspended in the air. Charlie returned her stare. "Food poisoning," Charlie said plainly. The woman's face went pale, and Charlie walked out the door.

When they got out to her car, John sat down in the passenger's seat and looked at Charlie expectantly. "You're sure you're okay?"

"It's been a rough day, that's all. I'm sorry."

"What happened?"

Tell him what happened, Charlie thought.

"I want to go to my dad's—my old house," she said instead, surprising herself. *Be honest*, her inner voice said harshly. *You know what kind of creature is doing this, and you know who built it. Stay focused.*

"Right," he said, his voice softening. "You haven't seen it since the storm." She nodded. *He thinks I want to see the damage.* She'd forgotten about the storm until now, but the sudden kindness in John's voice made her nervous. *Is there anything left?* She imagined the house razed to the ground and felt a sudden *wrongness*, like a part of her had been ripped away. She'd never thought of the house as anything but a house, but now, as she drove toward what was left of it, she felt a painful knot in her stomach. It was where all her clearest memories of her father were kept: his rough hands building her toys, showing her his new creations in his workshop, and holding her close when she was afraid. They'd lived there together, just the two of them, and it was the place where he had finally died. Charlie felt as if the joy, the sorrow, the love, and the anguish of their two lifetimes had poured off into the very bones of the old house. The idea of it being wrecked by a storm was an utter violation.

She shook her head and gripped the wheel tighter, suddenly aware of how angry she was. Her love of the house, even of her father, could never be simple. They had both betrayed her. But now there was a new monster out there. She clenched her jaw, trying to fight the tears that welled up in her eyes. *Dad, what did you do?*

As soon as they were out of the town center, Charlie sped up. Clay would be tied up dealing with the newest victim for a while, but eventually he would think to come to her father's house as well. She could only hope that she'd connected the dots first. *You're on the same side.* Charlie put a hand to her head and rubbed her temple. The impulse to guard her father's reputation from what was coming was visceral, but it was also nonsensical.

Less than a mile from the house they passed a construction site. It was set back too far from the road for Charlie to see what it was, though it looked abandoned at the moment.

"I did a little work over there when I first got here," John said. "Some huge demolition project." He laughed. "You have some weird stuff out here; you wouldn't know by looking at it." He studied the countryside for a moment.

"Isn't that the truth," Charlie said, not sure if there was something else she was supposed to say. She was still trying to calm herself. Finally, they came to her driveway. She pulled in with her eyes on the gravel, the house only a dark smudge in her peripheral vision. The last time Charlie had been here she'd run in and out without pausing to look at anything. All she'd wanted was Theodore, and she had grabbed him and gone. Now she regretted her haste, wishing for some final mental image. *You're not here to say good-bye.* She turned the car off, steeled herself, and looked up.

The house was surrounded by trees, and at least three of them had fallen, striking the roof directly. One had landed squarely on the front corner, crushing the walls beneath its weight. Charlie could see through the broken beams and crumbled drywall, into the living room. Inside there was only debris.

The front door was intact, though the steps to it were splintered and split. They looked as if they'd give way as soon as they bore weight. Charlie got out of the car and headed toward them.

"What are you doing?" John's voice was alarmed. Charlie ignored him. She heard his door slam, and he caught her arm, wrenching her back.

"What?" she snapped.

"Charlie, look at this place. That house is going to fall over any day now."

"It's not going to fall," she said flatly, but she did gaze up again. The house seemed to be listing to the side, though it must have been an illusion; surely the foundation itself couldn't have sunk. "I'll be out before I get killed, I promise," she said more gently, and he nodded.

"Go slow," he said.

They carefully climbed the steps to the porch, staying close to the sides, but the wood was sturdier than it looked. They could have taken three steps to the right and walked through the open wall, but Charlie took out her key and unlocked the door as John waited patiently, letting her go through the unnecessary ritual.

Inside, she paused at the foot of the stairs to the second floor. The holes in the ceiling were beaming down shafts of thin sunlight, dimming as the sun began to wane. It made the place feel almost like some sort of shrine. Charlie tore her eyes away from the holes and started upstairs to her bedroom.

As with the outdoor steps, she kept to the side, holding on to the bannister. The water damage was visible everywhere. There were dark stains and soft spots in the wood. Charlie reached out to touch a place where the paint had bubbled out from the wall, leaving a pocket of air.

Suddenly a cracking sound came from behind her and she spun around. John grabbed the bannister, struggling to hold on as the stair gave way under him. Charlie reached out, but John braced himself unsteadily. He hissed and gritted his teeth.

"My foot's stuck," he said, nodding down. Charlie saw that his foot had gone clear through the wood, and now the jagged edges dug into his ankle.

"Okay, hold on," Charlie said. She crouched down until she could reach him on the step below her, though the awkward angle made it hard to maintain her balance. The wood was only rotting in some places, while in others it was still intact. She grabbed the smaller pieces and pulled them cautiously back from John's foot, her hands growing raw with the rough and splintered surface.

"I think I've got it," John said finally, flexing his ankle.

She looked up and grinned. "And you thought *I* was going to get myself killed."

John gave her a weak smile. "How about we both make it out alive?"

"Right."

They made their way up the rest of the stairs much more slowly, each of them testing their weight before they took the next step. "Careful," John warned as Charlie reached the top.

"We won't be here long," Charlie said. She was much more aware of the danger now. The house's instability grew more obvious with each step they took; the very foundation seemed to wobble from side to side as they moved.

Her old bedroom was on the undamaged side of the house—or the side not struck by trees, at least. Charlie stopped in the doorway, and John came up behind her. The floor was strewn with glass. One window had been broken by something, and the shattered glass had blown into the room.

She took a deep breath, and it was then that she saw Stanley. The animatronic unicorn had once run on a track around her bedroom. Now he was lying on his side. Charlie went to him and sat down, pulling his head into her lap and patting his rusty cheek. He looked as if he'd been torn violently from his track. His legs were twisted, his hooves missing chunks. When she looked around the room she saw the missing pieces, still attached to the grooves in the floor.

"Stanley has seen better days." John smiled ruefully.

"Yeah," Charlie said absently, as she set the toy's head back on the floor. "John, can you turn that wheel?" She pointed to a crank soldered together at the foot of her bed. He complied, crossing the floor agonizingly slowly. Charlie bit back her impatience. He turned the crank and she waited for the littlest closet door to open, but nothing happened. John looked at Charlie expectantly.

She stood and went to the wall where the three closets stood, closed and apparently untouched by the weather. Even the paint was bright and immaculate. Charlie hesitated, feeling as if she might be disturbing something that no longer belonged to her, then forced the smallest door open.

Ella was there, the doll who had been the same size as Charlie when she was much younger. She, like Stanley, had once run around on a track, and she seemed to still be attached to it. She was entirely undamaged. Her dress was clean, and the tray she held in front of her was firm in her motionless hands. Her wide eyes had been gazing into the darkness since the last time Charlie saw her.

"Hi, Ella," Charlie said softly. "I don't suppose you can

tell me what I'm looking for?" She scanned over the doll quickly and brushed at her dress. "You just want to stay in here from now on?" Charlie studied the tiny frame of the door. "I don't blame you." She closed the closet door again without saying good-bye.

"So," she said, turning back to John. He seemed lost in thought, staring at something in his hand.

"What is that?" Charlie asked.

"A photo of you, when you were no bigger than her." John smiled and gestured toward Ella's door, then handed the picture to Charlie.

It looked like a school photo. A short, chubby girl gave a toothy grin for the camera—minus one tooth. Charlie smiled back at her. "I don't remember this."

"That doll is a little creepy, standing in the closet," John said. "I'm a bit on edge, I won't lie."

"Waiting for a tea party," Charlie said acerbically. "How sinister." She started to leave the room, but as her hand touched the doorframe, she paused. *Doors.* She stepped back through into her bedroom, and looked for a long moment at each of the rectangular closet doors. "John," she whispered.

"What?" John looked up, trying to follow Charlie's gaze.

"Doors," Charlie whispered. She took several long steps back to study the whole wall at once. The scribbles all over her notebooks had been shaped like dozens—hundreds—of rectangles. She drew them without thinking, as if they were pushing up through her mind, trying to break out of her subconscious. Now they had. "They're doors," she repeated.

"Yes. Yes, I see." John tilted his head curiously. "Are you okay?"

"Yes, I'm fine. I mean, I'm not sure." She ran her eyes over the wall of closets again. *Doors. But not these doors.*

"Come on, let's go look at the workshop," John said. "Maybe we can find something else there."

"Right." She gave a pained smile. She looked back once more at the three closets that sat in silence.

John nodded, and they went cautiously back down the stairs, testing each step before they took it. Outside, they stopped by the car. The workshop was invisible from the driveway, hidden behind the house. The backyard had once been surrounded by trees, a small wood that acted as a fence.

"Don't go into the woods, Charlie," she said, then smiled at John. "That's what he always told me, like something out of a fairy tale." They walked a bit farther, twigs snapping under their feet. "But the woods were only ten feet deep," she said, still peering into the trees as though something might leap out. As a child these trees had seemed impenetrable, a forest she might be lost in forever, if she dared to wander in. She started toward what remained of them, then stopped dead when she saw where some of the fallen trees had landed.

Her father's workshop had been crushed. A massive trunk

had hit the workshop's roof dead center, and others had come with it on all sides. The wall closest to the house was still standing, but it was bowed beneath the sagging roof.

It had been a garage when they moved in, and then it had become her father's world: a place of light and shadow that smelled of hot metal and burnt plastic. Charlie peered down at the rotting wood and broken glass with careful attention, looking for something she might otherwise miss.

"We're definitely not going in there," John said.

But Charlie was already lifting a piece of sheet metal that had once belonged to the roof. She threw it violently to the side, and it hit the ground with a resounding clang. John startled and kept his distance as Charlie continued to throw things. "What are you—what are *we* looking for?"

Charlie wrestled a toy from under the debris and threw it carelessly to the ground behind her, continuing to lift sheets of metal and toss them aside. "Charlie," John whispered, picking up the delicate toy and cradling it. "He must have made this for you."

Charlie ignored him. "There's got to be something else in here." She fought her way deeper into the workshop, toppling a wooden beam out of her way. Her hand slipped on the wood, and she realized it was wet; her arm was bleeding. She wiped her hand on her jeans. From the corner of her eye, she saw John set the toy carefully on the ground and follow her in.

Amazingly, there were still shelves and tables standing upright, with tools and shreds of fabric where her father had last set them. Charlie glanced at them for a passing moment, then swept her arm across the table nearest her, knocking everything to the ground. She didn't pause to see what had fallen before moving to the shelves. She began picking things off the nearest shelf one item at a time, inspecting them and throwing them to the ground. When the shelf was empty, she grabbed the board itself with both hands, wrenching at it violently, trying to pull it from the wall. When it didn't come loose, she began pounding at it with her fists.

"Stop!" John ran to her and grabbed her hands, pinning them to her sides.

"There has to be something here!" she screamed. "I'm supposed to be *here*, but I don't know what it is that I'm supposed to find."

"What are you talking about? There's a lot left. Look at this stuff!" He held the toy up to her again.

"This isn't about the storm, John. It's not about happy memories, or closure, or whatever you think I need. This is about monsters. They're out there, and they're killing people. And you and I both know that there is only one place they could have come from: here."

"You don't know that," John began. Charlie looked at him with a stony rage, stopping him short.

"I'm surrounded by monsters, and murder, and death, and spirits." At the last word her fury ebbed, and she turned away from John, surveying the workshop. She wasn't sure now what damage the storm had done, and what had been her. "All I can think about is Sammy. I *feel* him. Right now, I can feel him in this place, but he's—cut off. It doesn't even make sense. He died before my father and I moved here. But I know I'm here for a reason. There's something that I'm supposed to find. It's all connected, but I don't know how. Maybe something to do with the doors . . . I don't know."

"Hey, okay. We'll find it together." John reached out for her. Charlie's strength gave way and she let him pull her close, pressing her face into his shirt. "I know it's hard to see everything torn apart like this," he said. Charlie's anger drained away, fading into exhaustion. She rested her head on John's shoulder, wishing she could stay like this just a little longer.

"Charlie," John said with alarm, and Charlie came back to attention. He was looking over her shoulder, in the direction of the house.

The entire back face of the house had been torn open, as if someone had taken a massive hammer to it; inside was only dark.

"That's right under your room, isn't it? We could have fallen through the floor," John said.

"That should be the living room," Charlie said, wiping her sleeve across her face.

"Yeah, but it's not." John looked at her expectantly.

"That's not even a part of the house," she said. A sudden spark of hope revived inside her. Something was out of place. That meant there was something to find.

Charlie approached the chasm, and John didn't try to stop her as she climbed up several large slabs of broken concrete. John stayed a step behind her, close enough to catch her if she slipped. Charlie turned to him before entering. "Thank you," she said. John nodded.

"I've never seen this room before," Charlie whispered as she crept into the hollow space. The walls were made of dark concrete, and the room was small and windowless, a box jammed into the house and sealed away between the rooms. There were no decorations, and nothing to indicate what was stored here. Just a dirt floor and three large holes, deep and oblong like graves.

"Those don't look like storm damage," John said.

"They're not." Charlie went up to the edge of the nearest hole, looking down.

"Were you . . . expecting to find these?"

These holes were deeper than the ones she'd found at Tracy Horton's house. Perhaps it was the shadowy room, but these looked like real graves. They were a foot or so deeper than the ones she'd found before and partially filled with loose dirt.

John was standing patiently behind her, waiting for her answer.

"I've seen them before," she admitted. "Behind the house of a dead woman."

"What are you talking about?"

Charlie sighed. "There was another body. I found her today, in a field. I called Clay, and then I went to her house while he waited for the rest of the cops to show up. There were holes like this in her backyard."

"That's what you wouldn't tell me? Another body?" John sounded hurt, but his wounded expression lasted only seconds before it cleared. He started scanning the room again, his eyes intent on the walls and floor.

That, and the fact that she looked like me, Charlie thought.

"So what do you think the holes are?" he asked finally.

Charlie barely heard him. Her gaze had fixed on the blank concrete wall on the far side of the room. It was empty, whitewashed then left to turn gray with dust and mildew. But something drew her to it. Leaving John alone by the open graves, Charlie walked slowly to it, drawn there by a sense of sudden recognition. It was like she'd just remembered a word that had been on the tip of her tongue for days.

She hesitated, holding her hands out flat, less than an inch from the wall, uncertain what was holding her back. She steeled herself and placed her palms against the wall. It was cold. She felt a slight shock of surprise, as though she'd expected to feel warmth from the other side. John was speaking, but to her it was only murmurs in the distance. She turned her head and delicately placed her ear against the surface, closing her eyes. *Movement?*

"Hey!" John's voice broke her focus, waking her as if from a trance. "Over here!"

She turned. John was bent over the mound of dirt next to the farthest grave. Charlie started toward him, but he put up a hand to stop her.

"No, come around the other way."

She carefully made her way around the perimeter of the little room until she was beside him. At first she couldn't tell what he was trying to show her. Something was almost visible, veiled in a thin layer of dirt, so that it blended into the ground as if deliberately camouflaged.

But eventually she saw it—rusted metal, and the glint of a staring, plastic eye. She glanced at John, who just looked back at her. This was her territory now. Carefully, Charlie poked the mostly buried head of the thing with the toe of her sneaker, then yanked her foot back. The thing didn't move.

"What the heck is this?" John asked, glancing around the room. "And why is it in here?"

"I've never seen this before," Charlie said. She knelt, curiosity overtaking her fear, then used her hand to scrape aside some of the dirt, clearing off a little more of the creature's face. Behind her, John drew a sharp breath. Charlie just stared down. The creature had no fur, and its face was smooth. It had a short muzzle and oval ears sticking out from the sides of the head. It had the general appearance of an animal's head, though much larger than the animatronic animals from Freddy's. Charlie couldn't guess what kind of animal it was supposed to be. Running down the center of its face was a long, straight split, exposing wires and a line of metal frame. A thick plastic material was stuck to the face in large patches. Maybe it had been encased in it at some point.

"Do you recognize it?" John asked quietly.

Charlie shook her head. "No," she managed to say after a moment. "Something's wrong with it." She brushed back more dirt and found it came away easily. The thing had only been partially buried beneath the floor; that, or it had almost escaped. She started digging her hands into the dirt, trying to pry it out of what remained of its grave.

"You've got to be kidding me." John groaned as he knelt to help, getting his hands around any part of it he could. In one concentrated effort, they heaved it upward, managing to pull most of the torso out of the dirt. They let it drop, then fell back on the ground to study it while they caught their breath.

Like the face, the body was smoother than the animatronics that Charlie was used to. It had no fur, and no tail or other animal appendages. It was too large for a human being to wear, probably eight feet tall when standing. Still, Charlie couldn't shake the feeling that she recognized this creature. *Foxy.*

There was something sick about the creature, a weirdness that gripped her at the most basic, primal level and cried, *This is wrong.* Charlie closed her eyes for a moment. Her skin felt strange, like something was crawling all over it. *It's just an oversized doll.* She took a deep, deliberate breath, opened her eyes, and inched forward to examine the thing.

As her hand touched the creature, a wave of nausea hit her, but it lasted only a split second. She continued. She turned the head to the side, its joints resisting. The left side of its skull had been crushed. Charlie could see that the insides were broken, half the wires torn out. Just behind the eye, on the side that had been completely buried, a piece of the casing was missing. She could see a mass of plastic with a tangle of wires running in and out of it. Something had melted one of the circuit boards. Moving slowly down the body, Charlie examined its joints: one arm seemed fine, but on the other both the shoulder and elbow joints had been bent out of shape. Charlie looked up at John, who was watching her with a worried expression.

"Anything familiar?"

"I don't recognize it. It's not something my dad ever showed me," Charlie said.

"Maybe we should put it back in the ground and get out of here. This feels like it was a mistake."

"But on the inside . . ." Charlie ignored him. "The hardware, the joints—it's older technology. Maybe he made them earlier? I don't know."

"How can you tell?"

"I recognize some of this as my dad's work." She frowned and pointed at the creature's head. "But then a lot of it is foreign to me. Someone else may have had a hand in it. I'm not sure if my dad made it or not, but I have a feeling he's the one who buried it."

"I can't imagine it was designed to be onstage. It's hideous." John was noticeably nervous, and now he placed his hand on Charlie's arm. "Let's get out of here. This place gives me the creeps."

"'Gives me the creeps,'" Charlie said lightly. "Who says that? I'm going to try and get it the rest of the way out. I just want to see . . ." She moved away from John's touch, leaning down to dig again by the creature's buried torso.

"Charlie!" John cried, just as a metal shriek rang out.

The animatronic's arms lifted, and its chest opened like an iron gate. Its metal pieces slid out of place to reveal a dark, gaping pit where sharp spikes and spring locks were just barely visible. It was a trap waiting to be triggered. Yet, disorientingly, something else about it had transformed at the same time. Its artificial skin took on a luminescence, and its movements were fluid and sure. Its casing suddenly appeared to have skin and fur, though they were blurry, flickering like a trick of the light.

Charlie jumped backward, but it was too late: the thing had her in its grip and lifted her high into the air. It was pulling her toward it. She beat against its bent and damaged arm, but the other arm steadily forced her closer to the chest cavity. John stumbled backward for a moment, bending forward with one hand over his mouth, as if struck by a wave of nausea.

Charlie struggled to break free, but her strength was no match for the creature. Out of the corner of her eye she could see John lunging toward the beast. He grabbed its head, wrenching at it, trying to force it sideways. Beneath Charlie, the animatronic began to spasm, a stuttering, uncontrolled movement. The creature's grip came loose and its arms swung around wildly. Charlie struggled to get to her feet, but her legs slid in the dirt. The creature seized her again, and its cold fingers drew her closer.

Charlie braced her shoe against the ground, trying to give herself leverage, but she was being pulled down by an overwhelming force. Suddenly she was face-to-face with the beast, her shoulder already inside its chest cavity. The thing pressed her closer, then suddenly it jerked and released her. She rolled away and heard the sound of snapping spring locks. The creature convulsed on the ground in front of her, headless. Charlie looked at John. He was holding the thing's head in his hands, his eyes wide with shock. He dropped it and kicked it across the floor.

"Are you okay?" John scrambled to her. Charlie nodded, staring at the broken animatronic head. It still seemed alive. Its fur bristled and skin moved, as if there were muscle and sinew underneath.

"What the heck just happened?"

John raised both hands in surrender.

Charlie carefully picked up the massive head and flipped it upside down, peering into it through the base where John had torn it off the neck.

"Ugh." John bent over, his hands on his knees. His face was pale. He stifled a retching sound.

Charlie started toward him, surprised. "What's wrong with you? You've seen worse than this."

"No, it's not that. I don't know what it is." He straightened, then stumbled toward the wall, bracing himself. "It's like there's some horrible smell in the air, but without the smell."

Charlie held her finger to her ear, listening. There was a tone in the air, so high-pitched and quiet it was almost imperceptible. "I think something is still . . . on," she said.

She set the giant head on the ground. John had a hand to his ear, listening, but when she looked at him he shook his head.

"I can't hear anything."

Charlie returned to the body of the creature and peered into its gaping chest cavity. "Are you okay?" she asked half-heartedly, not taking her eyes off the robot.

"Yeah, I feel better back here." He heaved and she turned. John's face was strained, and his arm was tight across his stomach. "I think it's passing," he said, then doubled over, barely getting out the last syllable.

"This thing." Charlie clenched her teeth and jerked her weight back and forth, trying to wrestle something loose from inside the chest cavity.

"Charlie get away from it!" John took a step toward her, then swayed back, as if he were tethered to the wall. "There is something *really* wrong with that thing."

"Now *this* I've seen before," Charlie said as she pulled the object out at last. It was a flat disc, about the size of a half-dollar coin. She held it up to her ear. "Wow, that's really high-pitched. I can barely hear it. The sound is why you feel sick."

Charlie wedged her fingernail into a small groove on the side of the object and flipped a thin switch. John took several deep breaths, then stood upright again slowly, testing him-self. He looked at Charlie. "It stopped," she said.

"Charlie," John whispered, nodding toward the beast on the ground. Charlie looked, and a shock went through her.

The illusion of fur and flesh was gone. It was nothing more than a broken robot with unfinished features.

John picked up the head once again, turning it to face them. "That thing, it did something," John said, nodding toward the device in Charlie's hands. "Turn it back on." He lifted the creature's head a bit higher and stared into its lifeless round eyes.

Are you sure that's a good idea? she was about to say, but curiosity got the better of her. John could handle a little more nausea. She slipped her nail back into the groove and flipped the tiny switch. Before their eyes, the fractured and worn face became fluid and smooth, warping into something lifelike. John dropped the head and jumped backward.

"It's alive!"

"No, it's not," Charlie whispered, flipping the switch off again. She cradled the strange device in her hands, gazing down at it, mesmerized. "I want to know more about this. We have to get back to the dorm." She got to her feet. "I've seen something like this. When I came back here for Theodore, I grabbed a bunch of stuff and put it in a box to study later. I know I saw something like this."

For a long moment, John said nothing. Charlie felt a surge of shame. He was looking at her the way Jessica had, the way he had when he first saw her experiment. The little disc in Charlie's palm felt suddenly like the most vital thing in the world. She closed her hand on it.

"Okay, then," John said plainly. "Let's go." His tone was calm, and it caught Charlie off guard. John was being deliberately agreeable. She wasn't sure exactly why, but it was reassuring nonetheless.

"Okay." Charlie smiled.

CHAPTER SEVEN

When they got back to the college, Charlie headed for the dorm.

"Hey, slow down!" John struggled to catch up.

"You have that disc?"

"Of course." He patted his pocket.

"I know I've seen something like this before," she said. "I'll show you." She glanced at John as she let him into the room she shared with Jessica, but his face remained impassive. He'd already seen the mess. But John didn't look in the direction of Charlie's desk and the covered faces.

"You can clear off the chair," Charlie said as she shoved a stack of books out of the way. She crawled under the bed and emerged a moment later with a large cardboard box. John was standing beside the chair, looking perplexed. "I said you can clear it off," she said.

He laughed. "Clear it off to where?"

"Right." The chair had a stack of books on the seat, and a stack of T-shirts draped over the back. Charlie grabbed the shirts and threw them onto the bed. She set the box on the bed and settled herself cross-legged behind it, so that John would be able to look through it, too.

"So what is all of this?" He leaned slowly over the box as Charlie rummaged through it, pulling parts out one by one and setting them in a straight line on the bed.

"Stuff from my dad's house: electronics, mechanical parts. Things from the animatronics, from his work." She glanced at him nervously. "I know I said that I just went back for Theodore, and I did. But I may have grabbed a few things on the way out. I wanted to learn, and these classes—John, you know some of the tech my father was working with was ancient. It's practically ridiculous now. But he was making it up as he went along; he thought of stuff that's still unique, that no one else has thought of yet. I wanted all of it. I wanted to understand it. So, I went back to get what I could."

"You stripped the house for parts, I get it." John laughed as he picked up Theodore's severed paw and considered it for a moment. "Even your favorite toy? Don't you think that's a little . . . heartless?"

"Is it?" Charlie picked up a piece from the box, a metal

joint, and weighed it in her hands. "I took Theodore apart because I wanted to understand him, John. Isn't that the most loving thing there is?"

"Maybe I should reconsider this whole dating thing," John said, wide-eyed.

"He was important to me because my father made him for me, not because he was stitched up to look like a rabbit." She discarded the joint, setting it next to her on the bed. She turned her attention to the box, picking up pieces one by one and setting them in a row. She was sure she'd recognize what she needed when she saw it.

Charlie looked at circuitry and wires, metal joints and plastic casings, examining each piece carefully. Something would cry out to her, just like the animatronic beast had done, with that raw sense of *wrongness*. But after a while her neck grew sore from bending over the box. Her eyes were beginning to glaze over. She discarded the piece of metal tubing in her hand, tossing it onto the growing pile on her bed. At the clanking sound, John looked up.

"Where do you even sleep?" he asked, gesturing not only to the growing pile of electronic and mechanical parts, but to the clothing and books, and the smaller piles of electronic and mechanical parts.

Charlie shrugged. "There's always room for me," she said mildly. "Even if just barely."

"Yeah, but what about when you're married?" John's face

flushed before he'd even finished the sentence. Charlie looked up at him, one eyebrow hinged slightly higher than the other. "Someday," John said hastily. "To someone. Else." His face grew grimmer. Charlie felt her eyebrow lift higher of its own volition. "So, what are we looking for again?" John furrowed his brow and scooted his chair closer to the bed, peering into the box.

"This." Spotting a glimmer in the pile, Charlie took hold of a small disc and carefully placed it in the palm of her hand. She held it out so John could see. It looked just like the metallic disc they'd found in the body of the animatronic, but one side of it had been damaged, revealing a curious metal framework inside. Several wires extended, connecting to a black keypad not much larger than the disc itself.

"Funny." Charlie chuckled to herself.

"What?"

"The last time I held this, I was more interested in the keypad." She smiled. "This part is a common diagnostic tool. Someone must have been testing it."

"Or trying to find out what it was," John added. "That thing doesn't look like anything else in the box; just like that monster we found doesn't look like anything your dad made. I mean, it *kind of* looked like Foxy, but not the one your dad made. This was some sort of twisted version of Foxy."

She pulled a heavy metal joint from the box. "This doesn't belong here, either."

"What's wrong with it?"

"It's meant to be an elbow, but look." She bent the joint all the way over, then all the way back the other way, then looked at John expectantly.

He looked blank. "So?"

"My father wouldn't have used this. He always put stops so that the joints couldn't do things humans can't do."

"Maybe it's not finished?"

"It's finished. It's not just that, though, it's . . . it's the way the metal is cut, the way it's put together. It's like—you write things, right? So, you read other people's work?" He nodded. "If I ripped up some books and gave you a big pile of pages, and asked you to pick out the ones by your favorite author, could you do that, just based on the style?"

"Yeah, of course. I mean, I might be wrong about a few, but yeah."

"Well, it's the same thing here." She held the heavy piece up again to make her point. "My dad didn't *write* this."

"Okay, but what does it mean?" John asked. He unplugged the broken disc from the diagnostic keypad and took the second disc from the monster out of his pocket. He fiddled with it briefly, then managed to unhinge one side of it. Frowning with concentration, he attached the wires from the keypad to the new disc. When he was finished, he hesitated. "I don't want to flip any of the switches," he said. "I don't think my stomach can take it."

"Yeah, don't touch anything yet. After what happened at the house, we shouldn't assume that we know what any of this does." Charlie set the box on the floor and started shuffling through the parts again, looking at the patterns, trying to see something in them. "There has to be something else in here that I'm missing."

"Charlie," John said. "Sorry to interrupt your conversation with yourself, but look." He passed her the broken disc he'd just unhooked. "Look on the back."

The back had once been smooth, but it was scratched a lot since it was first made. Charlie stared at it for a minute, then finally saw it: there was writing along one edge. She had to bring the piece of plastic close to her face to make the letters out. They were tiny, and written in an old-fashioned, flowing script. They read: *Afton Robotics, LLC*. Charlie dropped the disc immediately.

"Afton? William Afton? That's my father's old partner. That's—"

"That's Dave's real name," John finished. Charlie sat silently for a moment, feeling as if something very large and unwieldy had been shoved into her head.

"I thought he was just a business partner for Freddy's," she said slowly.

"I guess he did a bit more than that."

"He's dead, though. It's not like we can ask him questions. We have to figure out what's happening now." She grabbed the cardboard box and swept the extraneous pieces—the pieces that had been her father's—into it, then shoved it back under the bed. John ducked out of her way as she maneuvered around the small space.

"And how do you think we should do that?" he asked. "What *is* happening now? There have been two bodies so far, both killed by something like what we just found."

"Three bodies," Charlie said, flushing slightly. John covered his face with his hands for a moment and took a deep breath.

"Okay, three. Are you sure it's not four?"

"I didn't see the third one. Clay just told me about it, after she was found. It had been out for a few days—she was the first one, I think."

"So why them? Are these robots just going on a killing spree? Why would they do that? Charlie, is there anything else about this that you're not telling me?" Charlie bit her lip, hesitant. "I'm serious. I'm in this with you, but if I don't know what's happening, I can't help you."

Charlie nodded. "I don't know if it means anything. Clay said it was just a coincidence. But the woman I found in the field—John, she looked like me."

His expression went dark. "What do you mean, looked like you?"

"Not exactly like me. Brown hair, same size, sort of. I don't know, if you described me to someone and asked them to pick me out of a crowd, they might come back with her. There was just this awful moment when I looked down at her, and it was like looking at me."

"Clay said it didn't mean anything?"

"He said it's a college town; there are a lot of brown-haired girls around. One of the other two victims was a man, so . . ."

"Probably a coincidence then," John offered.

"Yeah," Charlie said. "I guess it was just . . . unsettling."

"There must be something else that's linking them together. Another person, a job, a location maybe." John looked toward the window. Charlie caught him smiling, and John's expression sobered, looking suddenly self-conscious.

"You're enjoying this," she said.

"No." He shrugged. "I wouldn't put it that way. I don't want any more bodies. But—it's a mystery, and it's an excuse to spend some time with you." He smiled, but quickly made his face serious again. "So what about the bodies? Where were they found?"

"Well." Charlie brushed the hair off her face, slightly distracted. "They were all found in fields, miles apart. The first one—the one they just found—was over on the far side of Hurricane, and the girl I found today was left by the side of the road between Hurricane and here."

"Where on the road? How far from here?"

"About halfway . . ." Suddenly her eyes widened. "Forget

the fields. Or don't forget them, but they're not the point, or at least not the whole point. The holes were behind the woman's house. They take them from their homes. That's where they're starting; it's where we should start, too." She headed for the door, and John followed.

"Wait, what? Where are we going?"

"My car. I want to look at a map."

When they got to the car, Charlie pulled a stack of papers out of the glove compartment and rifled through them, then pulled out a map and handed it to John.

"Give me a pen." She held out her hand, and John pulled two from his front pocket, handing her one. Charlie spread the map out on the hood of the car and they bent over it.

"The woman's house was here," she said, circling the spot. "Clay gave me the addresses of the others." She pulled the now slightly grubby menu from her pocket and handed it to John. "You look for that one," she said quietly.

Even though they both knew the area, tracing the streets for the victim's houses took longer than Charlie had expected.

"Found it," John announced.

"1158 Oak Street is right . . . there." She circled the point and stepped back.

"What's that?" John said, pointing to something scribbled in the margin. Charlie picked up the corner of the map and her heart skipped. It was another drawing of a rectangle. She didn't remember making it. *It's a door. But what door?* She stared down at it. It had no knobs or latches, nothing to indicate how she would get inside. Or where it was. *What good is it to know what I'm looking for, if I don't know why, or how to find it?*

"Just a doodle," she said sternly, to redirect his attention. "Come on, concentrate."

"Yeah," John said. At least the pattern was instantly clear; the houses made a crooked line from Hurricane toward St. George, truncated halfway between.

"They're all about the same distance apart," Charlie said, a swell of dread rising in her chest. John was nodding as if he understood. "What does it mean?" she asked urgently.

"They're moving in a specific direction, and traveling roughly the same distance between." He paused. "Killing."

"Who's killing who?" A voice rang out behind them.

Charlie gasped and whirled around, her heart pounding. Jessica was behind her, holding a stack of books to her chest. Her eyes were wide and a grin of excitement broke across her face.

"We were just talking about the movie we saw last night," John said with a casual smile.

"Oh yeah, okay." Jessica gave him a quick look of faux seriousness and glanced at Charlie. "So, Charlie, what's the map for?" she asked, gesturing at it elaborately. "Oh, does it have to do with Freddy's?" she said with excitement in her voice. John looked at Charlie suspiciously.

"Did she tell you?" Jessica looked to John, and John looked back at Charlie, eager to hear the rest.

"Jessica, now probably isn't the best time," Charlie said feebly.

"We went to Freddy's yesterday," Jessica said in a hushed tone, although no one else was around.

"Oh, really? Funny, Charlie didn't mention that. Was that before or after all that shopping?" John folded his arms.

"I was going to tell you," Charlie murmured.

"Charlie, sometimes I think you're just trying to get yourself killed." John put his hand over his face.

"So what's the map for?" Jessica repeated. "What are we looking for?"

"Monsters," Charlie said. "New . . . animatronics. They're murdering people, seemingly at random," she continued, not fully convinced of what she'd just said.

Jessica's face grew grave, but her eyes still held a twinkle of eagerness as she walked around the side of the car to dump her books on the backseat. "How? Where did they come from? Freddy's?"

"No, not Freddy's. They came from my dad's house, we think. But they weren't his, Jessica. He didn't build them. We think it was Dave . . . Afton . . . whatever his name is." The words had come tumbling out all at once, nonsensical, and John stepped in to translate.

"She means that—"

"No, I get it," Jessica cut in. "You don't have to talk to me like I'm uninitiated. I was at Freddy's last year, too, remember? I've seen some crazy things. So, what are we going to do?" She looked at Charlie, her game face on. She looked far more together than Charlie felt.

"We don't know what any of it means for sure," John said. "We're still figuring it out."

"Why didn't you tell me?" Jessica asked. Charlie looked up at her hesitantly.

"I just didn't want it to be like last time," she said. "There's no need to put everyone at risk."

"Yeah, just me." John smirked.

"I get that," Jessica said. "But after what happened last time . . . I mean, we're in this together."

John leaned back against the car, glancing around for anyone who might be listening.

"So . . ." Jessica stepped around her to look at the map. "What are we doing?"

Charlie leaned in and squinted at the distance key on the map. "There's about three miles between each location." She studied the map again for a moment, then drew another circle. "That's my house—my dad's house." She looked up at John. "Whatever is out there killing people came from there. They must have . . ." Her voice trailed off.

"When the storm broke the wall," John muttered.

"What?" Jessica asked.

"A section of the house was sealed until the storm broke through."

With firm strokes, Charlie drew a straight line from her father's house, through the three houses of the victims, and continued the line across the map. "That can't be right," Jessica said when she saw where the line finally ended. John peered over Charlie's shoulder.

"Isn't that your college?" he asked.

"Yeah, it's our dorm." The excitement had left Jessica's voice. "That doesn't make any sense."

Charlie couldn't take her eyes off the paper. It felt a little like she had drawn the path to her own death. "It wasn't a coincidence," she said.

"What are you talking about?"

"Don't you get it?" She let out a faint laugh, unable to stop herself. "It's me. They're coming for me. They're *looking* for me!"

"What? Who are *they*?" Jessica looked to John.

"There were three empty . . . graves at her dad's house. So, there must be three of them out there somewhere."

"They move at night," Charlie said. "I mean they can't walk around in the daylight. So they find a place to bury themselves until nightfall."

"Even if you're right, and they're coming for you," John

said, bending down and trying to catch her eye, "now we know they're coming. And going by this, we can at least guess where they might go next."

"So, what are you saying? What does that matter?" Charlie heard her own voice break.

"It matters because those things are out there, right now, buried in someone's yard. And when the sun goes down they're going to kill again, in the most horrible way possible." Charlie said nothing, her head bowed. "Look." John straightened out the map and pushed it into Charlie's lap, so she couldn't help but see it. "Somewhere in here." He pointed to the next circled area on the line. "We can stop them if we can find them first," John said with urgency.

"Okay." Charlie took a breath. "We don't have much time, though."

John grabbed the map, and they all got into the car.

"Just tell me where to go," Charlie said grimly.

John peered down at the map. "So this is where we need to be?" he confirmed, pointing to the fifth circle, and Charlie nodded. He turned the map and squinted. "Turn left out of the parking lot, then take the next right. I know this place. I've driven past it. It's an apartment complex. It's pretty run-down from what I remember."

Jessica leaned forward, poking her head between the front seats. "Those circles don't look too precise; it could be anywhere in the area."

"Yeah, but I'm guessing it's going to be the place with the three fresh graves in the backyard," John said.

Charlie glanced at each of them for a second before fixing her eyes back on the road. There was safety in numbers. Last year when they were trapped at Freddy's together, Jessica was the one who had gotten them inside the restaurant in the first place. She was brave, even when she didn't want to be, and that meant more than whatever notion of romance John was entertaining.

"Charlie, turn right!" John exclaimed. She yanked the wheel, barely making the turn. *Focus. Imminent murder first, everything else later.*

Before them lay sprawling fields, lots marked out and prepared for construction and future development but never finished. Some had never even begun. Slabs of concrete were stacked here and there, almost completely obscured by overgrowth. A few lots away, steel beams had been erected to make a foundation that was never filled in. The place had decayed before it was completed.

In the farthest lot back was a cluster of what seemed to be finished apartment complexes. Grass and weeds grew rampant around them, however, climbing up their very walls; it looked like years of growth. It was hard to tell whether anyone lived inside. Years ago, the city had been diligently preparing for a population boom, one that never arrived.

"Are there even people out here?" Jessica was gazing out the window.

"There must be. There are parked cars." John craned his neck. "I think those are cars. I don't know where we're supposed to look, though."

"I think we just have to drive around." Charlie slowed the car as they traversed the road leading toward the buildings.

"Maybe not," John said. "I bet it's somewhere near the edge of the development. Most people would probably call the police if they saw eight-foot monsters digging holes in someone's backyard. There is a lot of visibility out here."

"Of course," Charlie said with dread in her voice. "They're buried, out of sight, and strategically placing themselves so as not to be found." She looked at John expectantly, but he just stared back. "They're intelligent," she explained. "I think I would have liked it better if they were just roaming the streets mindlessly. At least then someone could call the national guard or something." Charlie kept her eyes on the fields.

They drove around the outer edges of the development slowly, looking at the yards of each house. Some of the buildings looked abandoned, the windows boarded up or torn out completely, opening the apartments to the elements. The storm had done its damage, but little had been done to repair it. A tree had fallen across one cul-de-sac, blocking a building off completely. But it didn't look like anyone was trying to get in or out; the tree rotted where it lay. There was litter strewn in the abandoned streets, collecting in the gutters and bolstering the curbs. Maybe one apartment in five had curtains in the window.

Occasionally they passed a parked car or a toppled tricycle on the patchy grass. No one came outside, though Charlie thought she saw a curtain pull shut as they drove past. In two backyards there were aboveground pools filled by rainwater, and one had a large trampoline, its springs rusted and its canvas torn.

"Just a second." Charlie pulled to a stop, leaving the car running as she approached a tall wooden fence. It was too high to climb, but there was a single board that hung loose off its nail near the base. She squatted down and pried it away to peek inside.

Two round black eyes glared at her.

Charlie froze. The eyes belonged to a dog, a massive thing, which started to bark, its teeth gnashing and its chain clanking. Charlie slammed the board back in place and walked to the car. "Okay, let's keep going."

"Nothing?" Jessica asked dubiously, and Charlie shook her head. "Maybe they didn't make it this far."

"I think they did," Charlie said. "I think they're doing exactly what they mean to." She pulled the car over to the shoulder of the winding road and looked at the apartment buildings on either side. "This could have been a nice place to live," she said softly.

"Why are we stopping?" John looked confused.

Charlie leaned back in her seat and closed her eyes. *Locked in a box, a dark and cramped box, can't move, can't see, can't think. Let me out!* Her eyes flew open, and she grabbed the handle of the car door in a panic. She pulled against it hard.

"It's locked," John said. He leaned across her to pull up the button lock.

"I know that," she said angrily. She got out and closed the door. John moved to follow her, but Jessica placed her hand on his shoulder.

"Leave her alone for a minute," she said.

Charlie leaned over the trunk, propping her chin on her hands. *What am I missing, Dad?* She stood up straight and stretched her arms over her head, turning her whole body slowly to study her surroundings.

There was an empty lot beyond the development, not far from where they were. It was marked out with telephone poles, only one of which had wires. A breeze dragged the loose wires through the dirt, scattering gravel. It didn't look like it had ever been paved. There was a coil of barbed wire as tall as Charlie, sitting uselessly in a corner. Empty cans and fast-food wrappers littered the ground, the paper quivering and the cans rattling in the slight wind, like they sensed something awful. The wind rushed up behind Charlie and blew past her, straight toward the field, rustling the papers and cans and sending waves across the patches of brown grass. *Something wrong is planted there.*

Filled with a new energy, Charlie opened the car door just enough to lean inside.

"That lot. We have to go look."

"What do you see? It's kind of out of the way," John said.

Charlie nodded. "You said it yourself. If an eight-foot monster is digging up the neighbor's backyard, someone's going to notice. Besides, I just have . . . I have a feeling."

Jessica got out of the car and John followed at her heels. Charlie already had the trunk open. She pulled out a shovel, the big Maglite flashlight she always kept close by, and a crowbar.

"I've only got one shovel," she explained, making it clear she was keeping it for herself. Jessica took the flashlight and made a practice swing with it, as if hitting an invisible assailant.

"Why would you even have a shovel?" Jessica asked in a suspicious tone.

"Aunt Jen," John said by way of explanation.

Jessica laughed. "Well, you never know when you might have to dig up a robot."

"Come on," Charlie said, tossing John the crowbar and starting off. He caught it with ease and jogged beside her, leaning in so Jessica wouldn't hear.

"How come I don't get the shovel?"

"I figure you can swing a crowbar harder than I can," Charlie said.

He grinned. "Makes sense," he said confidently, gripping the crowbar with new purpose.

When they reached the edge of the lot, John and Jessica stopped, looking down at the ground before them, as though scared of what they might step on. Charlie went ahead across the loose dirt, gripping the shovel tightly. The field was mostly barren soil, studded with large mounds of gravel and dirt that had been left for so long that grass had begun growing on them.

"This must have been the dumping ground for when they were building," John said. He took a few steps into the lot, avoiding a broken glass bottle.

At the opposite edge was the tree line. Charlie studied it carefully, tracking its path back in the direction they'd come.

John knelt beside a pile of gravel and carefully poked at it with his crowbar, as though something might leap out. Jessica had wandered toward a cluster of bushes. She crouched to pick something up, then quickly dropped it and wiped her hands on her shirt. "Charlie, this place is disgusting!" she cried.

Charlie had reached the tree line and began walking alongside it, studying the ground.

"See anything?" John yelled from the other side of the lot.

Charlie ignored him. Deep grooves in the dirt extended from the trees, snaking around the bushes. The large rocks nearby were freshly marked with gashes and scrapes. "Not exactly footprints," Charlie whispered as she followed the grooves in the soil. Her foot touched soft ground, a sudden contrast to the hard-packed dirt of the rest of the lot. She stepped back. The dirt at her feet was discolored, familiar.

Charlie struck her shovel into the ground and started to dig, the metal rasping noisily on the gravel mixed in with the dirt. Jessica and John ran toward her.

"Careful," John warned as he approached. He hefted the crowbar in his hands like a baseball bat, ready to strike. Jessica hung back. Charlie saw that her knuckles were white on the flashlight's handle, but her face was calm and determined. The dirt was loose and came away easily. At last the blade of the shovel struck metal with a hollow *clunk*, and they all jumped. Charlie handed the shovel to John and knelt in the mess of scattered earth, brushing away the dirt with her hands.

"Careful!" Jessica said, her voice higher-pitched than usual, and John echoed her.

"This was a horrible idea," he murmured, scouting the area. "Where's a police car when you need one? Or any car?"

"It's still day for a little while longer," Charlie said absently, focused on the ground as her hands ran through it, prying away rocks and clods of dirt, digging to find what lay beneath.

"Yeah, it's day. It was also day when that twisted Foxy attacked you earlier, remember?" John said more urgently.

"Wait, WHAT?" Jessica exclaimed. "Charlie, get away from there! You didn't tell me that!" She turned on John accusingly.

"Look, a LOT has been going on, okay?" John raised his hands, palms out.

"Yeah, but if you're going to sign me up for this stuff, then you need to tell me about things like that! You were attacked?"

"Sign you up for this? You had one foot in the car at the first mention of murder! You practically invited yourself."

"Invited myself? You talk like I crashed your date, but you didn't exactly fall over yourself to refuse my help." Jessica planted her hands on her hips.

"Charlie," John sighed. "Can you please talk to—OH JEEZ." He jumped backward, and Jessica followed suit as soon as she looked down. Beneath them, gazing up from the loose dirt, was an enormous metal face, staring toward the sun. Charlie didn't say anything. She was still busy scooping away the soil from the edges, revealing two rounded ears on the sides of its head.

"Charlie. Is that . . . Freddy?" Jessica gasped.

"I don't know. I think it was supposed to be." Charlie heard the anxiety in her own voice as she stared down at the large, lifeless bear with its perpetual smile. The crude metal frame was covered with a layer of gelatinous plastic, giving it an organic appearance, almost embryonic.

"It's huge." John gasped. "And there's no fur . . ."

"Just like the other Foxy." Charlie's hands were getting sore. She cleared the hair from her face and stood up.

It was Freddy, but somehow not. The bear's eyes were open, glazed over with the inanimate look of lifelessness Charlie knew so well. This bear was dormant, for now.

"Charlie, we have to go," John said with a tone of warning. But he didn't move, still staring downward. He knelt beside the face and began to claw at the dirt above its forehead, clearing the earth away until he saw it: a filthy, battered black top hat. Charlie felt a smile tugging at her mouth, and she bit her lip.

"We should call Burke," Jessica said. "Now."

They all turned back toward the development as the wind rose again, rushing past them and making waves in the tall grass. The earth was still, and the sun was sinking lower behind the rolling hills in the distance.

CHAPTER EIGHT

harlie tossed her keys to John. "You go. There's a gas station a few miles back the way we came. You can call from there." He nodded, jangling the keys in his hand.

"I'll stay with you," Jessica said instantly.

"No," Charlie said, more forcefully than she intended. "Go with John." Jessica looked confused for a moment but finally nodded and headed off toward the car.

"Are you sure?" John asked. Charlie waved her hand at him dismissively.

"Someone needs to stay with it. I'll keep my distance. I promise. I won't disturb . . . it."

"Okay." Like Jessica, John hesitated for a moment. Then they left Charlie alone in the empty lot. After a minute, she heard the engine start, and the noise of the car faded as they drove off down the empty streets. She sat at the top of the mound where she had uncovered the misshapen bear and gazed down at it.

"What do you know?" she whispered. She stood and paced slowly over the other two plots of disturbed soil, wondering what lay beneath. The bear was frightening, misshapen, an imitation of Freddy created by someone else. It was a strange variation, into which her father had never breathed life. *But William Afton—Dave—did.* The man who designed these things was the same man who had stolen and murdered her brother.

A thought surfaced, a question that had visited her many times before: *Why did he take Sammy?* Charlie had asked herself, the wind, and her dreams that question endlessly. *Why did he take Sammy?* But she had always meant, *Why not me? Why was I the one who lived?* She stared down at the soil beneath her, envisioning the bear's strange, embryonic face. The children murdered at Freddy Fazbear's had lived on after death, their spirits lodged somehow inside the animatronic costumes that had killed them. Could Sammy's spirit be imprisoned somehow, behind a large, rectangular door?

Charlie shivered and stood up, suddenly wanting to put as much distance as possible between her and the twisted Freddy buried in the soil. The image of his face came to her again, and this time it made her skin crawl. Did the other two mounds hide similar creatures? Was there a malformed rabbit hidden in the dirt just there? A chicken clutching a cupcake to its grotesque chest? *But the thing that tried to kill me—tried to envelop me—it was designed to kill. There could be anything buried down there, waiting for nightfall.* She could look, dig up the other two mounds to see what lay slumbering beneath. But as soon as she thought it she could almost feel the lock of metal hands on her arms, forcing her inside that deathly, cavernous chest.

Charlie took a few deliberate steps back from the mounds, wishing just a little that she had allowed Jessica to stay.

"How has your visit with Charlie been?" Jessica asked in a conspiratorial tone as they made the final turn out of the development and onto the main road.

John didn't take his eyes off the road. "It's been fun to see her again. You, too," he added, and she laughed.

"Yes, you've always loved me. Don't worry, I know you're here to see her."

"I'm here for a job, actually."

"Right," Jessica said. She turned and looked out the window. "Do you think Charlie's changed?" she asked abruptly.

John was silent for a moment, picturing the bedroom Charlie had turned into a scrap heap and Theodore, ripped apart and strewn in pieces. He thought of her tendency to retreat into herself, losing whole minutes as if she were stepping briefly out of time. *Do I think she's changed?*

"No," he said finally.

"I don't think she has, either." Jessica sighed.

"What did you find at Freddy's?" John asked.

"Dave," Jessica said plainly, waiting for a moment before looking at John. "Right where we left him."

"And you're sure he was dead?" John looked down.

Jessica swallowed hard, suddenly seeing the body again. She pictured the discolored skin and the costume that had sunken into his rotting flesh, fusing the man to the mascot in a grotesque eternity.

"He was dead all right," she said hoarsely.

The gas station was just up ahead. John parked in the small lot and got out of the car without waiting for Jessica. She followed at his heels.

"What a dump." Jessica spun, marveling at the surroundings. "Surely there was a better place to . . ." Jessica stopped short, suddenly seeing the teenage boy behind the counter. He was staring into space, watching something just behind them and to the left.

"Excuse me," John said. "Do you have a public phone?" The boy shook his head.

"No, not public," he said, gesturing to it.

"Could we use it? Please?"

"Customers only."

"I'll pay for the call," John said. "Look, this is important." The boy looked at them, his eyes finally focusing, as if only just registering their presence. He nodded slowly.

"Okay, but you have to buy something while she makes the call." He shrugged, helpless against the rules of management.

"John, just give me the number," Jessica said. He dug it out of his pocket and handed it to her. As she went behind the counter, John scanned the shelves impatiently, looking for the cheapest item available.

"We have Popsicles," the kid said.

"No, thanks," John said.

"They're free." He pointed at the cooler.

"Well, how's that going to help me if they're free?"

"I'll let it count as a purchase." The boy winked.

John clenched his jaw and lifted the lid of the cooler, jerking slightly at the sight of the taxidermy coyote hidden inside.

"Brilliant. Did you stuff that yourself?" he asked loudly.

The boy laughed, a sudden, snorting sound. "Hey!" he yelled as John grabbed the carcass by the head and yanked it out of the cooler. "Hey! You can't do that!" John marched to the door, out into the parking lot, and hurled the dead thing into the road. "Hey!" The boy screamed again and ran out into the street, disappearing into a cloud of dust.

"John?" Jessica hurried out from around the counter. "Clay's on his way."

"Great." He followed her out to the car.

Charlie was still walking in circles, glancing up at the horizon every few seconds. She felt like a sentry, or the keeper of a vigil. She couldn't stop imagining the animatronics buried there, whatever they were. They weren't in boxes, not even shielded from the dirt; it would sink into their every pore and joint, it would fill them. They could open their mouths to scream, but the relentless dirt would just flow in, too fast for sound to escape.

Charlie shivered and rubbed her arms, looking up at the sky. It was turning orange, and shadows from the weeds began stretching out across the ground. Giving the mounds a sideways glance, she walked with deliberate steps to the other side of the lot where the only telephone pole with wires stood. They hung down from it like the branches of a weeping willow, dragging in the dirt. As Charlie got closer she saw small, dark shapes by its base. She approached slowly: they were rats, all lying stiff and dead. She stared down at them for a long moment, then whirled, startled, at the sounds of cars.

John and Jessica had returned, and Clay was just behind them. He must have already been in the area.

"Watch out for that pole," Charlie said by way of greeting. "I think the wires are live."

John laughed. "No one touch the wires. Glad you're okay."

Clay didn't speak; he was busy examining the patches of dirt. He walked around them as Charlie had, peering at them from every angle, then finally came to a stop when he'd made a full circle. "You dug one of these up?" he asked, and Charlie could hear the strain behind his level voice.

"No," John said hastily. "We just uncovered part of it, then covered it back up."

Clay looked down again. "I'm not sure if that makes it better or worse," he said, his eyes still on the mounds.

"It looked like Freddy," Charlie said urgently. "It looked like a strange, misshapen Freddy. There was something wrong with it."

"What was wrong?" Clay asked gently. He looked at her with serious eyes.

"I don't know," Charlie said helplessly. "But there's something wrong with all of them."

"Well, they're murdering people," Jessica offered. "I'd count that as something being wrong with them."

"Charlie," Clay said, still focused on her, "If you can tell me anything else about these things, then now's the time. We have to assume that, as Jessica told me over the phone, they're going to kill again tonight."

Charlie dropped to her knees in the place where they had dug up the twisted Freddy, and began digging again.

"What are you doing?" John protested.

"Clay needs to see it," she muttered.

"What in the . . ." Clay inched forward to study the face, then took a long step back to observe the disturbed plots of earth, measuring the size of the things buried at their feet.

"We have to evacuate these buildings," John said. "Otherwise, what are we going to do when these things get up? Ask them to go back to bed? There aren't that many apartments in this area that actually have people living in them. There's only one building in the whole block," he said, pointing, "maybe two, that looked occupied."

"Okay, I'm going to go check it out and see who's home. Keep watch over these things." Clay studied the row of buildings and made his way toward them.

"So we wait," John said.

Charlie continued watching the skyline. Dark clouds were rolling over the sun, making it appear as though night had fallen early.

"Do you hear that?" Jessica whispered.

Charlie knelt beside the metal face half-buried in the ground and turned her ear to it. "Charlie!" John startled. She lifted her head and stared at the face again. It had changed from one moment to the next. Its features had smoothed over, become less crude. She looked up at John, her eyes wide. "It's changing."

"Wait, what? What does that mean?" Jessica said, looking horrified.

"It means something is very wrong," he said. Jessica waited for him to explain.

"We're not at Freddy's anymore," was all he offered.

Clay returned from across the field.

"Everyone into the car," he said.

"My car?" Charlie asked.

Clay shook his head. "Mine." Charlie was about to protest, but Clay gave her a stern look. "Charlie, unless your car has a siren and you've had high-speed pursuit training, stand down." She nodded.

"What did you tell them?" Jessica asked suddenly.

"I told them there was a gas leak in the area," Clay said. "Scary enough to get them out, not so scary as to start a panic." Jessica nodded. She looked almost impressed, like she was taking mental notes.

They piled into Clay's car, Jessica quickly claiming the front seat, though Charlie suspected that she just wanted to leave her alone next to John. The cruiser sat at the edge of the lot, as far from the mounds as they could be without edging onto the road. As the sun sank below the horizon and the final streaks of light bled away into darkness, a single streetlight flickered on. It was old, the light almost orange, and it sputtered at intervals, as if it might fail at any moment. Charlie watched it for a while, empathizing.

John was busy staring out across the field, unblinking, but as the hour passed he began to slouch in his seat. He let out a yawn, then quickly brought himself back to alertness. An elbow poked him in the ribs and he turned to find Charlie with a mess of wires in her lap, studying something carefully. "What are you doing?" he asked, then turned his gaze back to the field.

"I'm trying to see what exactly this thing does." Charlie had the metal disc firmly in her hand. It was the one they'd wrestled from the monster that day. She was trying to connect it properly to the diagnostic tool's small keypad and display.

"Okay, John, don't puke on me." She smiled, her finger ready to flick the switch.

"I'll do my best," he grumbled and tried to concentrate on the dimly lit field.

"What is that?" Jessica whispered.

"We found it inside the animatronic that attacked us today," Charlie was eager to explain. Jessica leaned in closer to see. "It emits some kind of signal; we don't know what it is."

"It changes what those things look like." John turned his head from the window with a nauseated look.

"It changes our *perception* of what they look like," Charlie corrected.

"How?" Jessica seemed captivated.

"I'm not sure yet, but maybe we can find out." Charlie dug her nail into the groove and pulled the switch. "Ugh, I can hear it already."

John sighed. "And I can feel it."

"I can't . . ." Jessica tilted her head to listen. "Maybe I can. I don't know."

"It's very high-pitched." Charlie was busy turning small knobs on the handheld display, trying to get a readout from the device.

"It gets into your head." John rubbed his forehead. "This morning it almost made me sick."

"Of course," Charlie whispered. "It gets into your head."

"What?" Jessica turned toward her.

"These readings looked nonsensical at first. I thought something was wrong."

"And?" John said impatiently when Charlie suddenly went silent.

"In class we learned that when the brain is overstimulated, it fills in gaps for you. So, say you pass a red hexagonal sign on the road, and someone asks you what words were on it. You'd say 'STOP.' And you'd imagine that you saw it. You'd be able to picture that stop sign the way it should have been. That is, of course, if you were properly distracted and didn't notice an obviously blank sign. This thing distracts us. Somehow it makes our brains fill in blanks with previous experiences, the things we think we *should* be seeing."

"How does it do that? What's in the actual signal?" John glanced back again, only half listening.

"It's a pattern. Sort of." Charlie leaned back, letting her arms relax, the device cradled in her hands. "The disc emits five sound waves that continuously vary in frequency. First they match one another, then they don't; they go in and out of harmony, always on the edge of forming a predictable sequence, then branching away."

"I don't understand. So, it's *not* a pattern?" John said.

"It's not, but that's the whole point. It almost makes sense, but not quite." Charlie paused, thinking for a moment. "The tone fluctuations happen so fast that they're only detected by your subconscious. Your mind goes mad trying to make sense of it; it's immediately overwhelmed. It's like the opposite of white noise: you can't follow it, and you can't tune it out."

"So the animatronics aren't changing shape. We're just being distracted. What's the purpose of that, though?" John had turned away from the window, giving up the pretense of ignoring the conversation.

"To earn our trust. To look more friendly. To look more real." As the possibilities stacked up, a grim picture began to form in Charlie's mind.

John laughed. "To look more real, maybe. But they certainly don't strike me as friendly."

"To lure kids closer," Charlie continued. The car got quiet.

"Let's just focus on getting through the night, okay?" Clay said from the front seat. "I can't call this in as is. Right now it's just buried junk in a field. But if you're right, and something starts moving out there . . ." He didn't finish. John leaned against the car door, propping his head against the window so he could keep watching.

Charlie leaned her head back, letting her eyes close for just a few moments. Across the field, the orange bulb continued to flicker with a hypnotic pulse.

Minutes passed, and then almost another hour. Clay glanced at the teenagers. They had all fallen asleep. Charlie and John were awkwardly leaning on each other. Jessica had curled up with her feet on the seat beneath her and her head resting on the narrow window ledge. She looked like a cat, or a human who was going to wake up with neck problems. Clay shrugged his shoulders up and down, seized with the odd alertness he always felt when he was the only one awake. When Carlton had been a baby, he and Betty would take turns getting up with him. But while Betty had been exhausted by it, barely making it through the following day, Clay had found himself almost energized. There was something about walking through the world when no one else was stirring. It made him feel as if he could protect them all, as if he could make everything all right. *Oh, Betty.* He blinked, the orange streetlight suddenly shimmering as his eyes moistened. He took a deep breath, regaining control. *There was nothing I could say, was there?* Unbidden, the memory of their last conversation—their last fight—reared in his mind.

"*All hours of the night. It's not healthy. You're obsessed!*"

"*You're as consumed by your work as I am. It's something we have in common, remember? Something we love about each other.*"

"*This is different, Clay. This worries me.*"

"*You're being irrational.*"

She laughed, a sound like breaking glass. "*If you think that, then we're not living in the same reality.*"

"*Maybe we're not.*"

"*Maybe not.*"

The light changed. Clay glanced around, fully focused on the present again. The orange streetlight was fading, the flickering growing faster. As he watched, it gave a final heroic burst and went dark.

"Damn it," he said aloud. Jessica stirred in her sleep, making a small protesting noise. Quietly, but quickly, Clay exited the car, grabbing the flashlight from its place beside his seat. He closed the door and started toward the mounds, his frantic light shaking out across the field until it disappeared.

Charlie roused. Her heart was racing, but she couldn't tell if it was from the sudden awakening, or from the remnants of a dream she could no longer recall. She shook John.

"John, Jessica. Something's going on." Charlie was out of the car and running before they could answer, heading toward the mounds. "Clay!" she called. He jumped at the sound of her voice.

"They're gone." Charlie gasped, stumbling on the upturned earth. Clay was already running toward the apartment nearest him. "Go back to the car," he barked over his shoulder. Charlie ran after him, glancing back, trying to spot John and Jessica. Charlie's eyes weren't adjusted yet and Clay's flashlight seemed to sink into the darkness ahead of him. Charlie could only follow the sounds of his footsteps as he charged through the shallow grass.

She finally came to a brick wall and sprinted around it to the front of the apartment. Clay was at the door already. He banged against it and impatiently peered into the nearest window. No one answered; no one was inside.

A scream cut through the night, and Charlie froze. It was high-pitched and human, reverberating off the walls of the houses. It came again. Clay aimed his light in the direction of the sound.

"We missed someone!" he shouted. He darted around the side of the house, running blindly back across the field. The scream seemed to be in motion, making its way rapidly toward the black trees.

"Over here!" Charlie cried, breaking from behind Clay and running toward an indistinct movement in the dark.

"Charlie!" John's voice cut distantly through the night, but Charlie didn't wait for him. The sound of gravel under her feet was deafening. She came to an abrupt stop, realizing she'd lost her bearings. "Charlie!" someone yelled in the distance. The rest was lost in the rustle of the trees as a night wind swept through. She tried to keep her eyes open as grains of sand pelted her face. Then the wind finally calmed, and there was another rustle of branches nearby, this one unnatural. Charlie stumbled toward the sound, holding her arms in front of her until she could see again.

Then it was there. Just at the edge of the tree line, a misshapen figure stood hunched in the darkness. Charlie stopped short a few yards away, struck still, suddenly aware that she was alone. The thing lurched to the side, then stepped toward her, revealing a sleek snout. A wolf's mane ran over the top of its head and down its back. It was stooped over, one arm twisted downward while the other flailed up. Perhaps its control over its limbs was uncertain. It was looking at Charlie, and she met its eyes: they were piercing blue and self-illuminating. Yet while the eyes held a steady light, the rest of the creature was in flux, morphing in a disorienting fashion even as she watched. One moment it was a groomed and agile figure covered in silver hair, the next a tattered metal framework, partly coated in rubbery translucent skin. Its eyes were stark white bulbs. The creature flinched and convulsed, finally settling on its crude metal appearance. Charlie drew in a sharp breath, and the wolf broke its stare.

It spasmed alarmingly, doubling over. Its chest split open, folding outward like a horrid metal mouth. The parts made a grinding, abrasive sound. Charlie stifled a scream, rooted to the spot. It lurched again, and something fell from inside it, landing solidly on the ground. The wolf toppled forward beside it, shuddered, and went still.

"Oh no." Clay arrived from behind Charlie, staring at the human body that lay writhing in the grass.

Charlie remained motionless, captivated by the wolfish pinpoints of light that stared back at her. The thing tucked its head down, suddenly flowing again with a silver mane. It folded its long, silken ears, and slunk backward, disappearing into the woods. There was a rustling in the trees, and then it was gone.

No sooner had Jessica arrived than Clay was forcefully shoving the light into her hands. "Take it!" Clay knelt by the body doubled over in the grass and checked for a pulse. "She's alive," he said, but his voice was hard. He bent over her, looking for something else.

"Charlie!" It was John, tugging at her shoulder. "Charlie, come on, we have to get help!"

John took off running and Charlie followed more slowly, unable to take her eyes off the woman who seemed to be dying on the ground. Clay's voice faded into the darkness behind them.

"Miss, are you all right? Miss? Can you hear me?"

CHAPTER NINE

Professor Treadwell seemed restless. Her face was calm as ever, but as the students worked, she paced back and forth across the auditorium stage, the heels of her shoes making a repetitive click. Arty poked Charlie, nodded toward the professor, and quickly mimed screaming. Charlie smiled and turned back to her own work. She didn't mind the sound. The professor's sharp, regular steps were like a metronome, marking the time.

She reread the first question: *Describe the difference between a conditional loop and an infinite loop.* Charlie sighed. She knew the answer; it just seemed pointless to write it down. *A conditional loop happens only when certain conditions* she started, then scratched it out and sighed again, staring out over the heads of the other students.

She could see the face of the wolf again, shimmering back and forth between its two faces: the illusion and the frame beneath it. Its eyes stared into her own, as if reading something deep inside her. *Who are you? Who were you supposed to be?* she thought. She had never seen it before, and it worried her. Freddy Fazbear's Pizza didn't *have* a wolf.

Charlie had a near-photographic memory, she'd realized last year. It was the reason she had such recall of even her early childhood. But she didn't remember the wolf. *That's silly,* she told herself. *There's plenty you don't remember.* And yet her memories of her father's workshop were so strong: the smell, the heat. Her father bent over his workbench, and the place in the corner where she didn't like to look. It was all so present within her, so immediate. Even the things she didn't remember without prompting, like the old Fredbear's Family Diner, had been instantly familiar as soon as she'd seen them. Yet these creatures had no foothold in her memory. She didn't know them, but they clearly knew her.

Why were they entombed in the back of the house like that? Why not just destroyed? Her father's deep attachment to his creations had never outweighed his pragmatism. If something didn't work, he dismantled it for parts. He had done the same with Charlie's own toys.

She blinked, suddenly recalling.

He held it out to her, a little green frog with horn-rimmed glasses over its bulging eyes. Charlie looked at it skeptically.

173

"No," she said.

"Don't you want to see what he does?" her father protested, and she crossed her arms and shook her head.

"No," she mumbled. "I don't like the big eyes." Despite her protests, her father set the frog on the ground in front of her and pressed a button hidden beneath the plastic at its neck. It rotated its head from side to side, then suddenly leaped in the air. Charlie screamed and jumped back, and her father rushed to pick her up.

"I'm sorry, sweetheart. It's okay," he whispered. "I didn't mean for it to startle you."

"I don't like the eyes," she sobbed against his neck, and he held her for a long moment. Then set her down and picked up the frog. He put it on his workbench, took a short knife from the shelf, and sliced its skin along its entire length. Charlie clapped a hand over her mouth and made a small, squeaking sound, watching wide-eyed as he carelessly peeled the green casing off the robot. The plastic split with a loud cracking noise in the quiet workshop. The frog's legs kicked helplessly.

"I didn't mean it," she said hoarsely. "I'm sorry, I didn't mean it! Daddy!" She was speaking aloud, but it was mostly air. Her voice was somehow constrained, like in dreams where she tried to scream, but nothing came out. Her father was intent on his work and didn't seem to hear her.

The stripped-down robot lay prone before him on the bench. He prodded it and it made a horrible twitch, its back legs kicking out uselessly, repeating the motion of its leap into the air. It tried again, more frantically, like it was in pain.

"Wait. Daddy, don't hurt him," Charlie mouthed, trying and failing to force out the sound. Her father selected a tiny screwdriver and began to work at the frog's head, deftly unscrewing something on each side. He removed the back of the skull to reach inside. Its whole body convulsed. Charlie ran to her father's side and grabbed his leg, tugging at the knee of his pants. "Please!" she cried, her voice returning.

He disconnected something, and the skeleton went completely limp. Joints that had been stiff collapsed into a slump of parts. The eyes, which Charlie had not even noticed were lit, dimmed, flickered, and went dark. She let go of her father and moved back into the recess of the workshop, putting both hands over her mouth again so that he would not hear her cry as he began to methodically dismantle the frog.

Charlie shook her head, pulling herself back to the present. The child's guilt still clung to her, like a weight in her chest. She gently pressed her hand there. *My father was pragmatic,* she thought. *Parts were expensive, and he didn't waste them on things that didn't work.* She forced her mind to the problem at hand.

So why would he have buried them alive?

"Buried who alive?" Arty hissed, and she turned, startled.

"Shouldn't you be busy doing something?" she said hastily, mortified to have spoken aloud.

The creatures had been buried in a chamber like a mausoleum, hidden in the walls of the house. Her father hadn't wanted to destroy them for some reason, and he had wanted them nearby. *Why? So he could keep an eye on them? Or did he even know they were there? Did Dave somehow hide them there without his knowledge?* She shook her head. It didn't matter. What mattered was what the creatures were going to do next.

She closed her eyes again, trying to envision the wolflike creature. She'd only seen it for that moment, as it disgorged the woman inside it and hovered between states, its illusion flickering like a faulty lightbulb. Charlie held on to the image, kept it frozen in her mind. She'd been fixated first on the victim, then on the wolf's eyes, but she had still seen the rest of it. Now she pictured the scene, ignoring the wolf's gaze, ignoring the panic that had seized her, the others shouting and running around her. She watched it happen again and again, picturing the chest sliding open one tooth-like rib at a time, then the woman falling out.

She realized she had a better picture of the same thing stored away: the creature in the tomb, just before it tried to swallow her. She visualized its chest opening, searching her mind to see what lay beyond the hideous mouth, inside the cavernous chest. Then she bent her head over her exam book and began to draw.

"Time," called one of the graduate students. The other three began to march up the aisles, collecting blue books one by one. Charlie only had half a sentence in answer to the first question, and it was crossed out—the rest of the book was a mess of mechanisms and monsters. Just before the teaching assistant reached her, she quietly tucked the book under her arm. She exited the row, blending in with the students who had already finished. She didn't speak to anyone on the way out, drifting more than walking, focused on her own thoughts as her body carried her aimlessly down the familiar hallway. She found a bench and sat. She looked around at the passing students, chatting to one another or lost in thoughts of their own. It was as if a wall had risen up, circling only her, completely isolating her from everything around her.

She opened her book again, to the page where she'd spent her test time scribbling. There, staring back at her, were the faces she understood: the faces of monsters and murderers, with blank eyes that pierced right through her, even from her own sketches. *What are you trying to tell me?* She stood, clenching her book, then took one last look at her surroundings.

It felt as though she were saying good-bye to a chapter of her life, another passage that would become nothing more than a haunting memory.

"Charlie," John's voice said from nearby. She glanced around, trying to find him through the thick flow of students exiting the building.

She finally spotted him off to the side of the stairs. "Oh, hey," she called and made her way over. "What are you doing here? Not that I'm not glad to see you, I just thought you had to work," she added hastily, trying to settle the whirling thoughts in her head.

"Clay called me. He tried your dorm, but you were here I guess. The woman we . . . from last night. She's going to be okay. He said he went to the next area, the next spot on the map, and drove around." John glanced at the crowd of students streaming past them and lowered his voice. "You know, the next place they're going to—"

"I know," Charlie said quickly, forestalling the explanation. "What did he find?"

"Well, it's a lot of empty space and fields mostly. One plot for future development, but it's vacant. He thinks we should focus on tomorrow instead. He has a plan." Charlie looked at him blankly.

"We're going to have to fight them," he said at last. "We both know that. But it won't be tonight."

Charlie nodded. "So what do we do tonight then?" she asked helplessly.

"Dinner?" John suggested.

"You can't be serious." Charlie's tone dropped.

"I know there's a lot going on, but we still need to eat, right?"

Charlie stared at the ground, collecting her thoughts. "Sure. Dinner." She smiled. "This is all pretty awful. It might be nice to get my mind off it, even if just for an evening."

"Okay," he said, and shifted awkwardly. "I'm going to run home and change then. I won't be long."

"John, none of this has to involve you," Charlie said softly. She gripped the straps of her backpack with both hands, as if they were tethering her to the ground.

"What are you talking about?" John looked at her, his self-consciousness gone.

"It doesn't have to involve anybody. It's me they're looking for."

"We don't know that for sure," he said, and put a hand on her shoulder. "You have to get that out of your head for a while. You'll drive yourself crazy." John smiled briefly, but he still looked worried. "Try to do something relaxing for a bit, take a nap or something. I'll see you for dinner, okay? Same restaurant at seven?"

"Okay," she echoed. He looked at her helplessly and gave a distressed smile, then turned and went.

Jessica was gone when Charlie got back to the dorm. She closed the door behind her with a sense of relief. She needed quiet. She needed to think, and she needed to move. She looked around, paralyzed for a moment. Her system of piling everything up as she used it was functional day-to-day, but when searching for something she hadn't touched in weeks, the system broke down.

"Where is it?" she muttered, scanning the room. Her eyes lit on Theodore's head, lying tumbled up against the leg of her bed. She picked it up and brushed off the dust, stroking his long ears until they were clean, if matted and patchy. "You used to be so soft," she told the rabbit's head. She set it on the bed, propped up on her pillow. "I guess I did, too," she added and sighed.

"Have you seen my duffel bag?" she asked the dismembered toy. "Maybe under the bed?" She got down on her knees to check. It was there, all the way at the far side, crushed by a pile of books and clothing that had fallen through the space between the bed and the wall. Charlie wriggled under the bed until she could snag the strap, then dragged it out and set it on top.

It was empty—she'd dumped out the contents as soon as she arrived, a harbinger of the messy habits to follow. She grabbed her toothbrush and toothpaste and zipped them into the bag's side pocket.

"I lied to John," she said. "No, that's not right. I let him lie to me. He has to know it's me they're coming for. We all do. And this isn't going to stop." She picked up clothing from what she thought was the clean pile, pulling out a T-shirt and jeans, socks and underwear, and shoving them emphatically into her bag as she spoke. "Why else would they be coming in this direction?" she asked the rabbit. "But . . . how would they even know?" She threw two textbooks into the bag and patted her pocket, reassuring herself that the disc and the diagnostic keyboard were there. She zipped up the bag and tilted her head, meeting Theodore's plastic eyes.

"It's not just that," she said. "This thing . . ." She measured the disc in her hand and studied it anew. "It made John sick. But it sings a song to me." She broke off, unsure of what that meant about her. "I don't know if I've ever known anything with quite such certainty," she said quietly. "But I have to do this. Afton made them. And Afton took Sammy. When I was with John, I could feel . . . something in the house. It had to be him; it was like the missing part of me was *there*, closer than it had ever been. I just couldn't quite reach it. And I think those monsters are the only things in the world that might have answers."

Theodore stared back at her, unmoved.

"It's me they want. No one else is going to die because of me." She sighed. "At least I have you to protect me, right?" She slung the bag over her back and turned to go, then paused. She grabbed Theodore's head by the ears and held him up to her own eye level. "I think today I need all the support I can get," she whispered. She shoved him into her bag, then hurried out of the dorm to her car.

The map was in the glove compartment. Charlie took it out and spread it in front of her, glancing at it momentarily then putting it away with confidence. She drove slowly out of the lot. Though she passed people and other cars on her way, she felt as though she was just part of the background, unseen to the world. By the time she and her car slipped out of sight, she'd already be forgotten.

The sky was cloudy; it gave the world a sense of waiting. It seemed like Charlie had the road to herself, and peacefulness overtook her. She'd been preoccupied with isolation today, but the speed and openness were comforting. She didn't feel alone. The tree line seemed to race across the field when she watched it from the window, an illusion made by the speeding car. She began to feel as though there were something in the woods matching her speed, darting through the blur of branches, a silent companion, someone coming to tell her everything that she ever wanted to know. *I'm coming*, she whispered.

The street dwindled from a highway to a country road, then to a gravel path. It rose up a long hill, and as Charlie slowly ascended, she could see clusters of houses and cars in distant, more populated areas. She turned a corner and left it all behind: there were no more houses, no more cars. The rows of trees had been replaced with lines of stumps and piles of brush, accompanied by the occasional blank billboard that, presumably, would someday announce what was to come. Slabs of concrete and half-paved driveways interrupted the countryside, and an abandoned bulldozer sat in the distance. Charlie took Theodore's head from her bag and set it on the passenger seat.

"Stay alert," she said.

Then she saw it: a single ranch-style house stood at the center of it all, surrounded by bulldozed land and the bare rib cages of half-built houses jutting from the ground. It was out of place: painted, fenced, and even planted with flowers in the garden. That's when it made sense. *A show house.*

The road stopped a few yards into the development, replaced by worn-down tracks in the dirt where the machinery came in and out. Charlie slowed the car to a stop. "Even you can't follow me this time," she said to the rabbit's head, then got out and closed the door, giving Theodore a smile through the window.

Charlie walked the trail slowly. The hulking, unfinished frames of the houses seemed to watch her reproachfully as she trespassed. The gravel crunched under her feet in the silence. There wasn't even a breeze; everything was still. She stopped when she reached higher ground and surveyed her surroundings for a moment. Everything was disturbed. Everything was upturned. She glanced above her as a single bird passed overhead, barely visible from its soaring height. Her eyes returned to the wasteland. "You're here somewhere, aren't you?"

At last she reached the lone finished house. It was set at the center of a neat square of perfectly trimmed grass, towering above its stooped, half-constructed neighbors. Charlie stared at the lawn for a moment before realizing that it must be fake, just like whatever furniture was inside.

She didn't try the door right away, instead going around to the backyard. It was laid out in a neat square of AstroTurf, just like the front, but here the illusion had been ruined. Ragged strips of grass had been torn up. The place radiated a sense of distress, now eerily familiar. Charlie just stared for a moment, certainty pulsing through her. She clenched her jaw, then went back around to the front door. It opened easily, without even a whisper of sound, and Charlie went inside.

It was dark in the house. She flipped a light switch experimentally, and it illuminated the whole place in an instant. A fully furnished living room greeted her, complete with leather chairs and a couch, and even candles on the fireplace mantle. She started to close the front door behind her, then hesitated, leaving it ajar. She walked farther into the living room, where there was an L-shaped couch and a wide-screen TV. *I'm surprised it hasn't been stolen*, she thought. But when she went closer she saw why—it wasn't real. There were no cords or cables coming from it. The whole place had a surreal quality, almost of mockery.

She walked slowly into the dining room, her feet clapping against the polished hardwood floor. Inside was a beautiful, mahogany dining set. Charlie bent over to look at the underside of the table. "Balsa wood," she said, grinning to herself. It was a light, airy wood, made for model airplanes, not furniture; she could probably lift the table over her head if she wanted to. Down a short hallway from the dining room was a kitchen with gleaming new appliances, or at least imitations of them. There was also a back door in the kitchen. She unlocked it and pushed it open halfway, leaning outside and looking again at the expansive, tortured landscape. There were several stone steps here, leading down into a small garden. She stepped back inside, being sure to leave the door hanging slightly open.

There was a second long hall off the living room. This led to bedrooms and a small room fashioned into an office or den, complete with tall bookshelves, a desk, and an inbox tray full of empty file folders. Charlie sat down in the desk chair, finding herself enchanted by the utterly surface imitation of life. She spun the chair once, then stood again, not wanting to get distracted. There was a door to the outside here, too, though it was oddly placed beside the desk. Charlie opened it, fiddling with the latch until she was sure it would stay open. She continued on her way, walking through the house systematically, unlocking and opening each window she came to. Then she went down to the basement, where a storm cellar hung over a set of steep stone stairs. She opened that as well, leaving the doors gaping wide. Outside, dark had fallen.

There were several bedrooms, each furnished and made up with bright curtains and silk sheets, and a large bathroom with marble sinks. Charlie turned the faucet to see if there was water, but nothing happened, not even the grinding of pipes trying and failing. There was a master bedroom with an enormous bed, a guest room that somehow looked even less lived-in than the rest of the house, and a nursery with a life-size menagerie painted on the wall and a mobile hanging above a crib. Charlie glanced inside each, then went back into the master bedroom.

The bed was wide and covered in a light canopy of white mosquito netting. The covers were white as well, and the moon shone through the window to illuminate the pillows. It had an uncanny effect, as if whoever slept there would be on display. Charlie went to the window and leaned out, breathing in the soothing, cool night air. She looked up at the sky. It was still cloudy; there were only a few stars visible. She'd been moving with such grim, impulsive energy until now, but this part would be agonizing. Long hours might pass before anything happened, and all she could do was wait. A nervous fluttering had begun to fill her stomach. She wanted to pace, or even to run away, but she closed her eyes and clenched her jaw. *It's me they want.*

At last, Charlie pulled herself away from the window. She'd packed pajamas in the bag out in the car, but this sterile house full of props and imitations felt too strange for her to actually dress for bed. Instead she just took off her sneakers and considered her bedtime rituals complete. She laid down on the bed and tried to conjure her nightmares, gathering up those final moments with Sammy and holding them close to her like a talisman. *Hold on*, she thought. *I'm coming.*

John checked his watch. *She's just running late. But she was late last time, too.* The waitress caught his eye, and he shook his head. *Of course, last time she showed up covered in filth.* He'd already called her dorm room, but the phone just rang and rang. He'd seen what he'd thought was an answering machine when he was there, but realized only as he was waiting for it to pick up that it could have been one of Charlie's projects, or some piece of discarded junk. The waitress refilled his water glass, and he smiled at her.

She shook her head. "Same girl?" she asked gently.

John let out an involuntary laugh. "Yes, same girl," he said. "But it's okay. She's not standing me up, she's just . . . busy. College life, you know."

"Of course. Let me know if you want to order." She gave him another look of pity and went away. He shook his head.

Suddenly, he saw Charlie's hands on her backpack straps, holding on so tight that her knuckles had gone white. *They're coming for me*, she'd said. Charlie wasn't the type to wait around patiently for something to happen to her.

He got up and walked urgently to the pay phone at the back of the restaurant. Clay picked up on the first ring.

"Clay, it's John. Have you heard from Charlie?"

"No. What's wrong?"

"Nothing," John said reflexively. "I mean, I don't know. She was supposed to meet me, and she's—twenty-four minutes late. I know it's not a lot, but she said something earlier that's bothering me. I think she might do something stupid."

"Where are you?" John gave him the address. "I'll be right there," Clay said and hung up before John could reply.

F or the first few minutes, Charlie kept her eyes shut, feigning sleep, but after a little while they began to flutter of their own accord. She squeezed her eyes shut, trying to force them to stay closed, but it became unbearable. She opened them into the darkness and at once felt relief.

The house had grown cool with night. The open window let in fresh, clean air. She breathed deeply, trying with each exhalation to make herself calm. She wasn't anxious so much as impatient. *Hurry up*, she thought. *I know you're out there.*

But there was only silence, and stillness.

She took the disc out of her pocket and looked at it. It was too dark to see any details, not that there was anything on it she hadn't already memorized. A little light shone in from the moon outside, but the shadows in the corners were deep, like there was something hidden there eating up the light. She rubbed the side of the disc with her thumb, feeling the bumps of the letters. If she didn't know they were there, they'd be scarcely noticeable.

Afton Robotics, LLC. She'd seen pictures of William Afton, the man who Dave had been: pictures of him with her father, smiling and laughing. But she only remembered him as the man in the rabbit suit. *My father must have trusted him. He must not have suspected. He would never have built a second restaurant with the man who murdered one of his children. But those crea- tures—he had to have known they were buried beneath our house.* Charlie clenched her teeth, stifling a sudden delirious urge to smile. "Of course there was a secret robot graveyard under my bedroom," she murmured. "Of course that's where it would be." She covered her face in her hands. All the threads were tangling in her mind.

She pictured it unwillingly. *The creature in the doorway. At first he was a shadow, blocking the light, then he was a man in a rabbit suit, and even then it didn't occur to Charlie to be afraid. She knew this rabbit. Sammy hadn't even noticed him yet. He continued to play with his toy truck, running it back and forth hypnotically across the floor. Charlie stared up at the thing in the doorway, and a coldness began to gather in the pit of her stomach. This was* not *the rabbit she knew. Its eyes shifted back and forth subtly between the twins, taking its time: making its choice. When the eyes settled on Charlie, the cold feeling spread all through her, then he looked away again, at Sammy, who still hadn't turned around. Then a sudden movement, and the costumes on their hangers all leaped together, covering her so she couldn't see. She heard the toy truck hit the ground and spin in place for a moment, then everything was still.*

She was alone, a vital part of her cut away.

Charlie sat up, shaking herself to try and set the memories loose. She'd grown accustomed to sharing a room with Jessica. It was a long time since she'd been completely alone with her thoughts in the dark.

"I forgot how hard it is to be quiet," she whispered, her voice as soft as breath. She glared down at the strange disc in her hand, as if it was bringing these visions on her. She tossed it across the room and into a dark corner, out of sight.

Then she heard it. Something was inside the house.

Whatever it was, it was being cautious. She heard creaks from somewhere distant, but they were slow and muted. Silence followed; whatever moved was hoping the sound would be forgotten. Charlie crept from the bed and approached the door carefully, pushing it farther open and leaning out agonizingly slowly, until she could see deep into the living room, and the dining room beyond that. A part of her kept returning to the thought that she was in someone else's house, that she was the intruder.

"Hello?" she called, almost hoping for an answer, even an

angry one demanding to know what she was doing there. Maybe John would answer, happy to have found her, and come running from the darkness.

Only silence returned her call, but Charlie knew she wasn't alone anymore.

Her eyes widened, her heartbeat drumming in her throat, making it hard to breathe. She took careful steps over the stone tiles, down the short hall to just outside the living room, where she stood to listen again. A clock chimed the hours in a different room. Charlie walked to the edge of the living room and stopped again. She could see most of the house from here, and she scanned the area for anything out of place. Doorways surrounded her like gaping mouths, breathing night air from the windows she'd opened.

There was a long hall leading from the farthest corner of the living room to a different bedroom. It was one of the few places she didn't have a clear line of sight into. She edged around the leather sofa in front of her and across the circular rug that filled the room. As she walked, she could see more of the hall slowly revealing itself. It stretched out, farther and farther.

Charlie stopped midstep. She could see into the far bedroom now. It was full of windows and blue moonlight, and there was something obstructing her view, something she hadn't noticed while she was moving. Now its silhouette was unmistakable. Charlie carefully looked around again, her eyes adjusting to her surroundings. To her right, another large door led down a single step and into the large den. Bookcases stretched up to the ceiling, and a putrid air emanated from inside. Beyond the bookcases was another shadow that didn't belong. Charlie bumped into a lamp and startled. She hadn't even realized she was moving backward.

The front door was open wide. Charlie nearly bolted toward it to escape, but she stopped herself. She took a breath and stepped softly back toward the bedroom, checking over her shoulder as she went. She went back to the bed, sliding her bare feet on the wood floor so her steps would make no sound, and eased herself slowly onto the mattress, cautious to keep the springs from creaking. Charlie lay back, closed her eyes, and waited.

Her eyes twitched, every instinct she had shouting the same thing: *Open your eyes! Run!* Charlie breathed steadily in and out, trying to make her body go limp, trying to look asleep. *Something is moving.* She counted the steps. *One, two, one, two—no.* They were slightly asynchronous: there was more than one of them. Two, maybe all three, were inside the house. One set of footsteps passed her door, and she let her eyes flutter open for an instant, just in time to see an indistinct shadow cross before the crack in the door.

Another set of footsteps sounded like they were in the side hallway, while a third . . .

She screwed her eyes shut tight. The steps fell still outside her door. Her breath was shuddering; she almost hiccupped as she inhaled and she bit her lips together. The door was gliding open. Her lungs tightened, pressing her for air, but she refused. She hung on to that single breath as if it were the last one she'd ever get. *I'll find you.* She clenched her fists, determined to remain still.

The footsteps were through the door now, crossing the floor with a heavy tread. She kept still. The air above her stirred, and through her closed eyelids, the darkness grew even darker. Charlie opened her eyes, and breathed in.

The space above her was empty; nothing was looking down at her.

She turned her head slowly, peering into the open hall to her left. The noises had all stopped.

Suddenly the blankets were yanked off her, pulled from the foot of the bed. Charlie shot up and finally saw what had come for her. An enormous head rested its chin at her feet. It looked like something from a carnival game, its eyes rolling from side to side, clicking each time they moved. A pitch-black top hat was perched on its head, cocked slightly to one side, and the giant cheeks and button nose gave him away immediately. *Freddy.*

It was no longer the sleek and featureless head she had unearthed in the abandoned lot. His head was lively and full of movement, covered in wavy brown fur and bouncy cheeks. Yet there was something disjointed about it all, as though every part of his face was moving independently.

Charlie fought to remain still, but her body was acting of its own accord, squirming and pulling to get away from the mouth opening up toward her. Freddy's face slid across the bed like a python. His head lost its shape as it folded outward, taking hold of her feet and beginning to swallow, moving slowly upward as she fought not to scream or fight. A giant arm reached up and clapped the side of the bed, shaking the room as it anchored itself and pulled the giant torso higher. Freddy's jaw made motions of chewing as the distorted face pulled Charlie's legs inside it. His cheeks and chin dislocating further. It no longer resembled a living thing.

Panic took hold and Charlie screamed. She clenched her fists, but there was no longer a face to strike. There was only a squeezing and spiraling vortex of fur, teeth, and wire. Before she could struggle further, her arms were pinned to her side, trapped inside the thing. Only her head remained free. She gasped for a last breath, then was violently scooped up, consumed by the creature.

Clay Burke stopped the car without slowing down. The brakes screeched as they fishtailed in the dirt. John was out of the car before Clay had gotten it under control, running up the hill toward the house.

"Around back," Clay said, catching up to John, his voice low and tight. They made their way around the house to the back door, which was gaping open. "Check that way." Clay gestured to his right as he ran left. John stuck close to the wall, peering into doorways as he passed them.

"Charlie!" he cried.

"Charlie!" Clay echoed, entering the master bedroom.

"CHARLIE!" John ran from room to room, moving faster. "CHARLIE!" He arrived at the front door. He swung it wide open and stepped outside, half expecting to catch someone fleeing the scene.

"Clay, did you find her?" he shouted as he raced back inside.

Clay walked briskly back into the living room, shaking his head. "No, but she was here. The bed was unmade and there was dirt all over the floor. And these . . ." He held up Charlie's sneakers. John nodded grimly, only now noticing the trails of dirt strewn through the house. He glanced again to the front door.

"She's gone," John said, his voice catching in his throat. He looked at the older man. "Now what?" he asked.

Clay just stared at the floor, and said nothing.

lay!" John repeated. His alarm grew as the older man stared down at the dirty floorboards, apparently lost in thought. John put a hand on his arm, and Clay startled. He looked as if just he'd realized he wasn't alone. "We have to find her," John said urgently.

Clay nodded, springing back to life. He broke into a run and John followed close at heel, barely making it into the passenger's seat before Clay started the engine and took off, speeding down the half-made road.

"Where are we going?" John shouted. He was still struggling to close the door against the wind. It flapped like a massive wing, pulling against him as Clay swerved down the hill. Finally John yanked it shut.

"I don't know," Clay said grimly. "But we know about

how far they can get." He drove wildly back down the hill and out to the main road, flipping on his police lights. They went less than a mile before he turned quickly onto a small, unpaved lane.

John's shoulder banged hard against the door. He gripped his seat belt as they barreled down the trail, high brush scraping the sides of the car and thumping the windshield.

"They have to come through here," Clay said. "This field is right in the middle of the path between that house and the next area on the map. We just have to wait for them." He stopped the car abruptly and John jerked forward.

Together they got out of the car. Clay had stopped at the edge of an open field. There were trees scattered here and there, and the grass was tall, but there were no crops, and no livestock grazed. John walked out into the open, watching the grass ripple like water in the wind.

"You really think they'll come by here?" John asked.

"If they keep moving the direction they've been going," Clay said. "They have to."

Long minutes passed. John paced back and forth in front of the car. Clay positioned himself closer to the middle of the field, ready to run in any direction at a moment's notice.

"They should have been here by now," John said. "Something's wrong." He glanced at Clay, who nodded.

The sound of a car engine rose from the distance, growing louder. They both froze. Whoever it was, they were coming fast; John could hear branches whipping against the car's body in an irregular percussion. After a few seconds the car shot out from the lane and screeched to a halt.

"Jessica." John walked toward the car.

"Where's Charlie?" Jessica asked, stepping out onto the grass.

"How did you find us?" Clay demanded.

"I called her," John put in quickly. "From the restaurant, right after I talked to you."

"I've been driving all over the place. I'm lucky I found you. Why are we stopped here?"

"Their route crosses through here," John explained, but she looked skeptical.

"What does that mean? How do you know?"

John glanced at Clay, neither of them looking confident.

"They have her already, right?" Jessica said. "So why would they keep going toward her dorm?" Clay closed his eyes, putting a hand to his temples.

"They wouldn't," he said. He looked up at the sky, the wind battering across his upturned face with a raw touch.

"So they could be going anywhere now," Jessica added.

"We can't predict what they're doing anymore," John said. "They got what they wanted."

"And she wanted this? She planned this?" Jessica said, her voice rising. "What's *wrong* with you, Charlie?" She turned back to John. "They might not have even wanted *her*. It could have been anyone! So why did she have to go up there, like some kind of—of—"

"Sacrifice," John said quietly.

"She can't be dead," Jessica muttered, her voice shaky even under her breath.

"We can't think like that," John said sternly.

"We'll form a perimeter," Clay said. "Jessica, you and John take your car and start driving that way." He pointed. "I'll loop back the other direction. We'll make circles and hope we catch them. I can't think of any other way." He looked at the teenagers helplessly. No one moved, despite Clay's new plan. John could feel it in the air; they had all surrendered. "I don't know what else to do." Clay's voice had lost its strength.

"I might," John said abruptly, the idea forming even as he spoke. "Maybe we can ask them."

"You want to ask them?" Jessica said sarcastically. "Let's call them and leave a message. 'Please call us back with your murderous plot at your earliest convenience!'"

"Exactly," John said. "Clay, the mascots from Freddy's: Are they *all* gone? When you say you threw them out, what does that mean? Can we get access to them?" He turned to Jessica. "They helped us before, or at least they tried to, once they stopped trying to kill us. They might know something, I don't know, even if they're on a scrap heap somewhere, there must be something left. Clay?"

Clay had turned his face up to the sky again. Jessica gave him a sharp look. "You know, don't you?" she said. "You know where they are."

Clay sighed. "Yeah, I know where they are." He hesitated. "I couldn't let them be dismantled," he went on. "Not knowing what they are, who they had been. And I didn't dare let them be casually tossed out, considering what they're capable of doing." Jessica opened her mouth, about to ask a question, then stopped herself. "I . . . I kept them," Clay said. There was a rare note of uncertainty in his voice.

"You what?" John stepped forward, suddenly on guard.

"I kept them. All of them. I don't know about asking them any questions, though. Ever since that night, they haven't moved an inch. They're broken, or at least they're doing a good impression of it. They've been sitting in my basement for over a year now. I've been careful to leave them alone. It just seemed like they shouldn't be disturbed."

"Well, we have to disturb them," Jessica said. "We have to try to find Charlie."

John scarcely heard her. He was staring searchingly at Clay.

"Come on," Clay said. He set off toward his car with a heavy look, as if something had just been taken from him.

John and Jessica exchanged a glance, then followed. Before they reached Jessica's car, Clay was already heading toward the main road. Jessica stepped on the gas, catching up just as Clay made a sharp right turn.

They didn't speak. Jessica was intent on the road, and John was slouched in his seat, thinking things through. Ahead of them, Clay had switched on his flashing lights, though he left off the siren.

John stared into the darkness as they drove. Maybe he'd spot Charlie just by chance. He kept his hand loose on the door handle, ready to jump out, to run and save her. But there were only endless trees, scattered with the orange windows of distant houses, which hung on the hills like Christmas lights.

"We're here," Jessica said, sooner than John had expected. John pushed himself upright and peered out the window.

She made a left turn and slowed the car down, and as she did John recognized it. A few yards ahead was Carlton's house, surrounded by a cove of trees. Clay pulled into the driveway and they came in behind him. Jessica stopped the car inches from his bumper.

Clay jangled his keys nervously as they approached the house; he looked like an altered man, no longer the assured police chief in control of every situation. He unlocked the door, but John hung back. He wanted Clay to go in first.

Clay led them into the living room, and Jessica made a noise of surprise. Clay gave her a sheepish look. "Sorry for the mess," he said.

John glanced around. The room was mostly the same as he remembered, full of couches and chairs all fanned around a fireplace. But both couches were piled with open files and stacks of newspapers, and what looked like dirty laundry. Six coffee mugs sat crowded together on a single end table. John's heart sank as he noticed two bottles of whiskey lying on their sides between an armchair and the hearth. He cast his eyes around quickly, spotting two more. One had rolled under a couch; the other was still half-full, sitting beside a glass with a distinct yellow tinge. John snuck a look at Jessica, who bit her lip.

"What happened here?" she asked.

"Betty left," Clay said shortly.

"Oh."

"I'm sorry," John offered. Clay waved a hand at him, staving off further attempts at comfort. He cleared his throat.

"She was right, I guess. Or at least she did what was right for her." He forced a laugh and gestured at the mess that surrounded him. "We all do what we have to do." He sat down in a green armchair, the only seat completely free of paperwork and debris, and shook his head.

"Can I move these?" John asked, pointing to the papers that filled the couch opposite Clay. Clay didn't respond, so John stacked them up and put them to one side, careful not to let anything fall. He sat, and after a moment so did Jessica, though she eyed the couch as if she thought it might be carrying the plague.

"Clay—" John started, but the older man started talking again, as if he'd never stopped.

"After all of you left—after all of you were safe—I went back for them. Betty and I had decided it might be a good time for Carlton to get out of town for a while, so she took him to stay with her sister for a few weeks. To be honest, I don't remember if she suggested it, or if it was me who put the idea in her mind. But as soon as I saw them pull down the driveway and out of sight, I got to work.

"Freddy's was locked up. They'd taken away Officer Dunn's body and completed their search, under my careful guidance, of course. They took some samples, but nothing else had been removed from the premises, not yet. They were waiting on me to give the go-ahead. The place wasn't even under guard—after all, there was nothing dangerous inside, right? So, I waited for things to calm down. Then I drove to St. George and rented a U-Haul.

"It was raining when I picked up the truck, and by the time I got to Freddy's there was a full-on thunderstorm, even though the forecast had been clear. I had keys this time; all the locks were police-issue now, so I just walked right into the place. I knew where I would find them—or at least, I knew where I'd left them and prayed they were still here. They were all piled together in that room with the little stage."

"Pirate's Cove," Jessica said, her voice barely a whisper.

"I half expected them to be gone, but they were sitting patiently, like they'd been waiting for me. They're immense, you know. Hundreds of pounds of metal and whatever else was in there, so I had to drag them one by one. I loaded them all up eventually. I figured I would bring them down through the storm cellar, but when I got back home the lights were on and Betty's car was in the driveway. She'd come back from her trip early, it seemed."

"What did you do?" Jessica asked. She was hunched over, her chin in her palms. John shook his head, mildly amused. She was enjoying the story.

"I waited across the street. I watched the lights, staking out my own house. When the last light went out, I pulled into the driveway and started dragging those things again, lowering them down into the cellar one by one. I drove the truck back to St. George and came back home, all without anyone seeing me. It would have never worked if I hadn't had the cover of thunder and lightning to mask what I was doing. When I came in, I was soaking wet and my whole body ached. All I wanted was to go upstairs to bed, next to my wife . . ." He cleared his throat. "But I didn't dare. I took a blanket and I slept in front of the basement door, just in case something tried to come out."

"Did it?" Jessica asked. Clay shook his head slowly back and forth, like it had taken on extra weight.

"In the morning, they were exactly the way I'd left them. Every night after that, I went down there when Betty was asleep. I watched them, sometimes I even . . . talked to them, trying to provoke them somehow. I wanted to make sure they weren't going to kill us in our sleep. I went back over the case files, trying to figure out how we'd missed Afton. How had he managed to come back without anyone suspecting?

"Betty could tell something was wrong. A few weeks later, she woke up and came looking for me—she found me, and them." Burke closed his eyes. "I don't remember exactly how the conversation went, but the next morning she was gone again, and this time she didn't come back."

John shifted on the couch restlessly. "They haven't moved since then?"

"They're just sitting there like broken dolls. I don't even think about them anymore."

"Clay, Charlie's in danger," John said, standing. "We have to go see them."

Clay nodded. "Well, then let's go see them." He stood and gestured toward the kitchen.

The last time John had stood in the Burkes' kitchen was the morning after they'd all escaped from Freddy's. Clay had been making pancakes and kidding around. Betty, Carlton's mother, was sitting next to her son as if she were afraid to leave his side. They were all giddy with relief that the ordeal was over, but John could tell that each of them, in their own particular ways, was struggling with other emotions, too. Someone might stop talking in midsentence, forgetting the rest, or stare for several moments at the empty air in front of them. They were all just barely recovering. But the kitchen had been bright. Light sparkled off the counters, and the smells of coffee and pancakes were reassuring, a connection to reality.

Now, John was struck hard by the contrast. There was a rank smell, and he could see immediately what it was: the counters and table were strewn with dirty dishes, all crusted with leftover meals. Most had scarcely been eaten. There were two more empty bottles in the kitchen sink.

Clay opened the door to what looked like a closet, but turned out to be the basement steps. He flipped a light switch, illuminating a dim bulb right above the stairs, and motioned them in. Jessica started forward, but John put a hand lightly on her arm, stopping her. Clay went first, leading their descent, and John followed, guiding Jessica behind him.

The stairs were narrow and a little too steep. Each time John stepped down he felt a slight lurch, his body unprepared for the distance. Two steps down the air changed: it was damp and moldy.

"Watch out for that one," Clay said. John looked down to see that one of the boards was missing. He stepped over it carefully and turned, offering Jessica a hand as she made the awkward jump. "One of many things that's on my to-do list," Clay said offhandedly.

The basement itself was unfinished. The floor and walls were nothing but the unpainted inner surface of the foundation. Clay gestured to a dark corner where the boiler lurked heavily. Jessica gasped.

They were all there, lined up in a row against the wall. At the end of the line, Bonnie slumped against the boiler. The gigantic rabbit's blue fur was stained and matted, and his long ears drooped forward, almost obscuring his wide, square face. He still held a red bass guitar in one enormous hand, though it was battered and broken. Half of his bright red bow tie had torn off, giving his face a lopsided look. Beside him sat Freddy Fazbear. His top hat and matching black bow tie were undamaged, their material only a little scuffed. And though his brown fur was bedraggled, he still smiled for an absent audience. His blue eyes were wide and his eyebrows raised, like something exciting was about to happen. His microphone was missing, and he held his arms out stiffly before him, grasping at nothing. Chica leaned against Freddy, her head drooping to the side. The weight of her yellow body—inexplicably covered in fur, not feathers—seemed to rest entirely on him. Her long, orange chicken legs were splayed out in front of her, and for the first time John noticed the silver talons on her feet, inches long and sharp as knives. The bib she always wore had been torn. It had read: LET'S EAT!!!, but it was faded by time, along with the damp and mildew of the basement.

John squinted at her. Something else was missing.

"The cupcake," Jessica said, echoing his thoughts.

Then he spotted it. "There on the floor," he said. It was sitting alone beside Chica, almost huddled, its evil grin maniacal and pathetic.

Set a little apart from the three was the yellow Freddy, the one that had saved all their lives. He looked like Freddy Fazbear, and yet he did not. There was something different about him besides the color, but if someone had asked John what it was, he knew he wouldn't be able to name it. Jessica and John looked at it for a long moment. John felt a sense of quiet awe as he studied the yellow bear. *I never got to thank you*, he wanted to say. But he found he was too scared to approach it.

"Where's—" Jessica started, then cut herself off. She pointed to the corner where Foxy was propped against the wall, clothed in shadows but still visible. John knew what he would see: a robotic skeleton covered with dark red fur, but only from the knees up. It had been tattered even when the restaurant was open. Foxy had his own stage in Pirate's Cove. As John peered at him now, he thought he could see more places where the fur covering was ripped, and the metal frame showed through. Foxy's eye patch was still fixed in place above his eye. While one hand drooped at his side, the arm with the large, sharpened hook was raised above his head, poised for a downward slash.

"Is this how you left them?" John asked.

"Yep. Exactly how I left them," Clay answered, but he sounded suspicious of his own words.

Jessica approached Bonnie cautiously and crouched down to make her eyes level with the enormous rabbit. "Are you in there?" she whispered. There was no response. Jessica reached out slowly to touch his face. John watched, tensing, but as Jessica petted the rabbit, not even dust stirred in the mildewed basement. Finally she straightened and took a step back, then looked helplessly at John. "There's nothing—"

"Shh," he interrupted. A noise caught his attention.

"What is it?"

John bent his head, craning closer to the sound, though he couldn't tell exactly where it was coming from. It was like a voice on the wind, words swept away before he could catch them, so that he couldn't be sure it was a voice at all. "Is anyone . . . here?" he murmured. He looked at Freddy Fazbear, but as he tried to focus his attention, the sound situated itself. He turned to the yellow Freddy suit.

"You're here, aren't you?" he asked the bear. He went to the animatronic and crouched in front of it, but he didn't try to touch it. John looked into its shining eyes, searching for any of the spark of life he had seen that night, when the golden bear entered the room and they all knew as irrefutable fact that Michael, their childhood friend, was inside. John couldn't remember precisely how that knowledge had come: there was nothing behind the plastic eyes, nothing different physically. It was just pure certainty. He closed his eyes, trying to call it back. Maybe by recalling that essence of *Michael*, he could conjure him again. But he couldn't catch it, couldn't sense the presence of his friend as he had that night.

John opened his eyes and looked at all the animatronics one by one, remembering them alive and mobile. Once, the children stolen by William Afton had watched him back from inside. Were they still inside now, dormant? It was horrible to think of them moldering down here, staring into the darkness.

Something flickered in the yellow bear's eye, almost imperceptibly, and John drew in a sharp breath. He glanced behind, checking for a light that might have glanced off the hard plastic surface, but there was no obvious source. *Come back*, he pled silently, hoping to see the spark again.

"John." Jessica's voice pulled him back to reality. "John, I'm not sure that this was a good idea." He turned toward her voice, then stood, his legs cramping. How long had he been there, staring into the blind eyes of the mascot?

"I think there's still someone in there," he said slowly.

"Maybe so, but this doesn't feel right." She looked down from John toward the suits again.

Their heads had moved; they tilted up unnaturally, facing John and Jessica.

Jessica screamed and John heard himself shout something unintelligible, leaping back as if he'd been stung. They were all looking directly at him. John took three experimental steps to the left, and they appeared to track him: their eyes stayed fixed on him, and him alone.

Clay had grabbed a shovel and was holding it like a baseball bat, ready to strike. "I think it's time to go." He stepped forward.

"Stop, it's okay!" John exclaimed. "They know that we aren't enemies. We're here because we need their help." John opened his palms toward the creatures.

Clay lowered the shovel, though he kept it in his hand. John looked at Jessica, who nodded rapidly.

John turned back to the mascots. "We're here because we need your help," he said again. They gazed back at him blankly. "Remember me?" he asked awkwardly. They continued to stare, as frozen in their new poses as they'd been before. "Please listen," he went on. "Charlie, you remember her, right? You must. She's been taken by . . . creatures like you, but not like you." He glanced at Jessica, but she was watching anxiously, trusting this to him.

"They were animatronic suits, buried under Charlie's house. We don't know why they were there." He took a deep breath. "We don't think they were built by Henry; we think they were built by William Afton."

As soon as John said the name, the robots all began to shudder, convulsing where they sat. It was as if their machinery was being jump-started by a current too powerful for their systems to absorb.

"John!" Jessica cried. Clay stepped forward and grabbed John by the shoulder.

"We have to get out of here," Jessica said urgently. The mascots were seizing wildly, their arms and legs jerking. Their heads banged against the back wall with painful clanks. John stood rooted to the spot, torn between the impulse to run *to* them, to try and help, and the urge to run away.

"Go, now!" Clay shouted over the noise, pulling John backward. They made their way back up the basement stairs, Clay followed behind with the shovel raised defensively. John watched the mascots convulsing on the ground until they were out of sight.

"We need your help to find Charlie!" he shouted one last time, as Clay slammed the basement door and snapped three shiny new deadbolts shut.

"Come on," Clay said. They followed him, chased by hideous clanking and banging noises, only slightly muffled by the floor beneath. He led them back through the living room to a small study branching off from it, where he shut the door and bolted it.

"They're coming up," John said, pacing and watching the ground beneath his feet. Metal ground against metal; something crashed like it was slammed against the wall. The echo reverberated through the floor.

"Block the door," Clay ordered, grabbing one side of the desk in the corner. John grabbed the other side as Jessica cleared a path for them, yanking two chairs and a lamp out of the way. They dropped it in front of the door as, beneath them, something scraped across the concrete like it was being dragged.

Heavy footsteps shook the foundation of the house. The high-pitched whine of malfunctioning electronics filled the air, almost too high to hear. Jessica rubbed her ears. "Are they coming for *us*?"

"No. I mean, I don't think so," John said. He looked to Clay for reassurance, but Clay's eyes were on the door. The whine intensified and Jessica clapped her hands over her ears. The footsteps grew louder. There was a noise like cracking wood.

"At the door," Clay whispered. There was a loud thud, and then another. John, Jessica, and Clay sank down behind the desk, as if it would better hide them. Another thud resounded, then a sound of splintering wood. The earth-shaking footsteps came closer. John tried to count them, to see if the creatures were all together, but there was too much overlap. They layered one over another, rattling his teeth and shaking through his chest. It felt like the sound alone might break him to pieces.

Then, quickly, the footsteps faded and were gone. For a long moment no one moved. John gasped to breathe, realizing only now that he'd been holding his breath. He looked at the others. Jessica's eyes were closed, and she gripped her hands together so tightly that her fingertips had gone white. John reached out and touched her shoulder and she jumped, her eyes flying open. Clay was already standing, tugging at the desk. "Come on, John," he said. "Help me get this out of the way."

"Right," he said unsteadily. Together they shoved it aside and hurried out into the hall. The front door stood wide open to the night. John rushed out to look.

The grass outside had been torn up where the mascots shuffled through it. The tracks were obvious and easy to follow, leading straight into the woods. John broke into a run, chasing after them, Clay and Jessica at his heels. When they reached the cover of trees they slowed. In the distance, John saw a blur of movement for only an instant, and he motioned the others to hold back. They would follow, but they didn't dare be seen by whatever was leading the way.

CHAPTER TWELVE

The world thundered around Charlie, shaking her rhythmically back and forth, strange objects digging harder into her each time she was jostled. Charlie opened her eyes, and remembered where she was. Or rather, what she was inside. The awful image of the malformed Freddy sucking her into its mouth like some kind of snake hit her, and she closed her eyes again, biting her lips together so that she wouldn't scream. The thuds were footsteps, she realized: the animatronics were on the move.

Her head throbbed with each blow, making it hard to think straight. *I must have been knocked unconscious when it threw me in here*, she thought. The torso of the thing was connected to the head by a wide neck, which was almost level with her own, though its head stretched up another foot above her. It was like looking at the inside of a mask: the hollow of a protruding snout, the blank spheres that were the backs of the eyes. When she carefully tilted her head up, she could even see the bolt that attached the black top hat.

Charlie's legs were cramped and bent at odd angles, wedged between pieces of machinery. She must have been stuck this way for some time, but she had no way of knowing how long. Her arms were constrained, suspended away from her body into the arms of the suit. Her whole body was covered in small points of pain, bruises and cuts from tiny pieces of plastic and metal that deepened each time they banged against her. Charlie could feel blood trickling down her skin in half a dozen places. She itched to wipe it away but had no idea how much she could struggle without triggering the springs. Her mind flashed to the first murder victim, the lacerations that covered his body almost decoratively. She thought of Dave's screams as he died, and the bloated corpse beneath the stage at Pirate's Cove. *That can't be me. I can't die like that!*

Charlie had told Clay what she knew about the spring-lock suits. The animatronic parts were either recoiled, making room for a person inside to use it as a costume, or fully extended, so the mascot would work as a robot. But that was what Charlie knew from Fredbear's Family Diner— this creature was different. She was inside a cavity made for a human being, but the suit was moving with complete autonomy. Its insides were full of metal architecture and wires, all except for the space that Charlie occupied.

The animatronic lurched unexpectedly to the side, and Charlie was smacked against the jagged wall again with greater force. She cried out this time, unable to help herself, but there was no break in Freddy's stride. Either the creature hadn't heard, or it didn't care. She clenched her teeth, trying to quell the pounding in her head.

Where are we going? She craned her neck this way and that, looking through the holes in the animatronic's battered suit. There were only a few holes, small and on either side of the thing's torso. All she could make out was the forest: trees rushing by in the darkness as they hurried to their mysterious destination. Charlie sighed in frustration, tears welling up. *Where are you? Am I getting closer to you? Sammy, is it you?*

She gave up looking for hints outside and stared straight ahead at the inside of the suit. *Stay calm*, Aunt Jen's voice said in her head. *Always stay calm. It's the only way to keep your head clear.* She stared up into the mask, at the inside-out features of the twisted Freddy.

Suddenly, the blank spheres rolled back and the eyes flipped in, staring straight down at her with an impassive, plastic gaze. Charlie screamed and jerked back. Something behind her snapped, lashing a whiplike piece of metal into her side. She froze in terror. *No, please no.* Nothing else triggered, and after a moment she cautiously settled herself in place, trying not to meet the shiny blue eyes above her. Her side where the piece of metal had hit her shocked with pain each time she breathed. She wondered, alarmed, if a rib had broken. Before she could be sure, the animatronic lurched to the side again, and Charlie fell with it, hitting her head so hard that the blow reverberated through her body. Her vision darkened, closing to a tunnel, and as she faded into unconsciousness again, all she could see were Freddy's watching eyes.

John's lungs were beginning to burn, his legs turning rubbery as they ran on and on through the forest. They had been running for what felt like hours, though he knew it couldn't be. That was just his exhaustion playing tricks on his mind. The trail had faded. When they entered the forest, the trees had been their guide. They followed ripped, ragged bark and broken branches, and even torn roots where massive, careless feet had stepped.

But the signs had grown farther between, then stopped entirely. Now John ran on in the direction the creatures seemed to have been headed.

Truthfully, he might have been lost.

As he darted around trees, trekked up and down small hills, and stumbled on uneven ground, John began to lose his sense of direction entirely. Ahead of him, Jessica ran confidently onward. He followed, but for all he knew they could be running in an endless circle.

Behind him, Clay's steps were slowing, his breathing heavy. Jessica, a few paces ahead, doubled back, jogging in place as she waited for them to catch up.

"Come on, guys, we're almost there!" she said energetically.

"Almost where?" John asked, struggling to keep his tone even.

"I'm just trying to be encouraging," she said. "I was on my high school cross-country team for three years."

"Well, I was always more of a heavy-lifter, you know," John panted, suddenly defensive.

"Clay, come on, you can do it!" Jessica called. John glanced back. Clay had stopped running and was doubled over with his hands on his knees, taking gasping breaths. With relief, John slowed to a walk and turned back. Jessica let out a frustrated sound and followed him to Clay.

"Are you all right?" John asked.

The older man nodded, waving him back. "Fine," he said. "Go ahead, I'll catch up."

"There's nowhere to 'go ahead' to," John said. "We're running blind. When's the last time you saw tracks?"

"A while back," Clay said, "but they were heading this way, and it's all we have to go on."

"But it's nothing to go on!" John's voice rose in frustration. "There's no reason to think they went this way!"

"We're losing them," Jessica said urgently. She was still running in place, her ponytail bouncing like a little nervous animal behind her. Clay shook his head.

"No, we've already lost them."

Jessica stopped running, but she kept shifting from one foot to the other. "So now what?"

Something rustled in the trees ahead of them. Jessica grabbed John's arm, then released it quickly, looking embarrassed. The sound came again, and John started toward it, raising a hand to signal the others to stay. He made his way cautiously through the trees, glancing back once and noting that Jessica and Clay were close behind, despite his attempt to keep them back.

A few feet farther on, the trees broke into an open field; they had reached the far side of the woods. Jessica gasped, and a split second later John saw it. Halfway across the clearing a figure stood in the darkness. It was almost featureless and flat, scarcely distinct from the shadows. John squinted, trying to get hold of the image, to assure himself he was really seeing it. Heavy, black electrical wires stretched above the field like a canopy, but besides the wires, the field was clear. Though it was dark, there was no way for them to sneak closer to the figure without being seen.

So John straightened his shoulders and began to walk slowly and openly toward it.

The field was untended, and tall grass brushed John's knees as he walked. Behind him, Jessica and Clay made rustling sounds with every step. The wind whipped the grass against their legs, blowing more ferociously with each step they took. Almost halfway across the field, John stopped, puzzled. The figure was still there, but it seemed as far away from them as when they'd started. He glanced back at Jessica.

"Is it moving?" she whispered. He nodded and started walking again, not taking his eyes from the shadowy figure. "John, it looks like . . . Freddy?"

"I don't know what it is," John answered cautiously. "But I think it wants us to follow."

I can't breathe. Charlie coughed and gagged, coming suddenly awake. She lay on her back, dirt pouring down onto her. It filled her mouth, clogging her nose and covering her eyes. She spat, shaking her head and blinking rapidly. She tried to raise her hands but couldn't move them. She remembered suddenly that they were trapped inside the arms of the suit and would be mutilated if she struggled to free them.

Buried alive! I'm being buried alive. She opened her mouth to scream and more dirt fell in, hitting the back of her throat and making her gag again. Charlie could feel her pulse in her throat, choking her from the inside as surely as the dirt from outside. Her heart was beating too fast and she felt lightheaded. She took faster breaths, trying in vain to fill her lungs, but she only stirred up the dirt and inhaled it. She spat, gargling at the back of her throat to catch it before she swallowed, and turned her head to the side, away from the soil that fell like rain. She took a shuddering breath that shook her chest, and then another. *You're hyperventilating*, she told herself sternly. *You have to stop. You have to calm down. You need your head clear.* The last thought came in Aunt Jen's voice. She stared at the now-familiar side of the suit and took deep breaths, ignoring the dirt settling in her ear and sliding down her neck, until her fluttering heart slowed, and she could breathe almost normally again.

Charlie closed her eyes. *You have to get your arms free.* She concentrated all her attention on her left arm. Her T-shirt left the skin of her arms bare against the suit, so she could feel everything that touched her. With her eyes still closed, Charlie began to draw a map. *There's something at the shoulder joints on either side, and a space just below. Spikes in a line all the way down to my elbow on the outside, and the inside has—what is that?* She rocked her arm slowly, gently, back and forth against the objects, trying to envision them. *They're not spring locks.* She froze, focusing again on the place where the arm joined the torso. *THOSE are spring locks. Okay, I'll get to it. Hands.* She flexed her fingers slightly: the sleeves were wide, and her hands—which reached roughly to the creature's elbows—were less constrained than anything else. She spat out dirt again, trying not to notice that it was still pouring in steadily, piling up all around her. *Breathe. While you still can.* She clenched her jaw, envisioning the sleeve that encased her arm, and slowly began to work her way out of it. She dipped down her shoulder, rotated forward, held her breath—and pulled her arm three inches out. Charlie let out a shuddering sigh. Her shoulder was free of the spring locks. *That was the hardest part. The rest of my arm won't touch them if I'm careful.* She kept going, avoiding the things she thought might snap or stab her. When she was halfway out, her elbow at the shoulder seam, she twisted her arm too quickly and heard a snap. She stared horrified at the suit's shoulder, but it wasn't the spring lock. Something smaller inside had triggered, and now she could feel the burn of a fresh cut. *Okay. It's okay.* She got back to work.

Minutes later, her arm was free. She flexed it back and forth in the small space, feeling a little like she had never had an arm before. *Now the other one.* She wiped her face with her hand, smearing away the dirt, closed her eyes, and began again with her right arm.

The second sleeve took less time to get out of, but fatigue and the growing mounds of dirt around her made Charlie careless. Twice she triggered small mechanisms that bruised her painfully, but didn't break her skin. She yanked herself free too fast, bumping the spring locks and only barely snatching her hand away before they cracked open. The arm jumped and jolted as the robotic skeleton inside it unfolded with a noise like firecrackers. Charlie clutched her hand to her chest, cradling it against her pounding heart as she watched. *That could have been . . . It wasn't. It wasn't me. Focus. Legs.*

Her legs weren't pinned in place as her arms had been. They'd simply been awkwardly positioned, wedged between metal rods that ran through the body of the mascot. Without the weight of her body resting on them, she was able to maneuver. Cautiously, Charlie lifted her right leg into the air, pulling it over the rod and into the center of the torso. Nothing triggered, and she did the same with her left.

Her limbs freed, Charlie looked down the length of the animatronic, at the door to the chest cavity. The latch was on the outside, but these creatures were old; their parts were rusted and weak. She reached out and put her hands against the metal, feeling for springs and other devices. She couldn't quite see from where her head was stuck, and she couldn't move down safely. *Unless.*

The dirt had piled up almost a foot on either side of her head, and it covered the lower half of her body. Charlie abandoned the door momentarily, and began to slowly move the dirt. She lifted her head slightly and brushed at the mound with her hands, pushing soil into the space she left. She rocked her body back and forth, using her hands to sweep dirt under her, until she lay on it like a thin bed. It wouldn't protect her from the suit if she triggered it, but it would give her an extra cushion, make it slightly harder for her to jostle something and be skewered alive. She glanced at the arm of the suit that had been triggered, now filled with metal spines and hard plastic parts. A shiver went down her back.

Now she inched down until she could see the chest plates, placed her hands in the center, and began to push upward with all her might. After a moment they came apart and a rush of dirt cascaded in. Charlie coughed and turned her head, but she kept pushing as the dirt rained down on her. She managed to get the plates a foot apart, then crouched beneath them and paused for a moment. *How deep am I?* she thought for the first time. If she'd been buried six feet down, she might be escaping only to suffocate in the home stretch. *What else am I going to do?* Charlie closed her eyes, took a deep breath, and held it. Then she pressed herself up to the doors and began to claw her way out of the grave.

The dirt wasn't packed tightly, but it still took effort: she scratched and scraped at it with her bare hands, wishing for a tool as her fingernails split and bled. As she hacked at the dirt, her lungs began to burn and clench, trying to get her to breathe. She scrunched her face up as hard as she could and scratched harder. *Are you out there? I'm coming, but help me, please, I have to get out of this. Please, I can't die here, buried ali—*

Her hand broke the surface, and she drew it back in shock. *Air.* She gasped gratefully until she no longer felt starved of oxygen. Then she closed her eyes and battered her fists at the tiny hole above her head, breaking the sides until it was large enough to wriggle through. Charlie stood up, her feet still planted in the chest cavity of the suit. There had been little more than a foot of dirt covering her. She braced her feet on the half-open doors and clambered out of the hole, hauling herself up. She collapsed beside it, shaking with exhaustion. *You're not safe yet*, she scolded herself. *You have to get up.* But she couldn't bring herself to move. She stared, horrified, at the hole she had escaped from, her face wet with tears.

Time passed, minutes or hours; she lost track completely. Finally mustering her strength, Charlie pushed herself up to a sitting position, wiping her face. She couldn't tell where she was, but the air was cool and still. She was indoors, and somewhere in the distance was the sound of rushing water. With the adrenaline gone, her head ached again, throbbing along with her heartbeat. It wasn't just her head—everything hurt. She was covered in bruises, her clothing was stained with blood, and now that she wasn't suffocating, she was aware again of the stabbing sensation in her rib cage every time she inhaled. Charlie prodded her ribs, trying to feel if anything seemed out of place. The bruises were already brightly colored, especially where parts of the suit had struck her, but nothing was broken.

Charlie stood up, the pain receding enough to at least move and get her bearings. As she looked around, her blood went cold.

It was Freddy Fazbear's Pizza.

It can't be. The wave of panic rose again. She glanced around wildly, backing up, away from the hole in the ground. *The tables, the carousel in the corner, the stage—the tablecloths are blue.* "The tablecloths at Freddy's weren't blue," she said, but her relief was quickly washed away by confusion. *Then what is this place?*

The dining room was larger than the one at Freddy's, though there were fewer tables. The floor was black and white tile, except for large patches where the tiles were missing, revealing plots of packed dirt. It was oddly incongruous with everything else, which looked finished and brand-new, if dusty. As she turned to the opposite wall, she saw that she was being watched. Large plastic eyes stared back from the dark, glaring down at Charlie, seeming to identify her as an intruder. Fur and beaks and eyes stood poised like a small army halfway up the wall.

For a long moment she stood stock-still, bracing herself. But the animatronics didn't move. Charlie took a small step to one side, then the other; the eyes did not track her. The creatures looked forward, unseeing, at their fixed points. Some of their faces were animals, and some seemed to be painted like clowns. Others appeared disturbingly human.

Charlie moved closer and saw what it was they were perched on. All along the wall, arcade games and carnival attractions were lined up, each with its guardian beast or a giant face mounted on top. Their mouths were wide open, as if they were all laughing and cheering some invisible spectacle. As Charlie peered through the darkness, she saw that the animals were unnaturally posed, their bodies twisted in ways no animal should be able to twist. She scanned the wide-mouthed faces again and shivered. With their bodies so torturously bent, they looked like they were screaming in pain.

Charlie took deep breaths. As she calmed herself she realized that there was music playing through the speakers overhead. It was quiet; familiar, but she couldn't name it.

She approached the nearest of the games. A massive, contorted birdlike creature with a wide, curved beak presided over a large cabinet with a fake pond. Rows of ducks sat still in paper water, waiting for rubber balls to knock them down. Charlie looked up again at the creature perched on top of the game. Its wings stretched wide, and its head was thrown upward in the midst of an elaborate dance. It cast a shadow in front of the game, right where the player would stand. Charlie turned, not stepping any closer. Besides the duck pond, there were three arcade consoles lined up next to one another, their screens dusty. Three large chimpanzees squatted atop them, the tips of their toes gripping the edges above the screen. Their arms were raised, frozen in motion, and their teeth were bared in mirth, rage, or fear. Charlie stared for a moment at the teeth; they were long and yellow.

Something about the arcade games nagged at her. She looked them up and down carefully, but nothing tripped her memory. None were turned on, and none of them were games she had ever seen before. She wiped the dust from the screen of the central console, revealing a glossy black screen. Her face, distorted in the curved glass, showed only a little bruising and a few visible cuts. Charlie self-consciously smoothed her hair.

Wait. At Freddy's Pizza, ghostly images had been burned into the arcade screens after years of play. She pressed a couple of buttons experimentally. They were stiff and shiny—untouched.

"That's why it feels so empty," she said to the chimp above her. "No one's ever been here, have they?" The great ape didn't respond. Charlie glanced around. There was a doorway to her left, the bluish glow of an unseen black light emanating from the room beyond. Charlie went toward the light, through the door, and into another room of games and attractions. Here, too, they were all guarded by mascots, some more identifiable than others. Charlie staggered for a moment and put her hand on her forehead. "Strange," she whispered, regaining her balance. She looked back the way she'd come. *It must be the light making me dizzy*, she thought.

"Hello?" someone called faintly in the distance. Charlie whirled around as if someone had shouted in her ear. She held her breath, waiting for it to come again. The voice had been high and scared, a child. The sudden impression of life in this place shook her, as if waking her from a dream.

"Hello!" she called back. "Hello, are you all right? I won't hurt you." She glanced around the room. The sound of rushing water was louder here, making it hard to judge how far away the voice had come from. She moved quickly through the room, ignoring the wide-eyed creatures and the strange and garish games. A simple, skirted table in the corner caught her attention, and she went to it swiftly. Charlie crouched down, careful to keep her balance, and lifted the cloth. Eyes stared back at her and she startled, then steadied herself.

"It's okay," she whispered, flipping the cloth up over the table. The glimmer of the eyes faded with the rush of light. There was no one there after all.

Charlie put her hands on her forehead and pressed hard for a moment, trying to ward off the growing pain in her temples.

She went through another door, now unsure which way she'd come from, and discovered the source of the running water. Springing from the center of the wall to her left was a waterfall. It cascaded down over a rock face protruding several feet out, and joined with a riverbed below. The water rushed from a wide pipe only partly concealed by the rock.

The stream below was maybe three feet wide. It crossed the room, splitting the floor in two, and disappeared into the open mouth of a cave.

Charlie watched it for a moment, mesmerized by the water. After a moment, she noticed a narrow gap in the rock face behind the waterfall, just big enough for a person to walk through. "Hello?" Charlie called again, but only half-heartedly; here the white noise of the water was louder than anywhere else. She realized after a second that it was a recording, overpowering the sound of the actual water.

She surveyed the rest of the room: except for the water-fall and the little river it was empty, but she noticed the floor had a gray border. *No, it's a path.* It was narrower than a sidewalk, paved with square gray cobblestones. It ran along-side the curved wall, tracing the way to the waterfall, and led through a narrow passage under the fall itself. Charlie crouched down to touch the stones: they felt like hard plastic given a rough finish. The path was likely there for a time when the place would be filled with other attractions; she could probably just walk straight across the room. *Probably.*

Charlie stepped onto the cobblestones carefully, expecting them to give way under her weight, but they held. The man-ufactured coarseness of the rocks' surface was sharp—it hurt a little to walk on it. Charlie dutifully followed the walkway, keeping close to the wall. She had a vague sense that step-ping off onto the open floor might be dangerous.

When she reached the waterfall, she went to the gap and gingerly touched the rock surface. It was the same plastic as the cobblestones. Like the path, the cliff was hard plastic, solid, but because it looked like rocks it felt insubstantial when she touched it. Charlie took her hands away and wiped them on her jeans. She stepped carefully sideways, scooting through the hole behind the waterfall. The cavern was only a few feet long, but she stopped for a moment at the center. She felt trapped in the darkness, though she could see light on either side. *Trapped.* Her chest tightened, and she screwed her eyes shut. *Calm down. Focus on what's around you*, she thought. Charlie took a long, steadying breath and listened.

Standing beneath the waterfall, the tape recording was muffled. She thought she could hear the water itself, rushing over her head and spilling down in front of her, though she couldn't see it. There was something else as well, quiet but distinct. From above her, or maybe behind, Charlie could hear the cranking of gears. A machine was churning the water, keeping it flowing in a giant cycle, making the whole thing work. The sound of the machine at work calmed her; the rising panic subsided, and she opened her eyes.

She took another sideways step, moving closer to the light, and stubbed her toe on something hard. A shock of pain jolted her. The object tipped over, making a sloshing sound as it fell. Grinding her teeth, she waited a moment for her toe to stop hurting, then maneuvered herself into a crouch. It was a fuel can. *For the waterfall*, she realized as the machinery ground on overhead. There were several more, all neatly arranged along the wall, but this one had been in the middle of the path. If she had been going faster, she would have fallen over it. Charlie set it firmly beside the others, and stepped quickly into the other half of the room.

"Hello?" The voice again, this time a little louder. Charlie stood up straight, immediately on alert. It had come from ahead. She didn't respond this time but moved carefully toward it, staying on the path and keeping close to the wall.

The hallway opened out into another room. The lights were dimmer here. In the corner opposite Charlie was a small carousel, but there seemed to be little else. Charlie scanned the room, and then her breath caught. The child was there, motionless, almost hidden in the shadows in the far corner of the room.

Charlie approached slowly, apprehensive of what she might find. She blinked and shook her head hard, her dizziness resurging. The room seemed to spin around her. *Who are you? Are you all right?* she wanted to ask but kept silent. She stepped closer, and the figure came into focus. It was just another animatronic, or perhaps just a normal doll, made to look like a little boy selling balloons.

He was perhaps four feet tall, with a round head and a round body, his arms almost as long as his stout legs. He wore a red-and-blue striped shirt, and a matching propeller beanie on his head. He was made of plastic, but his shiny face had something old-fashioned about it. Its features mimicked fairy-tale dolls carved from wood. His nose was a triangle and his cheeks were made rosy with two raised circles of dusky pink. His blue eyes were enormous, wide, and staring, and his mouth was open in a grin that bared all his even white teeth. His hands were fingerless balls, each gripping an object. In one he held a red and yellow balloon nearly half his size on a stick. In the other he raised a wooden sign reading BALLOONS!

He was nothing like the creatures Charlie's father had made, nothing even like the animatronics that had kidnapped her. They were horrible, but she recognized them as twisted copies of her father's work. This boy was something new. She circled around him, tempted to poke and prod, but she held back. *Don't chance triggering anything.*

"You're not so bad," Charlie murmured, cautious not to take her eyes off him. He just kept grinning, wide-eyed, into the darkness. Turning her attention to the rest of the room, Charlie looked thoughtfully at the carousel, the only thing there besides the boy. She was too far away to make out the animals.

"Hello?" said the voice, right behind her. She spun back just in time to see the boy turn toward her with a single, swinging step. Charlie screamed and ran back the way she came from, but beneath her feet the dirt began to stir. It jolted, as if something were bumping upward. She scrambled backward as the dirt rose again, and something broke through the surface.

Charlie ran for the carousel, the only cover in the room. She ducked behind it, lying down on her stomach so her body would be hidden behind its base. She stared down at the ground and listened to muffled scratches and beating sounds as some creature climbed free of its grave. The spinning sensation took hold of her again. The black-and-white tiles swam beneath her. She tried to push herself up to peek over the carousel, but her head felt leaden. The weight of it held her down, threatening to pin her back to the ground. *There's something wrong with this room.* Charlie gritted her teeth and yanked her head up; she scrambled to her feet, steadying herself against the carousel, and ran back the way she came, not looking back.

The room with the games and the harsh black light was dizzying as well, and it sprawled out in all directions. Everything seemed farther apart than before, the walls miles away. Her mind was numb. She fumbled to remember where she was, unable to tell which way was which. She stumbled forward, and another mound of earth rose ahead of her. Something glimmered. Her eyes lit on the silhouettes of arcade machines, their reflective surfaces acting as beacons in the dark.

She staggered toward them, her head swaying, so heavy she could hardly stay upright. The walls were crawling with activity. Small things skittered disjointedly all over the ceiling, but she couldn't see what they were—they were wriggling *under* the paint. The surface undulated chaotically. There was a strange ringing in the air, and though she only now registered it, she realized it had been sounding all along. She stopped in her tracks and looked desperately for the source, but her vision was clouding and her thoughts were slow. She could barely name the things she saw. *Rectangle*, she thought fuzzily. *Circle. No. Sphere.* She looked from one indistinct shape to another, trying to remember what they were called. The effort distracted her from staying on her feet, and she fell to the ground again with a hard thud. Charlie was sitting upright, but her head dragged at her, threatening to pull her over.

Hello? A voice called again. She put her hands on her head, forcing it back, and looked up to see several children standing around her, all with plump little bodies and broad smiling faces. *Sammy?* She moved toward them instinctively. They were blurred, and she couldn't see their features. She blinked, but her vision didn't clear. *Don't trust your senses. Something is wrong.*

"Stay back!" Charlie screamed at them. She forced herself unsteadily to her feet and stumbled toward the shadows cast by the arcade towers. There, at least, she might be hidden from whatever worse things lurked in the room.

The children went with her, rushing in trails of color around her and sweeping in and out of view. They seemed more to float than walk. Charlie kept her eyes on the towers; the children were distracting, but she knew there was something worse nearby. She could hear the sickening grind of metal, and plastic twisting, and a rasping noise she recognized. Sharp feet scraped against the floor, digging grooves into the tile.

She crouched low, fixing her eyes on the nearest open door, and was struck with a certainty that this was the way she had come. She crawled desperately toward it, moving as fast as she could without fully standing. Finally, she collapsed under her own weight and lay flat on the tile again. *You have to get up, now!* Charlie let out a scream and clambered to her feet. She ran headlong into the next room, barely keeping her balance, and skidded to a stop. The room was full of dining tables and carnival games; it was where she'd started, but something had changed.

All the eyes were tracking her. The creatures were moving, their skin stretching organically, their mouths snapping. Charlie ran for the dining table in the center of the room, the largest one with a tablecloth that almost reached the floor on all sides. She slid to the ground and crawled under it, curling herself into a ball and pulling her legs tight against her. For a moment, there was only silence, and then the voices began again. *Hello?* a voice called from somewhere nearby. The tablecloth rustled.

Charlie held her breath. She looked at the thin gap between the tablecloth and the floor, but she could see only a sliver of the black-and-white tile. Something shot by, too fast to see, and she gasped and drew back, forgetting to be silent. The cloth rustled again, swinging gently inward. Someone outside was prodding it. Charlie maneuvered herself onto her hands and knees, feeling as if she had too many arms and legs. The cloth moved again, and this time a swirl of color appeared and vanished in the gap. *The children.* They had found her. The tablecloth swung again, but now it was moving on all sides, jouncing up and down as the children brushed against it. The strange, colorful trails of movement appeared and vanished all around the edges of her hiding place, surrounding her like a wall of living paper dolls.

Hello? Hello? Hello? More than one spoke at a time now, but not in a chorus. Their voices overlapped until the word became a meaningless layer of sound, blurred like the floating children themselves.

She turned her face to the side. One of the children stared back—it was under the cloth and gazing at her with a fixed grin and motionless eyes. Charlie jumped up, banging her head on the tabletop. She looked around wildly. She was surrounded: a smiling, blurry face was staring at her from every side. *One, two, three, four, four, four.* She turned in an awkward circle on her hands and knees. Two of the children feinted at her, making little jumps as if they were about to spring. She turned again, and the next one leaped at her, swimming under the cloth in a bright streak of blue and yellow. Charlie froze. *What do I do?* She scrabbled at her sluggish brain, trying desperately to revive it. Another sweep of color whooshed at her, all purple, and her brain awoke: *RUN.*

Charlie scrambled to the tablecloth on her hands and knees and grabbed it, yanking it off the table as she stood. She threw it down behind her and ran, not looking back as someone called again, *Hello?*

She raced toward a sign propped up in the middle of the room, knocking it over behind her as she ran past. Then a shadow near the stage caught her attention, and she swerved. She tripped over a chair and just barely managed to catch herself on another table. Her head was still too heavy. It jerked her forward, and she shoved the table aside, managing to stay upright. She arrived at the stage, and in the shadow there was a door.

Charlie fumbled with the knob, but it was spongy, too soft to turn. She grabbed it with both hands, putting the whole force of her body behind it, and it moved at last: the door opened. She hurried through and slammed it shut behind her, feeling for some kind of latch. She found one and snapped it shut, and as she did her hand brushed a light switch.

A bulb flickered for a moment, then came on dimly, a single glowing strand of orange illuminating the room. Charlie stared at it for a minute, waiting for the rest of the light. No more appeared.

She leaned back against a cabinet beside the door and slid down to sit, putting her hands on her temples and trying to shove her head back to a normal size. The relative darkness steadied her. She stared down at the floor, hoping whatever was happening to her was almost over. She looked up, and the room shifted nauseatingly. *It's not over.* Charlie closed her eyes, took a deep breath of the stale air, and opened them again.

Fur. Claws. Eyes. She clapped a hand over her mouth to stop herself from screaming. A jolt of adrenaline cut briefly through the fuzziness. The room was full of creatures, but she couldn't make sense of them. The dark fur of a simian arm lay on the floor, inches from her feet, but out of it spilled coils and bare wire. The rest of the ape was nowhere to be seen.

There was something large and gray right in front of her, a torso with arms and webbed, amphibious hands, but there was no head. Instead, someone had balanced a large cardboard box where the neck would have been. Past the torso were standing figures, a phalanx of shadows. As she stared at them, they resolved into something comprehensible. They were unfinished mascots, as distorted as the ones outside.

A rabbit stood at the back. Its head was brown like a jack-rabbit and its ears were swept back, but its eyes were just empty holes. The rabbit's body was hunched to the side, and its arms were short, held up as if in surrender. Two metal frames stood in front of it. One was headless, and the other topped with the head of a red-eyed, slavering black dog, whose fangs stuck out from its mouth. Charlie kept her eyes on it for a moment, but it didn't move. Beside it—

Charlie cringed and ducked her head, covering her face with her arms. Nothing happened. Cautiously, she lowered her hands and looked again.

It was Freddy—the misshapen Freddy that had been buried. Charlie glanced at the door, then back at Freddy. He stared straight ahead, his eyes blank and his hat askew. *It can't be him*, she told herself. *It's just another costume*. But she shrank back, trying to make herself smaller.

Something delicately stroked the top of her head. Charlie screamed and yanked herself away. She turned to see a disembodied human arm on the shelf above where she'd been sitting. Its hand stuck out at just the right height to brush her head. Other arms were stacked beside it and on top of it, some covered in fur and others not. Some had fingers, some simply ended, cut off at what would have been the wrist. The other shelves were stacked with similar things: one with pelts of fur, another with piles of detached feet. One just had dozens of extension cords tangled up in an ugly nest.

From outside the door Charlie heard the voice again. *Hello?* The doorknob rattled. She squeezed past the mutilated arcade games and chopped-off parts, gritting her teeth as she crawled over soft things that squelched beneath her weight. As she stepped back, her shoulder crashed into one of the standing metal frames, the headless one. It rocked on its ungrounded feet, threatening to topple. She tried to pull away, but the frame followed, swaying for a moment as she fought to free her hands. She yanked them back and ducked as more metal frames came crashing to the ground.

She squatted down beside one of the large arcade cabinets. The plastic casing was cracked so badly the words and pictures were entirely obscured. Right beside her, inches away, were Freddy's stocky legs. Charlie huddled down, pressing against the game as if she could blend in with it. *Don't turn around*, she thought, eyeing the motionless bear. The dim light seemed to be moving like a spotlight. It glinted off the dog's red eyes, then the gleaming tusk, then off something sharp-cornered at the back of the rabbit's hollow socket.

Just out of her line of sight, something moved. Charlie whipped her head around, but there was nothing there. From the corner of her eye, she saw the rabbit straighten its spine. She turned frantically back toward it but found it hunched in its same agonized posture as before. Slowly,

Charlie looked around her in a half circle, keeping her back pressed against the console.

Hello? The doorknob rattled again. She closed her eyes and pressed her fists to her temples. *No one's here, no one's here.* Something rustled in front of her, and Charlie's eyes snapped open. Scarcely breathing, she watched as Freddy came alive. A sickly twisting sound filled the room, and Freddy's torso began to turn. *Hello?* Her eyes shifted to the door for a split second, and when she looked back again Freddy was still. *I have to get out of here.*

She took a moment to measure the path, looking first to the door, then to Freddy in front of her, mapping a blurry route. At last she went, looking down at her hands and nothing else as she crawled steadily around the motionless legs of the standing animatronics, and past the half-bestial games. *Don't look up.* Something brushed against her leg as she passed it, and she pressed on, her head down. Then something grabbed her ankle.

Charlie screamed and flailed, trying to kick herself free, but the iron grip tightened. She looked frantically over her shoulder: Freddy was crouched behind her, the light glinting off his face and making him seem to smile. Charlie yanked her foot back with all her strength, and Freddy pulled even harder, dragging her closer. Charlie grabbed the leg of a pinball game and hoisted herself up to her knees. As Freddy tried again to drag her back, the game shook and rattled like it was about to fall. Clutching at it with all her might, Charlie jerked her body up and forward. Freddy's claws tore her skin as she wrenched herself free, and the pinball machine collapsed under her weight.

Freddy lurched forward. That horrible mouth unhinged again like an enormous snake. He crouched down, coming toward her in a sinuous motion. She scrambled over the broken game toward the door. Behind her, something rustled and scraped, but she didn't look back. Her hand on the doorknob, Charlie stopped as the room around her swayed. The noise behind her grew louder, closer, and she turned to see Freddy crawling toward her in a predatory crouch. His mouth was widening. Dirt poured out of it in a steady stream.

"Hello? Charlie?" came a voice from outside. But this voice was different; it wasn't the animatronic child. Charlie fumbled at the knob, the spinning sensation in her head worsening as Freddy came slowly, purposefully closer. The room swayed again, and her hand closed on the knob and turned it. She shoved the door open and stumbled into the light.

"Charlie!" someone cried, but she didn't look up. The sudden brightness was piercing, and she held up a hand to shield her eyes as she forced the door shut again. The ringing hadn't stopped while she was in the closet, but now it was louder. It filled her ears like a skewer, plunging into her swollen brain. She fell to her knees, wrapping her arms around her head, trying to protect it. "Charlie, are you okay?" Something touched her, and she shied away, her eyes screwed shut against the light. "Charlie, it's John," the voice said, cutting through the awful noise, and something in her went still.

"John?" she whispered, her voice raspy. The dust from the grave had settled in her throat.

"Yeah." She turned her head and peered up through the shield of her arms. Slowly, the blazing light calmed, and she saw a human face. *John.*

"Are you real?" she asked, uncertain what kind of answer would convince her. He touched her again, a hand on her arm, and she didn't pull away. She blinked, and her vision cleared a little. She looked up, feeling as if she were opening herself to attack. Her eyes lit on two more people, and her halting mind slowly named them. "Jessica . . . ? Clay?"

"Yeah," John said. She put her hand on his and tried to focus. She could see Jessica, who was doubled over, her hands over her own ears.

"The noise," Charlie said. "She hears the noise, too. Do you?" It grew louder, drowning out John's response, and Charlie grabbed his hand. *Real. This is real.* "The children!" she cried out suddenly, as a swath of undulating colors rose from underneath the tables. They flew, their feet not touching the ground, their bodies leaving comet-like trails of color behind them. "Do you see?" Charlie whispered to John.

"Jessica!" he shouted. "Look out!" Jessica straightened, dropping her hands, and yelled something indistinct. The children converged on her in a swarm, dancing around her, darting in close, then back out again, as if it were a game, or an ambush. Two rushed on Clay, who stared them down until they shriveled and swirled back to join the circle around Jessica.

"The lights!" Jessica cried, her voice rising above the painful ringing noise. "Clay, it's coming from the lights on the walls!" She pointed up, where Charlie could just make out a long row of decorative colored lights, evenly spaced.

A gunshot cut through the clamor, and Charlie gripped John's hand tighter. Jessica's hands were on her ears again. The children were still in motion, but it was a nervous, shimmering movement. They'd stopped in place. Clay stood with his back to them all, his gun pointed at the wall. Charlie watched, wide-eyed, as he took aim again, and shot out the bulb of the second light fixture. The room dimmed slightly, and he moved on to the third, then the next, then the next. As one shot rang out after another, Charlie's head began to equalize, like whatever stuff had filled her to the point of bursting was slowly being drained. The room darkened, one bulb at a time. *Bang.* She looked up at John, and his face was clear. "It's really you," she said, her voice still choked with dust. *Bang.*

"It's really me," he agreed.

Bang.

The children's shimmering slowed, giving glimpses of arms and legs and faces. Jessica took her hands from her ears.

Bang.

Clay shot the last light, and the children stopped shimmering. They wavered briefly on the edge of solidity, a sickening ripple of lights in a scattered harmony, and then they were still. The room was silent. It was still lit by the overhead lights, but all the others were dead. Jessica looked around her, bafflement and horror taking turns on her face. The children were no longer children. They were wind-up toys, plastic boys in striped shirts, wearing plastic smiles and propeller beanies, and offering balloons.

"Jessica, come here," Clay said in a low voice, holding out his hand. She stepped toward him, glancing warily at the balloon boys as she moved between them. He took her hand to help her through, as if he were pulling her out of a chasm. Charlie slowly let go of John's hand and put hers to her temples, checking to make sure everything was still there. Her head no longer ached; her vision was clear. Whatever had come over her was gone.

"Charlie," Jessica said. "Are you all right? What's going on in here? I feel . . . drugged."

"These things aren't real." Charlie steadied herself and slowly got to her feet. "I mean, they're real, but not how we're seeing them. This whole place is an illusion. It's twisted somehow. Those things . . ." She gestured toward the wall where Clay had shot out the lights. "Those things are like the disc we found. They emit some kind of signal that distorts how we see." Charlie shook her head. "We have to get out of here," she said. "There's something worse here than these."

She pushed over a balloon boy, and it toppled easily. Its head popped off as it hit the ground, and it rolled across the floor. *Hello?* it muttered, much quieter than before.

CHAPTER THIRTEEN

ohn prodded the plastic balloon boy's head with his toe. It rolled a little farther, but did not speak again.

"Charlie?" Jessica said shakily. "Where are they? The big ones."

"I don't know. My head is still spinning." Charlie glanced around quickly, then drew closer to the others as they surveyed the room. Everything had changed when Clay shattered the fixtures. The realistic beasts and vicious-looking creatures were gone, replaced with strange, hairless versions of themselves. They no longer had eyes, only smooth, raised bumps of blank plastic.

"They look like corpses," John said softly.

"Or some kind of mold," Clay said thoughtfully. "They don't look finished."

"It's the lights," Charlie said. "They were creating an illusion, like the chip."

"What are you talking about?" Jessica said. "What chip?"

"It's—it's some kind of transmitter, embedded in a disc," Charlie said. "It scrambles your brain, cluttering it with nonsense so that you see what you expect to see."

"Then why don't they look like that?" Clay pointed to posters on the walls depicting a very cheerful Freddy Fazbear with rosy cheeks and a warm smile.

"Or that." John had found another, depicting Bonnie jovially strumming a bright red guitar so shiny it looked like it was made from candy.

Charlie looked thoughtful for a moment. "Because we didn't come here first." She walked toward the posters. "If you were a little kid and you saw the cute commercials, then saw these posters and toys and all that stuff, then I think that's exactly what they would have looked like."

"Because you already have those images in your head," John said. He tore the Freddy poster off the wall and stared at it momentarily before letting it fall to the ground. "But we know better. We know they're monsters."

"And we're afraid of them," Charlie said.

"And so we're seeing them for exactly what they are," John concluded.

Clay went up to the arcade mascots again, his gun still

drawn. He walked back and forth in front of the displays, looking at them from different angles.

"How did you find me?" Charlie asked suddenly. "You showed up like the cavalry—just in time. How did you know I was here? How did you know any of this was here?"

No one answered right away. John and Jessica looked to Clay, who was casting his eyes around the room purposefully; he looked like he was searching for something specific. "We followed . . ." He trailed off.

Charlie looked at each of the three of them in turn. "Who?" she demanded. But just as she spoke, the closet door burst open, banging against the wall with a ringing clatter. The twisted Freddy who had taken Charlie came crashing out, his mouth still unhinged and swinging unnaturally. He was a nightmarish version of the Freddy they'd known as kids, with searing red eyes and the musculature of a monster. He turned his elongated head from side to side wildly, his jaw bouncing in place.

"Run!" Clay yelled, waving his arms and trying to usher them together toward the door. Charlie was rooted to the ground, unable to take her eyes off the maw of the beast.

"Wait!" Jessica cried suddenly. "Clay, these aren't possessed like the others—they're not the lost children!"

"What?" he said, momentarily stopping his frantic movement and looking thoroughly confused.

"Shoot it!" Jessica screamed. Clay clenched his jaw, then raised the gun and aimed at Freddy's gaping mouth. He fired once. The shot was only a few feet from Charlie's ear, and it was deafening. Freddy jerked back, the python-like jaw contracting, and for a split second his image blurred and distorted. The unnaturally stretched mouth began to close, but before it could, Clay fired again, three more times in quick succession. With each shot the creature seemed to glitch: it blurred, sputtering around the edges. Freddy's mouth curled in on itself, not quite closing but shrinking inward, as the bear hunched forward around its wounds. Clay fired one last time, aiming for Freddy's head. Finally, the animatronic toppled forward, a misshapen heap on the ground.

Freddy's image flickered like static on a television screen. The color faded from his fur, then everything that made him *Freddy* winked out, leaving only a smooth plastic figure in his place. It looked like the rest of the animals in the room, a blank mannequin stripped of its characteristics. Charlie approached the thing that had been Freddy cautiously. The ringing in her ears was beginning to fade. She crouched down next to the creature, tilting her head to the side.

"It's not like the other mascots from Freddy's," she said. "These aren't made of fur and fabric, they're made of us—by twisting our minds." The words came out with a revulsion she hadn't expected.

"Charlie," John said softly. He stepped forward, but she ignored him. She touched the creature's smooth skin. It felt like something between plastic and human skin: a strange, malleable substance that was a little too soft, a little too slick. The feeling of it made her nauseous. Charlie leaned over the body, ignoring her disgust, and plunged her fingers into one of the bullet holes. She dug around in the slippery, inorganic stuff of the chest cavity, pretending not to hear Jessica and Clay's protests, and then she found it. Her fingers touched the disc, which was bent in half, almost broken. Charlie pried out a second piece of metal that was wedged beside it.

She stood up and held it out to the others; a bullet rested in her palm.

"You shot the chip," she said. "You killed the illusion."

No one spoke. In the momentary quiet, Charlie was suddenly aware of the racket they had just made, in this place so accustomed to stillness. The silence was broken by a clicking sound: the noise of claws on tile.

They all whirled to see, and from what had appeared to be a dark and empty corner, a wolflike figure split away from the shadows and stalked toward them, upright but hunched forward, as if uncertain whether to walk as a beast or a human.

They backed away as one. Charlie saw Clay about to trip on Freddy's collapsed body. She shouted, "Look out!" He stopped, turning to see, and his eyes widened at something behind Charlie.

"There!" he cried, and fired a shot into the dark. They turned: an eight-foot, misshapen Bonnie, the rabbit counterpart to the creature on the floor, was blocking the doorway behind them. Its head was too large for its body, with eyes glowing white-hot in the dark. Its mouth was open, revealing several rows of gleaming teeth. Clay fired again, but the bullet had no effect.

"How many bullets do you have left?" John said, measuring up the two threats still in the room.

Clay fired off three more shots at Bonnie, then lowered the gun.

"Three," he said dryly. "I had three." From the corner of her eye, Charlie saw John and Jessica draw closer together, moving a little behind Clay. She stayed where she was as the others retreated, transfixed by the two advancing figures: the wolf and the rabbit. She started to walk toward them.

"Charlie," John said with a warning tone. "What are you doing? Come back!"

"Why did you bring me here?" Charlie asked, looking from one creature to the other. Her chest was tight and her eyes ached, like she'd been holding back tears for hours. "What do you want from me?" she shouted. They looked back at her with implacable plastic eyes. "What is this place? *What do you know about my brother?*" she screamed, her throat raw. She flung herself at the wolf, hurtling toward the gigantic beast, as if she could tear it apart with her bare hands. Someone caught her by the waist. Human hands lifted her up and pulled her back, and Clay spoke quietly into her ear.

"Charlie, we need to go, *now.*" She pulled herself out of his grasp, but remained where she was. Her breath was unsteady. She wanted to scream until her lungs gave out. She wanted to close her eyes and sit very still, and never emerge from the darkness.

Instead she looked again from Bonnie to the nameless wolf and asked, her voice so calm it chilled her to hear it, "Why do you want me?"

"They don't care about you. I'm the one that brought you here." A voice spoke from the same shadowed corner the wolf had emerged from. The rabbit and the wolf straightened their posture, as if responding to the speaker's command.

"I know that voice," Jessica whispered. A figure began to limp forward, obscured by darkness. No one moved. Charlie realized she was holding her breath, but she didn't hear anyone else breathing in the silence, either, just the uneven shuffle of whatever was coming. Whatever it was, it was the size of a man. Its body was contorted, sloping to one side as it lurched toward the group.

"You have something that belongs to me," said the voice, and then the figure stepped into the light.

Charlie gasped and heard John's sharp intake of breath. "Impossible," Charlie whispered. She felt John move up to stand beside her, but she didn't dare take her eyes off the man who stood before them.

His face was dark, the color mottled, and it was swollen with fluid; cheeks that had been hollow were now distended with the bloat of decay. His eyes were bloodshot, the burst capillaries threading through eyeballs that looked just a little too translucent. Something inside them had gone bad, jelly-like. At the base of his neck, Charlie could see two pieces of metal gleaming. They extended from within his neck, rectangular lumps standing out from his mottled skin. He wore what had once been a mascot suit of yellow fur, though what remained was now green with mold.

"Dave?" Jessica breathed.

"Don't call me that," he snarled. "I haven't been Dave for a long time." He held out his new hands: blood-soaked and forever sealed inside a rotting suit.

"William Afton, then? Of Afton Robotics?"

"Wrong again," he hissed. "I've accepted the new life that you gave me. You've made me one with my creation. My name is Springtrap!" The man who had once been Dave cried the name with a hoarse glee, then scrunched his gnarled face back into a glare. "I'm more than Afton ever was, and *far* more than Henry."

"Well, you smell terrible," Jessica quipped.

"Ever since Charlie remade me, set me free to my destiny, I've been master of all these creatures." He crooked his fingers and made a sharp gesture forward. Bonnie and the wolf took two steps forward, in unison. "See? All the animatronics are linked together; it was a system designed to control the choreography for the shows. Now, I control the system. I control the choreography. All of this belongs to me."

Springtrap shuffled forward, and Charlie shrank back. "I owe you both another debt of gratitude as well," he said. "I was imprisoned in that tomb beneath the stage, scarcely able to move, only able to see through the eyes of my creatures."

He gestured at the two who stood behind him. "But for all that I could see, I was trapped. Eventually *they* would have broken me out, but having you do it yourself was a delightful surprise." He met Charlie's eyes, and a muscle twitched in her cheek.

Get away from me, don't come any closer. As if reading her thoughts, he sidled nearer to her. She would have felt his breath on her face, if he still breathed.

Springtrap raised a bent hand. The fabric suit was ragged, revealing his human skin through the gaps. She could see the places where metal pins and rods had buried themselves alongside his bones and tendons, into a rusted shadow-skeleton. He touched the back of his hand to Charlie's face, stroking her cheek like a beloved child. From the corner of her eye, she saw John start forward.

"No, it's okay," she forced herself to say.

"I won't hurt your friends, but I need something from you."

"You have to be kidding," she said, her voice brittle.

His mouth twisted into something that grotesquely resembled a smile.

John heard a faint click, and turned just in time to see Clay loading one bullet quietly into his gun. Clay shrugged. "You never know when a corpse may wander out of the shadows wearing a rabbit suit." He raised his arm, steadied himself, and fired.

Springtrap recoiled. "Kids!" Clay shouted, "the door!" Charlie jerked her eyes away from Springtrap almost painfully, as if he had been exerting some hypnotic force on her. Bonnie had abandoned the exit, leaving it clear. Clay, John, and Jessica began to run. Charlie glanced back, reluctant to go, then joined the others.

They ran back the way they'd come from, Clay leading the way as they wound through the carnival games and looming, featureless mascots. He strode purposefully ahead, as if he knew the way. Charlie remembered her question that no one had answered. *How did you find me?*

They were chased by sounds: scraping metal and the clack

of the wolf's claws. In the open space, the noises echoed strangely, seeming to come from every side. It was as if an army pursued them. Charlie quickened her step. She glanced up at John, seeking reassurance, but his eyes were on Clay ahead of them.

They reached the room with the waterfall, and again Clay knew the path. He headed directly for the passage beneath the cliff, where the water emerged. They pressed through it one by one. Clay and John were too tall to walk through without bending over, and Charlie felt a quick pang of relief. *The monsters won't fit.* Halfway through the passage, Clay paused, standing motionless in an awkward position. He craned his neck, studying something just out of view. "Clay!" Charlie hissed.

"I have an idea," he said. Two shadows emerged from the far side of the room. Jessica glanced at the black-lit tunnel beside them, ready to run for it. But Clay shook his head. Instead, he guided the group backward, none of them taking their eyes off the monsters. All that shielded them now was the river that bisected the room. The animatronics were approaching the water hesitantly. The wolf sniffed at it and shook his fur, and Bonnie simply bent down and stared. "Don't run," Clay said sternly.

"They can't cross that thing, right?" Charlie said.

As if responding to her cue, the two mascots stepped unsteadily into the river. Jessica gasped, and Charlie took an

involuntary step back. Slowly and deliberately, the animatronics continued toward them through the waist-high
water. The wolf slipped on the smooth bottom and fell. It
dunked completely under the water for a moment, before
scrambling to the side, thrashing violently. Bonnie lost his
footing as well but managed to grab the riverbank and steady
himself, then continued forward.

"That's not possible," Charlie said. Behind her came a peal
of laughter, and she whirled around.

It was Springtrap, his eyes scarcely visible, peering through
the black-lit tunnel nearby. "Was that your plan?" he said
incredulously. "Did you think *my* robots would be as poorly
designed as your father's?"

"Well then, I'm sure you made them fireproof as well!"
Clay called out. His voice reverberated in the cavernous,
empty room. Springtrap frowned, puzzled, then looked at
the water in the stream. It was glistening in the dim light,
color dancing on its surface in gleaming swirls, like—

"Gasoline." Charlie turned to face Springtrap. Open gas
cans lined the walls, some lying on their sides; all were empty.

Clay flicked a lighter and flung it into the water. The
top of the river caught fire, a flame billowing up like a
tidal wave, obscuring the animatronics in the middle. The
creatures struggled to the side of the river, emitting guttural,
high-pitched shrieks. They managed to crawl onto the bank,
but it was too late. Their illusions deactivated. Their plastic

skin was exposed, liquefying and falling from their bodies into little flaming pools on the floor. Charlie and the others watched as the dissolving creatures fell, writhing in agonized screams.

They all stood frozen, mesmerized by the gruesome spectacle. Then, from behind her, Charlie heard a quiet scraping sound. She whirled around to see Springtrap vanish into the mouth of the narrow, black-lit cave. She took off after him, running into the eerie light.

"Charlie!" Clay called. He began to chase her, but the flaming creatures had crawled across the floor—perhaps trying to reach their master, perhaps in mindless desperation—and now they blocked the mouth of the cave with their blazing remains. Charlie set her eyes on the path ahead. She couldn't afford to look back.

The passage was narrow, and it smelled damp and ancient. The floor felt like rock beneath her bare feet, but though it was uneven, it wasn't painful. The surface was worn and smooth. As soon as the dark of the cave closed over her, she felt a spark from her dreams: the tug of something so like her that it *was* her, blood calling to blood.

"Sammy?" she whispered. His name glanced off the cave walls, shrouding her in the sound of it. The absence inside her pulled her forward, drawing her toward the promise of completion. *It has to be you.* Charlie ran faster, following a call that came from deep inside her.

She could hear the distant echo of Springtrap's laughter at intervals, but she couldn't spot him ahead of her. Occasionally she thought she caught glimpses of him, but he was always gone before her eyes had time to focus in the disorienting glow of the black light. The cave twisted and turned until she had no idea which direction she was headed, but she ran on.

Charlie blinked as something moved at the corner of her eye, just out of sight. She shook her head and ran on, but then it happened again. An unnatural shape, neon-bright, slithered out of the wall and wriggled past her.

Charlie stopped, clapping a hand over her mouth so she wouldn't scream. The thing undulated up the wall, moving like an eel though it was climbing rock. When it reached the ceiling, it vanished, but she couldn't see a break in the rock where it might have gone. *Just keep going.* She started to run again, but suddenly more of them poured out of the seam at the base of the wall. Dozens of wriggling shapes swam and danced, moving along the floor of the cave like it was the floor of the sea. Three of them headed right for Charlie. They rippled over her feet and she screamed, then realized as they circled her, nibbling curiously at her toes, that she felt nothing. "You aren't real," she said. She kicked at them, and her foot passed straight through empty air: the creatures had vanished. Charlie gritted her teeth and ran onward.

Ahead of her, large glowing creatures like dancers made

of mist appeared and vanished one after another. They dashed across the passage, as if they were running along a path that just happened to intersect with this one. When Charlie was almost close enough to touch them, the one nearest sputtered and faded out. She ran on, listening for the sound of Springtrap's maniacal giggle, hoping that it was enough to guide her.

She turned a corner, then the passage angled sharply the other way. Charlie ran straight into the wall, catching herself with her hands at the last second. She spun around, looking for the way forward. The jolt had been enough to distract her. She couldn't tell which way she had come from. Charlie took a deep breath and closed her eyes. She could hear a soft voice in the air. *Left.* She started running again.

A burst of blue light nearly blinded her as a massive shape rose in the darkness. Charlie screamed, flinging herself back against the wall of the cave and throwing her arms up to shield her face. The thing before her was a gaping mouth full of teeth, all glowing blue. The enormous maw bore down over her.

"It's an illusion," Charlie whispered. She ducked and tried to roll away in the narrow space. Her shoulder struck a rock and her arm went numb. Charlie clutched it instinctively and looked up: nothing was there.

She pressed her back against the wall of the cave, taking deep breaths as feeling slowly returned to her arm. "It's another transmitter," she said quietly. "Nothing I see here is real." Her voice was thin in the rocky passage, but saying the words aloud was enough to make her stand again. She closed her eyes. The connection she had felt was growing stronger as she ran, the sense that she was running toward a missing piece of herself. It was unbearable, stronger than the urge to fight or flee from danger. It was greater than hunger, deeper than thirst, and it pulled at the core of her being. She could no more turn back than she could choose to stop breathing. She set off again, hurtling farther into the cavern.

Far in the distance, Springtrap's laughter still echoed.

"Charlie!" John called again, but it was hopeless. She was long out of sight, deep into the cave, and what remained of Bonnie and the wolf still burned in front of the opening.

"We have to go!" Clay shouted. "We can find another way!" Jessica grabbed John's arm and he gave in, following Clay toward the arcade entrance.

Just as they reached the door, the twisted Freddy lunged out of the shadows, almost falling to the ground. Jessica screamed and John froze, struck still at the sight of him. His illusion sputtered on and off in pieces. An arm flickered away, exposing the smooth plastic underneath. Then the fur returned and his torso went blank, revealing the gunshot holes, and the ugly, twisted metal beneath the plastic shell.

Worse was the face: not only was the illusion missing, but the material underneath. From his chin to his forehead, the left half of Freddy's face had been ripped away, revealing metal plates and gnarled wires. His left eye glowed red amid the exposed machinery, while his right eye was completely dark.

A noise behind them broke John from his horrified reverie. He looked back to see that Bonnie and the wolf had gotten to their feet, still smoldering. Their plastic casings had almost entirely melted away, still dribbling slowly off their bodies, but the robotic works beneath seemed intact. They approached steadily, moving into position, so that John, Clay, and Jessica were surrounded.

"Do you have any bullets left?" John asked Clay in a low voice. Clay slowly shook his head. He was turning in a cautious circle, shifting his gaze from one animatronic to the next, as if trying to gauge which would make the first strike.

Charlie ran steadily on, keeping her eyes on the path. She turned another corner and blinked. Something was glowing blue ahead of her. *It's not real*, she told herself. She paused for a moment, but the glowing shapes didn't move. She kept going, realizing as she drew closer that the passageway was widening, opening out finally into a small alcove where the blue glow became clear.

The floor was spotted with patches of mushrooms, their caps glowing an intense neon blue under the black light. She slowed her pace, went to the nearest grouping and bent to touch the mushrooms. She snapped her hand back in surprise when she felt a spongy substance. "They're real, sort of," she said.

"Yes," said a voice beside her ear, and then she was choking. Springtrap grabbed her by the neck, crushing her windpipe. Charlie only panicked for a moment before anger returned to her, giving her clarity. She reached her arm out forward as far as she could, then jammed it back, striking her elbow into his solar plexus with as much force as she could muster. His hands dropped from her throat and she leaped free, turning to face him as he clutched his injured gut.

"Things have changed since you died," Charlie said, surprised by the calm disdain in her voice. "For one thing, I've been doing sit-ups!"

"I think this is it," Jessica said quietly, spinning in place as the three monsters approached, leaving no avenue of retreat. John felt his chest clench, his body protesting the idea. But she was right. He put a hand on her shoulder.

"Maybe we can play dead," he said.

"I don't think we'll have to play," Jessica said resignedly.

"Backs together," Clay barked, and they backed up into a

tiny triangle, each facing one of the creatures. The wolf was crouched, ready to spring. John met its eyes. They were sputtering in and out: dark and malevolent, then completely blank. The thing drew back, and John steeled himself. Jessica grabbed his hand, and he clenched hers tightly. The wolf leaped—and then fell to the ground screeching as something knocked it viciously on its face. The figure, invisible in the shadows, grabbed the wolf's feet and yanked it backward, dragging it away from its human prey as it howled, scrabbling at the floor with its claws. It kicked its hind legs, freeing itself, and began its attack again. Jessica screamed, and John shouted with her, then watched, breathless, as the wolf was caught by its feet again. The thing that held it flipped it onto its back and jumped on top of it. The new predator paused for an instant, meeting their eyes with a silver glow, and Jessica gasped.

"Foxy," John breathed. As if spurred on by hearing his name, Foxy plunged his hook into the wolf's chest and began to tear at its exposed machinery. The screeches of metal ripping apart metal ground at their ears. Foxy continued to dig furiously, burrowing into the wolf as wires and parts fell from the sky. He snapped his jaws in the air, then tore at the wolf's stomach, wrenching out its insides and flinging them aside with a brutal efficiency. The wolf was overpowered, its limbs flailing helplessly before falling heavily to the ground.

Behind them came another inhuman scream. John whipped around in time to see the fire-ravaged Bonnie on its stomach, being dragged steadily into the shadows. Its eyes blinked on and off in a panicked, meaningless pattern. It screamed again as, with a horrible grinding sound, it was torn to pieces by whatever lurked in the shadows. Pieces of metal and shredded plastic scattered across the floor, skittering out in front of the prone rabbit, so that it could see the remnants of its own lower half. It screamed again, anchoring its claws into the tile in a last, futile defense, only to be pulled screeching into the dark as though through a grinder. In the shadows, four lights glowed. John blinked, realizing they were eyes. He nudged Jessica.

"I can see them," he whispered. "Chica and Bonnie! *Our* Chica and Bonnie!" Beside the river, Foxy had torn the wolf's limbs from its body. He leaped from the ravaged torso and took an attack posture toward the large, twisted Freddy, which twitched and flickered for a moment, then lowered its massive head and charged. Foxy leaped, hitting the twisted Freddy's face with full force and knocking it onto its back, then tearing into its head cavity, slashing at what was left of the twisted face with enthusiasm.

Something grabbed John and he snapped out of his trance. The twisted Bonnie grabbed him with an arm of exposed metal, but the eyes in the dark rose suddenly behind it. The original Bonnie grabbed the torso of the twisted Bonnie and threw it aside to where Chica waited; she grabbed the misshapen rabbit's head and wrenched it off in a burst of sparks.

John shielded his eyes. When the smoke settled, all that remained was the hollow, burnt corpse of an unidentifiable monster. Bonnie and Chica had vanished into the shadows.

Charlie ran for the mouth of the passage, but Springtrap leaped on her with preternatural speed. He knocked her to the ground and reached again for her neck with his swollen hands. Charlie rolled out of the way, and something jabbed her hard in the back. She snatched at it, and a mushroom cap came away in her hands. She leaped to her knees as Springtrap got to his feet, circling her, looking for an opening. She glanced down: a sturdy, metal spike had held the mushroom cap in place. She wrapped her hand around its base, blocking it from Springtrap's sight with her body.

Charlie looked up at him, meeting his gelatinous eyes, silently daring him to attack. As if on cue, he sprang at her, leaping with his arms thrust out, stretching again toward her throat. At the last moment, Charlie ducked her head and thrust the spike upward with all her might. It stopped with a jolt as it hit his chest, but she drove it in, ignoring his sputtering cries as he tried uselessly to beat her away. She stood, her hands shaking as she shoved the stake in as far as it would go. He toppled backward, and she knelt swiftly beside him, giving the metal spike another thrust.

"Tell me why," she hissed. It was the question that consumed her, the thing that kept coming back in her nightmares. Now he said nothing, and she rocked the stake back and forth in his chest. He made a gagging cry of pain. *"Tell me why you took him! Why did you choose him? Why did you take Sammy?"*

"Into the cave!" John shouted. "We have to get Charlie!"

They hurried to the opening, but from inside the cave came a strange, overwhelming clatter. They all stepped back as a horde of the balloon boys emerged from the cave, shaking back and forth on unsteady feet, their pointed teeth chattering loudly as they wobbled forward with staring eyes.

"Not again! I hate these things!" Jessica cried. Clay took up a fighting stance, but John could see they would be overwhelmed. There was something different about the children now, something coordinated. Though they shook and wobbled, it no longer seemed like a sign of weakness. Instead, John thought of warriors rattling their shields: the threat before the battle.

"We have to get away," he said. "Clay!"

Something shook the earth—pounding, even footsteps—as a shadow loomed above them. John looked up and saw a smiling Freddy Fazbear approaching, his hat at a jaunty angle and his massive limbs swinging. "Oh no! He's back!" Jessica screeched.

"No, wait! That's *our* Freddy!" John grabbed Jessica and shielded her with his arms. Freddy lumbered past them and into the crowd of balloon boys. With a single lunge he smashed both arms into the crowd, creating a deafening shatter of metal and plastic. The air was filled with arms, legs, and broken shrapnel. Freddy got to his feet and grabbed one of the balloon boys, lifting it up like it weighed nothing. He crushed its head with one hand. Freddy tossed the body to the ground and stomped on it, pursuing the others as they ran. They scattered, but Freddy was moving swiftly, and the room resounded with the noise of cracking plastic.

"Come on, into the cave!" Clay yelled over the din, and they ran for the passage. They hurried down the narrow path, Clay at the front and John taking up the rear, glancing behind to make sure they weren't being followed. Suddenly Clay halted, and Jessica and John nearly ran into him. Crowding up beside him, they saw why he'd stopped: the path split, and there was no trace of Charlie.

"There," Jessica said suddenly. "There's a light!"

John blinked. It was dim, but he saw it. Somewhere down the passage there was a blue glow, though it was impossible to tell how far away it was. "Come on," he said grimly, pressing past Clay to take the lead.

"Why did you take Sammy?!" Charlie cried again. Springtrap wheezed and smiled but did not speak. She grabbed his head with both hands, desperate with fury. She lifted his head and brought it crashing against the rock where it lay. He made another sharp grunt of pain, and she did it again. This time something began to ooze from the back of his head, running thickly down the rock. "What did you do to him?" Charlie demanded. "Why did you take him? Why did you choose *him*?" He looked up at her; one of his pupils had swallowed the iris of his eye. He smiled vaguely.

"I didn't choose him."

Hands grabbed Charlie's shoulders, dragging her up and away from the semiconscious Springtrap. She shouted and turned to fight back, only stopping herself when she saw that it was Clay. The others were behind him. She turned back, shaking with rage.

"I'll kill you!" she cried. She lifted Springtrap up by the shoulders and shoved him back against the rock. His head bounced and lolled to the side. "What do you mean you didn't choose him?" Charlie said, leaning in close to him, as if she might read the answers in his battered face. "You took him from me! Why did you take him?"

Springtrap's mismatched eyes seemed to focus for a moment, and even he seemed to have difficulty muttering his next words.

"I didn't take him. I took you."

Charlie stared, her fingers going lax, loosening on Springtrap's moldy suit. *What?* The rage that had filled her to the breaking point drained away all at once. She felt like she'd lost too much blood and was going into shock. Springtrap didn't try to get away; he just lay there coughing and sputtering, his eyes once more unfocused, staring into a void Charlie couldn't see.

Suddenly the floor rattled beneath them. The walls rocked inward as the whole cave shook, and something mechanical roared on the other side of the wall. The sounds of grinding metal filled the air.

"It's a battle royale out there!" Clay shouted. "This whole place is coming down!" Charlie glanced at him, and as soon as her head was turned she felt Springtrap slip from her fingers. She whipped back around, just in time to see him roll through an open trap door at the base of an enormous rock a few feet away. Charlie leaped up to follow him, but the floor quaked violently. She lost her footing, nearly falling as half the cave wall came tumbling down. She stopped, glancing around in confusion: real rock and dirt cascaded all around them. "It's not the fake cave that's collapsing!" she shouted to the rest. "It's the whole building!"

"Is everyone okay?" Clay shouted. Charlie nodded, and saw that John and Jessica were still on their feet. "We have to go!" Light shone through a crack in the wall ahead. Clay started for it, motioning the others to follow. Charlie hesitated, unable to take her eyes from the last place she'd seen Springtrap. John put a hand on her arm.

The walls of the fake cavern had almost completely fallen, and now they could see the actual interior of the complex.

"That way!" Clay shouted, pointing to a narrow maintenance hall that seemed to stretch off endlessly into the distance. "None of these things will be able to fit through there!" Clay and Jessica ran for the entrance to the corridor, but Charlie faltered.

"Charlie, we can deal with him another day," John shouted over the din. "But we need to survive this one first!" The ground shook again and John looked at Charlie. She nodded, and they ran.

Clay led them racing through the tunnel as the sound of its collapse chased them. The air was filled with dust, obscuring the path ahead. Charlie looked back once, but the ruins were lost in the haze. Eventually the rumble of falling rock was reduced to a distant thunder. The clean, narrow hallway began to feel removed from the madness behind them.

"Clay we have to stop," Jessica cried, holding her side like she was in pain.

"I see something up ahead. I think we're almost to the end

of this. There!" The hallway ended in a heavy metal door, partially cracked, and Clay beckoned John to help him open it. It squealed and protested, then gave way at last, opening into a simple room of dark stone. One wall of it had been knocked down, and the room gaped open, the cool night air pouring in.

John looked at Charlie. "We're out! We're okay!" He laughed.

"Don't you see where we are?" she whispered. Slowly, she walked the length of the room, gesturing to the four enormous pits in the floor, one of which contained a headless, half-buried robot. "John, this is my dad's house. It's the room we found."

"Come on, Jessica." Clay was helping Jessica through the gap in the collapsed wall. He paused and looked back to John.

"It's okay," John said. "We'll be right there." Clay nodded. He helped Jessica through and moved out of sight.

"What is this?" Charlie put her hand on her stomach, a sudden unease settling over her.

"What's wrong?" John asked. Something flickered all around them, a disorienting flash, too fast to even tell where it had come from. A thunderous crash echoed from the hall they'd just broken out of. "Charlie, I think we should go with Clay."

"Yeah, I'm coming." Charlie followed John to the gap in the wall as he climbed through it.

"Okay, come on," John shouted, holding out his hand to her from what had once been her own backyard. She started forward, then stopped as the lights flickered again. *What is that?*

It was the walls. The whitewashed concrete was blinking in and out of existence, shivering like a dying bulb. It was the wall Charlie had been drawn to the first time they came to this place. Now she felt its pull as she had in the cave. It was stronger here than it had ever been, even in the dreams that left her drained and aching. *I'm here.* She took a step toward the far wall and felt another pang in her stomach. *Here. Yes, here.*

"Charlie!" John cried again. "Come on!"

"I have to," she said softly. She went to the wall and put her hands on it, as she'd done before. But this time the concrete was warm, and somehow smooth despite the rough finish. *I have to get inside.* For a moment, she felt like she was in two places at once: here, inside the little room, and on the other side of the wall, desperate to get through. She drew back suddenly, taking her hands off the wall as if it burned. The illusion flickered, then died altogether.

The concrete wall was made of metal, and at the center was a door.

Charlie stared, blank with shock. *This is the door.* She'd been drawing it without knowing what it was. Approximating over and over something she had never seen. She stepped forward again and put her hands on the surface. It was still warm. She pressed her cheek against it. "Are you in there?" she called softly. "I have to get you out."

Her heart was pounding, blood rushing in her ears so loudly she could scarcely hear anything else. "Charlie! Charlie!" John and Jessica were both calling her from outside, but their voices seemed as distant as memory. She stood, not taking her hands from the metal but tracing her fingers along it. It felt like letting go for even an instant would cause her pain. She brought her hands to the crack in the wall: it had no handle, no knob, and no hinges. It was just an outline, and now she ran her thumb up and down the side of it, trying to find a trip, some trick that would make the door open and let her through.

She heard John climb back inside and slowly approach her, keeping his distance, as though he might scare her away.

"Charlie, if you don't get out of here, you'll die. Whatever's behind that door, it can't give you back your family. You still have *us*." Charlie looked at John. His eyes were wide and frightened. She took a small step toward him.

"We've lost enough. Please, don't make me lose you, too," John pleaded. Charlie stared at the ceiling as it trembled; clouds of smoke were pouring out of the corridor they'd come from. John coughed heavily; he was choking. She looked at him. He was terrified, unwilling to draw closer than he already was.

She turned again, and the world around her faded; she couldn't hear John behind her, or smell the smoke filling the air. She laid her hand flat against the wall. *A heartbeat. I feel a heartbeat.* Though she made no intentional movement, her body turned to the side. She tensed, committing to remain where she stood, without ever making the decision. Something began to hiss: the steady, gentle sound of air being released. From the base of the door came a rhythmic clicking. Charlie closed her eyes.

"Charlie!" John grabbed her and turned her forcefully toward him, shaking her out of her stupor. "Look at me. I'm not leaving you here."

"I have to stay."

"No, you have to come with us!" he cried. "You have to come with *me*."

"No, I . . ." Charlie felt her voice trail off; she was losing strength.

"I love you," John said. Charlie's eyes stopped drifting: she fixed them on him. "I'm taking you with me, right now." He grabbed her hand roughly. He was strong enough to pull her away by force, she knew, but he was waiting for her to acknowledge him.

She looked into his eyes, trying to let them bring her back. It felt like trying to awaken from a dream. John's gaze was an anchor, and she held it, letting him keep her steady, draw her back to him. "Okay," she said quietly.

"Okay," John repeated, heaving the words out in a sigh. He'd been holding his breath. He walked backward, guiding her as he went.

She climbed to the top of the broken wall and paused, bracing herself against the insistent pull of the door and what lay behind it. She took a deep breath—then was torn backward by a colossal force. She ripped back through the rocks, her arms pinned to her sides. Charlie screamed, struggling to get away. Dimly she heard John shouting close by.

As she whipped her body back and forth against its grip, Charlie glimpsed the immense thing that had caught her. The twisted Freddy stared blankly forward, or at least what remained of it. It held her with one arm; the other was gone, and wires hung from its shoulder like extra bits of sinew. Its plastic casing had melted away, and what remained were metal plates and stays, a skeleton with unnatural bulges and gaps in its frame where the collapse had mangled it. Its face was a gaping hole, spilling teeth and wire that hung in shapeless masses. Charlie couldn't see it legs, and after a second she realized they were gone. It had dragged itself, one-armed, through the rubble. Wires spilled out of its body like guts, and when she saw its stomach, Charlie went cold with terror.

Its chest had parted at the middle. Sharp, uneven teeth lined both sides. Charlie kicked at the animatronic, but it did no good: it forced her instantly into the chasm. The thing embraced her, pushing her deeper inside its chest as they toppled backward together. The metal rib cage snapped shut: she was caught.

"Charlie!" John was kneeling beside her, and she reached out through the metal stays. He grabbed her hand. "Clay!" he shouted, "Jessica!" Jessica was there in seconds; Charlie could see Clay struggling back through the narrow opening.

"Wait!" Charlie cried as Jessica tried to pry the chest open. "The spring locks, they'll kill me if you touch the wrong thing!"

"But if we don't get you out, you'll die anyway!" Jessica shouted. Charlie saw for the first time that the mouth wasn't finished closing. It was layered somehow, and metal plates began folding over her like petals of a horrid flower. John started to stand, but Charlie tightened her hand around his.

"Don't let go of me!" she cried, panicked. He dropped back to his knees and pulled her hand to his chest. She stared at him, even as the metal plates closed over her, threatening to seal her off. Jessica tried to jam them delicately, without setting off the spring locks. "John—" Charlie gasped.

"Don't," he said roughly. "I've got you!"

The plates continued to slide down and meet in the center. Charlie's arm was trapped in the corner of the strange mouth, protruding from the only gap where the plates didn't meet. She looked around wildly: another layer was closing. She was wedged into the suit haphazardly, her whole body crammed into Freddy's torso, and she could see nothing but dimming figures as more layers of metal and plastic closed over her. Above her, Jessica was trying to stop the next layer from emerging, and she felt Freddy's mutilated body lurch.

"Jessica! Look out!" she screamed at the top of her lungs. Jessica leaped back just in time to avoid Freddy's violently swinging arm. The animatronic was on its back, but it struck out randomly, beating Jessica and Clay away. Its body rocked back and forth, and Charlie eyed the springs and robotic parts all around her: she drew her knees up to her chest, trying to make herself smaller.

John let go of her hand, and she grabbed at his absence. She could no longer see outside. "John!"

Freddy's body shook, struck by a massive blow.

"Let go of her!" John screamed. Clay hefted a metal beam from the ground and struck at Freddy's head. The twisted bear tried to strike with its remaining arm. Clay ducked out of the way and hit it again from the other side, out of reach. Jessica was still at the creature's chest, trying to find an opening to pry at, but each layer melded seamlessly together. There was nothing to catch at. John moved in next to her, trying to help. Clay struck at the head over and over, making Freddy's whole body jolt with every blow.

"I can't get to her!" Jessica yelled. "She's going to suffocate!" She tried to steady Charlie's trembling hand. Clay hit

Freddy's head once more with a resounding crash, and they heard metal cracking as the head was knocked off the creature's body.

"Can we get her out through the neck?" John asked urgently. Freddy's arm continued to flail, but it had weakened, and was just rising and falling, seeming to swing without purpose.

"Clay, help!" Jessica cried. He ran to take over, digging his fingers between the plates to pry them open. Jessica continued holding Charlie's hand, which had gone limp. "Charlie!" Jessica cried. Charlie's hand closed over hers again, and Jessica gasped with relief. "John, Clay, she's okay! Hurry! Charlie, can you hear me? It's Jessica." There was no sound from inside Freddy's sealed chest, but Charlie held on tightly to Jessica's hand as the others grimly worked to free her.

Suddenly a single high-pitched click reverberated through the air. John and Clay froze, their hands still hovering above Freddy's chest. For a moment, the air stood still, then the metal body convulsed violently. It launched itself off the ground, and a ghastly crunch of metal pierced the air. All three pulled back instinctively. Clay and John jumped away from the thing, and Jessica scrambled backward, dropping Charlie's hand.

The suit fell again and was still. The arm was splayed on the ground at an awkward angle. The room was silent. "Charlie?" John said softly, then his face went white. He ran to the place where her arm was exposed, falling hard on his knees, and grabbed her hand in both his own. It was limp. John turned it over and tapped her palm with his fingers. "Charlie? Charlie!"

"John," Jessica said very quietly. "The blood." He looked up at her, confused, still holding on to Charlie. Then something wet dripped onto his hand. There was blood running out of the suit and down Charlie's arm. Her skin was slick and red, except the hand he held. He watched, unable to look away, as it dripped steadily from the suit, pooling on the ground and beginning to seep into his jeans. It covered his hand and hers, until his skin was slippery and he began to lose his grip. She was sliding away from him.

Sirens were suddenly nearby, and John realized vaguely that he'd been hearing them in the distance. He looked dazedly up at Clay.

"I radioed them," he said. "We aren't safe in here." Clay took his eyes off the suit and looked up to study the ceiling. It was bowed and cracking, on the verge of collapse. John didn't move. People were shouting outside, and flashlights bobbed up and down as they ran toward the crumbling building. Jessica touched his shoulder. Breaks and cracks resounded through the space.

"John, we have to." As if to mark her point, the floor shook again beneath them and something crashed loudly not far away. Charlie's hand didn't move.

A uniformed officer pressed through the crack in the wall. "Chief Burke?"

"Thomson. We have to get the kids out, now." Thomson nodded and motioned to Jessica.

"Come on, miss."

"John, come on," Jessica managed to say, and a thunderous clatter sounded from behind them. Clay looked to the officer again.

"Get them out of here." Thomson took hold of Jessica's arm and she tried to shove him away.

"Don't touch me!" she shouted, but the officer firmly pulled her up and over the rubble, half dragging her outside. John only half heard the commotion, then someone's hands were on his shoulders as well. He batted them away, not looking around.

"We're leaving," Clay said in a low voice.

"Not without Charlie," John responded. Clay took a deep breath.

John saw him signal someone from the corner of his eye, then he was grabbed forcefully by two large men and dragged toward the opening.

"No!" he shouted. "Let me go!" They shoved him roughly over the broken wall, then Clay struggled out behind them.

"Is everyone out?" a female officer called.

"Yes," Clay said hesitantly, but with the ring of authority.

"NO!" John shouted. He broke free of the officers holding him back and ran for the opening again. He had one foot through the gap, then stopped dead as a sweeping flashlight briefly illuminated the room in front of him.

A dark-haired woman knelt in the pool of blood, holding Charlie's limp hand. She looked up sharply and met his eyes with a piercing black gaze. Before John could move or speak, hands grabbed his shoulders again and drew him back, and then the whole house collapsed before them.

We don't know for sure," Jessica said, firmly setting down the fork she'd been playing with on the diner table. It made a disappointing click.

"Don't do this," John warned. He didn't look up from the menu, though he hadn't read a word since he picked it up.

"It's just, all that we saw was, you know, blood. People can survive a lot of things. Dave—Springtrap, whatever he wants to call himself—he survived one of those suits, *twice*. For all we know she might be trapped in the rubble. We should go back. We could—"

"Jessica, *stop*." John closed the menu and put it down on the table. "Please. I can't listen to this. We both saw it happen. We both know she couldn't have . . ." Jessica opened her mouth again, about to interrupt. "I said, *stop*. Don't you think that I *want* to believe that she's okay? I cared about her, too. I cared about her a lot. There is nothing I want more than for her to somehow have escaped. For her to drive up in that ancient car and get out all furious and say, 'Hey, why'd you leave me behind?' But we saw the blood: there was too much. I held her hand, and it didn't feel like anything. As soon as I touched her, I just—Jessica, I *knew*. And you know it, too."

Jessica picked up her fork again and twirled it between her fingers, not meeting his eyes. "I feel like we're waiting for something to happen," she said quietly.

John picked up the menu again. "I know. But I think that's just how this feels." From behind him, he heard the waitress approach for the third time. "We don't know yet," he said without looking up. "Why am I even looking at this?" John set the menu back down and covered his face with his hands.

"Can I join you?" John looked up. An unfamiliar, brown-haired young man slid into the booth next to Jessica and across from John.

"Hey, Arty," Jessica said with a weak smile.

"Hey," he said, glancing from her to John and back again. John said nothing. "Everyone okay?" Arty asked finally. "I heard there was some kind of accident. Where's Charlie?"

Jessica looked down, tapping the fork on the table. John met the newcomer's eyes, then shook his head. Arty blanched, and John looked out the window. The parking lot outside blurred as he fixed his gaze on the smudged and streaky glass.

"The last thing she said to me was . . ." John lightly touched his fist to the table. "'Don't let go of me.'" He turned back to the window.

"John," Jessica whispered.

"And I did. I let go of her. And she died alone." There was silence for a few moments.

"I can't believe it," Arty said, his brow furrowed. "We had just started dating, you know?"

Jessica kept her face smooth, and John turned his thousand-yard stare on Arty. The boy faltered. "I mean, we were going to. I think. She really liked me, anyway." He looked to Jessica, who nodded.

"She liked you, Arty," she said. John turned back to the window.

"I'm sure she did," he said evenly.

Random thoughts swirled through his mind. The mess of her room. The pang of concern when he saw her childhood toy, Theodore the stuffed rabbit, torn apart. *Charlie, what was wrong?* There was so much more he wanted to ask her. Those blind faces with their smooth, nearly featureless faces and their couplet word games. Something—everything—about them had disturbed him, and now that he pictured them again, he was bothered for another reason. *They looked like William Afton's designs—the blank faces with no eyes. Charlie, what made you think of that?*

Jessica made an indistinct cry, and John startled back to the present to see her racing to the door, where Marla had appeared. He got up more slowly and followed her, with a sense of déjà vu. He was waiting his turn as Marla hugged Jessica close, stroking her hair and whispering something John couldn't hear.

Marla released Jessica and turned to him. "John," she said, taking both his hands. The sorrow in her eyes was what broke him. He leaned in and hugged her close, hiding his face in her hair until he could compose himself. When his breathing had steadied, she pushed him gently back and took his arm. They all went back to the table where Arty waited, peering uncertainly over the side of the booth. They sat down again. Marla slid in next to John and looked from him to Jessica. "You have to tell me what happened," she said quietly. Jessica nodded, letting her hair fall over her face for a minute in a shiny brown curtain.

"Yeah, I want to know, too," Arty piped up, and Marla glanced at him as if only just registering his presence.

"Hi," she said, sounding slightly puzzled. "I'm Marla."

"Arty. Charlie and I were—" He glanced at John. "We were good friends."

Marla nodded. "Well, I wish we were meeting under different circumstances. Jessica? John? Please, tell me."

They glanced at each other. John looked to the window again. He was content to let Jessica do the talking but felt an obligation—not to talk to Marla, but to talk *about* Charlie. "Charlie was chasing something from her past," John said, his voice calm. "She found it, and it didn't let her leave."

"There was a building collapse," Jessica added. "Her father's house."

"Charlie didn't make it out," John said roughly. He cleared his throat and reached for the glass of water in front of him.

John vaguely heard Marla and Jessica exchanging words of comfort, but his mind was elsewhere. *The woman, kneeling in the pool of Charlie's blood, holding her hand.* He had only glimpsed her for a moment; she had looked almost as surprised to see him as he was to see her. But there was something familiar about her.

He turned away from the others again and closed his eyes, trying to picture it. *Dark hair, dark eyes. She looked severe and unafraid, even with the ground shaking and the building tumbling down over her head. I know her.* The woman he remembered looked different, younger, but her face was the same . . . Suddenly he had it. *The last day I saw you, Charlie, back when we were kids. She came to pick you up from school, and the next day you weren't there, and the next day, and the day after that. Then even us kids began to hear the rumors, that your father had done what he did. And that's when I realized I would never see you again.* John shivered.

"John, what's wrong?" Marla said sharply, then blushed. "I mean, what are you thinking?"

"Her aunt was there," he said slowly. "Her aunt Jen."

"What?" Marla said. "Where?"

"They hadn't spoken in months," Jessica said doubtfully.

"I know," John said. "But she was there. When I ran back, just before they pulled me away, I *saw* her. With Charlie."

The thought struck him like a blow across the chest, and he looked out the window again so that he wouldn't have to meet anyone's eyes. "Charlie's aunt Jen was there," he repeated to the dirty pane of glass.

"Maybe Clay called her," Jessica offered. John didn't respond. No one spoke for a long moment.

"I think it's best not to look for more mysteries," Marla said slowly. "Charlie was—"

"Are you all ready to order?" The waitress asked brightly. John turned to look at her with impatience in his eyes, but Marla cut him off.

"Four coffees," she said firmly. "Four eggs and toast, scrambled."

"Thanks, Marla," John whispered. "I'm not sure if I can eat, though."

She glanced at the rest of them. Arty looked briefly as if he wanted to say something, then he cast his eyes down at the table. The woman departed, and Marla looked around. "We all have to eat. And you can't sit around in a diner all day without ordering anything."

"I'm glad you're here, Marla," John said. She nodded.

"We all love Charlie," she said, looking at each of them in turn. "There's never a right thing to say, is there? Nothing ever makes it okay, because it's not."

"All those crazy experiments," Jessica said suddenly. "I didn't understand, but she was so excited about them, and now she'll never get to finish."

"It's not fair," Marla said softly.

"So what do we do?" Jessica said with a plaintive note in her voice. She looked at Marla like she must have the answer.

"Jessica, sweetie," Marla said. "All anyone can do is hold on to the Charlie that we all loved."

"It's over," John said hoarsely, turning away from the window abruptly. "That . . . that psychopath murdered her, just like he did Michael and all those other kids. She was the most fascinating, the most amazing person I have ever known, and she died for *nothing*."

"She did *not* die for nothing!" Marla snapped, leaning in

toward him. Rage flashed in her eyes. "No one dies for nothing, John. Everyone's life has a meaning. Everyone has a death, and I hate it that this was hers. Do you hear me? I *hate* it! But we can't change it. All we can do is remember Charlie, and honor Charlie's life, from the beginning to the very end."

John held her stormy gaze for a long moment, then broke away and looked down at his folded hands on the table. She mirrored the movement and placed one hand over his.

Jessica gasped, and he turned back to the table wearily. "What, Jessica?" John asked. Her nervous energy was beginning to exhaust him. She didn't answer, but gave him an incredulous look, and turned back to the window. Marla leaned past John, craning her neck to see. Reluctantly he looked, too, letting his eyes focus for the first time on the parking lot outside the window, and not the pane of glass itself.

It was a car. The woman driving killed the engine and got out. She was slim and tall, with long, straight brown hair that glistened in the sun. She was wearing a bright red, knee-length dress with black combat boots, and she strode purposefully toward the diner. They all watched motionless, as if the slightest sound might rupture the illusion and send her away. The woman was almost at the door. Arty said it first:

"Charlie?"

Marla shook her head. She leaped up and turned, calling from the seat, "Charlie!"

She ran for the door, and Jessica was quick on her heels, crying out after her. They rushed to the doorway to meet her just as she walked in.

John stayed where he was, craning his neck to see the door. Arty seemed confused, his mouth open slightly and his brow furrowed. John watched for a steady moment, then turned away decisively, facing across the table with a grave expression. He didn't speak until Arty met his gaze.

"That's not Charlie."

About Scott Cawthon

Scott Cawthon is the author of the best-selling video game series Five Nights at Freddy's, and while he is a game designer by trade, he is first and foremost a storyteller at heart. He is a graduate of The Art Institute of Houston and lives in Texas with his wife and four sons.

About Kira Breed-Wrisley

Kira Breed-Wrisley has been writing stories since she could first pick up a pen and has no intention of stopping. She is the author of seven plays for Central New York teen theater company The Media Unit, and has developed several books with Kevin Anderson & Associates. She is a graduate of Cornell University, and lives in Brooklyn, NY.